PENGUIN BO

Author's Choice: Fo

GRAHAM GI

Graham Greene was born in 1904 and educated at Berkhamsted School, where his father was headmaster. On coming down from Balliol College, Oxford, where he published a book of verse, he worked for four years as a sub-editor on *The Times*. He established his reputation with his fourth novel, *Stamboul Train*, which he classed as an 'entertainment' in order to distinguish it from more serious work. In 1935 he made a journey across Liberia, described in *Journey Without Maps*, and on his return was appointed film critic of the *Spectator*. In 1926 he had been received into the Roman Catholic Church and was commissioned to visit Mexico in 1938 and report on the religious persecution there. As a result he wrote *The Lawless Roads* and, later, *The Power and the Glory*.

Brighton Rock was published in 1938 and in 1940 he became literary editor of the *Spectator*. The next year he undertook work for the Foreign Office and was sent out to Sierra Leone in 1941–3. One of his major post-war novels, *The Heart of the Matter*, is set in West Africa and is considered by many to be his finest book. This was followed by *The End of the Affair, The Quiet American*, a story set in Vietnam, *Our Man in Havana*, and *A Burnt-Out Case*. Many of his novels have been filmed, as have two of his short stories, and *The Third Man* was written as a film treatment. His other publications include *The Pleasure Dome* (1972), *The Honorary Consul* (1973), *An Impossible Woman: The Memories of Dottoressa Moor of Capri* (edited 1975), *The Human Factor* (1978), *Doctor Fischer of Geneva or The Bomb Party* (1980), *Monsignor Quixote* (1982), *J'Accuse: The Dark Side of Nice* (1982) and *The Tenth Man* (1985), an early novel recently rediscovered. His first volume of autobiography was *A Sort of Life* (1971), and *Ways of Escape*, a second autobiographical volume, was published in 1980.

In all, Graham Greene has written some thirty novels, many of which have been published in Penguins, 'entertainments', plays, children's books, travel books, and collections of essays and short stories. He was made a Companion of Honour in 1966.

Author's Choice: Four Novels by

GRAHAM GREENE

The Power and the Glory

The Quiet American

Travels with my Aunt

The Honorary Consul

Penguin Books

Penguin Books Ltd, Harmondsworth, Middlesex, England
Viking Penguin Inc., 40 West 23rd Street, New York, New York 10010, U.S.A.
Penguin Books Australia Ltd, Ringwood, Victoria, Australia
Penguin Books Canada Ltd, 2801 John Street, Markham, Ontario, Canada L3R 1B4
Penguin Books (N.Z.) Ltd, 182–190 Wairau Road, Auckland 10, New Zealand

The Power and the Glory

First published in Great Britain under the title *The Power and the Glory* by William Heinemann Ltd 1940
Published in Penguin Books in association with William Heinemann Ltd in Great Britain 1962
First published in the United States of America under the title *The Labyrinthine Ways* by The Viking Press 1940
Reissued under its original British title by The Viking Press 1946

The Quiet American

First published in Great Britain by William Heinemann Ltd 1955
Published by Penguin Books in association with William Heinemann Ltd in Great Britain 1962
First published in the United States of America by The Viking Press 1956

Travels with my Aunt

First published in Great Britain by The Bodley Head 1969
Published by Penguin Books in association with The Bodley Head 1971
First published in the United States of America by The Viking Press 1970

The Honorary Consul

First published by The Bodley Head 1973
Published in Penguin Books 1974

First published in one volume as *Author's Choice: Four Novels by Graham Greene* 1985

Typeset in 9/11pt Linotron Times by
Rowland Phototypesetting Ltd
Bury St Edmunds, Suffolk

Printed in Great Britain by
Cox and Wyman Ltd, Reading

Contents

Introduction	7
The Power and the Glory	9
The Quiet American	191
Travels with my Aunt	337
The Honorary Consul	547

INTRODUCTION

I have chosen these four novels to represent different aspects of my work. *The Power and the Glory* represents my treatment of a Catholic theme which incidentally displeased the Holy Office, though not Pope Paul VI! In *The Quiet American* I used in a novel some personal experiences of the French war in Vietnam. I attempted in *Travels with my Aunt* to treat humorously a serious theme, old age and death. A Swedish critic described it as 'laughter in the shadow of the gallows'. *The Honorary Consul* is my personal favourite as it combines my religious interest with my political interest, and I think I have succeeded here as nowhere else in creating two characters – the Doctor and the Consul – who change and develop in the course of the novel – not an easy thing to do.

Graham Greene

THE POWER AND THE GLORY

Th' inclosure narrow'd; the sagacious power
Of hounds and death drew nearer every hour.

DRYDEN

For Gervase

PART ONE

Chapter 1: The Port

Mr Tench went out to look for his ether cylinder, into the blazing Mexican sun and the bleaching dust. A few vultures looked down from the roof with shabby indifference: he wasn't carrion yet. A faint feeling of rebellion stirred in Mr Tench's heart, and he wrenched up a piece of the road with splintering finger-nails and tossed it feebly towards them. One rose and flapped across the town: over the tiny plaza, over the bust of an ex-president, ex-general, ex-human being, over the two stalls which sold mineral water, towards the river and the sea. It wouldn't find anything there: the sharks looked after the carrion on that side. Mr Tench went on across the plaza.

He said '*Buenos días*' to a man with a gun who sat in a small patch of shade against a wall. But it wasn't like England: the man said nothing at all, just stared malevolently up at Mr Tench, as if he had never had any dealings with the foreigner, as if Mr Tench were not responsible for his two gold bicuspid teeth. Mr Tench went sweating by, past the Treasury which had once been a church, towards the quay. Half-way across he suddenly forgot what he had come out for – a glass of mineral water? That was all there was to drink in this prohibition state – except beer, but that was a government monopoly and too expensive except on special occasions. An awful feeling of nausea gripped Mr Tench in the stomach – it couldn't have been mineral water he wanted. Of course his ether cylinder . . . the boat was in. He had heard its exultant piping while he lay on his bed after lunch. He passed the barbers' and two dentists' and came out between a warehouse and the customs on to the river bank.

The river went heavily by towards the sea between the banana plantations; the *General Obregon* was tied up to the bank, and beer was being unloaded – a hundred cases were already stacked upon the quay. Mr Tench stood in the shade of the customs house and thought:

what am I here for? Memory drained out of him in the heat. He gathered his bile together and spat forlornly into the sun. Then he sat down on a case and waited. Nothing to do. Nobody would come to see him before five.

The *General Obregon* was about thirty yards long. A few feet of damaged rail, one lifeboat, a bell hanging on a rotten cord, an oil-lamp in the bow, she looked as if she might weather two or three more Atlantic years, if she didn't strike a Norther in the gulf. That, of course, would be the end of her. It didn't really matter: everybody was insured when he bought a ticket, automatically. Half a dozen passengers leant on the rail, among the hobbled turkeys, and stared at the port, the warehouse, the empty baked street with the dentists and the barbers.

Mr Tench heard a revolver holster creak just behind him and turned his head. A customs officer was watching him angrily. He said something which Mr Tench did not catch. 'Pardon me,' Mr Tench said.

'My teeth,' the customs man said indistinctly.

'Oh,' Mr Tench said, 'yes, your teeth.' The man had none: that was why he couldn't talk clearly. Mr Tench had removed them all. He was shaken with nausea – something was wrong – worms, dysentery . . . He said, 'The set is nearly finished. Tonight,' he promised wildly. It was, of course, quite impossible; but that was how one lived, putting off everything. The man was satisfied: he might forget, and in any case what could he *do*? He had paid in advance. That was the whole world to Mr Tench: the heat and the forgetting, the putting off till tomorrow, if possible cash down – for what? He stared out over the slow river: the fin of a shark moved like a periscope at the river's mouth. In the course of years several ships had stranded and they now helped to prop up the bank, the smoke-stacks leaning over like guns pointing at some distant objective across the banana trees and the swamps.

Mr Tench thought: ether cylinder: I nearly forgot. His mouth fell open and he began moodily to count the bottles of Cerveza Moctezuma. A hundred and forty cases. Twelve times a hundred and forty: the heavy phlegm gathered in his mouth: twelve fours are forty-eight. He said aloud in English, 'My God, a pretty one': twelve hundred, sixteen hundred and eighty: he spat, staring with vague interest at a girl in the bows of the *General Obregon* – a fine thin figure, they were generally so thick, brown eyes, of course, and the inevitable gleam of the gold tooth, but something fresh and young . . . Sixteen hundred and eighty bottles at a peso a bottle.

Somebody whispered in English, 'What did you say?'

Mr Tench swivelled round. 'You English?' he asked in astonishment, but at the sight of the round and hollow face charred with a three-days' beard, he altered his question: 'You speak English?'

Yes, the man said, he spoke a little English. He stood stiffly in the shade, a small man dressed in a shabby dark city suit, carrying a small attaché case. He had a novel under his arm: bits of an amorous scene stuck out, crudely coloured. He said, 'Excuse me. I thought just now you were talking to me.' He had protuberant eyes; he gave an impression of unstable hilarity, as if perhaps he had been celebrating a birthday, alone.

Mr Tench cleared his mouth of phlegm. 'What did I say?' He couldn't remember a thing.

'You said my God a pretty one.'

'Now what could I have meant by that?' He stared up at the merciless sky. A vulture hung there, an observer. 'What? Oh just the girl I suppose. You don't often see a pretty piece round here. Just one or two a year worth looking at.'

'She is very young.'

'Oh, I don't have intentions,' Mr Tench said wearily. 'A man may look. I've lived alone for fifteen years.'

'Here?'

'Hereabouts.'

They fell silent and time passed, the shadow of the customs house shifted a few inches farther towards the river: the vulture moved a little, like the black hand of a clock.

'You came in *her*?' Mr Tench asked.

'No.'

'Going in her?'

The little man seemed to evade the question, but then as if some explanation were required: 'I was just looking,' he said. 'I suppose she'll be sailing quite soon?'

'To Vera Cruz,' Mr Tench said. 'In a few hours.'

'Without calling anywhere?'

'Where could she call?' He asked, 'How did you get here?'

The stranger said vaguely, 'A canoe.'

'Got a plantation, eh?'

'No.'

'It's good hearing English spoken,' Mr Tench said. 'Now you learnt yours in the States?'

The man agreed. He wasn't very garrulous.

'Ah, what wouldn't I give,' Mr Tench said, 'to be there now.' He said in a low anxious voice, 'You don't happen, do you, to have a drink in that case of yours? Some of you people back there – I've known one or two – a little for medical purposes.'

'Only medicine,' the man said.

'You a doctor?'

The bloodshot eyes looked slyly out of their corners at Mr Tench. 'You would call me perhaps a – quack?'

'Patent medicines? Live and let live,' Mr Tench said.

'Are *you* sailing?'

'No, I came down here for –. . . oh well, it doesn't matter anyway.' He put his hand on his stomach and said, 'You haven't got any medicine, have you, for – oh hell. I don't know what. It's just this bloody land. You can't cure me of that. No one can.'

'You want to go home?'

'Home,' Mr Tench said, 'my home's here. Did you see what the peso stands at in Mexico City? Four to the dollar. Four. O God. *Ora pro nobis*.'

'Are you a Catholic?'

'No, no. Just an expression. I don't believe in anything like that.' He said irrelevantly, 'It's too hot anyway.'

'I think I must find somewhere to sit.'

'Come up to my place,' Mr Tench said. 'I've got a spare hammock. The boat won't leave for hours – if you want to watch it go.'

The stranger said, 'I was expecting to see someone. The name was Lopez.'

'Oh, they shot him weeks ago,' Mr Tench said.

'Dead?'

'You know how it is round here. Friend of yours?'

'No, no,' the man protested hurriedly. 'Just a friend of a friend.'

'Well, that's how it is,' Mr Tench said. He brought up his bile again and spat it out into the hard sunlight. 'They say he used to help . . . oh, undesirables . . . well, to get out. His girl's living with the Chief of Police now.'

'His girl? Do you mean his daughter?'

'He wasn't married. I mean the girl he lived with.' Mr Tench was momentarily surprised by an expression on the stranger's face. He said again, 'You know how it is.' He looked across at the *General Obregon*. 'She's a pretty bit. Of course, in two years she'll be like all the rest. Fat and stupid. O God, I'd like a drink. *Ora pro nobis*.'

'I have a little brandy,' the stranger said.

Mr Tench regarded him sharply. 'Where?'

The hollow man put his hand to his hip – he might have been

indicating the source of his odd nervous hilarity. Mr Tench seized his wrist. 'Careful,' he said. 'Not here.' He looked down the carpet of shadow: a sentry sat on an empty crate asleep beside his rifle. 'Come to my place,' Mr Tench said.

'I meant,' the little man said reluctantly, 'just to see her go.'

'Oh, it will be hours yet,' Mr Tench assured him again.

'Hours? Are you certain? It's very hot in the sun.'

'You'd better come home.'

Home: it was a phrase one used to mean four walls behind which one slept. There had never been a home. They moved across the little burnt plaza where the dead General grew green in the damp and the gaseosa stalls stood under the palms. Home lay like a picture postcard on a pile of other postcards: shuffle the pack and you had Nottingham, a Metroland birthplace, an interlude in Southend. Mr Tench's father had been a dentist too – his first memory was finding a discarded cast in a wastepaper basket – the rough toothless gaping mouth of clay, like something dug up in Dorset – Neanderthal or Pithecanthropus. It had been his favourite toy: they tried to tempt him with Meccano, but fate had struck. There is always one moment in childhood when the door opens and lets the future in. The hot wet river-port and the vultures lay in the wastepaper basket, and he picked them out. We should be thankful we cannot see the horrors and degradations lying around our childhood, in cupboards and bookshelves, everywhere.

There was no paving; during the rains the village (it was really no more) slipped into the mud. Now the ground was hard under the feet like stone. The two men walked in silence past barbers' shops and dentists'; the vultures on the roofs looked contented, like domestic fowls: they searched under wide dusty wings for parasites. Mr Tench said, 'Excuse me,' stopping at a little wooden hut, one storey high, with a veranda where a hammock swung. The hut was a little larger than the others in the narrow street which petered out two hundred yards away in swamp. He said, nervously, 'Would you like to take a look around? I don't want to boast, but I'm the best dentist here. It's not a bad place. As places go.' Pride wavered in his voice like a plant with shallow roots.

He led the way inside, locking the door behind him, through a dining-room where two rocking-chairs stood on either side of a bare table: an oil lamp, some copies of old American papers, a cupboard. He said, 'I'll get the glasses out, but first I'd like to show you – you're an educated man . . .' The dentist's operating-room looked out on a yard where a few turkeys moved with shabby nervous pomp: a drill which worked with a pedal, a dentist's chair gaudy in bright red plush, a glass cupboard in which instruments were dustily jumbled. A forceps stood in a cup, a broken spirit-lamp was pushed into a corner, and gags of cotton-wool lay on all the shelves.

'Very fine,' the stranger commented.

'It's not so bad, is it,' Mr Tench said, 'for this town. You can't imagine the difficulties. That drill,' he continued bitterly, 'is made in Japan. I've only had it a month and it's wearing out already. But I can't afford American drills.'

'The window,' the stranger said, 'is very beautiful.'

One pane of stained glass had been let in: a Madonna gazed out through the mosquito wire at the turkeys in the yard. 'I got it,' Mr Tench said, 'when they sacked the church. It didn't feel right – a dentist's room without some stained glass. Not civilized. At home – I mean in England – it was generally the Laughing Cavalier – I don't know why – or else a Tudor rose. But one can't pick and choose.'

He opened another door and said, 'My workroom.' The first thing one saw was a bed under a mosquito tent. Mr Tench said, 'You understand – I'm pressed for room.' A ewer and basin stood at one end of a carpenter's bench, and a soap-dish: at the other a blow-pipe, a tray of sand, pliers, a little furnace. 'I cast in sand,' Mr Tench said. 'What else can I do in this place?' He picked up the case of a lower jaw. 'You can't always get them accurate,' he said. 'Of course, they complain.' He laid it down, and nodded at another object on the bench – something stringy and intestinal in appearance, with two little bladders of rubber. 'Congenital fissure,' he said. 'It's the first time I've tried. The Kingsley cast. I doubt if I can do it. But a man must try to keep abreast of things.' His mouth fell open: the look of vacancy returned: the heat in the small room was overpowering. He stood there like a man lost in a cavern among the fossils and instruments of an age of which he knows very little. The stranger said, 'If we could sit down . . .'

Mr Tench stared at him blankly.

'We could open the brandy.'

'Oh yes, the brandy.'

Mr Tench got two glasses out of a cupboard under the bench, and wiped off traces of sand. Then they went and sat in rocking-chairs in the front room. Mr Tench poured out.

'Water?' the stranger asked.

'You can't trust the water,' Mr Tench said. 'It's got me here.' He put his hand on his stomach and took a long draught. 'You don't look too well yourself,' he said. He took a longer look. 'Your teeth.' One canine had gone, and the front teeth were yellow with tartar and carious. He said, 'You want to pay attention to them.'

'What is the good?' the stranger said. He held a small spot of brandy in his glass warily – as if it was an animal to which he gave shelter, but not trust. He had the air, in his hollowness and neglect, of somebody of no account who had been beaten up incidentally, by ill-health or restlessness. He sat on the very edge of the rocking-chair, with his small attaché case balanced on his knee and the brandy staved off with guilty affection.

'Drink up,' Mr Tench encouraged him (it wasn't his brandy). 'It will do you good.' The man's dark suit and sloping shoulders reminded him uncomfortably of a coffin, and death was in his carious mouth already. Mr Tench poured himself out another glass. He said, 'It gets lonely here. It's good to talk English, even to a foreigner. I wonder if you'd like to see a picture of my kids.' He drew a yellow snapshot out of his note-case and handed it over. Two small children struggled over the handle of a watering-can in a back garden. 'Of course,' he said, 'that was sixteen years ago.'

'They are young men now.'

'One died.'

'Oh, well,' the other replied gently, 'in a Christian country.' He took a gulp of his brandy and smiled at Mr Tench rather foolishly.

'Yes, I suppose so,' Mr Tench said with surprise. He got rid of his phlegm and said, 'It doesn't seem to me, of course, to matter much.' He fell silent, his thoughts ambling away; his mouth fell open, he looked grey and vacant, until he was recalled by a pain in the stomach and helped himself to some more brandy. 'Let me see. What was it we were talking about? The kids . . . oh yes, the kids. It's funny what a man remembers. You know, I can remember that watering-can better than I can remember the kids. It cost three and elevenpence three farthings, green; I could lead you to the shop where I bought it. But as for the kids,' he brooded over his glass into the past, 'I can't remember much else but them crying.'

'Do you get news?'

'Oh, I gave up writing before I came here. What was the use? I couldn't send any money. It wouldn't surprise me if the wife had married again. Her mother would like it – the old sour bitch: she never cared for me.'

The stranger said in a low voice, 'It is awful.'

Mr Tench examined his companion again with surprise. He sat there like a black question mark, ready to go, ready to stay, poised on his chair. He looked disreputable in his grey three-days' beard, and weak: somebody you could command to do anything. He said, 'I mean the world. The way things happen.'

'Drink up your brandy.'

He sipped at it. It was like an indulgence. He said, 'You remember this place before – before the Red Shirts came?'

'I suppose I do.'

'How happy it was then.'

'Was it? I didn't notice.'

'They had at any rate – God.'

'There's no difference in the teeth,' Mr Tench said. He gave himself some more of the stranger's brandy. 'It was always an awful place. Lonely. My God. People at home would have said romance. I thought: five years here, and then I'll go. There was plenty of work. Gold teeth. But then the peso dropped. And now I can't get out. One day I will.' He said, 'I'll retire. Go home. Live as a gentleman ought to live. This' – he gestured at the bare base room – 'I'll forget all this. Oh, it won't be long now. I'm an optimist,' Mr Tench said.

The stranger asked suddenly, 'How long will she take to Vera Cruz?'

'Who?'

'The boat.'

Mr Tench said gloomily, 'Forty hours from now and we'd be there. The Diligencia. A good hotel. Dance places too. A gay town.'

'It makes it seem close,' the stranger said. 'And a ticket, how much would that be?'

'You'd have to ask Lopez,' Mr Tench said. 'He's the agent.'

'But Lopez . . .'

'Oh yes, I forgot. They shot him.'

Somebody knocked on the door. The stranger slipped the attaché case under his chair, and Mr Tench went cautiously up towards the window. 'Can't be too careful,' he said. 'Any dentist who's worth the name has enemies.'

A faint voice implored them, 'A friend,' and Mr Tench opened up. Immediately the sun came in like a white-hot bar.

A child stood in the doorway asking for a doctor. He wore a big hat and had stupid brown eyes. Behind him two mules stamped and whistled on the hot beaten road. Mr Tench said he was not a doctor: he was a dentist. Looking round he saw the stranger crouched in the rocking-chair, gazing with an effect of prayer, entreaty . . . The child said there was a new doctor in town: the old one had fever and wouldn't stir. His mother was sick.

A vague memory stirred in Mr Tench's brain. He said with an air of discovery, 'Why, you're a doctor, aren't you?'

'No, no. I've got to catch that boat.'

'I thought you said . . .'

'I've changed my mind.'

'Oh well, it won't leave for hours yet,' Mr Tench said. 'They're never on time.' He asked the child how far. The child said it was six leagues away.

'Too far,' Mr Tench said. 'Go away. Find someone else.' He said to the stranger, 'How things get around. Everyone must know you are in town.'

'I could do no good,' the stranger said anxiously: he seemed to be asking for Mr Tench's opinion, humbly.

'Go away,' Mr Tench commanded. The child did not stir. He stood in the hard sunlight looking in with infinite patience. He said his mother was dying. The brown eyes expressed no emotion: it was a fact. You were born, your parents died, you grew old, you died yourself.

'If she's dying,' Mr Tench said, 'there's no point in a doctor seeing her.'

But the stranger got up as though unwillingly he had been summoned to an occasion he couldn't pass by. He said sadly, 'It always seems to happen. Like this.'

'You'll have a job not to miss the boat.'

'I shall miss it,' he said. 'I am meant to miss it.' He was shaken by a tiny rage. 'Give me my brandy.' He took a long pull at it, with his eyes on the impassive child, the baked street, the vultures moving in the sky like indigestion spots.

'But if she's dying . . .' Mr Tench said.

'I know these people. She will be no more dying than I am.'

'You can do no good.'

The child watched them as if he didn't care. The argument in a foreign language going on in there was something abstract: He wasn't concerned. He would just wait here till the doctor came.

'You know nothing,' the stranger said fiercely. 'That is what everyone says all the time – you do no good.' The brandy had affected him. He said with monstrous bitterness, 'I can hear them saying it all over the world.'

'Anyway,' Mr Tench said, 'there'll be another boat. In a fortnight. Or three weeks. You are lucky. You can get out. You haven't got your capital here.' He thought of his capital: the Japanese drill, the dentist's chair, the spirit-lamp and the pliers and the little oven for the gold fillings: a stake in the country.

'Vamos,' the man said to the child. He turned back to Mr Tench and told him that he was grateful for the rest out of the sun. He had the kind of dwarfed dignity Mr Tench was accustomed to – the dignity of people afraid of a little pain and yet sitting down with some firmness in his chair. Perhaps he didn't care for mule travel. He said with an effect of old-fashioned ways, 'I will pray for you.'

'You were welcome,' Mr Tench said. The man got up on to the mule, and the child led the way, very slowly under the bright glare, towards the swamp, the interior. It was from there the man had emerged this morning to take a look at the *General Obregon*: now he was going back. He swayed very slightly in his saddle from the effect of the brandy. He became a minute disappointed figure at the end of the street.

It had been good to talk to a stranger, Mr Tench thought, going back into his room, locking the door behind him (one never knew). Loneliness faced him there, vacancy. But he was as accustomed to both as to his own face in the glass. He sat down in the rocking-chair and moved up and down, creating a faint breeze in the heavy air. A narrow column of ants moved across the room to the little patch on the floor where the stranger had spilt some brandy: they milled in it, then moved on in an orderly line to the opposite wall and disappeared. Down in the river the *General Obregon* whistled twice, he didn't know why.

The stranger had left his book behind. It lay under his rocking-chair: a woman in Edwardian dress crouched sobbing upon a rug embracing a man's brown polished pointed shoes. He stood above her disdainfully with a little waxed moustache. The book was called *La Eterna Mártir*. After a time Mr Tench picked it up. When he opened it he was taken aback – what was printed inside didn't seem to belong; it was Latin. Mr Tench grew thoughtful: he shut the book up and carried it into his workroom. You couldn't burn a book, but it might be as well to hide it if you were not sure – sure, that is, of what it was all about. He put it inside the little oven for gold alloy. Then he stood by the carpenter's bench, his mouth hanging open: he had remembered what had taken him to the quay – the ether cylinder which should have come down-river in the *General Obregon*. Again the whistle blew from the river, and Mr Tench ran without his hat into the sun. He had said the boat would not go before morning, but you could never trust these people *not* to keep to time-table, and sure enough, when he came out on to the bank between the customs and the warehouse, the *General Obregon* was already ten feet off in the sluggish river, making for the sea. He bellowed after it, but it wasn't any good: there was no sign of a cylinder anywhere on the quay. He shouted once again, and then didn't trouble any more. It didn't matter so much after all: a little additional pain was hardly noticeable in the huge abandonment.

On the *General Obregon* a faint breeze became evident: banana plantations on either side, a few wireless aerials on a point, the port slipped behind. When you looked back you could not have told that it had ever existed at all. The wide Atlantic opened up; the great grey cylindrical waves lifted the bows, and the hobbled turkeys shifted on the deck. The captain stood in the tiny deck-house with a toothpick in his hair. The land went backward at a low even roll, and the dark came quite suddenly, with a sky of low and brilliant stars. One oil-lamp was lit in the bows, and the girl whom Mr Tench had spotted from the bank began to sing gently – a melancholy, sentimental, and contented song about a rose which had been stained with true love's blood. There was an enormous sense of freedom and air upon the gulf with the low tropical shoreline buried in darkness as deeply as any mummy in a tomb. I am happy, the young girl said to herself without considering why, I am happy.

Far back inside the darkness the mules plodded on. The effect of the brandy had long ago worn off, and the man bore in his brain along the marshy tract, which, when the rains came, would be quite impassable, the sound of the *General Obregon*'s siren. He knew what it meant: the ship had kept to timetable: he was abandoned. He felt an unwilling hatred of the child ahead of him and the sick woman – he was unworthy of what he carried. A smell of damp came up all round him; it was as if this part of the world had never been dried in the flame when the world spun off into space: it had absorbed only the mist and cloud of those awful regions. He began to pray, bouncing up and down to the lurching slithering mule's stride, with his brandied tongue: 'Let me be caught soon . . . Let me be caught.' He had tried to escape, but he was like the King of a West African tribe, the slave of his people, who may not even lie down in case the winds should fail.

Chapter 2: THE CAPITAL

THE squad of police made their way back to the station. They walked raggedly with rifles slung anyhow: ends of cotton where buttons should have been: a puttee slipping down over the ankle: small men with black secret Indian eyes. The little plaza on the hill-top was lighted with globes strung together in threes and joined by trailing overhead wires. The Treasury, the Presidencia, a dentist's, the prison – a low white colonnaded building which dated back three hundred years – and then the steep street down past the back wall of a ruined church: whichever way you went you came ultimately to water and to river. Pink classical façades peeled off and showed the mud beneath, and the mud slowly reverted to mud. Round the plaza the evening parade went on – women in one direction, men in the other; young men in red shirts milled boisterously round the gaseosa stalls.

The lieutenant walked in front of his men with an air of bitter distaste. He might have been chained to them unwillingly – perhaps the scar on his jaw was the relic of an escape. His gaiters were polished, and his pistol-holster: his buttons were all sewn on. He had a sharp crooked nose jutting out of a lean dancer's face; his neatness gave an effect of inordinate ambition in the shabby city. A sour smell came up to the plaza from the river and the vultures were bedded on the roofs, under the tent of their rough black wings. Sometimes, a little moron head peered out and down and a claw shifted. At nine-thirty exactly all the lights in the plaza went out.

A policeman clumsily presented arms and the squad marched into barracks; they waited for no order, hanging up their rifles by the officers' room, lurching on into the courtyard, to their hammocks or the excusados. Some of them kicked off their boots and lay down. Plaster was peeling off the mud walls; a generation of policemen had scrawled messages on the whitewash. A few peasants waited on a bench, hands between their knees. Nobody paid them any attention. Two men were fighting in the lavatory.

'Where is the jefe?' the lieutenant asked. No one knew for certain: they thought he was playing billiards somewhere in the town. The lieutenant sat down with dapper irritation at the chief's table; behind his head two hearts were entwined in pencil on the whitewash. 'All right,' he said, 'what are you waiting for? Bring in the prisoners.' They came in bowing, hat in hand, one behind the other. 'So-and-so drunk and disorderly.' 'Fined five pesos.' 'But I can't pay, your excellency.' 'Let him clean out the lavatory and the cells then.' 'So-and-so. Defaced an election poster.' 'Fined five pesos.' 'So-and-so found wearing a holy medal under his shirt.' 'Fined five pesos.' The duty drew to a close: there was nothing of importance. Through the open door the mosquitoes came whirring in.

Outside the sentry could be heard presenting arms. The Chief of Police came breezily in, a stout man with a pink fat face, dressed in white flannels with a wide-awake hat and a cartridge-belt and a big pistol clapping his thigh. He held a handkerchief to his mouth: he was in distress. 'Toothache again,' he said, 'toothache.'

'Nothing to report,' the lieutenant said with contempt.

'The Governor was at me again today,' the chief complained.

'Liquor?'

'No, a priest.'

'The last was shot weeks ago.'

'He doesn't think so.'

'The devil of it is,' the lieutenant said, 'we haven't photographs.' He glanced along the wall to the picture of James Calver, wanted in the United States for bank robbery and homicide: a tough uneven face taken at two angles: description circulated to every station in Central America: the low forehead and the fanatic bent-on-one-thing eyes. He looked at it with regret: there was so little chance that he would ever get south; he would be picked up in some dive at the border – in Juarez or Piedras Negras or Nogales.

'He says we have,' the chief complained. 'My tooth, oh, my tooth.' He tried to find something in his hip-pocket, but the holster got in the way. The lieutenant tapped his polished boot impatiently. 'There,' the chief said. A large number of people sat round a table: young girls in white muslin: older women with untidy hair and harassed expressions: a few men peered shyly and solicitously out of the background. All the faces were made up of small dots. It was a newspaper photograph of a first communion party taken years ago; a youngish man in a Roman collar sat among the women. You could imagine him petted with small delicacies, preserved for their use in the stifling atmosphere of intimacy and respect. He sat there, plump, with protuberant eyes, bubbling with harmless feminine jokes. 'It was taken years ago.'

'He looks like all the rest,' the lieutenant said. It was obscure, but you could read into the smudgy photograph a well-shaved, well-powdered jowl much too developed for his age. The good things of life had come to him too early – the respect of his contemporaries, a safe livelihood. The trite religious word upon the tongue, the joke to ease the way, the ready acceptance of other people's homage . . . a happy man. A natural hatred as between dog and dog stirred in the lieutenant's bowels. 'We've shot him half a dozen times,' he said.

'The Governor has had a report . . . he tried to get away last week to Vera Cruz.'

'What are the Red Shirts doing that he comes to *us*?'

'Oh, they missed him, of course. It was just luck that he didn't catch the boat.'

'What happened to him?'

'They found his mule. The Governor says he must have him this month. Before the rains come.'

'Where was his parish?'

'Concepción and the villages around. But he left there years ago.'

'Is anything known?'

'He can pass as a gringo. He spent six years at some American seminary. I don't know what else. He was born in Carmen – the son of a storekeeper. Not that that helps.'

'They all look alike to me,' the lieutenant said. Something you could almost have called horror moved him when he looked at the white muslin dresses – he remembered the smell of incense in the churches of his boyhood, the candles and the laciness and the self-esteem, the immense demands made from the altar steps by men who didn't know the meaning of sacrifice. The old peasants knelt there before the holy images with their arms held out in the attitude of the cross: tired by the long day's labour in the plantations they squeezed out a further mortification. And the priest came round with the collecting-bag taking their centavos, abusing them for their small comforting sins, and sacrificing nothing at all in return – except a little sexual indulgence. And that was easy, the lieutenant thought, easy. Himself he felt no need of women. He said, 'We will catch him. It is only a question of time.'

'My tooth,' the chief wailed again. He said, 'It poisons the whole of life. Today my biggest break was twenty-five.'

'You will have to change your dentist.'

'They are all the same.'

The lieutenant took the photograph and pinned it on the wall. James

Calver, bank robber and homicide, stared in harsh profile towards the first communion party. 'He is a man at any rate,' the lieutenant said with approval.

'Who?'

'The gringo.'

The chief said, 'You heard what he did in Houston. Got away with ten thousand dollars. Two G men were shot.'

'G men?'

'It's an honour – in a way – to deal with such people.' He slapped furiously out at a mosquito.

'A man like that,' the lieutenant said, 'does no real harm. A few men dead. We all have to die. The money – somebody has to spend it. We do more good when we catch one of these.' He had the dignity of an idea, standing in the little whitewashed room with his polished boots and his venom. There was something disinterested in his ambition: a kind of virtue in his desire to catch the sleek respected guest of the first communion party.

The chief said mournfully, 'He must be devilishly cunning if he's been going on for years.'

'Anybody could do it,' the lieutenant said. 'We haven't really troubled about them – unless they put themselves in our hands. Why, I could guarantee to fetch this man in, inside a month if . . .'

'If what?'

'If I had the power.'

'It's easy to talk,' the chief said. 'What would you do?'

'This is a small state. Mountains on the north, the sea on the south. I'd beat it as you beat a street, house by house.'

'Oh, it sounds easy,' the chief moaned indistinctly with his handkerchief against his mouth.

The lieutenant said suddenly, 'I will tell you what I'd do. I would take a man from every village in the state as a hostage. If the villagers didn't report the man when he came, the hostage would be shot – and then we'd take another.'

'A lot of them would die, of course.'

'Wouldn't it be worth it?' the lieutenant demanded. 'To be rid of those people for ever.'

'You know,' the chief said, 'you've got something there.'

The lieutenant walked home through the shuttered town. All his life had lain here: the Syndicate of Workers and Peasants had once been a school. He had helped to wipe out that unhappy memory. The whole town was changed: the cement playground up the hill near the cemetery where iron swings stood like gallows in the moony darkness was the site of the cathedral. The new children would have new memories: nothing would ever be as it was. There was something of a priest in his intent observant walk – a theologian going back over the errors of the past to destroy them again.

He reached his own lodging. The houses were all one-storeyed, whitewashed, built round small patios, with a well and a few flowers. The windows on the street were barred. Inside the lieutenant's room there was a bed made of old packing-cases with a straw mat laid on top, a cushion and a sheet. There was a picture of the President on the wall, a calendar, and on the tiled floor a table and a rocking-chair. In the light of a candle it looked as comfortless as a prison or a monastic cell.

The lieutenant sat down upon his bed and began to take off his boots. It was the hour of prayer. Black-beetles exploded against the walls like crackers. More than a dozen crawled over the tiles with injured wings. It infuriated him to think that there were still people in the state who believed in a loving and merciful God. There are mystics who are said to have experienced God directly. He was a mystic, too, and what he had experienced was vacancy – a complete certainty in the existence of a dying, cooling world, of human beings who had evolved from animals for no purpose at all. He knew.

He lay down in his shirt and breeches on the bed and blew out the candle. Heat stood in the room like an enemy. But he believed against the evidence of his senses in the cold empty ether spaces. A radio was playing somewhere: music from Mexico City, or perhaps even from London or New York, filtered into this obscure neglected state. It seemed to him like a weakness: this was his own land, and he would have walled it in if he could with steel until he had eradicated from it everything which reminded him of how it had once appeared to a miserable child. He wanted to destroy everything: to be alone without any memories at all. Life began five years ago.

The lieutenant lay on his back with his eyes open while the beetles detonated on the ceiling. He remembered the priest the Red Shirts had shot against the wall of the cemetery up the hill, another little fat man with popping eyes. He was a monsignor, and he thought that would protect him. He had a sort of contempt for the lower clergy, and right up to the last he was explaining his rank. Only at the very end had he remembered his prayers. He knelt down and they had given him time for a short act of contrition. The lieutenant had watched: he wasn't directly concerned. Altogether they had shot about five priests – two or three had escaped, the bishop was safely in Mexico City, and one man had conformed to the Governor's law that all priests must marry. He lived now near the river with his housekeeper. That, of course, was the best solution of all, to leave the living witness to the weakness of their faith. It showed the deception they had practised all these years. For if they really believed in heaven or hell, they wouldn't mind a little pain now, in return for what immensities . . . The lieutenant, lying on his hard bed, in the damp hot dark, felt no sympathy at all with the weakness of the flesh.

In the back room of the Academia Commercial a woman was reading to her family. Two small girls of six and ten sat on the edge of their bed, and a boy of fourteen leant against the wall with an expression of intense weariness.

'Young Juan,' the mother read, 'from his earliest years was noted for his humility and piety. Other boys might be rough and revengeful; young Juan followed the precept of Our Lord and turned the other cheek. One day his father thought that he had told a lie and beat him. Later he learnt that his son had told the truth, and he apologized to Juan. But Juan said to him, "Dear father, just as our Father in heaven has the right to chastise when he pleases . . ."'

The boy rubbed his face impatiently against the whitewash and the mild voice droned on. The two little girls sat with beady intense eyes, drinking in the sweet piety.

'We must not think that young Juan did not laugh and play like other children, though there were times when he would creep away with a holy picture-book to his father's cow-house from a circle of his merry playmates.'

The boy squashed a beetle with his bare foot and thought gloomily that after all everything had an end – some day they would reach the last chapter and young Juan would die against a wall shouting, '*Viva el Christo Rey*.' But then, he supposed, there would be another book; they were smuggled in every month from Mexico City: if only the customs men had known where to look.

'No, young Juan was a true young Mexican boy, and if he was more thoughtful than his fellows, he was also always the first when any play-acting was afoot. One year his class acted a little play before the bishop, based on the persecution of the early Christians, and no one was more amused than Juan when he was chosen to play the part of Nero. And what comic spirit he put into his acting – this child, whose young manhood was to be cut short by a ruler far worse than Nero. His class-mate, who later became Father Miguel Cerra, S.J., writes: "None of us who were there will ever forget that day . . ."'

One of the little girls licked her lips secretively. This was life.

'The curtain rose on Juan wearing his mother's best bathrobe, a charcoal moustache and a crown made from a tin biscuit-box. Even the good old bishop smiled when Juan strode to the front of the little home-made stage and began to declaim . . .'

The boy strangled a yawn against the whitewashed wall. He said wearily, 'Is he really a saint?'

'He will be, one day soon, when the Holy Father pleases.'

'And are they all like that?'

'Who?'

'The martyrs.'

'Yes. All.'

'Even Padre José?'

'Don't mention him,' the mother said. 'How dare you? That despicable man. A traitor to God.'

'He told me he was more of a martyr than the rest.'

'I've told you many times not to speak to him. My dear child, oh, my dear child . . .'

'And the other one – the one who came to see us?'

'No, he is not – exactly – like Juan.'

'Is he despicable?'

'No, no. Not despicable.'

The smallest girl said suddenly, 'He smelt funny.'

The mother went on reading: 'Did any premonition touch young Juan that night that he, too, in a few short years, would be numbered among the martyrs? We cannot say, but Father Miguel Cerra tells how that evening Juan spent longer than usual upon his knees, and when his class-mates teased him a little, as boys will . . .'

The voice went on and on, mild and deliberate, inflexibly gentle; the small girls listened intently, framing in their minds little pious sentences with which to surprise their parents, and the boy yawned against the whitewash. Everything has an end.

Presently the mother went in to her husband. She said, 'I am so worried about the boy.'

'Why not about the girls? There is worry everywhere.'

'They are two little saints already. But the boy – he asks such questions – about that whisky priest. I wish we had never had him in the house.'

'They would have caught him if we hadn't, and then he would have been one of your martyrs. They would write a book about him and you would read it to the children.'

'That man – never.'

'Well, after all,' her husband said, 'he carries on. I don't believe all that they write in these books. We are all human.'

'You know what I heard today? About a poor woman who took to him her son to be baptized. She wanted him called Pedro – but he was drunk that he took no notice at all and baptized the boy Brigitta. Brigitta!'

'Well, it's a good saint's name.'

'There are times,' the mother said, 'when I lose all patience with you. And now the boy has been talking to Padre José.'

'This is a small town,' her husband said. 'And there is no use pretending. We have been abandoned here. We must get along as best we can. As for the Church – the Church is Padre José and the whisky priest – I don't know of any other. If we don't like the Church, well, we must leave it.'

He watched her with patience. He had more education than his wife; he could use a typewriter and knew the elements of book-keeping: once he had been to Mexico City: he could read a map. He knew the extent of their abandonment – the ten hours down-river to the port, the forty-two hours on the Gulf to Vera Cruz – that was one way out. To the north the swamps and rivers petering out against the mountains which divided them from the next state. And on the other side no roads – only mule-tracks and an occasional unreliable plane: Indian villages and the huts of herds: two hundred miles away, the Pacific.

She said, 'I would rather die.'

'Oh,' he said, 'of course. That goes without saying. But we have to go on living.'

The old man sat on a packing-case in the little dry patio. He was very fat and short of breath; he panted a little as if after great exertion in the heat. Once he had been something of an astronomer and now he tried to pick out the constellations, staring up into the night sky. He wore only a shirt and trousers; his feet were bare, but there remained something unmistakably clerical in his manner. Forty years of the priesthood had branded him. There was complete silence over the town: everybody was asleep.

The glittering worlds lay there in space like a promise – the world was not the universe. Somewhere Christ might not have died. He could not believe that to a watcher there *this* world could shine with such brilliance: it would roll heavily in space under its fog like a burning and abandoned ship. The whole globe was blanketed with his own sin.

A woman called from the only room he possessed, 'José, José.' He crouched like a galley-slave at the sound; his eyes left the sky, and the constellations fled upwards: the beetles crawled over the patio. 'José, José.' He thought with envy of the men who had died: it was over so soon. They were taken up there to the cemetery and shot against the wall: in two minutes life was extinct. And they called that martyrdom. Here life went on and on; he was only sixty-two. He might live to ninety. Twenty-eight years – that immeasurable period between his birth and his first parish: all childhood and youth and the seminary lay there.

'José. Come to bed.' He shivered: he knew that he was a buffoon. An old man who married was grotesque enough, but an old priest . . . He stood outside himself and wondered whether he was even fit for hell. He was just a fat old impotent man mocked and taunted between the sheets. But then he remembered the gift he had been given which nobody could take away. That was what made him worthy of damnation – the power he still had of turning the wafer into the flesh and blood of God. He was a sacrilege. Wherever he went, whatever he did, he defiled God. Some mad renegade Catholic, puffed up with the Governor's politics, had once broken into a church (in the days when there were still churches) and seized the Host. He had spat on it, trampled it, and then the people had got him and hung him as they did the stuffed Judas on Holy Thursday from the belfry. He wasn't so bad a man, Padre José thought – he would be forgiven, he was just a politician; but he himself, he was worse than that – he was like an obscene picture hung here every day to corrupt children with.

He belched on his packing-case shaken by wind. 'José. What are you doing? You come to bed.' There was never anything to do at all – no daily Office, no Masses, no Confessions, and it was no good praying any longer at all: a prayer demanded an act and he had no intention of acting. He had lived for two years now in a continuous state of mortal sin with no one to hear his Confession: nothing to do at all but to sit and eat – eat far too much; she fed him and fattened him and preserved him like a prize boar. 'José.' He began to hiccup with nerves at the thought of facing for the seven hundred and thirty-eighth time his harsh housekeeper – his wife. There she would be lying in the big shameless bed that filled half the room, a bony shadow within the mosquito-tent, a lanky jaw and a short grey pigtail and an absurd bonnet. She thought she had a position to keep up: a Government pensioner: the wife of the only married priest. She was proud of it. 'José.' 'I'm – hic – coming, my love,' he said and lifted himself from the crate. Somebody somewhere laughed.

He lifted little pink eyes like those of a pig conscious of the slaughter-room. A high child's voice said, 'José.' He stared in a bewildered way around the patio. At a barred window opposite three children watched him with deep gravity. He turned his back and took a step or two towards his door, moving very slowly because of his bulk. 'José,' somebody squeaked again. 'José.' He looked back over his shoulder and caught the faces out in expressions of wild glee; his little pink eyes showed no anger – he had no right to be angry: he moved his mouth into a ragged, baffled, disintegrated smile, and as if that sign of weakness gave them all the licence they needed, they squealed back at him without disguise, 'José, José. Come to bed, José.' Their little shameless voices filled the patio, and he smiled humbly and sketched small gestures for silence, and there was no respect anywhere left for him in his home, in the town, in the whole abandoned star.

Chapter 3: THE RIVER

CAPTAIN FELLOWS sang loudly to himself, while the little motor chugged in the bows of the canoe. His big sunburned face was like the map of a mountain region – patches of varying brown with two small blue lakes that were his eyes. He composed his songs as he went, and his voice was quite tuneless. 'Going home, going home, the food will be good for me-e-e. I don't like the food in the bloody citee.' He turned out of the main stream into a tributary: a few alligators lay on the sandy margin. 'I don't like your snouts, O trouts. I don't like your snouts, O trouts.' He was a happy man.

The banana plantations came down on either bank: his voice boomed under the hard sun: that and the churr of the motor were the only sounds anywhere – he was completely alone. He was borne up on a big tide of boyish joy – doing a man's job, the heart of the wild: he felt no responsibility for anyone. In only one other country had he felt more happy, and that was in wartime France, in the ravaged landscape of trenches. The tributary cork-screwed farther into the marshy overgrown state, and a vulture lay spread out in the sky; Captain Fellows opened a tin box and ate a sandwich – food never tasted so good as out of doors. A monkey made a sudden chatter at him as he went by, and Captain Fellows felt happily at one with nature – a wide shallow kinship with all the world moved with the blood-stream through the veins: he was at home anywhere. The artful little devil, he thought, the artful little devil. He began to sing again – somebody else's words a little jumbled in his friendly unretentive memory. 'Give to me the life I love, bread I dip in the river, under the wide and starry sky, the hunter's home from the sea.' The plantations petered out, and far behind the mountains came into view, heavy black lines drawn low-down across the sky. A few bungalows rose out of the mud. He was home. A very slight cloud marred his happiness.

He thought: after all, a man likes to be welcomed.

He walked up to his bungalow; it was distinguished from the others which lay along the bank by a tiled roof, a flagpost without a flag, a plate on the door with the title 'Central American Banana Company'. Two hammocks were strung up on the veranda, but there was nobody about. Captain Fellows knew where to find his wife. He burst boisterously through a door and shouted, 'Daddy's home.' A scared thin face peeked at him through a mosquito-net; his boots ground peace into the floor; Mrs Fellows flinched away into the white muslin tent. He said, 'Pleased to see me, Trix?' and she drew rapidly on her face the outline of her frightened welcome. It was like a trick you do with a blackboard. Draw a dog in one line without lifting the chalk – and the answer, of course, is a sausage.

'I'm glad to be home,' Captain Fellows said, and he believed it. It was his one firm conviction – that he really felt the correct emotions of love and joy and grief and hate. He had always been a good man at zero hour.

'All well at the office?'

'Fine,' Fellows said, 'fine.'

'I had a bit of fever yesterday.'

'Ah, you need looking after. You'll be all right now,' he said vaguely, 'that I'm home.' He shied merrily away from the subject of fever – clapping his hands, a big laugh, while she trembled in her tent. 'Where's Coral?'

'She's with the policeman,' Mrs Fellows said.

'I hoped she'd meet me,' he said, roaming aimlessly about the little interior room, full of boot-trees, while his brain caught up with her. 'Policeman? What policeman?'

'He came last night and Coral let him sleep on the veranda. He's looking for somebody, she says.'

'What an extraordinary thing. *Here?*'

'He's not an ordinary policeman. He's an officer. He left his men in the village – Coral says.'

'I do think you ought to be up,' he said. 'I mean – these fellows, you can't trust them.' He felt no conviction when he added, 'She's just a kid.'

'I tell you I had fever,' Mrs Fellows wailed, 'I felt so terribly ill.'

'You'll be all right. Just a touch of the sun. You'll see – now *I'm* home.'

'I had such a headache. I couldn't read or sew. And then this man . . .'

Terror was always just behind her shoulder: she was wasted by the effort of not turning round. She dressed up her fear, so that she could look at it – in the form of fever, rats, unemployment. The real thing was taboo – death coming nearer every year in the strange place: everybody packing up and leaving, while she stayed in a cemetery no one visited, in a big above-ground tomb.

He said, 'I suppose I ought to go and see the man.' He sat down on the bed and put his hand upon her arm. They had something in common – a kind of diffidence. He said absent-mindedly, 'That dago secretary of the boss has gone.'

'Where?'

'West.' He could feel her arm go stiff: she strained away from him towards the wall. He had touched the taboo – the bond was broken, he couldn't tell why. 'Headache, darling?'

'Hadn't you better see the man?'

'Oh yes, yes. I'll be off.' But he didn't stir: it was the child who came to him.

She stood in the doorway watching them with a look of immense responsibility. Before her serious gaze they became a boy you couldn't trust and a ghost you could almost puff away, a piece of frightened air. She was very young – about thirteen – and at that age you are not afraid of many things, age and death, all the things which may turn up, snake-bite and fever and rats and a bad smell. Life hadn't got at her yet; she had a false air of impregnability. But she had been reduced already, as it were, to the smallest terms – everything was there but on the thinnest lines. That was what the sun did to a child, reduced it to a framework. The gold bangle on the bony wrist was like a padlock on a canvas door which a fist could break. She said, 'I told the policeman you were home.'

'Oh yes, yes,' Captain Fellows said. 'Got a kiss for your old dad?'

She came solemnly across the room and kissed him formally upon the forehead – he could feel the lack of meaning. She had other things to think about. She said, 'I told cook that Mother would not be getting up for dinner.'

'I think you ought to make the effort, dear,' Captain Fellows said.

'Why?' Coral asked.

'Oh, well . . .'

Coral said, 'I want to talk to you alone.' Mrs Fellows shifted inside her tent. Common sense was a horrifying quality she had never possessed: it was common sense which said, 'The dead can't hear' or 'She can't know now' or 'Tin flowers are more practical'.

'I don't understand,' Captain Fellows said uneasily, 'why your mother shouldn't hear.'

'She wouldn't want to. It would only scare her.'

Coral – he was accustomed to it by now – had an answer to everything. She never spoke without deliberation; she was prepared – but sometimes the answers she had prepared seemed to him of a wildness . . . They were based on the only life she could remember, the swamp and vultures and no children anywhere, except a few in the village with bellies swollen by worms who ate dirt from the bank, inhumanly. A child is said to draw parents together, and certainly he felt an immense unwillingness to entrust himself to this child. Her answers might carry him anywhere. He felt through the net for his wife's hand, secretively: they were adults together. This was the stranger in their house. He said boisterously, 'You're frightening us.'

'I don't think,' the child said, with care, 'that *you'll* be frightened.'

He said weakly, pressing his wife's hand, 'Well, my dear, our daughter seems to have decided . . .'

'First you must see the policeman. I want him to go. I don't like him.'

'Then he must go, of course,' Captain Fellows said, with a hollow unconfident laugh.

'I told him that. I said we couldn't refuse him a hammock for the night when he arrived so late. But now he must go.'

'And he disobeyed you?'

'He said he wanted to speak to you.'

'He little knew,' Captain Fellows said, 'he little knew.' Irony was his only defence, but it was not understood; nothing was understood which was not clear – like an alphabet or a simple sum or a date in history. He relinquished his wife's hand and allowed himself to be led unwillingly into the afternoon sun. The police officer stood in front of the veranda, a motionless olive figure; he wouldn't stir a foot to meet Captain Fellows.

'Well, lieutenant?' Captain Fellows said breezily. It occurred to him that Coral had more in common with the policeman than with himself.

'I am looking for a man,' the lieutenant said. 'He has been reported in this district.'

'He can't be here.'

'Your daughter tells me the same.'

'She knows.'

'He is wanted on a very serious charge.'

'Murder?'

'No. Treason.'

'Oh, treason,' Captain Fellows said, all his interest dropping; there was so much treason everywhere – it was like petty larceny in a barracks.

'He is a priest. I trust you will report at once if he is seen.' The lieutenant paused. 'You are a foreigner living under the protection of our laws. We expect you to make a proper return for our hospitality. You are not a Catholic?'

'No.'

'Then I can trust you to report?' the lieutenant said.

'I suppose so.'

The lieutenant stood there like a little dark menacing question-mark in the sun: his attitude seemed to indicate that he wouldn't even accept the benefit of shade from a foreigner. But he had used a hammock; that, Captain Fellows supposed, he must have regarded as a requisition. 'Have a glass of gaseosa?'

'No. No, thank you.'

'Well,' Captain Fellows said, 'I can't offer you anything else, can I? It's treason to drink spirits.'

The lieutenant suddenly turned on his heel as if he could no longer bear the sight of them and strode away along the path which led to the village: his gaiters and his pistol holster winked in the sunlight. When he had gone some way they could see him pause and spit; he had not been discourteous, he had waited till he supposed that they no longer watched him before he got rid of his hatred and contempt for a different way of life, for ease, safety, toleration, and complacency.

'I wouldn't want to be up against him,' Captain Fellows said.

'Of course he doesn't trust us.'

'They don't trust anyone.'

'I think,' Coral said, 'he smelt a rat.'

'They smell them everywhere.'

'You see, I wouldn't let him search the place.'

'Why ever not?' Captain Fellows asked, and then his vague mind went off at a tangent. 'How did you stop him?'

'I said I'd loose the dogs on him – and complain to the Minister. He hadn't any right . . .'

'Oh, right,' Captain Fellows said. 'They carry their right on their hips. It wouldn't have done any harm to let him look.'

'I gave him my word.' She was as inflexible as the lieutenant: small and black and out of place among the banana groves. Her candour made allowances for nobody: the future, full of compromises, anxieties, and shame, lay outside. But at any moment now a word, a gesture, the most trivial act might be her sesame – to what? Captain Fellows was touched with fear; he was aware of an inordinate love which robbed him of authority. You cannot control what you love – you watch it driving recklessly towards the broken bridge, the torn-up track, the horror of seventy years ahead. He closed his eyes – he was a happy man – and hummed a tune.

Coral said, 'I shouldn't have liked a man like that to catch me out – lying, I mean.'

'Lying? Good God,' Captain Fellows said, 'you don't mean he's here.'

'Of course he's here,' Coral said.

'Where?'

'In the big barn,' she explained gently. 'We couldn't let them catch him.'

'Does your mother know about this?'

She said with devastating honesty, 'Oh no. I couldn't trust *her*.' She was independent of both of them: they belonged together in the past. In forty years' time they would be dead as last year's dog. He said, 'You'd better show me.'

He walked slowly; happiness drained out of him more quickly and completely than out of an unhappy man: an unhappy man is always prepared. As she walked in front of him, her two meagre tails of hair bleaching in the sunlight, it occurred to him for the first time that she was of an age when Mexican girls were ready for their first man. What was to happen? He flinched away from problems which he had never dared to confront. As they passed the window of his bedroom he caught sight of a thin shape lying bunched and bony and alone in a mosquito-net. He remembered with self-pity and nostalgia his happiness on the river, doing a man's job without thinking of other people. If I had never married . . . He wailed like a child at the merciless immature back, 'We've no business interfering with politics.'

'This isn't politics,' she said gently. 'I know about politics. Mother and I are doing the Reform Bill.' She took a key out of her pocket and unlocked the big barn in which they stored bananas before sending them down the river to the port. It was very dark inside after the glare. There was a scuffle in a corner. Captain Fellows picked up an electric torch and shone it on somebody in a torn dark suit – a small man who blinked and needed a shave.

'*Quién es usted?*' Captain Fellows said.

'I speak English.' He clutched a small attaché case to his side, as if he were waiting to catch a train he must on no account miss.

'You've no business here.'

'No,' the man said, 'no.'

'It's nothing to do with us,' Captain Fellows said. 'We are foreigners.'

The man said, 'Of course. I will go.' He stood with his head a little bent like a man in an orderly-room listening to an officer's decision. Captain Fellows relented a little. He said, 'You'd better wait till dark. You don't want to be caught.'

'No.'

'Hungry?'

'A little. It does not matter.' He said with a rather repulsive humility, 'If you would do me a favour . . .'

'What?'

'A little brandy.'

'I'm breaking the law enough for you as it is,' Captain Fellows said. He strode out of the barn, feeling twice the size, leaving the small bowed figure in the darkness among the bananas. Coral locked the door and followed him. 'What a religion,' Captain Fellows said. 'Begging for brandy. Shameless.'

'But you drink it somctimes.'

'My dear,' Captain Fellows said, 'when you are older you'll understand the difference between drinking a little brandy after dinner and – well, needing it.'

'Can I take him some beer?'

'*You* won't take him anything.'

'The servants wouldn't be safe.'

He was powerless and furious. He said, 'You see what a hole you've put us in.' He stumped back into the house and into his bedroom, roaming aimlessly among the boot-trees. Mrs Fellows slept uneasily, dreaming of weddings. Once she said aloud, 'My train. Be careful of my train.'

'What's that?' he asked petulantly. 'What's that?'

Dark fell like a curtain: one moment the sun was there, the next it had gone. Mrs Fellows woke to another night. 'Did you speak, dear?'

'It was you who spoke,' he said. 'Something about trains.'

'I must have been dreaming.'

'It will be a long time before they have trains here,' he said, with gloomy satisfaction. He came and sat on the bed, keeping away from the window; out of sight, out of mind. The crickets were beginning to chatter and beyond the mosquito wire fireflies moved like globes. He put his heavy, cheery, needing-to-be-reassured hand on the shape under the sheet and said, 'It's not such a bad life, Trixy. Is it now? Not a bad life?' But he could feel her stiffen: the word 'life' was taboo: it reminded you of death. She turned her face away from him towards the wall and then hopelessly back again – the phrase 'turn to the wall' was taboo too. She lay panic-stricken, while the boundaries of her fear widened to include every relationship and the whole world of inanimate things: it was like an infection. You could look at nothing for long without becoming aware that it, too, carried the germ . . . the word 'sheet' even. She threw the sheet off her and said, 'It's so hot, it's so hot.' The usually happy and the always unhappy one watched the night thicken from the bed with distrust. They were companions cut off from all the world: there was no meaning anywhere outside their own hearts: they were carried like children in a coach through the huge spaces without any knowledge of their destination. He began to hum with desperate cheerfulness a song of the war years; he wouldn't listen to the footfall in the yard outside, going in the direction of the barn.

Coral put down the chicken legs and tortillas on the ground and unlocked the door. She carried a bottle of Cerveza Moctezuma under her arm. There was the same scuffle in the dark: the noise of a frightened man. She said, 'It's me,' to quieten him, but she didn't turn on the torch. She said, 'There's a bottle of beer here, and some food.'

'Thank you. Thank you.'

'The police have gone from the village – south. You had better go north.'

He said nothing.

She asked, with the cold curiosity of a child, 'What would they do to you if they found you?'

'Shoot me.'

'You must be very frightened,' she said with interest.

He felt his way across the barn towards the door and the pale starlight. He said, 'I *am* frightened,' and stumbled on a bunch of bananas.

'Can't you escape from here?'

'I tried. A month ago. The boat was leaving and then I was summoned.'

'Somebody needed you?'

'She didn't need me,' he said bitterly. She could just see his face now, as the world swung among the stars: what her father would call an untrustworthy face. He said, 'You see how unworthy I am. Talking like this.'

'Unworthy of what?'

He clasped his little attaché case closely and said, 'Could you tell me what month it is. Is it still February?'

'No. It's the seventh of March.'

'I don't often meet people who know. That means another month – six weeks – before the rains.' He went on, 'When the rains come I am nearly safe. You see, the police can't get about.'

'The rains are best for you?' she asked: she had a keen desire to learn. The Reform Bill and Senlac and a little French lay like treasure-trove in her brain. She expected answers to every question, and she absorbed them hungrily.

'Oh no, no. They mean another six months living like this.' He tore at a chicken leg. She could smell his breath: it was disagreeable, like something which has lain about too long in the heat. He said, 'I'd rather be caught.'

'But can't you,' she said logically, 'just give yourself up?'

He had answers as plain and understandable as her questions. He said, 'There's the pain. To choose pain like that – it's not possible. And it's my duty not to be caught. You see, my bishop is no longer here.' Curious pedantries moved him. 'This is my parish.' He found a tortilla and began to eat ravenously.

She said solemnly. 'It's a problem.' She could hear a gurgle as he drank out of the bottle. He said, 'I try to remember how happy I was once.' A firefly lit his face like a torch and then went out – a tramp's face: what could ever have made it happy? He said, 'In Mexico City now they are saying Benediction. The Bishop's there . . . Do you imagine he ever thinks . . . ? They don't even know I'm alive.'

She said, 'Of course you could – renounce.'

'I don't understand.'

'Renounce your faith,' she explained, using the words of her European History.

He said, 'It's impossible. There's no way. I'm a priest. It's out of my power.'

The child listened intently. She said, 'Like a birthmark.' She could hear him sucking desperately at the bottle. She said, 'I think I could find my father's brandy.'

'Oh no, you mustn't steal.' He drained the beer: a long glassy whistle in the darkness: the last drop must have gone. He said, 'I must leave. At once.'

'You can always come back here.'

'Your father would not like it.'

'He needn't know,' she said. 'I could look after you. My room is just opposite this door. You would just tap at my window. Perhaps,' she went seriously on, 'it would be better to have a code. You see, somebody else might tap.'

He said in a horrified voice, 'Not a man?'

'Yes. You never know. Another fugitive from justice.'

'Surely,' he asked in bewilderment, 'that is not likely?'

She said airily, 'These things do happen.'

'Before today?'

'No, but I expect they will again. I want to be prepared. You must tap three times. Two long taps and a short one.'

He giggled suddenly like a child. 'How do you tap a long tap?'

'Like this.'

'Oh, you mean a loud one?'

'I call them long taps – because of Morse.' He was hopelessly out of his depth. He said, 'You are very good. Will you pray for me?'

'Oh,' she said, 'I don't believe in that.'

'Not in praying?'

'You see, I don't believe in God. I lost my faith when I was ten.'

'Well, well,' he said. 'Then I will pray for you.'

'You can,' she said patronizingly, 'if you like. If you come again I shall teach you the Morse code. It would be useful to you.'

'How?'

'If you were hiding in the plantation I could flash to you with my mirror news of the enemy's movements.'

He listened seriously. 'But wouldn't they see you?'

'Oh,' she said, 'I would invent an explanation.' She moved logically forward a step at a time, eliminating all objections.

'Good-bye, my child,' he said.

He lingered by the door. 'Perhaps – you do not care for prayers. Perhaps you would like . . . I know a good conjuring trick.'

'I like tricks.'

'You do it with cards. Have you any cards?'

'No.'

He sighed, 'Then that's no good,' and giggled – she could smell the beer on his breath – 'I shall just have to pray for you.'

She said, 'You don't sound afraid.'

'A little drink,' he said, 'will work wonders in a cowardly man. With a little brandy, why, I'd defy – the devil.' He stumbled in the doorway.

'Good-bye,' she said. 'I hope you'll escape.' A faint sigh came out of the darkness. She said gently, 'If they kill you I shan't forgive them – ever.' She was ready to accept any responsibility, even that of vengeance, without a second thought. It was her life.

Half a dozen huts of mud and wattle stood in a clearing; two were in ruins. A few pigs routed round, and an old woman carried a burning ember from hut to hut, lighting a little fire on the centre of each floor to fill the hut with smoke and keep mosquitoes away. Women lived in two of the huts, the pigs in another; in the last unruined hut where maize was stored, an old man and a boy and a tribe of rats. The old man stood in the clearing watching the fire being carried round; it flickered through the darkness like a ritual repeated at the same hour for a lifetime. White hair, a white stubbly beard, and hands brown and fragile as last year's leaves, he gave an effect of immense permanence. Living on the edge of subsistence nothing much could ever change him. He had been old for years.

The stranger came into the clearing. He wore what used to be town shoes, black and pointed; only the uppers were left, so that he walked to all intents barefoot. The shoes were symbolic, like the cobwebbed flags in churches. He wore a shirt and a pair of black torn trousers and he carried his attaché case, as if he were a season-ticket holder. He had nearly reached the state of permanency too, but he carried about with him the scars of time – the damaged shoes implied a different past, the lines of his face suggested hopes and fears of the future. The old woman with the ember stopped between two huts and watched him. He came on into the clearing with his eyes on the ground and his shoulders hunched, as if he felt exposed. The old man advanced to meet him; he took the stranger's hand and kissed it.

'Can you let me have a hammock for the night?'

'Ah, father, for a hammock you must go to a town. Here you must take only the luck of the road.'

'Never mind. Anywhere to lie down. Can you give me – a little spirit?'

'Coffee, father. We have nothing else.'

'Some food.'

'We have no food.'

'Never mind.'

The boy came out of the hut and watched them: everybody watched. It was like a bull-fight. The animal was tired and they waited for the next move. They were not hard-hearted; they were watching the rare spectacle of something worse off than themselves. He limped on towards the hut. Inside it was dark from the knees upwards; there was no flame on the floor, just a slow burning away. The place was half filled by a stack of maize, and rats rustled among the dry outer leaves. There was a bed made of earth with a straw mat on it, and two packing-cases made a table. The stranger lay down, and the old man closed the door on them both.

'Is it safe?'

'The boy will watch. He knows.'

'Were you expecting me?'

'No, father. But it is five years since we have seen a priest . . . it was bound to happen one day.'

He fell uneasily asleep, and the old man crouched on the floor, fanning the fire with his breath. Somebody tapped on the door and the priest jerked upright. 'It is all right,' the old man said. 'Just your coffee, father.' He brought it to him – grey maize coffee smoking in a tin mug, but the priest was too tired to drink. He lay on his side perfectly still: a rat watched him from the maize.

'The soldiers were here yesterday,' the old man said. He blew on the fire. The smoke poured up and filled the hut. The priest began to cough, and the rat moved quickly like the shadow of a hand into the stack.

'The boy, father, has not been baptized. The last priest who was here wanted two pesos. I had only one peso. Now I have only fifty centavos.'

'Tomorrow,' the priest said wearily.

'Will you say Mass, father, in the morning?'

'Yes, yes.'

'And confession, father, will you hear our confessions?'

'Yes, but let me sleep first.' He turned on his back and closed his eyes to keep out the smoke.

'We have no money, father, to give you. The other priest, Padre José . . .'

'Give me some clothes instead,' he said impatiently.

'But we have only what we wear.'

'Take mine in exchange.'

The old man hummed dubiously to himself, glancing sideways at what the fire showed of the black torn cloth. 'If I must, father,' he said. He blew quietly at the fire for a few minutes. The priest's eyes closed again.

'After five years there is so much to confess.'

The priest sat up quickly. 'What was that?' he said.

'You were dreaming, father. The boy will warn us if the soldiers come. I was only saying –'

'Can't you let me sleep for five minutes?' He lay down again. Somewhere, in one of the women's huts, someone was singing – 'I went down to my field and there I found a rose.'

The old man said softly, 'It would be a pity if the soldiers came before we had time . . . such a burden on poor souls, father . . .' The priest shouldered himself upright against the wall and said furiously, 'Very well. Begin. I will hear your confession.' The rats scuffled in the maize. 'Go on then,' he said. 'Don't waste time. Hurry. When did you last . . . ?' The old man knelt beside the fire, and across the clearing the woman sang: 'I went down to my field and the rose was withered.'

'Five years ago.' He paused and blew at the fire. 'It's hard to remember, father.'

'Have you sinned against purity?'

The priest leant against the wall with his legs drawn up beneath him, and the rats accustomed to the voices moved again in the maize. The old man picked out his sins with difficulty, blowing at the fire. 'Make a good act of contrition,' the priest said, 'and say – say – have you a rosary? – then say the Joyful Mysteries.' His eyes closed, his lips and tongue stumbled over the absolution, failed to finish . . . he sprang awake again.

'Can I bring the women?' the old man was saying. 'It is five years . . .'

'Oh, let them come. Let them all come,' the priest cried angrily. 'I am your servant.' He put his hand over his eyes and began to weep. The old man opened the door: it was not completely dark outside under the enormous arc of starry ill-lit sky. He went across to the women's huts and knocked. 'Come,' he said. 'You must say your confessions. It is only polite to the father.' They wailed at him that they were tired . . . the morning would do. 'Would you insult him?' he said. 'What do you think he has come here for? He is a very holy father. There he is in my hut now weeping for our sins.' He hustled them out; one by one they picked their way across the clearing towards the hut, and the old man set off down the path towards the river to take the place of the boy who watched the ford for soldiers.

Chapter 4: The Bystanders

It was years since Mr Tench had written a letter. He sat before the work-table sucking at a steel nib; an odd impulse had come to him to project this stray letter towards the last address he had – in Southend. Who knew who was alive still? He tried to begin. It was like breaking the ice at a party where you knew nobody. He started to write the envelope – Mrs Henry Tench, care of Mrs Marsdyke, 3 The Avenue, Westcliff. It was her mother's house: the dominating interfering creature who had induced him to set up his place in Southend for a fatal while. 'Please forward,' he wrote. She wouldn't do it if she knew, but she had probably forgotten his handwriting by this time.

He sucked the inky nib – how to go on? It would have been easier if there had been some purpose behind it other than the vague desire to put on record to somebody that he was still alive. It might prove awkward if she had married again, but in that case she wouldn't hesitate to tear the letter up. He wrote: *Dear Sylvia*, in a big clear immature script, listening to the furnace purring on the bench. He was making a gold alloy – there were no depots here where he could buy his material ready-made. Besides, the depots didn't favour 14-carat gold for dental work, and he couldn't afford finer material.

The trouble was – nothing ever happened here. His life was as sober, respectable, regular as even Mrs Marsdyke could require.

He took a look at the crucible. The gold was on the point of fusion with the alloy, so he flung in a spoonful of vegetable charcoal to protect the mixture from the air, took up his pen again and sat mooning over the paper. He couldn't remember his wife clearly – only the hats she wore. How surprised she would be at hearing from him after this long while; there had been one letter written by each of them since the little boy died. The years really meant nothing to him – they drifted fairly rapidly by without changing a habit. He had meant to leave six years ago, but the peso dropped with a revolution, and so he had come south. Now he had more money saved, but a month ago the peso dropped again – another revolution somewhere. There was nothing to do but wait . . . the nib went back between his teeth and memory melted in the little hot room. Why write at all? He couldn't remember now what had given him the odd idea. Somebody knocked at the outer door and he left the letter on the bench – *Dear Sylvia*, staring up, big and bold and hopeless. A boat's bell rang by the riverside: it was the *General Obregon* back from Vera Cruz. A memory stirred. It was as if something alive and in pain moved in the little front room among the rocking-chairs – 'an interesting afternoon: what happened to him, I wonder, when' – then died, or got away. Mr Tench was used to pain: it was his profession. He waited cautiously till a hand beat on the door again and a voice said, '*Con amistad*' – there was no trust anywhere – before he drew the bolts and opened up, to admit a patient.

Padre José went in, under the big classical gateway marked in black letters 'Silencio' to what people used to call the Garden of God. It was like a building estate where nobody had paid attention to the architecture of the next house. The big stone tombs of above-ground burial were any height and any shape; sometimes an angel stood on the roof with lichenous wings: sometimes through a glass window you could see some rusting metal flowers upon a shelf – it was like looking into the kitchen of a house whose owners have moved on, forgetting to clean the vases out. There was a sense of intimacy – you could go anywhere and see anything. Life here had withdrawn altogether.

He walked very slowly because of his bulk among the tombs; he could be alone here, there were no children about, and he could waken a faint sense of homesickness which was better than no feeling at all. He had buried some of these people. His small inflamed eyes turned here and there. Coming round the huge grey bulk of the Lopez tomb – a merchant family which fifty years ago had owned the only hotel in the capital – he found he was not alone. A grave was being dug at the edge of the cemetery next to the wall: two men were rapidly at work: a woman stood by and an old man. A child's coffin lay at their feet – it took no time at all in the spongy soil to get down far enough. A little water collected. That was why those who could afford it lay above ground.

They all paused a moment and looked at Padre José, and he sidled back towards the Lopez tomb as if he were an intruder. There was no sign of grief anywhere in the bright hot day: a vulture sat on a roof outside the cemetery. Somebody said, 'Father.'

Padre José put up his hand deprecatingly as if he were trying to indicate that he was not there, that he was gone, away, out of sight.

The old man said, 'Padre José.' They all watched him hungrily; they had been quite resigned until he had appeared, but now they were anxious, eager . . . He ducked and dodged away from them. 'Padre José,' the old man repeated. 'A prayer?' They smiled at him, waiting. They were quite accustomed to people dying, but an unforeseen hope of happiness had bobbed up among the tombs: they could boast after this that one at least of their family had gone into the ground with an official prayer.

'It's impossible,' Padre José said.

'Yesterday was her saint's day,' the woman said, as if that made a difference. 'She was five.' She was one of those garrulous women who show to strangers the photographs of their children, but all she had to show was a coffin.

'I am sorry.'

The old man pushed the coffin aside with his foot the better to approach Padre José; it was small and light and might have contained nothing but bones. 'Not a whole service, you understand – just a prayer. She was – innocent,' he said. The word in the little stony town sounded odd and archaic and local, outdated like the Lopez tomb, belonging only here.

'It is against the law.'

'Her name,' the woman went on, 'was Anita. I was sick when I had her,' she explained, as if to excuse the child's delicacy which had led to all this inconvenience.

'The law . . .'

The old man put his finger to his nose. 'You can trust us. It is just the case of a short prayer. I am her grandfather. This is her mother, her father, her uncle. You can trust us.'

But that was the trouble – he could trust no one. As soon as they got back home one or other of them would certainly begin to boast. He walked backwards all the time, weaving his plump fingers, shaking his head, nearly bumping into the Lopez tomb. He was scared, and yet a curious pride bubbled in his throat because he was being treated as a priest again, with respect. 'If I could,' he said, 'my children . . .'

Suddenly and unexpectedly there was agony in the cemetery. They had been used to losing children, but they hadn't been used to what the rest of the world knows best of all – the hope which peters out. The woman began to cry, dryly, without tears, the trapped noise of something wanting to be released; the old man fell on his knees with his hands held out. 'Padre José,' he said, 'there is no one else . . .' He looked as if he were asking for a miracle. An enormous temptation came to Padre José to take the risk and say a prayer over the grave. He felt the wild attraction of doing one's duty and stretched a sign of the cross in the air; then fear came back, like a drug. Contempt and safety waited for him down by the quay: he wanted to get away. He sank hopelessly down on his knees and entreated them: 'Leave me alone.' He said, 'I am unworthy. Can't you see? – I am a coward.' The two old men faced each other on their knees among the tombs, the small coffin shoved aside like a pretext – an absurd spectacle. He knew it was absurd: a lifetime of self-analysis enabled him to see himself as he was, fat and ugly and old and humiliated. It was as if a whole seducing choir of angels had silently withdrawn and left the voices of the children in the patio – 'Come to bed, José, come to bed,' sharp and shrill and worse than they had ever been. He knew he was in the grip of the unforgivable sin, despair.

'At last the blessed day arrived,' the mother read aloud, 'when the days of Juan's novitiate were over. Oh, what a joyful day was that for his mother and sisters. And a little sad too, for the flesh cannot always be strong, and how could they help mourning a while in their hearts for the loss of a small son and an elder brother? Ah, if they had known that they were gaining that day a saint in heaven to pray for them.'

The younger girl on the bed said, 'Have *we* got a saint?'

'Of course.'

'Why did they want another saint?'

The mother went on reading: 'Next day the whole family received communion from the hands of a son and brother. Then they said a fond good-bye – they little knew that it was the last – to the new soldier of Christ and returned to their homes in Morelos. Already clouds were darkening the heavens, and President Calles was discussing the anti-Catholic laws in the Palace at Chapultepec. The devil was ready to assail poor Mexico.'

'Is the shooting going to begin soon?' the boy asked, moving restlessly against the wall. His mother went relentlessly on: 'Juan unknown to all but his confessor was preparing himself for the evil days ahead with the most rigorous mortifications. His companions suspected nothing, for he was always the heart and soul of every merry conversation, and on the feast-day of the founder of the Order it was he . . .'

'I know, I know,' the boy said. 'He acted a play.'

The little girls opened astounded eyes.

'And why not, Luis?' the mother said, pausing with her finger on the prohibited book. He stared sullenly back at her. 'And why not, Luis?' she repeated. She waited a while, and then read on; the little girls watched their brother with horror and admiration. 'It was he,' she said, 'who obtained permission to perform a little one-act play founded on . . .'

'I know, I know,' the boy said, 'the catacombs.'

The mother, compressing her lips, continued: '. . . the persecution of the early Christians. Perhaps he remembered that occasion in his boyhood when he acted Nero before the good old bishop, but this time he insisted on taking the comic part of a Roman fishmonger . . .'

'I don't believe a word of it,' the boy said, with sullen fury, 'not a word of it.'

'How dare you!'

'Nobody could be such a fool.'

The little girls sat motionless, their eyes large and brown and pious.

'Go to your father.'

'Anything to get away from this – this –' the boy said.

'Tell him what you've told me.'

'This . . .'

'Leave the room.'

He slammed the door behind him. His father stood at the barred window of the *sala*, looking out; the beetles detonated against the oil-lamp and crawled with broken wings across the stone floor. The boy said, 'My mother told me to tell you that I told her that I didn't believe that the book she's reading . . .'

'What book?'

'The holy book.'

He said sadly, 'Oh that.' Nobody passed in the street, nothing happened; it was after nine-thirty and all the lights were out. He said, 'You must make allowances. For us, you know, everything seems over. That book – it is like our own childhood.'

'It sounds so silly.'

'You don't remember the time when the Church was here. I was a bad Catholic, but it meant – well, music, lights, a place where you could sit out of this heat – and for your mother, well, there was always something for her to do. If we had a theatre, anything at all instead, we shouldn't feel so – left.'

'But this Juan,' the boy said. 'He sounds so silly.'

'He was killed, wasn't he?'

'Oh, so were Villa, Obregon, Madero . . .'

'Who tells you about them?'

'We all of us play them. Yesterday I was Madero. They shot me in the plaza – the law of flight.' Somewhere in the heavy night a drum beat. The sour river smell filled the room: it was familiar like the taste of soot in cities. 'We tossed up. I was Madero: Pedro had to be Huerta. He fled to Vera Cruz down by the river. Manuel chased him – he was Carranza.' His father struck a beetle off his shirt, staring into the street: the sound of marching feet came nearer. He said, 'I suppose your mother's angry.'

'You aren't,' the boy said.

'What's the good? It's not your fault. We have been deserted.'

The soldiers went by, returning to barracks, up the hill near what had once been the cathedral; they marched out of step in spite of the drum-beat, they looked undernourished, they hadn't yet made much of war. They passed lethargically by in the dark street and the boy watched them out of sight with excited and hopeful eyes.

Mrs Fellows rocked backwards and forwards, backwards and forwards. 'And so Lord Palmerston said if the Greek Government didn't do right to Don Pacifico . . .' She said, 'My darling, I've got such a headache I think we must stop today.'

'Of course. I have a little one too.'

'I expect yours will be better soon. Would you mind putting the books away?' The little shabby books had come by post from a firm in Paternoster Row called Private Tutorials, Ltd – a whole education which began with 'Reading Without Tears' and went methodically on to the Reform Bill and Lord Palmerston and the poems of Victor Hugo. Once every six months an examination paper was delivered, and Mrs Fellows laboriously worked through the answers and awarded marks. These she sent back to Paternoster Row, and there, weeks later, they were filed: once she had forgotten her duty when there was shooting in Zapata, and had received a printed slip beginning: 'Dear Parent, I regret to see . . .' The trouble was they were years ahead of schedule by now – there were so few other books to read – and so the examination papers were years behind. Sometimes the firm sent embossed certificates for framing, announcing that Miss Coral Fellows had passed third with honours into the second grade, signed with a rubber stamp Henry Beckley, B.A., Director of Private Tutorials, Ltd, and sometimes there would be little personal letters typewritten, with the same blue smudgy signature, saying: *Dear Pupil, I think you should pay more attention this week to . . .* The letters were always six weeks out of date.

'My darling,' Mrs Fellows said, 'will you see the cook and order lunch? Just yourself. I can't eat a thing, and your father's out on the plantation.'

'Mother,' the child said, 'do you believe there's a God?'

The question scared Mrs Fellows. She rocked furiously up and down and said, 'Of course.'

'I mean the Virgin Birth – and everything.'

'My dear, what a thing to ask. Who have you been talking to?'

'Oh,' she said. 'I've been thinking, that's all.' She didn't wait for any further answer; she knew quite well there would be none – it was always her job to make decisions. Henry Beckley, B.A., had put it all into an early lesson – it hadn't been any more difficult to accept then than the giant at the top of the beanstalk, and at the age of ten she had discarded both relentlessly. By that time she was starting algebra.

'Surely your father hasn't . . .'

'Oh no.'

She put on her sun-helmet and went out into the blazing ten o'clock heat to find the cook – she looked more fragile than ever and more indomitable. When she had given her orders she went to the warehouse to inspect the alligator skins tacked out on a wall, then to the stables to see that the mules were in good shape. She carried her responsibilities carefully like crockery across the hot yard: there was no question she wasn't prepared to answer; the vultures rose languidly at her approach.

She returned to the house and her mother. She said, 'It's Thursday.'

'Is it, dear?'

'Hasn't father got the bananas down to the quay?'

'I'm sure I don't know, dear.'

She went briskly back into the yard and rang a bell. An Indian came. No, the bananas were still in the store; no orders had been given. 'Get them down,' she said, 'at once, quickly. The boat will be here soon.' She fetched her father's ledger and counted the bunches as they were carried out – a hundred bananas or more to a bunch which was worth a few pence. It took more than two hours to empty the store; somebody had got to do the work, and once before her father had forgotten the day. After half an hour she began to feel tired – she wasn't used to weariness so early in the day. She leant against the wall and it scorched her shoulder-blades. She felt no resentment at all at being there, looking after things: the word 'play' had no meaning to her at all – the whole of life was adult. In one of Henry Beckley's early reading-books there had been a picture of a doll's tea-party: it was incomprehensible like a ceremony she hadn't learned: she couldn't see the point of pretending. Four hundred and fifty-six. Four hundred and fifty-seven. The sweat poured down the peons' bodies steadily like a shower-bath. An awful pain took her suddenly in the stomach – she missed a load and tried to catch up in her calculations: she felt the sense of responsibility for the first time like a load borne for too many years. Five hundred and twenty-five. It was a new pain (not worms this time), but it didn't scare her; it was as if her body had expected it, had grown up to it, as the mind grows up to the loss of tenderness. You couldn't call it childhood draining out of her: of childhood she had never really been conscious.

'Is that the last?' she said.

'Yes, señorita.'

'Are you sure?'

'Yes, señorita.'

But she had to see for herself. Never before had it occurred to her to do a job unwillingly – if she didn't do a thing nobody would – but today she wanted to lie down, to sleep: if all the bananas didn't get away it was her father's fault. She wondered whether she had fever, her feet felt so cold on the hot ground. Oh well, she thought, and went patiently into the barn, found the torch, and switched it on. Yes, the place seemed empty enough, but she never left a job half done. She advanced towards the back wall, holding the torch in front of her. An empty bottle rolled away – she dropped the light on it: Cerveza Moctezuma. Then the torch lit the back wall: low down near the ground somebody had scrawled in chalk – she came closer: a lot of little crosses leant in the circle of light. He must have lain down among the bananas and tried to relieve his fear by writing something, and this was all he could think of. The child stood in her woman's pain and looked at them: a horrible novelty enclosed her whole morning: it was as if today everything were memorable.

The Chief of Police was in the cantina playing billiards when the lieutenant found him. He had a handkerchief tied all round his face with some idea that it relieved the toothache. He was chalking his cue for a difficult shot as the lieutenant pushed through the swing door. On the shelves behind were nothing but gaseosa bottles and a yellow liquid called Sidral – warranted non-alcoholic. The lieutenant stood protestingly in the doorway. The situation was ignoble; he wanted to eliminate anything in the state at which a foreigner might have cause to sneer. He said, 'Can I speak to you?' The jefe winced at a sudden jab of pain and came with unusual alacrity towards the door; the lieutenant glanced at the score, marked in rings strung on a cord across the room – the jefe was losing. 'Back – moment,' the jefe said, and explained to the lieutenant, 'Don't want open mouth.' As they pushed the door somebody raised a cue and surreptitiously pushed back one of the jefe's rings.

They walked up the street side by side, the fat one and the lean. It was a Sunday and all the shops closed at noon – that was the only relic of the old time. No bells rang anywhere. The lieutenant said, 'Have you seen the Governor?'

'You can do anything,' the jefe said, 'anything.'

'He leaves it to us?'

'On conditions,' he winced.

'What are they?'

'He'll hold you – responsible – if – not caught before – rains.'

'As long as I'm not responsible for anything else . . . .' the lieutenant said moodily.

'You asked for it. You got it.'

'I'm glad.' It seemed to the lieutenant that all the world he cared about now lay at his feet. They passed the new hall built for the Syndicate of Workers and Peasants: through the window they could see the big bold clever murals – of one priest caressing a woman in the confessional, another tippling on the sacramental wine. The lieutenant said, 'We will soon make these unnecessary.' He looked at the pictures with the eye of a foreigner: they seemed to him barbarous.

'One day they'll forget there ever was a Church here.'

The jefe said nothing. The lieutenant knew he was thinking, what a fuss about nothing. He said sharply, 'Well, what are my orders?'

'Orders?'

'You are my chief.'

The jefe was silent. He studied the lieutenant unobtrusively with little astute eyes. Then he said, 'You know I trust you. Do what you think best.'

'Will you put that in writing?'

'Oh – not necessary. We know each other.'

All the way up the road they fenced warily for positions.

'Didn't the Governor give you anything in writing?' the lieutenant asked.

'No. He said we knew each other.'

It was the lieutenant who gave way because it was he who really cared. He was indifferent to his personal future. He said, 'I shall take hostages from every village.'

'Then he won't stay in the villages.'

'Do you imagine,' the lieutenant asked bitterly, 'that they don't know where he is? He has to keep some touch – or what good is he?'

'Just as you like,' the jefe said.

'And I shall shoot as often as it's necessary.'

The jefe said with facetious brightness, 'A little blood never hurt anyone. Where will you start?'

'His parish, I think, Concepción, and then – perhaps – his home.'

'Why there?'

'He may think he's safe there.' He brooded past the shuttered shops. 'It's worth a few deaths, but will *he*, do you think, support me if they make a fuss in Mexico City?'

'It isn't likely, is it?' the jefe said. 'But it's what –' he was stopped by a stab of pain.

'It's what I wanted,' the lieutenant said for him.

He made his way on alone towards the police station, and the chief went back to billiards. There were few people about; it was too hot. If only, he thought, we had a proper photograph – he wanted to know the features of his enemy. A swarm of children had the plaza to themselves. They were playing some obscure and intricate game from bench to bench. An empty gaseosa bottle sailed through the air and smashed at the lieutenant's feet. His hand went to his holster and he turned; he caught a look of consternation on a boy's face.

'Did you throw that bottle?'

The heavy brown eyes stared sullenly back at him.

'What were you doing?'

'It was a bomb.'

'Were you throwing it at me?'

'No.'

'What then?'

'A gringo.'

The lieutenant smiled – an awkward movement of the lips. 'That's right, but you must aim better.' He kicked the broken bottle into the road and tried to think of words which would show these children that they were on the same side. He said, 'I suppose the gringo was one of those rich Yankees . . .' and surprised an expression of devotion in the boy's face; it called for something in return, and the lieutenant became aware in his own heart of a sad and unsatisfiable love. He said, 'Come here.' The child approached, while his companions stood in a scared semicircle and watched from a safe distance. 'What is your name?'

'Luis.'

'Well,' the lieutenant said, at a loss for words, 'you must learn to aim properly.'

The boy said passionately, 'I wish I could.' He had his eye on the holster.

'Would you like to see my gun?' the lieutenant asked. He pulled his heavy automatic from the holster and held it out: the children drew cautiously in. He said, 'This is the safety-catch. Lift it. So. Now it's ready to fire.'

'Is it loaded?' Luis asked.

'It's always loaded.'

The tip of the boy's tongue appeared: he swallowed. Saliva came from the glands as if he smelt food. They all stood close in now. A daring child put out his hand and touched the holster. They ringed the lieutenant round: he was surrounded by an insecure happiness as he fitted the gun back on his hip.

'What is it called?' Luis asked.

'A Colt ·38.'

'How many bullets?'

'Six.'

'Have you killed somebody with it?'

'Not yet,' the lieutenant said.

They were breathless with interest. He stood with his hand on his holster and watched the brown intent patient eyes: it was for these he was fighting. He would eliminate from their childhood everything which had made him miserable, all that was poor, superstitious, and corrupt. They deserved nothing less than the truth – a vacant universe and a cooling world, the right to be happy in any way they chose. He was quite prepared to make a massacre for their sakes – first the Church and then the foreigner and then the politician – even his own chief would one day have to go. He wanted to begin the world again with them, in a desert.

'Oh,' Luis said, 'I wish . . . I wish . . .' as if his ambition were too vast for definition. The lieutenant put out his hand in a gesture of affection – a touch, he didn't know what to do with it. He pinched the boy's ear and saw him flinch away with the pain; they scattered from him like birds and he went on alone across the plaza to the police station, a little dapper figure of hate carrying his secret of love. On the wall of the office the gangster still stared stubbornly in profile towards the first communion party. Somebody had inked round the priest's head to detach him from the girls' and the women's faces: the unbearable grin peeked out of a halo. The lieutenant called furiously out into the patio, 'Is there nobody here?' Then he sat down at the desk while the gun-butts scraped the floor.

PART TWO

Chapter 1

THE mule suddenly sat down under the priest. It was not an unnatural thing to do, for they had been travelling through the forest for nearly twelve hours. They had been going west, but news of soldiers met them there and they had turned east; the Red Shirts were active in that direction, so they had tacked north, wading through the swamps, diving into the mahogany darkness. Now they were both tired out and the mule simply sat down. The priest scrambled off and began to laugh. He was feeling happy. It is one of the strange discoveries a man can make that life, however you lead it, contains moments of exhilaration; there are always comparisons which can be made with worse times: even in danger and misery the pendulum swings.

He came cautiously out of the belt of trees into a marshy clearing. The whole state was like that, river and swamp and forest. He knelt down in the late sunlight and bathed his face in a brown pool which reflected back at him like a piece of glazed pottery the round, stubbly and hollow features. They were so unexpected that he grinned at them – with the shy evasive untrustworthy smile of a man caught out. In the old days he often practised a gesture a long while in front of a glass so that he had come to know his own face as well as an actor does. It was a form of humility – his own natural face hadn't seemed the right one. It was a buffoon's face, good enough for mild jokes to women, but unsuitable at the altar-rail. He had tried to change it – and indeed, he thought, indeed I have succeeded, they'll never recognize me now, and the cause of his happiness came back to him like the taste of brandy, promising temporary relief from fear, loneliness, a lot of things. He was being driven by the presence of soldiers to the very place where he most wanted to be. He had avoided it for six years, but now it wasn't his fault – it was his duty to go there – it couldn't count as sin. He went back to his mule and kicked it gently, 'Up, mule, up,' a small gaunt man in torn peasant's clothes going for the first time in many years, like any ordinary man, to his home.

In any case, even if he could have gone south and avoided the village, it was only one more surrender. The years behind him were littered with similar surrenders – feast days and fast days and days of abstinence had been the first to go: then he had ceased to trouble more than occasionally about his breviary – and finally he had left it behind altogether at the port in one of his periodic attempts at escape. Then the altar stone went – too dangerous to carry with him. He had no business to say Mass without it; he was probably liable to suspension, but penalties of the ecclesiastical kind began to seem unreal in a state where the only penalty was the civil one of death. The routine of his life like a dam was cracked and forgetfulness came dribbling through, wiping out this and that. Five years ago he had given way to despair – the unforgivable sin – and he was going back now to the scene of his despair with a curious lightening of the heart. For he had got over despair too. He was a bad priest, he knew it. They had a word for his kind – a whisky priest, but every failure dropped out of sight and mind: somewhere they accumulated in secret – the rubble of his failures. One day they would choke up, he supposed, altogether the source of grace. Until then he carried on, with spells of fear, weariness, with a shamefaced lightness of heart.

The mule splashed across the clearing and they entered the forest again. Now that he no longer despaired it didn't mean, of course, that he wasn't damned – it was simply that after a time the mystery became too great, a damned man putting God into the mouths of men: an odd sort of servant, that, for the devil. His mind was full of a simplified mythology: Michael dressed in armour slew a dragon, and the angels fell through space like comets with beautiful streaming hair because they were jealous, so one of the Fathers had said, of what God intended for men – the enormous privilege of life – this life.

There were signs of cultivation; stumps of trees and the ashes of fires where the ground was being cleared for a crop. He stopped beating the mule on; he felt a curious shyness . . . A woman came out of a hut and watched him lagging up the path on the tired mule. The tiny village, not more than two dozen huts round a dusty plaza, was made to pattern, but it was a pattern which lay close to his heart. He felt secure – he was confident of a welcome, confident that in this place there would be at least one person he could trust not to betray him to the police. When he was quite close the mule sat down again – this time he had to roll on the ground to escape. He picked himself up and the woman watched him as if he were an enemy. 'Ah, Maria,' he said, 'and how are you?'

'Well,' she exclaimed, 'it is you, father?'

He didn't look directly at her: his eyes were sly and cautious. He said, 'You didn't recognize me?'

'You've changed.' She looked him up and down with a kind of contempt. She said, 'When did you get those clothes, father?'

'A week ago.'

'What did you do with yours?'

'I gave them in exchange.'

'Why? They were good clothes.'

'They were very ragged – and conspicuous.'

'I'd have mended them and hidden them away. It's a waste. You look like a common man.'

He smiled, looking at the ground, while she chided him like a housekeeper: it was just as in the old days when there was a presbytery and meetings of the Children of Mary and all the guilds and gossip of a parish, except of course that . . . He said gently, not looking at her, with the same embarrassed smile, 'How's Brigitta?' His heart jumped at the name: a sin may have enormous consequences: it was six years since he had been – home.

'She's as well as the rest of us. What did you expect?'

He had his satisfaction, but it was connected with his crime; he had no business to feel pleasure at anything attached to that past. He said mechanically, 'That's good,' while his heart beat with its secret love. He said, 'I'm very tired. The police were about near Zapata . . .'

'Why didn't you make for Monte Cristo?'

He looked quickly up with anxiety. It wasn't the welcome that he had expected; a small knot of people had gathered between the huts and watched him from a safe distance – there was a little decaying bandstand and a single stall for gaseosas – people had brought their chairs out for the evening. Nobody came forward to kiss his hand and ask his blessing. It was as if he had descended by means of his sin into the human struggle to learn other things besides despair and love, that a man can be unwelcome even in his own home. He said, 'The Red Shirts were there.'

'Well, father,' the woman said, 'we can't turn you away. You'd better come along.' He followed her meekly, tripping once in the long peon's trousers, with the happiness wiped off his face and the smile somehow left behind like the survivor of a wreck. There were seven or eight men, two women, half a dozen children: he came among them like a beggar. He couldn't help remembering the last time . . . the excitement, the gourds of spirit brought out of holes in the ground . . . his guilt had still been fresh, yet how he had been welcomed. It was as if he had returned to them in their vicious prison as one of themselves – an émigré who comes back to his native place enriched.

'This is the father,' the woman said. Perhaps it was only that they hadn't recognized him, he thought, and waited for their greetings. They came forward one by one and kissed his hand and then stood back and watched him. He said, 'I am glad to see you . . .' he was going to say 'my children', but then it seemed to him that only the childless man has the right to call strangers his children. The real children were coming up now to kiss his hand, one by one, under the pressure of their parents. They were too young to remember the old days when the priests dressed in black and wore Roman collars and had soft superior patronizing hands; he could see they were mystified at the show of respect to a peasant like their parents. He didn't look at them directly, but he was watching them closely all the same. Two were girls – a thin washed-out child – of five, six, seven? he couldn't tell, and one who had been sharpened by hunger into an appearance of devilry and malice beyond her age. A young woman stared out of the child's eyes. He watched them disperse again, saying nothing: they were strangers.

One of the men said, 'Will you be here long, father?'

He said, 'I thought, perhaps . . . I could rest . . . a few days.'

One of the other men said, 'Couldn't you go a bit farther north, father, to Pueblito?'

'We've been travelling for twelve hours, the mule and I.'

The woman suddenly spoke for him, angrily, 'Of course he'll stay here tonight. It's the least we can do.'

He said, 'I'll say Mass for you in the morning,' as if he were offering them a bribe, but it might almost have been stolen money from their expressions of shyness and unwillingness.

Somebody said, 'If you don't mind, father, very early . . . in the night perhaps.'

'What is the matter with you all?' he asked. 'Why should you be afraid?'

'Haven't you heard . . . ?'

'Heard?'

'They are taking hostages now – from all the villages where they think you've been. And if people don't tell . . . somebody is shot . . . and then they take another hostage. It happened in Concepción.'

'Concepción?' One of his lids began to twitch up and down, up and down. He said, 'Who?' They looked at him stupidly. He said furiously, 'Who did they murder?'

'Pedro Montez.'

He gave a little yapping cry like a dog's – the absurd short-hand of grief. The old-young child laughed. He said, 'Why don't they catch me? The fools. Why don't they catch *me*?' The little girl laughed again; he stared at her sightlessly, as if he could hear the sound but couldn't see the face. Happiness was dead again before it had had time to breathe; he was like a woman with a stillborn child – bury it quickly and forget and begin again. Perhaps the next would live.

'You see, father,' one of the men said, 'why . . .'

He felt as a guilty man does before his judges. He said 'Would you rather that I was like . . . like Padre José in the capital . . . you have heard of him . . . ?'

They said unconvincingly, 'Of course not that, father.'

He said, 'What am I saying now? It's not what you want or what I want.' He continued sharply, with authority, 'I will sleep now . . . You can wake me an hour before dawn . . . half an hour to hear your confessions . . . then Mass, and I will be gone.'

But where? There wouldn't be a village in the state to which he wouldn't be an unwelcome danger now.

The woman said, 'This way, father.'

He followed her into a small room where all the furniture had been made out of packing-cases – a chair, a bed of boards tacked together and covered with a straw mat, a crate on which a cloth had been laid and on the cloth an oil-lamp. He said, 'I don't want to turn anybody out of here.'

'It's mine.'

He looked at her doubtfully. 'Where will you sleep?' He was afraid of claims. He watched her covertly: was this all there was in marriage, this evasion and suspicion and lack of ease? When people confessed to him in terms of passion, was this all they meant – the hard bed and the busy woman and the not talking about the past?

'When you are gone.'

The light flattened out behind the forest and the long shadows of the trees pointed towards the door. He lay down upon the bed, and the woman busied herself somewhere out of sight: he could hear her scratching at the earth floor. He couldn't sleep. Had it become his duty then to run away? He had tried to escape several times, but he had always been prevented . . . now they wanted him to go. Nobody would stop him, saying a woman was ill or a man dying. He was a sickness now.

'Maria,' he said. 'Maria, what are you doing?'

'I have saved a little brandy for you.'

He thought: if I go, I shall meet other priests: I shall go to confession: I shall feel contrition and be forgiven: eternal life will begin for me all over again. The Church taught that it was every man's first duty to save his own soul. The simple ideas of hell and heaven moved in his brain; life without books, without contact with educated men, had peeled away from his memory everything but the simplest outline of the mystery.

'There,' the woman said. She carried a small medicine bottle filled with spirit.

If he left them, they would be safe, and they would be free from his example. He was the only priest the children could remember: it was from him they would take their ideas of the faith. But it was from him too they took God – in their mouths. When he was gone it would be as if God in all this space between the sea and the mountains ceased to exist. Wasn't it his duty to stay, even if they despised him, even if they were murdered for his sake? even if they were corrupted by his example? He was shaken with the enormity of the problem. He lay with his hands over his eyes: nowhere, in all the wide flat marshy land, was there a single person he could consult. He raised the brandy to his mouth.

He said shyly, 'And Brigitta . . . is she . . . well?'

'You saw her just now.'

'No.' He couldn't believe that he hadn't recognized her. It was making light of his mortal sin: you couldn't do a thing like that and then not even recognize . . .

'Yes, she was there.' Maria went to the door and called, 'Brigitta, Brigitta,' and the priest turned on his side and watched her come in out of the outside landscape of terror and lust – that small malicious child who had laughed at him.

'Go and speak to the father,' Maria said. 'Go on.'

He made an attempt to hide the brandy bottle, but there was nowhere . . . he tried to minimize it in his hands, watching her, feeling the shock of human love.

'She knows her catechism,' Maria said, 'but she won't say it . . .'

The child stood there, watching him with acuteness and contempt. They had spent no love in her conception: just fear and despair and half a bottle of brandy and the sense of loneliness had driven him to an act which horrified him – and this scared shame-faced overpowering love was the result. He said, 'Why not? Why won't you say it?' taking quick secret glances, never meeting her gaze, feeling his heart pound in his breast unevenly, like an old donkey engine, with the baulked desire to save her from – everything.

'Why should I?'

'God wishes it.'

'How do you know?'

He was aware of an immense load of responsibility: it was indistinguishable from love. This, he thought, must be what all parents feel: ordinary men go through life like this crossing their fingers, praying against pain, afraid . . . This is what we escape at no cost at all, sacrificing an unimportant motion of the body. For years, of course, he had been responsible for souls, but that was different . . . a lighter thing. You could trust God to make allowances, but you couldn't trust smallpox, starvation, men . . . He said, 'My dear,' tightening his grip upon the brandy bottle . . . He had baptized her at his last visit: she had been like a rag doll with a wrinkled aged face – it had seemed unlikely that she would live long . . . He had felt nothing but a regret; it was difficult even to feel shame where no one blamed him. He was the only priest most of them had ever known – they took their standard of the priesthood from him. Even the women.

'Are you the gringo?'

'What gringo?'

The woman said, 'The silly little creature. It's because the police have been looking for a man.' It seemed odd to hear of any other man they wanted but himself.

'What has he done?'

'He's a Yankee. He murdered some people in the north.'

'Why should he be here?'

'They think he's making for Quintana Roo – the chiceli plantations.' It was where many criminals in Mexico ended up: you could work on a plantation and earn good money and nobody interfered.

'Are you the gringo?' the child repeated.

'Do I look like a murderer?'

'I don't know.'

If he left the state, he would be leaving her too, abandoned. He said humbly to the woman, 'Couldn't I stay a few days here?'

'It's too dangerous, father.'

He caught the look in the child's eyes which frightened him – it was again as if a grown woman was there before her time, making her plans, aware of far too much. It was like seeing his own mortal sin look back at him, without contrition. He tried to find some contact with the child and not the woman; he said, 'My dear, tell me what games you play . . .' The child sniggered. He turned his face quickly away and stared up at the roof, where a spider moved. He remembered a proverb – it came out of the recesses of his own childhood: his father had used it – 'The best smell is bread, the best savour salt, the best love that of children.' It had been a happy childhood, except that he had been afraid of too many things, and had hated poverty like a crime; he had believed that when he was a priest he would be rich and proud – that was called having a vocation. He thought of the immeasurable distance a man travels – from the first whipping-top to this bed, on which he lay clasping the brandy. And to God it was only a moment. The child's snigger and the first mortal sin lay together more closely than two blinks of the eye. He put out his hand as if he could drag her back by force from – something; but he was powerless. The man or the woman waiting to complete her corruption might not yet have been born. How could he guard her against the non-existent?

She started out of his reach and put her tongue out at him. The woman said, 'You little devil you,' and raised her hand.

'No,' the priest said. 'No.' He scrambled into a sitting position. 'Don't you dare . . .'

'I'm her mother.'

'We haven't any right.' He said to the child, 'If only I had some cards I could show you a trick or two. You could teach your friends . . .' He had never known how to talk to children except from the pulpit. She stared back at him with insolence. He asked, 'Do you know how to send messages with taps – long, short, long . . .?'

'What on earth, father!' the woman exclaimed.

'It's a game children play. I know.' He said to the child, 'Have you any friends?'

The child suddenly laughed again knowingly. The seven-year-old body was like a dwarf's: it disguised an ugly maturity.

'Get out of here,' the woman said. 'Get out before I teach you . . .'

She made a last impudent malicious gesture and was gone – perhaps for ever as far as he was concerned. You do not always say good-bye to those you love beside a deathbed, in an atmosphere of leisure and incense. He said, 'I wonder what *we* can teach . . .' He thought of his own death and her life going on; it might be his hell to watch her rejoining him gradually through the debasing years, sharing his weakness like tuberculosis . . . He lay back on the bed and turned his head away from the draining light; he appeared to be sleeping, but he was wide awake. The woman busied herself with small jobs, and as the sun went down the mosquitoes came out, flashing through the air to their mark unerringly, like sailors' knives.

'Shall I put up a net, father?'

'No. It doesn't matter.' He had had more fevers in the last ten years than he could count: he had ceased to bother: they came and went and made no difference – they were part of his environment.

Presently she left the hut and he could hear her voice gossiping outside. He was astonished and a bit relieved by her resilience. Once for five minutes seven years ago they had been lovers – if you could give that name to a relationship in which she had never used his baptismal name: to her it was just an incident, a scratch which heals completely in the healthy flesh: she was even proud of having been the priest's woman. He alone carried a wound, as though a whole world had died.

It was dark: no sign as yet of the dawn. Perhaps two dozen people sat on the earth floor of the largest hut while he preached to them. He couldn't see them with any distinctness. The candles on the packing-case smoked steadily upwards – the door was shut and there was no current of air. He was talking about heaven, standing between them and the candles in the ragged peon trousers and the torn shirt. They grunted and moved restlessly. He knew they were longing for the Mass to be over: they had woken him very early, because there were rumours of police . . .

He said, 'One of the Fathers has told us that joy always depends on pain. Pain is part of joy. We are hungry and then think how we enjoy our food at last. We are thirsty . . .' He stopped suddenly, with his eyes glancing away into the shadows, expecting the cruel laugh that did not come. He said, 'We deny ourselves so that we can enjoy. You have heard of rich men in the north who eat salted foods, so that they can be thirsty – for what they call the cocktail. Before the marriage, too, there is the long betrothal . . .' Again he stopped. He felt his own unworthiness like a weight at the back of the tongue. There was a smell of hot wax from where a candle drooped in the nocturnal heat; people shifted on the hard floor in the shadows. The smell of unwashed human beings warred with the wax. He cried out stubbornly in a voice of authority, 'That is why I tell you that heaven is here: this is a part of heaven just as pain is a part of pleasure.' He said, 'Pray that you will suffer more and more and more. Never get tired of suffering. The police watching you, the soldiers gathering taxes, the beating you always get from the jefe because you are too poor to pay, smallpox and fever, hunger . . . that is all part of heaven – the preparation. Perhaps without them, who can tell, you wouldn't enjoy heaven so much. Heaven would not be complete. And heaven. What is heaven?' Literary phrases from what seemed now to be another life altogether – the strict quiet life of the seminary – became confused on his tongue: the names of precious stones: Jerusalem the Golden. But these people had never seen gold.

He went rather stumbling on, 'Heaven is where there is no jefe, no unjust laws, no taxes, no soldiers and no hunger. Your children do not die in heaven.' The door of the hut opened and a man slipped in. There was whispering out of the range of the candlelight. 'You will never be afraid there – or unsafe. There are no Red Shirts. Nobody grows old. The crops never fail. Oh, it is easy to say all the things that there will *not* be in heaven: what is there is God. That is more difficult. Our words are made to describe what we know with our senses. We say "light", but we are thinking only of the sun, "love" . . .' It was not easy to concentrate: the police were not far away. The man had probably brought news. 'That means perhaps a child . . .' The door opened again: he could see another day drawn across like a grey slate outside. A voice whispered urgently to him, 'Father.'

'Yes?'

'The police are on the way. They are only a mile off, coming through the forest.'

This was what he was used to: the words not striking home, the hurried close, the expectation of pain coming between him and his faith. He said stubbornly, 'Above all remember this – heaven is here.' Were they on horseback or on foot? If they were on foot, he had twenty minutes left to finish Mass and hide. 'Here now, at this minute, your fear and my fear are part of heaven, where there will be no fear any more for ever.' He turned his back on them and began very quickly to recite the Credo. There was a time when he had approached the Canon of the Mass with actual physical dread – the first time he had consumed the body and blood of God in a state of mortal sin. But then life bred its excuses – it hadn't after a while seemed to matter very much, whether he was damned or not, so long as these others . . .

He kissed the top of the packing-case and turned to bless. In the inadequate light he could just see two men kneeling with their arms stretched out in the shape of a cross – they would keep that position until the consecration was over, one more mortification squeezed out of their harsh and painful lives. He felt humbled by the pain ordinary men bore voluntarily; his pain was forced on him. 'Oh Lord, I have loved the beauty of thy house . . .' The candles smoked and the people shifted on their knees – an absurd happiness bobbed up in him again before anxiety returned: it was as if he had been permitted to look in from the outside at the population of heaven. Heaven must contain just such scared and dutiful and hunger-lined faces. For a matter of seconds he felt an immense satisfaction that he could talk of suffering to them now without hypocrisy – it is hard for the sleek and well-fed priest to praise poverty. He began the prayer for the living: the long list of the Apostles and Martyrs fell like footsteps – Cornelii, Cypriani, Laurentii, Chrysogoni – soon the police would reach the clearing where his mule had sat down under him and he had washed in the pool. The Latin words ran into each other on his hasty tongue: he could feel impatience all round him. He began the Consecration of the Host (he had finished the wafers long ago – it was a piece of bread from Maria's oven); impatience abruptly died away: everything in time became a routine but this – 'Who the day before he suffered took Bread into his holy and venerable hands . . .' Whoever moved outside on the forest path, there was no movement here – '*Hoc est enim Corpus Meum.*' He could hear the sigh of breaths released: God was here in the body for the first time in six years. When he raised the Host he could imagine the faces lifted like famished dogs. He began the Consecration of the Wine – in a chipped cup. That was one more surrender – for two years he had carried a chalice around with him; once it would have cost him his life, if the police officer who opened his case had not been a Catholic. It may very well have cost the officer his life, if anybody had discovered the evasion – he didn't know; you went round making God knew what martyrs – in Concepción or elsewhere – when you yourself were without grace enough to die.

The Consecration was in silence: no bell rang. He knelt by the packing-case exhausted, without a prayer. Somebody opened the door: a voice whispered urgently, 'They're here.' They couldn't have come on foot then, he thought vaguely. Somewhere in the absolute stillness of the dawn – it couldn't have been more than a quarter of a mile away – a horse whinnied.

He got to his feet – Maria stood at his elbow. She said, 'The cloth, father, give me the cloth.' He put the Host hurriedly into his mouth and drank the wine: one had to avoid profanation: the cloth was whipped away from the packing-case. She nipped the candles, so that the wick should not leave a smell . . . The room was already cleared, only the owner hung by the entrance waiting to kiss his hand. Through the door the world was faintly visible, and a cock in the village crowed.

Maria said, 'Come to the hut quickly.'

'I'd better go.' He was without a plan. 'Not be found here.'

'They are all round the village.'

Was this the end at last, he wondered? Somewhere fear waited to spring at him, he knew, but he wasn't afraid yet. He followed the woman, scurrying across the village to her hut, repeating an act of contrition mechanically as he went. He wondered when the fear would start. He had been afraid when the policeman opened his case – but that was years ago. He had been afraid hiding in the shed among the bananas, hearing the child argue with the police officer – that was only a few weeks away. Fear would undoubtedly begin again soon. There was no sign of the police – only the grey morning, and the chickens and turkeys astir, flopping down from the trees in which they had roosted during the night. Again the cock crew. If they were so careful, they must know beyond the shadow of doubt that he was here. It *was* the end.

Maria plucked at him. 'Get in. Quick. On to the bed.' Presumably she had an idea – women were appallingly practical: they built new plans at once out of the ruins of the old. But what was the good? She said, 'Let me smell your breath. O God, anyone can tell . . . wine . . . what would we be doing with wine?' She was gone again, inside, making a lot of bother in the peace and quiet of the dawn. Suddenly, out of the forest, a hundred yards away, an officer rode. In the absolute stillness you could hear the creaking of his revolver-holster as he turned and waved.

All round the little clearing the police appeared – they must have marched very quickly, for only the officer had a horse. Rifles at the trail, they approached the small group of huts – an exaggerated and rather absurd show of force. One man had a puttee trailing behind him – it had probably caught on something in the forest. He tripped on it and fell with a great clatter of cartridge-belt on gunstock: the lieutenant on the horse looked round and then turned his bitter and angry face upon the silent huts.

The woman was pulling at him from inside the hut. She said, 'Bite this. Quick. There's no time . . .' He turned his back on the advancing police and came into the dusk of the room. She had a small raw onion in her hand. 'Bite it,' she said. He bit it and began to weep. 'Is that better?' she said. He could hear the pad, pad of the cautious horse hoofs advancing between the huts.

'It's horrible,' he said with a giggle.

'Give it to me.' She made it disappear somewhere into her clothes: it was a trick all women seemed to know. He asked, 'Where's my case?'

'Never mind your case. Get on to the bed.'

But before he could move a horse blocked the doorway. They could see a leg in riding-boots piped with scarlet: brass fittings gleamed: a hand in a glove rested on the high pommel. Maria put a hand upon his arm – it was as near as she had ever come to a movement of affection: affection was taboo between them. A voice cried, 'Come on out, all of you.' The horse stamped and a little pillar of dust went up. 'Come on out, I said.' Somewhere a shot was fired. The priest left the hut.

The dawn had really broken: light feathers of colour were blown up the sky: a man still held his gun pointed upwards: a little balloon of grey smoke hung at the muzzle. Was this how the agony would start?

Out of all the huts the villagers were reluctantly emerging – the children first: they were inquisitive and unfrightened. The men and women had the air already of people condemned by authority – authority was never wrong. None of them looked at the priest. They stared at the ground and waited. Only the children watched the horse as if it were the most important thing there.

The lieutenant said, 'Search the huts.' Time passed very slowly; even the smoke of the shot seemed to remain in the air for an unnatural period. Some pigs came grunting out of a hut, and a turkey-cock paced with evil dignity into the centre of the circle, puffing out its dusty feathers and tossing the long pink membrane from its beak. A soldier came up to the lieutenant and saluted sketchily. He said, 'They're all here.'

'You've found nothing suspicious?'

'No.'

'Then look again.'

Once more time stopped like a broken clock. The lieutenant drew out a cigarette-case, hesitated and put it back again. Again the policeman approached and reported, 'Nothing.'

The lieutenant barked out, 'Attention. All of you. Listen to me.' The outer ring of police closed in, pushing the villagers together into a small group in front of the lieutenant: only the children were left free. The priest saw his own child standing close to the lieutenant's horse; she could just reach above his boot: she put up her hand and touched the leather. The lieutenant said, 'I am looking for two men – one is a gringo, a yankee, a murderer. I can see very well he is not here. There is a reward of five hundred pesos for his capture. Keep your eyes open.' He paused and ran his eye over them. The priest felt his gaze come to rest; he looked down like the others at the ground.

'The other,' the lieutenant said, 'is a priest.' He raised his voice: 'You know what that means – a traitor to the republic. Anyone who shelters him is a traitor too.' Their immobility seemed to anger him. He said, 'You're fools if you still believe what the priests tell you. All they want is your money. What has God ever done for you? Have you got enough to eat? Have your children got enough to eat? Instead of food they talk to you about heaven. Oh, everything will be fine after you are dead, they say. I tell you – everything will be fine when *they* are dead, and you must help.' The child had her hand on his boot. He looked down at her with dark affection. He said with conviction, 'This child is worth more than the Pope in Rome.' The police leant on their guns; one of them yawned; the turkey-cock went hissing back towards the hut. The lieutenant said, 'If you've seen this priest speak up. There's a reward of seven hundred pesos . . .' Nobody spoke.

The lieutenant yanked his horse's head round towards them. He said, 'We know he's in this district. Perhaps you don't know what happened to a man in Concepción. One of the women began to weep. He said, 'Come up – one after the other – and let me have your names. No, not the women, the men.'

They filed sullenly up and he questioned them, 'What's your name? What do you do? Married? Which is your wife? Have you heard of this priest?' Only one man now stood between the priest and the horse's head. He recited an act of contrition silently with only half a mind – '. . . my sins, because they have crucified my loving Saviour . . . but above all because they have offended . . .' He was alone in front of the lieutenant – 'I hereby resolve never more to offend Thee . . .' It was a formal act, because a man had to be prepared: it was like making your will and might be as valueless.

'Your name?'

The name of the man in Concepción came back to him. He said, 'Montez.'

'Have you ever seen the priest?'

'No.'

'What do you do?'

'I have a little land.'

'Are you married?'

'Yes.'

'Which is your wife?'

Maria suddenly broke out, 'I'm his wife. Why do you want to ask so many questions? Do you think *he* looks like a priest?'

The lieutenant was examining something on the pommel of his saddle: it seemed to be an old photograph. 'Let me see your hands,' he said.

The priest held them up: they were as hard as a labourer's. Suddenly the lieutenant leant down from the saddle and sniffed at his breath. There was complete silence among the villagers – a dangerous silence, because it seemed to convey to the lieutenant a fear . . . He stared back at the hollow stubbled face, looked back at the photograph. 'All right,' he said, 'next,' and then as the priest stepped aside, 'Wait.' He put his hand down to Brigitta's head and gently tugged at her black stiff hair. He said, 'Look up. You know everyone in this village, don't you?'

'Yes,' she said.

'Who's that man, then? What's his name?'

'I don't know,' the child said. The lieutenant caught his breath. 'You don't know his name?' he said. 'Is he a stranger?'

Maria cried, 'Why, the child doesn't know her own name. Ask her who her father is.'

'Who's your father?'

The child stared up at the lieutenant and then turned her knowing eyes upon the priest . . . 'Sorry and beg pardon for all my sins,' he was repeating to himself with his fingers crossed for luck. The child said, 'That's him. There.'

'All right,' the lieutenant said, 'Next.' The interrogations went on: name? work? married? while the sun came up above the forest. The priest stood with his hands clasped in front of him: again death had been postponed. He felt an enormous temptation to throw himself in front of the lieutenant and declare himself – 'I am the one you want.' Would they shoot him out of hand? A delusive promise of peace tempted him. Far up in the sky a vulture watched; they must appear from that height as two groups of carnivorous animals who might at any time break into conflict, and it waited there, a tiny black spot, for carrion. Death was not the end of pain – to believe in peace was a kind of heresy.

The last man gave his evidence.

The lieutenant said, 'Is no one willing to help?'

They stood silent beside the decayed bandstand. He said, 'You heard what happened at Concepción. I took a hostage there . . . and when I found that this priest had been in the neighbourhood I put the man against the nearest tree. I found out because there's always someone who changes his mind – perhaps because somebody in Concepción loved the man's wife and wanted him out of the way. It's not my business to look into reasons. I only know we found wine later in Concepción . . . Perhaps there's somebody in this village who wants your piece of land – or your cow. It's much safer to speak now. Because I'm going to take a hostage from here too.' He paused. Then he said, 'There's no need even to speak, if he's here among you. Just look at him. No one will know then that it was you who gave him away. He won't know himself if you're afraid of his curses. Now . . . This is your last chance.'

The priest looked at the ground – he wasn't going to make it difficult for the man who gave him away.

'Right,' the lieutenant said, 'then I shall choose my man. You've brought it on yourselves.'

He sat on his horse watching them – one of the policemen had leant his gun against the bandstand and was doing up a puttee. The villagers still stared at the ground; everyone was afraid to catch his eye. He broke out suddenly, 'Why won't you trust me? I don't want any of you to die. In my eyes – can't you understand – you are worth far more than he is. I want to give you' – he made a gesture with his hands which was valueless, because no one saw him – 'everything.' He said in a dull voice, 'You. You there. I'll take you.'

A woman screamed. 'That's my boy. That's Miguel. You can't take my boy.'

He said dully, 'Every man here is somebody's husband or somebody's son. I know that.'

The priest stood silently with his hands clasped; his knuckles whitened as he gripped . . . He could feel all round him the beginning of hate. Because he was no one's husband or son. He said, 'Lieutenant . . .'

'What do you want?'

'I'm getting too old to be much good in the fields. Take me.'

A rout of pigs came rushing round the corner of a hut, taking no notice of anybody. The soldier finished his puttee and stood up. The sunlight coming up above the forest winked on the bottles of the gaseosa stall.

The lieutenant said, 'I'm choosing a hostage, not offering free board and lodging to the lazy. If you are no good in the fields, you are no good as a hostage.' He gave an order. 'Tie the man's hands and bring him along.'

It took no time at all for the police to be gone – they took with them two or three chickens, a turkey and the man called Miguel. The priest said aloud, 'I did my best.' He went on, 'It's *your* job – to give me up. What do you expect me to do? It's my job not to be caught.'

One of the men said, 'That's all right, father. Only will you be careful . . . to see that you don't leave any wine behind . . . like you did at Concepción?'

Another said, 'It's no good staying, father. They'll get you in the end. They won't forget your face again. Better go north, to the mountains. Over the border.'

'It's a fine state over the border,' a woman said. 'They've still got churches there. Nobody can go in them, of course – but they are there. Why, I've heard that there are priests too in the towns. A cousin of mine went over the mountains to Las Casas once and heard Mass – in a house, with a proper altar, and the priest all dressed up like in the old days. You'd be happy there, father.'

The priest followed Maria to the hut. The bottle of brandy lay on the table; he touched it with his fingers – there wasn't much left. He said, 'My case, Maria? Where's my case?'

'It's too dangerous to carry that around any more,' Maria said.

'How else can I take the wine?'

'There isn't any wine.'

'What do you mean?'

She said, 'I'm not going to bring trouble on you and everyone else. I've broken the bottle. Even if it brings a curse . . .'

He said gently and sadly, 'You mustn't be superstitious. That was simply – wine. There's nothing sacred in wine. Only it's hard to get hold of here. That's why I kept a store of it in Concepción. But they've found that.'

'Now perhaps you'll go – go away altogether. You're no good any more to anyone,' she said fiercely. 'Don't you understand, father? We don't want you any more.'

'Oh yes,' he said. 'I understand. But it's not what you want – or I want . . .'

She said savagely, 'I know about things. I went to school. I'm not like these others – ignorant. I know you're a bad priest. That time we were together – that wasn't all you've done. I've heard things, I can tell you. Do you think God wants you to stay and die – a whisky priest like you?' He stood patiently in front of her, as he had stood in front of the lieutenant, listening. He hadn't known she was capable of all this thought. She said, 'Suppose you die. You'll be a martyr, won't you? What kind of a martyr do you think you'll be? It's enough to make people mock.'

That had never occurred to him – that anybody would consider him a martyr. He said, 'It's difficult. Very difficult. I'll think about it. I wouldn't want the Church to be mocked . . .'

'Think about it over the border then . . .'

'Well . . .'

She said, 'When you-know-what happened, I was proud. I thought the good days would come back. It's not everyone who's a priest's woman. And the child . . . I thought you could do a lot for her. But you might as well be a thief for all the good . . .'

He said vaguely, 'There've been a lot of good thieves.'

'For God's sake take this brandy and go.'

'There was one thing,' he said. 'In my case . . . there was something . . .'

'Go and find it yourself on the rubbish-tip then. I won't touch it again.'

'And the child,' he said, 'you're a good woman, Maria. I mean – you'll try and bring her up well . . . as a Christian.'

'She'll never be good for anything, you can see that.'

'She can't be very bad – at her age,' he implored her.

'She'll go on the way she's begun.'

He said, 'The next Mass I say will be for her.'

She wasn't even listening. She said, 'She's bad through and through.' He was aware of faith dying out between the bed and the door – the Mass would soon mean no more to anyone than a black cat crossing the path. He was risking all their lives for the sake of spilt salt or a crossed finger. He began, 'My mule . . .'

'They are giving it maize now.'

She added, 'You'd better go north. There's no chance to the south any more.'

'I thought perhaps Carmen . . .'

'They'll be watching there.'

'Oh, well . . .' He said sadly, 'Perhaps one day . . . when things are better . . .' He sketched a cross and blessed her, but she stood impatiently before him, willing him to be gone for ever.

'Well, good-bye, Maria.'

'Good-bye.'

He walked across the plaza with his shoulders hunched; he felt that there wasn't a soul in the place who wasn't watching him with satisfaction – the trouble-maker who for obscure and superstitious reasons they preferred not to betray to the police. He felt envious of the unknown gringo whom they wouldn't hesitate to trap – he at any rate had no burden of gratitude to carry round with him.

Down a slope churned up with the hoofs of mules and ragged with tree-roots there was the river – not more than two feet deep, littered with empty cans and broken bottles. A notice, which hung on a tree, read, 'It is forbidden to deposit rubbish . . .' Underneath all the refuse of the village was collected and slid gradually down into the river. When the rains came it would be washed away. He put his foot among the old tins and the rotting vegetables and reached for his case. He sighed: it had been quite a good case: one more relic of the quiet past . . . Soon it would be difficult to remember that life had ever been any different. The lock had been torn off: he felt inside the silk lining . . .

The papers were there; reluctantly he let the case fall – a whole important and respected youth dropped among the cans – he had been given it by his parishioners in Concepción on the fifth anniversary of his ordination . . . Somebody moved behind a tree. He lifted his feet out of the rubbish – flies burred round his ankles. With the papers hidden in his fist he came round the trunk to see who was spying . . . The child sat on a root, kicking her heels against the bark. Her eyes were shut tight fast. He said, 'My dear, what is the matter with you . . . ?' They came open quickly then – red-rimmed and angry, with an expression of absurd pride.

She said, 'You . . . you . . .'

'Me?'

'You are the matter.'

He moved towards her with infinite caution, as if she were an animal who distrusted him. He felt weak with longing. He said, 'My dear, why me . . . ?'

She said furiously, 'They laugh at me.'

'Because of me?'

She said, 'Everyone else has a father . . . who works.'

'I work too.'

'You're a priest, aren't you?'

'Yes.'

'Pedro says you aren't a man. You aren't any good for women.' She said, 'I don't know what he means.'

'I don't suppose he knows himself.'

'Oh, yes he does,' she said. 'He's ten. And I want to know. You're going away, aren't you?'

'Yes.'

He was appalled again by her maturity, as she whipped up a smile from a large and varied stock. She said, 'Tell me –' enticingly. She sat there on the trunk of the tree by the rubbish-tip with an effect of abandonment. The world was in her heart already, like the small spot of decay in a fruit. She was without protection – she had no grace, no charm to plead for her; his heart was shaken by the conviction of loss. He said, 'My dear, be careful . . .'

'What of? Why are you going away?'

He came a little nearer; he thought – a man may kiss his own daughter, but she started away from him. 'Don't you touch me,' she screeched at him in her ancient voice and giggled. Every child was born with some kind of knowledge of love, he thought; they took it with the milk at the breast: but on parents and friends depended the kind of love they knew – the saving or the damning kind. Lust too was a kind of love. He saw her fixed in her life like a fly in amber – Maria's hand raised to strike: Pedro talking prematurely in the dusk: and the police beating the forest – violence everywhere. He prayed silently, 'O God, give me any kind of death – without contrition, in a state of sin – only save this child.'

He was a man who was supposed to save souls. It had seemed quite simple once, preaching at Benediction, organizing the guilds, having coffee with elderly ladies behind barred windows, blessing new houses with a little incense, wearing black gloves . . . It was as easy as saving money: now it was a mystery. He was aware of his own desperate inadequacy.

He went down on his knees and pulled her to him, while she giggled and struggled to be free: 'I love you. I am your father and I love you. Try to understand that.' He held her tightly by the wrist and suddenly she stayed still, looking up at him. He said, 'I would give my life, that's nothing, my soul . . . my dear, my dear, try to understand that you are – so important.' That was the difference, he had always known, between his faith and theirs, the political leaders of the people who cared only for things like the state, the republic: this child was more important than a whole continent. He said, 'You must take care of yourself because you are so – necessary. The president up in the capital goes guarded by men with guns – but my child, you have all the angels of heaven –' She stared back at him out of dark and unconscious eyes; he had a sense that he had come too late. He said, 'Good-bye, my dear,' and clumsily kissed her – a silly infatuated ageing man, who as soon as he released her and started padding back to the plaza could feel behind his hunched shoulders the whole vile world coming round the child to ruin her. His mule was there, saddled, by the gaseosa stall. A man said, 'Better go north, father,' and stood waving his hand. One mustn't have human affections – or rather one must love every soul as if it were one's own child. The passion to protect must extend itself over a world – but he felt it tethered and aching like a hobbled animal to the tree trunk. He turned his mule south.

He was travelling in the actual track of the police. So long as he went slowly and didn't overtake any stragglers it seemed a fairly safe route. What he wanted now was wine. Without it he was useless; he might as well escape north into the mountains and the safe state beyond, where the worst that could happen to him was a fine and a few days in prison because he couldn't pay. But he wasn't ready yet for the final surrender – every small surrender had to be paid for in a further endurance, and now he felt the need of somehow ransoming his child. He would stay another month, another year . . . Jogging up and down on the mule he tried to bribe God with promises of firmness . . . The mule suddenly dug in its hoofs and stopped dead: a tiny green snake raised itself on the path and then hissed away into the grass like a match-flame. The mule went on.

When he came near a village he would stop the mule and advance as close as he could on foot – the police might have stopped there. Then he would ride quickly through, speaking to nobody beyond a '*Buenos días*', and again on the forest path he would pick up the track of the lieutenant's horse. He had no clear idea now about anything; he only wanted to put as great a distance as possible between him and the village where he had spent the night. In one hand he still carried the crumpled ball of paper. Somebody had tied a bunch of about fifty bananas to his saddle, beside the machete and the small bag which contained his store of candles, and every now and then he ate one – ripe, brown, and sodden, tasting of soap. It left a smear like a moustache over his mouth.

After six hours' travelling he came to La Candelaria, which lay, a long mean tin-roofed village, beside one of the tributaries of the Grijalva River.. He came cautiously out into the dusty street – it was early afternoon. The vultures sat on the roofs with their small heads hidden from the sun, and a few men lay in hammocks in the narrow shade the houses cast. The mule plodded forward very slowly through the heavy day. The priest leant forward on his pommel.

The mule came to a stop of its own accord beside a hammock. A man lay in it, bunched diagonally, with one leg trailing to keep the hammock moving, up and down, up and down, making a tiny current of air. The priest said, '*Buenas tardes*.' The man opened his eyes and watched him.

'How far is it to Carmen?'

'Three leagues.'

'Can I get a canoe across the river?'

'Yes.'

'Where?'

The man waved a languid hand – as much as to say anywhere but here. He had only two teeth left, canines which stuck yellowly out at either end of his mouth like the teeth you find enclosed in clay which have belonged to long-extinct animals.

'What were the police doing here?' the priest asked, and a cloud of flies came down, settling on the mule's neck; he poked at them with a stick and they rose heavily, leaving a small trickle of blood, and dropped again on the tough grey skin. The mule seemed to feel nothing, standing in the sun with his head drooping.

'Looking for someone,' the man said.

'I've heard,' the priest said, 'that there's a reward out – for a gringo.'

The man swung his hammock back and forth. He said, 'It's better to be alive and poor than rich and dead.'

'Can I overtake them if I go towards Carmen?'

'They aren't going to Carmen.'

'No?'

'They are making for the city.'

The priest rode on. Twenty yards farther he stopped again beside a gaseosa stall and asked the boy in charge, 'Can I get a boat across the river?'

'There isn't a boat.'

'No boat?'

'Somebody stole it.'

'Give me a sidral.' He drank down the yellow bubbly chemical liquid: it left him thirstier than before. He said, 'How do I get across?'

'Why do you want to get across?'

'I'm making for Carmen. How did the police get over?'

'They swam.'

'*Mula, Mula,*' the priest said, urging the mule on, past the inevitable bandstand and a statue in florid taste of a woman in a toga waving a wreath. Part of the pedestal had been broken off and lay in the middle of the road – the mule went round it. The priest looked back; far down the street the mestizo was sitting upright in the hammock watching him. The mule turned off down a steep path to the river, and again the priest looked back – the half-caste was still in the hammock, but he had both feet upon the ground. An habitual uneasiness made the priest beat at the mule – '*Mula, Mula,*' but the mule took its time, sliding down the bank towards the river.

By the riverside it refused to enter the water. The priest split the end of his stick with his teeth and jabbed a sharp point into the mule's flank. It waded reluctantly in, and the water rose to the stirrups and then to the knees; the mule began to swim, splayed out flat with only the eyes and nostrils visible, like an alligator. Somebody shouted from the bank.

The priest looked round. At the river's edge the mestizo stood and called, not very loudly: his voice didn't carry. It was as if he had a secret purpose which nobody but the priest must hear. He waved his arm, summoning the priest back, but the mule lurched out of the water and up the bank beyond and the priest paid no attention – uneasiness was lodged in his brain. He urged the mule forward through the green half-light of a banana grove, not looking behind. All these years there had been two places to which he could always return and rest safely in hiding – one had been Concepción, his old parish, and that was closed to him now: the other was Carmen, where he had been born and where his parents were buried. He had imagined there might be a third, but he would never go back now . . . He turned the mule's head towards Carmen, and the forest took them again. At this rate they would arrive in the dark, which was what he wanted. The mule unbeaten went with extreme langour, head drooping, smelling a little of blood. The priest, leaning forward on the high pommel, fell asleep. He dreamed that a small girl in stiff white muslin was reciting her Catechism – somewhere in the background, there was a bishop and a group of Children of Mary, elderly women with grey hard pious faces wearing pale blue ribbons. The bishop said, 'Excellent . . . Excellent,' and clapped his hands, plop, plop. A man in a morning coat said, 'There's a deficit of five hundred pesos on the new organ. We propose to hold a special musical performance, when it is hoped . . .' He remembered with appalling suddenness that he oughtn't to be there at all . . . he was in the wrong parish . . . he should be holding a retreat at Concepción. The man Montez appeared behind the child in white muslin, gesticulating, reminding him . . . Something had happened to Montez, he had a dry wound on his forehead. He felt with dreadful certainty a threat to the child. He said, 'My dear, my dear,' and woke to the slow rolling stride of the mule and the sound of footsteps.

He turned. It was the mestizo, padding behind him, dripping water: he must have swum the river. His two teeth stuck out over his lower lip, and he grinned ingratiatingly. 'What do you want?' the priest asked sharply.

'You didn't tell me you were going to Carmen.'

'Why should I?'

'You see, I want to go to Carmen, too. It's better to travel in company.' He was wearing a shirt, a pair of white trousers, and gym shoes through which one big toe showed – plump and yellow like something which lives underground. He scratched himself under the armpits and came chummily up to the priest's stirrup. He said, 'You are not offended, señor?'

'Why do you call me señor?'

'Anyone can tell you're a man of education.'

'The forest is free to all,' the priest said.

'Do you know Carmen well?' the man asked.

'Not well. I have a few friends.'

'You're going on business, I suppose?'

The priest said nothing. He could feel the man's hand on his foot, a light and deprecating touch. The man said, 'There's a *finca* off the road two leagues from here. It would be as well to stay the night.'

'I am in a hurry,' the priest said.

'But what good would it be reaching Carmen at one, two in the morning? We could sleep at the *finca* and be there before the sun was high.'

'I do what suits me.'

'Of course, señor, of course.' The man was silent for a little while, and then said, 'It isn't wise travelling at night if the señor hasn't got a gun. It's different for a man like me . . .'

'I am a poor man,' the priest said. 'You can see for yourself. I am not worth robbing.'

'And then there's the gringo – they say he's a wild kind of a man, a real *pistolero*. He comes up to you and says in his own language – Stop: what is the way to – well, some place, and you do not understand what he is saying and perhaps you make a movement and he shoots you dead. But perhaps you know Americano, señor?'

'Of course I don't. How should I? I am a poor man. But I don't listen to every fairy-tale.'

'Do you come from far?'

The priest thought a moment: 'Concepción.' He could do no more harm there.

The man for the time being seemed satisfied. He walked along by the mule, a hand on the stirrup. Every now and then he spat. When the priest looked down he could see the big toe moving like a grub along the ground – he was probably harmless. It was the general condition of life that made for suspicion. The dusk fell and then almost at once the dark. The mule moved yet more slowly. Noise broke out all round them; it was like a theatre when the curtain falls and behind in the wings and passages hubbub begins. Things you couldn't put a name to – jaguars perhaps – cried in the undergrowth, monkeys moved in the upper boughs, and the mosquitoes hummed all round like sewing machines. 'It's thirsty walking,' the man said. 'Have you by any chance, señor, got a little drink . . . ?'

'No.'

'If you want to reach Carmen before three, you will have to beat the mule. Shall I take the stick . . . ?'

'No, no, let the brute take its time. It doesn't matter to me . . .' he said drowsily.

'You talk like a priest.'

He came quickly awake, but under the tall dark trees he could see nothing. He said, 'What nonsense you talk.'

'I am a very good Christian,' the man said, stroking the priest's foot.

'I dare say. I wish I were.'

'Ah, you ought to be able to tell which people you can trust.' He spat in a comradely way.

'I have nothing to trust anyone with,' the priest said. 'Except these trousers – they are very torn. And this mule – it isn't a good mule; you can see for yourself.'

There was silence for a while, and then, as if he had been considering the last statement, the half-caste went on, 'It wouldn't be a bad mule if you treated it right. Nobody can teach me anything about mules. I can see for myself it's tired out.'

The priest looked down at the grey swinging stupid head. 'Do you think so?'

'How far did you travel yesterday?'

'Perhaps twelve leagues.'

'Even a mule needs rest.'

The priest took his bare feet from out of the deep leather stirrups and scrambled to the ground. The mule for less than a minute took a longer stride and then dropped to a yet slower pace. The twigs and roots of the forest path cut the priest's feet – after five minutes he was bleeding. He tried in vain not to limp. The half-caste exclaimed, 'How delicate your feet are. You should wear shoes.'

Stubbornly he reasserted, 'I am a poor man.'

'You will never get to Carmen at this rate. Be sensible, man. If you don't want to go as far off the road as the *finca*, I know a little hut less than half a league from here. We can sleep a few hours and still reach Carmen at daybreak.' There was a rustle in the grass beside the path – the priest thought of snakes and his unprotected feet. The mosquitoes jabbed at his wrists; they were like little surgical syringes filled with poison and aimed at the bloodstream. Sometimes a firefly held its lighted globe close to the half-caste's face, turning it on and off like a torch. He said accusingly, 'You don't trust me. Just because I am a man who likes to do a good turn to strangers, because I try to be a Christian, you don't trust me.' He seemed to be working himself into a little artificial rage. He said, 'If I wanted to rob you, couldn't I have done it already? You're an old man.'

'Not so very old,' the priest said mildly. His conscience began automatically to work: it was like a slot machine into which any coin could be fitted, even a cheater's blank disk. The words proud, lustful, envious, cowardly, ungrateful – they all worked the right springs – he was all these things. The half-caste said, 'Here I have spent many hours guiding you to Carmen – I don't want any reward because I am a good Christian. I have probably lost money by it at home – never mind that . . .'

'I thought you said you had business in Carmen?' the priest said gently.

'When did I say that?' It was true – he couldn't remember . . . perhaps he was unjust too . . . 'Why should I say a thing which isn't true? No, I give up a whole day to helping you, and you pay no attention when your guide is tired . . .'

'I didn't need a guide,' he protested mildly.

'You say that when the road is plain, but if it wasn't for me, you'd have taken the wrong path a long time ago. You said yourself you didn't know Carmen well. That was why I came.'

'But of course,' the priest said, 'if you are tired, we will rest.' He felt guilty at his own lack of trust, but all the same, it remained like a growth only a knife could rid him of.

After half an hour they came to the hut. Made of mud and twigs, it had been set up in a minute clearing by a small farmer whom the forest must have driven out, edging in on him, an unstayable natural force which he couldn't defeat with his machete and his small fires. There were still signs in the blackened ground of an attempt to clear the brushwood for some meagre and inadequate crop. The man said, 'I will see to the mule. You go in and lie down and rest.'

'But it is you who are tired.'

'Me tired?' the half-caste said. 'What makes you say that? I am never tired.'

With a heavy heart the priest took off his saddlebag, pushed at the door and went in to complete darkness. He struck a light – there was no furniture; only a raised dais of hard earth and a straw mat too torn to have been worth removing. He lit a candle and stuck it in its own wax on the dais: then sat down and waited: the man was a long time. In one fist he still carried the ball of paper salvaged from his case – a man must retain some sentimental relics if he is to live at all. The argument of danger only applies to those who live in relative safety. He wondered whether the mestizo had stolen his mule, and reproached himself for the necessary suspicion. Then the door opened and the man came in – the two yellow canine teeth, the finger-nails scratching in the armpit. He sat down on the earth, with his back against the door, and said, 'Go to sleep. You are tired. I'll wake you when we need to start.'

'I'm not very sleepy.'

'Blow out the candle. You'll sleep better.'

'I don't like darkness,' the priest said. He was afraid.

'Won't you say a prayer, father, before we sleep?'

'Why do you call me that?' he asked sharply, peering across the shadowy floor to where the half-caste sat against the door.

'Oh, I guessed, of course. But you needn't be afraid of me. I'm a good Christian.'

'You're wrong.'

'I could easily find out, couldn't I?' the half-caste said. 'I'd just have to say – father, hear my confession. You couldn't refuse a man in mortal sin.'

The priest said nothing, waiting for the demand to come: the hand which held the papers twitched. 'Oh, you needn't fear me,' the mestizo went carefully on. 'I wouldn't betray you. I'm a Christian. I just thought a prayer . . . would be good . . .'

'You don't need to be a priest to know a prayer.' He began, '*Pater noster qui es in coelis* . . .' while the mosquitoes came droning towards the candle-flame. He was determined not to sleep – the man had some plan. His conscience ceased to accuse him of uncharity. He knew. He was in the presence of Judas.

He leant his head back against the wall and half closed his eyes – he remembered Holy Week in the old days when a stuffed Judas was hanged from the belfry and boys made a clatter with tins and rattles as he swung out over the door. Old staid members of the congregation had sometimes raised objections: it was blasphemous, they said, to make this guy out of Our Lord's betrayer; but he had said nothing and let the practice continue – it seemed to him a good thing that the world's traitor should be made a figure of fun. It was too easy otherwise to idealize him as a man who fought with God – a Prometheus, a noble victim in a hopeless war.

'Are you awake?' a voice whispered from the door. The priest suddenly giggled, as if this man, too, were absurd with stuffed straw legs and a painted face and an old straw hat who would presently be burnt in the plaza while people made political speeches and the fireworks went off.

'Can't you sleep?'

'I was dreaming,' the priest whispered. He opened his eyes and saw the man by the door was shivering – the two sharp teeth jumped up and down on the lower lip. 'Are you ill?'

'A little fever,' the man said. 'Have you any medicine?'

'No.'

The door creaked as the man's back shook. He said, 'It was getting wet in the river . . .' He slid farther down upon the floor and closed his eyes – mosquitoes with singed wings crawled over the earth bed. The priest thought: I mustn't sleep, it's dangerous, I must watch him. He opened his fist and smoothed out the paper. There were faint pencil lines visible – single words, the beginnings and ends of sentences, figures. Now that his case was gone, it was the only evidence left that life had ever been different: he carried it with him as a charm, because if life had been like that once, it might be so again. The candle-flame in the hot marshy lowland air burned to a smoky point vibrating . . . The priest held the paper close to it and read the words Altar Society, Guild of the Blessed Sacrament, Children of Mary, and then looked up again and across the dark hut saw the yellow malarial eyes of the mestizo watching him. Christ would not have found Judas sleeping in the garden: Judas could watch more than one hour.

'What's that paper . . . father?' he said enticingly, shivering against the door.

'Don't call me father. It is a list of seeds I have to buy in Carmen.'

'Can you write?'

'I can read.'

He looked at the paper again and a little mild impious joke stared up at him in faded pencil – something about 'of one substance'. He had been referring to his corpulency and the good dinner he had just eaten: the parishioners had not much relished his humour.

It had been a dinner given at Concepción in honour of the tenth anniversary of his ordination. He sat in the middle of the table with – who was it on his right hand? There were twelve dishes – he had said something about the Apostles, too, which was not thought to be in the best of taste. He was quite young and he had been moved by a gentle devilry, surrounded by all the pious and middle-aged and respectable people of Concepción, wearing their guild ribbons and badges. He had drunk just a little too much; in those days he wasn't used to liquor. It came back to him now suddenly who was on his right hand – it was Montez, the father of the man they had shot.

Montez had talked at some length. He had reported the progress of the Altar Society in the last year – they had a balance in hand of twenty-two pesos. He had noted it down for comment – there it was, AS 22. Montez had been very anxious to start a branch of the Society of St Vincent de Paul, and some woman had complained that bad books were being sold in Concepción, fetched in from the capital by mule: her child had got hold of one called *A Husband for a Night*. In his speech he said he would write to the Governor on the subject.

The moment he had said that the local photographer had set off his flare, and so he could remember himself at that instant, just as if he had been a stranger looking in from the outside – attracted by the noise – on some happy and festal and strange occasion: noticing with envy, and perhaps a little amusement, the fat youngish priest who stood with one plump hand splayed authoritatively out while the tongue played pleasantly with the word 'Governor'. Mouths were open all round fishily, and the faces glowed magnesium-white, with the lines and individuality wiped out.

That moment of authority had jerked him back to seriousness – he had ceased to unbend and everybody was happier. He said, 'The balance of twenty-two pesos in the accounts of the Altar Society – though quite revolutionary for Concepción – is not the only cause for congratulation in the last year. The Children of Mary have increased their membership by nine – and the Guild of the Blessed Sacrament last autumn made our annual retreat more than usually successful. But we mustn't rest on our laurels, and I confess I have got plans you may find a little startling. You already think me a man, I know, of inordinate ambitions – well, I want Concepción to have a better school – and that means a better presbytery too, of course. We are a big parish and the priest has a position to keep up. I'm not thinking of myself but of the Church. And we shall not stop there – though it will take a good many years, I'm afraid, even in a place the size of Concepción, to raise the money for that.' As he talked a whole serene life lay ahead – he *had* ambition: he saw no reason why one day he might not find himself in the state capital, attached to the cathedral, leaving another man to pay off the debts in Concepción. An energetic priest was always known by his debts. He went on, waving a plump and eloquent hand, 'Of course, many dangers here in Mexico threaten our dear Church. In this state we are unusually lucky – men have lost their lives in the north and we must be prepared' – he refreshed his dry mouth with a draught of wine – 'for the worst. Watch and pray,' he went vaguely on, 'watch and pray. The devil like a raging lion –' The Children of Mary stared up at him with their mouths a little open, the pale blue ribbons slanting across their dark best blouses.

He talked for a long while, enjoying the sound of his own voice: he had discouraged Montez on the subject of the St Vincent de Paul Society, because you had to be careful not to encourage a layman too far, and he had told a charming story about a child's deathbed – she was dying of consumption very firm in her faith at the age of eleven. She asked who it was standing at the end of her bed, and they had said, 'That's Father So-and-so,' and she had said, 'No, no. I know Father So-and-so. I mean the one with the golden crown.' One of the Guild of the Blessed Sacrament had wept. Everybody was very happy. It was a true story too, though he couldn't quite remember where he had heard it. Perhaps he had read it in a book once. Somebody refilled his glass. He took a long breath and said, 'My children . . .'

. . . and as the mestizo stirred and grunted by the door he opened his eyes and the old life peeled away like a label: he was lying in torn peon trousers in a dark unventilated hut with a price upon his head. The whole world had changed – no church anywhere: no brother priest, except Padre José, the outcast, in the capital. He lay listening to the heavy breathing of the half-caste and wondered why he had not gone the same road as Padre José and conformed to the laws. I was too ambitious, he thought, that was it. Perhaps Padre José was the better man – he was so humble that he was ready to accept any amount of mockery; at the best of times he had never considered himself worthy of the priesthood. There had been a conference once of the parochial clergy in the capital, in the happy days of the old governor, and he could remember Padre José slinking in at the tail of every meeting, curled up half out of sight in a back row, never opening his mouth. It was not, like some more intellectual priests, that he was over-scrupulous: he had been simply filled with an overwhelming sense of God. At the Elevation of the Host you could see his hands trembling – he was not like St Thomas who needed to put his hands into the wounds in order to believe: the wounds bled anew for him over every altar. Once Padre José had said to him in a burst of confidence, 'Every time . . . I have such fear.' His father had been a peon.

But it was different in his case – he had ambition. He was no more an intellectual than Padre José, but his father was a storekeeper, and he knew the value of a balance of twenty-two pesos and how to manage mortgages. He wasn't content to remain all his life the priest of a not very large parish. His ambitions came back to him now as something faintly comic, and he gave a little gulp of astonished laughter in the candlelight. The half-caste opened his eyes and said, 'Are you still not asleep?'

'Sleep yourself,' the priest said, wiping a little sweat off his face with his sleeve.

'I am so cold.'

'Just a fever. Would you like this shirt? It isn't much, but it might help.'

'No, no. I don't want anything of yours. You don't trust me.'

No, if he had been humble like Padre José, he might be living in the capital now with Maria on a pension. This was pride, devilish pride, lying here offering his shirt to the man who wanted to betray him. Even his attempts at escape had been half-hearted because of his pride – the sin by which the angels fell. When he was the only priest left in the state his pride had been all the greater; he thought himself the devil of a fellow carrying God around at the risk of his life; one day there would be a reward . . . He prayed in the half-light: 'O God, forgive me – I am a proud, lustful, greedy man. I have loved authority too much. These people are martyrs – protecting me with their own lives. They deserve a martyr to care for them – not a man like me, who loves all the wrong things. Perhaps I had better escape – if I tell people how it is over here, perhaps they will send a good man with a fire of love . . .' As usual his self-confession dwindled away into the practical problem – what am I to do?

Over by the door the mestizo was uneasily asleep.

How little his pride had to feed on – he had celebrated only four Masses this year, and he had heard perhaps a hundred confessions. It seemed to him that the dunce of any seminary could have done as well

. . . or better. He raised himself very carefully and began to move on his naked toes across the floor. He must get to Carmen and away again quickly before this man . . . the mouth was open, showing the pale hard toothless gums. In his sleep he was grunting and struggling; then he collapsed upon the floor and lay still.

There was a sense of abandonment, as if he had given up every struggle from now on and lay there a victim of some power . . . The priest had only to step over his legs and push the door – it opened outwards.

He put one leg over the body and a hand gripped his ankle. The mestizo stared up at him. 'Where are you going?'

'I want to relieve myself,' the priest said.

The hand still held his ankle. 'Why can't you do it here?' the man whined at him. 'What's preventing you, father? You are a father, aren't you?'

'I have a child,' the priest said, 'if that's what you mean.'

'You know what I mean. You understand about God, don't you?' The hot hand clung. 'Perhaps you've got him there – in a pocket. You carry him around, don't you, in case there's anybody sick . . . Well, I'm sick. Why don't you give him to me? or do you think he wouldn't have anything to do with me . . . if he knew?'

'You're feverish.'

But the man wouldn't stop. The priest was reminded of an oil-gusher which some prospectors had once struck near Concepción – it wasn't a good enough field apparently to justify further operations, but there it had stood for forty-eight hours against the sky, a black fountain spouting out of the marshy useless soil and flowing away to waste – fifty thousand gallons an hour. It was like the religious sense in man, cracking suddenly upwards, a black pillar of fumes and impurity, running to waste. 'Shall I tell you what I've done? – It's your business to listen. I've taken money from women to do you know what, and I've given money to boys . . .'

'I don't want to hear.'

'It's your business.'

'You're mistaken.'

'Oh no, I'm not. You can't deceive me. Listen. I've given money to boys – you know what I mean. And I've eaten meat on Fridays.' The awful jumble of the gross, the trivial, and the grotesque shot up between the two yellow fangs, and the hand on the priest's ankle shook and shook with the fever. 'I've told lies, I haven't fasted in Lent for I don't know how many years. Once I had two women – I'll tell you what I did . . .' He had an immense self-importance; he was unable to picture a world of which he was only a typical part – a world of treachery, violence, and lust in which his shame was altogether insignificant. How often the priest had heard the same confession – Man was so limited he hadn't even the ingenuity to invent a new vice: the animals knew as much. It was for this world that Christ had died; the more evil you saw and heard about you, the greater glory lay around the death. It was too easy to die for what was good or beautiful, for home or children or a civilization – it needed a God to die for the half-hearted and the corrupt. He said, 'Why do you tell me all this?'

The man lay exhausted, saying nothing; he was beginning to sweat, his hand loosed its hold on the priest's ankle. He pushed the door open and went outside – the darkness was complete. How to find the mule? He stood listening – something howled not very far away. He was frightened. Back in the hut the candle burned – there was an odd bubbling sound: the man was weeping. Again he was reminded of oil land, the little black pools and the bubbles blowing slowly up and breaking and beginning again.

The priest struck a match and walked straight forward – one, two, three paces into a tree. A match in that immense darkness was of no more value than a firefly. He whispered, '*Mula, mula*,' afraid to call out in case the half-caste heard him; besides, it was unlikely that the stupid beast would make any reply. He hated it – the lurching mandarin head, the munching greedy mouth, the smell of blood and ordure. He struck another match and set off again, and again after a few paces he met a tree. Inside the hut the gaseous sound of grief went on. He had got to get to Carmen and away before that man found a means of communicating with the police. He began again, quartering the clearing – one, two, three, four – and then a tree. Something moved under his foot, and he thought of scorpions. One, two, three, and suddenly the grotesque cry of the mule came out of the dark; it was hungry, or perhaps it smelt some animal.

It was tethered a few yards behind the hut – the candle-flame swerved out of sight. His matches were running low, but after two more attempts he found the mule. The half-caste had stripped it and hidden the saddle. He couldn't waste time looking any more. He mounted, and only then realized how impossible it was to make it move without even a piece of rope round the neck; he tried twisting its ears, but they had no more sensitivity than door-handles: it stood planted there like an equestrian statue. He struck a match and held the flame against its side – it struck up suddenly with its back hooves and he dropped the match; then it was still again, with drooping sullen head and great antediluvian haunches. A voice said accusingly, 'You are leaving me here to die.'

'Nonsense,' the priest said. 'I am in a hurry. You will be all right in the morning, but I can't wait.'

There was a scuffle in the darkness and then a hand gripped his naked foot. 'Don't leave me alone,' the voice said. 'I appeal to you – as a Christian.'

'You won't come to any harm here.'

'How do you know with the gringo somewhere about?'

'I don't know anything about the gringo. I've met nobody who has seen him. Besides, he's only a man – like one of us.'

'I won't be left alone. I have an instinct . . .'

'Very well,' the priest said wearily, 'find the saddle.'

When they had saddled the mule they set off again, the mestizo holding the stirrup. They were silent – sometimes the half-caste stumbled, and the grey false dawn began; a small coal of cruel satisfaction glowed at the back of the priest's mind – this was Judas sick and unsteady and scared in the dark. He had only to beat the mule on to leave him stranded in the forest once he dug in the point of his stick and forced it forward at a weary trot, and he could feel the pull, pull of the half-caste's arm on the stirrup holding him back. There was a groan – it sounded like 'Mother of God', and he let the mule slacken its pace. He prayed silently, 'God forgive me.' Christ had died for this man too: how could he pretend with his pride and lust and cowardice to be any more worthy of that death than the half-caste? This man intended to betray him for money which he needed, and he had betrayed God for what? Not even for real lust. He said, 'Are you sick?' and there was no reply. He dismounted and said, 'Get up. I'll walk for a while.'

'I'm all right,' the man said in a tone of hatred.

'Better get up.'

'You think you're very fine,' the man said. 'Helping your enemies. That's Christian, isn't it?'

'Are you my enemy?'

'That's what you think. You think I want seven hundred pesos – that's the reward. You think a poor man like me can't afford not to tell the police . . .'

'You're feverish.'

The man said in a sick voice of cunning, 'You're right, of course.'

'Better mount.' The man nearly fell: he had to shoulder him up. He leant hopelessly down from the mule with his mouth almost on a level with the priest's, breathing bad air into the other's face. He said, 'A poor man has no choice, father. Now if I was a rich man – only a little rich – I should be good.'

The priest suddenly – for no reason – thought of the Children of Mary eating pastries. He giggled and said, 'I doubt it.' If that were goodness . . .

'What was that you said, father? You don't trust me,' he went ambling on, 'because I'm poor, and because you don't trust me –' he collapsed over the pommel of the saddle, breathing heavily and shivering. The priest held him on with one hand and they proceeded slowly towards Carmen. It was no good; he couldn't stay there now. It would be unwise even to enter the village, for if it became known, somebody would lose his life – they would take a hostage. Somewhere a long way off a cock crew. The mist came up knee-high out of a spongy ground, and he thought of the flashlight going off in the bare church hall among the trestle tables. What hour did the cocks crow? One of the oddest things about the world these days was that there were no clocks – you could go a year without hearing one strike. They went with the churches, and you were left with the grey slow dawns and the precipitate nights as the only measurements of time.

Slowly, slumped over the pommel, the half-caste became visible, the yellow canines jutting out of the open mouth; really, the priest thought, he deserved his reward – seven hundred pesos wasn't so much, but he could probably live on it – in that dusty hopeless village – for a whole year. He giggled again; he could never take the complications of destiny quite seriously, and it was just possible, he thought, that a year without anxiety might save this man's soul. You only had to turn up the underside of any situation and out came scuttling these small absurd contradictory situations. He had given way to despair – and out of that had emerged a human soul and love – not the best love, but love all the same. The mestizo said suddenly, 'It's fate. I was told once by a fortune-teller . . . a reward . . .'

He held the half-caste firmly in the saddle and walked on. His feet were bleeding, but they would soon harden. An odd stillness dropped over the forest, and welled up in the mist from the ground. The night had been noisy, but now all was quiet. It was like an armistice with the guns silent on either side: you could imagine the whole world listening to what they had never heard before – peace.

A voice said 'You *are* the priest, aren't you?'

'Yes.' It was as if they had climbed out of their opposing trenches and met to fraternize among the wires in No Man's Land. He remembered stories of the European war – how during the last years men had sometimes met on an impulse between the lines.

'Yes,' he said again, and the mule plodded on. Sometimes, instructing children in the old days, he had been asked by some black lozenge-eyed Indian child, 'What is God like?' and he would answer facilely with references to the father and the mother, or perhaps more ambitiously he would include brother and sister and try to give some idea of all loves and relationships combined in an immense and yet personal passion . . . But at the centre of his own faith there always stood the convincing mystery – that we were made in God's image. God was the parent, but He was also the policeman, the criminal, the priest, the maniac, and the judge. Something resembling God dangled from the gibbet or went into odd attitudes before the bullets in a prison yard or contorted itself like a camel in the attitude of sex. He would sit in the confessional and hear the complicated dirty ingenuities which God's image had thought out, and God's image shook now, up and down on the mule's back, with the yellow teeth sticking out over the lower lip, and God's image did its despairing act of rebellion with Maria in the hut among the rats. He said, 'Do you feel better now? Not so cold, eh? Or so hot?' and pressed his hand with a kind of driven tenderness upon the shoulders of God's image.

The man didn't answer, as the mule's backbone slid him first to one side, then the other.

'It isn't more than two leagues now,' the priest said encouragingly – he had to make up his mind. He carried around with him a clearer picture of Carmen than any other village or town in the state: the long slope of grass which led up from the river to the cemetery on a tiny hill where his parents were buried. The wall of the burial-ground had fallen in: one or two crosses had been smashed by enthusiasts: an angel had lost one of its stone wings, and what gravestones were left undamaged leant at an acute angle in the long marshy grass. One image of the Mother of God had lost ears and arms and stood like a pagan Venus over the grave of some rich forgotten timber merchant. It was odd – this fury to deface, because, of course, you could never deface enough. If God had been like a toad, you could have rid the globe of toads, but when God was like yourself, it was no good being content with stone figures – you had to kill yourself among the graves.

He said, 'Are you strong enough now to hold on?' He took away his hand. The path divided – one way led to Carmen, the other west. He pushed the mule on, down the Carmen path, flogging at its haunches. He said, 'You'll be there in two hours,' and stood watching the mule go on towards his home with the informer humped over the pommel.

The half-caste tried to sit upright. 'Where are you going?'

'You'll be my witness,' the priest said. 'I haven't been in Carmen. But if you mention me, they'll give you food.'

'Why . . . why . . .' The half-caste tried to wrench round the mule's head, but he hadn't enough strength: it just went on. The priest called out, 'Remember. I haven't been in Carmen.' But where else now could he go? The conviction came to him that there was only one place in the whole state where there was no danger of an innocent man being taken as a hostage – but he couldn't go there in these clothes . . . The half-caste held hard on to the pommel and swivelled his yellow eyes beseechingly, 'You wouldn't leave me here – alone.' But it was more than the half-caste he was leaving behind on the forest track: the mule stood sideways like a barrier, nodding a stupid head, between him and the place where he had been born. He felt like a man without a passport who is turned away from every harbour.

The half-caste was calling after him, 'Call yourself a Christian.' He had somehow managed to get himself upright. He began to shout abuse – a meaningless series of indecent words which petered out in the forest like the weak blows of a hammer. He whispered, 'If I see you again, you can't blame *me* . . .' Of course, he had every reason to be angry: he had lost seven hundred pesos. He shrieked hopelessly, 'I don't forget a face.'

Chapter 2

THE young men and women walked round and round the plaza in the hot electric night, the men one way, the girls another, never speaking to each other. In the northern sky the lightning flapped. It was like a religious ceremony which had lost all meaning, but at which they still wore their best clothes. Sometimes a group of older women would join in the procession with a little more excitement and laughter, as if they retained some memory of how things used to go before all the books were lost. A man with a gun on his hip watched from the Treasury steps, and a small withered soldier sat by the prison door with a gun between his knees and the shadows of the palms pointed at him like a zareba of sabres. Lights were burning in a dentist's window, shining on the swivel chair and the red plush cushions and the glass for rinsing on its little stand and the child's chest-of-drawers full of fittings. Behind the wire-netted windows of the private houses grandmothers swung back and forth in rocking-chairs, among the family photographs – nothing to do, nothing to say, with too many clothes on, sweating a little. This was the capital city of a state.

The man in the shabby drill suit watched it all from a bench. A squad of armed police went by to their quarters walking out of step, carrying their rifles anyhow. The plaza was lit at each corner by clusters of three globes joined by ugly trailing overhead wires, and a beggar worked his way from seat to seat without success.

He sat down next to the man in drill and started a long explanation. There was something confidential, and at the same time threatening, in his manner. On every side the streets ran down towards the river and the port and the marshy plain. He said that he had a wife and so many children, and that during the last few weeks they had eaten so little – he broke off and fingered the cloth of the other's drill suit. 'And how much,' he said, 'did this cost?'

'You'd be surprised how little.'

Suddenly as a clock struck nine-thirty all the lights went out. The beggar said, 'It's enough to make a man desperate.' He looked this way and that as the parade drifted away down hill. The man in drill got up, and the other got up too, tagging after him towards the edge of the plaza: his flat bare feet went slap, slap on the pavement. He said, 'A few pesos wouldn't make any difference to you . . .'

'Ah, if you knew what a difference they would make.'

The beggar was put out. He said, 'A man like me sometimes feels that he would do anything for a few pesos.' Now that the lights were out all over town, they stood intimately in the shadow. He said, 'Can you blame me?'

'No, no. It would be the last thing I would do.'

Everything he said seemed to feed the beggar's irritation. 'Sometimes,' the beggar said, 'I feel as if I could kill . . .'

'That, of course, would be very wrong.'

'Would it be wrong if I got a man by the throat . . . ?'

'Well, a starving man has got the right to save himself, certainly.'

The beggar watched with rage, while the other talked on as if he were considering a point of academic interest. 'In my case, of course, it would hardly be worth the risk. I possess exactly fifteen pesos seventy-five centavos in the world. I haven't eaten myself for forty-eight hours.'

'Mother of God,' the beggar said, 'you're as hard as a stone. Haven't you a heart?'

The man in the drill suit suddenly giggled. The other said, 'You're lying. Why haven't you eaten – if you've got fifteen pesos?'

'You see, I want to spend them on drink.'

'What sort of drink?'

'The kind of drink a stranger doesn't know how to get in a place like this.'

'You mean spirits?'

'Yes – and wine.'

The beggar came very close. His leg touched the leg of the other man, he put a hand upon the other's sleeve. They might have been great friends or even brothers standing intimately together in the dark. Even the lights in the houses were going out now, and the taxis, which during the day waited half-way down the hill for fares that never seemed to come, were already dispersing – a tail-lamp winked and went out past the police barracks. The beggar said, 'Man, this is your lucky day. How much would you pay me . . . ?'

'For some drink?'

'For an introduction to someone who could let you have a little brandy – real fine Vera Cruz brandy.'

'With a throat like mine,' the man in drill explained, 'it's wine I really want.'

'Pulque or mescal – he's got everything.'

'Wine?'

'Quince wine.'

'I'd give everything I've got,' the other swore solemnly and exactly, '– except the centavos, that's to say – for some real genuine grape wine.' Somewhere down the hill by the river a drum was beating, one-two, one-two, and the sound of marching feet kept a rough time: the soldiers – or the police – were going home to bed.

'How much?' the beggar repeated impatiently.

'Well, I would give you the fifteen pesos and you would get the wine for me for what you cared to spend.'

'You come with me.'

They began to go down the hill. At the corner where one street ran up past the chemist's shop towards the barracks and another ran down to the hotel, the quay, the warehouse of the United Banana Company, the man in drill stopped. The police were marching up, rifles slung at ease. 'Wait a moment.' Among them walked a half-caste with two fang-like teeth jutting out over his lip. The man in drill standing in the shadow watched him go by: once the mestizo turned his head and their eyes met. Then the police went by, up into the plaza. 'Let's go. Quickly.'

The beggar said, 'They won't interfere with us. They're after bigger game.'

'What was that man doing with them, do you think?'

'Who knows? A hostage perhaps.'

'If he had been a hostage, they would have tied his hands, wouldn't they?'

'How do I know?' He had the grudging independence you find in countries where it is the right of a poor man to beg. He said, 'Do you want the spirits or don't you?'

'I want wine.'

'I can't say he'll have this or that. You must take what comes.'

He led the way down towards the river. He said, 'I don't even know if he's in town.' The beetles were flocking out and covering the pavements; they popped under the feet like puff-balls, and a sour green smell came up from the river. The white bust of a general glimmered in a tiny public garden, all hot paving and dust, and an electric dynamo throbbed on the ground floor of the only hotel. Wide wooden stairs crawling with beetles ran up to the first floor. 'I've done my best,' the beggar said, 'a man can't do more.'

On the first floor a man dressed in formal dark trousers and a white skin-tight vest came out of a bedroom with a towel over his shoulder. He had a little grey aristocratic beard and he wore braces as well as a belt. Somewhere in the distance a pipe gurgled, and the beetles detonated against a bare globe. The beggar was talking earnestly, and once as he talked the light went off altogether and then flickered unsatisfactorily on again. The head of the stairs was littered with wicker rocking-chairs, and on a big slate were chalked the names of the guests – three only for twenty rooms.

The beggar turned back to his companion. 'The gentleman,' he said, 'is not in. The manager says so. Shall we wait for him?'

'Time to me is of no account.'

They went into a big bare bedroom with a tiled floor. The little black iron bedstead was like something somebody has left behind by accident when moving out. They sat down on it side by side and waited, and the beetles came popping in through the gaps in the mosquito wire. 'He is a very important man,' the beggar said. 'He is the cousin of the

Governor – he can get anything for you, anything at all. But, of course, you must be introduced by someone he trusts.'

'And he trusts you?'

'I worked for him once.' He added frankly, 'He has to trust me.'

'Does the Governor know?'

'Of course not. The Governor is a hard man.'

Every now and then the water-pipes swallowed noisily.

'And why should he trust me?'

'Oh, anyone can tell a drinker. You'll want to come back for more. It's good stuff he sells. Better give me the fifteen pesos.' He counted them carefully twice. He said, 'I'll get you a bottle of the best Vera Cruz brandy. You see if I don't.' The light went off, and they sat in the dark; the bed creaked as one of them shifted.

'I don't want brandy,' a voice said. 'At least – not very much.'

'What do you want then?'

'I told you – wine.'

'Wine's expensive.'

'Never mind that. Wine or nothing.'

'Quince wine?'

'No, no. French wine.'

'Sometimes he has Californian wine.'

'That would do.'

'Of course himself – he gets it for nothing. From the Customs.'

The dynamo began throbbing again below and the light came dimly on. The door opened and the manager beckoned the beggar; a long conversation began. The man in the drill suit leant back on the bed. His chin was cut in several places where he had been shaving too closely; his face was hollow and ill – it gave the impression that he had once been plump and round-faced but had caved in. He had the appearance of a business man who had fallen on hard times.

The beggar came back. He said, 'The gentleman's busy, but he'll be back soon. The manager sent a boy to look for him.'

'Where is he?'

'He can't be interrupted. He's playing billiards with the Chief of Police.' He came back to the bed, squashing two beetles under his naked feet. He said, 'This is a fine hotel. Where do you stay? You're a stranger, aren't you?'

'Oh, I'm just passing through.'

'This gentleman is very influential. It would be a good thing to offer him a drink. After all, you won't want to take it all away with you. You may as well drink here as anywhere else.'

'I should like to keep a little – to take home.'

'It's all one. I say that home is where there is a chair and a glass.'

'All the same –' Then the light went out again, and on the horizon the lightning bellied out. The sound of thunder came through the mosquito-net from very far away like the noise you hear from the other end of a town when the Sunday bull-fight is on.

The beggar said confidentially, 'What's your trade?'

'Oh, I pick up what I can – where I can.'

They sat in silence together listening to the sound of feet on the wooden stairs. The door opened, but they could see nothing. A voice swore resignedly and asked, 'Who's there?' Then a match was struck and showed a large blue jaw and went out. The dynamo churned away and the light went on again. The stranger said wearily, 'Oh, it's you.'

'It's me.'

He was a small man with a too large pasty face and he was dressed in a tight grey suit. A revolver bulged under his waistcoat. He said, 'I've got nothing for you. Nothing.'

The beggar padded across the room and began to talk earnestly in a very low voice: once he gently squeezed the other's polished shoe with his bare toes. The man sighed and blew out his cheeks and watched the bed closely as if he feared they had designs on it. He said sharply to the one in the drill suit, 'So you want some Vera Cruz brandy, do you? It's against the law.'

'Not brandy. I don't want brandy.'

'Isn't beer good enough for you?'

He came fussily and authoritatively into the middle of the room, his shoes squeaking on the tiles – the Governor's cousin. 'I could have you arrested,' he threatened.

The man in the drill suit cringed formally. He said, 'Of course, your Excellency . . .'

'Do you think I've got nothing better to do than slake the thirst of every beggar who chooses . . . ?'

'I would never have troubled you if this man had not . . .'

The Governor's cousin spat on the tiles.

'But if your Excellency would rather I went away . . .'

He said sharply, 'I'm not a hard man. I always try to oblige my fellows . . . when it's in my power and does no harm. I have a position, you understand. These drinks come to me quite legally.'

'Of course.'

'And I have to charge what they cost me.'

'Of course.'

'Otherwise I'd be a ruined man.' He walked delicately to the bed as if his shoes were cramping him and began to unmake it. 'Are you a talker?' he asked over his shoulder.

'I know how to keep a secret.'

'I don't mind you telling the right people.' There was a large rent in the mattress; he pulled out a handful of straw and put his fingers in again. The man in drill gazed out with false indifference at the public gardens, the dark mud-banks and the masts of sailing ships; the lightning flapped behind them, and the thunder came nearer.

'There,' said the Governor's cousin, 'I can spare you that. It's good stuff.'

'It wasn't really brandy I wanted.'

'You must take what comes.'

'Then I think I'd rather have my fifteen pesos back.'

The Governor's cousin exclaimed sharply, '*Fifteen* pesos.' The beggar began rapidly to explain that the gentleman wanted to buy a little wine as well as brandy: they began to argue fiercely by the bed in low voices about prices. The Governor's cousin said, 'Wine's very difficult to get. I can let you have two bottles of brandy.'

'One of brandy and one of . . .'

'It's the best Vera Cruz brandy.'

'But I am a wine drinker . . . you don't know how I long for wine . . .'

'Wine costs me a great deal of money. How much more can you pay?'

'I have only seventy-five centavos left in the world.'

'I could let you have a bottle of tequila.'

'No, no.'

'Another fifty centavos then . . . It will be a large bottle.' He began to scrabble in the mattress again, pulling out straw. The beggar winked at the man in drill and made the motions of drawing a cork and filling a glass.

'There,' the Governor's cousin said, 'take it or leave it.'

'Oh, I will take it.'

The Governor's cousin suddenly lost his surliness. He rubbed his hands and said, 'A stuffy night. The rains are going to be early this year, I think.'

'Perhaps your Excellency would honour me by taking a glass of brandy to toast our business.'

'Well, well . . . perhaps . . .' The beggar opened the door and called briskly for glasses.

'It's a long time,' the Governor's cousin said, 'since I had a glass of wine. Perhaps it would be more suitable for a toast.'

'Of course,' the man in drill said, 'as your Excellency chooses.' He watched the cork drawn with a look of painful anxiety. He said, 'If you will excuse me, I think I will have brandy,' and smiled raggedly, with an effort, watching the wine level fall.

They toasted each other, all three sitting on the bed – the beggar drank brandy. The Governor's cousin said, 'I'm proud of this wine. It's good wine. The best Californian.' The beggar winked and motioned and the man in drill said, 'One more glass, your Excellency – or can I recommend this brandy?'

'It's good brandy – but I think another glass of wine.' They refilled their glasses. The man in drill said, 'I'm going to take some of that wine back – to my mother. She loves a glass.'

'She couldn't do better,' the Governor's cousin said emptying his own. He said, 'So you have a mother?'

'Haven't we all?'

'Ah, you're lucky. Mine's dead. His hand strayed towards the bottle, grasped it. 'Sometimes I miss her. I called her "my little friend".' He tilted the bottle. 'With your permission?'

'Of course, your Excellency,' the other said hopelessly, taking a long draught of brandy. The beggar said, 'I too have a mother.'

'Who cares?' the Governor's cousin said sharply. He leant back and the bed creaked. He said, 'I have often thought a mother is a better friend than a father. Her influence is towards peace, goodness, charity . . . Always on the anniversary of her death I go to her grave with flowers.'

The man in drill caught a hiccup politely. He said, 'Ah, if I could too . . .'

'But you said your mother was alive?'

'I thought you were speaking of your grandmother.'

'How could I? I can't remember my grandmother.'

'Nor can I.'

'I can,' the beggar said.

The Governor's cousin said, 'You talk too much.'

'Perhaps I could send him to have this wine wrapped up. . . . For your Excellency's sake I mustn't be seen . . .'

'Wait, wait. There's no hurry. You are very welcome here. Anything in this room is at your disposal. Have a glass of wine.'

'I think brandy . . .'

'Then with your permission . . .' He tilted the bottle: a little of it splashed over on to the sheets. 'What were we talking about?'

'Our grandmothers.'

'I don't think it can have been that. I can't even remember mine. The earliest thing I can remember . . .'

The door opened. The manager said, 'The Chief of Police is coming up the stairs.'

'Excellent. Show him in.'

'Are you sure?'

'Of course. He's a good fellow.' He said to the others. 'But at billiards you can't trust him.'

A large stout man in a singlet, white trousers and a revolver-holster appeared in the doorway. The Governor's cousin said, 'Come in. Come in. How is your toothache? We were talking about our grandmothers.' He said sharply to the beggar, 'Make room for the jefe.'

The jefe stood in the doorway, watching them with dim embarrassment. He said, 'Well, well . . .'

'We're having a little private party. Will you join us? It would be an honour.'

The jefe's face suddenly lit up at the sight of the wine. 'Of course – a little beer never comes amiss.'

'That's right. Give the jefe a glass of beer.' The beggar filled his own glass with wine and held it out. The jefe took his place upon the bed and drained the glass: then he took the bottle himself. He said, 'It's good beer. Very good beer. Is this the only bottle?' The man in drill watched him with frigid anxiety.

'I'm afraid the only bottle.'

'*Salud!*'

'And what,' the Governor's cousin said, 'were we talking about?'

'About the first thing you could remember,' the beggar said.

'The first thing I can remember,' the jefe began, with deliberation, '– but this gentleman is not drinking.'

'I will have a little brandy.'

'*Salud!*'

'*Salud!*'

'The first thing I can remember with any distinctness is my first communion. Ah, the thrill of the soul, my parents round me . . .'

'How many parents then have you got?'

'Two, of course.'

'They could not have been around you – you would have needed at least four – ha, ha.'

'*Salud!*'

'*Salud!*'

'No, but as I was saying – life has such irony. It was my painful duty to watch the priest who gave me that communion shot – an old man. I am not ashamed to say that I wept. The comfort is that he is probably a saint and that he prays for us. It is not everyone who earns a saint's prayers.'

'An unusual way . . .'

'But then life is mysterious.'

'*Salud!*'

The man in drill said, 'A glass of brandy, jefe?'

'There is so little in this bottle that I may as well . . .'

'I was very anxious to take a little back for my mother.'

'Oh, a drop like this. It would be an insult to take it. Just the dregs.' He turned it up over his glass and chuckled, 'If you can talk of beer having dregs.' Then he stopped with the bottle held over the glass and said with astonishment, 'Why, man, you're crying.' All three watched the man in drill with their mouths a little open. He said, 'It always takes me like this – brandy. Forgive me, gentlemen. I get drunk very easily and then I see . . .'

'See what?'

'Oh, I don't know, all the hope of the world draining away.'

'Man, you're a poet.'

The beggar said, 'A poet is the soul of his country.'

Lightning filled the windows like a white sheet, and thunder crashed suddenly overhead. The one globe flickered and faded up near the ceiling. 'This is bad news for my men,' the jefe said, stamping on a beetle which had crawled too near.

'Why bad news?'

'The rains coming so early. You see they are on a hunt.'

'The gringo . . . ?'

'He doesn't really matter, but the Governor's found there's still a priest, and you know what he feels about that. If it was me, I'd let the poor devil alone. He'd starve or die of fever or give up. He can't be doing any good – or any harm. Why, nobody even noticed he was about till a few months ago.'

'You'll have to hurry.'

'Oh, he hasn't any real chance. Unless he gets over the border. We've got a man who knows him. Spoke to him, spent a night with him. Let's talk of something else. Who wants to be a policeman?'

'Where do you think he is?'

'You'd be surprised.'

'Why?'

'He's here – in this town, I mean. That's deduction. You see since we started taking hostages from the villages, there's really nowhere else . . . They turn him away, they won't have him. So we've set this man I told you about loose like a dog – he'll run into him one day or another – and then . . .'

The man in drill said, 'Have you had to shoot many hostages?'

'Not yet. Three or four perhaps. Well, here goes the last of the beer. *Salud!*' He put the glass regretfully down. 'Perhaps now I could have just a drop of your – sidral, shall we say?'

'Yes. Of course.'

'Have I met you before? Your face somehow . . .'

'I don't think I've had the honour.'

'That's another mystery,' the jefe said, stretching out a long fat limb and gently pushing the beggar towards the bed-knobs, 'how you think you've seen people – and places – before. Was it in a dream or in a past life? I once heard a doctor say it was something to do with the focusing of the eyes. But he was a Yankee. A materialist.'

'I remember once . . .' the Governor's cousin said. The lightning shot down over the harbour and the thunder beat on the roof; this was the atmosphere of a whole state – the storm outside and the talk just going on – words like 'mystery' and 'soul' and 'the source of life' came in over and over again, as they sat on the bed talking, with nothing to do and nothing to believe and nowhere better to go.

The man in drill said, 'I think perhaps I had better be moving on.'

'Where to?'

'Oh . . . friends,' he said vaguely, sketching widely with his hands a whole world of fictitious friendships.

'You'd better take your drink with you,' the Governor's cousin said. He admitted, 'After all you paid for it.'

'Thank you, Excellency.' He picked up the brandy bottle. Perhaps there were three fingers left. The bottle of wine, of course, was quite empty.

'Hide it, man, hide it,' the Governor's cousin said sharply.

'Oh, of course, Excellency, I will be careful.'

'You don't have to call him Excellency,' the jefe said. He gave a bellow of laughter and thrust the beggar right off the bed on to the floor.

'No, no, that is . . .' He sidled cautiously out, with a smudge of tears under his red sore eyes and from the hall heard the conversation begin again – 'mystery', 'soul' – going interminably on to no end.

*

The beetles had disappeared; the rain had apparently washed them away: it came perpendicularly down, with a sort of measured intensity, as if it were driving nails into a coffin lid. But the air was no clearer: sweat and rain hung together on the clothes. The priest stood for a few seconds in the doorway of the hotel, the dynamo thudding behind him, then he darted a few yards into another doorway and hesitated, staring over past the bust of the general to the tethered sailing boats and one old barge with a tin funnel. He had nowhere to go. Rain hadn't entered into his calculations: he had believed that it would be possible just to hang on somehow, sleeping on benches or by the river.

A couple of soldiers arguing furiously came down the street towards the quay – they just let the rain fall on them, as if it didn't matter, as if things were so bad anyway you couldn't notice . . . The priest pushed the wooden door against which he stood, a cantina door coming down only to the knees, and went in out of the rain: stacks of gaseosa bottles and a single billiard table with the score strung on rings, three or four men – somebody had laid his holster on the bar. The priest moved too quickly and jolted the elbow of a man who was making a shot. He turned furiously: 'Mother of God!' He was a Red Shirt. Was there no safety anywhere, even for a moment?

The priest apologized humbly, edging back towards the door but, again he was too quick – his pocket caught against the wall and the brandy bottle chinked. Three or four faces looked at him with malicious amusement: he was a stranger and they were going to have fun. 'What's that you've got in your pocket?' the Red Shirt asked. He was a youth not out of his teens, with gold teeth and a jesting conceited mouth.

'Lemonade,' the priest said.

'What do you want to carry lemonade with you for?'

'I take it at night – with my quinine.'

The Red Shirt swaggered up and poked the pocket with the butt of his cue. 'Lemonade, eh?'

'Yes, lemonade.'

'Let's have a look at the lemonade.' He turned proudly to the others and said, 'I can scent a smuggler at ten paces.' He thrust his hand into the priest's pocket and hauled at the brandy bottle. 'There,' he said. 'Didn't I tell you –' The priest flung himself against the swing door and burst out into the rain. A voice shouted, 'Catch him.' They were having the time of their lives.

He was off up the street towards the plaza, turned left and right again – it was lucky the streets were dark and the moon obscured. As long as he kept away from lighted windows he was almost invisible –

he could hear them calling to each other. They were not giving up: it was better than billiards: somewhere a whistle blew – the police were joining in.

This was the town to which it had been his ambition to be promoted, leaving the right kind of debts behind at Concepción: he thought of the cathedral and Montez and a Monsignor he once knew, as he doubled this way and that. Something buried very deep, the will to escape, cast a momentary and appalling humour over the whole situation – he giggled and panted and giggled again. He could hear them hallooing and whistling in the dark, and the rain came down; it drove and jumped upon the cement floor of the useless frontón which had once been the cathedral (it was too hot to play pelota and a few iron swings stood like gallows at its edge). He worked his way downhill again: he had an idea.

The shouts came nearer, and then up from the river a new lot of men approached; these were pursuing the hunt methodically – he could tell it by their slow pace, the police, the official hunters. He was between the two – the amateurs and the professionals. But he knew the door – he pushed it open, came quickly through into the patio and closed it behind him.

He stood in the dark and panted, hearing the steps come nearer up the street, while the rain drove down. Then he realized that somebody was watching him from the window, a small dark withered face, like one of the preserved heads tourists buy. He came up to the grill and said, 'Padre José?'

'Over there.' A second face appeared behind the other's shoulder, lit uncertainly by a candle-flame, then a third face: faces sprouted like vegetables. He could feel them watching him as he splashed back across the patio and banged on a door.

He didn't for a second or two recognize Padre José in the absurd billowing nightshirt, holding a lamp. The last time he had seen him was at the conference, sitting in the back row, biting his nails, afraid to be noticed. It hadn't been necessary: none of the busy cathedral clergy even knew what he was called. It was odd to think that now he had won a kind of fame superior to theirs. He said 'José' gently, winking up at him from the splashing dark.

'Who are you?'

'Don't you remember me? Of course, it's years now . . . don't you remember the conference at the cathedral . . . ?'

'O God,' Padre José said.

'They are looking for me. I thought perhaps just for tonight you could perhaps . . .'

'Go away,' Padre José said, 'go away.'

'They don't know who I am. They think I'm a smuggler – but up at the police station they'll know.'

'Don't talk so loud. My wife . . .'

'Just show me some corner,' he whispered. He was beginning to feel fear again. Perhaps the effect of the brandy was wearing off (it was impossible in this hot damp climate to stay drunk for long: alcohol came out again under the armpits: it dripped from the forehead), or perhaps it was only that the desire of life which moves in cycles was returning – any sort of life.

In the lamplight Padre José's face wore an expression of hatred. He said, 'Why come to me? Why should you think . . . ? I'll call the police if you don't go. You know what sort of a man I am.'

He pleaded gently. 'You're a good man, José. I've always known that.'

'I'll shout if you don't go.'

He tried to remember some cause of hatred. There were voices in the street – arguments, a knocking – were they searching the houses? He said, 'If I ever offended you, José, forgive me. I was conceited, proud, overbearing – a bad priest. I always knew in my heart you were the better man.'

'Go,' José screeched at him, 'go. I don't want martyrs here. I don't belong any more. Leave me alone. I'm all right as I am.' He tried to gather up his venom into spittle and shot it feebly at the other's face: it didn't even reach, but fell impotently through the air. He said, 'Go and die quickly. That's your job,' and slammed the door to. The door of the patio came suddenly open and the police were there. He caught a glimpse of Padre José peering through a window and then an enormous shape in a white nightshirt engulfed him and drew him away – whisked him off, like a guardian spirit, from the disastrous human struggle. A voice said, 'That's him.' It was the young Red Shirt. He let his fist open and dropped by Padre José's wall a little ball of paper: it was like the final surrender of a whole past.

He knew it was the beginning of the end – after all these years. He began to say silently an act of contrition, while they picked the brandy bottle out of his pocket, but he couldn't give his mind to it. That was the fallacy of the death-bed repentance – penitence was the fruit of long training and discipline: fear wasn't enough. He tried to think of his child with shame, but he could only think of her with a kind of famished love – what would become of her? And the sin itself was so old that like an ancient picture the deformity had faded and left a kind of grace. The Red Shirt smashed the bottle on the stone paving and the smell of spirit rose all round them – not very strongly: there hadn't been much left.

Then they took him away. Now that they had caught him they treated him in a friendly way, poking fun at his attempt to escape, except the Red Shirt whose shot he had spoiled. He couldn't find any answer to their jokes: self-preservation lay across his brain like a horrifying obsession. When would they discover who he really was? When would he meet the half-caste, or the lieutenant who had interrogated him already? They moved in a bunch slowly up the hill to the plaza. A rifle-butt grounded outside the station as they came in. A small lamp fumed against the dirty white-washed wall; in the courtyard hammocks swung, bunched around sleeping bodies like the nets in which poultry are tied. 'You can sit down,' one of the men said, and pushed him in a comradely way towards a bench. Everything now seemed irrevocable; the sentry passed back and forth outside the door, and in the courtyard among the hammocks the ceaseless murmur of sleep went on.

Somebody had spoken to him: he gaped helplessly up. 'What?' There seemed to be an argument in progress between the police and the Red Shirt as to whether somebody should be disturbed. 'But it's his duty,' the Red Shirt kept on repeating: he had rabbity front teeth. He said, 'I'll report it to the Governor.'

A policeman said, 'You plead guilty, don't you?'

'Yes,' the priest said.

'There. What more do you want? It's a fine of five pesos. Why disturb anybody?'

'And who gets the five pesos, eh?'

'That's none of your business.'

The priest said suddenly, 'No one gets them.'

'No one?'

'I have only twenty-five centavos in the world.'

The door of an inner room opened and the lieutenant came out. He said. 'What in God's name is all the noise . . . ?' The police came raggedly and unwillingly to attention.

'I've caught a man carrying spirits,' the Red Shirt said.

The priest sat with his eyes on the ground . . . 'because it has crucified . . . crucified . . . crucified . . .' contrition stuck hopelessly over the formal words. He felt no emotion but fear.

'Well,' the lieutenant said, 'what is it to do with you? We catch dozens.'

'Shall we bring him in?' one of the men asked.

The lieutenant took a look at the bowed servile figure on the bench. 'Get up,' he said. The priest rose. Now, he thought, now . . . he raised his eyes. The lieutenant looked away, out of the door where the sentry slouched to and fro. His dark pinched face looked rattled, harassed . . .

'He has no money,' one of the policemen said.

'Mother of God,' the lieutenant said, 'can I never teach you . . . ?' He took two steps towards the sentry and turned, 'Search him. If he has no money, put him in a cell. Give him some work . . .' He went outside and suddenly raising his open hand he struck the sentry on the ear. He said, 'You're asleep. March as if you have some pride . . . pride,' he repeated again, while the small acetylene lamp fumed up the whitewashed wall and the smell of urine came up out of the yard and the men lay in their hammocks netted and secured.

'Shall we take his name?' a sergeant asked.

'Yes, of course,' the lieutenant said, not looking at him, walking briskly and nervously back past the lamp into the courtyard; he stood there unsheltered, looking round while the rain fell on his dapper uniform. He looked like a man with something on his mind: it was as if he were under the influence of some secret passion which had broken up the routine of his life. Back he came. He couldn't keep still.

The sergeant pushed the priest ahead into the inner room. A bright commercial calendar hung on the flaking whitewash – a dark-skinned mestizo girl in a bathing-dress advertised some gaseous water; somebody had pencilled in a neat pedagogic hand a facile and over-confident statement about man having nothing to lose but his chains.

'Name?' the sergeant said. Before he could check himself he had replied, 'Montez.'

'Home?'

He named a random village: he was absorbed in his own portrait. There he sat among the white-starched dresses of the first communicants. Somebody had put a ring round his face to pick it out. There was another picture on the wall too – the gringo from San Antonio, Texas, wanted for murder and bank robbery.

'I suppose,' the sergeant said cautiously, 'that you bought the drink from a stranger . . .'

'Yes.'

'Whom you can't identify?'

'No.'

'That's the way,' the sergeant said approvingly: it was obvious he didn't want to start anything. He took the priest quite confidingly by the arm and led him out and across the courtyard; he carried a large key like the ones used in morality plays or fairy stories as a symbol. A few men moved in the hammocks – a large unshaven jaw hung over the side like something left unsold on a butcher's counter: a big torn ear: a naked black-haired thigh. He wondered when the mestizo's face would appear, elated with recognition.

The sergeant unlocked a small grated door and let out with his boot at something straddled across the entrance. He said, 'They are all good fellows, all good fellows here,' kicking his way in. A heavy smell lay on the air and somebody in the absolute darkness wept.

The priest lingered on the threshold trying to see. He said, 'I am so dry. Could I have water?' the stench poured up his nostrils and he retched.

'In the morning,' the sergeant said, 'you've drunk enough now,' and laying a large considerate hand upon the priest's back, he pushed him in, then slammed the door to. He trod on a hand, an arm, and pressing his face against the grill, protested, 'There's no room. I can't see. Who are these people?' Outside among the hammocks the sergeant began to laugh. 'Hombre,' he said, 'hombre, have you never been in jail before?'

Chapter 3

A VOICE near his foot said, 'Got a cigarette?'

He drew quickly back and trod on an arm. A voice said imperatively, 'Water, quick,' as if whoever it was thought he could take a stranger unawares, and make him fork out.

'Got a cigarette?'

'No.' He said weakly, 'I have nothing at all,' and imagined he could feel enmity fuming up all round him. He moved again. Somebody said, 'Look out for the bucket.' That was where the stench came from. He stood perfectly still and waited for his sight to return. Outside the rain began to stop: it dropped haphazardly and the thunder moved away. You could count forty now between the lightning flash and the roll. Halfway to the sea, or halfway to the mountains. He felt around with his foot, trying to find enough space to sit down but there seemed to be no room at all. When the lightning went on he could see the hammocks at the edge of the courtyard.

'Got something to eat?' a voice asked, and when he didn't answer, 'Got something to eat?'

'No.'

'Got any money?' another voice said.

'No.'

Suddenly, from about five feet away, there came a tiny scream – a woman's. A tired voice said, 'Can't you be quiet?' Among the furtive movements came again the muffled painless cries. He realized that pleasure was going on even in this crowded darkness. Again he put out his foot and began to edge his way inch by inch away from the grill. Behind the human voices another noise went permanently on: it was like a small machine, an electric belt set at a certain tempo. It filled any silences that there were louder than human breath. It was the mosquitoes.

He had moved perhaps six feet from the grill, and his eyes began to distinguish heads – perhaps the sky was clearing: they hung around him like gourds. A voice said, 'Who are you?' He made no reply, feeling panic, edging in. Suddenly he found himself against the back wall: the stone was wet against his hand – the cell could not have been more than twelve feet deep. He found he could just sit down if he kept his feet drawn up under him. An old man lay slumped against his shoulder; he told his age from the featherweight lightness of the bones, the feeble uneven flutter of the breath. He was either somebody close to birth or death – and he could hardly be a child in this place. The old man said suddenly, 'Is that you, Catarina?' and his breath went out in a long patient sigh, as if he had been waiting a long while and could afford to wait a lot longer.

The priest said, 'No. Not Catarina.' When he spoke everybody came suddenly silent, listening, as if what he said had importance: then the voices and movements began again. But the sound of his own voice, the sense of communication with a neighbour, calmed him.

'You wouldn't be,' the old man said. 'I didn't really think you were. She'll never come.'

'Is she your wife?'

'What's that you're saying? I haven't got a wife.'

'Catarina?'

'She's my daughter.' Everybody was listening except the two invisible people who were concerned only in their cramped pleasure.

'Perhaps they won't allow her here.'

'She'll never try,' the old hopeless voice pronounced with absolute conviction. The priest's feet began to ache, drawn up under his haunches. He said, 'If she loves you . . .' Somewhere across the huddle of dark shapes the woman cried again – that finished cry of protest and abandonment and pleasure.

'It's the priests who've done it,' the old man said.

'The priests?'

'The priests.'

'Why the priests?'

'The priests.'

A low voice near his knees said, 'The old man's crazy. What's the use of asking him questions?'

'Is that you, Catarina?' He added, 'I don't really believe it, you know. It's just a question.'

'Now *I've* got something to complain about,' the voice went on. 'A man's got to defend his honour. You'll admit that, won't you?'

'I don't know anything about honour.'

'I was in the cantina and the man I'm telling you about came up to me and said, "Your mother's a whore." Well, I couldn't do anything about it: he'd got his gun on him. All I could do was wait. He drank too much beer – I knew he would – and when he was staggering I followed him out. I had a bottle and I smashed it against a wall. You see, I hadn't got my gun. His family's got influence with the jefe or I'd never be here.'

'It's a terrible thing to kill a man.'

'You talk like a priest.'

'It was the priests who did it,' the old man said. 'You're right there.'

'What does he mean?'

'What does it matter what an old man like that means? I'd like to tell you about something else . . .'

A woman's voice said, 'They took the child away from him.'

'Why?'

'It was a bastard. They acted quite correctly.'

At the word 'bastard' his heart moved painfully, as when a man in love hears a stranger name a flower which is also the name of his woman. 'Bastard!' the word filled him with miserable happiness. It brought his own child nearer: he could see her under the tree by the rubbish-dump, unguarded. He repeated 'Bastard?' as he might have repeated her name – with tenderness disguised as indifference.

'They said he was no fit father. But, of course, when the priests fled, she had to go with him. Where else could she go?' It was like a happy ending until she said, 'Of course she hated him. They'd taught her about things.' He could imagine the small set mouth of an educated woman. What was she doing here?

'Why is he in prison?'

'He had a crucifix.'

The stench from the pail got worse all the time; the night stood round them like a wall, without ventilation, and he could hear somebody making water, drumming on the tin sides. He said, 'They had no business . . .'

'They were doing what was right, of course. It was a mortal sin.'

'No right to make her hate him.'

'They knew what's right.'

He said, 'They were bad priests to do a thing like that. The sin was over. It was their duty to teach – well, love.'

'You don't know what's right. The priests know.'

He said after a moment's hesitation, very distinctly, 'I am a priest.'

It was like the end: there was no need to hope any longer. The ten years' hunt was over at last. There was silence all round him. This place was very like the world: overcrowded with lust and crime and unhappy love, it stank to heaven; but he realized that after all it was possible to find peace there, when you knew for certain that the time was short.

'A priest?' the woman said at last.

'Yes.'

'Do *they* know?'

'Not yet.'

He could feel a hand fumbling at his sleeve. A voice said, 'You shouldn't have told us. Father, there are all sorts here. Murderers . . .'

The voice which had described the crime to him said, 'You've no cause to abuse me. Because I kill a man it doesn't mean . . .' Whispering started everywhere. The voice said bitterly, 'I'm not an informer just because when a man says "Your mother was a whore . . ."'

The priest said, 'There's no need for anyone to inform on me. That would be a sin. When it's daylight they'll discover for themselves.'

'They'll shoot you, father,' the woman's voice said.

'Yes.'

'Are you afraid?'

'Yes. Of course.'

A new voice spoke, in the corner from which the sounds of pleasure had come. It said roughly and obstinately, 'A man isn't afraid of a thing like that.'

'No?' the priest asked.

'A bit of pain. What do you expect? It has to come.'

'All the same,' the priest said, 'I *am* afraid.'

'Toothache is worse.'

'We can't all be brave men.'

The voice said with contempt, 'You believers are all the same. Christianity makes you cowards.'

'Yes. Perhaps you are right. You see I am a bad priest and a bad man. To die in a state of mortal sin' – he gave an uneasy chuckle – 'it makes you think.'

'There. It's as I say. Believing in God makes cowards.' The voice was triumphant, as if it had proved something.

'So then?' the priest said.

'Better not to believe – and be a brave man.'

'I see – yes. And of course, if one believed the Governor did not exist or the jefe, if we could pretend that this prison was not a prison at all but a garden, how brave we could be then.'

'That's just foolishness.'

'But when we found that the prison was a prison, and the Governor up there in the square undoubtedly existed, well, it wouldn't much matter if we'd been brave for an hour or two.'

'Nobody could say that this prison was not a prison.'

'No? You don't think so? I can see you don't listen to the politicians.' His feet were giving him great pain: he had cramp in the soles, but he could bring no pressure on the muscles to relieve them. It was not yet midnight; the hours of darkness stretched ahead interminably.

The woman said suddenly, 'Think. We have a martyr here . . .'

The priest giggled: he couldn't stop himself. He said, 'I don't think martyrs are like this.' He became suddenly serious, remembering Maria's words – it wouldn't be a good thing to bring mockery on the Church. He said, 'Martyrs are holy men. It is wrong to think that just because one dies . . . no. I tell you I am in a state of mortal sin. I have done things I couldn't talk to you about. I could only whisper them in the confessional.' Everybody, when he spoke, listened attentively to him as if he were addressing them in church. He wondered where the inevitable Judas was sitting now, but he wasn't aware of Judas as he had been in the forest hut. He was moved by an irrational affection for the inhabitants of this prison. A phrase came to him: 'God so loved the world . . .' He said, 'My children, you must never think the holy martyrs are like me. You have a name for me. Oh, I've heard you use it before now. I am a whisky priest. I am in here now because they found a bottle of brandy in my pocket.' He tried to move his feet from under him: the cramp had passed: now they were lifeless: all feeling gone. Oh well, let them stay. He wouldn't have to use them often again.

The old man was muttering and the priest's thoughts went back to Brigitta. The knowledge of the world lay in her like the dark explicable spot in an X-ray photograph; he longed – with a breathless feeling in the breast – to save her, but he knew the surgeon's decision – the ill was incurable.

The woman's voice said pleadingly, 'A little drink, father . . . it's not so important.' He wondered why she was here – probably for having a holy picture in her house. She had the tiresome intense note of a pious woman. They were extraordinarily foolish over pictures. Why not burn them? One didn't need a picture . . . He said sternly, 'Oh, I am not only a drunkard.' He had always been worried by the fate of pious women. As much as politicians, they fed on illusion. He was frightened for them: they came to death so often in a state of invincible complacency, full of uncharity. It was one's duty, if one could, to rob them of their sentimental notions of what was good . . . He said in hard accents, 'I have a child.'

What a worthy woman she was! Her voice pleaded in the darkness; he couldn't catch what she said, but it was something about the Good Thief. He said, 'My child, the thief repented. I haven't repented.' He remembered her coming into the hut, the dark malicious knowing look with the sunlight at her back. He said, 'I don't know how to repent.' That was true: he had lost the faculty. He couldn't say to himself that he wished his sin had never existed, because the sin seemed to him now so unimportant and he loved the fruit of it. He needed a confessor to draw his mind slowly down the drab passages which led to grief and repentance.

The woman was silent now: he wondered whether after all he had been too harsh with her. If it helped her faith to believe that he was a martyr . . . But he rejected the idea: one was pledged to truth. He shifted an inch or two on his hams and said, 'What time does it get light?'

'Four . . . five . . .' a man replied. 'How can we tell, father? We haven't clocks.'

'Have you been here long?'

'Three weeks.'

'Are you kept here all day?'

'Oh no. They let us out to clean the yard.'

He thought: that is when I shall be discovered – unless it's earlier, for surely one of these people will betray me first. A long train of thought began, which led him to announce after a while, 'They are offering a reward for me. Five hundred, six hundred pesos, I'm not sure.' Then he was silent again. He couldn't urge any man to inform against him – that would be tempting him to sin – but at the same time if there was an informer here, there was no reason why the wretched creature should be bilked of his reward. To commit so ugly a sin – it must count as murder – and to have no compensation in this world . . . He thought: it wouldn't be fair.

'Nobody here,' a voice said, 'wants their blood money.'

Again he was touched by an extraordinary affection. He was just one criminal among a herd of criminals . . . He had a sense of companionship which he had never experienced in the old days when pious people came kissing his black cotton glove.

The pious woman's voice leapt hysterically out at him, 'It is so stupid to tell them that. You don't know the sort of wretches who are here, father. Thieves, murderers . . .'

'Well,' an angry voice said, 'why are you here?'

'I had good books in my house,' she announced, with unbearable pride. He had done nothing to shake her complacency. He said, 'They are everywhere. It's no different here.'

'Good books?'

He giggled. 'No, no. Thieves, murderers . . . Oh, well, my child, if you had more experience you would know there are worse things to be.' The old man seemed to be uneasily asleep; his head lay sideways against the priest's shoulder, and he muttered angrily. God knows, it had never been easy to move in this place, but the difficulty seemed to increase as the night wore on and limbs stiffened. He couldn't twitch his shoulder now without waking the old man to another night of suffering. Well, he thought, it was my kind who robbed him: it's only fair to be made a little uncomfortable . . . He sat silent and rigid against the damp wall, with his dead feet under his haunches. The mosquitoes droned on; it was no good defending yourself by striking at the air: they pervaded the whole place like an element. Somebody as well as the old man had fallen asleep and was snoring, a curious note of satisfaction, as though he had eaten and drunk well at a good dinner and was now taking a snooze . . . The priest tried to calculate the hour: how much time had passed since he had met the beggar in the plaza? It was probably not long after midnight: there would be hours more of this.

It was, of course, the end, but at the same time you had to be prepared for everything, even escape. If God intended him to escape He could snatch him away from in front of a firing-squad. But God was merciful. There was only one reason, surely, which would make Him refuse His peace – if there was any peace – that he could still be of use in saving a soul, his own or another's. But what good could he do now? They had him on the run; he dared not enter a village in case somebody else should pay with his life – perhaps a man who was in mortal sin and unrepentant. It was impossible to say what souls might not be lost simply because he was obstinate and proud and wouldn't admit defeat. He couldn't even say Mass any longer – he had no wine. It had gone down the dry gullet of the Chief of Police. It was appallingly complicated. He was still afraid of death, he would be more afraid of death yet when the morning came, but it was beginning to attract him by its simplicity.

The pious woman was whispering to him. She must have somehow edged her way nearer. She was saying, 'Father, will you hear my confession?'

'My dear child, here! It's quite impossible. Where would be the secrecy?'

'It's been so long . . .'

'Say an Act of Contrition for your sins. You must trust God, my dear, to make allowances . . .'

'I wouldn't mind suffering . . .'

'Well, you are here.'

'That's nothing. In the morning my sister will have raised the money for my fine.'

Somewhere against the far wall pleasure began again; it was unmistakable: the movements, the breathlessness, and then the cry. The pious woman said aloud with fury, 'Why won't they stop it? The brutes, the animals!'

'What's the good of your saying an Act of Contrition now in this state of mind?'

'But the ugliness . . .'

'Don't believe that. It's dangerous. Because suddenly we discover that our sins have so much beauty.'

'Beauty,' she said with disgust. 'Here. In this cell. With strangers all round.'

'Such a lot of beauty. Saints talk about the beauty of suffering. Well, we are not saints, you and I. Suffering to us is just ugly. Stench and crowding and pain. *That* is beautiful in that corner – to them. It needs a lot of learning to see things with a saint's eye: a saint gets a subtle taste for beauty and can look down on poor ignorant palates like theirs. But we can't afford to.'

'It's mortal sin.'

'We don't know. It may be. But I'm a bad priest, you see. I know – from experience – how much beauty Satan carried down with him when he fell. Nobody ever said the fallen angels were the ugly ones. Oh no, they were just as quick and light and . . .'

Again the cry came, an expression of intolerable pleasure. The woman said, 'Stop them. It's a scandal.' He felt fingers on his knee, grasping, digging. He said, 'We're all fellow prisoners. I want drink at this moment more than anything, more than God. That's a sin too.'

'Now,' the woman said, 'I can see you're a bad priest. I wouldn't believe it before. I do now. You sympathize with these animals. If your bishop heard you . . .'

'Ah, he's a very long way off.' He thought of the old man now in Mexico City, living in one of those ugly comfortable pious houses, full of images and holy pictures, saying Mass on Sundays at one of the cathedral altars.

'When I get out of here, I shall write . . .'

He couldn't help laughing: she had no sense of how life had changed. He said, 'If he gets the letter he'll be interested to hear I'm alive.' But again he became serious. It was more difficult to feel pity for her than for the half-caste who a week ago had tagged him through the forest, but her case might be worse. The other had so much excuse – poverty and fever and innumerable humiliations. He said, 'Try not to be angry. Pray for me instead.'

'The sooner you are dead the better.'

He couldn't see her in the darkness, but there were plenty of faces he could remember from the old days which fitted the voice. When you visualized a man or woman carefully, you could always begin to feel pity – that was a quality God's image carried with it. When you saw the lines at the corners of the eyes, the shape of the mouth, how the hair grew, it was impossible to hate. Hate was just a failure of imagination. He began to feel an overwhelming responsibility for this pious woman. 'You and Father José,' she said. 'It's people like you who make people mock – at real religion.' She had, after all, as many excuses as the half-caste. He saw the kind of salon in which she spent her days, with the rocking-chair and the photographs, meeting no one. He said gently, 'You are not married, are you?'

'Why do you want to know?'

'And you never had a vocation?'

'They wouldn't believe it,' she said bitterly.

He thought: poor woman, she's had nothing, nothing at all. If only one could find the right word . . . He leant hopelessly back, moving carefully so as not to waken the old man. But the right words never came to him. He was more out of touch with her kind than he had ever been; he would have known what to say to her in the old days, feeling no pity at all, speaking with half a mind a platitude or two. Now he felt useless. He was a criminal and ought only to talk to criminals; he had done wrong again, trying to break down her complacency. He might just as well have let her go on thinking him a martyr.

His eyes closed and immediately he began to dream. He was being pursued; he stood outside a door banging on it, begging for admission, but nobody answered – there was a word, a password, which would save him, but he had forgotten it. He tried desperately at random – cheese and child, California, excellency, milk, Vera Cruz. His feet had gone to sleep and he knelt outside the door. Then he knew why he wanted to get in: he wasn't being pursued after all: that was a mistake. His child lay beside him bleeding to death and this was a doctor's house. He banged on the door and shouted, 'Even if I can't think of the right word, haven't you a heart?' The child was dying and looked up at him with middle-aged complacent wisdom. She said, 'You animal,' and he woke again crying. He couldn't have slept for more than a few seconds because the woman was still talking about the vocation the nuns had refused to recognize. He said, 'That made you suffer, didn't it? To suffer like that – perhaps it was better than being a nun and happy,' and immediately after he had spoken he thought: a silly remark, what does it mean? Why can't I find something to say to her which she could remember?

He didn't sleep again: he was striking yet another bargain with God. This time, if he escaped from the prison, he would escape altogether. He would go north, over the border. His escape was so improbable that, if it happened, it couldn't be anything else but a sign – an indication that he was doing more harm by his example than good by his occasional confessions. The old man moved against his shoulder and the night just stayed around them. The darkness was always the same and there were no clocks – there was nothing to indicate time passing. The only punctuation of the night was the sound of urination.

Suddenly, he realized that he could see a face, and then another; he had begun to forget that it would ever be another day, just as one forgets that one will ever die. It comes suddenly on one in a screeching brake or a whistle in the air, the knowledge that time moves and comes to an end. All the voices slowly became faces – there were no surprises. The confessional teaches you to recognize the shape of a voice – the loose lip of the weak chin and the false candour of the too straight forward eyes. He saw the pious woman a few feet away, uneasily dreaming with her prim mouth open, showing strong teeth like tombs: the old man: the boaster in the corner, and his woman asleep untidily across his knees. Now that the day was at last here, he was the only one awake, except for a small Indian boy who sat cross-legged near the door with an expression of interested happiness, as if he had never known such friendly company. Over the courtyard the whitewash became visible upon the opposite wall. He began formally to pay his farewell to the world: he couldn't put any heart in it. His corruption was less evident to his senses than his death. One bullet, he thought, is almost certain to go directly through the heart – a squad must contain one accurate marksman. Life would go out in a 'fraction of a second' (that was the phrase), but all night he had been realizing that time depends on clocks and the passage of light. There were no clocks and the light wouldn't change. Nobody really knew how long a second of pain could be. It might last a whole purgatory – or for ever. For some reason he thought of a man he had once shrived who was on the point of death with cancer – his relatives had had to bandage their faces, the smell of the rotting interior was so appalling. He wasn't a saint. Nothing in life was as ugly as death.

A voice in the yard called 'Montez.' He sat on upon his dead feet; he thought automatically: This suit isn't good for much more. It was smeared and fouled by the cell floor and his fellow prisoners. He had obtained it at great risk in a store down by the river, pretending to be a small farmer with ideas above his station. Then he remembered he wouldn't need it much longer – it came with an odd shock, like locking the door of one's house for the last time. The voice repeated impatiently, 'Montez.'

He remembered that that, for the moment, was his name. He looked up from his ruined suit and saw the sergeant unlocking the cell door. 'Here, Montez.' He let the old man's head fall gently back against the sweating wall and tried to stand up, but his feet crumpled like pastry. 'Do you want to sleep all night?' the sergeant complained testily: something had irritated him: he wasn't as friendly as he had been the night before. He let out a kick at a sleeping man and beat on the cell door, 'Come on. Wake up all of you. Out into the yard.' Only the

Indian boy obeyed, sliding unobtrusively out with his look of alien happiness. The sergeant complained, 'The dirty hounds. Do they want us to wash them? You, Montez.' Life began to return painfully to his feet. He managed to reach the door.

The yard had come sluggishly to life. A queue of men were bathing their faces at a single tap; a man in a vest and pants sat on the ground hugging a rifle. 'Get out into the yard and wash,' the sergeant yelled at them, but when the priest stepped out he snapped at him, 'Not you, Montez.'

'Not me?'

'We've got other plans for you,' the sergeant said.

The priest stood waiting while his fellow prisoners filed out into the yard. One by one they went past him; he looked at their feet and not their faces, standing like a temptation at the door. Nobody said a word: a woman's feet went draggingly by in black worn low-heeled shoes. He was shaken by the sense of his own uselessness. He whispered without looking up, 'Pray for me.'

'What's that you said, Montez?'

He couldn't think of a lie; he felt as if ten years had exhausted his whole stock of deceit.

'What's that you said?'

The shoes had stopped moving. The woman's voice said, 'He was begging.' She added mercilessly, 'He ought to have more sense. I've nothing for him.' Then she went on, flat-footed into the yard.

'Did you sleep well, Montez?' the sergeant badgered him.

'Not very well.'

'What do you expect?' the sergeant said. 'It'll teach you to like brandy too well, won't it?'

'Yes.' He wondered how much longer all these preliminaries would take.

'Well, if you spend all your money on brandy, you've got to do a bit of work in return for a night's lodging. Fetch the pails out of the cells and mind you don't spill them – this place stinks enough as it is.'

'Where do I take them to?'

The sergeant pointed to the door of the *excusados* beyond the tap. 'Report to me when you've finished that,' he said, and went bellowing orders back into the yard.

The priest bent down and took the pail. It was full and very heavy: he went bowed with the weight across the yard. Sweat got into his eyes. He wiped them free and saw one behind the other in the washing queue faces he knew – the hostages. There was Miguel, whom he had seen taken away; he remembered the mother screaming out and the lieutenant's tired anger and the sun coming up. They saw him at the same time; he put down the heavy pail and looked at them. Not to recognize them would have been like a hint, a claim, a demand to them to go on suffering and let him escape. Miguel had been beaten up: there was a sore under his eye – flies buzzed round it as they buzz round a mule's raw flank. Then the queue moved on; they looked on the ground and passed him; strangers took their place. He prayed silently: Oh God, send them someone more worthwhile to suffer for. It seemed to him a damnable mockery that they should sacrifice themselves for a whisky priest with a bastard child. The soldier sat in his pants with the gun between his knees paring his nails and biting off the loose skin. In an odd way he felt abandoned because they had shown no sign of recognition.

The *excusados* was a cesspool with two planks across it on which a man could stand. He emptied the pail and went back across the yard to the row of cells. There were six: one by one he took the pails: once he had to stop and retch: splash, splash, to and fro across the yard. He came to the last cell. It wasn't empty; a man lay back against the wall; the early sun just reached his feet. Flies buzzed around a mound of vomit on the floor. The eyes opened and watched the priest stooping over the pail: two fangs protruded . . .

The priest moved quickly and splashed the floor. The half-caste said in that too-familiar nagging tone, 'Wait a moment. You can't do that in here.' He explained proudly, 'I'm not a prisoner. I'm a guest.' The priest made a motion of apology (he was afraid to speak) and moved again. 'Wait a moment,' the half-caste commanded him again. 'Come here.'

The priest stood stubbornly, half-turned away, near the door.

'Come here,' the half-caste said. 'You're a prisoner, aren't you? – and I'm a guest – of the Governor. Do you want me to shout for a policeman? Then do as you're told: come here.'

It seemed as if God were deciding . . . finally. He came, pail in hand, stood beside the large flat naked foot, and the half-caste looked up at him from the shadow of the wall, asking him sharply and anxiously, 'What are you doing here?'

'Cleaning up.'

'You know what I mean.'

'I was caught with a bottle of brandy,' the priest said, trying to roughen his voice.

'I know you,' the half-caste said. 'I couldn't believe my eyes, but when you speak . . .'

'I don't think . . .'

'That priest's voice,' the half-caste said with disgust. He was like a dog of a different breed: he couldn't help his hackles rising. The big toe moved plumply and inimically. The priest put down the pail. He argued hopelessly, 'You're drunk.'

'Beer, beer,' the half-caste said, 'nothing but beer. They promised me the best of everything, but you can't trust them. Don't I know the jefe's got his own brandy locked away?'

'I must empty the pail.'

'If you move, I'll shout. I've got so many things to think about,' the half-caste complained bitterly. The priest waited: there was nothing else to do; he was at the man's mercy – a silly phrase, for those malarial eyes had never known what mercy was. He was saved at any rate from the indignity of pleading.

'You see,' the mestizo carefully explained, 'I'm comfortable here.' His yellow toes curled luxuriously beside the vomit. 'Good food, beer, company, and this roof doesn't leak. You don't have to tell me what'll happen after – they'll kick me out like a dog, like a dog.' He became shrill and indignant. 'What have they got you here for? That's what I want to know. It looks crooked to me. It's my job, isn't it, to find you. Who's going to have the reward if they've got you already? The jefe, I shouldn't wonder, or that bastard sergeant.' He brooded unhappily. 'You can't trust a soul these days.'

'And there's a Red Shirt,' the priest said.

'A Red Shirt?'

'He really caught me.'

'Mother of God,' the mestizo said, 'and they all have the ear of the Governor.' He looked up beseechingly. He said, 'You're an educated man. Advise me.'

'It would be murder,' the priest said, 'a mortal sin.'

'I don't mean that. I mean about the reward. You see as long as they don't *know*, well, I'm comfortable here. A man deserves a few weeks' holiday. And you can't escape far, can you? It would be better, wouldn't it, to catch you out of here. In the town somewhere. I mean nobody else could claim . . .' He said furiously, 'A poor man has so much to think about.'

'I dare say,' the priest said, 'they'd give you *something* even here.'

'Something,' the mestizo said, levering himself up against the wall, 'why shouldn't I have it all?'

'What's going on in here?' the sergeant asked. He stood in the doorway, in the sunlight, looking in.

The priest said slowly, 'He wanted me to clear up his vomit. I said you hadn't told me . . .'

'Oh, he's a guest,' the sergeant said. 'He's got to be treated right. You do as he says.'

The mestizo smirked. He said, 'And another bottle of beer, sergeant?'

'Not yet,' the sergeant said. 'You've got to look round the town first.'

The priest picked up the pail and went back across the yard, leaving them arguing. He felt as if a gun were levelled at his back. He went into the *excusados* and emptied the pail, then came out again into the sun – the gun was levelled at his breast. The two men stood in the cell door talking. He walked across the yard: they watched him come. The sergeant said to the mestizo, 'You say you're bilious and can't see properly this morning. You clean up your own vomit then. If you don't do *your* job . . .' Behind the sergeant's back the mestizo gave him a cunning and unreassuring wink. Now that the immediate fear was over, he felt only regret. God had decided. He had to go on with life, go on making decisions, acting on his own advice, making plans . . .

It took him another half-hour to finish cleaning the cells, throwing a bucket of water over each floor; he watched the pious woman go off through the archway to where her sister waited with the fine; they were both tied up in black shawls like things bought in the market, things hard and dry and second-hand. Then he reported again to the sergeant, who inspected the cells and criticized his work and ordered him to throw more water down, and then suddenly got tired of the whole business and told him he could go to the jefe for permission to leave. So he waited another hour on the bench outside the jefe's door, watching the sentry move lackadaisically to and fro in the hot sun.

And when at last a policeman led him in, it wasn't the jefe who sat at the desk but the lieutenant. The priest stood not far from his own portrait on the wall and waited. Once he glanced quickly and nervously up at the old crumpled newspaper cutting and thought, It's not very like me now. What an unbearable creature he must have been in those days – and yet in those days he had been comparatively innocent. That was another mystery: it sometimes seemed to him that venial sins – impatience, an unimportant lie, pride, a neglected opportunity – cut you off from grace more completely than the worst sins of all. Then, in his innocence, he had felt no love for anyone; now in his corruption he had learnt . . .

'Well,' the lieutenant asked, 'has he cleaned up the cells?' He didn't take his eyes from his papers. He went on, 'Tell the sergeant I want two dozen men with properly cleaned rifles – within two minutes.' He looked abstractedly up at the priest and said, 'Well, what are you waiting for?'

'For permission, Excellency, to go away.'

'I am not an excellency. Learn to call things by their right names.' He said sharply, 'Have you been here before?'

'Never.'

'Your name is Montez. I seem to come across too many people of that name in these days. Relations of yours?' He sat watching him closely, as if memory were beginning to work.

The priest said hurriedly, 'My cousin was shot at Concepción.'

'That was not my fault.'

'I only meant – we were much alike. Our fathers were twins. Not half an hour between them. I thought your Excellency seemed to think . . .'

'As I remember him, he was quite different. A tall thin man . . . narrow shoulders . . .'

The priest said hurriedly, 'Perhaps only to the family eye . . .'

'But then I only saw him once.' It was almost as if the lieutenant had something on his conscience, as he sat with his dark Indian-blooded hands restless on the pages, brooding. . . . He asked, 'Where are you going?'

'God knows.'

'You are all alike, you people. You never learn the truth – that God knows nothing.' Some tiny scrap of life like a grain of smut went racing across the page in front of him; he pressed his finger down on it and said, 'You had no money for your fine?' and watched another smut edge out between the leaves, scurrying for refuge: in this heat there was no end to life.

'No.'

'How will you live?'

'Some work perhaps . . .'

'You are getting too old for work.' He put his hand suddenly in his pocket and pulled out a five-peso piece. 'There,' he said. 'Get out of here, and don't let me see your face again. Mind that.'

The priest held the coin in his fist – the price of a Mass. He said with astonishment, 'You're a good man.'

Chapter 4

It was still very early in the morning when he crossed the river and came dripping up the other bank. He wouldn't have expected anybody to be about. The bungalow, the tin-roofed shed, the flagstaff: he had an idea that all Englishmen lowered their flag at sunset and sang 'God Save the King'. He came carefully round the corner of the shed and the door gave to his pressure. He was inside in the dark where he had been before: how many weeks ago? He had no idea. He only remembered that then the rains were a long way off: now they were beginning to break. In another week only an aeroplane would be able to cross the mountains.

He felt around him with his foot; he was so hungry that even a few bananas would be better than nothing – he had had no food for two days – but there were none here, none at all. He must have arrived on a day when the crop had gone down-river. He stood just inside the door trying to remember what the child had told him – the Morse code, her window: across the dead-white dusty yard the mosquito wire caught the sun. He was reminded suddenly of an empty larder. He began to listen anxiously. There wasn't a sound anywhere; the day here hadn't yet begun with that first sleepy slap of a shoe on a cement floor, the claws of a dog scratching as it stretched, the knock-knock of a hand on a door. There was just nothing, nothing at all.

What was the time? How many hours of light had there been? It was impossible to tell. Suppose, after all, it was not very early – it might be six, seven . . . He realized how much he had counted on this child. She was the only person who could help him without endangering herself. Unless he got over the mountains in the next few days he was trapped – he might as well hand himself over to the police, because how could he live through the rains with nobody daring to give him food or shelter? It would have been better, quicker, if he had been recognized in the police station a week ago: so much less trouble. Then he heard a sound; it was like hope coming tentatively back: a scratching and a whining. This was what one meant by dawn – the noise of life. He waited for it – hungrily – in the doorway.

And it came: a mongrel bitch dragging herself across the yard, an ugly creature with bent ears, trailing a wounded or a broken leg, whimpering. There was something wrong with her back. She came very slowly. He could see her ribs like an exhibit in a natural history museum. It was obvious that she hadn't had food for days: she had been abandoned.

Unlike him, she retained a kind of hope. Hope is an instinct only the reasoning human mind can kill. An animal never knows despair. Watching her wounded progress he had a sense that this had happened daily – perhaps for weeks; he was watching one of the well-rehearsed effects of the new day, like bird-song in happier regions. She dragged herself up to the veranda door and began to scratch with one paw, lying oddly spreadeagled. Her nose was down to a crack: she seemed to be breathing in the unused air of empty rooms; then she whined impatiently, and once her tail beat as if she heard something move inside. At last she began to howl.

The priest could bear it no longer. He knew now what it meant: he might as well let his eyes see. He came out into the yard and the animal turned awkwardly – the parody of a watchdog – and began to bark at him. It wasn't anybody she wanted: she wanted what she was used to: she wanted the old world back.

He looked in through the window – perhaps this was the child's room. Everything had been removed from it except the useless or the broken. There was a cardboard box full of torn paper and a small chair which had lost a leg. There was a large nail in the whitewashed wall where a mirror perhaps had been hung or a picture. There was a broken shoe-horn.

The bitch was dragging itself along the veranda growling: instinct is like a sense of duty – one can confuse it with loyalty very easily. He avoided the animal simply by stepping out into the sun; it couldn't turn quickly enough to follow him. He pushed at the door and it opened – nobody had bothered to lock up. An ancient alligator's skin which had been badly cut and inefficiently dried hung on the wall. There was a snuffle behind him and he turned; the bitch had two paws over the threshold, but now that he was established in the house, she didn't mind him. He was there, in possession, the master, and there were all kinds of smells to occupy her mind. She pushed herself across the floor, making a wet noise.

The priest opened a door on the left – perhaps it had been the bedroom. In a corner lay a pile of old medicine bottles. There were medicines for headaches, stomach-aches, medicines to be taken after meals and before meals. Somebody must have heen very ill to need so many? There was a hairslide, broken, and a ball of hair-combings – very fair hair turning dusty white. He thought with relief: It was her mother, only her mother.

He tried another room which faced, through the mosquito wire, the slow and empty river. This had been the living-room, for they had left behind the table, a folding card-table of plywood bought for a few shillings which hadn't been worth taking with them wherever they'd gone. Had the mother been dying, he wondered? They had cleared the crop perhaps, and gone to the capital where there was a hospital. He left that room and entered another: this was the one he had seen from the outside – the child's. He turned over the contents of the wastepaper box with sad curiosity. He felt as if he were clearing up after a death, deciding what would be too painful to keep.

He read, 'The immediate cause of the American War of Independence was what is called the Boston Tea Party.' It seemed to be part of an essay written in large firm letters, carefully. 'But the real issue' (the word was spelt wrongly, crossed out and re-written) 'was whether it was right to tax people who were not represented in Parliament.' It must have been a rough copy – there were so many corrections. He picked out another scrap at random – it was about people called Whigs and Tories – the words were incomprehensible to him. Something like a duster flopped down off the roof into the yard: it was a vulture. He read on, 'If five men took three days to mow a meadow of four acres five roods, how much would two men mow in one day?' There was a neat line ruled under the question, and then the calculations began – a hopeless muddle of figures which didn't work out. There was a hint of heat and irritation in the crumpled paper tossed aside. He could see her very clearly, dispensing with that question decisively: the neat accurately moulded face with the two pinched pigtails. He remembered her readiness to swear eternal enmity against anyone who hurt him, and he remembered his own child enticing him by the rubbish-dump.

He shut the door carefully behind him as if he were preventing an escape. He could hear the bitch – somewhere – growling, and followed her into what had once been the kitchen. She lay in a deathly attitude over a bone with her old teeth bared. An Indian's face hung outside the mosquito wire like something hooked up to dry – dark, withered, and unappetizing. He had his eyes on the bone as if he coveted it. He looked up as the priest came across the kitchen and immediately was gone as if he had never been there, leaving the house just as abandoned. The priest, too, looked at the bone.

There was a lot of meat on it still. A small cloud of flies hung above it a few inches from the bitch's mouth, and the bitch kept her eye fixed, now that the Indian was gone, on the priest. They were all in competition. The priest advanced a step or two and stamped twice. 'Go,' he said, 'go,' flapping his hands, but the mongrel wouldn't move, flattened above the bone, with all the resistance left in the broken body concentrated in the yellow eyes, burring between her teeth. It was like hate on a deathbed. The priest came cautiously forward; he wasn't yet used to the idea that the animal couldn't spring. One associates a dog with action, but this creature, like any crippled human being, could only think. You could see the thoughts – hunger and hope and hatred – stuck on the eyeball.

The priest put out his hand towards the bone and the flies buzzed upwards. The animal became silent, watching. 'There, there,' the priest said cajolingly; he made little enticing movements in the air and the animal stared back. Then the priest turned and moved away as if he were abandoning the bone; he droned gently to himself a phrase from the Mass, elaborately paying no attention. Then he switched quickly round again. It hadn't worked. The bitch watched him, screwing round her neck to follow his ingenious movements.

For a moment he became furious – that a mongrel bitch with a broken back should steal the only food. He swore at it – popular expressions picked up beside bandstands: he would have been surprised in other circumstances that they came so readily to his tongue. Then suddenly he laughed: this was human dignity disputing with a bitch over a bone. When he laughed the animal's ears went back, twitching at the tips, apprehensive. But he felt no pity – her life had no importance beside that of a human being. He looked round for something to throw, but the room had been cleared of nearly everything except the bone. Perhaps, who knows? it might have been left deliberately for this mongrel; he could imagine the child remembering, before she left with the sick mother and the stupid father: he had the impression that it was always she who had to think. He could find for his purpose nothing better than a broken wire rack which had been used for vegetables.

He advanced again towards the bitch and struck her lightly on the head. She snapped at the wire with her old broken teeth and wouldn't move. He beat at her again more fiercely and she caught the wire – he had to rasp it away. He struck again and again before he realized that she couldn't, except with great exertion, move at all: she was unable to escape his blows or leave the bone. She just had to endure, her eyes yellow and scared and malevolent shining back at him between the blows.

So then he changed his method; he used the vegetable rack as a kind of muzzle, holding back the teeth with it, while he bent and captured the bone. One paw tugged at it and gave way; he lowered the wire and jumped back – the animal tried without success to follow him, then lapsed upon the floor. The priest had won: he had his bone. The bitch no longer tried to growl.

The priest tore off some raw meat with his teeth and began to chew: no food had ever tasted so good, and now that for the moment he was happy he began to feel a little pity. He thought: I will eat just so much and she can have the rest. He marked mentally a point upon the bone and tore off another piece. The nausea he had felt for hours now began to die away and leave an honest hunger; he ate on and the bitch watched him. Now that the fight was over she seemed to bear no malice; her tail began to beat the floor, hopefully, questioningly. The priest reached the point he had marked, but now it seemed to him that his previous hunger had been imaginary: this was hunger, what he felt now. A man's need was greater than a dog's: he would leave that knuckle of meat at the joint. But when the moment came he ate that too – after all, the dog had teeth: it would eat the bone itself. He dropped it and left the kitchen.

He made one more progress through the empty rooms. A broken shoe-horn: medicine bottles: an essay on the American War of Independence – there was nothing to tell him why they had gone away. He came out on to the veranda and saw through a gap in the planks that a book had fallen to the ground and lay between the rough pillars of brick which raised the house out of the track of ants. It was months since he had seen a book. It was almost like a promise, mildewing there under the piles, of better things to come – life going on in private houses with wireless sets and bookshelves and beds made ready for the night and a cloth laid for food. He knelt down on the ground and reached for it. He suddenly realized that when once the long struggle was over and he had crossed the mountains and the state line, life might, after all, be enjoyed again.

It was an English book, but from his years in an American seminary he retained enough English to read it, with a little difficulty. Even if he had been unable to understand a word, it would still have been a book. It was called *Jewels Five Words Long: A Treasury of English Verse*, and on the fly-leaf was pasted a printed certificate – Awarded to . . . and then the name of Coral Fellows filled up in ink . . . for proficiency in English Composition, Third Grade. There was an obscure coat of arms, which seemed to include a griffon and oak leaf, a Latin motto, '*Virtus Laudata Crescit*,' and a signature from a rubber stamp, Henry Beckley, B.A., Principal of Private Tutorials, Ltd.

The priest sat down on the veranda steps. There was silence everywhere – no life around the abandoned banana station except the vulture which hadn't yet given up hope. The Indian might never have existed at all. After a meal, the priest thought with sad amusement, a little reading, and opened the book at random. Coral – so that was the child's name. He thought of the shops in Vera Cruz full of it – the hard brittle jewellery which was thought for some reason so suitable for young girls after their first communion.

> 'I come,' he read, 'from haunts of coot and hern,
> I make a sudden sally,
> And sparkle out among the fern,
> To bicker down a valley.'

It was a very obscure poem, full of words which were like Esperanto. He thought: So this is English poetry: how odd. The little poetry he knew dealt mainly with agony, remorse, and hope. These verses ended on a philosophical note – 'For men may come and men may go, But I go on for ever.' The triteness and untruth of 'for ever' shocked him a little: a poem like this ought not to be in a child's hands. The vulture came picking its way across the yard, a dusty and desolate figure; every now and then it lifted sluggishly from the earth and flapped down twenty yards on. The priest read:

> '"Come back! Come back!" he cried in grief
> Across the stormy water:
> "And I'll forgive your Highland chief –
> My daughter, O my daughter."'

That sounded to him more impressive – though hardly perhaps, any more than the other, stuff for children. He felt in the foreign words the ring of genuine passion and repeated to himself on his hot and lonely perch the last line – 'My daughter, O my daughter.' The words seemed to contain all that he felt himself of repentance, longing and unhappy love.

It was an odd thing that ever since that hot and crowded night in the cell he had passed into a region of abandonment – almost as if he had died there with the old man's head on his shoulder and now wandered in a kind of limbo, because he wasn't good or bad enough . . . Life didn't exist any more: it wasn't merely a matter of the banana station. Now as the storm broke and he scurried for shelter he knew quite well what he would find – nothing.

The huts leapt up in the lightning and stood there shaking, then disappeared again in the rumbling darkness. The rain hadn't come yet: it was sweeping up from Campeche Bay in great sheets, covering the whole state in its methodical advance. Between the thunder-breaks he could imagine that he heard it – a gigantic rustle moving across towards the mountains which were now so close to him – a matter of twenty miles.

He reached the first hut; the door was open, and as the lightning quivered he saw as he expected nobody at all. Just a pile of maize and the indistinct grey movement of – perhaps – a rat. He dashed for the next hut, but it was the same as ever (the maize and nothing else), just as if all human life were receding before him, as if Somebody had determined that from now on he was to be left alone – altogether alone. As he stood there the rain reached the clearing; it came out of the forest like thick white smoke and moved on. It was as if an enemy were laying a gas-cloud across a whole territory, carefully, to see that nobody escaped. The rain spread and stayed just long enough, as though the enemy had his stopwatch out and knew to a second the limit of the lungs' endurance. The roof held the rain out for a while and then let it through – the twigs bent under the weight of water and shot apart; it came through in half a dozen places, pouring down in black funnels; then the downpour stopped and the roof dripped and the rain moved on, with the lightning quivering on its flanks like a protective barrage. In a few minutes it would reach the mountains: a few more storms like this and they would be impassable.

He had been walking all day and he was very tired; he found a dry spot and sat down. When the lightning struck he could see the clearing. All around was the gentle noise of the dripping water. It was nearly like peace, but not quite. For peace you needed human company – his aloneness was like a threat of things to come. Suddenly he remembered – for no apparent reason – a day of rain at the American seminary, the glass windows of the library steamed over with the central heating, the tall shelves of sedate books, and a young man – a stranger from Tuscon – drawing his initials on the pane with his finger – that was peace. He looked at it from the outside: he couldn't believe that he would ever again get in. He had made his own world, and this was it – the empty broken huts, the storm going by, and fear again – fear because he was not alone after all.

Somebody was moving outside, cautiously. The footsteps would come a little way and then stop. He waited apathetically, and the roof dripped behind him. He thought of the mestizo padding around the city, seeking a really cast-iron occasion for his betrayal. A face peered round the hut door at him and quickly withdrew – an old woman's face, but you could never tell with Indians – she mightn't have been more than twenty. He got up and went outside. She scampered back from before him in her heavy sack-like skirt, her black plaits swinging heavily. Apparently his loneliness was only to be broken by these evasive faces, creatures who looked as if they had come out of the Stone Age, who withdrew again quickly.

He was stirred by a sort of sullen anger – this one should not withdraw. He pursued her across the clearing, splashing in the pools, but she had a start and no sense of shame and she got into the forest before him. It was useless looking for her there, and he returned towards the nearest hut. It wasn't the hut which he had been sheltering in before, but it was just as empty. What had happened to these people? He knew well enough that these more or less savage encampments were temporary only; the Indians would cultivate a small patch of ground and when they had exhausted the soil for the time being, they would simply move away. They knew nothing about the rotation of crops, but when they moved they would take their maize with them. This was more like flight, from force or disease. He had heard of such flights in the case of sickness, and the horrible thing, of course, was that they carried the sickness with them wherever they moved; sometimes they became panicky like flies against a pane, but discreetly, letting nobody know, muting their hubbub. He turned moodily again to stare out at the clearing, and there was the Indian woman creeping back towards the hut where she had sheltered. He called out to her sharply and again she fled, shambling, towards the forest. Her clumsy progress reminded him of a bird feigning a broken wing . . . He made no movement to follow her, and before she reached the trees she stopped and watched him; he began to move slowly back towards the other hut. Once he turned: she was following him at a distance, keeping her eyes on him. Again he was reminded of something animal or bird-like, full of anxiety. He walked on, aiming directly at the hut. Far away beyond it the lightning stabbed down, but you could hardly hear the thunder; the sky was clearing overhead and the moon came out. Suddenly he heard an odd artificial cry, and turning he saw the woman making back towards the forest; then she stumbled, flung up her arms and fell to the ground, like the bird offering herself.

He felt quite certain now that something valuable was in the hut, perhaps hidden among the maize, and he paid her no attention, going in. Now that the lightning had moved on, he couldn't see – he felt across the floor until he reached the pile of maize. Outside the padding footsteps came nearer. He began to feel all over it – perhaps food was hidden there – and the dry crackle of the leaves was added to the drip of water and the cautious footsteps, like the faint noises of people busy about their private businesses. Then he put his hand on a face.

He couldn't be frightened any more by a thing like that – it was something human he had his fingers on. They moved down the body; it was a child's which lay completely quiet under his hand. In the doorway the moonlight showed the woman's face indistinctly. She was probably convulsed with anxiety, but you couldn't tell. He thought – I must get this into the open where I can see . . .

It was a male child – perhaps three years old: a withered bullet head with a mop of black hair: unconscious, but not dead: he could feel the faintest movement in the breast. He thought of disease again until he took out his hand and found that the child was wet with blood, not sweat. Horror and disgust touched him – violence everywhere: was there no end to violence? He said to the woman sharply, 'What happened?' It was as if man in all this state had been left to man.

The woman knelt two or three feet away, watching his hands. She knew a little Spanish, because she replied, '*Americano*.' The child wore a kind of brown one-piece smock. He lifted it up to the neck: the child had been shot in three places. Life was going out of him all the time: there was nothing – really – to be done, but one had to try . . . He said 'Water' to the woman, 'Water,' but she didn't seem to understand, squatting there, watching him. It was a mistake one easily made, to think that just because the eyes expressed nothing there was no grief. When he touched the child he could see her move on her haunches – she was ready to attack him with her teeth if the child so much as moaned.

He began to speak slowly and gently (he couldn't tell how much she understood): 'We must have water. To wash him. You needn't be afraid of me. I will do him no harm.' He took off his shirt and began to tear it into strips – it was hopelessly insanitary, but what else was there to do? except pray, of course, but one didn't pray for life, this life. He repeated again, 'Water.' The woman seemed to understand – she gazed hopelessly round at where the rain stood in pools – that was all there was. Well, he thought, the earth's as clean as any vessel would have been. He soaked a piece of his shirt and leant over the child; he could hear the woman slide closer along the ground – a menacing approach. He tried to reassure her again, 'You needn't be afraid of me. I am a priest.'

The word 'priest' she understood; she leant forward and grabbed at the hand which held the wet scrap of shirt and kissed it. At that moment, while her lips were on his hand, the child's face wrinkled, the eyes opened and glared at them, the tiny body shook with a kind of fury of pain; they watched the eyeballs roll up and suddenly become fixed, like marbles in a solitaire-board, yellow and ugly with death. The woman let go his hand and scrambled to a pool of water, cupping her fingers for it. The priest said, 'We don't need that any more,' standing up with his hands full of wet shirt. The woman opened her fingers and let the water fall. She said 'Father' imploringly, and he wearily went down on his knees and began to pray.

He could feel no meaning any longer in prayers like these. The Host was different: to lay that between a dying man's lips was to lay God. That was a fact – something you could touch, but this was no more than a pious aspiration. Why should anyone listen to *his* prayers? Sin was a constriction which prevented their escape; he could feel his prayers weigh him down like undigested food.

When he had finished he lifted up the body and carried it back into the hut; it seemed a waste of time to have taken it out, like a chair you carry out into the garden and back again because the grass is wet. The woman followed him meekly; she didn't seem to want to touch the body, just watched him put it back in the dark upon the maize. He sat down on the ground and said slowly, 'It will have to be buried.'

She understood that, nodding.

He said, 'Where is your husband? Will he help you?'

She began to talk rapidly. It might have been Camacho she was speaking: he couldn't understand more than an occasional Spanish word here and there. The word '*Americano*' occurred again, and he remembered the wanted man whose portrait had shared the wall with his. He asked her, 'Did *he* do this?' She shook her head. What had happened? he wondered. Had the man taken shelter here and had the soldiers fired into the huts? It was not unlikely. He suddenly had his attention caught. She had said the name of the banana station – but there had been no dying person there: no sign of violence, unless silence and desertion were signs. He had assumed the mother had been taken ill, but it might be something worse – and he imagined that stupid Captain Fellows taking down his gun, presenting himself clumsily armed to a man whose chief talent it was to draw quickly or to shoot directly from the pocket. That poor child . . . what responsibilities she had perhaps been forced to undertake.

He shook the thought away and said, 'Have you a spade?' She didn't understand that, and he had to go through the motions of digging. Another roll of thunder came between them. A second storm was coming up, as if the enemy had discovered that the first barrage after all had left a few survivors – this would flatten them. Again he could hear the enormous breathing of the rain miles away. He realized the woman had spoken the one word 'church'. Her Spanish consisted of isolated words. He wondered what she meant by that. Then the rain reached them. It came down like a wall between him and escape, fell altogether in a heap and built itself up around them. All the light went out except when the lightning flashed.

The roof couldn't keep out *this* rain. It came dripping through everywhere: the dry maize leaves where the dead child lay crackled like burning wood. He shivered with cold; he was probably on the edge of fever – he must get away before he was incapable of moving at all. The woman (he couldn't see her now) said '*Iglesia*' again imploringly. It occurred to him that she wanted the child buried near a church or perhaps only taken to an altar, so that he might be touched by the feet of a Christ. It was a fantastic notion.

He took advantage of a long quivering stroke of blue light to describe with his hands his sense of the impossibility. 'The soldiers,' he said, and she replied immediately, '*Americano*.' That word always came up, like one with many meanings which depends on the accent whether it is to be taken as an explanation, a warning or a threat. Perhaps she meant that the soldiers were all occupied in the chase, but even so, this rain was ruining everything. It was still twenty miles to the border, and the mountain paths after the storm were probably impassable – and a church – he hadn't the faintest idea of where there would be a church. He hadn't so much as seen such a thing for years now; it was difficult to believe that they still existed only a few days' journey off. When the lightning went on again he saw the woman watching him with stony patience.

For the last thirty hours they had only had sugar to eat – large brown lumps of it the size of a baby's skull; they had seen no one, and they had exchanged no words at all. What was the use when almost the only words they had in common were '*Iglesia*' and '*Americano*'? The woman followed at his heels with the dead child strapped on her back. She never seemed to tire. A day and a night brought them out of the marshes to the foothills; they slept fifty feet up above the slow green river, under a projecting piece of rock where the soil was dry – everywhere else was deep mud. The woman sat with her knees drawn up, and her head down. She showed no emotion, but she put the child's body behind her as if it needed protection from marauders like other possessions. They had travelled by the sun until the black wooded bar of mountain told them where to go. They might have been the only survivors of a world which was dying out; they carried the visible marks of the dying with them.

Sometimes he wondered whether he was safe, but when there are no visible boundaries between one state and another – no passport examination or customs house – danger just seems to go on, travelling with you, lifting its heavy feet in the same way as you do. There seemed to be so little progress: the path would rise steeply, perhaps five hundred feet, and fall again, clogged with mud. Once it took an enormous hairpin bend, so that after three hours they had returned to a point opposite their starting-place, less than a hundred yards away.

At sunset on the second day they came out on to a wide plateau covered with short grass. A grove of crosses stood up blackly against the sky, leaning at different angles – some as high as twenty feet, some not much more than eight. They were like trees that had been left to seed. The priest stopped and stared at them. They were the first Christian symbols he had seen for more than five years publicly exposed – if you could call this empty plateau in the mountains a public place. No priest could have been concerned in the strange rough group; it was the work of Indians and had nothing in common with the tidy vestments of the Mass and the elaborately worked out symbols of the liturgy. It was like a short cut to the dark and magical heart of the faith – to the night when the graves opened and the dead walked. There was a movement behind him and he turned.

The woman had gone down on her knees and was shuffling slowly across the cruel ground towards the group of crosses; the dead baby rocked on her back. When she reached the tallest cross she unhooked the child and held the face against the wood and afterwards the loins; then she crossed herself, not as ordinary Catholics do, but in a curious and complicated pattern which included the nose and ears. Did she expect a miracle? and if she did, why should it not be granted her, the priest wondered? Faith, one was told, could move mountains, and here was faith – faith in the spittle that healed the blind man and the voice that raised the dead. The evening star was out: it hung low down over the edge of the plateau – it looked as if it was within reach – and a small hot wind stirred. The priest found himself watching the child for some movement. When none came, it was as if God had missed an opportunity. The woman sat down, and taking a lump of sugar from her bundle began to eat, and the child lay quietly at the foot of the cross. Why, after all, should we expect God to punish the innocent with more life?

'*Vamos*,' the priest said, but the woman scraped the sugar with her sharp front teeth, paying no attention. He looked up at the sky and saw the evening star blotted out by black clouds. '*Vamos*.' There was no shelter anywhere on this plateau.

The woman never stirred; the broken snub-nosed face between the black plaits was completely passive: it was as if she had fulfilled her duty and could now take up her everlasting rest. The priest suddenly shivered; the ache which had pressed like a stiff hat-rim across his forehead all day dug deeper in. He thought: I have to get to shelter – a man's first duty is to himself – even the Church taught that, in a way. The whole sky was blackening. The crosses stuck up like dry and ugly cacti. He made off to the edge of the plateau. Once, before the path led down, he looked back – the woman was still biting at the lump of sugar, and he remembered that it was all the food they had.

The way was very steep – so steep that he had to turn and go down backwards; on either side trees grew perpendicularly out of the grey rock, and five hundred feet below the path climbed up again. He began to sweat and he had an appalling thirst, and when the rain came it was at first a kind of relief. He stayed where he was, hunched back against a boulder. There was no shelter before he reached the bottom of the barranca, and it hardly seemed worth while to make that effort. He was shivering now more or less continuously, and the ache seemed no longer inside his head – it was something outside, almost anything, a noise, a thought, a smell. The senses were jumbled up together. At one moment the ache was like a tiresome voice explaining to him that he had taken the wrong path. He remembered a map he had once seen of the two adjoining states. The state from which he was escaping was peppered with villages – in the hot marshy land people bred as readily as mosquitoes, but in the next state – in the north-west corner – there was hardly anything but blank white paper. You're on that blank paper now, the ache told him. But there's a path, he argued wearily. Oh, a path, the ache said, a path may take you fifty miles before it reaches anywhere at all: you know you won't last that distance. There's just white paper all around.

At another time the ache was a face. He became convinced that the

American was watching him – he had a skin all over spots like a newspaper photograph. Apparently he had followed them because he wanted to kill the mother as well as the child: he was sentimental in that respect. It was necessary to do something. The rain was like a curtain behind which almost anything might happen. He thought: I shouldn't have left her alone like that. God forgive me. I have no sense of responsibility: what can you expect of a whisky priest? and he struggled to his feet and began to climb back towards the plateau. He was tormented by ideas; it wasn't only the woman: he was responsible for the American as well: the two faces – his own and the gunman's – were hanging together on the police station wall, as if they were brothers in a family portrait gallery. You didn't put temptation in a brother's way.

Shivering and sweating and soaked with rain he came up over the edge of the plateau. There was nobody there – a dead child was not someone, just a useless object abandoned at the foot of one of the crosses. The mother had gone home. She had done what she wanted to do. The surprise lifted him, as it were, out of his fever before it dropped him back again. A small lump of sugar – all that was left – lay by the child's mouth – in case a miracle should happen or for the spirit to eat? The priest bent down with an obscure sense of shame and took it: the dead child couldn't growl back at him like a broken dog: but who was he to disbelieve in miracles? He hesitated, while the rain poured down; then he put the sugar in his mouth. If God chose to give back life, couldn't He give food as well?

Immediately he began to eat, the fever returned: the sugar stuck in his throat: he felt an appalling thirst. Crouching down he tried to lick some water from the uneven ground; he even sucked at his soaked trousers. The child lay under the streaming rain like a dark heap of cattle dung. The priest moved away again, back to the edge of the plateau and down the barranca side; it was loneliness he felt now – even the face had gone, he was moving alone across that blank white sheet, going deeper every moment into the abandoned land.

Somewhere, in some direction, there were towns, of course: go far enough and you reached the coast, the Pacific, the railway track to Guatemala; there were roads there and motor-cars. He hadn't seen a railway train for ten years. He could imagine the black line following the coast along the map, and he could see the fifty, hundred miles of unknown country. That was where he was: he had escaped too completely from men. Nature would kill him now.

All the same, he went on; there was no point in going back towards the deserted village, the banana station with its dying mongrel and its shoe-horn. There was nothing you could do except put one foot forward and then the other, scrambling down and then scrambling up; from the top of the barranca, when the rain passed on, there was nothing to see except a huge crumpled land, forest and mountain, with the grey wet veil moving over. He looked once and never looked again. It was too like watching despair.

It must have been hours later that he ceased to climb. It was evening and forest; monkeys crashed invisibly among the trees with an effect of clumsiness and recklessness, and what were probably snakes hissed away like match-flames through the grass. He wasn't afraid of them. They were a form of life, and he could feel life retreating from him all the time. It wasn't only people who were going, even the animals and the reptiles moved away; presently he would be left alone with nothing but his own breath. He began to recite to himself, 'O God, I have loved the beauty of Thy house,' and the smell of soaked and rotting leaves and the hot night and the darkness made him believe that he was in a mine shaft, going down into the earth to bury himself. Presently he would find his grave.

When a man came towards him carrying a gun he did nothing at all. The man approached cautiously; you didn't expect to find another person underground. He said, 'Who are you?' with his gun ready.

The priest gave his name to a stranger for the first time in ten years because he was tired and there seemed no object in going on living.

'A priest?' the man asked, with astonishment. 'Where have you come from?'

The fever lifted again: a little reality seeped back. He said, 'It is all right. I will not bring you any trouble. I am going on.' He screwed up all his remaining energy and walked on. A puzzled face penetrated his fever and receded: there were going to be no more hostages, he assured himself aloud. Footsteps followed him, he was like a dangerous man you see safely off an estate before you go home. He repeated aloud, 'It is all right. I am not staying here. I want nothing.'

'Father . . .' the voice said, humbly and anxiously.

'I will go right away.' He tried to run and came suddenly out of the forest on to a long slope of grass. There were lights and huts below, and up there at the edge of the forest a big whitewashed building – a barracks? Were there soldiers? He said, 'If I have been seen I will give myself up. I assure you no one shall get into trouble because of me.'

'Father . . .' He was racked with his headache, he stumbled and put his hand against the wall for support. He felt immeasurably tired. He asked, 'The barracks?'

'Father,' the voice said, puzzled and worried, 'it is our church.'

'A church?' The priest ran his hands incredulously over the wall like a blind man trying to recognize a particular house, but he was too tired to feel anything at all. He heard the man with the gun babbling out of sight, 'Such an honour, father. The bell must be rung . . .' and he sat down suddenly on the rain-drenched grass, and leaning his head against the white wall, he fell asleep, with home behind his shoulder-blades.

His dream was full of a jangle of cheerful noise.

PART THREE

Chapter 1

THE middle-aged woman sat on the veranda darning socks; she wore pince-nez and she had kicked off her shoes for further comfort. Mr Lehr, her brother, read a New York magazine – it was three weeks old, but that didn't really matter: the whole scene was like peace.

'Just help yourself to water,' Miss Lehr said, 'when you want it.'

A huge earthenware jar stood in a cool corner with a ladle and a tumbler. 'Don't you have to boil the water?' the priest asked.

'Oh no, *our* water's fresh and clean,' Miss Lehr said primly, as if she couldn't answer for anybody else's.

'Best water in the state,' her brother said. The shiny magazine leaves crackled as they turned, covered with photographs of big clean-shaven mastiff jowls – Senators and Congressmen. Pasture stretched away beyond the garden fence, undulating gently towards the next mountain range, and a tulipan tree blossomed and faded daily at the gate.

'You certainly are looking better, father,' Miss Lehr said. They both spoke rather guttural English with slight American accents – Mr Lehr had left Germany when he was a boy to escape military service: he had a shrewd, lined and idealistic face. You needed to be shrewd in this country if you were going to retain any ideals at all and he was cunning in the defence of the good life.

'Oh,' Mr Lehr said, 'he only needed to rest up a few days.' He was quite incurious about this man whom his foreman had brought in on a mule in a state of collapse three days before. All he knew the priest had told him. That was another thing this country taught you – never ask questions or to look ahead.

'So I can go on,' the priest said.

'You don't have to hurry,' said Miss Lehr, turning over her brother's sock, looking for holes.

'It's so quiet here.'

'Oh,' Mr Lehr said, 'we've had our troubles.' He turned a page and said, 'That Senator – Hiram Long – they ought to control him. It doesn't do any good insulting other countries.'

'Haven't they tried to take your land?'

The idealistic face turned his way: it wore a look of innocent craft. 'Oh, I gave them as much as they asked for – five hundred acres of barren land. I saved a lot on taxes. I never could get anything to grow there.' He nodded towards the veranda posts. 'That was the last *real* trouble. See the bullet-holes. Villa's men.'

The priest got up again and drank more water. He wasn't very thirsty; he was satisfying a sense of luxury. He asked, 'How long will it take me to get to Las Casas?'

'You could do it in four days,' Mr Lehr said.

'Not in *his* condition,' Miss Lehr said. 'Six.'

'It will seem so strange,' the priest said. 'A city with churches, a university . . .'

'Of course,' Mr Lehr said, 'my sister and I are Lutherans. We don't hold with your Church, father. Too much luxury, it seems to me, while the people starve.'

Miss Lehr said, 'Now, dear, it isn't the father's fault.'

'Luxury?' the priest asked. He stood by the earthenware jar, glass in hand, trying to collect his thoughts, staring out over the long peaceful glassy slopes. 'You mean . . .' Perhaps Mr Lehr was right; he had lived very easily once and here he was, already settling down to idleness again.

'All the gold leaf in the churches.'

'It's often just paint, you know,' the priest murmured conciliatingly. He thought: yes, three days and I've done nothing, nothing, and he looked down at his feet elegantly shod in a pair of Mr Lehr's shoes, his legs in Mr Lehr's spare trousers. Mr Lehr said, 'He won't mind my speaking my mind. We're all Christians here.'

'Of course. I like to hear . . .'

'It seems to me you people make a lot of fuss about inessentials.'

'Yes? You mean . . .'

'Fasting . . . fish on Friday . . .'

Yes, he remembered like something in his childhood that there had been a time when he had observed these rules. He said, 'After all, Mr Lehr, you're a German. A great military nation.'

'I was never a soldier. I disapprove . . .'

'Yes, of course, but still you understand – discipline is necessary. Drills may be no good in battle, but they form the character. Otherwise you get – well, people like me.' He looked down with sudden hatred at the shoes – they were like the badge of a deserter. 'People like me,' he repeated with fury.

There was a good deal of embarrassment; Miss Lehr began to say something, 'Why, father . . .', but Mr Lehr forestalled her, laying down the magazine and its load of well-shaved politicians. He said in his German–American voice with its guttural precision, 'Well, I guess it's time for a bath now. Will you be coming, father?' and the priest obediently followed him into their common bedroom. He took off Mr Lehr's clothes and put on Mr Lehr's mackintosh and followed Mr Lehr barefoot across the veranda and the field beyond. The day before he had asked apprehensively, 'Are there no snakes?' and Mr Lehr had grunted contemptuously that if there were any snakes they'd pretty soon get out of the way. Mr Lehr and his sister had combined to drive out savagery by simply ignoring anything that conflicted with an ordinary German–American homestead. It was, in its way, an admirable mode of life.

At the bottom of the field there was a little shallow stream running over brown pebbles. Mr Lehr took off his dressing-gown and lay down flat on his back. There was something upright and idealistic even in the thin elderly legs with their scrawny muscles. Tiny fishes played over his chest and made little tugs at his nipples undisturbed. This was the skeleton of the youth who had disapproved of militarism to the point of flight. Presently he sat up and began carefully to soap his lean thighs. The priest afterwards took the soap and followed suit. He felt it was expected of him, though he couldn't help thinking it was a waste of time. Sweat cleaned you as effectively as water. But this was the race which had invented the proverb that cleanliness was next to godliness – cleanliness, not purity.

All the same, one did feel an enormous luxury lying there in a little cold stream while the sun sank . . . He thought of the prison cell with the old man and the pious woman, the half-caste lying across the hut door, the dead child, and the abandoned station. He thought with shame of his daughter left to her knowledge and her ignorance by the rubbish-dump. He had no right to such luxury.

Mr Lehr said, 'Would you mind – the soap?'

He had heaved over on his face, and now he set to work on his back.

The priest said, 'I think perhaps I should tell you – tomorrow I am saying Mass in the village. Would you prefer me to leave your house? I do not wish to make trouble for you.'

Mr Lehr splashed seriously, cleaning himself. He said, 'Oh, they won't bother me. But you had better be careful. You know, of course, that it's against the law.'

'Yes,' the priest said. 'I know that.'

'A priest I knew was fined four hundred pesos. He couldn't pay and they sent him to prison for a week. What are you smiling at?'

'Only because it seems so . . . peaceful here. Prison for a week!'

'Well, I've always heard you people get your own back when it comes to collections. Would you like the soap?'

'No, thank you. I have finished.'

'We'd better be drying ourselves then. Miss Lehr likes to have her bath before sunset.'

As they came back to the bungalow in single file they met Miss Lehr, very bulky under her dressing-gown. She asked mechanically, like a clock with a very gentle chime, 'Is the water nice today?' and her brother answered, as he must have answered a thousand times, 'Pleasantly cool, dear,' and she slopped down across the grass in bedroom slippers, stooping slightly with short sight.

'If you wouldn't mind,' Mr Lehr said, shutting the bedroom door, 'staying in here till Miss Lehr comes back. One can see the stream – you understand – from the front of the house.' He began to dress, tall and bony and a little stiff. Two brass bedsteads, a single chair and a wardrobe – the room was monastic, except that there was no cross – no 'inessentials' as Mr Lehr would have put it. But there was a Bible. It lay on the floor beside one of the beds in a black oilskin cover. When the priest had finished dressing he opened it.

On the flyleaf there was a label which stated that the book was furnished by the Gideons. It went on: 'A Bible in every Hotel Guest Room. Winning Commercial Men for Christ. Good news.' There was then a list of texts. The priest read with some astonishment:

If you are in trouble	*read*	Psalm 34.
If trade is poor		Psalm 37.
If very prosperous		I Corinthians, x, 2.
If overcome and backsliding		James I. Hosea xiv, 4–9.
If tired of sin		Psalm 51. Luke xviii, 9–14.
If you desire peace, power and plenty		John 14.
If you are lonesome and discouraged		Psalms 23 and 27.
If you are losing confidence in men		I Corinthians, xiii.
If you desire peaceful slumbers		Psalm 121.

He couldn't help wondering how it had got here – with its ugly type and its over-simple explanations – into a hacienda in Southern Mexico. Mr Lehr turned away from his mirror with a big coarse hairbrush in his hand and explained carefully, 'My sister ran a hotel once. For drummers. She sold it to join me when my wife died, and she brought one of those from the hotel. You wouldn't understand that, father. You don't like people to read the Bible.' He was on the defensive all the time about his faith, as if he were perpetually conscious of some friction, like that of an ill-fitting shoe.

The priest asked, 'Is your wife buried here?'

'In the paddock,' Mr Lehr said bluntly. He stood listening, brush in hand, to the gentle footsteps outside. 'That's Miss Lehr,' he said, 'come up from her bath. We can go out now.'

The priest got off Mr Lehr's old horse when he reached the church and threw the rein over a bush. This was his first visit to the village since the night he collapsed beside the wall. The village ran down below him in the dusk: tin-roofed bungalows and mud huts faced each other over a single wide grass-grown street. A few lamps had been lit and fire was being carried round among the poorest huts. He walked slowly, conscious of peace and safety. The first man he saw took off his hat and knelt and kissed the priest's hand.

'What is your name?' the priest asked.

'Pedro, father.'

'Good night, Pedro.'

'Is there to be Mass in the morning, father?'

'Yes. There is to be Mass.'

He passed the rural school. The schoolmaster sat on the step: a plump young man with dark brown eyes and horn-rimmed glasses. When he saw the priest coming he looked ostentatiously away. He was the law-abiding element: he wouldn't recognize criminals. He began to talk pedantically and priggishly to someone behind him – something about the infant class. A woman kissed the priest's hand; it was odd to be wanted again, not to feel himself the carrier of death. She asked, 'Father, will you hear our confessions?'

He said, 'Yes. Yes. In Señor Lehr's barn. Before the Mass. I will be there at five. As soon as it is light.'

'There are so many of us, father . . .'

'Well tonight too then . . . At eight.'

'And, father, there are many children to be baptized. There has not been a priest for three years.'

'I am going to be here for two more days.'

'What will you charge, father?'

'Well – two pesos is the usual charge.' He thought: I must hire two mules and a guide. It will cost me fifty pesos to reach Las Casas. Five pesos for the Mass – that left forty-five.

'We are very poor here, father,' she haggled gently. 'I have four children myself. Eight pesos is a lot of money.'

'Four children are a lot of children – if the priest was here only three years ago.'

He could hear authority, the old parish intonation coming back into his voice, as if the last years had been a dream and he had never really been away from the Guilds, the Children of Mary, and the daily Mass. He asked sharply, 'How many children are there here – unbaptized?'

'Perhaps a hundred, father.'

He made calculations: there was no need to arrive in Las Casas then as a beggar; he could buy a decent suit of clothes, find a respectable lodging, settle down . . . He said, 'You must pay one peso fifty a head.'

'One peso, father. We are very poor.'

'One peso fifty.' A voice from years back said firmly into his ear: they don't value what they don't pay for. It was the old priest he had succeeded at Concepción who had explained to him: 'They will always tell you they are poor, starving, but they will always have a little store of money buried somewhere, in a pot.' The priest said, 'You must bring the money – and the children – to Señor Lehr's barn tomorrow at two in the afternoon.'

She said, 'Yes, father.' She seemed quite satisfied; she had brought him down by fifty centavos a head. The priest walked on. Say a hundred children, he was thinking, that means a hundred and sixty pesos with tomorrow's Mass. Perhaps I can get the mules and the guide for forty pesos. Señor Lehr will give me food for three days. I shall have a hundred and twenty pesos left. After all these years, it was like wealth. He felt respect all the way up the street: men took off their hats as he passed: it was as if he had got back to the days before the persecution. He could feel the old life hardening round him like a habit, a stony cast which held his head high and dictated the way he walked, and even formed his words. A voice from the cantina said, 'Father.'

The man was very fat, with three commercial chins: he wore a waistcoat in spite of the great heat, and a watch-chain. 'Yes?' the priest said. Behind the man's head stood bottles of mineral waters, beer, spirits . . . The priest came in out of the dusty street to the heat of the lamp. He asked, 'What is it?' with his new-old manner of authority and impatience.

'I thought, father, you might be in need of a little sacramental wine.'

'Perhaps . . . but you will have to give me credit.'

'A priest's credit, father, is always good enough for me. I am a religious man myself. This is a religious place. No doubt you will be holding a baptism.' He leant avidly forward with a respectful and impertinent manner, as if they were two people with the same ideas, educated men.

'Perhaps . . .'

The man smiled understandingly. Between people like ourselves, he seemed to indicate, there is no need of anything explicit: we understand each other's thoughts. He said, 'In the old days, when the church was open, I was treasurer to the Guild of the Blessed Sacrament. Oh, I am a good Catholic, father. The people, of course, are very ignorant.' He asked, 'Would you perhaps honour me by taking a glass of brandy?' He was in his way quite sincere.

The priest said doubtfully, 'It is kind . . .' The two glasses were already filled. He remembered the last drink he had had, sitting on the bed in the dark, listening to the Chief of Police, and seeing, as the light went on, the last wine drain away . . . The memory was like a hand, pulling away the cast, exposing him. The smell of brandy dried his mouth. He thought: what a play-actor I am. I have no business here, among good people. He turned the glass in his hand, and all the other glasses turned too: he remembered the dentist talking of his children and Maria unearthing the bottle of spirits she had kept for him – the whisky priest.

He took a reluctant drink. 'It's good brandy, father,' the man said.

'Yes. Good brandy.'

'I could let you have a dozen bottles for sixty pesos.'

'Where would I find sixty pesos?' He thought that in some ways it was better over there, across the border. Fear and death were not the worst things. It was sometimes a mistake for life to go on.

'I wouldn't make a profit out of you, father. Fifty pesos.'

'Fifty, sixty. It's all the same to me.'

'Go on. Have another glass, father. It's good brandy.' The man leant engagingly forward across the counter and said, 'Why not half a dozen, father, for twenty-four pesos?' He said slyly, 'After all, father – there are the baptisms.'

It was appalling how easily one forgot and went back; he could still hear his own voice speaking in the street with the Concepción accent – unchanged by mortal sin and unrepentance and desertion. The brandy was musty on the tongue with his own corruption. God might forgive cowardice and passion, but was it possible to forgive the habit of piety? He remembered the woman in the prison and how impossible it had been to shake her complacency. It seemed to him that he was another of the same kind. He drank the brandy down like damnation: men like the half-caste could be saved, salvation could strike like lightning at the evil heart, but the habit of piety excluded everything but the evening prayer and the Guild meeting and the feel of humble lips on your gloved hand.

'Las Casas is a fine town, father. They say you can hear Mass every day.'

This was another pious person. There were a lot of them about in the world. He was pouring a little more brandy, but going carefully – not too much. He said, 'When you get there, father, look up a compadre of mine in Guadalupe Street. He has the cantina nearest the church – a good man. Treasurer of the Guild of the Blessed Sacrament – just like I was in this place in the good days. He'll see you get what you want cheap. Now, what about some bottles for the journey?'

The priest drank. There was no point in not drinking. He had the habit now – like piety and the parish voice. He said, 'Three bottles. For eleven pesos. Keep them for me here.' He finished what was left and went back into the street; the lamps were lit in windows and the wide street stretched like a prairie in between. He stumbled in a hole and felt a hand upon his sleeve. 'Ah, Pedro. That was the name wasn't it? Thank you, Pedro.'

'At your service, father.'

The church stood in the darkness like a block of ice: it was melting away in the heat. The roof had fallen in at one place, a coign above the doorway had crumbled. The priest took a quick sideways look at Pedro, holding his breath in case it smelt of brandy, but he could see only the outlines of the face. He said – with a feeling of cunning as though he were cheating a greedy prompter inside his own heart – 'Tell the people, Pedro, that I only want one peso for the baptisms . . .' There would still be enough for the brandy then, even if he arrived at Las Casas like a beggar. There was silence for as long as two seconds and then the wily village voice began to answer him, 'We are poor, father. One peso is a lot of money. I – for example – I have three children. Say seventy-five centavos, father.'

*

Miss Lehr stretched out her feet in their easy slippers and the beetles came up over the veranda from the dark outside. She said, 'In Pittsburgh once . . .' Her brother was asleep with an ancient newspaper across his knee: the mail had come in. The priest gave a little sympathetic giggle as in the old days; it was a try-out which didn't come off. Miss Lehr stopped and sniffed. 'Funny. I thought I smelt – spirits.'

The priest held his breath, leaning back in the rocking-chair. He thought, how quiet it is, how safe. He remembered townspeople who couldn't sleep in country places because of the silence: silence can be like noise, dinning against the eardrums.

'What was I saying father?'

'In Pittsburgh once . . .'

'Of course. In Pittsburgh . . . I was waiting for the train. You see I had nothing to read. Books are so expensive. So I thought I'd buy a paper – any paper, the news is just the same. But when I opened it – it was called something like *Police News*. I never knew such dreadful things were printed. Of course, I didn't read more than a few lines. I think it was the most dreadful thing that's ever happened to me. It . . . well, it opened my eyes.'

'Yes.'

'I've never told Mr Lehr. He wouldn't think the same of me, I do believe, if he knew.'

'But there was nothing wrong . . .'

'It's knowing, isn't it . . . ?'

Somewhere a long way off a bird of some kind called; the lamp on the table began to smoke, and Miss Lehr leant over and turned down the wick: it was as if the only light for miles around had been lowered. The brandy returned on his palate like the smell of ether that reminds a man of a recent operation before he's used to life: it tied him to another state of being. He didn't yet belong to this deep tranquillity. He told himself. In time it will be all right, I shall pull up, I only ordered three bottles this time. They will be the last I'll ever drink, I won't need drink there – he knew he lied. Mr Lehr woke suddenly and said, 'As I was saying . . .'

'You were saying nothing, dear. You were asleep.'

'Oh no, we were talking about that scoundrel Hoover.'

'I don't think so, dear. Not for a long while.'

'Well,' Mr Lehr said, 'it's been a long day. The father will be tired too . . . after all that confessing,' he added with slight distaste.

There had been a continuous stream of penitents from eight to ten – two hours of the worst evil a small place like this could produce after three years. It hadn't amounted to very much – a city would have made a better show – or would it? There isn't much a man can do. Drunkenness, adultery, uncleanness: he sat there tasting the brandy all the while, sitting on a rocking-chair in a horse-box, not looking at the face of the one who knelt at his side. The others had waited, kneeling in an empty stall – Mr Lehr's stable had been depopulated these last few years. He had only one old horse left, which blew windily in the dark as the sins came whimpering out.

'How many times?'

'Twelve, father. Perhaps more,' and the horse blew.

It is astonishing the sense of innocence that goes with sin – only the hard and careful man and the saint are free of it. These people went out of the stable clean; he was the only one left who hadn't repented, confessed, and been absolved. He wanted to say to this man, 'Love is not wrong, but love should be happy and open – it is only wrong when it is secret, unhappy . . . It can be more unhappy than anything but the loss of God. It *is* the loss of God. You don't need a penance, my child, you have suffered quite enough,' and to this other, 'Lust is not the worst thing. It is because any day, any time, lust may turn into love that we have to avoid it. And when we love our sin then we are damned indeed.' But the habit of the confessional reasserted itself: it was as if he were back in the little stuffy wooden boxlike coffin in which men bury their uncleanness with their priest. He said, 'Mortal sin . . . danger . . . self-control,' as if those words meant anything at all. He said, 'Say three Our Fathers and three Hail Marys.'

He whispered wearily, 'Drink is only the beginning . . .' He found he had no lesson he could draw against even that common vice unless it was himself smelling of brandy in the stable. He gave out the penance, quickly, harshly, mechanically. The man would go away, saying, 'A bad priest,' feeling no encouragement, no interest . . .

He said, 'Those laws were made for man. The Church doesn't expect . . . if you can't fast, you must eat, that's all.' The old woman prattled on and on, while the penitents stirred restlessly in the next stall and the horse whinnied, prattled of abstinence days broken, of evening prayers curtailed. Suddenly, without warning, with an odd sense of homesickness, he thought of the hostages in the prison yard, waiting at the water-tap, not looking at him – the suffering and the endurance which went on everywhere the other side of the mountains. He interrupted the woman savagely, 'Why don't you confess properly to me? I'm not interested in your fish supply or in how sleepy you are at night . . . remember your real sins.'

'But I'm a good woman, father,' she squeaked at him with astonishment.

'Then what are you doing here, keeping away the bad people?' He said, 'Have you any love for anyone but yourself?'

'I love God, father,' she said haughtily. He took a quick look at her in the light of the candle burning on the floor – the hard old raisin eyes under the black shawl – another of the pious – like himself.

'How do you know? Loving God isn't any different from loving a man – or a child. It's wanting to be with Him, to be near Him.' He made a hopeless gesture with his hands. 'It's wanting to protect Him from yourself.'

When the last penitent had gone away he walked back across the yard to the bungalow; he could see the lamp burning, and Miss Lehr knitting, and he could smell the grass in the paddock, wet with the first rains. It ought to be possible for a man to be happy here, if he were not so tied to fear and suffering – unhappiness too can become a habit like piety. Perhaps it was his duty to break it, his duty to discover peace. He felt an immense envy of all those people who had confessed to him and been absolved. In six days, he told himself, in Las Casas, I too . . . But he couldn't believe that anyone anywhere would rid him of his heavy heart. Even when he drank he felt bound to his sin by love. It was easier to get rid of hate.

Miss Lehr said, 'Sit down, father. You must be tired. I've never held, of course, with confession. Nor has Mr Lehr.'

'No?'

'I don't know how you can stand sitting there, listening to all the horrible things . . . I remember in Pittsburgh once . . .'

The two mules had been brought in overnight, so that he could start early immediately after Mass – the second that he had said in Mr Lehr's barn. His guide was sleeping somewhere, probably with the mules, a thin nervous creature, who had never been to Las Casas; he simply knew the route by hearsay. Miss Lehr had insisted the night before that she must call him, although he woke of his own accord before it was light. He lay in bed and heard the alarm go off in another room – dinning like a telephone – and presently he heard the slop, slop of Miss Lehr's bedroom-slippers in the passage outside and a knock-knock on the door. Mr Lehr slept on undisturbed upon his back with the thin rectitude of a bishop upon a tomb.

The priest had lain down in his clothes and he opened the door before Miss Lehr had time to get away; she gave a small squeal of dismay, a bunchy figure in a hair-net.

'Excuse me.'

'Oh, it's quite all right. How long will Mass take, father?'

'There will be a great many communicants. Perhaps three-quarters of an hour.'

'I will have some coffee ready for you – and sandwiches.'

'You must not bother.'

'Oh, we can't send you away hungry.'

She followed him to the door, standing a little behind him, so as not to be seen by anything or anybody in the wide empty early world. The grey light uncurled across the pastures; at the gate the tulipán tree bloomed for yet another day; very far off, beyond the little stream where he had bathed, the people were walking up from the village on the way to Mr Lehr's barn – they were too small at that distance to be human. He had a sense of expectant happiness all round him, waiting for him to take part, like an audience of children at a cinema or a rodeo; he was aware of how happy he might have been if he had left nothing behind him across the range except a few bad memories. A man should always prefer peace to violence, and he was going towards peace.

'You have been very good to me, Miss Lehr.'

How odd it had seemed at first to be treated as a guest, not as a criminal or a bad priest. These were heretics – it never occurred to them that he was not a good man: they hadn't the prying insight of fellow Catholics.

'We've enjoyed having you, father. But you'll be glad to be away. Las Casas is a fine city. A very moral place, as Mr Lehr always says. If you meet Father Quintana you must remember us to him – he was here three years ago.'

A bell began to ring. They had brought the church bell down from the tower and hung it outside Mr Lehr's barn; it was like any Sunday anywhere.

'I've sometimes wished,' Miss Lehr said, 'that I could go to church.'

'Why not?'

'Mr Lehr wouldn't like it. He's very strict. But it happens so seldom nowadays – I don't suppose there'll be another service now for another three years.'

'I will come back before then.'

'Oh no,' Miss Lehr said. 'You won't do that. It's a hard journey and Las Casas is a fine city. They have electric light in the streets: there are two hotels. Father Quintana promised to come back – but there are Christians everywhere, aren't there? Why should he come back here? It isn't even as if we were really badly off.'

A little group of Indians passed the gate, gnarled tiny creatures of the Stone Age. The men in short smocks walked with long poles, and the women with black plaits and knocked-about faces carried their babies on their backs. 'The Indians have heard you are here,' Miss Lehr said. 'They've walked fifty miles – I shouldn't be surprised.' They stopped at the gate and watched him; when he looked at them they went down on their knees and crossed themselves – the strange elaborate mosaic touching the nose and ears and chin. 'My brother gets so angry,' Miss Lehr said, 'if he sees somebody go on his knees to a priest, but I don't see that it does any harm.'

Round the corner of the house the mules were stamping – the guide must have brought them out to give them their maize. They were slow feeders, you had to give them a long start. It was time to begin Mass and be gone. He could smell the early morning. The world was still fresh and green, and in the village below the pastures a few dogs barked. The alarm clock tick-tocked in Miss Lehr's hand. He said, 'I must be going now.' He felt an odd reluctance to leave Miss Lehr and the house and the brother sleeping in the inside room. He was aware of a mixture of tenderness and dependence. When a man wakes after a dangerous operation he puts a special value upon the first face he sees as the anaesthetic wears away.

He had no vestments, but the Masses in this village were nearer to the old parish days than any he had known in the last eight years – there was no fear of interruption, no hurried taking of the sacraments as the police approached. There was even an altar stone brought from the locked church. But because it was so peaceful he was all the more aware of his own sin as he prepared to take the Elements – 'Let not the participation of thy Body, O Lord Jesus Christ, which I, though unworthy, presume to receive, turn to my judgement and condemnation.' A virtuous man can almost cease to believe in Hell, but he carried Hell about with him. Sometimes at night he dreamed of it. *Domine, non sum dignus . . . domine, non sum dignus . . .* Evil ran like malaria in his veins. He remembered a dream he had had of a big grassy arena lined with the statues of the saints – but the saints were alive, they turned their eyes this way and that, waiting for something. He waited, too, with an awful expectancy. Bearded Peters and Pauls, with Bibles pressed to their breasts, watched some entrance behind his back he couldn't see – it had the menace of a beast. Then a marimba began to play, tinkly and repetitive, a firework exploded, and Christ danced into the arena – danced and postured with a bleeding painted face, up and down, up and down, grimacing like a prostitute, smiling and suggestive. He woke with the sense of complete despair that a man might feel finding the only money he possessed was counterfeit.

'. . . and we saw his glory, the glory as of the only-begotten of the Father, full of grace and truth.' Mass was over.

In three days, he told himself, I shall be in Las Casas: I shall have confessed and been absolved, and the thought of the child on the rubbish-heap came automatically back to him with painful love. What was the good of confession when you loved the result of your crime?

The people knelt as he made his way down the barn. He saw the little group of Indians: women whose children he had baptized: Pedro: the man from the cantina was there too, kneeling with his face buried in his plump hands, a chain of beads falling between the fingers. He looked a good man: perhaps he was a good man. Perhaps, the priest thought, I have lost the faculty of judging – that woman in prison may have been the best person there. A horse cried in the early day, tethered to a tree, and all the freshness of the morning came in through the open door.

Two men waited beside the mules; the guide was adjusting a stirrup, and beside him, scratching under the arm-pit, awaiting his coming with a doubtful and defensive smile, stood the half-caste. He was like the small pain that reminds a man of his sickness, or perhaps like the unexpected memory which proves that love after all isn't dead. 'Well,' the priest said, 'I didn't expect you here.'

'No, father, of course not.' He scratched and smiled.

'Have you brought the soldiers with you?'

'What things you do say, father,' he protested with a callow giggle. Behind him, across the yard and through an open door, the priest could see Miss Lehr putting up his sandwiches. She had dressed, but she still wore her hair-net. She was wrapping the sandwiches carefully in grease-proof paper, and her sedate movements had a curious effect of unreality. It was the half-caste who was real. He said, 'What trick are you playing now?' Had he perhaps bribed his guide to lead him back across the border? He could believe almost anything of that man.

'You shouldn't say things like that, father.'

Miss Lehr passed out of sight, with the soundlessness of a dream.

'No?'

'I'm here, father,' the man seemed to take a long breath for his surprising stilted statement, 'on an errand of mercy.'

The guide finished with one mule and began on the next, shortening the already short Mexican stirrup; the priest giggled nervously. 'An errand of mercy?'

'Well, father, you're the only priest this side of Las Casas, and the man's dying . . .'

'What man?'

'The Yankee.'

'What are you talking about?'

'The one the police wanted. He robbed a bank. You know the one I mean.'

'He wouldn't need me,' the priest said impatiently, remembering the photograph on the peeling wall watching the first communion party.

'Oh, he's a good Catholic, father.' Scratching under his arm-pit, he didn't look at the priest. 'He's dying, and you and I wouldn't like to have on our conscience what that man . . .'

'We shall be lucky if we haven't worse.'

'What do you mean, father?'

The priest said, 'He only killed and robbed. He hasn't betrayed his friends.'

'Holy Mother of God, I've never . . .'

'We both have,' the priest said. He turned to the guide. 'Are the mules ready?'

'Yes, father.'

'We'll start then.' He had forgotten Miss Lehr completely; the other world had stretched a hand across the border, and he was again in the atmosphere of flight.

'Where are you going?' the half-caste said.

'To Las Casas.' He climbed stiffly on to his mule. The half-caste held on to his stirrup-leather, and he was reminded of their first meeting: there was the same mixture of complaint, appeal, abuse. 'You're a fine priest,' he wailed up to him. 'Your bishop ought to hear of this. A man's dying, wants to confess, and just because you want to get to the city . . .'

'Why do you think me such a fool?' the priest said. 'I know why you've come. You're the only one they've got who can recognize me, and they can't follow me into this state. Now if I ask you where this American is, you'll tell me – I know – you don't have to speak – that he's just the other side.'

'Oh no, father, you're wrong there. He's just this side.'

'A mile or two makes no difference.'

'It's an awful thing, father,' the half-caste said, 'never to be believed. Just because once – well, I admit it –'

The priest kicked his mule into motion. They passed out of Mr Lehr's yard and turned south; the half-caste trotted at his stirrup.

'I remember,' the priest said, 'that you told me you'd never forget my face.'

'And I haven't,' the man put in triumphantly, 'or I wouldn't be here, would I? Listen, father, I'll admit a lot. You don't know how a reward will tempt a poor man like me. And when you wouldn't trust me, I thought, well, if that's how he feels – I'll show him. But I'm a good Catholic, father, and when a dying man wants a priest . . .'

They climbed the long slope of Mr Lehr's pastures which led to the next range of hills. The air was still fresh, at six in the morning, at three thousand feet; up there tonight it would be very cold – they had another six thousand feet to climb. The priest said uneasily, 'Why should I put my head in your noose?' It was too absurd.

'Look, father.' The half-caste was holding up a scrap of paper: the familiar writing caught the priest's attention – the large deliberate handwriting of a child. The paper had been used to wrap up food; it was smeared and greasy. He read, 'The Prince of Denmark is wondering whether he should kill himself or not, whether it is better to go on suffering all the doubts about his father, or by one blow . . .'

'Not that, father, on the other side. That's nothing.'

The priest turned the paper and read a single phrase written in English in blunt pencil: 'For Christ's sake, father . . .' The mule, unbeaten, lapsed into a slow heavy walk; the priest made no attempt to urge it on: this piece of paper left no doubt whatever.

He asked, 'How did this come to you?'

'It was this way, father. I was with the police when they shot him. It was in a village the other side. He picked up a child to act as a screen, but, of course, the soldiers didn't pay any attention. It was only an Indian. They were both shot, but he escaped.'

'Then how . . . ?'

'It was this way, father.' He positively prattled. It appeared that he was afraid of the lieutenant, who resented the fact that the priest had escaped, and so he planned to slip across the border, out of reach. He got his chance at night, and on the way – it was probably on this side of the state line, but who knew where one state began or another ended? – he came on the American. He had been shot in the stomach . . .

'How could he have escaped then?'

'Oh, father, he is a man of superhuman strength. He was dying, he wanted a priest . . .'

'How did he tell you that?'

'It only needed two words, father.' Then, to prove the story, the man had found enough strength to write this note, and so . . . the story had as many holes in it as a sieve. But what remained was this note, like a memorial stone you couldn't overlook.

The half-caste bridled angrily again. 'You don't trust me, father.'

'Oh no,' the priest said. 'I don't trust you.'

'You think I'm lying.'

'Most of it is lies.'

He pulled the mule up and sat thinking, facing south. He was quite certain that this was a trap – probably the half-caste had suggested it – but it was a fact that the American was there, dying. He thought of the deserted banana station where something had happened and the Indian child lay dead on the maize: there was no question at all that he was needed. A man with all that on his soul . . . The oddest thing of all was that he felt quite cheerful; he had never really believed in this peace. He had dreamed of it so often on the other side that now it meant no more to him than a dream. He began to whistle a tune – something he had heard somewhere once. 'I found a rose in my field': it was time he woke up. It wouldn't really have been a good dream – that confession in Las Casas when he would have had to admit, as well as everything else, that he had denied confession to a dying man.

He asked, 'Will the man still be alive?'

'I think so, father,' the half-caste caught him eagerly up.

'How far is it?'

'Four – five hours, father.'

'You can take it in turns to ride the other mule.'

The priest turned his mule back and called out to the guide. The man dismounted and stood inertly there, while he explained. The only remark he made was to the half-caste, motioning him into the saddle, 'Be careful of that saddle-bag. The father's brandy's there.'

They rode slowly back: Miss Lehr was at her gate. She said, 'You forgot the sandwiches, father.'

'Oh yes. Thank you.' He stole a quick look round – it didn't mean a thing to him. He said, 'Is Mr Lehr still asleep?'

'Shall I wake him?'

'No, no. But you will thank him for his hospitality?'

'Yes. And perhaps, father, in a few years we shall see you again? As you said.' She looked curiously at the half-caste, and he stared back through his yellow insulting eyes.

The priest said, 'It's possible,' glancing away with a sly secretive smile.

'Well, good-bye, father. You'd better be off, hadn't you? The sun's getting high.'

'Good-bye, my dear Miss Lehr.' The mestizo slashed impatiently at his mule and stirred it into action.

'Not that way, my man,' Miss Lehr called.

'I have to pay a visit first,' the priest explained, and breaking into an uncomfortable trot he bobbed down behind the mestizo's mule towards the village. They passed the white-washed church – that too belonged to a dream. Life didn't contain churches. The long untidy village street opened ahead of them. The schoolmaster was at his door and waved an ironic greeting, malicious and horn-rimmed. 'Well, father, off with your spoils?'

The priest stopped his mule. He said to the half-caste, 'Really . . . I had forgotten . . .'

'You did well out of the baptisms,' the schoolmaster said. 'It pays to wait a few years, doesn't it?'

'Come on, father,' the half-caste urged him. 'Don't listen to him.' He spat. 'He's a bad man.'

The priest said, 'You know the people here better than anyone. If I leave a gift, will you spend it on things that do no harm – I mean food, blankets – not books?'

'They need food more than books.'

'I have forty-five pesos here . . .'

The mestizo wailed, 'Father, what are you doing . . . ?'

'Conscience money?' the schoolmaster said.

'Yes.'

'All the same, of course I thank you. It's good to see a priest with a conscience. It's a stage in evolution,' he said, his glasses flashing in the sunlight, a plump embittered figure in front of his tin-roofed shack, an exile.

They passed the last houses, the cemetery, and began to climb. 'Why, father, why?' the half-caste protested.

'He's not a bad man, he does his best, and I shan't need money again, shall I?' the priest asked, and for quite a while they rode without speaking, while the sun came blindingly out, and the mules' shoulders strained on the steep rocky paths, and the priest began to whistle again – 'I have a rose' – the only tune he knew. Once the half-caste started a complaint about something, 'The trouble with you, father, is . . .' but it petered out before it was defined because there wasn't really anything to complain about as they rode steadily north towards the border.

'Hungry?' the priest asked at last.

The half-caste muttered something that sounded angry or derisive.

'Take a sandwich,' the priest said, opening Miss Lehr's packet.

Chapter 2

'THERE,' the half-caste said, with a sort of whinny of triumph, as though he had lain innocently all these seven hours under the suspicion of lying. He pointed across the barranca to a group of Indian huts on a peninsula of rock jutting out across the chasm. They were perhaps two hundred yards away, but it would take another hour at least to reach them, winding down a thousand feet and up another thousand.

The priest sat on his mule watching intently; he could see no movement anywhere. Even the look-out, the little platform of twigs built on a mound above the huts, was empty. He said, 'There doesn't seem to be anybody about.' He was back in the atmosphere of desertion.

'Well,' the half-caste said, 'you didn't expect anybody, did you? Except him. He's there. You'll soon find that.'

'Where are the Indians?'

'There you go again,' the man complained. 'Suspicion. Always suspicion. How should I know where the Indians are? I told you he was quite alone, didn't I?'

The priest dismounted. 'What are you doing now?' the half-caste cried despairingly.

'We shan't need the mules any more. They can be taken back.'

'Not need them? How are you going to get away from here?'

'Oh,' the priest said, 'I won't have to think about that, will I?' He counted out forty pesos and said to the muleteer, 'I hired you for Las Casas. Well, this is your good luck. Six days' pay.'

'You don't want me any more, father?'

'No, I think you'd better get away from here quickly. Leave you-know-what behind.'

The half-caste said excitedly, 'We can't walk all that way, father. Why, the man's dying.'

'We can go just as quickly on our own hooves. Now, friend, be off.' The mestizo watched the mules pick their way along the narrow stony path with a look of wistful greed; they disappeared round a shoulder of rock – crack, crack, crack, the sound of their hooves contracted into silence.

'Now,' the priest said briskly, 'we won't delay any more,' and he started down the path, with a small sack slung over his shoulder. He could hear the half-caste panting after him: his wind was bad. They had probably let him have far too much beer in the capital, and the priest thought, with an odd touch of contemptuous affection, of how much had happened to them both since that first encounter in a village of which he didn't even know the name – the half-caste lying there in the hot noonday rocking his hammock with one naked yellow foot. If he had been asleep at that moment, this wouldn't have happened. It was really shocking bad luck for the poor devil that he was to be burdened with a sin of such magnitude. The priest took a quick look back and saw the big toes protruding like slugs out of the dirty gym shoes; the man picked his way down, muttering all the time – his perpetual grievance didn't help his wind. Poor man, the priest thought, he isn't really bad enough . . .

And he wasn't strong enough either for *this* journey. By the time the priest had reached the bottom of the barranca he was fifty yards behind. The priest sat down on a boulder and mopped his forehead, and the half-caste began to complain long before he was down to his level, 'There isn't so much hurry as all that.' It was almost as though the nearer he got to his treachery the greater the grievance against his victim became.

'Didn't you say he was dying?' the priest asked.

'Oh yes, dying, of course. But that can take a long time.'

'The longer the better for all of us,' the priest said. 'Perhaps you are right. I'll take a rest here.'

But now, like a contrary child, the half-caste wanted to start again. He said, 'You do nothing in moderation. Either you run or you sit.'

'Can I do nothing right?' the priest teased him, and then he put in sharply and shrewdly, 'They will let me see him, I suppose?'

'Of course,' the half-caste said and immediately checked himself. 'They, they? Who are you talking about now? First you complain that the place is empty, and then you talk of "they".' He said with tears in his voice, 'You may be a good man, but why won't you talk plainly, so that a man can understand you? It's enough to make a man a bad Catholic.'

The priest said, 'You see this sack here. We don't want to carry that any farther. It's heavy. I think a little drink will do us both good. We both need courage, don't we?'

'Drink, father?' the half-caste asked with excitement, and watched the priest unpack a bottle. He never took his eyes away while the priest drank. His two fangs stuck greedily out, quivering slightly on the lower lip. Then he too fastened on the mouth. 'It's illegal, I suppose,' the priest said with a giggle, 'on this side of the border – if we are on this side.' He had another draw himself and handed it back: it was soon exhausted – he took the bottle and threw it at a rock and it exploded like shrapnel. The half-caste started. He said, 'Be careful. People might think you'd got a gun.'

'As for the rest,' the priest said, 'we won't need that.'

'You mean there's more of it?'

'Two more bottles – but we can't drink any more in this heat. We'd better leave it here.'

'Why didn't you say it was heavy, father? I'll carry it for you. You've only to ask me to do a thing. I'm willing. Only you just won't ask.'

They set off again uphill, the bottles clinking gently; the sun shone vertically down on the pair of them. It took them the best part of an hour to reach the top of the barranca. Then the watch-tower gaped over their path like an upper jaw and the tops of the huts appeared over the rocks above them. Indians do not build their settlements on a mule path; they prefer to stand aside and see who comes. The priest wondered how soon the police would appear; they were keeping very carefully hidden.

'This way, father.' The half-caste took the lead, scrambling away from the path up the rocks to the little plateau. He looked anxious, almost as if he had expected something to happen before this. There were about a dozen huts; they stood quiet, like tombs against the heavy sky. A storm was coming up.

The priest felt a nervous impatience; he had walked into this trap, the least they could do was to close it quickly, finish everything off. He wondered whether they would suddenly shoot him down from one of the huts. He had come to the very edge of time: soon there would be no tomorrow and no yesterday, just existence going on for ever. He began to wish he had taken a little more brandy. His voice broke uncertainly when he said, 'Well, we are here. Where is this Yankee?'

'Oh yes, the Yankee,' the half-caste said, jumping a little. It was as if for a moment he had forgotten the pretext. He stood there, gaping at the huts, wondering too. He said, 'He was over there when I left him.'

'Well, he couldn't have moved, could he?'

If it hadn't been for that letter he would have doubted the very existence of the American – and if he hadn't seen the dead child too, of course. He began to walk across the little silent clearing towards the hut: would they shoot him before he got to the entrance? It was like walking a plank blindfold: you didn't know at what point you would step off into space for ever. He hiccuped once and knotted his hands behind his back to stop them trembling. He had been glad in a way to turn from Miss Lehr's gate – he had never really believed that he would ever get back to parish work and the daily Mass and the careful appearances of piety, but all the same you needed to be a little drunk to die. He got to the door – not a sound anywhere; then a voice said, 'Father.'

He looked round. The mestizo stood in the clearing with his face contorted: the two fangs jumped and jumped; he looked frightened.

'Yes, what is it?'

'Nothing, father.'

'Why did you call me?'

'I said nothing,' he lied.

The priest turned and went in.

The American was there all right. Whether he was alive was another matter. He lay on a straw mat with his eyes closed and his mouth open and his hands on his belly, like a child with stomach-ache. Pain alters a face – or else successful crime has its own falsity like politics or piety. He was hardly recognizable from the news picture on the police station wall; that was tougher, arrogant, a man who had made good. This was just a tramp's face. Pain had exposed the nerves and given the face a kind of spurious intelligence.

The priest knelt down and put his face near the man's mouth, trying to hear the breathing. A heavy smell came up to him – a mixture of vomit and cigar smoke and stale drink; it would take more than a few lilies to hide this corruption. A very faint voice close to his ear said in English, 'Beat it, father.' Outside the door, in the stormy sunlight, the mestizo stood, staring towards the hut, a little loose about the knees.

'So you're alive, are you?' the priest said briskly. 'Better hurry. You haven't got long.'

'Beat it, father.'

'You wanted me, didn't you? You're a Catholic?'

'Beat it,' the voice whispered again, as if those were the only words it could remember of a lesson learnt some while ago.

'Come now,' the priest said. 'How long is it since you went to confession?'

The eyelids rolled up and astonished eyes looked up at him. The man said in a puzzled voice, 'Ten years, I guess. What are you doing here anyway?'

'You asked for a priest. Come now. Ten years is a long time.'

'You got to beat it, father,' the man said. He was remembering the lesson now; lying there flat on the mat with his hands folded on his stomach, any vitality that was left had accumulated in the brain: he was like a reptile crushed at one end. He said in a strange voice, 'That bastard . . .' The priest said furiously, 'What sort of a confession is this? I make a five hours' journey . . . and all I get out of you are evil words.' It seemed to him horribly unfair that his uselessness should return with his danger – he couldn't do anything for a man like this.

'Listen, father . . .' the man said.

'I am listening.'

'You beat it out of here quick. I didn't know . . .'

'I haven't come all this way to talk about myself,' the priest said. 'The sooner your confession's done, the sooner I will be gone.'

'You don't need to trouble about me. I'm through.'

'You mean damned?' the priest said angrily.

'Sure. Damned,' the man replied, licking blood away from his lips.

'You listen to me,' the priest said, leaning closer to the stale and nauseating smell, 'I have come here to listen to your confession. Do you want to confess?'

'No.'

'Did you when you wrote that note . . . ?'

'Maybe.'

'I know what you want to tell me. I know it, do you understand? Let that be. Remember you are dying. Don't depend too much on God's mercy. He has given you this chance. He may not give you another. What sort of a life have you led all these years? Does it seem so grand now? You've killed a lot of people – that's about all. Anybody can do that for a while, and then he is killed too. Just as you are killed. Nothing left except pain.'

'Father.'

'Yes?' The priest gave an impatient sigh, leaning closer. He hoped for a moment that at last he had got the man started on some meagre train of sorrow.

'You take my gun, father. See what I mean? Under my arm.'

'I haven't any use for a gun.'

'Oh yes, you have.' The man detached one hand from his stomach and began to move it slowly up his body. So much effort: it was unbearable to watch. The priest said sharply, 'Lie still. It's not there.' He could see the holster empty under the arm-pit.

'Bastards,' the man said, and his hand lay wearily where it had got to, over his heart; he imitated the prudish attitude of a female statue, one hand over the breast and one upon the stomach. It was very hot in the hut; the heavy light of the storm lay over them.

'Listen, father . . .' The priest sat hopelessly at the man's side; nothing would shift that violent brain towards peace: once, hours ago perhaps, when he wrote that message – but the chance had come and gone. He was whispering now something about a knife. There was a legend believed by many criminals that dead eyes held the picture of what they had last seen – a Christian could believe that the soul did the same, held absolution and peace at the final moment, after a lifetime of the most hideous crime: or sometimes pious men died suddenly in brothels unabsolved and what had seemed a good life went out with the permanent stamp on it of impurity. He had heard men talk of the unfairness of a death-bed repentance – as if it was an easy thing to break the habit of a life whether to do good or evil. One suspected the good of the life that ended badly – or the viciousness that ended well. He made another desperate attempt. He said 'You believed once. Try and understand – this is your chance. At the last moment. Like the thief. You have murdered men – children perhaps,' he added, remembering the little black heap under the cross. 'But that need not be so important. It only belongs to this life, a few years – it's over already. You can drop it all here, in this hut, and go on for ever . . .' He felt sadness and longing at the vaguest idea of a life he couldn't lead himself . . . words like peace, glory, love.

'Father,' the voice said urgently, 'you let me be. You look after yourself. You take my knife . . .' The hand began its weary march again – this time towards the hip. The knees crooked up in an attempt to roll over, and then the whole body gave up the effort, the ghost, everything.

The priest hurriedly whispered the words of conditional absolution, in case, for one second before it crossed the border, the spirit had repented, but it was more likely that it had gone over still seeking its knife, bent on vicarious violence. He prayed: 'O merciful God, after all he was thinking of me, it was for my sake . . .' but he prayed without conviction. At the best, it was only one criminal trying to aid the escape of another – whichever way you looked, there wasn't much merit in either of them.

Chapter 3

A VOICE said, 'Well, have you finished now?'

The priest got up and made a small scared gesture of assent. He recognized the police officer who had given him money at the prison, a dark smart figure in the doorway with the storm-light glinting on his leggings. He had one hand on his revolver and he frowned sourly in at the dead gunman. 'You didn't expect to see me,' he said.

'Oh, but I did,' the priest said. 'I must thank you.'

'Thank me, what for?'

'For letting me stay alone with him.'

'I am not a barbarian,' the officer said. 'Will you come out now, please? It's no use at all your trying to escape. You can see that,' he added, as the priest emerged and looked round at the dozen armed men who surrounded the hut.

'I've had enough of escaping,' he said. The half-caste was no longer in sight; the heavy clouds were piling up the sky: they made the real mountains look like little bright toys below them. He sighed and giggled nervously. 'What a lot of trouble I had getting across those mountains, and now . . . here I am . . .'

'I never believed you would return.'

'Oh well, lieutenant, you know how it is. Even a coward has a sense of duty.' The cool fresh wind which sometimes blows across before a storm breaks touched his skin. He said with badly-affected ease, 'Are you going to shoot me now?'

The lieutenant said again sharply, 'I am not a barbarian. You will be tried . . . properly.'

'What for?'

'For treason.'

'I have to go all the way back there?'

'Yes. Unless you try to escape.' He kept his hand on his gun as if he didn't trust the priest a yard. He said, 'I could swear that somewhere . . .'

'Oh yes,' the priest said. 'You have seen me twice. When you took a hostage from my village . . . you asked my child: "Who is he?" She said: "My father," and you let me go.' Suddenly the mountains ceased to exist: it was as if somebody had dashed a handful of water into their faces.

'Quick,' the lieutenant said, 'into that hut.' He called out to one of the men. 'Bring us some boxes so that we can sit.'

The two of them joined the dead man in the hut as the storm came up all round them. A soldier dripping with rain carried in two packing-cases. 'A candle,' the lieutenant said. He sat down on one of the cases and took out his revolver. He said, 'Sit down, there, away from the door, where I can see you.' The soldier lit a candle and stuck it in its own wax on the hard earth floor, and the priest sat down, close to the American; huddled up in his attempt to get at his knife he gave an effect of wanting to reach his companion, to have a word or two in private. They looked two of a kind, dirty and unshaved: the lieutenant seemed to belong to a different class altogether. He said with contempt, 'So you have a child?'

'Yes,' the priest said.

'You – a priest?'

'You mustn't think they are all like me.' He watched the candlelight blink on the bright buttons. He said, 'There are good priests and bad priests. It is just that I am a bad priest.'

'Then perhaps we will be doing your Church a service . . .'

'Yes.'

The lieutenant looked sharply up as if he thought he was being mocked. He said, 'You told me twice. That I had seen you twice.'

'Yes, I was in prison. And you gave me money.'

'I remember.' He said furiously, 'What an appalling mockery. To have had you and then to let you go. Why, we lost two men looking for you. They'd be alive today . . .' The candle sizzled as the drops of rain came through the roof. 'This American wasn't worth two lives. He did no real harm.'

The rain poured ceaselessly down. They sat in silence. Suddenly the lieutenant said, 'Keep your hand away from your pocket.'

'I was only feeling for a pack of cards. I thought perhaps it would help to pass the time . . .'

'I don't play cards,' the lieutenant said harshly.

'No, no. Not a game. Just a few tricks I can show you. May I?'

'All right. If you wish to.'

Mr Lehr had given him an old pack of cards. The priest said, 'Here, you see, are three cards. The ace, the king, and the jack. Now,' he spread them fanwise out on the floor, 'tell me which is the ace.'

'This, of course,' the lieutenant said grudgingly, showing no interest.

'But you are wrong,' the priest said, turning it up. 'That is the jack.'

The lieutenant said contemptuously, 'A game for gamblers – or children.'

'There is another trick,' the priest said, 'called Fly-away Jack. I cut the pack into three – so. And I take this Jack of Hearts and I put it into the centre pack – so. Now I tap the three packs.' His face lit up as he spoke – it was such a long time since he had handled cards – he forgot the storm, the dead man and the stubborn unfriendly face opposite him. 'I say Fly-away Jack' – he cut the left-hand pack in half and disclosed the jack – 'and there he is.'

'Of course there are two jacks.'

'See for yourself.' Unwillingly the lieutenant leant forward and inspected the centre pack. He said, 'I suppose you tell the Indians that that is a miracle of God.'

'Oh no,' the priest giggled, 'I learnt it from an Indian. He was the richest man in the village. Do you wonder? with such a hand. No, I used to show the tricks at any entertainments we had in the parish – for the Guilds, you know.'

A look of physical disgust crossed the lieutenant's face. He said, 'I remember those Guilds.'

'When you were a boy?'

'I was old enough to know . . .'

'Yes?'

'The trickery.' He broke out furiously with one hand on his gun, as though it had crossed his mind that it would be better to eliminate this beast, now, at this instant, for ever. 'What an excuse it all was, what a fake. Sell all and give to the poor – that was the lesson, wasn't it? and Señora So-and-so, the druggist's wife, would say the family wasn't really deserving of charity, and Señor This, That and the Other would say that if they starved, what else did they deserve, they were Socialists anyway, and the priest – you – would notice who had done his Easter duty and paid his Easter offering.' His voice rose – a policeman looked into the hut anxiously and withdrew again through the lashing rain. 'The Church was poor, the priest was poor, therefore everyone should sell all and give to the Church.'

The priest said, 'You are so right.' He added quickly, 'Wrong too, of course.'

'How do you mean?' the lieutenant asked savagely. 'Right? Won't you even defend . . . ?'

'I felt at once that you were a good man when you gave me money at the prison.'

The lieutenant said, 'I only listen to you because you have no hope. No hope at all. Nothing you say will make any difference.'

'No.'

He had no intention of angering the police officer, but he had had very little practice the last eight years in talking to any but a few peasants and Indians. Now something in his tone infuriated the lieutenant. He said, 'You're a danger. That's why we kill you. I have nothing against you, you understand, as a man.'

'Of course not. It's God you're against. I'm the sort of man you shut up every day – and give money to.'

'No, I don't fight against a fiction.'

'But I'm not worth fighting, am I? You've said so. A liar, a drunkard. That man's worth a bullet more than I am.'

'It's your ideas.' The lieutenant sweated a little in the hot steamy air. He said, 'You are so cunning, you people. But tell me this – what have you ever done in Mexico for *us?* Have you ever told a landlord he shouldn't beat his peon – oh yes, I know, in the confessional perhaps, and it's your duty, isn't it, to forget it at once. You come out and have dinner with him and it's your duty not to know that he has murdered a peasant. That's all finished. He's left it behind in your box.'

'Go on,' the priest said. He sat on the packing-case with his hands on his knees and his head bent; he couldn't, though he tried, keep his mind on what the lieutenant was saying. He was thinking – forty-eight hours to the capital. Today is Sunday. Perhaps on Wednesday I shall be dead. He felt it as a treachery that he was more afraid of the pain of bullets than of what came after.

'Well, we have ideas too,' the lieutenant was saying. 'No more money for saying prayers, no more money for building places to say prayers in. We'll give people food instead, teach them to read, give them books. We'll see they don't suffer.'

'But if they want to suffer . . .'

'A man may want to rape a woman. Are we to allow it because he wants to? Suffering is wrong.'

'And you suffer all the time,' the priest commented, watching the sour Indian face behind the candle-flame. He said, 'It sounds fine, doesn't it? Does the jefe feel like that too?'

'Oh, we have our bad men.'

'And what happens afterwards? I mean after everybody has got enough to eat and can read the right books – the books you let them read?'

'Nothing. Death's a fact. We don't try to alter facts.'

'We agree about a lot of things,' the priest said, idly dealing out his cards. 'We have facts, too, we don't try to alter – that the world's unhappy whether you are rich or poor – unless you are a saint, and there aren't many of those. It's not worth bothering too much about a little pain here. There's one belief we both of us have – that we'll all be dead in a hundred years.' He fumbled, trying to shuffle, and bent the cards: his hands were not steady.

'All the same, you're worried now about a little pain,' the lieutenant said maliciously, watching his fingers.

'But I'm not a saint,' the priest said. 'I'm not even a brave man.' He looked up apprehensively: light was coming back: the candle was no longer necessary. It would soon be clear enough to start the long journey back. He felt a desire to go on talking, to delay even by a few minutes the decision to start. He said, 'That's another difference between us. It's no good your working for your end unless you're a good man yourself. And there won't always be good men in your party. Then you'll have all the old starvation, beating, get-rich-anyhow. But it doesn't matter so much my being a coward – and all the rest. I can put God into a man's mouth just the same – and I can give him God's pardon. It wouldn't make any difference to that if every priest in the Church was like me.'

'That's another thing I don't understand,' the lieutenant said, 'why you – of all people – should have stayed when the others ran.'

'They didn't all run,' the priest said.

'But why did you stay?'

'Once,' the priest said, 'I asked myself that. The fact is, a man isn't presented suddenly with two courses to follow: one good and one bad. He gets caught up. The first year – well, I didn't believe there was really any cause to run. Churches have been burnt before now. You know how often. It doesn't mean much. I thought I'd stay till next month, say, and see if things were better. Then – oh, you don't know how time can slip by.' It was quite light again now: the afternoon rain was over: life had to go on. A policeman passed the entrance of the hut and looked in curiously at the pair of them. 'Do you know I suddenly realized that I was the only priest left for miles around? The law which made priests marry finished them. They went: they were quite right to go. There was one priest in particular – he had always disapproved of me. I have a tongue, you know, and it used to wag. He said – quite rightly – that I wasn't a firm character. He escaped. It felt – you'll laugh at this – just as it did at school when a bully I had been afraid of – for years – got too old for any more teaching and was turned out. You see, I didn't have to think about anybody's opinion any more. The people – they didn't worry me. They liked me.' He gave a weak smile, sideways, towards the humped Yankee.

'Go on,' the lieutenant said moodily.

'You'll know all there is to know about me at this rate,' the priest said, with a nervous giggle, 'by the time I get to, well, prison.'

'It's just as well. To know an enemy, I mean.'

'That other priest was right. It was when he left I began to go to pieces. One thing went after another. I got careless about my duties. I began to drink. It would have been much better, I think, if I had gone too. Because pride was at work all the time. Not love of God.' He sat bowed on the packing-case, a small plump man in Mr Lehr's cast-off clothes. He said, 'Pride was what made the angels fall. Pride's the worst thing of all. I thought I was a fine fellow to have stayed when the others had gone. And then I thought I was so grand I could make my own rules. I gave up fasting, daily Mass. I neglected my prayers – and one day because I was drunk and lonely – well, you know how it was, I got a child. It was all pride. Just pride because I'd stayed. I wasn't any use, but I stayed. At least, not much use. I'd got so that I didn't have a hundred communicants a month. If I'd gone I'd have given God to twelve times that number. It's a mistake one makes – to think just because a thing is difficult or dangerous . . .' He made a flapping motion with his hands.

The lieutenant said in a tone of fury, 'Well, you're going to be a martyr – you've got that satisfaction.'

'Oh no. Martyrs are not like me. They don't think all the time – if I had drunk more brandy I shouldn't be so afraid.'

The lieutenant said sharply to a man in the entrance, 'Well, what is it? What are you hanging round for?'

'The storm's over, lieutenant. We wondered when we were to start?'

'We start immediately.'

He got up and put back the pistol in his holster. He said, 'Get a horse ready for the prisoner. And have some men dig a grave quickly for the Yankee.'

The priest put the cards in his pocket and stood up. He said, 'You have listened very patiently . . .'

'I am not afraid,' the lieutenant said, 'of other people's ideas.'

Outside the ground was steaming after the rain: the mist rose nearly to their knees: the horses stood ready. The priest mounted, but before they had time to move a voice made the priest turn – the same sullen whine he had heard so often. 'Father.' It was the half-caste.

'Well, well,' the priest said. 'You again.'

'Oh, I know what you're thinking,' the half-caste said. 'There's not much charity in you, father. You thought all along I was going to betray you.'

'Go,' the lieutenant said sharply. 'You've done your job.'

'May I have one word, lieutenant?' the priest asked.

'You're a good man, father,' the mestizo cut quickly in, 'but you think the worst of people. I just want your blessing, that's all.'

'What is the good? You can't sell a blessing,' the priest said.

'It's just because we won't see each other again. And I didn't want you to go off there thinking ill things . . .'

'You are so superstitious,' the priest said. 'You think my blessing will be like a blinker over God's eyes. I can't stop him knowing all about it. Much better go home and pray. Then if he gives you grace to feel sorry, give away the money . . .'

'What money, father?' The half-caste shook his stirrup angrily. 'What money? There you go again . . .'

The priest sighed. He felt empty with the ordeal. Fear can be more tiring than a long monotonous ride. He said, 'I'll pray for you,' and beat his horse into position beside the lieutenant's.

'And I'll pray for you, father,' the half-caste announced complacently. Once the priest looked back as his horse poised for the steep descent between the rocks. The half-caste stood alone among the huts, his mouth a little open, showing the two long fangs. He might have been snapped in the act of shouting some complaint or some claim – that he was a good Catholic perhaps; one hand scratched under the arm-pit. The priest waved his hand; he bore no grudge because he expected nothing else of anything human and he had one cause at least for satisfaction – that yellow and unreliable face would be absent 'at the death'.

'You're a man of education,' the lieutenant said. He lay across the entrance of the hut with his head on his rolled cape and his revolver by his side. It was night, but neither man could sleep. The priest, when he shifted, groaned a little with stiffness and cramp. The lieutenant was in a hurry to get home, and they had ridden till midnight. They were down off the hills and in the marshy plain. Soon the whole State would be subdivided by swamp. The rains had really begun.

'I'm not that. My father was a storekeeper.'

'I mean, you've been abroad. You can talk like a Yankee. You've had schooling.'

'Yes.'

'I've had to think things out for myself. But there are some things which you don't have to learn in a school. That there are rich and poor.' He said in a low voice, 'I've shot three hostages because of you. Poor men. It made me hate you.'

'Yes,' the priest admitted, and tried to stand to ease the cramp in his right thigh. The lieutenant sat up quickly, gun in hand: 'What are you doing?'

'Nothing. Just cramp. That's all.' He lay down again with a groan.

The lieutenant said, 'Those men I shot. They were my own people. I wanted to give them the whole world.'

'Well, who knows? Perhaps that's what you did.'

The lieutenant spat suddenly, viciously, as if something unclean had got upon his tongue. He said, 'You always have answers which mean nothing.'

'I was never any good at books,' the priest said. 'I haven't any memory. But there was one thing always puzzled me about men like yourself. You hate the rich and love the poor. Isn't that right?'

'Yes.'

'Well, if I hated you, I wouldn't want to bring up my child to be like you. It's not sense.'

'That's just twisting . . .'

'Perhaps it is. I've never got your ideas straight. We've always said the poor are blessed and the rich are going to find it hard to get into heaven. Why should we make it hard for the poor man too? Oh, I know we are told to give to the poor, to see they are not hungry – hunger can make a man do evil just as much as money can. But why should we give the poor power? It's better to let him die in dirt and wake in heaven – so long as we don't push his face in the dirt.'

'I hate your reasons,' the lieutenant said. 'I don't want reasons. If you see somebody in pain, people like you reason and reason. You say – pain's a good thing, perhaps he'll be better for it one day. I want to let my heart speak.'

'At the end of a gun.'

'Yes. At the end of a gun.'

'Oh well, perhaps when you're my age you'll know the heart's an untrustworthy beast. The mind is too, but it doesn't talk about love. Love. And a girl puts her head under water or a child's strangled, and the heart all the time says love, love.'

They lay quiet for a while in the hut. The priest thought the lieutenant was asleep until he spoke again. 'You never talk straight. You say one thing to me – but to another man, or a woman, you say, "God is love." But you think that stuff won't go down with me, so you say different things. Things you think I'll agree with.'

'Oh,' the priest said, 'that's another thing altogether – God *is* love. I don't say the heart doesn't feel a taste of it, but what a taste. The smallest glass of love mixed with a pint pot of ditch-water. We wouldn't recognize *that* love. It might even look like hate. It would be enough to scare us – God's love. It set fire to a bush in the desert, didn't it, and smashed open graves and set the dead walking in the dark. Oh, a man like me would run a mile to get away if he felt that love around.'

'You don't trust him much, do you? He doesn't seem a grateful kind of God. If a man served me as well as you've served him, well, I'd recommend him for promotion, see he got a good pension . . . if he was in pain, with cancer, I'd put a bullet through his head.'

'Listen,' the priest said earnestly, leaning forward in the dark, pressing on a cramped foot, 'I'm not as dishonest as you think I am. Why do you think I tell people out of the pulpit that they're in danger of damnation if death catches them unawares? I'm not telling them fairy stories I don't believe myself. I don't know a thing about the mercy of God: I don't know how awful the human heart looks to Him. But I do know this – that if there's ever been a single man in this state damned, then I'll be damned too.' He said slowly, 'I wouldn't want it to be any different. I just want justice, that's all.'

'We'll be in before dark,' the lieutenant said. Six men rode in front and six behind; sometimes, in the belts of forest between the arms of the river, they had to ride in single file. The lieutenant didn't speak much, and once, when two of his men struck up a song about a fat shopkeeper and his woman, he told them savagely to be silent. It wasn't a very triumphal procession. The priest rode with a weak grin fixed on his face; it was like a mask he had stuck on, so that he could think quietly without anyone noticing. What he thought about mostly was pain.

'I suppose,' the lieutenant said, scowling ahead, 'you're hoping for a miracle.'

'Excuse me. What did you say?'

'I said I suppose you're hoping for a miracle.'

'No.'

'You believe in them, don't you?'

'Yes. But not for me. I'm no more good to anyone, so why should God keep me alive?'

'I can't think how a man like you can believe in those things. The Indians, yes. Why, the first time they see an electric light they think it's a miracle.'

'And I dare say the first time you saw a man raised from the dead you might think so too.' He giggled unconvincingly behind the smiling mask. 'Oh, it's funny, isn't it? It isn't a case of miracles not happening – it's just a case of people calling them something else. Can't you see the doctors round the dead man? He isn't breathing any more, his pulse has stopped, his heart's not beating: he's dead. Then somebody gives him back his life, and they all – what's the expression? – reserve their opinion. They won't say it's a miracle, because that's a word they don't like. Then it happens again and again perhaps – because God's about on earth – and they say: these aren't miracles, it is simply that we have enlarged our conception of what life is. Now we know you can be alive without pulse, breath, heart-beats. And they invent a new word to describe that state of life, and they say science has disproved a miracle.' He giggled again. 'You can't get round them.'

They were out of the forest track on to a hard-beaten road, and the lieutenant dug in his spur and the whole cavalcade broke into a canter. They were nearly home now. The lieutenant said grudgingly, 'You aren't a bad fellow. If there's anything I can do for you . . .'

'If you would give permission for me to confess . . .'

The first houses came into sight, little hard-baked houses of earth falling into ruin, a few classical pillars just plaster over mud, and a dirty child playing in the rubble.

The lieutenant said, 'But there's no priest.'

'Padre José.'

'Oh, Padre José,' the lieutenant said with contempt, 'he's no good for you.'

'He's good enough for me. It's not likely I'd find a saint here, is it?'

The lieutenant rode on for a little while in silence; they came to the cemetery, full of chipped angels, and passed the great portico with its black letters, 'Silencio'. He said, 'All right. You can have him.' He wouldn't look at the cemetery as they went by – there was the wall where prisoners were shot. The road went steeply downhill towards the river; on the right, where the cathedral had been, the iron swings stood empty in the hot afternoon. There was a sense of desolation everywhere, more of it than in the mountains because a lot of life had once existed here. The lieutenant thought: No pulse, no breath, no heart-beat, but it's still life – we've only got to find a name for it. A small boy watched them pass; he called out to the lieutenant, 'Lieutenant, have you got him?' and the lieutenant dimly remembered the face – one day in the plaza – a broken bottle, and he tried to smile back, an odd sour grimace, without triumph or hope. One had to begin again with that.

Chapter 4

THE lieutenant waited till after dark and then he went himself. It would be dangerous to send another man because the news would be around the city in no time that Padre José had been permitted to carry out a religious duty in the prison. It was wiser not to let even the jefe know. One didn't trust one's superiors when one was more successful than they were. He knew the jefe wasn't pleased that he had brought the priest in – an escape would have been better from his point of view.

In the patio he could feel himself watched by a dozen eyes. The children clustered there ready to shout at Padre José if he appeared. He wished he had promised the priest nothing, but he was going to keep his word – because it would be a triumph for that old corrupt God-ridden world if it could show itself superior on any point – whether of courage, truthfulness, justice . . .

Nobody answered his knock; he stood darkly in the patio like a petitioner. Then he knocked again, and a voice called, 'A moment. A moment.'

Padre José put his face against the bars of his window and asked, 'Who's there?' He seemed to be fumbling at something near the ground.

'Lieutenant of police.'

'Oh,' Padre José squeaked. 'Excuse me. It is my trousers. In the dark.' He seemed to heave at something and there was a sharp crack, as if his belt or braces had given way. Across the patio the children began to squeak, 'Padre José. Padre José.' When he came to the door he wouldn't look at them, muttering tenderly, 'The little devils.'

The lieutenant said, 'I want you to come to the police station.'

'But I've done nothing. Nothing. I've been so careful.'

'Padre José,' the children squeaked.

He said imploringly, 'If it's anything about a burial, you've been misinformed. I wouldn't even say a prayer.'

'Padre José. Padre José.'

The lieutenant turned and strode across the patio. He said furiously to the faces at the grid, 'Be quiet. Go to bed. At once. Do you hear me?' They dropped out of sight one by one, but immediately the lieutenant's back was turned, they were there again watching.

Padre José said, 'Nobody can do anything with those children.'

A woman's voice said, 'Where are you, José?'

'Here, my dear. It is the police.'

A huge woman in a white nightdress came billowing out at them. It wasn't much after seven; perhaps she lived, the lieutenant thought, in that dress – perhaps she lived in bed. He said, 'Your husband,' dwelling on the term with satisfaction, 'your husband is wanted at the station.'

'Who says so?'

'I do.'

'He's done nothing.'

'I was just saying, my dear . . .'

'Be quiet. Leave the talking to me.'

'You can both stop jabbering,' the lieutenant said. 'You're wanted at the station to see a man – a priest. He wants to confess.'

'To me?'

'Yes. There's no one else.'

'Poor man,' Padre José said. His little pink eyes swept the patio. 'Poor man.' He shifted uneasily, and took a quick furtive look at the sky where the constellations wheeled.

'You won't go,' the woman said.

'It's against the law, isn't it?' Padre José asked.

'You needn't trouble about that.'

'Oh, we needn't, eh?' the woman said. 'I can see through you. You don't want my husband to be let alone. You want to trick him. I know your work. You get people to ask him to say prayers – he's a kind man. But I'd have you remember this – he's a pensioner of the government.'

The lieutenant said slowly, 'This priest – he has been working for years secretly – for *your* Church. We've caught him and, of course, he'll be shot tomorrow. He's not a bad man, and I told him he could see you. He seems to think it will do him good.'

'I know him,' the woman interrupted, 'he's a drunkard. That's all he is.'

'Poor man,' Padre José said. 'He tried to hide here once.'

'I promise you,' the lieutenant said, 'nobody shall know.'

'Nobody know?' the woman cackled. 'Why, it will be all over town. Look at those children there. They never leave José alone.' She went on, 'There'll be no end of it – everybody will be wanting to confess, and the Governor will hear of it, and the pension will be stopped.'

'Perhaps, my dear,' José said, 'it's my duty . . .'

'You aren't a priest any more,' the woman said, 'you're my husband.' She used a coarse word. 'That's your duty now.'

The lieutenant listened to them with acid satisfaction. It was like rediscovering an old belief. He said, 'I can't wait here while you argue. Are you going to come with me?'

'He can't make you,' the woman said.

'My dear, it's only that . . . well . . . I *am* a priest.'

'A priest,' the woman cackled, 'you a priest.' She went off into a peal of laughter, which was taken up tentatively by the children at the window. Padre José put his fingers up to his pink eyes as if they hurt. He said, 'My dear . . .' and the laughter went on.

'Are you coming?'

Padre José made a despairing gesture – as much as to say, what does one more failure matter in a life like this? He said, 'I don't think it's – possible.'

'Very well,' the lieutenant said. He turned abruptly – he hadn't any more time to waste on mercy, and heard Padre José's voice speak imploringly, 'Tell him I shall pray.' The children had gained confidence; one of them called out sharply, 'Come to bed, José,' and the lieutenant laughed once – a poor unconvincing addition to the general laughter which now surrounded Padre José, chiming up all round towards the disciplined constellations he had once known by name.

The lieutenant opened the cell door. It was very dark inside. He shut the door carefully behind him and locked it, keeping his hand on his gun. He said, 'He won't come.'

A little bunched figure in the darkness was the priest. He crouched on the floor like a child playing. He said, 'You mean – not tonight?'

'I mean he won't come at all.'

There was silence for some while, if you could talk of silence where there was always the drill-drill of mosquitoes and the little crackling explosions of beetles against the wall. At last the priest said, 'He was afraid, I suppose . . .'

'His wife wouldn't let him come.'

'Poor man.' He tried to giggle, but no sound could have been more miserable than the half-hearted attempt. His head drooped between his knees; he looked as if he had abandoned everything and been abandoned.

The lieutenant said, 'You had better know everything. You've been tried and found guilty.'

'Couldn't I have been present at my own trial?'

'It wouldn't have made any difference.'

'No.' He was silent, preparing an attitude. Then he asked with a kind of false jauntiness, 'And when, if I may ask . . . ?'

'Tomorrow.' The promptness and brevity of the reply called his bluff. His head went down again and he seemed, as far as it was possible to see in the dark, to be biting his nails.

The lieutenant said, 'It's bad being alone on a night like this. If you would like to be transferred to the common cell . . .'

'No, no. I'd rather be alone. I've got plenty to do.' His voice failed, as though he had a heavy cold. He wheezed, 'So much to think about.'

'I should like to do something for you,' the lieutenant said. 'I've brought you some brandy.'

'Against the law?'

'Yes.'

'It's very good of you.' He took the small flask. 'You wouldn't need this, I dare say. But I've always been afraid of pain.'

'We have to die some time,' the lieutenant said. 'It doesn't seem to matter so much when.'

'You're a good man. You've got nothing to be afraid of.'

'You have such odd ideas,' the lieutenant complained. He said, 'Sometimes I feel you're just trying to talk me round.'

'Round to what?'

'Oh, to letting you escape perhaps – or to believing in the Holy Catholic Church, the communion of saints . . . how does that stuff go?'

'The forgiveness of sins.'

'You don't believe much in that, do you?'

'Oh yes, I believe,' the little man said obstinately.

'Then what are you worried about?'

'I'm not ignorant, you see. I've always known what I've been doing. And I can't absolve myself.'

'Would Father José coming here have made all that difference?'

He had to wait a long while for his answer, and then he didn't understand it when it came. 'Another man . . . it makes it easier . . .'

'Is there nothing more I can do for you?'

'No. Nothing.'

The lieutenant reopened the door; mechanically putting his hand again upon his revolver he felt moody, as though now the last priest was under lock and key, there was nothing left to think about. The spring of action seemed to be broken. He looked back on the weeks of hunting as a happy time which was over now for ever. He felt without a purpose, as if life had drained out of the world. He said with bitter kindness (he couldn't summon up any hate of the small hollow man), 'Try to sleep.'

He was closing the door when a scared voice spoke. 'Lieutenant.'

'Yes.'

'You've seen people shot. People like me.'

'Yes.'

'Does the pain go on – a long time?'

'No, no. A second,' he said roughly, and closed the door, and picked his way back across the whitewashed yard. He went into the office. The pictures of the priest and the gunman were still pinned up on the wall: he tore them down – they would never be wanted again. Then he sat at his desk and put his head upon his hands and fell asleep with utter weariness. He couldn't remember afterwards anything of his dreams except laughter, laughter all the time, and a long passage in which he could find no door.

The priest sat on the floor, holding the brandy-flask. Presently he unscrewed the cap and put his mouth to it. The spirit didn't do a thing to him – it might have been water. He put it down again and began some kind of a general confession, speaking in a whisper. He said, 'I have committed fornication.' The formal phrase meant nothing at all: it was like a sentence in a newspaper: you couldn't feel repentance over a thing like that. He started again, 'I have lain with a woman,' and tried to imagine the other priest asking him, 'How many times? Was she married?' 'No.' Without thinking what he was doing, he took another drink of brandy.

As the liquid touched his tongue he remembered his child, coming in out of the glare: the sullen unhappy knowledgeable face. He said, 'Oh God, help her. Damn me, I deserve it, but let her live for ever.' This was the love he should have felt for every soul in the world: all the fear and the wish to save concentrated unjustly on the one child. He began to weep; it was as if he had to watch her from the shore drown slowly because he had forgotten how to swim. He thought: This is what I should feel all the time for everyone, and he tried to turn his brain away towards the half-caste, the lieutenant, even a dentist he had once sat with for a few minutes, the child at the banana station, calling up a long succession of faces, pushing at his attention as if it were a heavy door which wouldn't budge. For those were all in danger too. He prayed, 'God help them,' but in the moment of prayer he switched back to his child beside the rubbish-dump, and he knew it was for her only that he prayed. Another failure.

After a while he began again: 'I have been drunk – I don't know how many times; there isn't a duty I haven't neglected; I have been guilty of pride, lack of charity . . .' The words were becoming formal again, meaning nothing. He had no confessor to turn his mind away from the formula to the fact.

He took another drink of brandy, and getting up with pain because of his cramp he moved to the door and looked through the bars at the hot moony square. He could see the police asleep in their hammocks, and one man who couldn't sleep lazily rocking up and down, up and down. There was an odd silence everywhere, even in the other cells; it was as if the whole world had tactfully turned away to avoid seeing him die. He felt his way back along the wall to the farthest corner and sat down with the flask between his knees. He thought: If I hadn't been so useless, useless . . . The eight hard hopeless years seemed to him to be only a caricature of service: a few communions, a few confessions, and an endless bad example. He thought: If I had only one soul to offer, so that I could say, Look what I've done . . . People had died for him, they had deserved a saint, and a tinge of bitterness spread across his mind for their sake that God hadn't thought fit to send them one. Padre José and me, he thought, Padre José and me, and he took a drink again from the brandy flask. He thought of the cold faces of the saints rejecting him.

The night was slower than the last he had spent in prison because he was alone. Only the brandy, which he finished about two in the morning, gave him any sleep at all. He felt sick with fear, his stomach ached, and his mouth was dry with the drink. He began to talk aloud to himself because he couldn't stand the silence any more. He complained miserably, 'It's all very well . . . for saints,' and later, 'How does he know it only lasts a second? How long's a second?' Then he began to cry, beating his head gently against the wall. They had given a chance to Padre José, but they had never given him a chance at all. Perhaps they had got it all wrong – just because he had escaped them for such a time. Perhaps they really thought he would refuse the conditions Padre José had accepted, that he would refuse to marry, that he was proud. Perhaps if he suggested it himself, he would escape yet. The hope calmed him for a while, and he fell asleep with his head against the wall.

He had a curious dream. He dreamed he was sitting at a café table in front of the high altar of the cathedral. About six dishes were spread before him, and he was eating hungrily. There was a smell of incense and an odd sense of elation. The dishes – like all food in dreams – did not taste of much, but he had a sense that when he had finished them, he would have the best dish of all. A priest passed to and fro before the altar saying Mass, but he took no notice: the service no longer seemed to concern him. At last the six plates were empty; someone out of sight rang the sanctus bell, and the serving priest knelt before he raised the Host. But *he* sat on, just waiting, paying no attention to the God over the altar, as though that were a God for other people and not for him. Then the glass by his plate began to fill with wine, and looking up he saw that the child from the banana station was serving him. She said, 'I got it from my father's room.'

'You didn't steal it?'

'Not exactly,' she said in her careful and precise voice.

He said, 'It is very good of you. I had forgotten the code – what did you call it?'

'Morse.'

'That was it. Morse. Three long taps and one short one,' and immediately the taps began: the priest by the altar tapped, a whole invisible congregation tapped along the aisles – three long and one short. He asked, 'What is it?'

'News,' the child said, watching him with a stern, responsible and interested gaze.

When he woke up it was dawn. He woke with a huge feeling of hope which suddenly and completely left him at the first sight of the prison yard. It was the morning of his death. He crouched on the floor with the empty brandy-flask in his hand trying to remember an Act of Contrition. 'O God, I am sorry and beg pardon for all my sins . . . crucified . . . worthy of thy dreadful punishments.' He was confused, his mind was on other things: it was not the good death for which one always prayed. He caught sight of his own shadow on the cell wall; it had a look of surprise and grotesque unimportance. What a fool he had been to think that he was strong enough to stay when others fled. What an impossible fellow I am, he thought, and how useless. I have done nothing for anybody. I might just as well have never lived. His parents were dead – soon he wouldn't even be a memory – perhaps after all he was not at the moment afraid of damnation – even the fear of pain was in the background. He felt only an immense disappointment because he had to go to God empty-handed, with nothing done at all. It seemed to him, at that moment, that it would have been quite easy to have been a saint. It would only have needed a little self-restraint and a little courage. He felt like someone who has missed happiness by seconds at an appointed place. He knew now that at the end there was only one thing that counted – to be a saint.

PART FOUR

MRS FELLOWS lay in bed in the hot hotel room, listening to the siren of a boat on the river. She could see nothing because she had a handkerchief soaked in eau-de-Cologne over her eyes and forehead. She called sharply out, 'My dear. My dear,' but nobody replied. She felt that she had been prematurely buried in this big brass family tomb, all alone on two pillows, under a canopy. 'Dear,' she said again sharply, and waited.

'Yes, Trixy?' It was Captain Fellows. He said, 'I was asleep, dreaming . . .'

'Put some more Cologne on this handkerchief, dear. My head's splitting.'

'Yes, Trixy.'

He took the handkerchief away; he looked old and tired and bored – a man without a hobby, walking over to the dressing-table.

'Not too much, dear. It will be days before we can get any more.'

He didn't answer, and she said sharply, 'You heard what I said, dear, didn't you?'

'Yes.'

'You are so silent these days. You don't realize what it is to be ill and alone.'

'Well,' Captain Fellows said, 'you know how it is.'

'But we agreed, dear, didn't we, that it was better just to say nothing at all, ever. We mustn't be morbid.'

'No.'

'We've got our own life to lead.'

'Yes.'

He came across to the bed and laid the handkerchief over his wife's eyes. Then sitting down on a chair, he slipped his hand under the net and felt for her hand. They gave an odd effect of being children, lost in a strange town, without adult care.

'Have you got the tickets?' she asked.

'Yes, dear.'

'I must get up later and pack, but my head hurts so. Did you tell them to collect the boxes?'

'I forgot.'

'You really must try to think of things,' she said weakly and sullenly, 'there's no one else,' and they both sat silent at a phrase they should have avoided. He said suddenly, 'There's a lot of excitement in town.'

'Not a revolution?'

'Oh no. They caught a priest and he's being shot this morning, poor devil. I can't help wondering whether it's the man Coral – I mean the man we sheltered.'

'It's not likely.'

'No.'

'There are so many priests.'

He let go of her hand and going to the window looked out. Boats on the river, a small stony public garden with a bust and vultures everywhere.

Mrs Fellows said, 'It will be good to be back home. I sometimes thought I should die in this place.'

'Of course not, dear.'

'Well, people do.'

'Yes, they do,' he said glumly.

'Now, dear,' Mrs Fellows said sharply, 'your promise.' She gave a long sigh, 'My poor head.'

'Would you like some aspirin?'

'I don't know where I've put it. Somehow nothing is ever in its place.'

'Shall I go out and get you some more?'

'No, dear, I can't bear to be left alone.' She went on with dramatic brightness, 'I expect I shall be all right when we get home. I'll have a proper doctor then. I sometimes think it's more than a headache. Did I tell you that I'd heard from Norah?'

'No.'

'Get me my glasses, dear, and I'll read you – what concerns us.'

'They're on your bed.'

'So they are.' One of the sailing-boats cast off and began to drift down the wide sluggish stream, going towards the sea. She read with satisfaction, 'Dear Trix: how you have suffered. That scoundrel . . .' She broke abruptly off. 'Oh yes, and then she goes on: "Of course, you and Charles must stay with us for a while until you have found somewhere to live. If you don't mind semi-detached . . ."'

Captain Fellows said suddenly and harshly, 'I'm not going back.'

'"The rent is only fifty-six pounds a year, exclusive, and there's a maid's bathroom."'

'I'm staying.'

'"A cookanheat." What on earth are you saying, dear?'

'I'm not going back.'

'We've been over that so often, dear. You know it would kill me to stay.'

'You needn't stay.'

'But I couldn't go alone,' Mrs Fellows said. 'What on earth would Norah think? Besides – oh, it's absurd.'

'A man here can do a job of work.'

'Picking bananas,' Mrs Fellows said. She gave a little cold laugh. 'And you weren't much good at that.'

He turned furiously towards the bed. 'You don't mind,' he said, 'do you – running away and leaving *her* . . .'

'It wasn't my fault. If you'd been at home . . .' She began to cry hunched up under the mosquito-net. She said, 'I'll never get home alive.'

He came wearily over to the bed and took her hand again. It was no good. They had both been deserted. They had to stick together. 'You won't leave me alone, will you, dear?' she asked. The room reeked of eau-de-Cologne.

'No, dear.'

'You do realize how absurd it is?'

'Yes.'

They sat in silence for a long while, as the morning sun climbed outside and the room got stiflingly hot. Mrs Fellows said at last, 'A penny, dear. '

'What?'

'For your thoughts.'

'I was just thinking of that priest. A queer fellow. He drank. I wonder if it's him.'

'If it is, I expect he deserves all he gets.'

'But the odd thing is – the way she went on afterwards – as if he'd told her things.'

'Darling,' Mrs Fellows repeated, with harsh weakness from the bed, 'your promise.'

'Yes, I'm sorry. I was trying, but it seems to come up all the time.'

'We've got each other, dear,' Mrs Fellows said, and the letter from Norah rustled as she turned her head, swathed in handkerchief, away from the hard outdoor light.

*

Mr Tench bent over the enamel basin washing his hands with pink soap. He said in his bad Spanish, 'You don't need to be afraid. You can tell me directly it hurts.'

The jefe's room had been fixed up as a kind of temporary dentistry – at considerable expense, for it had entailed transporting not only Mr Tench himself but Mr Tench's cabinet, chair, and all sorts of mysterious packing-cases which seemed to contain little but straw and which were unlikely to return empty.

'I've had it for months,' the jefe said. 'You can't imagine the pain . . .'

'It was foolish of you not to call me in sooner. Your mouth's in a very bad state. You are lucky to have escaped pyorrhoea.'

He finished washing and suddenly stood, towel in hand, thinking of something. 'What's the matter?' the jefe asked. Mr Tench woke with a jump, and coming forward to his cabinet, began to lay out the drill needles in a little metallic row of pain. The jefe watched with apprehension. He said, 'Your hand is very jumpy. Are you quite sure you are well enough this morning?'

'It's indigestion,' Mr Tench said. 'Sometimes I have so many spots in front of my eyes I might be wearing a veil.' He fitted a needle into the drill and bent the arm round. 'Now open your mouth very wide.' He began to stuff the jefe's mouth with plugs of cotton. He said, 'I've never seen a mouth as bad as yours – except once.'

The jefe struggled to speak. Only a dentist could have interpreted the muffled and uneasy question.

'He wasn't a patient. I expect someone cured him. You cure a lot of people in this country, don't you, with bullets?'

As he picked and picked at the tooth, he tried to keep up a running fire of conversation; that was how one did things at Southend. He said, 'An odd thing happened to me just before I came up the river. I got a letter from my wife. Hadn't so much as heard from her for – oh, twenty years. Then out of the blue she . . .' he leant closer and levered furiously with his pick: the jefe beat the air and grunted. 'Wash out your mouth,' Mr Tench said, and began grimly to fix his drill. He said, 'What was I talking about? Oh, the wife, wasn't it? Seems she had got religion of some kind. Some sort of a group – Oxford. What would she be doing in Oxford? Wrote to say that she had forgiven me and wanted to make things legal. Divorce, I mean. Forgiven *me*,' Mr Tench said, looking round the little hideous room, lost in thought, with his hand on the drill. He belched and put his other hand against his stomach, pressing, pressing, seeking an obscure pain which was nearly always there. The jefe leant back exhausted with his mouth wide open.

'It comes and goes,' Mr Tench said, losing the thread of his thought completely. 'Of course, it's nothing. Just indigestion. But it gets me locked.' He stared moodily into the mouth as though a crystal were concealed between the carious teeth. Then, as if he were exerting an awful effort of will, he leant forward, brought the arm of the drill round and began to pedal. Buzz and grate. Buzz and grate. The jefe stiffened all over and clutched the arms of the chair, and Mr Tench's foot went up and down, up and down. The jefe made odd sounds and waved his hands. 'Hold hard,' Mr Tench said, 'hold hard. There's just one tiny corner. Nearly finished. There she comes. There.' He stopped and said, 'Good God, what's that?'

He left the jefe altogether and went to the window. In the yard below a squad of police had just grounded their arms. With his hand on his stomach he protested, 'Not another revolution?'

The jefe levered himself upright and spat out a gag. 'Of course not,' he said. 'A man's being shot.'

'What for?'

'Treason.'

'I thought you generally did it,' Mr Tench said, 'up by the cemetery?' A horrid fascination kept him by the window: this was something he had never seen. He and the vultures looked down together on the little whitewashed courtyard.

'It was better not to this time. There might have been a demonstration. People are so ignorant.'

A small man came out of a side door: he was held up by two policemen, but you could tell that he was doing his best – it was only that his legs were not fully under his control. They paddled him across to the opposite wall; an officer tied a handkerchief round his eyes. Mr Tench thought: But I know him. Good God, one ought to do something. This was like seeing a neighbour shot.

The jefe said, 'What are you waiting for? The air gets into this tooth.'

Of course there was nothing to do. Everything went very quickly like a routine. The officer stepped aside, the rifles went up, and the little man suddenly made jerky movements with his arms. He was trying to say something: what was the phrase they were always supposed to use? That was routine too, but perhaps his mouth was too dry, because nothing came out except a word that sounded like 'Excuse'. The crash of the rifles shook Mr Tench: they seemed to vibrate inside his own guts: he felt sick and shut his eyes. Then there was a single shot, and opening them again he saw the officer stuffing his gun back into his holster, and the little man was a routine heap beside the wall –

something unimportant which had to be cleared away. Two knock-kneed men approached quickly. This was an arena, and the bull was dead, and there was nothing more to wait for any more.

'Oh,' the jefe moaned from the chair, 'the pain, the pain.' He implored Mr Tench, 'Hurry,' but Mr Tench was lost in thought beside the window, one hand automatically seeking in his stomach for the hidden uneasiness. He remembered the little man rising bitterly and hopelessly from his chair that blinding afternoon to follow the child out of town; he remembered a green watering-can, the photo of the children, that cast he was making out of sand for a split palate.

'The filling,' the jefe pleaded, and Mr Tench's eyes went to the gold on the glass dish. Currency – he would insist on foreign currency: this time he was going to clear out, clear out for good. In the yard everything had been tidied away; a man was throwing sand out of a spade, as if he were filling a grave. But there was no grave: there was nobody there: an appalling sense of loneliness came over Mr Tench, doubling him with indigestion. The little fellow had spoken English and knew about his children. He felt deserted.

'And now,' the woman's voice swelled triumphantly, and the two little girls with beady eyes held their breath, 'the great testing day had come.' Even the boy showed interest, standing by the window, looking out into the dark curfew-emptied street – this was the last chapter, and in the last chapter things always happened violently. Perhaps all life was like that – dull and then a heroic flurry at the end.

'When the Chief of Police came to Juan's cell he found him on his knees, praying. He had not slept at all, but had spent his last night preparing for martyrdom. He was quite calm and happy, and smiling at the Chief of Police, he asked him if he had come to lead him to the banquet. Even that evil man, who had persecuted so many innocent people, was visibly moved.'

If only it would get on towards the shooting, the boy thought: the shooting never failed to excite him, and he always waited anxiously for the *coup de grâce*.

'They led him out into the prison yard. No need to bind those hands now busy with his beads. In that short walk to the wall of execution, did young Juan look back on those few, those happy years he had so bravely spent? Did he remember days in the seminary, the kindly rebukes of his elders, the moulding discipline, days, too, of frivolity when he acted Nero before the old bishop? Nero was here beside him, and this the Roman amphitheatre.'

The mother's voice was getting a little hoarse: she fingered the remaining pages rapidly: it wasn't worth while stopping now, and she raced more and more rapidly on.

'Reaching the wall, Juan turned and began to pray – not for himself, but for his enemies, for the squad of poor innocent Indian soldiers who faced him and even for the Chief of Police himself. He raised the crucifix at the end of his beads and prayed that God would forgive them, would enlighten their ignorance, and bring them at last – as Saul the persecutor was brought – into his eternal kingdom.'

'Had they loaded?' the boy asked.

'What do you mean – "had they loaded"?'

'Why didn't they fire and stop him?'

'Because God decided otherwise.' She coughed and went on: 'The officer gave the command to present arms. In that moment a smile of complete adoration and happiness passed over Juan's face. It was as if he could see the arms of God open to receive him. He had always told his mother and sisters that he had a premonition that he would be in heaven before them. He would say with a whimsical smile to his mother, the good but over-careful housewife: "I will have tidied everything up for you." Now the moment had come, the officer gave the order to fire, and –' She had been reading too fast because it was past the little girls' bedtime and now she was thwarted by a fit of hiccups. 'Fire,' she repeated, 'and . . .'

The two little girls sat placidly side by side – they looked nearly asleep – this was the part of the book they never cared much about; they endured it for the sake of the amateur theatricals and the first communion, and of the sister who became a nun and paid a moving farewell to her family in the third chapter.

'Fire,' the mother tried again, 'and Juan, raising both arms above his head, called out in a strong brave voice to the soldiers and the levelled rifles, "Hail, Christ the King." Next moment he fell riddled with a dozen bullets and the officer, stooping over his body, put his revolver close to Juan's ear and pulled the trigger.'

A long sigh came from the window.

'No need to have fired another shot. The soul of the young hero had already left its earthly mansion, and the happy smile on the dead face told even those ignorant men where they would find Juan now. One of the men there that day was so moved by his bearing that he secretly soaked his handkerchief in the martyr's blood, and that handkerchief, cut into a hundred relics, found its way into many pious homes. And now,' the mother went rapidly on, clapping her hands, 'to bed.'

'And that one,' the boy said, 'they shot today. Was he a hero too?'

'Yes.'

'The one who stayed with us that time?'

'Yes. He was one of the martyrs of the Church.'

'He had a funny smell,' one of the little girls said.

'You must never say that again,' the mother said. 'He may be one of the saints.'

'Shall we pray to him then?'

The mother hesitated. 'It would do no harm. Of course, before we *know* he is a saint, there will have to be miracles . . .'

'Did he call "*Viva el Cristo Rey*"?' the boy asked.

'Yes. He was one of the heroes of the faith.'

'And a handkerchief soaked in blood?' the boy went on. 'Did anyone do that?'

The mother said ponderously, 'I have reason to believe . . . Señora Jiminez told me . . . I think if your father will give me a little money, I shall be able to get a relic.'

'Does it cost money?'

'How else could it be managed? Everybody can't have a piece.'

'No.'

He squatted beside the window, staring out, and behind his back came the muffled sound of small girls going to bed. It brought it home to one – to have had a hero in the house, though it had only been for twenty-four hours. And he was the last. There were no more priests and no more heroes. He listened resentfully to the sound of booted feet coming up the pavement. Ordinary life pressed round him. He got down from the window-seat and picked up his candle – Zapata, Villa, Madeor, and the rest, they were all dead, and it was people like the man out there who killed them. He felt deceived.

The lieutenant came along the pavement; there was something brisk and stubborn about his walk, as if he were saying at every step, 'I have done what I have done.' He looked in at the boy holding the candle with a look of indecisive recognition. He said to himself, 'I would do much more for him and them, more more; life is never going to be again for them what it was for me,' but the dynamic love which used to move his trigger-finger felt flat and dead. Of course, he told himself, it will come back. It was like love of a woman and went in cycles: he had satisfied himself that morning, that was all. This was satiety. He smiled painfully at the child through the window and said, '*Buenas noches*.' The boy was looking at his revolver-holster and he remembered an incident in the plaza when he had allowed a child to touch his gun

– perhaps this boy. He smiled again and touched it too – to show he remembered, and the boy crinkled up his face and spat through the window bars, accurately, so that a little blob of spittle lay on the revolver-butt.

The boy went across the patio to bed. He had a little dark room with an iron bedstead that he shared with his father. He lay next to the wall and his father would lie on the outside, so that he could come to bed without waking his son. He took off his shoes and undressed glumly by candlelight. He could hear the whispering of prayers in the other room; he felt cheated and disappointed because he had missed something. Lying on his back in the heat he stared up at the ceiling, and it seemed to him that there was nothing in the world but the store, his mother reading, and silly games in the plaza.

But very soon he went to sleep. He dreamed that the priest whom they had shot that morning was back in the house dressed in the clothes his father had lent him and laid out stiffly for burial. The boy sat beside the bed and his mother read out of a very long book all about how the priest had acted in front of the bishop the part of Julius Caesar: there was a fish basket at her feet, and the fish were bleeding, wrapped in her handkerchief. He was very bored and very tired and somebody was hammering nails into a coffin in the passage. Suddenly the dead priest winked at him – an unmistakable flicker of the eyelid, just like that.

He woke and there was the crack, crack on the knocker on the outer door. His father wasn't in bed and there was complete silence in the other room. Hours must have passed. He lay listening. He was frightened, but after a short interval the knocking began again, and nobody stirred anywhere in the house. Reluctantly, he put his feet on the ground – it might be only his father locked out; he lit the candle and wrapped a blanket round himself and stood listening again. His mother might hear it and go, but he knew very well that it was *his* duty. He was the only man in the house.

Slowly he made his way across the patio towards the outer door. Suppose it was the lieutenant come back to revenge himself for the spittle . . . He unlocked the heavy iron door and swung it open. A stranger stood in the street, a tall pale thin man with a rather sour mouth, who carried a small suitcase. He named the boy's mother and asked if this were the señora's house. Yes, the boy said, but she was asleep. He began to shut the door, but a pointed shoe got in the way.

The stranger said, 'I have only just landed. I came up the river tonight. I thought perhaps . . . I have an introduction for the señora from a great friend of hers.'

'She is asleep,' the boy repeated.

'If you would let me come in,' the man said with an odd frightened smile, and suddenly lowering his voice he said to the boy, 'I am a priest.'

'You?' the boy exclaimed.

'Yes,' he said gently. 'My name is Father –' But the boy had already swung the door open and put his lips to his hand before the other could give himself a name.

THE QUIET AMERICAN

'I do not like being moved: for the will is excited; and
  action
Is a most dangerous thing; I tremble for something
  factitious,
Some malpractice of heart and illegitimate process;
We're so prone to these things, with our terrible
  notions of duty.'

A. H. Clough

'This is the patent age of new inventions
  For killing bodies, and for saving souls,
All propagated with the best intentions.'

Byron

Dear Réné and Phuong,

I have asked permission to dedicate this book to you not only in memory of the happy evenings I have spent with you in Saigon over the last five years, but also because I have quite shamelessly borrowed the location of your flat to house one of my characters, and your name, Phuong, for the convenience of readers because it is simple, beautiful and easy to pronounce, which is not true of all your country-women's names. You will both realize I have borrowed little else, certainly not the characters of anyone in Viet Nam. Pyle, Granger, Fowler, Vigot, Joe – these have had no originals in the life of Saigon or Hanoi, and General Thé is dead: shot in the back, so they say. Even the historical events have been in at least one case rearranged. For example, the big bomb near the Continental preceded and did not follow the bicycle bombs. I have no scruples about such small changes. This is a story and not a piece of history, and I hope that as a story about a few imaginary characters it will pass for both of you one hot Saigon evening.

Yours affectionately,
Graham Greene

PART ONE

Chapter 1

AFTER dinner I sat and waited for Pyle in my room over the rue Catinat; he had said, 'I'll be with you at latest by ten,' and when midnight struck I couldn't stay quiet any longer and went down into the street. A lot of old women in black trousers squatted on the landing: it was February and I suppose too hot for them in bed. One trishaw driver pedalled slowly by towards the river-front and I could see lamps burning where they had disembarked the new American planes. There was no sign of Pyle anywhere in the long street.

Of course, I told myself, he might have been detained for some reason at the American Legation, but surely in that case he would have telephoned to the restaurant – he was very meticulous about small courtesies. I turned to go indoors when I saw a girl waiting in the next doorway. I couldn't see her face, only the white silk trousers and the long flowered robe, but I knew her for all that. She had so often waited for me to come home at just this place and hour.

'Phuong,' I said – which means Phoenix, but nothing nowadays is fabulous and nothing rises from its ashes. I knew before she had time to tell me that she was waiting for Pyle too. 'He isn't here.'

'*Je sais. Je t'ai vu seul à la fenêtre.*'

'You may as well wait upstairs,' I said. 'He will be coming soon.'

'I can wait here.'

'Better not. The police might pick you up.'

She followed me upstairs. I thought of several ironic and unpleasant jests I might make, but neither her English nor her French would have been good enough for her to understand the irony, and, strange to say, I had no desire to hurt her or even to hurt myself. When we reached the landing all the old women turned their heads, and as soon as we had passed their voices rose and fell as though they were singing together.

'What are they talking about?'

'They think I have come home.'

Inside my room the tree I had set up weeks ago for the Chinese New Year had shed most of its yellow blossoms. They had fallen between the keys of my typewriter. I picked them out. '*Tu es troublé*,' Phuong said.

'It's unlike him. He's such a punctual man.'

I took off my tie and my shoes and lay down on the bed. Phuong lit the gas stove and began to boil the water for tea. It might have been six months ago. 'He says you are going away soon now,' she said.

'Perhaps.'

'He is very fond of you.'

'Thank him for nothing,' I said.

I saw that she was doing her hair differently, allowing it to fall black and straight over her shoulders. I remembered that Pyle had once criticized the elaborate hairdressing which she thought became the daughter of a mandarin. I shut my eyes and she was again the same as she used to be: she was the hiss of steam, the clink of a cup, she was a certain hour of the night and the promise of rest.

'He will not be long,' she said as though I needed comfort for his absence.

I wondered what they talked about together. Pyle was very earnest and I had suffered from his lectures on the Far East, which he had known for as many months as I had years. Democracy was another subject of his – he had pronounced and aggravating views on what the United States was doing for the world. Phuong on the other hand was wonderfully ignorant; if Hitler had come into the conversation she would have interrupted to ask who he was. The explanation would be all the more difficult because she had never met a German or a Pole and had only the vaguest knowledge of European geography, though about Princess Margaret of course she knew more than I. I heard her put a tray down on the end of the bed.

'Is he still in love with you, Phuong?'

To take an Annamite to bed with you is like taking a bird: they twitter and sing on your pillow. There had been a time when I thought none of their voices sang like Phuong's. I put out my hand and touched her arm – their bones too were as fragile as a bird's.

'Is he, Phuong?'

She laughed and I heard her strike a match. 'In love?' – perhaps it was one of the phrases she didn't understand.

'May I make your pipe?' she asked.

When I opened my eyes she had lit the lamp and the tray was already prepared. The lamplight made her skin the colour of dark amber as she bent over the flame with a frown of concentration, heating the small paste of opium, twirling her needle.

'Does Pyle still not smoke?' I asked her.

'No.'

'You ought to make him or he won't come back.' It was a superstition among them that a lover who smoked would always return, even from France. A man's sexual capacity might be injured by smoking, but they would always prefer a faithful to a potent lover. Now she was kneading the little ball of hot paste on the convex margin of the bowl and I could smell the opium. There is no smell like it. Beside the bed my alarm-clock showed twelve-twenty, but already my tension was over. Pyle had diminished. The lamp lit her face as she tended the long pipe, bent over it with the serious attention she might have given to a child. I was fond of my pipe: more than two feet of straight bamboo, ivory at either end. Two-thirds of the way down was the bowl, like a convolvulus reversed, the convex margin polished and darkened by the frequent kneading of the opium. Now with a flick of the wrist she plunged the needle into the tiny cavity, released the opium and reversed the bowl over the flame, holding the pipe steady for me. The bead of opium bubbled gently and smoothly as I inhaled.

The practised inhaler can draw a whole pipe down in one breath, but I always had to take several pulls. Then I lay back, with my neck on the leather pillow, while she prepared the second pipe.

I said, 'You know, really, it's as clear as daylight. Pyle knows I smoke a few pipes before bed, and he doesn't want to disturb me. He'll be round in the morning.'

In went the needle and I took my second pipe. As I laid it down, I said, 'Nothing to worry about. Nothing to worry about at all.' I took a sip of tea and held my hand in the pit of her arm. 'When you left me,' I said, 'it was lucky I had this to fall back on. There's a good house in the rue d'Ormay. What a fuss we Europeans make about nothing. You shouldn't live with a man who doesn't smoke, Phuong.'

'But he's going to marry me,' she said. 'Soon now.'

'Of course, that's another matter.'

'Shall I make your pipe again?'

'Yes.'

I wondered whether she would consent to sleep with me that night if Pyle never came, but I knew that when I had smoked four pipes I would no longer want her. Of course it would be agreeable to feel her thigh beside me in the bed – she always slept on her back, and when I woke in the morning I could start the day with a pipe, instead of with my own company. 'Pyle won't come now,' I said. 'Stay here, Phuong.' She held the pipe out to me and shook her head. By the time I had drawn the opium in, her presence or absence mattered very little.

'Why is Pyle not here?' she asked.

'How do I know?' I said.

'Did he go to see General Thé?'

'I wouldn't know.'

'He told me if he could not have dinner with you, he wouldn't come here.'

'Don't worry. He'll come. Make me another pipe.' When she bent over the flame the poem of Baudelaire's came into my mind: '*Mon enfant, ma soeur* . . .' How did it go on?

> *Aimer à loisir,*
> *Aimer et mourir*
> *Au pays qui te ressemble.*

Out on the waterfront slept the ships, '*dont l'humeur est vagabonde*'. I thought that if I smelt her skin it would have the faintest fragrance of opium, and her colour was that of the small flame. I had seen the flowers on her dress beside the canals in the north, she was indigenous like a herb, and I never wanted to go home.

'I wish I were Pyle,' I said aloud, but the pain was limited and bearable – the opium saw to that. Somebody knocked on the door.

'Pyle,' she said.

'No. It's not his knock.'

Somebody knocked again impatiently. She got quickly up, shaking the yellow tree so that it showered its petals again over my typewriter. The door opened. 'Monsieur Fowlair,' a voice commanded.

'I'm Fowler,' I said. I was not going to get up for a policeman – I could see his khaki shorts without lifting my head.

He explained in almost unintelligible Vietnamese French that I was needed immediately – at once – rapidly – at the Sureté.

'At the French Sureté or the Vietnamese?'

'The French.' In his mouth the word sounded like '*Françung*'.

'What about?'

He didn't know: it was his orders to fetch me.

'*Toi aussi*,' he said to Phuong.

'Say *vous* when you speak to a lady,' I told him. 'How did you know she was here?'

He only repeated that they were his orders.

'I'll come in the morning.'

'*Sur le chung*.' he said, a little, neat, obstinate figure. There wasn't any point in arguing, so I got up and put on my tie and shoes. Here the police had the last word: they could withdraw my order of circulation: they could have me barred from Press Conferences: they could even, if they chose, refuse me an exit permit. These were the open legal methods, but legality was not essential in a country at war. I knew a man who had suddenly and inexplicably lost his cook – he had traced him to the Vietnamese Sureté, but the officers there assured him that he had been released after questioning. His family never saw him again. Perhaps he had joined the Communists; perhaps he had been enlisted in one of the private armies which flourished round Saigon – the Hoa-Haos or the Caodaists or General Thé. Perhaps he was in a French prison. Perhaps he was happily making money out of girls in Cholon, the Chinese suburb. Perhaps his heart had given way when they questioned him. I said, 'I'm not going to walk. You'll have to pay for a trishaw.' One had to keep one's dignity.

That was why I refused a cigarette from the French officer at the Sureté. After three pipes I felt my mind clear and alert: it could take such decisions easily without losing sight of the main question – what do they want from me? I had met Vigot before several times at parties – I had noticed him because he appeared incongruously in love with his wife, who ignored him, a flashy and false blonde. Now it was two in the morning and he sat tired and depressed in the cigarette smoke and the heavy heat, wearing a green eye-shade, and he had a volume of Pascal open on his desk to while away the time. When I refused to allow him to question Phuong without me he gave way at once, with a single sigh that might have represented his weariness with Saigon, with the heat, or with the whole human condition.

He said in English, 'I'm so sorry I had to ask you to come.'

'I wasn't asked. I was ordered.'

'Oh, these native police – they don't understand.' His eyes were on a page of *Les Pensées* as though he were still absorbed in those sad arguments. 'I wanted to ask you a few questions – about Pyle.'

'You had better ask him the questions.'

He turned to Phuong and interrogated her sharply in French. 'How long have you lived with Monsieur Pyle?'

'A month – I don't know,' she said.

'How much has he paid you?'

'You've no right to ask her that,' I said. 'She's not for sale.'

'She used to live with you, didn't she?' he asked abruptly. 'For two years.'

'I'm a correspondent who's supposed to report your war – when you let me. Don't ask me to contribute to your scandal sheet as well.'

'What do you know about Pyle? Please answer my questions, Monsieur Fowler. I don't want to ask them. But this is serious. Please believe me it is very serious.'

'I'm not an informer. You know all I can tell you about Pyle. Age thirty-two, employed in the Economic Aid Mission, nationality American.'

'You sound like a friend of his,' Vigot said, looking past me at Phuong. A native policeman came in with three cups of black coffee.

'Or would you rather have tea?' Vigot asked.

'I *am* a friend,' I said. 'Why not? I shall be going home one day, won't I? I can't take her with me. She'll be all right with him. It's a reasonable arrangement. And he's going to marry her, he says. He might, you know. He's a good chap in his way. Serious. Not one of those noisy bastards at the Continental. A quiet American,' I summed him precisely up as I might have said, 'a blue lizard', 'a white elephant'.

Vigot said, 'Yes.' He seemed to be looking for words on his desk with which to convey his meaning as precisely as I had done. 'A very quiet American.' He sat there in the little hot office waiting for one of us to speak. A mosquito droned to the attack and I watched Phuong. Opium makes you quick-witted – perhaps only because it calms the nerves and stills the emotions. Nothing, not even death, seems so important. Phuong, I thought, had not caught his tone, melancholy and final, and her English was very bad. While she sat there on the hard office-chair, she was still waiting patiently for Pyle. I had at that moment given up waiting, and I could see Vigot taking those two facts in.

'How did you meet him first?' Vigot asked me.

Why should I explain to him that it was Pyle who had met me? I had seen him last September coming across the square towards the bar of the Continental: an unmistakably young and unused face flung at us like a dart. With his gangly legs and his crew-cut and his wide campus gaze he seemed incapable of harm. The tables on the street were most of them full. 'Do you mind?' he had asked with serious courtesy. 'My name's Pyle. I'm new here,' and he had folded himself around a chair and ordered a beer. Then he looked quickly up into the hard noon glare.

'Was that a grenade?' he asked with excitement and hope.

'Most likely the exhaust of a car,' I said, and was suddenly sorry for his disappointment. One forgets so quickly one's own youth: once I was interested myself in what for want of a better term they call news. But grenades had staled on me; they were something listed on the back page of the local paper – so many last night in Saigon, so many in Cholon: they never made the European Press. Up the street came the lovely flat figures – the white silk trousers, the long tight jackets in pink and mauve patterns slit up the thigh. I watched them with the nostalgia I knew I would feel when I had left these regions for ever. 'They are lovely, aren't they?' I said over my beer, and Pyle cast them a cursory glance as they went up the rue Catinat.

'Oh, sure,' he said indifferently: he was a serious type. 'The Minister's very concerned about these grenades. It would be very awkward, he says, if there was an incident – with one of us, I mean.'

'With one of you? Yes, I suppose that would be serious. Congress wouldn't like it.' Why does one want to tease the innocent? Perhaps only ten days ago he had been walking back across the Common in Boston, his arms full of the books he had been reading in advance on the Far East and the problems of China. He didn't even hear what I said; he was absorbed already in the dilemmas of Democracy and the responsibilities of the West; he was determined – I learnt that very soon – to do good, not to any individual person but to a country, a continent, a world. Well, he was in his element now with the whole universe to improve.

'Is he in the mortuary?' I asked Vigot.

'How did you know he was dead?' It was a foolish policeman's question, unworthy of the man who read Pascal, unworthy also of the man who so strangely loved his wife. You cannot love without intuition.

'Not guilty,' I said. I told myself that it was true. Didn't Pyle always go his own way? I looked for any feeling in myself, even resentment at a policeman's suspicion, but I could find none. No one but Pyle was responsible. Aren't we all better dead? the opium reasoned within me. But I looked cautiously at Phuong, for it was hard on her. She must have loved him in her way: hadn't she been fond of me and hadn't she left me for Pyle? She had attached herself to youth and hope and seriousness and now they had failed her more than age and despair. She sat there looking at the two of us and I thought she had not yet understood. Perhaps it would be a good thing if I could get her away before the fact got home. I was ready to answer any questions if I could bring the interview quickly and ambiguously to an end, so that I might tell her later, in private, away from a policeman's eye and the hard office chairs and the bare globe where the moths circled.

I said to Vigot, 'What hours are you interested in?'

'Between six and ten.'

'I had a drink at the Continental at six. The waiters will remember. At six forty-five I walked down to the quay to watch the American planes unloaded. I saw Wilkins of the Associated News by the door of the Majestic. Then I went into the cinema next door. They'll probably remember – they had to get me change. From there I took a trishaw to the Vieux Moulin – I suppose I arrived about eight thirty – and had dinner by myself. Granger was there – you can ask him. Then I took a trishaw back about a quarter to ten. You could probably find the driver. I was expecting Pyle at ten, but he didn't turn up.'

'Why were you expecting him?'

'He telephoned me. He said he had to see me about something important.'

'Have you any idea what?'

'No. Everything was important to Pyle.'

'And this girl of his? – do you know where she was?'

'She was waiting for him outside at midnight. She was anxious. She knows nothing. Why, can't you see she's waiting for him still?'

'Yes,' he said.

'And you can't really believe I killed him for jealousy – or she for what? He was going to marry her.'

'Yes.'

'Where did you find him?'

'He was in the water under the bridge to Dakow.'

The Vieux Moulin stood beside the bridge. There were armed police on the bridge and the restaurant had an iron grille to keep out grenades. It wasn't safe to cross the bridge at night for all the far side of the river was in the hands of the Vietminh after dark. I must have dined within fifty yards of his body.

'The trouble was,' I said, 'he got mixed up.'

'To speak plainly,' Vigot said, 'I am not altogether sorry. He was doing a lot of harm.'

'God save us always,' I said, 'from the innocent and the good.'

'The good?'

'Yes, good. In his way. You're a Roman Catholic. You wouldn't recognize his way. And anyway, he was a damned Yankee.'

'Would you mind identifying him? I'm sorry. It's a routine, not a very nice routine.'

I didn't bother to ask him why he didn't wait for someone from the American Legation, for I knew the reason. French methods are a little old-fashioned by our cold standards: they believe in the conscience, the sense of guilt, a criminal should be confronted with his crime, for he may break down and betray himself. I told myself again I was innocent, while he went down the stone stairs to where the refrigerating plant hummed in the basement.

They pulled him out like a tray of ice-cubes, and I looked at him. The wounds were frozen into placidity. I said, 'You see, they don't re-open in my presence.'

'*Comment?*'

'Isn't that one of the objects? Ordeal by something or other? But you've frozen him stiff. They didn't have deep freezes in the Middle Ages.'

'You recognize him?'

'Oh yes.'

He looked more than ever out of place: he should have stayed at home. I saw him in a family snapshot album, riding on a dude ranch, bathing on Long Island, photographed with his colleagues in some apartment on the twenty-third floor. He belonged to the skyscraper and the express elevator, the ice-cream and the dry Martinis, milk at lunch, and chicken sandwiches on the Merchant Limited.

'He wasn't dead from this,' Vigot said, pointing at a wound in the chest. 'He was drowned in the mud. We found the mud in his lungs.'

'You work quickly.'

'One has to in this climate.'

They pushed the tray back and closed the door. The rubber padded.

'You can't help us at all?' Vigot asked.

'Not at all.'

I walked back with Phuong towards my flat. I was no longer on my dignity. Death takes away vanity – even the vanity of the cuckold who mustn't show his pain. She was still unaware of what it was about, and I had no technique for telling her slowly and gently. I was a correspondent: I thought in headlines. 'American official murdered in Saigon.' Working on a newspaper one does not learn the way to break bad news, and even now I had to think of my paper and to ask her, 'Do you mind stopping at the cable office?' I left her in the street and sent my wire and came back to her. It was only a gesture: I knew too well that the French correspondents would already be informed, or if Vigot had played fair (which was possible), then the censors would hold my telegram till the French had filed theirs. My paper would get the news first under a Paris date-line. Not that Pyle was very important. It wouldn't have done to cable the details of his true career, that before he died he had been responsible for at least fifty deaths, for it would have damaged Anglo-American relations, the Minister would have been upset. The Minister had a great respect for Pyle – Pyle had taken a good degree in – well, one of those subjects Americans can take degrees in: perhaps public relations or theatrecraft, perhaps even Far Eastern studies (he had read a lot of books).

'Where is Pyle?' Phuong asked. 'What did they want?'

'Come home,' I said.

'Will Pyle come?'

'He's as likely to come there as anywhere else.'

The old women were still gossiping on the landing, in the relative cool. When I opened my door I could tell my room had been searched: everything was tidier than I ever left it.

'Another pipe?' Phuong asked.

'Yes.'

I took off my tie and my shoes; the interlude was over; the night was nearly the same as it had been. Phuong crouched at the end of the bed and lit the lamp. *Mon enfant, ma soeur* – skin the colour of amber. *Sa douce langue natale.*

'Phuong,' I said. She was kneading the opium on the bowl. '*Il est mort*, Phuong.' She held the needle in her hand and looked up at me like a child trying to concentrate, frowning. '*Tu dis*?'

'Pyle *est mort. Assassiné*.'

She put the needle down and sat back on her heels, looking at me. There was no scene, no tears, just thought – the long private thought of somebody who has to alter a whole course of life.

'You had better stay here tonight,' I said.

She nodded and taking up the needle again began to heat the opium. That night I woke from one of those short deep opium sleeps, ten minutes long, that seem a whole night's rest, and found my hand where it had always lain at night, between her legs. She was asleep and I could hardly hear her breathing. Once again after so many months I was not alone, and yet I thought suddenly with anger, remembering Vigot and his eye-shade in the police station and the quiet corridors of the Legation with no one about and the soft hairless skin under my hand, 'Am I the only one who really cared for Pyle?'

Chapter 2

1

THE morning Pyle arrived in the square by the Continental I had seen enough of my American colleagues of the Press, big, noisy, boyish and middle-aged, full of sour cracks against the French, who were, when all was said, fighting this war. Periodically, after an engagement had been tidily finished and the casualties removed from the scene, they would be summoned to Hanoi, nearly four hours' flight away, addressed by the Commander-in-Chief, lodged for one night in a Press Camp where they boasted that the barman was the best in Indo-China, flown over the late battlefield at a height of 3,000 feet (the limit of a heavy machine-gun's range) and then delivered safely and noisily back, like a school-treat, to the Continental Hotel in Saigon.

Pyle was quiet, he seemed modest, sometimes that first day I had to lean forward to catch what he was saying. And he was very, very serious. Several times he seemed to shrink up within himself at the noise of the American Press on the terrace above – the terrace which was popularly believed to be safer from hand-grenades. But he criticized nobody.

'Have you read York Harding?' he asked.

'No. No, I don't think so. What did he write?'

He gazed at a milk-bar across the street and said drearily, 'That looks like a soda-fountain.' I wondered what depth of homesickness lay behind his odd choice of what to observe in a scene so unfamiliar. But hadn't I on my first walk up the rue Catinat noticed first the shop with the Guerlain perfume and comforted myself with the thought that, after all, Europe was only distant thirty hours? He looked reluctantly away from the milk-bar and said, 'York wrote a book called *The Advance of Red China*. It's a very profound book.'

'I haven't read it. Do you know him?'

He nodded solemnly and lapsed into silence. But he broke it again a moment later to modify the impression he had given. 'I don't know him well,' he said. 'I guess I only met him twice.' I liked him for that

– to consider it was boasting to claim acquaintance with – what was his name? – York Harding. I was to learn later that he had an enormous respect for what he called serious writers. That term excluded novelists, poets and dramatists unless they had what he called a contemporary theme, and even then it was better to read the straight stuff as you got it from York.

I said, 'You know, if you live in a place for long you cease to read about it.'

'Of course I always like to know what the man on the spot has to say,' he replied guardedly.

'And then check it with York?'

'Yes.' Perhaps he had noticed the irony, because he added with his habitual politeness, 'I'd take it as a very great privilege if you could find time to brief me on the main points. You see, York was here more than two years ago.'

I liked his loyalty to Harding – whoever Harding was. It was a change from the denigrations of the Pressmen and their immature cynicism. I said, 'Have another bottle of beer and I'll try to give you an idea of things.'

I began, while he watched me intently like a prize pupil, by explaining the situation in the north, in Tonkin, where the French in those days were hanging on to the delta of the Red River, which contained Hanoi and the only northern port, Haiphong. Here most of the rice was grown, and when the harvest was ready the annual battle for the rice always began.

'That's the north,' I said. 'The French may hold, poor devils, if the Chinese don't come to help the Vietminh. A war of jungle and mountain and marsh, paddy fields where you wade shoulder-high and the enemy simply disappear, bury their arms, put on peasant dress. But you can rot comfortably in the damp in Hanoi. They don't throw bombs there. God knows why. You could call it a regular war.'

'And here in the south?'

'The French control the main roads until seven in the evening: they control the watch towers after that, and the towns – part of them. That doesn't mean you are safe, or there wouldn't be iron grilles in front of the restaurants.'

How often I had explained all this before. I was a record always turned on for the benefit of newcomers – the visiting Member of Parliament, the new British Minister. Sometimes I would wake up in the night saying, 'Take the case of the Caodaists.' Or the Hoa-Haos or the Binh Xuyen, all the private armies who sold their services for money or revenge. Strangers found them picturesque, but there is nothing picturesque in treachery and distrust.

'And now,' I said, 'there's General Thé. He was Caodaist Chief of Staff, but he's taken to the hills to fight both sides, the French, the Communists . . .'

'York,' Pyle said, 'wrote that what the East needed was a Third Force.' Perhaps I should have seen that fanatic gleam, the quick response to a phrase, the magic sound of figures: Fifth Column, Third Force, Seventh Day. I might have saved all of us a lot of trouble, even Pyle, if I had realized the direction of that indefatigable young brain. But I left him with arid bones of background and took my daily walk up and down the rue Catinat. He would have to learn for himself the real background that held you as a smell does: the gold of the rice-fields under a flat late sun: the fishers' fragile cranes hovering over the fields like mosquitoes: the cups of tea on an old abbot's platform, with his bed and his commercial calendars, his buckets and broken cups and the junk of a life-time washed up around his chair: the mollusc hats of the girls repairing the road where a mine had burst: the gold and the young green and the bright dresses of the south, and in the north the deep browns and the black clothes and the circle of enemy mountains and the drone of planes. When I first came I counted the days of my assignment, like a schoolboy marking off the days of term; I thought I was tied to what was left of a Bloomsbury square and the 73 bus passing the portico of Euston and springtime in the local in Torrington Place. Now the bulbs would be out in the square garden, and I didn't care a damn. I wanted a day punctuated by those quick reports that might be car-exhausts or might be grenades, I wanted to keep the sight of those silk-trousered figures moving with grace through the humid noon, I wanted Phuong, and my home had shifted its ground eight thousand miles.

I turned at the High Commissioner's house, where the Foreign Legion stood on guard in their white képis and their scarlet epaulettes, crossed by the Cathedral and came back by the dreary wall of the Vietnamese Sureté that seemed to smell of urine and injustice. And yet that too was a part of home, like the dark passages on upper floors one avoided in childhood. The new dirty magazines were out on the bookstalls near the quay – *Tabu* and *Illusion*, and the sailors were drinking beer on the pavement, an easy mark for a home-made bomb. I thought of Phuong, who would be haggling over the price of fish in the third street down on the left before going for her elevenses to the milk-bar (I always knew where she was in those days), and Pyle ran easily and naturally out of my mind. I didn't even mention him to Phuong, when we sat down to lunch together in our room over the rue Catinat and she wore her best flowered silk robe because it was two years to a day since we had met in the Grand Monde in Cholon.

2

Neither of us mentioned him when we woke on the morning after his death. Phuong had risen before I was properly awake and had our tea ready. One is not jealous of the dead, and it seemed easy to me that morning to take up our old life together.

'Will you stay tonight?' I asked Phuong over the *croissants* as casually as I could.

'I will have to fetch my box.'

'The police may be there,' I said. 'I had better come with you.' It was the nearest we came that day to speaking of Pyle.

Pyle had a flat in a new villa near the rue Duranton, off one of those main streets which the French continually subdivided in honour of their generals – so that the rue de Gaulle became after the third intersection the rue Leclerc, and that again sooner or later would probably turn abruptly into the rue de Lattre. Somebody important must have been arriving from Europe by air, for there was a policeman facing the pavement every twenty yards along the route to the High Commissioner's Residence.

On the gravel drive to Pyle's apartment were several motorcycles and a Vietnamese policeman examined my press-card. He wouldn't allow Phuong into the house, so I went in search of a French officer. In Pyle's bathroom Vigot was washing his hands with Pyle's soap and drying them on Pyle's towel. His tropical suit had a stain of oil on the sleeve – Pyle's oil, I supposed.

'Any news?' I asked.

'We found his car in the garage. It's empty of petrol. He must have gone off last night in a trishaw – or in somebody else's car. Perhaps the petrol was drained away.'

'He might even have walked,' I said. 'You know what Americans are.'

'Your car was burnt, wasn't it?' he went thoughtfully on. 'You haven't a new one yet?'

'No.'

'It's not an important point.'

'No.'

'Have you any views?' he asked.

'Too many,' I said.

'Tell me.'

'Well, he might have been murdered by the Vietminh. They have murdered plenty of people in Saigon. His body was found in the river by the bridge to Dakow – Vietminh territory when your police withdraw at night. Or he might have been killed by the Vietnamese Sureté – it's been known. Perhaps they didn't like his friends. Perhaps he was killed by Caodaists because he knew General Thé.'

'Did he?'

'They say so. Perhaps he was killed by General Thé because he knew the Caodaists. Perhaps he was killed by the Hoa-Haos for making passes at the General's concubines. Perhaps he was just killed by someone who wanted his money.'

'Or a simple case of jealousy,' Vigot said.

'Or perhaps by the French Sureté,' I continued, 'because they didn't like his contacts. Are you really looking for the people who killed him?'

'No,' Vigot said. 'I'm just making a report, that's all. So long as it's an act of war – well, there are thousands killed every year.'

'You can rule me out,' I said. 'I'm not involved. Not involved,' I repeated. It had been an article of my creed. The human condition being what it was, let them fight, let them love, let them murder, I would not be involved. My fellow journalists called themselves correspondents; I preferred the title of reporter. I wrote what I saw. I took no action – even an opinion is a kind of action.

'What are you doing here?'

'I've come for Phuong's belongings. Your police wouldn't let her in.'

'Well, let us go and find them.'

'It's nice of you, Vigot.'

Pyle had two rooms, a kitchen and bathroom. We went to the bedroom. I knew where Phuong would keep her box – under the bed. We pulled it out together; it contained her picture books. I took her few spare clothes out of the wardrobe, her two good robes and her spare trousers. One had a sense that they had been hanging there for a few hours only and didn't belong, they were in passage like a butterfly in a room. In a drawer I found her small triangular *culottes* and her collection of scarves. There was really very little to put in the box, less than a week-end visitor's at home.

In the sitting-room there was a photograph of herself and Pyle. They had been photographed in the botanical gardens beside a large stone dragon. She held Pyle's dog on a leash – a black chow with a black tongue. A too black dog. I put the photograph in her box. 'What's happened to the dog?' I said.

'It isn't here. He may have taken it with him.'

'Perhaps it will return and you can analyse the earth on its paws.'

'I'm not Lecoq, or even Maigret, and there's a war on.'

I went across to the bookcase and examined the two rows of books – Pyle's library. *The Advance of Red China*, *The Challenge to Democracy*, *The Rôle of the West* – these, I suppose, were the complete works of York Harding. There were a lot of Congressional Reports, a Vietnamese phrase book, a history of the War in the Philippines, a Modern Library Shakespeare. On what did he relax? I found his light reading on another shelf: a portable Thomas Wolfe and a mysterious anthology called *The Triumph of Life* and a selection of American poetry. There was also a book of chess problems. It didn't seem much for the end of the working day, but, after all, he had had Phuong. Tucked away behind the anthology there was a paper-backed book called *The Physiology of Marriage*. Perhaps he was studying sex, as he had studied the East, on paper. And the keyword was marriage. Pyle believed in being involved.

His desk was quite bare. 'You've made a clean sweep,' I said.

'Oh,' Vigot said, 'I had to take charge of these on behalf of the American Legation. You know how quickly rumour spreads. There might have been looting. I had all his papers sealed up.' He said it seriously without even smiling.

'Anything damaging?'

'We can't afford to find anything damaging against an ally,' Vigot said.

'Would you mind if I took one of these books – as a keepsake?'

'I'll look the other way.'

I chose York Harding's *The Rôle of the West* and packed it in the box with Phuong's clothes.

'As a friend,' Vigot said, 'is there nothing you could tell me in confidence? My report's all tied up. He was murdered by the Communists. Perhaps the beginning of a campaign against American aid. But between you and me – listen, it's dry talking, what about a vermouth cassis round the corner?'

'Too early.'

'He didn't confide anything to you the last time he saw you?'

'No.'

'When was that?'

'Yesterday morning. After the big bang.'

He paused to let my reply sink in – to my mind, not to his: he interrogated fairly. 'You were out when he called on you last night?'

'Last night? I must have been. I didn't think . . .'

'You may be wanting an exit visa. You know we could delay it indefinitely.'

'Do you really believe,' I said, 'that I want to go home?'

Vigot looked through the window at the bright cloudless day. He said sadly, 'Most people do.'

'I like it here. At home there are – problems.'

'*Merde*,' Vigot said, 'here's the American Economic Attaché.' He repeated with sarcasm, 'Economic Attaché.'

'I'd better be off. He'll want to seal me up too.'

Vigot said wearily, 'I wish you luck. He'll have a terrible lot to say to me.'

The Economic Attaché was standing by his Packard when I came out, trying to explain something to his driver. He was a stout middle-aged man with an exaggerated bottom and a face that looked as if it never needed a razor. He called out, 'Fowler. Could you explain to this darned driver . . . ?'

I explained.

He said, 'But that's just what I told him, but he always pretends not to understand French.'

'It may be a matter of accent.'

'I was three years in Paris. My accent's good enough for one of these darned Vietnamese.'

'The voice of Democracy,' I said.

'What's that?'

'I expect it's a book by York Harding.'

'I don't get you.' He took a suspicious look at the box I carried. 'What've you got there?' he said.

'Two pairs of white silk trousers, two silk robes, some girl's underpants – three pairs, I think. All home products. No American aid.'

'Have you been up there?' he asked.

'Yes.'

'You heard the news?'

'Yes.'

'It's a terrible thing,' he said, 'terrible.'

'I expect the Minister's very disturbed.'

'I should say. He's with the High Commissioner now, and he's asked for an interview with the President.' He put his hand on my arm and walked me away from the cars. 'You knew young Pyle well, didn't you?

I can't get over a thing like that happening to him. I knew his father. Professor Harold C. Pyle – you'll have heard of him?'

'No.'

'He's the world authority on underwater erosion. Didn't you see his picture on the cover of *Time* the other month?'

'Oh, I think I remember. A crumbling cliff in the background and gold-rimmed glasses in the foreground.'

'That's him. I had to draft the cable home. It was terrible. I loved that boy like he was my son.'

'That makes you closely related to his father.'

He turned his wet brown eyes on me. He said, 'What's getting you? That's not the way to talk when a fine young fellow . . .'

'I'm sorry,' I said. 'Death takes people in different ways.' Perhaps he had really loved Pyle. 'What did you say in your cable?' I asked.

He replied seriously and literally, '"Grieved to report your son died a soldier's death in cause of Democracy." The Minister signed it.'

'A soldier's death,' I said. 'Mightn't that prove a bit confusing? I mean to the folks at home. The Economic Aid Mission doesn't sound like the Army. Do you get Purple Hearts?'

He said in a low voice, tense with ambiguity, 'He had special duties.'

'Oh yes, we all guessed that.'

'He didn't talk, did he?'

'Oh no,' I said, and Vigot's phrase came back to me, 'He was a very quiet American.'

'Have you any hunch,' he asked, 'why they killed him? and who?'

Suddenly I was angry; I was tired of the whole pack of them with their private stores of Coca-Cola and their portable hospitals and their too wide cars and their not quite latest guns. I said, 'Yes. They killed him because he was too innocent to live. He was young and ignorant and silly and he got involved. He had no more of a notion than any of you what the whole affair's about, and you gave him money and York Harding's books on the East and said, "Go ahead. Win the East for Democracy." He never saw anything he hadn't heard in a lecture-hall, and his writers and his lecturers made a fool of him. When he saw a dead body he couldn't even see the wounds. A Red menace, a soldier of democracy.'

'I thought you were his friend,' he said in a tone of reproach.

'I *was* his friend. I'd have liked to see him reading the Sunday supplements at home and following the baseball. I'd have liked to see him safe with a standardized American girl who subscribed to the Book Club.'

He cleared his throat with embarrassment. 'Of course,' he said, 'I'd forgotten that unfortunate business. I was quite on your side, Fowler. He behaved very badly. I don't mind telling you I had a long talk with him about the girl. You see, I had the advantage of knowing Professor and Mrs Pyle.'

I said, 'Vigot's waiting,' and walked away. For the first time he spotted Phuong and when I looked back at him he was watching me with pained perplexity: an eternal brother who didn't understand.

Chapter 3

1

THE first time Pyle met Phuong was again at the Continental, perhaps two months after his arrival. It was the early evening, in the momentary cool which came when the sun had just gone down, and the candles were lit on the stalls in the side streets. The dice rattled on the tables where the French were playing *Quatre Cent Vingt-et-un* and the girls in the white silk trousers bicycled home down the rue Catinat. Phuong was drinking a glass of orange juice and I was having a beer and we sat in silence, content to be together. Then Pyle came tentatively across, and I introduced them. He had a way of staring hard at a girl as though he hadn't seen one before and then blushing. 'I was wondering whether you and your lady,' Pyle said, 'would step across and join my table. One of our attachés . . .'

It was the Economic Attaché. He beamed down at us from the terrace above, a great warm welcoming smile, full of confidence, like the man who keeps his friends because he uses the right deodorants. I had heard him called Joe a number of times, but I had never learnt his surname. He made a noisy show of pulling out chairs and calling for the waiter, though all that activity could possibly produce at the Continental was a choice of beer, brandy-and-soda or vermouth cassis. 'Didn't expect to see you here, Fowler,' he said. 'We are waiting for the boys back from Hanoi. There seems to have been quite a battle. Weren't you with them?'

'I'm tired of flying four hours for a Press Conference,' I said.

He looked at me with disapproval. He said, 'These guys are real keen. Why, I expect they could earn twice as much in business or on the radio without any risk.'

'They might have to work,' I said.

'They seem to sniff the battle like war-horses,' he went on exultantly, paying no attention to words he didn't like. 'Bill Granger – you can't keep him out of a scrap.'

'I expect you're right. I saw him in one the other evening at the bar of the Sporting.'

'You know very well I didn't mean that.'

Two trishaw drivers came pedalling furiously down the rue Catinat and drew up in a photo-finish outside the Continental. In the first was Granger. The other contained a small, grey, silent heap which Granger now began to pull out on to the pavement. 'Oh, come on, Mick,' he said, 'come on.' Then he began to argue with his driver about the fare. 'Here,' he said, 'take it or leave it,' and flung five times the correct amount into the street for the man to stoop for.

The Economic Attaché said nervously, 'I guess these boys deserve a little relaxation.'

Granger flung his burden on to a chair. Then he noticed Phuong. 'Why,' he said, 'you old so-and-so, Joe. Where did you find her? Didn't know you had a whistle in you. Sorry, got to find the can. Look after Mick.'

'Rough soldierly manners,' I said.

Pyle said earnestly, blushing again, 'I wouldn't have invited you two over if I'd thought . . .'

The grey heap stirred in the chair and the head fell on the table as though it wasn't attached. It sighed, a long whistling sigh of infinite tedium, and lay still.

'Do you know him?' I asked Pyle.

'No. Isn't he one of the Press?'

'I heard Bill call him Mick,' the Economic Attaché said.

'Isn't there a new UP correspondent?'

'It's not him. I know him. What about your Economic Mission? You can't know all your people – there are hundreds of them.'

'I don't think he belongs,' the Economic Attaché said. 'I can't recollect him.'

'We might find his identity card,' Pyle suggested.

'For God's sake don't wake him. One drunk's enough. Anyway Granger will know.'

But he didn't. He came gloomily back from the lavatory. 'Who's the dame?' he asked morosely.

'Miss Phuong is a friend of Fowler's,' Pyle said stiffly. 'We want to know who . . .'

'Where'd he find her? You got to be careful in this town.' He added gloomily, 'Thank God for penicillin.'

'Bill,' the Economic Attaché said, 'we want to know who Mick is.'

'Search me.'

'But you brought him here.'

'The Frogs can't take Scotch. He passed out.'

'Is he French? I thought you called him Mick.'

'Had to call him something,' Granger said. He leant over to Phuong and said, 'Here. You. Have another glass of orange? Got a date tonight?'

I said, 'She's got a date every night.'

The Economic Attaché said hurriedly, 'How's the war, Bill?'

'Great victory north-west of Hanoi. French recaptured two villages they never told us they'd lost. Heavy Vietminh casualties. Haven't been able to count their own yet but will let us know in a week or two.'

The Economic Attaché said, 'There's a rumour that the Vietminh have broken into Phat Diem, burned the Cathedral, chased out the Bishop.'

'They wouldn't tell us about that in Hanoi. That's not a victory.'

'One of our medical teams couldn't get beyond Nam Dinh,' Pyle said.

'You didn't get down as far as that, Bill?' the Economiic Attaché asked.

'Who do you think I am? I'm a correspondent with an *Ordre de Circulation* which shows when I'm out of bounds. I fly to Hanoi airport. They give us a car to the Press Camp. They lay on a flight over the two towns they've recaptured and show us the tricolour flying. It might be any darned flag at that height. Then we have a Press Conference and a colonel explains to us what we've been looking at. Then we file our cables with the censor. Then we have drinks. Best barman in Indo-China. Then we catch the plane back.'

Pyle frowned at his beer.

'You underrate yourself, Bill,' the Economic Attaché said. 'Why, that account of Road 66 – what did you call it? Highway to Hell – that was worthy of the Pulitzer. You know the story I mean – the man with his head blown off kneeling in the ditch, and that other you saw walking in a dream . . .'

'Do you think I'd really go near their stinking highway? Stephen

Crane could describe a war without seeing one. Why shouldn't I? It's only a damned colonial war anyway. Get me another drink. And then let's go and find a girl. You've got a piece of tail. I want a piece of tail too.'

I said to Pyle, 'Do you think there's anything in the rumour about Phat Diem?'

'I don't know. Is it important? I'd like to go and have a look,' he said, 'if it's important.'

'Important to the Economic Mission?'

'Oh, well,' he said, 'you can't draw hard lines. Medicine's a kind of weapon, isn't it? These Catholics, they'd be pretty strong against the Communists, wouldn't they?'

'They trade with the Communists. The Bishop gets his cows and the bamboo for his building from the Communists. I wouldn't say they were exactly York Harding's Third Force,' I teased him.

'Break it up,' Granger was shouting. 'Can't waste the whole night here. I'm off to the House of Five Hundred Girls.'

'If you and Miss Phuong would have dinner with me . . .' Pyle said.

'You can eat at the Chalet,' Granger interrupted him, 'while I'm knocking the girls next door. Come on, Joe. Anyway you're a man.'

I think it was then, wondering what a man is, that I felt my first affection for Pyle. He sat a little turned away from Granger, twisting his beer mug, with an expression of determined remoteness. He said to Phuong, 'I guess you get tired of all this shop – about your country, I mean?'

'*Comment*?'

'What are you going to do with Mick?' the Economic Attaché asked.

'Leave him here,' Granger said.

'You can't do that. You don't even know his name.'

'We could bring him along and let the girls look after him.'

The Economic Attaché gave a loud communal laugh. He looked like a face on television. He said, 'You young people can do what you want, but I'm too old for games. I'll take him home with me. Did you say he was French?'

'He spoke French.'

'If you can get him into my car . . .'

After he had driven away, Pyle took a trishaw with Granger, and Phuong and I followed along the road to Cholon. Granger had made an attempt to get into the trishaw with Phuong, but Pyle diverted him. As they pedalled us down the long suburban road to the Chinese town a line of French armoured cars went by, each with its jutting gun and silent officer motionless like a figurehead under the stars and the black, smooth, concave sky – trouble again probably with a private army, the Binh Xuyen, who ran the Grand Monde and the gambling halls of Cholon. This was a land of rebellious barons. It was like Europe in the Middle Ages. But what were the Americans doing here? Columbus had not yet discovered their country. I said to Phuong, 'I like that fellow, Pyle.'

'He's quiet,' she said, and the adjective which she was the first to use stuck like a schoolboy name, till I heard even Vigot use it, sitting there with his green eye-shade, telling me of Pyle's death.

I stopped our trishaw outside the Chalet and said to Phuong, 'Go in and find a table. I had better look after Pyle.' That was my first instinct – to protect him. It never occurred to me that there was greater need to protect myself. Innocence always calls mutely for protection when we would be so much wiser to guard ourselves against it: innocence is like a dumb leper who has lost his bell, wandering the world, meaning no harm.

When I reached the House of the Five Hundred Girls, Pyle and Granger had gone inside. I asked at the military police post just inside the doorway, '*Deux Américains*?'

He was a young Foreign Legion corporal. He stopped cleaning his revolver and jutted his thumb towards the doorway beyond, making a joke in German. I couldn't understand it.

It was the hour of rest in the immense courtyard which lay open to the sky. Hundreds of girls lay on the grass or sat on their heels talking to their companions. The curtains were undrawn in the little cubicles around the square – one tired girl lay alone on a bed with her ankles crossed. There was trouble in Cholon and the troops were confined to quarters and there was no work to be done: the Sunday of the body. Only a knot of fighting, scrabbling, shouting girls showed me where custom was still alive. I remembered the old Saigon story of the distinguished visitor who had lost his trousers fighting his way back to the safety of the police post. There was no protection here for the civilian. If he chose to poach on military territory, he must look after himself and find his own way out.

I had learnt a technique – to divide and conquer. I chose one in the crowd that gathered round me and edged her slowly towards the spot where Pyle and Granger struggled.

'*Je suis un vieux*,' I said. '*Trop fatigué*.' She giggled and pressed. '*Mon ami*,' I said, '*il est très riche, très vigoureux*.'

'*Tu es sale*,' she said.

I caught sight of Granger flushed and triumphant; it was as though he took this demonstration as a tribute to his manhood. One girl had her arm through Pyle's and was trying to tug him gently out of the ring. I pushed my girl in among them and called to him, 'Pyle, over here.'

He looked at me over their heads and said, 'It's terrible. Terrible.' It may have been a trick of the lamplight, but his face looked haggard. It occurred to me that he was quite possibly a virgin.

'Come along, Pyle,' I said. 'Leave them to Granger.' I saw his hand move towards his hip pocket. I really believe he intended to empty his pockets of piastres and greenbacks. 'Don't be a fool, Pyle,' I called sharply. 'You'll have them fighting.' My girl was turning back to me and I gave her another push into the inner ring round Granger. '*Non, non*,' I said, '*je suis un Anglais, pauvre, très pauvre*.' Then I got hold of Pyle's sleeve and dragged him out, with the girl hanging on to his other arm like a hooked fish. Two or three girls tried to intercept us before we got to the gateway where the corporal stood watching, but they were half-hearted.

'What'll I do with this one?' Pyle said.

'She won't be any trouble,' and at that moment she let go his arm and dived back into the scrimmage round Granger.

'Will he be all right?' Pyle asked anxiously.

'He's got what he wanted – a bit of tail.'

The night outside seemed very quiet with only another squadron of armoured cars driving by like people with a purpose. He said, 'It's terrible. I wouldn't have believed . . .' He said with sad awe, 'They were so pretty.' He was not envying Granger, he was complaining that anything good – and prettiness and grace are surely forms of goodness – should be marred or ill-treated. Pyle could see pain when it was in front of his eyes. (I don't write that as a sneer; after all there are many of us who can't.)

I said, 'Come back to the Chalet. Phuong's waiting.'

'I'm sorry,' he said. 'I quite forgot. You shouldn't have left her.'

'*She* wasn't in danger.'

'I just thought I'd see Granger safely . . .' He dropped again into his thoughts, but as we entered the Chalet he said with obscure distress, 'I'd forgotten how many men there are . . .'

2

Phuong had kept us a table at the edge of the dance-floor and the orchestra was playing some tune which had been popular in Paris five years ago. Two Vietnamese couples were dancing, small, neat, aloof, with an air of civilization we couldn't match. (I recognized one, an accountant from the Banque de l'Indo-Chine and his wife.) They never, one felt, dressed carelessly, said the wrong word, were a prey to untidy passion. If the war seemed medieval, they were like the eighteenth-century future. One would have expected Mr Pham-Van-Tu to write Augustans in his spare time, but I happened to know he was a student of Wordsworth and wrote nature poems. His holidays he spent at Dalat, the nearest he could get to the atmosphere of the English lakes. He bowed slightly as he came round. I wondered how Granger had fared fifty yards up the road.

Pyle was apologizing to Phuong in bad French for having kept her waiting. '*C'est impardonable*,' he said.

'Where have you been?' she asked him.

He said, 'I was seeing Granger home.'

'Home?' I said and laughed, and Pyle looked at me as though I were another Granger. Suddenly I saw myself as he saw me, a man of middle age, with eyes a little bloodshot, beginning to put on weight, ungraceful in love, less noisy than Granger perhaps but more cynical, less innocent, and I saw Phuong for a moment as I had seen her first, dancing past my table at the Grand Monde in a white ball-dress, eighteen years old, watched by an elder sister who had been determined on a good European marriage. An American had bought a ticket and asked her for a dance: he was a little drunk – not harmfully, and I suppose he was new to the country and thought the hostesses of the Grand Monde were whores. He held her much too close as they went round the floor the first time, and then suddenly there she was, going back to sit with her sister, and he was left, stranded and lost among the dancers, not knowing what had happened or why. And the girl whose name I didn't know sat quietly there, occasionally sipping her orange juice, owning herself completely.

'*Peut-on avoir l'honneur?*' Pyle was saying in his terrible accent, and a moment later I saw them dancing in silence at the other end of the room, Pyle holding her so far away from him that you expected him at any moment to sever contact. He was a very bad dancer, and she had been the best dancer I had ever known in her days at the Grand Monde.

It had been a long and frustrating courtship. If I could have offered marriage and a settlement everything would have been easy, and the elder sister would have slipped quietly and tactfully away whenever we were together. But three months passed before I saw her so much as momentarily alone, on a balcony at the Majestic, while her sister in the next room kept on asking when we proposed to come in. A cargo boat from France was being unloaded in Saigon River by the light of flares, the trishaw bells rang like telephones, and I might have been a young and inexperienced fool for all I found to say. I went back hopelessly to my bed in the rue Catinat and never dreamed that four months later she would be lying beside me, a little out of breath, laughing as though with surprise because nothing had been quite what she expected.

'Monsieur Fowlair.' I had been watching them dance and hadn't seen her sister signalling to me from another table. Now she came over and I reluctantly asked her to sit down. We had never been friends since the night she was taken ill in the Grand Monde and I had seen Phuong home.

'I haven't seen you for a whole year,' she said.

'I am away so often at Hanoi.'

'Who is your friend?' she asked.

'A man called Pyle.'

'What does he do?'

'He belongs to the American Economic Mission. You know the kind of thing – electrical sewing machines for starving seamstresses.'

'Are there any?'

'I don't know.'

'But they don't use sewing machines. There wouldn't be any electricity where they live.' She was a very literal woman.

'You'll have to ask Pyle,' I said.

'Is he married?'

I looked at the dance floor. 'I should say that's as near as he ever got to a woman.'

'He dances very badly,' she said.

'Yes.'

'But he looks a nice reliable man.'

'Yes.'

'Can I sit with you for a little? My friends are very dull.'

The music stopped and Pyle bowed stiffly to Phuong, then led her back and drew out her chair. I could tell that his formality pleased her. I thought how much she missed in her relation to me.

'This is Phuong's sister,' I said to Pyle. 'Miss Hei.'

'I'm very glad to meet you,' he said and blushed.

'You come from New York?' she asked.

'No. From Boston.'

'That is in the United States too?'

'Oh yes. Yes.'

'Is your father a business man?'

'Not really. He's a professor.'

'A teacher?' she asked with a faint note of disappointment.

'Well, he's a kind of authority, you know. People consult him.'

'About health? Is he a doctor?'

'Not that sort of doctor. He's a doctor of engineering though. He understands all about underwater erosion. You know what that is?'

'No.'

Pyle said with a dim attempt at humour, 'Well, I'll leave it to Dad to tell you about that.'

'He is here?'

'Oh no.'

'But he is coming?'

'No. That was just a joke,' Pyle said apologetically.

'Have you got another sister?' I asked Miss Hei.

'No. Why?'

'It sounds as though you were examining Mr Pyle's marriageability.'

'I have only one sister,' Miss Hei said, and she clamped her hand heavily down on Phuong's knee, like a chairman with his gavel marking a point of order.

'She's a very pretty sister,' Pyle said.

'She is the most beautiful girl in Saigon,' Miss Hei said, as though she were correcting him.

'I can believe it.'

I said, 'It's time we ordered dinner. Even the most beautiful girl in Saigon must eat.'

'I am not hungry,' Phuong said.

'She is delicate,' Miss Hei went firmly on. There was a note of menace in her voice. 'She needs care. She deserves care. She is very, very loyal.'

'My friend is a lucky man,' Pyle said gravely.

'She loves children,' Miss Hei said.

I laughed and then caught Pyle's eye; he was looking at me with shocked surprise, and suddenly it occurred to me that he was genuinely interested in what Miss Hei had to say. While I was ordering dinner (though Phuong had told me she was not hungry, I knew she could manage a good steak tartare with two raw eggs and etceteras), I listened to him seriously discussing the question of children. 'I've always thought I'd like a lot of children,' he said. 'A big family's a wonderful interest. It makes for the stability of marriage. And it's good for the children too. I was an only child. It's a great disadvantage being an only child.' I had never heard him talk so much before.

'How old is your father?' Miss Hei asked with gluttony.

'Sixty-nine.'

'Old people love grandchildren. It is very sad that my sister has no parents to rejoice in her children. When the day comes,' she added with a baleful look at me.

'Nor you either,' Pyle said, rather unnecessarily I thought.

'Our father was of a very good family. He was a mandarin in Hué.'

I said, 'I've ordered dinner for all of you.'

'Not for me,' Miss Hei said. 'I must be going to my friends. I would like to meet Mr Pyle again. Perhaps you could manage that.'

'When I get back from the north,' I said.

'Are you going to the north?'

'I think it's time I had a look at the war.'

'But the Press are all back,' Pyle said.

'That's the best time for me. I don't have to meet Granger.'

'Then you must come and have dinner with me and my sister when Monsieur Fowlair is gone.' She added with morose courtesy, 'To cheer her up.'

After she had gone Pyle said, 'What a very nice cultivated woman. And she spoke English so well.'

'Tell him my sister was in business once in Singapore,' Phuong said proudly.

'Really? What kind of business?'

I translated for her. 'Import, export. She can do shorthand.'

'I wish we had more like her in the Economic Mission.'

'I will speak to her,' Phuong said. 'She would like to work for the Americans.'

After dinner they danced again. I am a bad dancer too and I hadn't the unselfconsciousness of Pyle – or had I possessed it, I wondered, in the days when I was first in love with Phuong? There must have been many occasions at the Grand Monde before the memorable night of Miss Hei's illness when I had danced with Phuong just for an opportunity to speak to her. Pyle was taking no such opportunity as they came round the floor again; he had relaxed a little, that was all, and was holding her less at arm's length, but they were both silent. Suddenly watching her feet, so light and precise and mistress of his shuffle, I was in love again. I could hardly believe that in an hour, two hours, she would be coming back to me to that dingy room with the communal closet and the old women squatting on the landing.

I wished I had never heard the rumour about Phat Diem, or that the rumour had dealt with any other town than the one place in the north where my friendship with a French naval officer would allow me to slip in, uncensored, uncontrolled. A newspaper scoop? Not in those days when all the world wanted to read about was Korea. A chance of death? Why should I want to die when Phuong slept beside me every night? But I knew the answer to that question. From childhood I had never believed in permanence, and yet I had longed for it. Always I was afraid of losing happiness. This month, next year, Phuong would leave me. If not next year, in three years. Death was the only absolute value in my world. Lose life and one would lose nothing again for ever. I envied those who could believe in a God and I distrusted them. I felt they were keeping their courage up with a fable of the changeless and the permanent. Death was far more certain than God, and with death there would be no longer the daily possibility of love dying. The nightmare of a future of boredom and indifference would lift. I could never have been a pacifist. To kill a man was surely to grant him an immeasurable benefit. Oh yes, people always, everywhere, loved their enemies. It was their friends they preserved for pain and vacuity.

'Forgive me for taking Miss Phuong from you,' Pyle's voice said.

'Oh, I'm no dancer, but I like watching her dance.' One always spoke of her like that in the third person as though she were not there. Sometimes she seemed invisible like peace.

The first cabaret of the evening began: a singer, a juggler, a comedian – he was very obscene, but when I looked at Pyle he obviously couldn't follow the argot. He smiled when Phuong smiled and laughed uneasily when I laughed. 'I wonder where Granger is now,' I said, and Pyle looked at me reproachfully.

Then came the turn of the evening: a troupe of female impersonators. I had seen many of them during the day in the rue Catinat walking up and down, in old slacks and sweaters, a bit blue about the chin, swaying their hips. Now in low-cut evening dresses, with false jewellery and false breasts and husky voices, they appeared at least as desirable as most of the European women in Saigon. A group of young Air Force officers whistled to them and they smiled glamorously back. I was astonished by the sudden violence of Pyle's protest. 'Fowler,' he said, 'let's go. We've had enough, haven't we? This isn't a bit suitable for *her*.'

Chapter 4

1

FROM the bell tower of the Cathedral the battle was only picturesque, fixed like a panorama of the Boer War in an old *Illustrated London News*. An aeroplane was parachuting supplies to an isolated post in the *calcaire*, those strange weather-eroded mountains on the Annam border that look like piles of pumice, and because it always returned to the same place for its glide, it might never have moved, and the parachute was always there in the same spot, half-way to earth. From the plain the mortar-bursts rose unchangingly, the smoke as solid as stone, and in the market the flames burnt palely in the sunlight. The tiny figures of the parachutists moved in single file along the canals, but at this height they appeared stationary. Even the priest who sat in a corner of the tower never changed his position as he read in his breviary. The war was very tidy and clean at that distance.

I had come in before dawn in a landing-craft from Nam Dinh. We couldn't land at the naval station because it was cut off by the enemy who completely surrounded the town at a range of six hundred yards, so the boat ran in beside the flaming market. We were an easy target in the light of the flames, but for some reason no one fired. Everything was quiet, except for the flop and crackle of the burning stalls. I could hear a Senegalese sentry on the river's edge shift his stance.

I had known Phat Diem well in the days before the attack – the one long narrow street of wooden stalls, cut up every hundred yards by a canal, a church and a bridge. At night it had been lit only by candles or small oil lamps (there was no electricity in Phat Diem except in the French officers' quarters), and day or night the street was packed and noisy. In its strange medieval way, under the shadow and protection of the Prince Bishop, it had been the most living town in all the country, and now when I landed and walked up to the officers' quarters it was the most dead. Rubble and broken glass and the smell of burnt paint and plaster, the long street empty as far as the sight could reach, it reminded me of a London thoroughfare in the early morning after an all-clear: one expected to see a placard, 'Unexploded Bomb'.

The front wall of the officers' house had been blown out, and the houses across the street were in ruins. Coming down the river from Nam Dinh I had learnt from Lieutenant Peraud what had happened. He was a serious young man, a Freemason, and to him it was like a judgement on the superstitions of his fellows. The Bishop of Phat Diem had once visited Europe and acquired there a devotion to Our Lady of Fatima – that vision of the Virgin which appeared, so Roman Catholics believe, to a group of children in Portugal. When he came home, he built a grotto in her honour in the Cathedral precincts, and he celebrated her feast-day every year with a procession. Relations with the colonel in charge of the French and Vietnamese troops had always been strained since the day when the authorities had disbanded the Bishop's private army. This year the colonel – who had some sympathy with the Bishop, for to each of them his country was more important than Catholicism – made a gesture of amity and walked with his senior officers in the front of the procession. Never had a greater crowd gathered in Phat Diem to do honour to Our Lady of Fatima. Even many of the Buddhists – who formed about half the population – could not bear to miss the fun, and those who had belief in neither God nor Buddha believed that somehow all these banners and incense-burners and the golden monstrance would keep war from their homes. All that was left of the Bishop's army – his brass band – led the procession, and the French officers, pious by order of the colonel, followed like choirboys through the gateway into the Cathedral precincts, past the white statue of the Sacred Heart that stood on an island in the little lake before the Cathedral, under the bell tower with spreading oriental wings and into the carved wooden Cathedral with its gigantic pillars formed out of single trees and the scarlet lacquer work of the altar, more Buddhist than Christian. From all the villages between the canals, from that Low Country landscape where young green rice-shoots and golden harvests take the place of tulips and churches of windmills, the people poured in.

Nobody noticed the Vietminh agents who had joined the procession too, and that night as the main Communist battalion moved through the passes in the *calcaire*, into the Tonkin plain, watched helplessly by the French outpost in the mountains above, the advance agents struck in Phat Diem.

Now after four days, with the help of parachutists, the enemy had been pushed back half a mile around the town. This was a defeat: no journalists were allowed, no cables could be sent, for the papers must carry only victories. The authorities would have stopped me in Hanoi if they had known of my purpose, but the further you get from headquarters, the looser becomes the control until, when you come within range of the enemy's fire, you are a welcome guest – what has been a menace for the *Etat Major* in Hanoi, a worry for the full colonel in Nam Dinh, to the lieutenant in the field is a joke, a distraction, a mark of interest from the outer world, so that for a few blessed hours he can dramatize himself a little and see in a false heroic light even his own wounded and dead.

The priest shut his breviary and said, 'Well, that's finished.' He was a European, but not a Frenchman, for the Bishop would not have tolerated a French priest in his diocese. He said apologetically, 'I have to come up here, you understand, for a bit of quiet from all those poor people.' The sound of the mortar-fire seemed to be closing in, or perhaps it was the enemy at last replying. The strange difficulty was to find them: there were a dozen narrow fronts, and between the canals, among the farm buildings and the paddy fields, innumerable opportunities for ambush.

Immediately below us stood, sat and lay the whole population of Phat Diem. Catholics, Buddhists, pagans, they had all packed their most valued possessions – a cooking-stove, a lamp, a mirror, a wardrobe, some mats, a holy picture – and moved into the Cathedral precincts. Here in the north it would be bitterly cold when darkness came, and already the Cathedral was full: there was no more shelter; even on the stairs to the bell tower every step was occupied, and all the time more people crowded through the gates, carrying their babies and household goods. They believed, whatever their religion, that here they would be safe. While we watched, a young man with a rifle in Vietnamese uniform pushed his way through: he was stopped by a priest, who took his rifle from him. The father at my side said in explanation, 'We are neutral here. This is God's territory.' I thought, 'It's a strange poor population God has in his kingdom, frightened, cold, starving – "I don't know how we are going to feed these people," the priest told me – you'd think a great King would do better than that.' But then I thought, 'It's always the same wherever one goes – it's not the most powerful rulers who have the happiest populations.'

Little shops had already been set up below. I said, 'It's like an enormous fair, isn't it, but without one smiling face.'

The priest said, 'They were terribly cold last night. We have to keep the monastery gates shut or they would swamp us.'

'You all keep warm in here?' I asked.

'Not very warm. And we would not have room for a tenth of them.' He went on, 'I know what you are thinking. But it is essential for some of us to keep well. We have the only hospital in Phat Diem, and our only nurses are these nuns.'

'And your surgeon?'

'I do what I can.' I saw then that his soutane was speckled with blood.

He said, 'Did you come up here to find me?'

'No. I wanted to get my bearings.'

'I asked you because I had a man up here last night. He wanted to go to confession. He had got a little frightened, you see, with what he had seen along the canal. One couldn't blame him.'

'It's bad along there?'

'The parachutists caught them in a cross-fire. Poor souls. I thought perhaps you were feeling the same.'

'I'm not a Roman Catholic. I don't think you could even call me a Christian.'

'It's strange what fear does to a man.'

'It would never do that to me. If I believed in any God at all, I should still hate the idea of confession. Kneeling in one of your boxes. Exposing myself to another man. You must excuse me, Father, but to me it seems morbid – unmanly even.'

'Oh,' he said lightly, 'I expect you are a good man. I don't suppose you've ever had much to regret.'

I looked along the churches, where they ran down evenly spaced between the canals, towards the sea. A light flashed from the second tower. I said, 'You haven't kept all your churches neutral.'

'It isn't possible,' he said. 'The French have agreed to leave the Cathedral precincts alone. We can't expect more. That's a Foreign Legion post you are looking at.'

'I'll be going along. Good-bye, Father.'

'Good-bye and good luck. Be careful of the snipers.'

I had to push my way through the crowd to get out past the lake and the white statue with its sugary outspread arms, into the long street. I could see for nearly three quarters of a mile each way, and there were only two living beings in all that length besides myself – two soldiers with camouflaged helmets going slowly away up the edge of the street, their sten guns at the ready. I say the living because one body lay in a doorway with its head in the road. The buzz of flies collecting there and the squelch of the soldiers' boots growing fainter and fainter were the only sounds. I walked quickly past the body, turning my head the other way. A few minutes later when I looked back I was quite alone with my shadow and there were no sounds except the sounds I made. I felt as though I were a mark on a firing range. It occurred to me that if something happened to me in this street it might be many hours before I was picked up: time for the flies to collect.

When I had crossed two canals, I took a turning that led to a church. A dozen men sat on the ground in the camouflage of parachutists, while two officers examined a map. Nobody paid me any attention when I joined them. One man, who wore the long antennae of a walkie-talkie, said, 'We can move now,' and everybody stood up.

I asked them in my bad French whether I could accompany them. An advantage of this war was that a European face proved in itself a passport on the field: a European could not be suspected of being an enemy agent. 'Who are you?' the lieutenant asked.

'I am writing about the war,' I said.

'American?'

'No, English.'

He said, 'It is a very small affair, but if you wish to come with us . . .' He began to take off his steel helmet. 'No, no,' I said, 'that is for combatants.'

'As you wish.'

We went out behind the church in single file, the lieutenant leading, and halted for a moment on a canal-bank for the soldier with the walkie-talkie to get contact with the patrols on either flank. The mortar shells tore over us and burst out of sight. We had picked up more men behind the church and were now about thirty strong. The lieutenant explained to me in a low voice, stabbing a finger at his map, 'Three hundred have been reported in this village here. Perhaps massing for tonight. We don't know. No one has found them yet.'

'How far?'

'Three hundred yards.'

Words came over the wireless and we went on in silence, to the right the straight canal, to the left low scrub and fields and scrub again. 'All clear,' the lieutenant whispered with a reassuring wave as we started. Forty yards on, another canal, with what was left of a bridge, a single plank without rails, ran across our front. The lieutenant motioned to us to deploy and we squatted down facing the unknown territory ahead, thirty feet off, across the plank. The men looked at the water and then, as though by a word of command, all together, they looked away. For a moment I didn't see what they had seen, but when I saw, my mind went back, I don't know why, to the Chalet and the female impersonators and the young soldiers whistling and Pyle saying, 'This isn't a bit suitable.'

The canal was full of bodies: I am reminded now of an Irish stew containing too much meat. The bodies overlapped: one head, seal-grey, and anonymous as a convict with a shaven scalp, stuck up out of the water like a buoy. There was no blood: I suppose it had flowed away a long time ago. I have no idea how many there were: they must have been caught in a cross-fire, trying to get back, and I suppose every man of us along the bank was thinking, 'Two can play at that game.' I too took my eyes away; we didn't want to be reminded of how little we counted, how quickly, simply and anonymously death came. Even though my reason wanted the state of death, I was afraid like a virgin of the act. I would have liked death to come with due warning, so that I could prepare myself. For what? I didn't know, nor how, except by taking a look around at the little I would be leaving.

The lieutenant sat beside the man with the walkie-talkie and stared at the ground between his feet. The instrument began to crackle instructions and with a sigh as though he had been roused from sleep he got up. There was an odd comradeliness about all their movements, as though they were equals engaged on a task they had performed together times out of mind. Nobody waited to be told what to do. Two men made for the plank and tried to cross it, but they were unbalanced by the weight of their arms and had to sit astride and work their way across a few inches at a time. Another man had found a punt hidden in some bushes down the canal and he worked it to where the lieutenant stood. Six of us got in and he began to pole towards the other bank, but we ran on a shoal of bodies and stuck. He pushed away with his pole, sinking it into this human clay, and one body was released and floated up all its length beside the boat like a bather lying in the sun. Then we were free again, and once on the other side we scrambled out, with no backward look. No shots had been fired: we were alive: death had withdrawn perhaps as far as the next canal. I heard somebody just behind me say with great seriousness, '*Gott sei dank.*' Except for the lieutenant they were most of them Germans.

Beyond was a group of farm-buildings; the lieutenant went in first, hugging the wall, and we followed at six-foot intervals in single file. Then the men, again without an order, scattered through the farm. Life had deserted it – not so much as a hen had been left behind, though hanging on the walls of what had been the living room were two hideous oleographs of the Sacred Heart and the Mother and Child which gave the whole ramshackle group of buildings a European air.

One knew what these people believed even if one didn't share their belief: they were human beings, not just grey drained cadavers.

So much of the war is sitting around and doing nothing, waiting for somebody else. With no guarantee of the amount of time you have left it doesn't seem worth starting even a train of thought. Doing what they had done so often before, the sentries moved out. Anything that stirred ahead of us now was enemy. The lieutenant marked his map and reported our position over the radio. A noonday hush fell: even the mortars were quiet and the air was empty of planes. One man doodled with a twig in the dirt of the farmyard. After a while it was as if we had been forgotten by war. I hoped that Phuong had sent my suits to the cleaners. A cold wind ruffled the straw of the yard, and a man went modestly behind a barn to relieve himself. I tried to remember whether I had paid the British Consul in Hanoi for the bottle of whisky he had allowed me.

Two shots were fired to our front, and I thought, 'This is it. Now it comes.' It was all the warning I wanted. I awaited, with a sense of exhilaration, the permanent thing.

But nothing happened. Once again I had 'over-prepared the event'. Only long minutes afterwards one of the sentries entered and reported something to the lieutenant. I caught the phrase, '*Deux civils*.'

The lieutenant said to me, 'We will go and see,' and following the sentry we picked our way along a muddy overgrown path between two fields. Twenty yards beyond the farm buildings, in a narrow ditch, we came on what we sought: a woman and a small boy. They were very clearly dead: a small neat clot of blood on the woman's forehead, and the child might have been sleeping. He was about six years old and he lay like an embryo in the womb with his little bony knees drawn up. '*Mal chance*,' the lieutenant said. He bent down and turned the child over. He was wearing a holy medal round his neck, and I said to myself, 'The juju doesn't work.' There was a gnawed piece of loaf under his body. I thought, 'I hate war.'

The lieutenant said, 'Have you seen enough?' speaking savagely, almost as though I had been responsible for these deaths. Perhaps to the soldier the civilian is the man who employs him to kill, who includes the guilt of murder in the pay-envelope and escapes responsibility. We walked back to the farm and sat down again in silence on the straw, out of the wind, which like an animal seemed to know that dark was coming. The man who had doodled was relieving himself, and the man who had relieved himself was doodling. I thought how in those moments of quiet, after the sentries had been posted, they must have believed it safe to move from the ditch. I wondered whether they had lain there long – the bread had been very dry. This farm was probably their home.

The radio was working again. The lieutenant said wearily, 'They are going to bomb the village. Patrols are called in for the night.' We rose and began our journey back, punting again around the shoal of bodies, filing past the church. We hadn't gone very far, and yet it seemed a long enough journey to have made with the killing of those two as the only result. The planes had gone up, and behind us the bombing began.

Dark had fallen by the time I reached the officers' quarters, where I was spending the night. The temperature was only a degree above zero, and the sole warmth anywhere was in the blazing market. With one wall destroyed by a bazooka and the doors buckled, canvas curtains couldn't shut out the draughts. The electric dynamo was not working, and we had to build barricades of boxes and books to keep the candles burning. I played *Quatre Cent Vingt-et-un* for Communist currency with a Captain Sorel: it wasn't possible to play for drinks as I was a guest of the mess. The luck went wearisomely back and forth. I opened my bottle of whisky to try to warm us a little, and the others gathered round. The colonel said, 'This is the first glass of whisky I have had since I left Paris.'

A lieutenant came in from his round of the sentries. 'Perhaps we shall have a quiet night,' he said.

'They will not attack before four,' the colonel said. 'Have you a gun?' he asked me.

'No.'

'I'll find you one. Better keep it on your pillow.' He added courteously, 'I am afraid you will find your mattress rather hard. And at three-thirty the mortar-fire will begin. We try to break up any concentrations.'

'How long do you suppose this will go on?'

'Who knows? We can't spare any more troops from Nam Dinh. This is just a diversion. If we can hold out with no more help than we got two days ago, it is, one may say, a victory.'

The wind was up again, prowling for an entry. The canvas curtain sagged (I was reminded of Polonius stabbed behind the arras) and the candle wavered. The shadows were theatrical. We might have been a company of barnstormers.

'Have your posts held?'

'As far as we know.' He said with an effect of great tiredness, 'This is nothing, you understand, an affair of no importance compared with what is happening a hundred kilometres away at Hoa Binh. That is a battle.'

'Another glass, Colonel?'

'Thank you, no. It is wonderful, your English whisky, but it is better to keep a little for the night in case of need. I think, if you will excuse me, I will get some sleep. One cannot sleep after the mortars start. Captain Sorel, you will see that Monsieur Fowlair has everything he needs, a candle, matches, a revolver.' He went into his room.

It was the signal for all of us. They had put a mattress on the floor for me in a small store-room and I was surrounded by wooden cases. I stayed awake only a very short time – the hardness of the floors was like rest. I wondered, but oddly without jealousy, whether Phuong was at the flat. The possession of a body tonight seemed a very small thing – perhaps that day I had seen too many bodies which belonged to no one, not even to themselves. We were all expendable. When I fell asleep I dreamed of Pyle. He was dancing all by himself on a stage, stiffly, with his arms held out to an invisible partner, and I sat and watched him from a seat like a music-stool with a gun in my hand in case anyone should interfere with his dance. A programme set up by the stage, like the numbers in an English music-hall, read, 'The Dance of Love. "A" certificate.' Somebody moved at the back of the theatre and I held my gun tighter. Then I woke.

My hand was on the gun they had lent me, and a man stood in the doorway with a candle in his hand. He wore a steel helmet which threw a shadow over his eyes, and it was only when he spoke that I knew he was Pyle. He said shyly, 'I'm awfully sorry to wake you up. They told me I could sleep in here.'

I was still not fully awake. 'Where did you get that helmet?' I asked.

'Oh, somebody lent it to me,' he said vaguely. He dragged in after him a military kitbag and began to pull out a wool-lined sleeping-bag.

'You are very well equipped,' I said, trying to recollect why either of us should be here.

'This is the standard travelling kit,' he said, 'of our medical aid teams. They lent me one in Hanoi.' He took out a thermos and a small spirit stove, a hair-brush, a shaving-set and a tin of rations. I looked at my watch. It was nearly three in the morning.

2

Pyle continued to unpack. He made a little ledge of cases, on which he put his shaving-mirror and tackle. I said, 'I doubt if you'll get any water.'

'Oh,' he said, 'I've enough in the thermos for the morning.' He sat down on his sleeping-bag and began to pull off his boots.

'How on earth did you get here?' I asked.

'They let me through as far as Nam Dinh to see our trachoma team, and then I hired a boat.'

'A boat?'

'Oh, some kind of a punt – I don't know the name for it. As a matter of fact I had to buy it. It didn't cost much.'

'And you came down the river by yourself?'

'It wasn't really difficult, you know. The current was with me.'

'You are crazy.'

'Oh no. The only real danger was running aground.'

'Or being shot up by a naval patrol, or a French plane. Or having your throat cut by the Vietminh.'

He laughed shyly. 'Well, I'm here anyway,' he said.

'Why?'

'Oh, there are two reasons. But I don't want to keep you awake.'

'I'm not sleepy. The guns will be starting soon.'

'Do you mind if I move the candle? It's a little too bright here.' He seemed nervous.

'What's the first reason?'

'Well, the other day you made me think this place was rather interesting. You remember when we were with Granger . . . and Phuong.'

'Yes?'

'I thought I ought to take a look at it. To tell you the truth, I was a little ashamed of Granger.'

'I see. As simple as all that.'

'Well, there wasn't any real difficulty, was there?' He began to play with his bootlaces, and there was a long silence. 'I'm not being quite honest,' he said at last.

'No?'

'I really came to see you.'

'You came here to see me?'

'Yes.'

'Why?'

He looked up from his bootlaces in an agony of embarrassment. 'I had to tell you – I've fallen in love with Phuong.'

I laughed. I couldn't help it. He was so unexpected and serious. I said, 'Couldn't you have waited till I got back? I shall be in Saigon next week.'

'You might have been killed,' he said. 'It wouldn't have been honourable. And then I don't know if I could have stayed away from Phuong all that time.'

'You mean, you *have* stayed away?'

'Of course. You don't think I'll tell *her* – without you knowing?'

'People do,' I said. 'When did it happen?'

'I guess it was that night at the Chalet, dancing with her.'

'I didn't think you ever got close enough.'

He looked at me in a puzzled way. If his conduct seemed crazy to me, mine was obviously inexplicable to him. He said, 'You know, I think it was seeing all those girls in that house. They were so pretty. Why, she might have been one of them. I wanted to protect her.'

'I don't think she's in need of protection. Has Miss Hei invited you out?'

'Yes, but I haven't gone. I've kept away.' He said gloomily, 'It's been terrible. I feel such a heel, but you do believe me, don't you, that if you'd been married – why, I wouldn't ever come between a man and his wife.'

'You seem pretty sure you *can* come between,' I said. For the first time he had irritated me.

'Fowler,' he said, 'I don't know your Christian name . . .?'

'Thomas. Why?'

'I can call you Tom, can't I? I feel in a way this has brought us together. Loving the same woman, I mean.'

'What's your next move?'

He sat up enthusiastically against the packing-cases. 'Everything seems different now that you know,' he said. 'I shall ask her to marry me, Tom.'

'I'd rather you called me Thomas.'

'She'll just have to choose between us, Thomas. That's fair enough.' But was it fair? I felt for the first time the premonitory chill of loneliness. It was all fantastic, and yet . . . He might be a poor lover, but I was the poor man. He had in his hand the infinite riches of respectability.

He began to undress and I thought, 'He has youth too.' How sad it was to envy Pyle.

I said, 'I can't marry her. I have a wife at home. She would never divorce me. She's High Church – if you know what that means.'

'I'm sorry, Thomas. By the way, my name's Alden, if you'd care . . .'

'I'd rather stick to Pyle,' I said. 'I think of you as Pyle.'

He got into his sleeping-bag and stretched his hand out for the candle. 'Whew,' he said, 'I'm glad that's over, Thomas. I've been feeling awfully bad about it.' It was only too evident that he no longer did.

When the candle was out, I could just see the outline of his crew-cut against the light of the flames outside. 'Goodnight, Thomas. Sleep well,' and immediately at those words like a bad comedy cue the mortars opened up, whirring, shrieking, exploding.

'Good God,' Pyle said, 'is it an attack?'

'They are trying to stop an attack.'

'Well, I suppose, there'll be no sleep for us now?'

'No sleep.'

'Thomas, I want you to know what I think of the way you've taken all this – I think you've been swell, swell, there's no other word for it.'

'Thank you.'

'You've seen so much more of the world than I have. You know, in some ways Boston is a bit – cramping. Even if you aren't a Lowell or a Cabot. I wish you'd advise me, Thomas.'

'What about?'

'Phuong.'

'I wouldn't trust my advice if I were you. I'm biased. I want to keep her.'

'Oh, but I know you're straight, absolutely straight, and we both have her interests at heart.'

Suddenly I couldn't bear his boyishness any more. I said, 'I don't care that for her interests. You can have her interests. I only want her body. I want her in bed with me. I'd rather ruin her and sleep with her than, than . . . look after her damned interests.'

He said, 'Oh,' in a weak voice, in the dark.

I went on, 'If it's only her interests you care about, for God's sake leave Phuong alone. Like any other woman she'd rather have a good . . .' The crash of a mortar saved Boston ears from the Anglo-Saxon word.

But there was a quality of the implacable in Pyle. He had determined I was behaving well and I had to behave well. He said, 'I know what you are suffering, Thomas.'

'I'm not suffering.'

'Oh yes, you are. I know what I'd suffer if I had to give up Phuong.'

'But I haven't given her up.'

'I'm pretty physical too, Thomas, but I'd give up all hope of that if I could see Phuong happy.'

'She is happy.'

'She can't be – not in her situation. She needs children.'

'Do you really believe all that nonsense her sister . . .'

'A sister sometimes knows better . . .'

'She was just trying to sell the notion to you, Pyle, because she thinks you have more money. And, my God, she has sold it all right.'

'I've only got my salary.'

'Well, you've got a favourable rate of exchange anyway.'

'Don't be bitter, Thomas. These things happen. I wish it had happened to anybody else but you. Are those our mortars?'

'Yes, "our" mortars. You talk as though she was leaving me, Pyle.'

'Of course,' he said without conviction, 'she may choose to stay with you.'

'What would you do then?'

'I'd apply for a transfer.'

'Why don't you just go away, Pyle, without causing trouble?'

'It wouldn't be fair to her, Thomas,' he said quite seriously. I never knew a man who had better motives for all the trouble he caused. He added, 'I don't think you quite understand Phuong.'

And waking that morning months later with Phuong beside me, I thought, 'And did you understand her either? Could you have anticipated this situation? Phuong so happily asleep beside me and you dead?' Time has its revenges, but revenges seem so often sour. Wouldn't we all do better not trying to understand, accepting the fact that no human being will ever understand another, not a wife a husband, a lover a mistress, nor a parent a child? Perhaps that's why men have invented God – a being capable of understanding. Perhaps if I wanted to be understood or to understand I would bamboozle myself into belief, but I am a reporter; God exists only for leader-writers.

'Are you sure there's anything much to understand?' I asked Pyle. 'Oh, for God's sake, let's have a whisky. It's too noisy to argue.'

'It's a little early,' Pyle said.

'It's damned late.'

I poured out two glasses and Pyle raised his and stared through the whisky at the light of the candle. His hand shook whenever a shell burst, and yet he had made that senseless trip from Nam Dinh.

Pyle said, 'It's a strange thing that neither of us can say "Good luck".' So we drank saying nothing.

Chapter 5

1

I HAD thought I would be only one week away from Saigon, but it was nearly three weeks before I returned. In the first place it proved more difficult to get out of the Phat Diem area than it had been to get in. The road was cut between Nam Dinh and Hanoi and aerial transport could not be spared for one reporter who shouldn't have been there anyway. Then when I reached Hanoi the correspondents had been flown up for briefing on the latest victory and the plane that took them back had no seat left for me. Pyle got away from Phat Diem the morning he arrived: he had fulfilled his mission – to speak to me about Phuong, and there was nothing to keep him. I left him asleep when the mortar-fire stopped at five-thirty and when I returned from a cup of coffee and some biscuits in the mess he wasn't there. I assumed that he had gone for a stroll – after punting all the way down the river from Nam Dinh a few snipers would not have worried him; he was as incapable of imagining pain or danger to himself as he was incapable of conceiving the pain he might cause others. On one occasion – but that was months later – I lost control and thrust his foot into it, into the pain I mean, and I remember how he turned away and looked at his stained shoe in perplexity and said, 'I must get a shine before I see the Minister.' I knew then he was already forming his phrases in the style he had learnt from York Harding. Yet he was sincere in his way: it was coincidence that the sacrifices were all paid by others, until that final night under the bridge to Dakow.

It was only when I returned to Saigon that I learnt how Pyle, while I drank my coffee, had persuaded a young naval officer to take him on a landing-craft which after a routine patrol dropped him surreptitiously at Nam Dinh. Luck was with him and he got back to Hanoi with his trachoma team twenty-four hours before the road was officially regarded as cut. When I reached Hanoi he had already left for the south, leaving me a note with the barman at the Press Camp.

'Dear Thomas,' he wrote, 'I can't begin to tell you how swell you were the other night. I can tell you my heart was in my mouth when I walked into that room to find you.' (Where had it been on the long boat-ride down the river?) 'There are not many men who would have taken the whole thing so calmly. You were great, and I don't feel half as mean as I did, now that I've told you.' (Was he the only one that mattered? I wondered angrily, and yet I knew that he didn't intend it that way. To him the whole affair would be happier as soon as he didn't feel mean – I would be happier, Phuong would be happier, the whole world would be happier, even the Economic Attaché and the Minister. Spring had come to Indo-China now that Pyle was mean no longer.) 'I waited for you here for twenty-four hours, but I shan't get back to Saigon for a week if I don't leave today, and my real work is in the south. I've told the boys who are running the trachoma teams to look you up – you'll like them. They are great boys and doing a man-size job. Don't worry in any way that I'm returning to Saigon ahead of you. I promise you I won't see Phuong until you return. I don't want you to feel later that I've been unfair in any way. Cordially yours, Alden.'

Again that calm assumption that 'later' it would be I who would lose Phuong. Is confidence based on a rate of exchange? We used to speak of sterling qualities. Have we got to talk now about a dollar love? A dollar love, of course, would include marriage and Junior and Mother's Day, even though later it might include Reno or the Virgin Islands or wherever they go nowadays for their divorces. A dollar love had good intentions, a clear conscience, and to Hell with everybody. But my love had no intentions: it knew the future. All one could do was try to make the future less hard, to break the future gently when it came, and even opium had its value there. But I never foresaw that the first future I would have to break to Phuong would be the death of Pyle.

I went – for I had nothing better to do – to the Press Conference. Granger, of course, was there. A young and too beautiful French colonel presided. He spoke in French and a junior officer translated. The French correspondents sat together like a rival football-team. I found it hard to keep my mind on what the colonel was saying: all the time it wandered back to Phuong and the one thought – suppose Pyle is right and I lose her: where does one go from here?

The interpreter said, 'The colonel tells you that the enemy has suffered a sharp defeat and severe losses – the equivalent of one complete battalion. The last detachments are now making their way back across the Red River on improvised rafts. They are shelled all the time by the Air Force.' The colonel ran his hand through his elegant yellow hair and, flourishing his pointer, danced his way down the long maps on the wall. An American correspondent asked, 'What are the French losses?'

The colonel knew perfectly well the meaning of the question – it was usually put at this stage of the conference, but he paused, pointer raised with a kind smile like a popular schoolmaster, until it was interpreted. Then he answered with patient ambiguity.

'The colonel says our losses have not been heavy. The exact number is not yet known.'

This was always the signal for trouble. You would have thought that sooner or later the colonel would have found a formula for dealing with his refractory class, or that the headmaster would have appointed a member of his staff more efficient at keeping order.

'Is the colonel seriously telling us,' Granger said, 'that he's had time to count the enemy dead and not his own?'

Patiently the colonel wove his web of evasion, which he knew perfectly well would be destroyed again by another question. The French correspondents sat gloomily silent. If the American correspondents stung the colonel into an admission they would be quick to seize it, but they would not join in baiting their countryman.

'The colonel says the enemy forces are being over-run. It is possible to count the dead behind the firing-line, but while the battle is still in progress you cannot expect figures from the advancing French units.'

'It's not what *we* expect,' Granger said, 'it's what the *Etat Major* knows or not. Are you seriously telling us that platoons do not report their casualties as they happen by walkie-talkie?'

The colonel's temper was beginning to fray. If only, I thought, he had called our bluff from the start and told us firmly that he knew the figures but wouldn't say. After all it was their war, not ours. We had no God-given right to information. We didn't have to fight Left-Wing deputies in Paris as well as the troops of Ho Chi Minh between the Red and the Black Rivers. We were not dying.

The colonel suddenly snapped out the information that French casualties had been in a proportion of one to three, then turned his back on us, to stare furiously at his map. These were his men who were dead, his fellow officers, belonging to the same class at St Cyr – not numerals as they were to Granger. Granger said, 'Now we are getting somewhere,' and stared round with oafish triumph at his fellows; the French with heads bent made their sombre notes.

'That's more than can be said in Korea,' I said with deliberate misunderstanding, but I had only given Granger a new line.

'Ask the colonel,' he said, 'what the French are going to do next? He says the enemy's on the run across the Black River . . .'

'Red River,' the interpreter corrected him.

'I don't care what the colour of the river is. What we want to know is what the French are going to do now.'

'The enemy are in flight.'

'What happens when they get to the other side? What are you going to do then? Are you just going to sit down on the other bank and say that's over?' The French officers listened with gloomy patience to Granger's bullying voice. Even humility is required today of the soldier. 'Are you going to drop them Christmas cards?'

The captain interpreted with care, even to the phrase, '*cartes de Noël*'. The colonel gave us a wintry smile. 'Not Christmas cards,' he said.

I think the colonel's youth and beauty particularly irritated Granger. The colonel wasn't – at least not by Granger's interpretation – a man's man. He said, 'You aren't dropping much else.'

The colonel spoke suddenly in English, good English. He said, 'If the supplies promised by the Americans had arrived, we should have more to drop.' He was really in spite of his elegance a simple man. He believed that a newspaper correspondent cared for his country's honour more than for news. Granger said sharply (he was efficient: he kept dates well in his head), 'You mean that none of the supplies promised for the beginning of September have arrived?'

'No.'

Granger had got his news: he began to write.

'I am sorry,' the colonel said, 'that is not for printing: that is for background.'

'But colonel,' Granger protested, 'that's news. We can help you there.'

'No, it is a matter for the diplomats.'

'What harm can it do?'

The French correspondents were at a loss: they could speak very little English. The colonel had broken the rules. They muttered angrily together.

'I am no judge,' the colonel said. 'Perhaps the American newspapers would say, "Oh, the French are always complaining, always begging." And in Paris the Communists would accuse, "The French are spilling their blood for America and America will not even send a second-hand helicopter." It does no good. At the end of it we should still have no helicopters, and the enemy would still be there, fifty miles from Hanoi.'

'At least I can print that, can't I, that you need helicopters bad?'

'You can say,' the colonel said, 'that six months ago we had three helicopters and now we have one. One,' he repeated with a kind of amazed bitterness. 'You can say that if a man is wounded in this fighting, not seriously wounded, just wounded, he knows that he is probably a dead man. Twelve hours, twenty-four hours perhaps, on a stretcher to the ambulance, then bad tracks, a breakdown, perhaps an ambush, gangrene. It is better to be killed outright.' The French correspondents leant forward, trying to understand. 'You can write that,' he said, looking all the more venomous for his physical beauty. '*Interprètez*,' he ordered, and walked out of the room leaving the captain the unfamiliar task of translating from English into French.

'Got him on the raw,' said Granger with satisfaction, and he went into a corner by the bar to write his telegram. Mine didn't take long: there was nothing I could write from Phat Diem that the censors would pass. If the story had seemed good enough I could have flown to Hong Kong and sent it from there, but was any news good enough to risk expulsion? I doubted it. Expulsion meant the end of a whole life, it meant the victory of Pyle, and there, when I returned to my hotel, waiting in my pigeon-hole, was in fact his victory, the end of the affair – a congratulatory telegram of promotion. Dante never thought up that turn of the screw for his condemned lovers. Paolo was never promoted to Purgatory.

I went upstairs to my bare room and the dripping cold-water tap (there was no hot water in Hanoi) and sat on the edge of my bed with the bundle of the mosquito-net like a swollen cloud overhead. I was to be the new foreign editor, arriving every afternoon at half past three, at that grim Victorian building near Blackfriars station with a plaque of Lord Salisbury by the lift. They had sent the good news on from Saigon, and I wondered whether it had already reached Phuong's ears. I was to be a reporter no longer: I was to have opinions, and in return for that empty privilege I was deprived of my last hope in the contest with Pyle. I had experience to match his virginity, age was as good a card to play in the sexual game as youth, but now I hadn't even the limited future of twelve more months to offer, and a future was trumps. I envied the most homesick officer condemned to the chance of death. I would have liked to weep, but the ducts were as dry as the hot-water pipes. Oh, they could have home – I only wanted my room in the rue Catinat.

It was cold after dark in Hanoi and the lights were lower than those of Saigon, more suited to the darker clothes of the women and the fact of war. I walked up the rue Gambetta to the Pax Bar – I didn't want to drink in the Metropole with the senior French officers, their wives and their girls, and as I reached the bar I was aware of the distant drumming of the guns out towards Hoa Binh. In the day they were drowned in traffic-noises, but everything was quiet now except for the tring of bicycle-bells where the trishaw drivers plied for hire. Pietri sat in his usual place. He had an odd elongated skull which sat on his shoulders like a pear on a dish; he was a Sureté officer and was married to a pretty Tonkinese who owned the Pax Bar. He was another man who had no particular desire to go home. He was a Corsican, but he preferred Marseilles, and to Marseilles he preferred any day his seat on the pavement in the rue Gambetta. I wondered whether he already knew the contents of my telegram.

'*Quatre Cent Vingt-et-un?*' he asked.

'Why not?'

We began to throw and it seemed impossible to me that I could ever have a life again, away from the rue Gambetta and the rue Catinat, the flat taste of vermouth cassis, the homely click of dice, and the gunfire travelling like a clock-hand around the horizon.

I said, 'I'm going back.'

'Home?' Pietri asked, throwing a four-to-one.

'No. England.'

PART TWO

Chapter 1

PYLE had invited himself for what he called a drink, but I knew very well he didn't really drink. After the passage of weeks that fantastic meeting in Phat Diem seemed hardly believable: even the details of the conversation were less clear. They were like the missing letters on a Roman tomb and I the archaeologist filling in the gaps according to the bias of my scholarship. It even occurred to me that he had been pulling my leg, and that the conversation had been an elaborate and humorous disguise for his real purpose, for it was already the gossip of Saigon that he was engaged in one of those services so ineptly called secret. Perhaps he was arranging American arms for a Third Force – the Bishop's brass band, all that was left of his young scared unpaid levies. The telegram that awaited me in Hanoi I kept in my pocket. There was no point in telling Phuong, for that would be to poison the few months we had left with tears and quarrels. I wouldn't even go for my exit-permit until the last moment in case she had a relation in the immigration-office.

I told her, 'Pyle's coming at six.'

'I will go and see my sister,' she said.

'I expect he'd like to see you.'

'He does not like me or my family. When you were away he did not come once to my sister, although she had invited him. She was very hurt.'

'You needn't go out.'

'If he wanted to see me, he would have asked us to the Majestic. He wants to talk to you privately – about business.'

'What is his business?'

'People say he imports a great many things.'

'What things?'

'Drugs, medicines . . .'

'Those are for the trachoma teams in the north.'

'Perhaps. The Customs must not open them. They are diplomatic parcels. But once there was a mistake – the man was discharged. The First Secretary threatened to stop all imports.'

'What was in the case?'

'Plastic.'

'You don't mean bombs?'

'No. Just plastic.'

When Phuong had gone, I wrote home. A man from Reuter's was leaving for Hong Kong in a few days and he could mail my letter from there. I knew my appeal was hopeless, but I was not going to reproach myself later for not taking every possible measure. I wrote to the Managing Editor that this was the wrong moment to change their correspondent. General de Lattre was dying in Paris: the French were about to withdraw altogether from Hoa Binh: the north had never been in greater danger. I wasn't suitable, I told him, for a foreign editor – I was a reporter, I had no real opinions about anything. On the last page I even appealed to him on personal grounds, although it was unlikely that any human sympathy could survive under the strip-light, among the green eye-shades and the stereotyped phrases – 'the good of the paper', 'the situation demands . . .'

I wrote: 'For private reasons I am very unhappy at being moved from Vietnam. I don't think I can do my best work in England, where there will be not only financial but family strains. Indeed, if I could afford it I would resign rather than return to the UK. I only mention this as showing the strength of my objection. I don't think you have found me a bad correspondent, and this is the first favour I have ever asked of you.' Then I looked over my article on the battle of Phat Diem, so that I could send it out to be posted under a Hong Kong dateline. The French would not seriously object now – the siege had been raised: a defeat could be played as a victory. Then I tore up the last page of my letter to the editor. It was no use – the 'private reasons' would become only the subject of sly jokes. Every correspondent, it was assumed, had his local girl. The editor would joke to the night-editor, who would take the envious thought back to his semi-detached villa in Streatham and climb into bed with it beside the faithful wife he had carried with him years back from Glasgow. I could see so well the kind of house that has no mercy – a broken tricycle stood in the hall and somebody had broken his favourite pipe; and there was a child's shirt in the living-room waiting for a button to be sewn on. 'Private reasons':

drinking in the Press Club I wouldn't want to be reminded by their jokes of Phuong.

There was a knock on the door. I opened it to Pyle and his black dog walked in ahead of him. Pyle looked over my shoulder and found the room empty. 'I'm alone,' I said, 'Phuong is with her sister.' He blushed. I noticed that he was wearing a Hawaii shirt, even though it was comparatively restrained in colour and design. I was surprised: had he been accused of un-American activities? He said, 'I hope I haven't interrupted . . .'

'Of course not. Have a drink?'

'Thanks. Beer?'

'Sorry. We haven't a frig – we send out for ice. What about a Scotch?'

'A small one, if you don't mind. I'm not very keen on hard liquor.'

'On the rocks?'

'Plenty of soda – if you aren't short.'

I said, 'I haven't seen you since Phat Diem.'

'You got my note, Thomas?'

When he used my Christian name, it was like a declaration that he hadn't been humorous, that he hadn't been covering up, that he was here to get Phuong. I noticed that his crew-cut had recently been trimmed; was even the Hawaii shirt serving the function of male plumage?

'I got your note,' I said. 'I suppose I ought to knock you down.'

'Of course,' he said, 'you've every right, Thomas. But I boxed at college – and I'm so much younger.'

'No, it wouldn't be a good move for me, would it?'

'You know, Thomas (I'm sure you feel the same), I don't like discussing Phuong behind her back. I thought she would be here.'

'Well, what shall we discuss – plastic?' I hadn't meant to surprise him.

He said, 'You know about that?'

'Phuong told me.'

'How could she . . . ?'

'You can be sure it's all over the town. What's so important about it? Are you going into the toy business?'

'We don't like the details of our aid to get around. You know what Congress is like – and then one has visiting Senators. We had a lot of trouble about our trachoma teams because they were using one drug instead of another.'

'I still don't understand the plastic.'

His black dog sat on the floor taking up too much room, panting; its tongue looked like a burnt pancake. Pyle said vaguely, 'Oh, you know, we want to get some of these local industries on their feet, and we have to be careful of the French. They want everything bought in France.'

'I don't blame them. A war needs money.'

'Do you like dogs?'

'No.'

'I thought the British were great dog-lovers.'

'We think Americans love dollars, but there must be exceptions.'

'I don't know how I'd get along without Duke. You know sometimes I feel so darned lonely . . .'

'You've got a great many companions in your branch.'

'The first dog I ever had was called Prince. I called him after the Black Prince. You know, the fellow who . . .'

'Massacred all the women and children in Limoges.'

'I don't remember that.'

'The history books gloss it over.'

I was to see many times that look of pain and disappointment touch his eyes and mouth when reality didn't match the romantic ideas he cherished, or when someone he loved or admired dropped below the impossible standard he had set. Once, I remember, I caught York Harding out in a gross error of fact, and I had to comfort him: 'It's human to make mistakes.' He had laughed nervously and said, 'You must think me a fool, but – well, I almost thought him infallible.' He added, 'My father took to him a lot the only time they met, and my father's darned difficult to please.'

The big black dog called Duke, having panted long enough to establish a kind of right to the air, began to poke about the room. 'Could you ask your dog to be still?' I said.

'Oh, I'm so sorry. Duke. Duke. Sit down, Duke.' Duke sat down and began noisily to lick his private parts. I filled our glasses and managed in passing to disturb Duke's toilet. The quiet lasted a very short time; he began to scratch himself.

'Duke's awfully intelligent,' said Pyle.

'What happened to Prince?'

'We were down on the farm in Connecticut and he got run over.'

'Were you upset?'

'Oh, I minded a lot. He meant a great deal to me, but one has to be sensible. Nothing could bring him back.'

'And if you lose Phuong, will you be sensible?'

'Oh yes, I hope so. And you?'

'I doubt it. I might even run amok. Have you thought about that, Pyle?'

'I wish you'd call me Alden, Thomas.'

'I'd rather not. Pyle has got – associations. Have you thought about it?'

'Of course I haven't. You're the straightest guy I've ever known. When I remember how you behaved when I barged in . . .'

'I remember thinking before I went to sleep how convenient it would be if there were an attack and you were killed. A hero's death. For Democracy.'

'Don't laugh at me, Thomas.' He shifted his long limbs uneasily. 'I must seem a bit dumb to you, but I know when you're kidding.'

'I'm not.'

'I know if you come clean you want what's best for her.'

It was then I heard Phuong's step. I had hoped against hope that he would have gone before she returned. He heard it too and recognized it. He said, 'There she is,' although he had had only one evening to learn her footfall. Even the dog got up and stood by the door, which I had left open for coolness, almost as though he accepted her as one of Pyle's family. I was an intruder.

Phuong said, 'My sister was not in,' and looked guardedly at Pyle.

I wondered whether she were telling the truth or whether her sister had ordered her to hurry back.

'You remember Monsieur Pyle?' I said.

'*Enchantée*.' She was on her best behaviour.

'I'm so pleased to see you again,' he said, blushing.

'*Comment?*'

'Her English is not very good,' I said.

'I'm afraid my French is awful. I'm taking lessons though. And I can understand – if Phuong will speak slowly.'

'I'll act as interpreter,' I said. 'The local accent takes some getting used to. Now what do you want to say? Sit down, Phuong. Monsieur Pyle has come specially to see you. Are you sure,' I added to Pyle, 'that you wouldn't like me to leave you two alone?'

'I want you to hear everything I have to say. It wouldn't be fair otherwise.'

'Well, fire away.'

He said solemnly, as though this part he had learned by heart, that he had a great love and respect for Phuong. He had felt it ever since the night he had danced with her. I was reminded a little of a butler showing a party of tourists over a 'great house'. The great house was his heart, and of the private apartments where the family lived we were given only a rapid and surreptitious glimpse. I translated for him with meticulous care – it sounded worse that way, and Phuong sat quiet with her hands in her lap as though she were listening to a movie.

'Has she understood that?' he asked.

'As far as I can tell. You don't want me to add a little fire to it, do you?'

'Oh no,' he said, 'just translate. I don't want to sway her emotionally.'

'I see.'

'Tell her I want to marry her.'

I told her.

'What was that she said?'

'She asked me if you were serious. I told her you were the serious type.'

'I suppose this is an odd situation,' he said. 'Me asking you to translate.'

'Rather odd.'

'And yet it seems so natural. After all you are my best friend.'

'It's kind of you to say so.'

'There's nobody I'd go to in trouble sooner than you,' he said.

'And I suppose being in love with my girl is a kind of trouble?'

'Of course. I wish it was anybody but you, Thomas.'

'Well, what do I say to her next. That you can't live without her?'

'No, that's too emotional. It's not quite true either. I'd have to go away, of course, but one gets over everything.'

'While you are thinking what to say, do you mind if I put in a word for myself?'

'No, of course not, it's only fair, Thomas.'

'Well, Phuong,' I said, 'are you going to leave me for him? He'll marry you. I can't. You know why.'

'Are you going away?' she asked and I thought of the editor's letter in my pocket.

'No.'

'Never?'

'How can one promise that? He can't either. Marriages break. Often they break quicker than an affair like ours.'

'I do not want to go,' she said, but the sentence was not comforting; it contained an unexpressed 'but'.

Pyle said, 'I think I ought to put all my cards on the table. I'm not rich. But when my father dies I'll have about fifty thousand dollars.

I'm in good health – I've got a medical certificate only two months old, and I can let her know my blood-group.'

'I don't know how to translate that. What's it for?'

'Well, to make certain we can have children together.'

'Is that how you make love in America – figures of income and blood-group?'

'I don't know, I've never done it before. Maybe at home my mother would talk to her mother.'

'About your blood-group?'

'Don't laugh at me, Thomas. I expect I'm old-fashioned. You know I'm a little lost in this situation.'

'So am I. Don't you think we might call it off and dice for her?'

'Now you are pretending to be tough, Thomas. I know you love her in your way as much as I do.'

'Well, go on, Pyle.'

'Tell her I don't expect her to love me right away. That will come in time, but tell her what I offer is security and respect. That doesn't sound very exciting, but perhaps it's better than passion.'

'She can always get passion,' I said, 'with your chauffeur when you are away at the office.'

Pyle blushed. He got awkwardly to his feet and said, 'That's a dirty crack. I won't have her insulted. You've no right . . .'

'She's not your wife yet.'

'What can you offer her?' he asked with anger. 'A couple of hundred dollars when you leave for England, or will you pass her on with the furniture?'

'The furniture isn't mine.'

'She's not either. Phuong, will you marry me?'

'What about the blood-group?' I said. 'And a health certificate. You'll need hers, surely? Maybe you ought to have mine too. And her horoscope – no, that's an Indian custom.'

'Will you marry me?'

'Say it in French,' I said, 'I'm damned if I'll interpret for you any more.'

I got to my feet and the dog growled. It made me furious. 'Tell your damned Duke to be quiet. This is my home, not his.'

'Will you marry me?' he repeated. I took a step towards Phuong and the dog growled again.

I said to Phuong, 'Tell him to go away and take his dog with him.'

'Come away with me now,' Pyle said. '*Avec moi.*'

'No,' Phuong said, 'no.' Suddenly all the anger in both of us vanished;

it was a problem as simple as that: it could be solved with a word of two letters. I felt an enormous relief; Pyle stood there with his mouth a little open and an expression of bewilderment on his face. He said, 'She said no.'

'She knows that much English.' I wanted to laugh now: what fools we had both made of each other. I said, 'Sit down and have another Scotch, Pyle.'

'I think I ought to go.'

'One for the road.'

'Mustn't drink all your whisky,' he muttered.

'I get all I want through the Legation.' I moved towards the table and the dog bared its teeth.

Pyle said furiously, 'Down, Duke. Behave yourself.' He wiped the sweat off his forehead. 'I'm awfully sorry, Thomas, if I said anything I shouldn't. I don't know what came over me.' He took the glass and said wistfully, 'The best man wins. Only please don't leave her, Thomas.'

'Of course I shan't leave her,' I said.

Phuong said to me, 'Would he like to smoke a pipe?'

'Would you like to smoke a pipe?'

'No, thank you. I don't touch opium and we have strict rules in the service. I'll just drink this up and be off. I'm sorry about Duke. He's very quiet as a rule.'

'Stay to supper.'

'I think, if you don't mind, I'd rather be alone.' He gave an uncertain grin. 'I suppose people would say we'd both behaved rather strangely. I wish you could marry her, Thomas.'

'Do you really?'

'Yes. Ever since I saw that place – you know, that house near the Chalet – I've been so afraid.'

He drank his unaccustomed whisky quickly, not looking at Phuong, and when he said good-bye he didn't touch her hand, but gave an awkward little bobbing bow. I noticed how her eyes followed him to the door and as I passed the mirror I saw myself: the top button of my trousers undone, the beginning of a paunch. Outside he said, 'I promise not to see her, Thomas. You won't let this come between us, will you? I'll get a transfer when I finish my tour.'

'When's that?'

'About two years.'

I went back to the room and I thought. 'What's the good? I might as well have told them both that I was going.' He had only to carry his bleeding heart for a few weeks as a decoration . . . My lie would even ease his conscience.

'Shall I make you a pipe?' Phuong asked.

'Yes, in a moment. I just want to write a letter.'

It was the second letter of the day, but I tore none of this up, though I had as little hope of a response. I wrote: 'Dear Helen, I am coming back to England next April to take the job of foreign editor. You can imagine I am not very happy about it. England is to me the scene of my failure. I had intended our marriage to last quite as much as if I had shared your Christian beliefs. To this day I'm not certain what went wrong (I know we both tried), but I think it was my temper. I know how cruel and bad my temper can be. Now I think it's a little better – the East has done that for me – not sweeter, but quieter. Perhaps it's simply that I'm five years older – at the end of life when five years becomes a high proportion of what's left. You have been very generous to me, and you have never reproached me once since our separation. Would you be even more generous? I know that before we married you warned me there could never be a divorce. I accepted the risk and I've nothing to complain of. At the same time I'm asking for one now.'

Phuong called out to me from the bed that she had the tray ready.

'A moment,' I said.

'I could wrap this up,' I wrote, 'and make it sound more honourable and more dignified by pretending it was for someone else's sake. But it isn't, and we always used to tell each other the truth. It's for my sake and only mine. I love someone very much, we have lived together for more than two years, she has been very loyal to me, but I know I'm not essential to her. If I leave her, she'll be a little unhappy I think, but there won't be any tragedy. She'll marry someone else and have a family. It's stupid of me to tell you this. I'm putting a reply into your mouth. But because I've been truthful so far, perhaps you'll believe me when I tell you that to lose her will be, for me, the beginning of death. I'm not asking you to be "reasonable" (reason is all on your side) or to be merciful. It's too big a word for my situation and anyway I don't particularly deserve mercy. I suppose what I'm really asking you is to behave, all of a sudden, irrationally, out of character. I want you to feel' (I hesitated over the word and then I didn't get it right) 'affection and to act before you have time to think. I know that's easier done over a telephone than over eight thousand miles. If only you'd just cable me "I agree"!'

When I had finished I felt as though I had run a long way and strained unconditioned muscles. I lay down on the bed while Phuong made my pipe. I said, 'He's young.'

'Who?'

'Pyle.'

'That's not so important.'

'I would marry you if I could, Phuong.'

'I think so, but my sister does not believe it.'

'I have just written to my wife and I have asked her to divorce me. I have never tried before. There is always a chance.'

'A big chance?'

'No, but a small one.'

'Don't worry. Smoke.'

I drew in the smoke and she began to prepare my second pipe. I asked her again, 'Was your sister really not at home, Phuong?'

'I told you – she was out.' It was absurd to subject her to this passion for truth, an Occidental passion, like the passion for alcohol. Because of the whisky I had drunk with Pyle, the effect of the opium was lessened. I said, 'I lied to you, Phuong. I have been ordered home.'

She put the pipe down. 'But you won't go?'

'If I refused, what would we live on?'

'I could come with you. I would like to see London.'

'It would be very uncomfortable for you if we were not married.'

'But perhaps your wife will divorce you.'

'Perhaps.'

'I will come with you anyway,' she said. She meant it, but I could see in her eyes the long train of thoughts begin, as she lifted the pipe again and began to warm the pellet of opium. She said, 'Are there skyscrapers in London?' and I loved her for the innocence of her question. She might lie from politeness, from fear, even for profit, but she would never have the cunning to keep her lie concealed.

'No,' I said, 'you have to go to America for them.'

She gave me a quick look over the needle and registered her mistake. Then as she kneaded the opium she began to talk at random of what clothes she would wear in London, where we should live, of the tube-trains she had read about in a novel, and the double-decker buses: would we fly or go by sea? 'And the Statue of Liberty . . .' she said.

'No, Phuong, that's American too.'

Chapter 2

1

AT least once a year the Caodaists hold a festival at the Holy See in Tanyin, which lies eighty kilometres to the north-west of Saigon, to celebrate such and such a year of Liberation, or of Conquest, or even a Buddhist, Confucian or Christian festival. Caodaism was always the favourite chapter of my briefing to visitors. Caodaism, the invention of a Cochin civil servant, was a synthesis of the three religions. The Holy See was at Tanyin. A Pope and female cardinals. Prophecy by planchette. Saint Victor Hugo. Christ and Buddha looking down from the roof of the Cathedral on a Walt Disney fantasia of the East, dragons and snakes in technicolour. Newcomers were always delighted with the description. How could one explain the dreariness of the whole business: the private army of twenty-five thousand men, armed with mortars made out of the exhaust-pipes of old cars, allies of the French who turned neutral at the moment of danger? To these celebrations, which helped to keep the peasants quiet, the Pope invited members of the Government (who would turn up if the Caodaists at the moment held office), the Diplomatic Corps (who would send a few second secretaries with their wives or girls) and the French Commander-in-Chief, who would detail a two-star general from an office job to represent him.

Along the route to Tanyin flowed a fast stream of staff and CD cars, and on the more exposed sections of the road Foreign Legionaries threw out cover across the rice-fields. It was always a day of some anxiety for the French High Command and perhaps a certain hope for the Caodaists, for what could more painlessly emphasize their own loyalty than to have a few important guests shot outside their territory?

Every kilometre a small mud watch tower stood up above the flat fields like an exclamation-mark, and every ten kilometres there was a larger fort manned by a platoon of Legionaries, Moroccans or Senegalese. Like the traffic into New York the cars kept one pace – and as with the traffic into New York you had a sense of controlled impatience, watching the next car ahead and in the mirror the car behind. Everybody wanted to reach Tanyin, see the show and get back as quickly as possible: curfew was at seven.

One passed out of the French-controlled rice-fields into the rice-fields of the Hoa-Haos and thence into the rice-fields of the Caodaists, who were usually at war with the Hoa-Haos: only the flags changed on the watch towers. Small naked boys sat on the buffaloes which waded genital-deep among the irrigated fields; where the gold harvest was ready the peasants in their hats like limpets winnowed the rice against little curved shelters of plaited bamboo. The cars drove rapidly by, belonging to another world.

Now the churches of the Caodaists would catch the attention of strangers in every village; pale blue and pink plasterwork and a big eye of God over the door. Flags increased: troops of peasants made their way along the road: we were approaching the Holy See. In the distance the sacred mountain stood like a green bowler hat above Tanyin – that was where General Thé held out, the dissident Chief of Staff who had recently declared his intention of fighting both the French and the Vietminh. The Caodaists made no attempt to capture him, although he had kidnapped a cardinal, but it was rumoured that he had done it with the Pope's connivance.

It always seemed hotter in Tanyin than anywhere else in the Southern Delta; perhaps it was the absence of water, perhaps it was the sense of interminable ceremonies which made one sweat vicariously, sweat for the troops standing to attention through the long speeches in a language they didn't understand, sweat for the Pope in his heavy chinoiserie robes. Only the female cardinals in their white silk trousers chatting to the priests in sun-helmets gave an impression of coolness under the glare; you couldn't believe it would ever be seven o'clock and cocktail-time on the roof of the Majestic, with a wind from Saigon river.

After the parade I interviewed the Pope's deputy. I didn't expect to get anything out of him and I was right: it was a convention on both sides. I asked him about General Thé.

'A rash man,' he said and dismissed the subject. He began his set speech, forgetting that I had heard it two years before – it reminded me of my own gramophone records for newcomers. Caodaism was a religious synthesis . . . the best of all religions . . . missionaries had been despatched to Los Angeles . . . the secrets of the Great Pyramid . . . He wore a long white soutane and he chain-smoked. There was something cunning and corrupt about him: the word 'love' occurred often. I was certain he knew that all of us were there to laugh at his movement; our air of respect was as corrupt as his phoney hierarchy, but we were less cunning. Our hypocrisy gained us nothing – not even a reliable ally, while theirs had procured arms, supplies, even cash down.

'Thank you, your Eminence.' I got up to go. He came with me to the door, scattering cigarette-ash.

'God's blessing on your work,' he said unctuously. 'Remember God loves the truth.'

'Which truth?' I asked.

'In the Caodaist faith all truths are reconciled and truth is love.'

He had a large ring on his finger and, when he held out his hand I really think he expected me to kiss it, but I am not a diplomat.

Under the bleak vertical sunlight I saw Pyle; he was trying in vain to make his Buick start. Somehow, during the last two weeks, at the bar of the Continental, in the only good bookshop in the rue Catinat, I had continually run into Pyle. The friendship which he had imposed from the beginning he now emphasized more than ever. His sad eyes would inquire with fervour after Phuong, while his lips expressed with even more fervour the strength of his affection and of his admiration – God save the mark – for me.

A Caodaist commandant stood beside the car talking rapidly. He stopped when I came up. I recognized him – he had been one of Thé's assistants before Thé took to the hills.

'Hullo, commandant,' I said, 'how's the General?'

'Which general?' he asked with a shy grin.

'Surely in the Caodaist faith,' I said, 'all generals are reconciled.'

'I can't make this car move, Thomas,' Pyle said.

'I will get a mechanic,' the commandant said, and left us.

'I interrupted you.'

'Oh, it was nothing,' Pyle said. 'He wanted to know how much a Buick cost. These people are so friendly when you treat them right. The French don't seem to know how to handle them.'

'The French don't trust them.'

Pyle said solemnly, 'A man becomes trustworthy when you trust him.' It sounded like a Caodaist maxim. I began to feel the air of Tanyin was too ethical for me to breathe.

'Have a drink,' Pyle said.

'There's nothing I'd like better.'

'I brought a thermos of lime-juice with me.' He leant over and busied himself with a basket in the back.

'Any gin?'

'No, I'm awfully sorry. You know,' he said encouragingly, 'lime-juice is very good for you in this climate. It contains – I'm not sure which vitamins.' He held out a cup to me and I drank.

'Anyway, it's wet,' I said.

'Like a sandwich? They're really awfully good. A new sandwich-spread called Vit-Health. My mother sent it from the States.'

'No, thanks, I'm not hungry.'

'It tastes rather like Russian salad – only sort of drier.'

'I don't think I will.'

'You don't mind if I do?'

'No, no, of course not.'

He took a large mouthful and it crunched and crackled. In the distance Buddha in white and pink stone rode away from his ancestral home and his valet – another statue – pursued him running. The female cardinals were drifting back to their house and the Eye of God watched us from above the Cathedral door.

'You know they are serving lunch here?' I said.

'I thought I wouldn't risk it. The meat – you have to be careful in this heat.'

'You are quite safe. They are vegetarian.'

'I suppose it's all right – but I like to know what I'm eating.' He took another munch at his Vit-Health. 'Do you think they have any reliable mechanics?'

'They know enough to turn your exhaust pipe into a mortar. I believe Buicks make the best mortars.'

The commandant returned and, saluting us smartly, said he had sent to the barracks for a mechanic. Pyle offered him a Vit-Health sandwich, which he refused politely. He said with a man-of-the-world air, 'We have so many rules here about food.' (He spoke excellent English.) 'So foolish. But you know what it is in a religious capital. I expect it is the same thing in Rome – or Canterbury,' he added with a neat natty little bow to me. Then he was silent. They were both silent. I had a strong impression that my company was not wanted. I couldn't resist the temptation to tease Pyle – it is, after all, the weapon of weakness and I was weak. I hadn't youth, seriousness, integrity, a future. I said, 'Perhaps after all I'll have a sandwich.'

'Oh, of course,' Pyle said, 'of course.' He paused before turning to the basket in the back.

'No, no,' I said. 'I was only joking. You two want to be alone.'

'Nothing of the kind,' Pyle said. He was one of the most inefficient liars I have ever known – it was an art he had obviously never practised.

He explained to the commandant, 'Thomas here's the best friend I have.'

'I know Mr Fowler,' the commandant said.

'I'll see you before I go, Pyle.' And I walked away to the Cathedral. I could get some coolness there.

Saint Victor Hugo in the uniform of the French Academy with the halo round his tricorn hat pointed at some noble sentiment Sun Yat Sen was inscribing on a tablet, and then I was in the nave. There was nowhere to sit except in the Papal chair, round which a plaster cobra coiled, the marble floor glittered like water and there was no glass in the windows. We make a cage for air with holes, I thought, and man makes a cage for his religion in much the same way – with doubts left open to the weather and creeds opening on innumerable interpretations. My wife had found her cage with holes and sometimes I envied her. There is a conflict between sun and air: I lived too much in the sun.

I walked the long empty nave – this was not the Indo-China I loved. The dragons with lion-like heads climbed the pulpit: on the roof Christ exposed his bleeding heart. Buddha sat, as Buddha always sits, with his lap empty. Confucius's beard hung meagrely down like a waterfall in the dry season. This was play-acting: the great globe above the altar was ambition: the basket with the movable lid in which the Pope worked his prophecies was trickery. If this Cathedral had existed for five centuries instead of two decades, would it have gathered a kind of convincingness with the scratches of feet and the erosion of weather? Would somebody who was convincible like my wife find here a faith she couldn't find in human beings? And if I had really wanted faith would I have found it in her Norman church? But I had never desired faith. The job of a reporter is to expose and record. I had never in my career discovered the inexplicable. The Pope worked his prophecies with a pencil in a movable lid and the people believed. In any vision somewhere you could find the planchette. I had no visions or miracles in my repertoire of memory.

I turned my memories over at random like pictures in an album: a fox I had seen by the light of an enemy flare over Orpington stealing along beside a fowl run, out of his russet place in the marginal country: the body of a bayoneted Malay which a Gurkha patrol had brought at the back of a lorry into a mining camp in Pahang, and the Chinese coolies stood by and giggled with nerves, while a brother Malay put a cushion under the dead head: a pigeon on a mantelpiece, poised for flight in a hotel bedroom: my wife's face at a window when I came home to say good-bye for the last time. My thoughts had begun and ended with her. She must have received my letter more than a week ago, and the cable I did not expect had not come. But they say if a jury remains out for long enough there is hope for the prisoner. In another week, if no letter arrived, could I begin to hope? All round me I could hear the cars of the soldiers and the diplomats revving up: the party was over for another year. The stampede back to Saigon was beginning, and curfew called. I went out to look for Pyle.

He was standing in a patch of shade with his commandant, and no one was doing anything to his car. The conversation seemed to be over, whatever it had been about, and they stood silently there, constrained by mutual politeness. I joined them.

'Well,' I said, 'I think I'll be off. You'd better be leaving too if you want to be in before curfew.'

'The mechanic hasn't turned up.'

'He will come soon,' the commandant said. 'He was in the parade.'

'You could spend the night,' I said. 'There's a special Mass – you'll find it quite an experience. It lasts three hours.'

'I ought to get back.'

'You won't get back unless you start now.' I added unwillingly, 'I'll give you a lift if you like and the commandant can have your car sent in to Saigon tomorrow.'

'You need not bother about curfew in Caodaist territory,' the commandant said smugly. 'But beyond . . . Certainly I will have your car sent tomorrow.'

'Exhaust intact,' I said, and he smiled brightly, neatly, efficiently, a military abbreviation of a smile.

2

The procession of cars was well ahead of us by the time we started. I put on speed to try to overtake it, but we had passed out of the Caodaist zone into the zone of the Hoa-Haos with not even a dust cloud ahead of us. The world was flat and empty in the evening.

It was not the kind of country one associates with ambush, but men could conceal themselves neck-deep in the drowned fields within a few yards of the road.

Pyle cleared his throat and it was the signal for an approaching intimacy. 'I hope Phuong's well,' he said.

'I've never known her ill.' One watch tower sank behind, another appeared, like weights on a balance.

'I saw her sister out shopping yesterday.'

'And I suppose she asked you to look in,' I said.

'As a matter of fact she did.'

'She doesn't give up hope easily.'

'Hope?'

'Of marrying you to Phuong.'

'She told me you are going away.'

'These rumours get about.'

Pyle said, 'You'd play straight with me, Thomas, wouldn't you?'

'Straight?'

'I've applied for a transfer,' he said. 'I wouldn't want her to be left without either of us.'

'I thought you were going to see your time out.'

He said without self-pity, 'I found I couldn't stand it.'

'When are you leaving?'

'I don't know. They thought something could be arranged in six months.'

'You can stand six months?'

'I've got to.'

'What reason did you give?'

'I told the Economic Attaché – you met him – Joe – more or less the facts.'

'I suppose he thinks I'm a bastard not to let you walk off with my girl.'

'Oh no, he rather sided with you.'

The car was spluttering and heaving – it had been spluttering for a minute, I think, before I noticed it, for I had been examining Pyle's innocent question: 'Are you playing straight?' It belonged to a psychological world of great simplicity, where you talked of Democracy and Honor without the *u* as it's spelt on old tombstones, and you meant what your father meant by the same words. I said, 'We've run out.'

'Gas?'

'There was plenty. I crammed it full before I started. Those bastards in Tanyin have syphoned it out. I ought to have noticed. It's like them to leave us enough to get out of their zone.'

'What shall we do?'

'We can just make the next watch tower. Let's hope they have a little.'

But we were out of luck. The car reached within thirty yards of the tower and gave up. We walked to the foot of the tower and I called up in French to the guards that we were friends, that we were coming up.

I had no wish to be shot by a Vietnamese sentry. There was no reply: nobody looked out. I said to Pyle, 'Have you a gun?'

'I never carry one.'

'Nor do I.'

The last colours of sunset, green and gold like the rice, were dripping over the edge of the flat world: against the grey neutral sky the watch tower looked as black as print. It must be nearly the hour of curfew. I shouted again and nobody answered.

'Do you know how many towers we passed since the last fort?'

'I wasn't noticing.'

'Nor was I.' It was probably at least six kilometres to the next fort – an hour's walk. I called a third time, and silence repeated itself like an answer.

I said, 'It seems to be empty: I'd better climb up and see.' The yellow flag with red stripes faded to orange showed that we were out of the territory of the Hoa-Haos and in the territory of the Vietnamese army.

Pyle said, 'Don't you think if we waited here a car might come?'

'It might, but *they* might come first.'

'Shall I go back and turn on the lights? For a signal.'

'Good God, no. Let it be.' It was dark enough now to stumble, looking for the ladder. Something cracked under foot; I could imagine the sound travelling across the fields of paddy, listened to by whom? Pyle had lost his outline and was a blur at the side of the road. Darkness, when once it fell, fell like a stone. I said, 'Stay there until I call.' I wondered whether the guard would have drawn up his ladder, but there it stood – though an enemy might climb it, it was their only way of escape. I began to mount.

I have read so often of people's thoughts in the moment of fear: of God, or family, or a woman. I admire their control. I thought of nothing, not even of the trap-door above me: I ceased, for those seconds, to exist: I was fear taken neat. At the top of the ladder I banged my head because fear couldn't count steps, hear, or see. Then my head came over the earth floor and nobody shot at me and fear seeped away.

3

A small oil lamp burned on the floor and two men crouched against the wall, watching me. One had a sten gun and one a rifle, but they were as scared as I'd been. They looked like schoolboys, but with the Vietnamese age drops suddenly like the sun – they are boys and then they are old men. I was glad that the colour of my skin and the shape of my eyes were a passport – they wouldn't shoot now even from fear.

I came up out of the floor, talking to reassure them, telling them that my car was outside, that I had run out of petrol. Perhaps they had a little I could buy. It didn't seem likely as I stared around. There was nothing in the little round room except a box of ammunition for the sten gun, a small wooden bed, and two packs hanging on a nail. A couple of pans with the remains of rice and some wooden chopsticks showed they had been eating without much appetite.

'Just enough to get us to the next fort?' I asked.

One of the men sitting against the wall – the one with the rifle – shook his head.

'If you can't we'll have to stay the night here.'

'*C'est défendu.*'

'Who by?'

'You are a civilian.'

'Nobody's going to make me sit out there on the road and have my throat cut.'

'Are you French?'

Only one man had spoken. The other sat with his head turned sideways, watching the slit in the wall. He could have seen nothing but a postcard of sky: he seemed to be listening and I began to listen too. The silence became full of sound: noises you couldn't put a name to – a crack, a creak, a rustle, something like a cough, and a whisper. Then I heard Pyle: he must have come to the foot of the ladder. 'You all right, Thomas?'

'Come up,' I called back. He began to climb the ladder and the silent soldier shifted his sten gun – I don't believe he'd heard a word of what we'd said: it was an awkward, jumpy movement. I realized that fear had paralysed him. I rapped out at him like a sergeant-major, 'Put that gun down!' and I used the kind of French obscenity I thought he would recognize. He obeyed me automatically. Pyle came up into the room. I said, 'We've been offered the safety of the tower till morning.'

'Fine,' Pyle said. His voice was a little puzzled. He said, 'Oughtn't one of those mugs to be on sentry?'

'They prefer not to be shot at. I wish you'd brought something stronger than lime-juice.'

'I guess I will next time,' Pyle said.

'We've got a long night ahead.' Now that Pyle was with me, I didn't hear the noises. Even the two soldiers seemed to have relaxed a little.

'What happens if the Viets attack them?' Pyle asked.

'They'll fire a shot and run. You read it every morning in the *Extrême Orient*. "A post south-west of Saigon was temporarily occupied last night by the Vietminh".'

'It's a bad prospect.'

'There are forty towers like this between us and Saigon. The chances always are that it's the other chap who's hurt.'

'We could have done with those sandwiches,' Pyle said. 'I do think one of them should keep a look-out.'

'He's afraid a bullet might look in.' Now that we too had settled on the floor, the Vietnamese relaxed a little. I felt some sympathy for them: it wasn't an easy job for a couple of ill-trained men to sit up here night after night, never sure of when the Viets might creep up on the road through the fields of paddy. I said to Pyle, 'Do you think they know they are fighting for Democracy? We ought to have York Harding here to explain it to them.'

'You always laugh at York,' said Pyle.

'I laugh at anyone who spends so much time writing about what doesn't exist – mental concepts.'

'They exist for him. Haven't you got any mental concepts? God, for instance?'

'I've no reason to believe in a God. Do you?'

'Yes. I'm a Unitarian.'

'How many hundred million Gods do people believe in? Why, even a Roman Catholic believes in quite a different God when he's scared or happy or hungry.'

'Maybe, if there is a God, he'd be so vast he'd look different to everyone.'

'Like the great Buddha in Bangkok,' I said. 'You can't see all of him at once. Anyway *he* keeps still.'

'I guess you're just trying to be tough,' Pyle said. 'There's something you must believe in. Nobody can go on living without some belief.'

'Oh, I'm not a Berkeleian. I believe my back's against this wall. I believe there's a sten gun over there.'

'I didn't mean that.'

'I believe what I report, which is more than most of your correspondents do.'

'Cigarette?'

'I don't smoke – except opium. Give one to the guards. We'd better stay friends with them.' Pyle got up and lit their cigarettes and came back. I said, 'I wish cigarettes had a symbolic significance like salt.'

'Don't you trust them?'

'No French officer,' I said, 'would care to spend the night alone with two scared guards in one of these towers. Why, even a platoon have been known to hand over their officers. Sometimes the Viets have a better success with a megaphone than a bazooka. I don't blame them. They don't believe in anything either. You and your like are trying to make a war with the help of people who just aren't interested.'

'They don't want Communism.'

'They want enough rice,' I said. 'They don't want to be shot at. They want one day to be much the same as another. They don't want our white skins around telling them what they want.'

'If Indo-China goes . . .'

'I know the record. Siam goes. Malaya goes. Indonesia goes. What does "go" mean? If I believed in your God and another life, I'd bet my future harp against your golden crown that in five hundred years there may be no New York or London, but they'll be growing paddy in these fields, they'll be carrying their produce to market on long poles wearing their pointed hats. The small hoys will be sitting on the buffaloes. I like the buffaloes, they don't like our smell, the smell of Europeans. And remember – from a buffalo's point of view you are a European too.'

'They'll be forced to believe what they are told, they won't be allowed a think for themselves.'

'Thought's a luxury. Do you think the peasant sits and thinks of God and Democracy when he gets inside his mud hut at night?'

'You talk as if the whole country were peasant. What about the educated? Are they going to be happy?'

'Oh no,' I said, 'we've brought them up in *our* ideas. We've taught them dangerous games, and that's why we are waiting here, hoping we don't get our throats cut. We deserve to have them cut. I wish your friend York was here too. I wonder how he'd relish it.'

'York Harding's a very courageous man. Why, in Korea . . .'

'He wasn't an enlisted man, was he? He had a return ticket. With a return ticket courage becomes an intellectual exercise, like a monk's flagellation. How much can I stick? Those poor devils can't catch a plane home. Hi,' I called to them, 'what are your names?' I thought that knowledge somehow would bring them into the circle of our conversation. They didn't answer: just lowered back at us behind the stumps of their cigarettes. 'They think we are French,' I said.

'That's just it,' Pyle said. 'You shouldn't be against York, you should be against the French. Their colonialism.'

'Isms and ocracies. Give me facts. A rubber planter beats his labourer

– all right, I'm against him. He hasn't been instructed to do it by the Minister of the Colonies. In France I expect he'd beat his wife. I've seen a priest, so poor he hasn't a change of trousers, working fifteen hours a day from hut to hut in a cholera epidemic, eating nothing but rice and salt fish, saying his Mass with an old cup – a wooden platter. I don't believe in God and yet I'm for that priest. Why don't you call that colonialism?'

'It *is* colonialism. York says it's often the good administrators who make it hard to change a bad system.'

'Anyway the French are dying every day – that's not a mental concept. They aren't leading these people on with half-lies like your politicians – and ours. I've been in India, Pyle, and I know the harm liberals do. We haven't a liberal party any more – liberalism's infected all the other parties. We are all either liberal conservatives or liberal socialists: we all have a good conscience. I'd rather be an exploiter who fights for what he exploits, and dies with it. Look at the history of Burma. We go and invade the country: the local tribes support us: we are victorious: but like you Americans we weren't colonialists in those days. Oh no, we made peace with the king and we handed him back his province and left our allies to be crucified and sawn in two. They were innocent. They thought we'd stay. But we were liberals and we didn't want a bad conscience.'

'That was a long time ago.'

'We shall do the same thing here. Encourage them and leave them with a little equipment and a toy industry.'

'Toy industry?'

'Your plastic.'

'Oh yes, I see.'

'I don't know what I'm talking politics for. They don't interest me and I'm a reporter. I'm not *engagé*.'

'Aren't you?' Pyle said.

'For the sake of an argument – to pass this bloody night, that's all. I don't take sides. I'll be still reporting, whoever wins.'

'If they win, you'll be reporting lies.'

'There's usually a way round, and I haven't noticed much regard for truth in our papers either.'

I think the fact of our sitting there talking encouraged the two soldiers: perhaps they thought the sound of our white voices – for voices have a colour too, yellow voice sing and black voices gargle, while ours just speak – would give an impression of numbers and keep the Viets away. They picked up their pans and began to eat again, scraping with their chopsticks, eyes watching Pyle and me over the rim of the pan.

'So you think we've lost?'

'That's not the point,' I said. 'I've no particular desire to see you win. I'd like those two poor buggers there to be happy – that's all. I wish they didn't have to sit in the dark at night scared.'

'You have to fight for liberty.'

'I haven't seen any Americans fighting around here. And as for liberty, I don't know what it means. Ask them.' I called across the floor in French to them. '*La liberté – qu'est ce que c'est la liberté?*' They sucked in the rice and stared back and said nothing.

Pyle said, 'Do you want everybody to be made in the same mould? You're arguing for the sake of arguing. You're an intellectual. You stand for the importance of the individual as much as I do – or York.'

'Why have we only just discovered it?' I said. 'Forty years ago no one talked that way.'

'It wasn't threatened then.'

'Ours wasn't threatened, oh no, but who cared about the individuality of the man in the paddy field – and who does now? The only man to treat him as a man is the political commissar. He'll sit in his hut and ask his name and listen to his complaints; he'll give up an hour a day to teaching him – it doesn't matter what, he's being treated like a man, like someone of value. Don't go on in the East with that parrot cry about a threat to the individual soul. Here you'd find yourself on the wrong side – it's they who stand for the individual and we just stand for Private 23987, unit in the global strategy.'

'You don't mean half what you are saying,' Pyle said uneasily.

'Probably three quarters. I've been here a long time. You know, it's lucky I'm not *engagé*, there are things I might be tempted to do – because here in the East – well, I don't like Ike. I like – well, these two. This is their country. What's the time? My watch has stopped.'

'It's turned eight-thirty.'

'Ten hours and we can move.'

'It's going to be quite chilly,' Pyle said and shivered. 'I never expected that.'

'There's water all round. I've got a blanket in the car. That will be enough.'

'Is it safe?'

'It's early for the Viets.'

'Let me go.'

'I'm more used to the dark.'

When I stood up the soldiers stopped eating. I told them, '*Je reviens, tout de suite*.' I dangled my legs over the trap door, found the ladder and went down. It is odd how reassuring conversation is, especially on abstract subjects: it seems to normalize the strangest surroundings. I was no longer scared: it was as though I had left a room and would be returning there to pick up the argument – the watch tower was the rue Catinat, the bar of the Majestic, or even a room off Gordon Square.

I stood below the tower for a minute to get my vision back. There was starlight, but no moonlight. Moonlight reminds me of a mortuary and the cold wash of an unshaded globe over a marble slab, but starlight is alive and never still, it is almost as though someone in those vast spaces is trying to communicate a message of good will, for even the names of the stars are friendly. Venus is any woman we love, the Bears are the bears of childhood, and I suppose the Southern Cross, to those, like my wife, who believe, may be a favourite hymn or a prayer beside the bed. Once I shivered as Pyle had done. But the night was hot enough, only the shallow stretch of water on either side gave a kind of icing to the warmth. I started out towards the car, and for a moment when I stood on the road I thought it was no longer there. That shook my confidence, even after I remembered that it had petered out thirty yards away. I couldn't help walking with my shoulders bent: I felt more unobtrusive that way.

I had to unlock the boot to get the blanket and the click and squeak startled me in the silence. I didn't relish being the only noise in what must have been a night full of people. With the blanket over my shoulder I lowered the boot more carefully than I had raised it, and then, just as the catch caught, the sky towards Saigon flared with light and the sound of an explosion came rumbling down the road. A bren spat and spat and was quiet again before the rumbling stopped. I thought, 'Somebody's had it,' and very far away heard voices crying with pain or fear or perhaps even triumph. I don't know why, but I had thought all the time of an attack coming from behind, along the road we had passed, and I had a moment's sense of unfairness that the Viets should be there ahead, between us and Saigon. It was as though we had been unconsciously driving towards danger instead of away from it, just as I was now walking in its direction, back towards the tower. I walked because it was less noisy than to run, but my body wanted to run.

At the foot of the ladder I called up to Pyle, 'It's me – Fowler.' (Even then I couldn't bring myself to use my Christian name to him.) The scene inside the hut had changed. The pans of rice were back on the floor; one man held his rifle on his hip and sat against the wall staring at Pyle and Pyle knelt a little way out from the opposite wall with his eyes on the sten gun which lay between him and the second guard. It was as though he had begun to crawl towards it but had been halted. The second guard's arm was extended towards the gun: no one had fought or even threatened, it was like that child's game when you mustn't be seen to move or you are sent back to base to start again.

'What's going on?' I said.

The two guards looked at me and Pyle pounced, pulling the sten to his side of the room.

'Is it a game?' I asked.

'I don't trust him with the gun,' Pyle said, 'if they are coming.'

'Ever used a sten?'

'No.'

'That's fine. Nor have I. I'm glad it's loaded – we wouldn't know how to reload it.'

The guards had quietly accepted the loss of the gun. The one lowered his rifle and laid it across his thighs; the other slumped against the wall and shut his eyes as though like a child he believed himself invisible in the dark. Perhaps he was glad to have no more responsibility. Somewhere far away the bren started again – three bursts and then silence. The second guard screwed his eyes closer shut.

'They don't know we can't use it,' Pyle said.

'They are supposed to be on our side.'

'I thought you didn't have a side.'

'*Touché*,' I said. 'I wish the Viets knew it.'

'What's happening out there?'

I quoted again tomorrow's *Extrême Orient*: 'A post fifty kilometres outside Saigon was attacked and temporarily captured last night by Vietminh irregulars.'

'Do you think it would be safer in the fields?'

'It would be terribly wet.'

'You don't seem worried,' Pyle said.

'I'm scared stiff – but things are better than they might be. They don't usually attack more than three posts in a night. Our chances have improved.'

'What's that?'

It was the sound of a heavy car coming up the road, driving towards Saigon. I went to the rifle slit and looked down, just as a tank went by.

'The patrol,' I said. The gun in the turret shifted now to this side, now to that. I wanted to call out to them, but what was the good? They hadn't room on board for two useless civilians. The earth floor shook a little as they passed, and they had gone. I looked at my watch – eight fifty-one, and waited, straining to read when the light flapped. It was like judging the distance of lightning by the delay before the thunder. It was nearly four minutes before the gun opened up. Once I thought I detected a bazooka replying, then all was quiet again.

'When they come back,' Pyle said, 'we could signal them for a lift to the camp.'

An explosion set the floor shaking. 'If they come back,' I said. 'That sounded like a mine.' When I looked at my watch again it had passed nine fifteen and the tank had not returned. There had been no more firing.

I sat down beside Pyle and stretched out my legs. 'We'd better try to sleep,' I said. 'There's nothing else we can do.'

'I'm not happy about the guards,' Pyle said.

'They are all right so long as the Viets don't turn up. Put the sten under your leg for safety.' I closed my eyes and tried to imagine myself somewhere else – sitting up in one of the fourth-class compartments the German railways ran before Hitler came to power, in the days when one was young and sat up all night without melancholy, when waking dreams were full of hope and not of fear. This was the hour when Phuong always set about preparing my evening pipes. I wondered whether a letter was waiting for me – I hoped not, for I knew what a letter would contain, and so long as none arrived I could day-dream of the impossible.

'Are you asleep?' Pyle asked.

'No.'

'Don't you think we ought to pull up the ladder?'

'I begin to understand why they don't. It's the only way out.'

'I wish that tank would come back.'

'It won't now.'

I tried not to look at my watch except at long intervals, and the intervals were never as long as they had seemed. Nine forty, ten five, ten twelve, ten thirty-two, ten forty-one.

'You awake?' I said to Pyle.

'Yes.'

'What are you thinking about?'

He hesitated. 'Phuong,' he said.

'Yes?'

'I was just wondering what she was doing.'

'I can tell you that. She'll have decided that I'm spending the night at Tanyin – it won't be the first time. She'll be lying on the bed with a joss stick burning to keep away the mosquitoes and she'll be looking at the pictures in an old *Paris-Match*. Like the French she has a passion for the Royal Family.'

He said wistfully, 'It must be wonderful to know exactly,' and I could imagine his soft dog's eyes in the dark. They ought to have called him Fido, not Alden.

'I don't really know – but it's probably true. There's no good in being jealous when you can't do anything about it. "No barricado for a belly."'

'Sometimes I hate the way you talk, Thomas. Do you know how she seems to me? She seems fresh, like a flower.'

'Poor flower,' I said. 'There are a lot of weeds around.'

'Where did you meet her?'

'She was dancing at the Grand Monde.'

'Dancing,' he exclaimed, as though the idea were painful.

'It's a perfectly respectable profession,' I said. 'Don't worry.'

'You have such an awful lot of experience, Thomas.'

'I have an awful lot of years. When you reach my age . . .'

'I've never had a girl,' he said, 'not properly. Not what you'd call a real experience.'

'A lot of energy with your people seems to go into whistling.'

'I've never told anybody else.'

'You're young. It's nothing to be ashamed of.'

'Have you had a lot of women, Fowler?'

'I don't know what a lot means. Not more than four women have had any importance to me – or me to them. The other forty-odd – one wonders why one does it. A notion of hygiene, of one's social obligations, both mistaken.'

'You think they *are* mistaken?'

'I wish I could have those nights back. I'm still in love, Pyle, and I'm a wasting asset. Oh, and there was pride, of course. It takes a long time before we cease to feel proud of being wanted. Though God knows why we should feel it, when we look around and see who is wanted too.'

'You don't think there's anything wrong with me, do you, Thomas?'

'No, Pyle.'

'It doesn't mean I don't *need* it, Thomas, like everybody else. I'm not – odd.'

'Not one of us needs it as much as we say. There's an awful lot of self-hypnosis around. Now I know I need nobody – except Phuong.

But that's a thing one learns with time. I could go a year without one restless night if she wasn't there.'

'But she *is* there,' he said in a voice I could hardly catch.

'One starts promiscuous and ends like one's grandfather, faithful to one woman.'

'I suppose it seems pretty naïve to start that way . . .'

'No.'

'It's not in the Kinsey Report.'

'That's why it's not naïve.'

'You know, Thomas, it's pretty good being here, talking to you like this. Somehow it doesn't seem dangerous any more.'

'We used to feel that in the blitz,' I said, 'when a lull came. But they always returned.'

'If somebody asked you what your deepest sexual experience had been, what would you say?'

I knew the answer to that. 'Lying in bed early one morning and watching a woman in a red dressing-gown brush her hair.'

'Joe said it was being in bed with a Chink and a negress at the same time.'

'I'd have thought that one up too when I was twenty.'

'Joe's fifty.'

'I wonder what mental age they gave him in the war.'

'Was Phuong the girl in the red dressing-gown?'

I wished that he hadn't asked that question.

'No,' I said, 'that woman came earlier. When I left my wife.'

'What happened?'

'I left her, too.'

'Why?'

Why indeed? 'We are fools,' I said, 'when we love. I was terrified of losing her. I thought I saw her changing – I don't know if she really was, but I couldn't bear the uncertainty any longer. I ran towards the finish just like a coward runs towards the enemy and wins a medal. I wanted to get death over.'

'Death?'

'It was a kind of death. Then I came east.'

'And found Phuong?'

'Yes.'

'But don't you find the same thing with Phuong?'

'Not the same. You see, the other one loved me. I was afraid of losing love. Now I'm only afraid of losing Phuong.' Why had I said that, I wondered? He didn't need encouragement from me.

'But she loves you, doesn't she?'

'Not like that. It isn't in their nature. You'll find that out. It's a cliché to call them children – but there's one thing which is childish. They love you in return for kindness, security, the presents you give them – they hate you for a blow or an injustice. They don't know what it's like – just walking into a room and loving a stranger. For an aging man, Pyle, it's very secure – she won't run away from home so long as the home is happy.'

I hadn't meant to hurt him. I only realized I had done it when he said with muffled anger, 'She might prefer greater security or more kindness.'

'Perhaps.'

'Aren't you afraid of that?'

'Not so much as I was of the other.'

'Do you love her at all?'

'Oh yes, Pyle, yes. But that other way I've only loved once.'

'In spite of the forty-odd women,' he snapped at me.

'I'm sure it's below the Kinsey average. You know, Pyle, women don't want virgins. I'm not sure *we* do, unless we are a pathological type.'

'I didn't mean I was a virgin,' he said. All my conversations with Pyle seemed to take grotesque directions. Was it because of his sincerity that they so ran off the customary rails? His conversation never took the corners.

'You can have a hundred women and still be a virgin, Pyle. Most of your GIs who were hanged for rape in the war were virgins. We don't have so many in Europe. I'm glad. They do a lot of harm.'

'I just don't understand you, Thomas.'

'It's not worth explaining. I'm bored with the subject anyway. I've reached the age when sex isn't the problem so much as old age and death. I wake up with these in mind and not a woman's body. I just don't want to be alone in my last decade, that's all. I wouldn't know what to think about all day long. I'd sooner have a woman in the same room – even one I didn't love. But if Phuong left me, would I have the energy to find another? . . .'

'If that's all she means to you . . .'

'All, Pyle? Wait until you're afraid of living ten years alone with no companion and a nursing home at the end of it. Then you'll start running in any direction, even away from that girl in the red dressing-gown, to find someone, anyone, who will last until you are through.'

'Why don't you go back to your wife, then?'

'It's not easy to live with someone you've injured.'

A sten gun fired a long burst – it couldn't have been more than a mile away. Perhaps a nervous sentry was shooting at shadows: perhaps another attack had begun. I hoped it was an attack – it increased our chances.

'Are you scared, Thomas?'

'Of course I am. With all my instincts. But with my reason I know it's better to die like this. That's why I came east. Death stays with you.' I looked at my watch. It had gone eleven. An eight-hour night and then we could relax. I said, 'We seem to have talked about pretty nearly everything except God. We'd better leave him to the small hours.'

'You don't believe in Him, do you?'

'No.'

'Things to me wouldn't make sense without Him.'

'They don't make sense to me with him.'

'I read a book once . . .'

I never knew what book Pyle had read. (Presumably it wasn't York Harding or Shakespeare or the anthology of contemporary verse or *The Physiology of Marriage* – perhaps it was *The Triumph of Life*.) A voice came right into the tower with us, it seemed to speak from the shadows by the trap – a hollow megaphone voice saying something in Vietnamese. 'We're for it,' I said. The two guards listened, their faces turned to the rifle slit, their mouths hanging open.

'What is it?' Pyle asked.

Walking to the embrasure was like walking through the voice. I looked quickly out: there was nothing to be seen – I couldn't even distinguish the road and when I looked back into the room the rifle was pointed, I wasn't sure whether at me or at the slit. But when I moved round the wall the rifle wavered, hesitated, kept me covered: the voice went on saying the same thing over again. I sat down and the rifle was lowered.

'What's he saying?' Pyle asked.

'I don't know. I expect they've found the car and are telling these chaps to hand us over or else. Better pick up that sten before they make up their minds.'

'He'll shoot.'

'He's not sure yet. When he is he'll shoot anyway.'

Pyle shifted his leg and the rifle came up.

'I'll move along the wall,' I said. 'When his eyes waver get him covered.'

Just as I rose the voice stopped: the silence made me jump. Pyle said sharply, 'Drop your rifle.' I had just time to wonder whether the sten was unloaded – I hadn't bothered to look – when the man threw his rifle down.

I crossed the room and picked it up. Then the voice began again – I had the impression that no syllable had changed. Perhaps they used a record. I wondered when the ultimatum would expire.

'What happens next?' Pyle asked, like a schoolboy watching a demonstration in the laboratory: he didn't seem personally concerned.

'Perhaps a bazooka, perhaps a Viet.'

Pyle examined his sten. 'There doesn't seem any mystery about this,' he said. 'Shall I fire a burst?'

'No, let them hesitate. They'd rather take the post without firing and it gives us time. We'd better clear out fast.'

'They may be waiting at the bottom.'

'Yes.'

The two men watched us – I write men, but I doubt whether they had accumulated forty years between them. 'And these?' Pyle asked, and he added with a shocking directness, 'Shall I shoot them?' Perhaps he wanted to try the sten.

'They've done nothing.'

'They were going to hand us over.'

'Why not?' I said. 'We've no business here. It's their country.'

I unloaded the rifle and laid it on the floor. 'Surely you're not leaving that,' he said.

'I'm too old to run with a rifle. And this isn't my war. Come on.'

It wasn't my war, but I wished those others in the dark knew that as well. I blew the oil-lamp out and dangled my legs over the trap, feeling for the ladder. I could hear the guards whispering to each other like crooners, in their language like a song. 'Make straight ahead,' I told Pyle, 'aim for the rice. Remember there's water – I don't know how deep. Ready?'

'Yes.'

'Thanks for the company.'

'Always a pleasure,' Pyle said.

I heard the guards moving behind us: I wondered if they had knives. The megaphone voice spoke peremptorily as though offering a last chance. Something shifted softly in the dark below us, but it might have been a rat. I hesitated. 'I wish to God I had a drink,' I whispered.

'Let's go.'

Something was coming up the ladder: I heard nothing, but the ladder shook under my feet.

'What's keeping you?' Pyle said.

I don't know why I thought of it as something, that silent stealthy approach. Only a man could climb a ladder, and yet I couldn't think of it as a man like myself – it was as though an animal were moving in to kill, very quietly and certainly with the remorselessness of another kind of creation. The ladder shook and shook and I imagined I saw its eyes glaring upwards. Suddenly I could bear it no longer and I jumped, and there was nothing there at all but the spongy ground, which took my ankle and twisted it as a hand might have done. I could hear Pyle coming down the ladder; I realized I had been a frightened fool who could not recognize his own trembling, and I had believed I was tough and unimaginative, all that a truthful observer and reporter should be. I got on my feet and nearly fell again with the pain. I started out for the field dragging one foot after me and heard Pyle coming behind me. Then the bazooka shell burst on the tower and I was on my face again.

4

'Are you hurt?' Pyle said.

'Something hit my leg. Nothing serious.'

'Let's get on,' Pyle urged me. I could just see him because he seemed to be covered with a fine white dust. Then he simply went out like a picture on the screen when the lamps of the projector fail: only the soundtrack continued. I got gingerly up on to my good knee and tried to rise without putting any weight on my bad left ankle, and then I was down again breathless with pain. It wasn't my ankle: something had happened to my left leg. I couldn't worry – pain took away care. I lay very still on the ground hoping that pain wouldn't find me again. I even held my breath, as one does with toothache. I didn't think about the Viets who would soon be searching the ruins of the tower: another shell exploded on it – they were making quite sure before they came in. What a lot of money it costs, I thought as the pain receded, to kill a few human beings – you can kill horses so much cheaper. I can't have been fully conscious, for I began to think I had strayed into a knacker's yard which was the terror of my childhood in the small town where I was born. We used to think we heard the horses whinnying with fear and the explosion of the painless killer.

It was some while since the pain had returned, now that I was lying still and holding my breath – that seemed to me just as important. I wondered quite lucidly whether perhaps I ought to crawl towards the fields. The Viets might not have time to search far. Another patrol would be out by now trying to contact the crew of the first tank. But I was more afraid of the pain than of the partisans, and I lay still. There was no sound anywhere of Pyle: he must have reached the fields. Then I heard someone weeping. It came from the direction of the tower, or what had been the tower. It wasn't like a man weeping: it was like a child who is frightened of the dark and yet afraid to scream. I supposed it was one of the two boys – perhaps his companion had been killed. I hoped that the Viets wouldn't cut his throat. One shouldn't fight a war with children and a little curled body in a ditch came back to mind. I shut my eyes – that helped to keep the pain away, too, and waited. A voice called something I didn't understand. I almost felt I could sleep in this darkness and loneliness and absence of pain.

Then I heard Pyle whispering, 'Thomas. Thomas.' He had learnt footcraft quickly; I had not heard him return.

'Go away,' I whispered back.

He found me then and lay down flat beside me. 'Why didn't you come? Are you hurt?'

'My leg. I think it's broken.'

'A bullet?'

'No, no. Log of wood. Stone. Something from the tower. It's not bleeding.'

'You've got to make an effort.'

'Go away, Pyle. I don't want to, it hurts too much.'

'Which leg?'

'Left.'

He crept round to my side and hoisted my arm over his shoulder. I wanted to whimper like the boy in the tower and then I was angry, but it was hard to express anger in a whisper. 'God damn you, Pyle, leave me alone. I want to stay.'

'You can't.'

He was pulling me half on to his shoulder and the pain was intolerable. 'Don't be a bloody hero. I don't want to go.'

'You've got to help,' he said, 'or we are both caught.'

'You . . .'

'Be quiet or they'll hear you.' I was crying with vexation – you couldn't use a stronger word. I hoisted myself against him and let my left leg dangle – we were like awkward contestants in a three-legged race and we wouldn't have stood a chance if, at the moment we set off, a bren had not begun to fire in quick short bursts somewhere down the road towards the next tower. Perhaps a patrol was pushing up or perhaps they were completing their score of three towers destroyed. It covered the noise of our slow and clumsy flight.

I'm not sure whether I was conscious all the time: I think for the last twenty yards Pyle must have almost carried my weight. He said, 'Careful here. We are going in.' The dry rice rustled around us and the mud squelched and rose. The water was up to our waists when Pyle stopped. He was panting and a catch in his breath made him sound like a bull-frog.

'I'm sorry,' I said.

'Couldn't leave you,' Pyle said.

The first sensation was relief; the water and mud held my leg tenderly and firmly like a bandage, but soon the cold set us chattering. I wondered whether it had passed midnight yet; we might have six hours of this if the Viets didn't find us.

'Can you shift your weight a little,' Pyle said, 'just for a moment?' And my unreasoning irritation came back – I had no excuse for it but the pain. I hadn't asked to be saved, or to have death so painfully postponed. I thought with nostalgia of my couch on the hard dry ground. I stood like a crane on one leg trying to relieve Pyle of my weight, and when I moved, the stalks of rice tickled and cut and crackled.

'You saved my life there,' I said, and Pyle cleared his throat for the conventional response, 'so that I could die here. I prefer dry land.'

'Better not talk,' Pyle said as though to an invalid.

'Who the hell asked you to save my life? I came east to be killed. It's like your damned impertinence . . .' I staggered in the mud and Pyle hoisted my arm around his shoulder. 'Ease it off,' he said.

'You've been seeing war-films. We aren't a couple of marines and you can't win a war-medal.'

'Sh-sh.' Footsteps could be heard, coming down to the edge of the field. The bren up the road stopped firing and there was no sound except the footsteps and the slight rustle of the rice when we breathed. Then the footsteps halted: they only seemed the length of a room away. I felt Pyle's hand on my good side pressing me slowly down; we sank together into the mud very slowly so as to make the least disturbance of the rice. On one knee, by straining my head backwards, I could just keep my mouth out of the water. The pain came back to my leg and I thought, 'If I faint here I drown' – I had always hated and feared the thought of drowning. Why can't one choose one's death? There was no sound now: perhaps twenty feet away they were waiting for a rustle, a cough, a sneeze – 'Oh God,' I thought, 'I'm going to sneeze.' If only he had left me alone, I would have heen responsible only for my own life – not his – and he wanted to live. I pressed my free fingers against my upper lip in that trick we learn when we are children playing at Hide and Seek, but the sneeze lingered, waiting to burst, and silent in the darkness the others waited for the sneeze. It was coming, coming, came . . .

But in the very second that my sneeze broke, the Viets opened with stens, drawing a line of fire through the rice – it swallowed my sneeze with its sharp drilling like a machine punching holes through steel. I took a breath and went under – so instinctively one avoids the loved thing, coquetting with death, like a woman who demands to be raped by her lover. The rice was lashed down over our heads and the storm passed. We came up for air at the same moment and heard the footsteps going away back towards the tower.

'We've made it,' Pyle said, and even in my pain I wondered what we'd made: for me, old age, an editor's chair, loneliness; and as for him, I know now that he spoke prematurely. Then in the cold we settled down to wait. Along the road to Tanyin a bonfire burst into life: it burnt merrily like a celebration.

'That's my car,' I said.

Pyle said, 'It's a shame, Thomas. I hate to see waste.'

'There must have been just enough petrol in the tank to set it going. Are you as cold as I am, Pyle?'

'I couldn't be colder.'

'Suppose we get out and lie flat on the road?'

'Let's give them another half hour.'

'The weight's on you.'

'I can stick it, I'm young.' He had meant the claim humorously, but it struck as cold as the mud. I had intended to apologize for the way my pain had spoken, but now it spoke again. 'You're young all right. You can afford to wait, can't you.'

'I don't get you, Thomas.'

We had spent what seemed to have been a week of nights together, but he could no more understand me than he could understand French. I said, 'You'd have done better to let me be.'

'I couldn't have faced Phuong,' he said, and the name lay there like a banker's bid. I took it up.

'So it was for her,' I said. What made my jealousy more absurd and humiliating was that it had to be expressed in the lowest of whispers – it had no tone, and jealousy likes histrionics. 'You think these heroics will get her. How wrong you are. If I were dead you could have had her.'

'I didn't mean that,' Pyle said. 'When you are in love you want to play the game, that's all.' That's true, I thought, but not as he innocently means it. To be in love is to see yourself as someone else sees you, it is to be in love with the falsified and exalted image of yourself. In love we are incapable of honour – the courageous act is no more than playing a part to an audience of two. Perhaps I was no longer in love but I remembered.

'If it had been you, I'd have left you,' I said.

'Oh no, you wouldn't, Thomas.' He added with unbearable complacency, 'I know you better than you do yourself.' Angrily I tried to move away from him and take my own weight, but the pain came roaring back like a train in a tunnel and I leant more heavily against him, before I began to sink into the water. He got both arms round me and held me up, and then inch by inch he began to edge me to the bank and the roadside. When he got me there he lowered me flat in the shallow mud below the bank at the edge of the field, and when the pain retreated and I opened my eyes and ceased to hold my breath, I could see only the elaborate cypher of the constellations – a foreign cypher which I couldn't read: they were not the stars of home. His face wheeled over me, blotting them out. 'I'm going down the road, Thomas, to find a patrol.'

'Don't be a fool,' I said. 'They'll shoot you before they know who you are. If the Viets don't get you.'

'It's the only chance. You can't lie in the water for six hours.'

'Then lay me in the road.'

'It's no good leaving you the sten?' he asked doubtfully.

'Of course it's not. If you are determined to be a hero, at least go slowly through the rice.'

'The patrol would pass before I could signal it.'

'You don't speak French.'

'I shall call out "*Je suis Frongçais*". Don't worry, Thomas. I'll be very careful.' Before I could reply he was out of a whisper's range – he was moving as quietly as he knew how, with frequent pauses. I could see him in the light of the burning car, but no shot came; soon he passed beyond the flames and very soon the silence filled the footprints. Oh yes, he was being careful as he had been careful boating down the river into Phat Diem, with the caution of a hero in a boy's adventure-story, proud of his caution like a Scout's badge and quite unaware of the absurdity and the improbability of his adventure.

I lay and listened for the shots from the Viets or a Legion patrol, but none came – it would probably take him an hour or even more before he reached a tower, if he ever reached it. I turned my head enough to see what remained of our tower, a heap of mud and bamboo and struts which seemed to sink lower as the flames of the car sank. There was peace when the pain went – a kind of Armistice Day of the nerves: I wanted to sing. I thought how strange it was that men of my profession would make only two news-lines out of all this night – it was just a common-or-garden night and I was the only strange thing about it. Then I heard a low crying begin again from what was left of the tower. One of the guards must still be alive.

I thought, 'Poor devil, if we hadn't broken down outside *his* post, he could have surrendered as they nearly all surrendered, or fled, at the first call from the megaphone. But we were there – two white men, and we had the sten and they didn't dare to move. When we left it was too late.' I was responsible for that voice crying in the dark: I had prided myself on detachment, on not belonging to this war, but those wounds had been inflicted by me just as though I had used the sten, as Pyle had wanted to do.

I made an effort to get over the bank into the road. I wanted to join him. It was the only thing I could do, to share his pain. But my own personal pain pushed me back. I couldn't hear him any more. I lay still and heard nothing but my own pain beating like a monstrous heart and held my breath and prayed to the God I didn't believe in, 'Let me die or faint. Let me die or faint'; and then I suppose I fainted and was aware of nothing until I dreamed that my eyelids had frozen together and someone was inserting a chisel to prise them apart, and I wanted to warn them not to damage the eyeballs beneath but couldn't speak and the chisel bit through and a torch was shining on my face.

'We made it, Thomas,' Pyle said. I remember that, but I don't remember what Pyle later described to others: that I waved my hand in the wrong direction and told them there was a man in the tower and they had to see to him. Anyway I couldn't have made the sentimental assumption that Pyle made. I know myself, and I know the depth of my selfishness. I cannot be at ease (and to be at ease is my chief wish) if someone else is in pain, visibly or audibly or tactually. Sometimes this is mistaken by the innocent for unselfishness, when all I am doing is sacrificing a small good – in this case postponement in attending to my hurt – for the sake of a far greater good, a peace of mind when I need think only of myself.

They came back to tell me the boy was dead, and I was happy – I didn't even have to suffer much pain after the hypodermic of morphia had bitten my leg.

Chapter 3

1

I CAME slowly up the stairs to the flat in the rue Catinat, pausing and resting on the first landing. The old women gossiped as they always had done, squatting on the floor outside the urinoir, carrying Fate in the lines of their faces as others on the palm. They were silent as I passed and I wondered what they might have told me, if I had known their language, of what had passed while I had been away in the Legion Hospital back on the road towards Tanyin. Somewhere in the tower and the fields I had lost my keys, but I had sent a message to Phuong which she must have received, if she was still there. That 'if' was the measure of my uncertainty. I had had no news of her in hospital, but she wrote French with difficulty, and I couldn't read Vietnamese. I knocked on the door and it opened immediately and everything seemed to be the same. I watched her closely while she asked how I was and touched my splinted leg and gave me her shoulder to lean on, as though one could lean with safety on so young a plant. I said, 'I'm glad to be home.'

She told me that she had missed me, which of course was what I wanted to hear: she always told me what I wanted to hear, like a coolie answering questions, unless by accident. Now I awaited the accident.

'How have you amused yourself?' I asked.

'Oh, I have seen my sister often. She has found a post with the Americans.'

'She has, has she? Did Pyle help?'

'Not Pyle. Joe.'

'Who's Joe?'

'You know him. The Economic Attaché.'

'Oh, of course, Joe.'

He was a man one always forgot. To this day I cannot describe him, except his fatness and his powdered clean-shaven cheeks and his big laugh; all his identity escapes me – except that he was called Joe. There are some men whose names are always shortened.

With Phuong's help I stretched myself on the bed. 'Seen any movies?' I asked.

'There is a very funny one at the Catinat,' and immediately she began to tell me the plot in great detail, while I looked around the room for the white envelope that might be a telegram. So long as I didn't ask, I could believe that she had forgotten to tell me, and it might be there on the table by the typewriter, or on the wardrobe, perhaps put for safety in the cupboard-drawer where she kept her collection of scarves.

'The postmaster – I think he was the postmaster, but he may have been the mayor – followed them home, and he borrowed a ladder from the baker and he climbed through Corinne's window, but, you see, she had gone into the next room with François, but he did not hear Mme Bompierre coming and she came in and saw him at the top of the ladder and thought . . .'

'Who was Mme Bompierre?' I asked, turning my head to see the wash-basin, where sometimes she propped reminders among the lotions.

'I told you. She was Corinne's mother and she was looking for a husband because she was a widow . . .'

She sat on the bed and put her hand inside my shirt. 'It was very funny,' she said.

'Kiss me, Phuong.' She had no coquetry. She did at once what I asked and she went on with the story of the film. Just so she would have made love if I had asked her to, straight away, peeling off her trousers without question, and afterwards have taken up the thread of Mme Bompierre's story and the postmaster's predicament.

'Has a call come for me?'

'Yes.'

'Why didn't you give it me?'

'It is too soon for you to work. You must lie down and rest.'

'This may not be work.'

She gave it me and I saw that it had been opened. It read: 'Four hundred words background wanted effect de Lattre's departure on military and political situation.'

'Yes,' I said. 'It *is* work. How did you know? Why did you open it?'

'I thought it was from your wife. I hoped that it was good news.'

'Who translated it for you?'

'I took it to my sister.'

'If it had been bad news would you have left me, Phuong?'

She rubbed her hand across my chest to reassure me, not realizing that it was words this time I required, however untrue. 'Would you like a pipe? There *is* a letter for you. I think perhaps it is from her.'

'Did you open that too?'

'I don't open your letters. Telegrams are public. The clerks read them.'

This envelope was among the scarves. She took it gingerly out and laid it on the bed. I recognized the hand-writing. 'If this is bad news what will you . . . ?' I knew well that it could be nothing else but bad. A telegram might have meant a sudden act of generosity: a letter could only mean explanation, justification . . . so I broke off my question, for there was no honesty in asking for the kind of promise no one can keep.

'What are you afraid of?' Phuong asked, and I thought, 'I'm afraid of the loneliness, of the Press Club and the bed-sitting room, I'm afraid of Pyle.'

'Make me a brandy-and-soda,' I said. I looked at the beginning of the letter, 'Dear Thomas,' and the end, 'Affectionately, Helen,' and waited for the brandy.

'It is from *her*?'

'Yes.' Before I read it I began to wonder whether at the end I should lie or tell the truth to Phuong.

'Dear Thomas,

'I was not surprised to get your letter and to know that you were not alone. You are not a man, are you? to remain alone for very long. You pick up women like your coat picks up dust. Perhaps I would feel more sympathy with your case if I didn't feel that you would find consolation very easily when you return to London. I don't suppose you'll believe me, but what gives me pause and prevents me cabling you a simple No is the thought of the poor girl. We are apt to be more involved than you are.'

I had a drink of brandy. I hadn't realized how open the sexual wounds remain over the years. I had carelessly – not choosing my words with skill – set hers bleeding again. Who could blame her for seeking my own scars in return? When we are unhappy we hurt.

'Is it bad?' Phuong asked.

'A bit hard,' I said. 'But she has the right . . .' I read on.

'I always believed you loved Anne more than the rest of us until you packed up and went. Now you seem to be planning to leave another woman because I can tell from your letter that you don't really expect a "favourable" reply. "I'll have done my best" – aren't you thinking that? What would you do if I cabled "Yes"? Would you actually marry her? (I have to write "her" – you don't tell me her name.) Perhaps you would. I suppose like the rest of us you are getting old and don't like living alone. I feel very lonely myself sometimes. I gather Anne has found another companion. But you left her in time.'

She had found the dried scab accurately. I drank again. An issue of blood – the phrase came into my mind.

'Let me make you a pipe,' Phuong said.

'Anything,' I said, 'anything.'

'That is one reason why I ought to say No. (We don't need to talk about the religious reason, because you've never understood or believed in that.) Marriage doesn't prevent you leaving a woman, does it? It only delays the process, and it would be all the more unfair to the girl in this case if you lived with her as long as you lived with me. You would bring her back to England where she would be lost and a stranger, and when you left her, how terribly abandoned she would feel. I don't suppose she even uses a knife and fork, does she? I'm being harsh because I'm thinking of her good more than I am of yours. But, Thomas dear, I do think of yours too.'

I felt physically sick. It was a long time since I had received a letter from my wife. I had forced her to write it and I could feel her pain in every line. Her pain struck at my pain: we were back at the old routine of hurting each other. If only it were possible to love without injury – fidelity isn't enough: I had been faithful to Anne and yet I had injured her. The hurt is in the act of possession: we are too small in mind and body to possess another person without pride or to be possessed without humiliation. In a way I was glad that my wife had struck out at me again – I had forgotten her pain for too long, and this was the only kind of recompense I could give her. Unfortunately the innocent are always involved in any conflict. Always, everywhere, there is some voice crying from a tower.

Phuong lit the opium lamp. 'Will she let you marry me?'

'I don't know yet.'

'Doesn't she say?'

'If she does, she says it very slowly.'

I thought, 'How much you pride yourself on being *dégagé*, the reporter, not the leader-writer, and what a mess you make behind the scenes. The other kind of war is more innocent than this. One does less damage with a mortar.'

'If I go against my deepest conviction and say "Yes", would it even be good for you? You say you are being recalled to England and I can realize how you will hate that and do anything to make it easier. I can see you marrying after a drink too many. The first time we really tried – you as well as me – and we failed. One doesn't try so hard the second time. You say it will be the end of life to lose this girl. Once you used exactly that phrase to me – I could show you the letter, I have it still – and I suppose you wrote in the same way to Anne. You say that we've always tried to tell the truth to each other, but, Thomas, your truth is always so temporary. What's the good of arguing with you, or trying to make you see reason? It's easier to act as my faith tells me to act – as you think unreasonably – and simply to write: I don't believe in divorce: my religion forbids it, and so the answer, Thomas, is no – no.'

There was another half-page, which I didn't read, before 'Affectionately, Helen'. I think it contained news of the weather and an old aunt of mine I loved.

I had no cause for complaint, and I had expected this reply. There was a lot of truth in it. I only wished that she had not thought aloud at quite such length, when the thoughts hurt her as well as me.

'She says "No"?'

I said with hardly any hesitation, 'She hasn't made up her mind. There's still hope.'

Phuong laughed. '–You say "hope" with such a long face.' She lay at my feet like a dog on a crusader's tomb, preparing the opium, and I wondered what I should say to Pyle. When I had smoked four pipes I felt more ready for the future and I told her the hope was a good one – my wife was consulting a lawyer. Any day now I would get the telegram of release.

'It would not matter so much. You could make a settlement,' she said, and I could hear her sister's voice speaking through her mouth.

'I have no savings,' I said. 'I can't outbid Pyle.'

'Don't worry. Something may happen. There are always ways,' she said. 'My sister says you could take out a life-insurance,' and I thought how realistic it was of her not to minimize the importance of money and not to make any great and binding declarations of love. I wondered how Pyle over the years would stand that hard core, for Pyle was a romantic; but then of course in his case there would be a good settlement, the hardness might soften like an unused muscle when the need for it vanished. The rich had it both ways.

That evening, before the shops had closed in the rue Catinat, Phuong bought three more silk scarves. She sat on the bed and displayed them to me, exclaiming at the bright colours, filling a void with her singing voice, and then folding them carefully she laid them with a dozen others in her drawer: it was as though she were laying the foundation of a modest settlement. And I laid the crazy foundation of mine, writing a letter that very night to Pyle with the unreliable clarity and foresight of opium. This was what I wrote – I found it again the other day tucked into York Harding's *Rôle of the West*. He must have been reading the book when my letter arrived. Perhaps he had used it as a bookmark and then not gone on reading.

'Dear Pyle,' I wrote, and was tempted for the only time to write, 'Dear Alden,' for, after all, this was a bread-and-butter letter of some importance and it differed from other bread-and-butter letters in containing a falsehood:

'Dear Pyle, I have been meaning to write from the hospital to say thank you for the other night. You certainly saved me from an uncomfortable end. I'm moving about again now with the help of a stick – I broke apparently in just the right place and age hasn't yet reached my bones and made them brittle. We must have a party together some time to celebrate.' (My pen stuck on that word, and then, like an ant meeting an obstacle, went round it by another route.) 'I've got something else to celebrate and I know you will be glad of this, too, for you've always said that Phuong's interests were what we both wanted. I found a letter from my wife waiting when I got back, and she's more or less agreed to divorce me. So you don't need to worry any more about Phuong' – it was a cruel phrase, but I didn't realize the cruelty until I read the letter over and then it was too late to alter. If I were going to scratch that out, I had better tear the whole letter up.

'Which scarf do you like best?' Phuong asked. 'I love the yellow.'

'Yes. The yellow. Go down to the hotel and post this letter for me.'

She looked at the address. 'I could take it to the Legation. It would save a stamp.'

'I would rather you posted it.'

Then I lay back and in the relaxation of the opium I thought, 'At least she won't leave me now before I go, and perhaps, somehow, tomorrow, after a few more pipes, I shall think of a way to remain.'

2

Ordinary life goes on – that has saved many a man's reason. Just as in an air-raid it proved impossible to be frightened all the time, so under the bombardment of routine jobs, of chance encounters, of impersonal anxieties, one lost for hours together the personal fear. The thoughts of the coming April, of leaving Indo-China, of the hazy future without Phuong, were affected by the day's telegrams, the bulletins of the Vietnam Press, and by the illness of my assistant, an Indian called Dominguez (his family had come from Goa by way of Bombay) who had attended in my place the less important Press Conferences, kept a sensitive ear open to the tones of gossip and rumour, and took my messages to the cable-offices and the censorship. With the help of Indian traders, particularly in the north, in Haiphong, Nam Dinh and Hanoi, he ran his own personal Intelligence Service for my benefit, and I think he knew more accurately than the French High Command the location of Vietminh battalions within the Tonkin delta.

And because we never used our information except when it became news, and never passed any reports to the French intelligence, he had the trust and the friendship of several Vietminh agents hidden in Saigon-Cholon. The fact that he was an Asiatic, in spite of his name, unquestionably helped.

I was fond of Dominguez. Where other men carry their pride like a skin-disease on the surface, sensitive to the least touch, his pride was deeply hidden, and reduced to the smallest proportion possible, I think, for any human being. All that you encountered in daily contact with him was gentleness and humility and an absolute love of truth: you would have had to be married to him to discover the pride. Perhaps truth and humility go together; so many lies come from our pride – in my profession a reporter's pride, the desire to file a better story than the other man's, and it was Dominguez who helped me not to care – to withstand all those telegrams from home asking why I had not covered so and so's story or the report of someone else which I knew to be untrue.

Now that he was ill I realized how much I owed him – why, he would even see that my car was full of petrol, and yet never once, with a phrase or a look, had he encroached on my private life. I believe he was a Roman Catholic, but I had no evidence for it beyond his name and the place of his origin – for all I knew from his conversation, he might have worshipped Krishna or gone on annual pilgrimages, pricked by a wire frame, to the Batu Caves. Now his illness came like a mercy, reprieving me from the treadmill of private anxiety. It was I now who had to attend the wearisome Press Conferences and hobble to my table at the Continental for a gossip with my colleagues; but I was less capable than Dominguez of telling truth from falsehood, and so I formed the habit of calling in on him in the evenings to discuss what I had heard. Sometimes one of his Indian friends was there, sitting beside the narrow iron bed in the lodgings Dominguez shared in one of the meaner streets off the Boulevard Galliéni. He would sit up straight in his bed with his feet tucked under him so that you had less the impression of visiting a sick man than of being received by a rajah or a priest. Sometimes when his fever was bad his face ran with sweat, but he never lost the clarity of his thought. It was as though his illness were happening to another person's body. His landlady kept a jug of fresh lime by his side, but I never saw him take a drink – perhaps that would have been to admit that it was his own thirst, and his own body which suffered.

Of all the days that I visited him I remember one in particular. I had given up asking him how he was for fear that the question sounded like a reproach, and it was always he who inquired with great anxiety about my health and apologized for the stairs I had to climb. Then he said, 'I would like you to meet a friend of mine. He has a story you should listen to.'

'Yes.'

'I have his name written down because I know you find it difficult to remember Chinese names. We must not use it, of course. He has a warehouse on the Quai Mytho for junk metal.'

'Important?'

'It might be.'

'Can you give me an idea?'

'I would rather you heard from him. There is something strange, but I don't understand it.' The sweat was pouring down his face, but he just let it run as though the drops were alive and sacred – there was that much of the Hindu in him, he would never have endangered the life of a fly. He said, 'How much do you know of your friend Pyle?'

'Not very much. Our tracks cross, that's all. I haven't seen him since Tanyin.'

'What job does he do?'

'Economic Mission, but that covers a multitude of sins. I think he's interested in home-industries – I suppose with an American business tie-up. I don't like the way they keep the French fighting and cut out their business at the same time.'

'I heard him talking the other day at a party the Legation was giving to visiting Congressmen. They had put him on to brief them.'

'God help Congress,' I said, 'he hasn't been in the country six months.'

'He was talking about the old colonial powers – England and France, and how you two couldn't expect to win the confidence of the Asiatics. That was where America came in now with clean hands.'

'Hawaii, Puerto Rico,' I said, 'New Mexico.'

'Then someone asked him some stock question about the chances of the Government here ever beating the Vietminh and he said a Third

Force could do it. There was always a Third Force to be found free from Communism and the taint of colonialism – national democracy he called it; you only had to find a leader and keep him safe from the old colonial powers.'

'It's all in York Harding,' I said. 'He had read it before he came out here. He talked about it his first week and he's learned nothing.'

'He may have found his leader,' Dominguez said.

'Would it matter?'

'I don't know. I don't know what he does. But go and talk to my friend on the Quai Mytho.'

I went home to leave a note for Phuong in the rue Catinat and then drove down past the port as the sun set. The tables and chairs were out on the *quai* beside the steamers and the grey naval boats, and the little portable kitchens burned and bubbled. In the Boulevard de la Somme the hairdressers were busy under the trees and the fortune-tellers squatted against the walls with their soiled packs of cards. In Cholon you were in a different city where work seemed to be just beginning rather than petering out with the daylight. It was like driving into a pantomime set: the long vertical Chinese signs and the bright lights and the crowd of extras led you into the wings, where everything was suddenly so much darker and quieter. One such wing took me down again to the *quai* and a huddle of sampans, where the warehouses yawned in the shadow and no one was about.

I found the place with difficulty and almost by accident, the godown gates were open, and I could see the strange Picasso shapes of the junk-pile by the light of an old lamp: bedsteads, bathtubs, ashcans, the bonnets of cars, stripes of old colour where the light hit. I walked down a narrow track carved in the iron quarry and called out for Mr Chou, but there was no reply. At the end of the godown a stair led up to what I supposed might be Mr Chou's house – I had apparently been directed to the back door, and I supposed that Dominguez had his reasons. Even the staircase was lined with junk, pieces of scrap-iron which might come in useful one day in this jackdaw's nest of a house. There was one big room on the landing and a whole family sat and lay about in it with the effect of a camp which might be struck at any moment. Small tea-cups stood about everywhere and there were lots of cardboard boxes full of unidentifiable objects and fibre suitcases ready strapped; there was an old lady sitting on a big bed, two boys and two girls, a baby crawling on the floor, three middle-aged women in old brown peasant-trousers and jackets, and two old men in a corner in blue silk mandarin coats playing mah jongg. They paid no attention to my coming; they played rapidly, identifying each piece by touch, and the noise was like shingle turning on a beach after a wave withdraws. No one paid any more attention than they did; only a cat leapt on to a cardboard box and a lean dog sniffed at me and withdrew.

'Monsieur Chou?' I asked, and two of the women shook their heads, and still no one regarded me, except that one of the women rinsed out a cup and poured tea from a pot which had been resting warm in its silk-lined box. I sat down on the end of the bed next to the old lady and a girl brought me the cup: it was as though I had been absorbed into the community with the cat and the dog – perhaps they had turned up the first time as fortuitously as I had. The baby crawled across the floor and pulled at my laces and no one reproved it: one didn't in the East reprove children. Three commercial calendars were hanging on the walls, each with a girl in gay Chinese costume with bright pink cheeks. There was a big mirror mysteriously lettered Café de la Paix – perhaps it had got caught up accidentally in the junk: I felt caught up in it myself.

I drank slowly the green bitter tea, shifting the handleless cup from palm to palm as the heat scorched my fingers, and I wondered how long I ought to stay. I tried the family once in French, asking when they expected Monsieur Chou to return, but no one replied: they had probably not understood. When my cup was empty they refilled it and continued their own occupations: a woman ironing, a girl sewing, the two boys at their lessons, the old lady looking at her feet, the tiny crippled feet of old China – and the dog watching the cat, which stayed on the cardboard boxes.

I began to realize how hard Dominguez worked for his lean living.

A Chinese of extreme emaciation came into the room. He seemed to take up no room at all: he was like the piece of greaseproof paper that divides the biscuits in a tin. The only thickness he had was in his striped flannel pyjamas. 'Monsieur Chou?' I asked.

He looked at me with the indifferent gaze of a smoker: the sunken cheeks, the baby wrists, the arms of a small girl – many years and many pipes had been needed to whittle him down to these dimensions. I said, 'My friend, Monsieur Dominguez, said that you had something to show me. You *are* Monsieur Chou?'

Oh yes, he said, he was Monsieur Chou and waved me courteously back to my seat. I could tell that the object of my coming had been lost somewhere within the smoky corridors of his skull. I would have a cup of tea? he was much honoured by my visit. Another cup was rinsed on to the floor and put like a live coal into my hands – the ordeal by tea. I commented on the size of his family.

He looked round with faint surprise as though he had never seen it in that light before. 'My mother,' he said, 'my wife, my sister, my uncle, my brother, my children, my aunt's children.' The baby had rolled away from my feet and lay on its back kicking and crowing. I wondered to whom it belonged. No one seemed young enough – or old enough – to have produced that.

I said. 'Monsieur Dominguez told me it was important.'

'Ah, Monsieur Dominguez. I hope Monsieur Dominguez is well?'

'He has had a fever.'

'It is an unhealthy time of year.' I wasn't convinced that he even remembered who Dominguez was. He began to cough, and under his pyjama jacket, which had lost two buttons, the tight skin twanged like a native drum.

'You should see a doctor yourself,' I said. A newcomer joined us – I hadn't heard him enter. He was a young man neatly dressed in European clothes. He said in English, 'Mr Chou has only one lung.'

'I am very sorry . . .'

'He smokes one hundred and fifty pipes every day.'

'That sounds a lot.'

'The doctor says it will do him no good, but Mr Chou feels much happier when he smokes.'

I made an understanding grunt.

'If I may introduce myself, I am Mr Chou's manager.'

'My name is Fowler. Mr Dominguez sent me. He said that Mr Chou had something to tell me.'

'Mr Chou's memory is very much impaired. Will you have a cup of tea?'

'Thank you, I have had three cups already.' It sounded like a question and an answer in a phrase-book.

Mr Chou's manager took the cup out of my hand and held it out to one of the girls, who after spilling the dregs on the floor again refilled it.

'That is not strong enough,' he said, and took it and tasted it himself, carefully rinsed it and refilled it from a second teapot. 'That is better?' he asked.

'Much better.'

Mr Chou cleared his throat, but it was only for an immense expectoration into a tin spittoon decorated with pink blooms. The baby rolled up and down among the tea-dregs and the cat leapt from a cardboard box on to a suitcase.

'Perhaps it would be better if you talked to me,' the young man said. 'My name is Mr Heng.'

'If you would tell me . . .'

'We will go down to the warehouse,' Mr Heng said. 'It is quieter there.'

I put out my hand to Mr Chou, who allowed it to rest between his palms with a look of bewilderment, then gazed around the crowded room as though he were trying to fit me in. The sound of the turning shingle receded as we went down the stairs. Mr Heng said, 'Be careful. The last step is missing,' and he flashed a torch to guide me.

We were back among the bedsteads and the bathtubs and Mr Heng led the way down a side aisle. When he had gone about twenty paces he stopped and shone his light on to a small iron drum. He said, 'Do you see that?'

'What about it?'

He turned it over and showed the trade mark: 'Diolacton.'

'It still means nothing to me.'

He said, 'I had two of those drums here. They were picked up with other junk at the garage of Mr Phan-Van-Muoi. You know him?'

'No, I don't think so.'

'His wife is a relation of General Thé.'

'I still don't quite see . . . ?'

'Do you know what this is?' Mr Heng asked, stooping and lifting a long concave object like a stick of celery which glistened chromium in the light of his torch.

'It might be a bath-fixture.'

'It is a mould,' Mr Heng said. He was obviously a man who took a tiresome pleasure in giving instruction. He paused for me to show my ignorance again. 'You understand what I mean by a mould?'

'Oh yes, of course, but I still don't follow . . .'

'This mould was made in USA. Diolacton is an American trade name. You begin to understand?'

'Frankly, no.'

'There is a flaw in the mould. That was why it was thrown away. But it should not have been thrown away with the junk – nor the drum either. That was a mistake. Mr Muoi's manager came here personally. I could not find the mould, but I let him have back the other drum. I said it was all I had, and he told me he needed them for storing chemicals. Of course, he did not ask for the mould – that would have given too much away – but he had a good search. Mr Muoi himself called later at the American Legation and asked for Mr Pyle.'

'You seem to have quite an Intelligence Service,' I said. I still couldn't imagine what it was all about.

'I asked Mr Chou to get in touch with Mr Dominguez.'

'You mean you've established a kind of connection between Pyle and the General,' I said. 'A very slender one. It's not news anyway. Everybody here goes in for Intelligence.'

Mr Heng beat his heel against the black iron drum and the sound reverberated among the bedsteads. He said, 'Mr Fowler, you are English. You are neutral. You have been fair to all of us. You can sympathize if some of us feel strongly on whatever side.'

I said, 'If you are hinting that you are a Communist, or a Vietminh, don't worry. I'm not shocked. I have no politics.'

'If anything unpleasant happens here in Saigon, it will be blamed on us. My Committee would like you to take a fair view. That is why I have shown you this and this.'

'What is Diolacton?' I said. 'It sounds like condensed milk.'

'It has something in common with milk.' Mr Heng shone his torch inside the drum. A little white powder lay like dust on the bottom. 'It is one of the American plastics,' he said.

'I heard a rumour that Pyle was importing plastics for toys.' I picked up the mould and looked at it. I tried in my mind to divine its shape. This was not how the object itself would look: this was the image in a mirror, reversed.

'Not for toys,' Mr Heng said.

'It is like parts of a rod.'

'The shape is unusual.'

'I can't see what it could be for.'

Mr Heng turned away. 'I only want you to remember what you have seen,' he said, walking back in the shadows of the junk-pile. 'Perhaps one day you will have a reason for writing about it. But you must not say you saw the drum here.'

'Nor the mould?' I asked.

'Particularly not the mould.'

3

It is not easy the first time to meet again one who has saved as they put it – one's life. I had not seen Pyle while I was in the Legion Hospital, and his absence and silence, easily accountable (for he was more sensitive to embarrassment than I), sometimes worried me unreasonably, so that at night before my sleeping drug had soothed me I would imagine him going up my stairs, knocking at my door, sleeping in my bed. I had been unjust to him in that, and so I had added a sense of guilt to my other more formal obligation. And then I suppose there was also the guilt of my letter. (What distant ancestors had given me this stupid conscience? Surely they were free of it when they raped and killed in their palaeolithic world.)

Should I invite my saviour to dinner, I sometimes wondered, or should I suggest a meeting for a drink in the bar of the Continental? It was an unusual social problem, perhaps depending on the value one attributed to one's life. A meal and a bottle of wine or a double whisky? – it had worried me for some days until the problem was solved by Pyle himself, who came and shouted at me through my closed door. I was sleeping through the hot afternoon, exhausted by the morning's effort to use my leg, and I hadn't heard his knock.

'Thomas, Thomas.' The call dropped into a dream I was having of walking down a long empty road looking for a turning which never came. The road unwound like a tape-machine with a uniformity that would never have altered if the voice hadn't broken in – first of all like a voice crying in pain from a tower and then suddenly a voice speaking to me personally, 'Thomas, Thomas.'

Under my breath I said, 'Go away, Pyle. Don't come near me. I don't want to be saved.'

'Thomas.' He was hitting at my door, but I lay possum as though I were back in the rice-field and he was an enemy. Suddenly I realized that the knocking had stopped, someone was speaking in a low voice outside and someone was replying. Whispers are dangerous. I couldn't tell who the speakers were. I got carefully off the bed and with the help of my stick reached the door of the other room. Perhaps I had moved too hurriedly and they had heard me, because a silence grew outside. Silence like a plant put out tendrils: it seemed to grow under the door and spread its leaves in the room where I stood. It was a silence I didn't like, and I tore it apart by flinging the door open. Phuong stood in the passage and Pyle had his hands on her shoulders: from their attitude they might have parted from a kiss.

'Why, come in,' I said, 'come in.'

'I couldn't make you hear,' Pyle said.

'I was asleep at first, and then I didn't want to be disturbed. But I *am* disturbed, so come in.' I said in French to Phuong, 'Where did you pick him up?'

'Here. In the passage,' she said. 'I heard him knocking, so I ran upstairs to let him in.'

'Sit down,' I said to Pyle. 'Will you have some coffee?'

'No, and I don't want to sit down, Thomas.'

'I must. This leg gets tired. You got my letter?'

'Yes. I wish you hadn't written it.'

'Why?'

'Because it was a pack of lies. I trusted you, Thomas.'

'You shouldn't trust anyone when there's a woman in the case.'

'Then you needn't trust me after this. I'll come sneaking up here when you go out, I'll write letters in typewritten envelopes. Maybe I'm growing up, Thomas.' But there were tears in his voice, and he looked younger than he had ever done. 'Couldn't you have won without lying?'

'No. This is European duplicity, Pyle. We have to make up for our lack of supplies. I must have been clumsy though. How did you spot the lies?'

'It was her sister,' he said. 'She's working for Joe now. I saw her just now. She knows you've been called home.'

'Oh, that,' I said with relief. 'Phuong knows it too.'

'And the letter from your wife? Does Phuong know about that? Her sister's seen it.'

'How?'

'She came here to meet Phuong when you were out yesterday and Phuong showed it to her. You can't deceive her. She reads English.'

'I see.' There wasn't any point in being angry with anyone – the offender was too obviously myself, and Phuong had probably only shown the letter as a kind of boast – it wasn't a sign of mistrust.

'You knew all this last night?' I asked Phuong.

'Yes.'

'I noticed you were quiet.' I touched her arm. 'What a fury you might have been, but you're Phuong – you are no fury.'

'I had to think,' she said, and I remembered how waking in the night I had told from the irregularity of her breathing that she was not asleep. I'd put my arm out to her and asked her '*Le caucheman*?' She used to suffer from nightmares when she first came to the rue Catinat, but last night she had shaken her head at the suggestion: her back was turned to me and I had moved my leg against her – the first move in the formula of intercourse. I had noticed nothing wrong even then.

'Can't you explain, Thomas, why . . .'

'Surely it's obvious enough. I wanted to keep her.'

'At any cost to her?'

'Of course.'

'That's not love.'

'Perhaps it's not your way of love, Pyle.'

'I want to protect her.'

'I don't. She doesn't need protection. I want her around, I want her in my bed.'

'Against her will?'

'She wouldn't stay against her will, Pyle.'

'She can't love you after this.' His ideas were as simple as that. I turned to look for her. She had gone through to the bedroom and was pulling the counterpane straight where I had lain; then she took one of her picture books from a shelf and sat on the bed as though she were quite unconcerned with our talk. I could tell what book it was – a pictorial record of the Queen's life. I could see upside-down the state coach on the way to Westminster.

'Love's a Western word,' I said. 'We use it for sentimental reasons or to cover up an obsession with one woman. These people don't suffer from obsessions. You're going to be hurt, Pyle, if you aren't careful.'

'I'd have beaten you up if it wasn't for that leg.'

'You should be grateful to me – and Phuong's sister, of course. You can go ahead without scruples now – and you are very scrupulous in some ways, aren't you, when it doesn't come to plastics.'

'Plastics?'

'I hope to God you know what you are doing there. Oh, I know your motives are good, they always are.' He looked puzzled and suspicious. 'I wish sometimes you had a few bad motives, you might understand a little more about human beings. And that applies to your country too, Pyle.'

'I want to give her a decent life. This place – smells.'

'We keep the smell down with joss sticks. I suppose you'll offer her a deep freeze and a car for herself and the newest television set and . . .'

'And children,' he said.

'Bright young American citizens ready to testify.'

'And what will you give her? You weren't going to take her home.'

'No, I'm not that cruel. Unless I can afford her a return ticket.'

'You'll just keep her as a comfortable lay until you leave.'

'She's a human being, Pyle. She's capable of deciding.'

'On faked evidence. And a child at that.'

'She's no child. She's tougher than you'll ever be. Do you know the kind of polish that doesn't take scratches? That's Phuong. She can survive a dozen of us. She'll get old, that's all. She'll suffer from childbirth and hunger and cold and rheumatism, but she'll never suffer like we do from thoughts, obsessions – she won't scratch, she'll only decay.' But even while I made my speech and watched her turn the page (a family group with Princess Anne), I knew I was inventing a character just as much as Pyle was. One never knows another human being; for all I could tell, she was as scared as the rest of us: she didn't have the gift of expression, that was all. And I remembered that first tormenting year when I had tried so passionately to understand her, when I had begged her to tell me what she thought and had scared her with my unreasoning anger at her silences. Even my desire had been a weapon, as though when one plunged one's sword towards the victim's womb, she would lose control and speak.

'You've said enough,' I told Pyle. 'You know all there is to know. Please go.'

'Phuong,' he called.

'Monsieur Pyle?' she inquired, looking up from the scrutiny of Windsor Castle, and her formality was comic and reassuring at that moment.

'He's cheated you.'

'*Je ne comprends pas.*'

'Oh, go away,' I said. 'Go to your Third Force and York Harding and the Rôle of Democracy. Go away and play with plastics.'

Later I had to admit that he had carried out my instructions to the letter.

PART THREE

Chapter 1

1

It was nearly a fortnight after Pyle's death before I saw Vigot again. I was going up the Boulevard Charner when his voice called to me from Le Club. It was the restaurant most favoured in those days by members of the Sureté, who, as a kind of defiant gesture to those who hated them, would lunch and drink on the ground-floor while the general public fed upstairs out of the reach of a partisan with a hand-grenade. I joined him and he ordered me a vermouth cassis. 'Play for it?'

'If you like,' and I took out my dice for the ritual game of *Quatre Cent Vingt-et-un*. How those figures and the sight of dice bring back to mind the war-years in Indo-China. Anywhere in the world when I see two men dicing I am back in the streets of Hanoi or Saigon or among the blasted buildings of Phat Diem, I see the parachutists, protected like caterpillars by their strange markings, patrolling by the canals, I hear the sound of the mortars closing in, and perhaps I see a dead child.

'*Sans vaseline*,' Vigot said, throwing a four-two-one. He pushed the last match towards me. The sexual jargon of the game was common to all the Sureté; perhaps it had been invented by Vigot and taken up by his junior officers, who hadn't however taken up Pascal. '*Sous-lieutenant*.' Every game you lost raised you a rank – you played till one or other became a captain or a commandant. He won the second game as well and while he counted out the matches, he said, 'We've found Pyle's dog.'

'Yes?'

'I suppose it had refused to leave the body. Anyway they cut its throat. It was in the mud fifty yards away. Perhaps it dragged itself that far.'

'Are you still interested?'

'The American Minister keeps bothering us. We don't have the same trouble, thank God, when a Frenchman is killed. But then those cases don't have rarity value.'

We played for the division of matches and then the real game started. It was uncanny how quickly Vigot threw a four-two-one. He reduced his matches to three and I threw the lowest score possible. '*Nanette*,' Vigot said, pushing me over two matches. When he had got rid of his last match he said, '*Capitaine*,' and I called the waiter for drinks. 'Does anybody ever beat you?' I asked.

'Not often. Do you want your revenge?'

'Another time. What a gambler you could be, Vigot. Do you play any other game of chance?'

He smiled miserably, and for some reason I thought of that blonde wife of his who was said to betray him with his junior officers.

'Oh well,' he said, 'there's always the biggest of all.'

'The biggest?'

'"Let us weigh the gain and loss," he quoted, "in wagering that God is, let us estimate these two chances. If you gain, you gain all; if you lose you lose nothing."'

I quoted Pascal back at him – it was the only passage I remembered. '"Both he who chooses heads and he who chooses tails are equally at fault. They are both in the wrong. True course is not to wager at all."'

'"Yes; but you must wager. It is not optional. You are embarked." You don't follow your own principles, Fowler. You're *engagé*, like the rest of us.'

'Not in religion.'

'I wasn't talking about religion. As a matter of fact,' he said, 'I was thinking about Pyle's dog.'

'Oh.'

'Do you remember what you said to me – about finding clues on its paws, analysing the dirt and so on?'

'And you said you weren't Maigret or Lecoq.'

'I've not done so badly after all,' he said. 'Pyle usually took the dog with him when he went out, didn't he?'

'I suppose so.'

'It was too valuable to let it stray by itself?'

'It wouldn't be very safe. They eat chows, don't they, in this country?' He began to put the dice in his pocket. 'My dice, Vigot.'

'Oh, I'm sorry. I was thinking . . .'

'Why did you say I was *engagé*?'

'When did you last see Pyle's dog, Fowler?'

'God knows. I don't keep an engagement-book for dogs.'

'When are you due to go home?'

'I don't know exactly.' I never like giving information to the police. It saves them trouble.

'I'd like – tonight – to drop in and see you. At ten? If you will be alone.'

'I'll send Phuong to the cinema.'

'Things all right with you again – with her?'

'Yes.'

'Strange. I got the impression that you are – well – unhappy.'

'Surely there are plenty of possible reasons for that Vigot.' I added bluntly, 'You should know.'

'Me?'

'You're not a very happy man yourself.'

'Oh, I've nothing to complain about. "A ruined house is not miserable."'

'What's that?'

'Pascal again. It's an argument for being proud of misery. "A tree is not miserable."'

'What made you into a policeman, Vigot?'

'There were a number of factors. The need to earn a living, a curiosity about people, and – yes, even that, a love of Gaboriau.'

'Perhaps you ought to have been a priest.'

'I didn't read the right authors for that – in those days.'

'You still suspect me, don't you, of being concerned?'

He rose and drank what was left of his vermouth cassis.

'I'd like to talk to you, that's all.'

I thought after he had turned and gone that he had looked at me with compassion, as he might have looked at some prisoner, for whose capture he was responsible, undergoing his sentence for life.

2

I *had* been punished. It was as though Pyle, when he left my flat, had sentenced me to so many weeks of uncertainty. Every time that I returned home it was with the expectation of disaster. Sometimes Phuong would not be there, and I found it impossible to settle to any work till she returned, for I always wondered whether she would ever return. I would ask her where she had been (trying to keep anxiety or suspicion out of my voice) and sometimes she would reply the market or the shops and produce her piece of evidence (even her readiness to confirm her story seemed at that period unnatural), and sometimes it was the cinema, and the stub of her ticket was there to prove it, and sometimes it was her sister's – that was where I believed she met Pyle. I made love to her in those days savagely as though I hated her, but what I hated was the future. Loneliness lay in my bed and I took loneliness into my arms at night. She didn't change; she cooked for me, she made my pipes, she gently and sweetly laid out her body for my pleasure (but it was no longer a pleasure), and just as in those early days I wanted her mind, now I wanted to read her thoughts, but they were hidden away in a language I couldn't speak. I didn't want to question her. I didn't want to make her lie (as long as no lie was spoken openly I could pretend that we were the same to each other as we had always been), but suddenly my anxiety would speak for me, and I said, 'When did you last see Pyle?'

She hesitated – or was it that she was really thinking back? 'When we came here,' she said.

I began – almost unconsciously – to run down everything that was American. My conversation was full of the poverty of American literature, the scandals of American politics, the beastliness of American children. It was as though she were being taken away from me by a nation rather than by a man. Nothing that America could do was right. I became a bore on the subject of America, even with my French friends who were ready enough to share my antipathies. It was as if I had been betrayed, but one is not betrayed by an enemy.

It was just at that time that the incident occurred of the bicycle bombs. Coming back from the Imperial Bar to an empty flat (was she at the cinema or with her sister?) I found that a note had been pushed under the door. It was from Dominguez. He apologized for being still sick and asked me to be outside the big store at the corner of the Boulevard Charner around ten-thirty the next morning. He was writing at the request of Mr Chou, but I suspected that Mr Heng was the more likely to require my presence.

The whole affair, as it turned out, was not worth more than a paragraph, and a humorous paragraph at that. It bore no relation to the sad and heavy war in the north, those canals in Phat Diem choked with the grey days-old bodies, the pounding of the mortars, the white glare of napalm. I had been waiting for about a quarter of an hour by a stall of flowers when a truck-load of police drove up with a grinding of brakes and a squeal of rubber from the direction of the Sureté Headquarters in the rue Catinat; the men disembarked and ran for the store, as though they were charging a mob, but there was no mob – only a zareba of bicycles. Every large building in Saigon is fenced in by them – no university city in the West contains so many bicycle-owners. Before I had time to adjust my camera the comic and inexplicable action had been accomplished. The police had forced their way among the bicycles and emerged with three which they carried over their heads into the boulevard and dropped into the decorative fountain. Before I could intercept a single policeman they were back in their truck and driving hard down the Boulevard Bonnard.

'*Operation Bicyclette*,' a voice said. It was Mr Heng.

'What is it?' I asked. 'A practice? For what?'

'Wait a while longer,' Mr Heng said.

A few idlers began to approach the fountain, where one wheel stuck up like a buoy as though to warn shipping away from the wrecks below: a policeman crossed the road shouting and waving his hands.

'Let's have a look,' I said.

'Better not,' Mr Heng said, and examined his watch. The hands stood at four minutes past eleven.

'You're fast,' I said.

'It always gains.' And at that moment the fountain exploded over the pavement. A bit of decorative coping struck a window and the glass fell like the water in a bright shower. Nobody was hurt. We shook the water and glass from our clothes. A bicycle wheel hummed like a top in the road, staggered and collapsed. 'It must be just eleven,' Mr Heng said.

'What on earth . . . ?'

'I thought you would be interested,' Mr Heng said. 'I *hope* you were interested.'

'Come and have a drink?'

'No, I am sorry. I must go back to Mr Chou's, but first let me show you something.' He led me to the bicycle park and unlocked his own machine. 'Look carefully.'

'A Raleigh,' I said.

'No, look at the pump. Does it remind you of anything?' He smiled patronizingly at my mystification and pushed off. Once he turned and waved his hand, pedalling towards Cholon and the warehouse of junk. At the Sureté, where I went for information, I realized what he meant. The mould I had seen in his warehouse had been shaped like a half-section of a bicycle-pump. That day all over Saigon innocent bicycle-pumps had proved to contain bombs which had gone off at the stroke of eleven, except where the police, acting on information that I suspect emanated from Mr Heng, had been able to anticipate the explosions. It was all quite trivial – ten explosions, six people slightly injured, and God knows how many bicycles. My colleagues – except for the correspondent of the *Extrême Orient*, who called it an 'outrage' – knew they could only get space by making fun of the affair. 'Bicycle Bombs' made a good headline. All of them blamed the Communists. I was the only one to write that the bombs were a demonstration on the part of General Thé, and my account was altered in the office. The General wasn't news. You couldn't waste space by identifying him. I sent a message of regret through Dominguez to Mr Heng – I had done my best. Mr Heng sent a polite verbal reply. It seemed to me then that he – or his Vietminh Committee – had been unduly sensitive; no one held the affair seriously against the Communists. Indeed, if anything could have done so, it would have given them the reputation for a sense of humour. 'What'll they think of next?' people said at parties, and the whole absurd affair was symbolized for me too in the bicycle-wheel gaily spinning like a top in the middle of the boulevard. I never even mentioned to Pyle what I had heard of his connection with the General. Let him play harmlessly with plastic moulds: it might keep his mind off Phuong. All the same, because I happened to be in the neighbourhood one evening, because I had nothing better to do, I called in at Mr Muoi's garage.

It was a small, untidy place, not unlike a junk warehouse itself, in the Boulevard de la Somme. A car was jacked up in the middle of the floor with its bonnet open, gaping like the cast of some pre-historic animal in a provincial museum which nobody ever visits. I don't believe anyone remembered it was there. The floor was littered with scraps of iron and old boxes – the Vietnamese don't like throwing anything away, any more than a Chinese cook partitioning a duck into seven courses will dispense with so much as a claw. I wondered why anybody had so wastefully disposed of the empty drums and the damaged mould – perhaps it was a theft by an employee making a few piastres, perhaps somebody had been bribed by the ingenious Mr Heng.

Nobody seemed about, so I went in. Perhaps, I thought, they are keeping away for a while in case the police call. It was possible that Mr Heng had some contact in the Sureté, but even then it was unlikely that the police would act. It was better from their point of view to let people assume that the bombs were Communist.

Apart from the car and the junk strewn over the concrete floor there was nothing to be seen. It was difficult to picture how the bombs could have been manufactured at Mr Muoi's. I was very vague about how one turned the white dust I had seen in the drum into plastic, but surely the process was too complex to be carried out here, where even the two petrol pumps in the street seemed to be suffering from neglect. I stood in the entrance and looked out into the street. Under the trees in the centre of the boulevard the barbers were at work: a scrap of mirror nailed to a tree-trunk caught the flash of the sun. A girl went by at a trot under her mollusc hat carrying two baskets slung on a pole. The fortune-teller squatting against the wall of Simon Frères had found a customer, an old man with a wisp of beard like Ho Chi Minh's who watched impassively the shuffling and turning of the ancient cards. What possible future had he got that was worth a piastre? In the Boulevard de la Somme you lived in the open; everybody here knew all about Mr Muoi, but the police had no key which would unlock their confidence. This was the level of life where everything was known, but you couldn't step down to that level as you could step into the street. I remembered the old women gossiping on our landing beside the communal lavatory: they heard everything too, but I didn't know what they knew.

I went back into the garage and entered a small office at the back. There was the usual Chinese commercial calendar, a littered desk – price-lists and a bottle of gum and an adding-machine, some paper-clips, a teapot and three cups and a lot of unsharpened pencils, and for some reason an unwritten picture-postcard of the Eiffel Tower. York Harding might write in graphic abstractions about the Third Force, but this was what it came down to – this was It. There was a door in the back wall; it was locked, but the key was on the desk among the pencils. I opened the door and went through.

I was in a small shed about the size of the garage. It contained one piece of machinery that at first sight seemed like a cage of rods and wires furnished with innumerable perches to hold some wingless adult bird – it gave the impression of being tied up with old rags, but the rags had probably been used for cleaning when Mr Muoi and his assistants had been called away. I found the name of a manufacturer – somebody in Lyons and a patent number – patenting what? I switched on the current and the old machine came alive: the rods had a purpose – the contraption was like an old man gathering his last vital force, pounding down his fist, pounding down . . . This thing was still a press, though in its own sphere it must have belonged to the same era as the nickelodeon, but I suppose that in this country where nothing was ever wasted, and where everything might be expected to come one day to finish its career (I remembered seeing that ancient movie *The Great*

Train Robbery jerking its way across a screen, giving entertainment, in a back-street in Nam Dinh), the press was still employable.

I examined the press more closely; there were traces of a white powder. Diolacton, I thought, something in common with milk. There was no sign of a drum or a mould. I went back into the office and into the garage. I felt like giving the old car a pat on the mudguard; it had a long wait ahead of it, perhaps, but it too one day . . . Mr Muoi and his assistants were probably by this time somewhere among the rice-fields on the way to the sacred mountain where General Thé had his headquarters. When now at last I raised my voice and called 'Monsieur Muoi!' I could imagine I was far away from the garage and the boulevard and the barbers, back among those fields where I had taken refuge on the road to Tanyin. 'Monsieur Muoi!' I could see a man turn his head among the stalks of rice.

I walked home and up on my landing the old women burst into their twitter of the hedges which I could understand no more than the gossip of the birds. Phuong was not in – only a note to say that she was with her sister. I lay down on the bed – I still tired easily – and fell asleep. When I woke I saw the illuminated dial of my alarm pointing to one twenty-five and I turned my head expecting to find Phuong asleep beside me. But the pillow was undented. She must have changed the sheet that day – it carried the coldness of the laundry. I got up and opened the drawer where she kept her scarves, and they were not there. I went to the bookshelf – the pictorial Life of the Royal Family had gone too. She had taken her dowry with her.

In the moment of shock there is little pain; pain began about three a.m. when I began to plan the life I had still somehow to live and to remember memories in order somehow to eliminate them. Happy memories are the worst, and I tried to remember the unhappy. I was practised. I had lived all this before. I knew I could do what was necessary, but I was so much older – I felt I had little energy left to reconstruct.

3

I went to the American Legation and asked for Pyle. It was necessary to fill in a form at the door and give it to a military policeman. He said, 'You haven't put the purpose of the visit.'

'He'll know,' I said.

'You're by appointment, then?'

'You can put it that way if you like.'

'Seems silly to you, I guess, but we have to be very careful. Some strange types come around here.'

'So I've heard.' He shifted his chewing-gum to another side and entered the lift. I waited. I had no idea what to say to Pyle. This was a scene I had never played before. The policeman returned. He said grudgingly, 'I guess you can go up. Room 12A. First floor.'

When I entered the room I saw that Pyle wasn't there. Joe sat behind the desk: the Economic Attaché: I still couldn't remember his surname. Phuong's sister watched me from behind a typing desk. Was it triumph that I read in those brown acquisitive eyes?

'Come in, come in, Tom,' Joe called boisterously. 'Glad to see you. How's your leg? We don't often get a visit from you to our little outfit. Pull up a chair. Tell me how you think the new offensive's going. Saw Granger last night at the Continental. He's for the north again. That boy's *keen*. Where there's news there's Granger. Have a cigarette. Help yourself. You know Miss Hei? Can't remember all these names – too hard for an old fellow like me. I call her "Hi, there!" – she likes it. None of this stuffy colonialism. What's the gossip of the market, Tom? You fellows certainly do keep your ears to the ground. Sorry to hear about your leg. Alden told me . . .'

'Where's Pyle?'

'Oh, Alden's not in the office this morning. Guess he's at home. Does a lot of his work at home.'

'I know what he does at home.'

'That boy's keen. Eh, what's that you said?'

'Anyway, I know one of the things he does at home.'

'I don't catch on, Tom. Slow Joe – that's me. Always was. Always will be.'

'He sleeps with my girl – your typist's sister.'

'I don't know what you mean.'

'Ask her. She fixed it. Pyle's taken my girl.'

'Look here, Fowler, I thought you'd come here on business. We can't have scenes in the office, you know.'

'I came here to see Pyle, but I suppose he's hiding.'

'Now, you're the very last man who ought to make a remark like that. After what Alden did for you.'

'Oh yes, yes, of course. He saved my life, didn't he? But I never asked him to.'

'At great danger to himself. That boy's got guts.'

'I don't care a damn about his guts. There are other parts of his body that are more à propos.

'Now we can't have any innuendoes like that, Fowler, with a lady in the room.'

'The lady and I know each other well. She failed to get her rake-off from me, but she's getting it from Pyle. All right. I know I'm behaving badly, and I'm going to go on behaving badly. This is a situation where people do behave badly.'

'We've got a lot of work to do. There's a report on the rubber output . . .'

'Don't worry, I'm going. But just tell Pyle if he phones that I called. He might think it polite to return the visit.' I said to Phuong's sister, 'I hope you've had the settlement witnessed by the notary public and the American Consul and the Church of Christ Scientist.'

I went into the passage. There was a door opposite me marked Men. I went in and locked the door and sitting with my head against the cold wall I cried. I hadn't cried until now. Even their lavatories were air-conditioned, and presently the temperate tempered air dried my tears as it dries the spit in your mouth and the seed in your body.

4

I left affairs in the hands of Dominguez and went north. At Haiphong I had friends in the Squadron Gascogne, and I would spend hours in the bar up at the airport, or playing bowls on the gravel-path outside. Officially I was at the front: I could qualify for keenness with Granger, but it was of no more value to my paper than had been my excursion to Phat Diem. But if one writes about war, self-respect demands that occasionally one shares the risks.

It wasn't easy to share them for even the most limited period, since orders had gone out from Hanoi that I was to be allowed only on horizontal raids – raids in this war as safe as a journey by bus, for we flew above the range of the heavy machine-gun; we were safe from anything but a pilot's error or a fault in the engine. We went out by time-table and came home by time-table: the cargoes of bombs sailed diagonally down and the spiral of smoke blew up from the road-junction or the bridge, and then we cruised back for the hour of the aperitif and drove our iron bowls across the gravel.

One morning in the mess in the town, as I drank brandies-and-sodas with a young officer who had a passionate desire to visit Southend Pier, orders for a mission came in. 'Like to come?' I said yes. Even a horizontal raid would be a way of killing time and killing thought. Driving out to the airport he remarked, 'This is a vertical raid.'

'I thought I was forbidden . . .'

'So long as you write nothing about it. It will show you a piece of country up near the Chinese border you will not have seen before. Near Lai Chau.'

'I thought all was quiet there – and in French hands?'

'It was. They captured this place two days ago. Our parachutists are only a few hours away. We want to keep the Viets head down in their holes until we have recaptured the post. It means low diving and machine-gunning. We can only spare two planes – one's on the job now. Ever dive-bombed before?'

'No.'

'It is a little uncomfortable when you are not used to it.'

The Gascogne Squadron possessed only small B26 bombers – the French called them prostitutes because with their short wing-span they had no visible means of support. I was crammed on to a little metal pad the size of a bicycle seat with my knees against the navigator's back. We came up the Red River, slowly climbing, and the Red River at this hour was really red. It was as though one had gone far back in time and saw it with the old geographer's eyes who had named it first, at just such an hour when the late sun filled it from bank to bank; then we turned away at 9,000 feet towards the Black River, really black, full of shadows, missing the angle of the light, and the huge majestic scenery of gorge and cliff and jungle wheeled around and stood upright below us. You could have dropped a squadron into those fields of green and grey and left no more trace than a few coins in a harvest-field. Far ahead of us a small plane moved like a midge. We were taking over.

We circled twice above the tower and the green-encircled village, then corkscrewed up into the dazzling air. The pilot – who was called Trouin – turned to me and winked. On his wheel were the studs that controlled the gun and the bomb-chamber. I had that loosening of the bowels, as we came into position for the dive, that accompanies any new experience – the first dance, the first dinner-party, the first love. I was reminded of the Great Racer at the Wembley Exhibition when it came to the top of the rise – there was no way to get out: you were trapped with your experience. On the dial I had just time to read 3,000 metres when we drove down. All was feeling now, nothing was sight. I was forced up against the navigator's back: it was as though something of enormous weight were pressing on my chest. I wasn't aware of the moment when the bombs were released; then the gun chattered and the cockpit was full of the smell of cordite, and the weight was off my chest as we rose, and it was the stomach that fell away, spiralling down like a suicide to the ground we had left. For forty seconds Pyle had not existed: even loneliness hadn't existed. As we climbed in a great arc I could see the smoke through the side window pointing at me. Before the second dive I felt fear – fear of humiliation, fear of vomiting over the navigator's back, fear that my ageing lungs would not stand the pressure. After the tenth dive I was aware only of irritation – the affair had gone on too long, it was time to go home. And again we shot steeply up out of machine-gun range and swerved away and the smoke pointed. The village was surrounded on all sides by mountains. Every time we had to make the same approach, through the same gap. There was no way to vary our attack. As we dived for the fourteenth time I thought, now that I was free from the fear of humiliation, 'They have only to fix one machine-gun into position.' We lifted our nose again into the safe air – perhaps they didn't even have a gun. The forty minutes of the patrol had seemed interminable, but it had been free from the discomfort of personal thought. The sun was sinking as we turned for home: the geographer's moment had passed: the Black River was no longer black, and the Red River was only gold.

Down we went again, away from the gnarled and fissured forest towards the river, flattening out over the neglected rice-fields, aimed like a bullet at one small sampan on the yellow stream. The cannon gave a single burst of tracer, and the sampan blew apart in a shower of sparks: we didn't even wait to see our victims struggling to survive, but climbed and made for home. I thought again as I had thought when I saw the dead child at Phat Diem, 'I hate war.' There had been something so shocking in our sudden fortuitous choice of a prey – we had just happened to be passing, one burst only was required, there was no one to return our fire, we were gone again, adding our little quota to the world's dead.

I put on my earphones for Captain Trouin to speak to me. He said, 'We will make a little detour. The sunset is wonderful on the *calcaire*. You must not miss it,' he added kindly, like a host who is showing the beauty of his estate, and for a hundred miles we trailed the sunset over the Baie d'Along. The helmeted Martian face looked wistfully out, down the golden groves among the great humps and arches of porous stone, and the wounds of murder ceased to bleed.

5

Captain Trouin insisted that night on being my host in the opium house, though he would not smoke himself. He liked the smell, he said, he liked the sense of quiet at the end of the day, but in his profession relaxation could go no further. There were officers who smoked, but they were Army men – he had to have his sleep. We lay in a small cubicle in a row of cubicles like a dormitory at school, and the Chinese proprietor prepared my pipes. I hadn't smoked since Phuong left me. Across the way a *métisse* with long and lovely legs lay coiled after her smoke reading a glossy woman's paper, and in the cubicle next to her two middle-aged Chinese transacted business, sipping tea, their pipes laid aside.

I said, 'That sampan – this evening – was it doing any harm?'

Trouin said, 'Who knows? In those reaches of the river we have orders to shoot up anything in sight.'

I smoked my first pipe. I tried not to think of all the pipes I had smoked at home. Trouin said, 'Today's affair – that is not the worst for someone like myself. Over the village they could have shot us down. Our risk was as great as theirs. What I detest is napalm bombing. From 3,000 feet, in safety.' He made a hopeless gesture. 'You see the forest catching fire. God knows what you would see from the ground. The poor devils are burnt alive, the flames go over them like water. They are wet through with fire.' He said with anger against a whole world that didn't understand, 'I'm not fighting a colonial war. Do you think I'd do these things for the planters of Terre Rouge? I'd rather be court-martialled. We are fighting all of your wars, but you leave us the guilt.'

'That sampan,' I said.

'Yes, that sampan too.' He watched me as I stretched out for my second pipe. 'I envy you your means of escape.'

'You don't know what I'm escaping from. It's not from the war. That's no concern of mine. I'm not involved.'

'You will all be. One day.'

'Not me.'

'You are still limping.'

'They had the right to shoot at me, but they weren't even doing that. They were knocking down a tower. One should always avoid demolition squads. Even in Piccadilly.'

'One day something will happen. You will take a side.'

'No, I'm going back to England.'

'That photograph you showed me once . . .'

'Oh, I've torn that one up. She left me.'

'I'm sorry.'

'It's the way things happen. One leaves people oneself and then the tide turns. It almost makes me believe in justice.'

'I do. The first time I dropped napalm I thought, this is the village where I was born. That is where M. Dubois, my father's old friend, lives. The baker – I was very fond of the baker when I was a child – is running away down there in the flames I've thrown. The men of Vichy did not bomb their own country. I felt worse than them.'

'But you still go on.'

'Those are moods. They come only with the napalm. The rest of the time I think that I am defending Europe. And you know, those others – they do some monstrous things also. When they were driven out of Hanoi in 1946 they left terrible relics among their own people – people they thought had helped us. There was one girl in the mortuary – they had not only cut off her breasts, they had mutilated her lover and stuffed his . . .'

'That's why I won't be involved.'

'It's not a matter of reason or justice. We all get involved in a moment of emotion and then we cannot get out. War and Love – they have always been compared.' He looked sadly across the dormitory to where the *métisse* sprawled in her great temporary peace. He said, 'I would not have it otherwise. *There* is a girl who was involved by her parents – what is her future when this port falls? France is only half her home . . .'

'Will it fall?'

'You are a journalist. You know better than I do that we can't win. You know the road to Hanoi is cut and mined every night. You know we lose one class of St Cyr every year. We were nearly beaten in '50. De Lattre has given us two years of grace – that's all. But we are professionals: we have to go on fighting till the politicians tell us to stop. Probably they will get together and agree to the same peace that we could have had at the beginning, making nonsense of all these years.' His ugly face which had winked at me before the dive wore a kind of professional brutality like a Christmas mask from which a child's eyes peer through the holes in the paper. 'You would not understand the nonsense, Fowler. You are not one of us.'

'There are other things in one's life which make nonsense of the years.'

He put his hand on my knee with an odd protective gesture as though he were the older man. 'Take her home,' he said. 'That is better than a pipe.'

'How do you know she would come?'

'I have slept with her myself, and Lieutenant Perrin. Five hundred piastres.'

'Expensive.'

'I expect she would go for three hundred, but under the circumstances one does not care to bargain.'

But his advice did not prove sound. A man's body is limited in the acts which it can perform and mine was frozen by memory. What my hands touched that night might be more beautiful than I was used to, but we are not trapped only by beauty. She used the same perfume, and suddenly at the moment of entry the ghost of what I'd lost proved more powerful than the body stretched at my disposal. I moved away and lay on my back and desire drained out of me.

'I am sorry,' I said, and lied, 'I don't know what is the matter with me.'

She said with great sweetness and misunderstanding, 'Don't worry. It often happens that way. It is the opium.'

'Yes,' I said, 'the opium.' And I wished to heaven that it had been.

Chapter 2

1

It was strange, this first return to Saigon with nobody to welcome me. At the airport I wished there were somewhere else to which I could direct my taxi than the rue Catinat. I thought to myself: 'Is the pain a little less than when I went away?' and tried to persuade myself that it was so. When I reached the landing I saw that the door was open, and I became breathless with an unreasonable hope. I walked very slowly towards the door. Until I reached the door hope would remain alive. I heard a chair creak, and when I came to the door I could see a pair of shoes, but they were not a woman's shoes. I went quickly in, and it was Pyle who lifted his awkward weight from the chair Phuong used to use.

He said, 'Hullo, Thomas.'

'Hullo, Pyle. How did you get in?'

'I met Dominguez. He was bringing your mail. I asked him to let me stay.'

'Has Phuong forgotten something?'

'Oh no, but Joe told me you'd been to the Legation. I thought it would be easier to talk here.'

'What about?'

He gave a lost gesture, like a boy put up to speak at some school function who cannot find the grown-up words. 'You've been away?'

'Yes. And you?'

'Oh, I've been travelling around.'

'Still playing with plastics?'

He grinned unhappily. He said, 'Your letters are over there.'

I could see at a glance there was nothing which could interest me now: there was one from my office in London and several that looked like bills, and one from my bank. I said, 'How's Phuong?'

His face lit up automatically like one of those electric toys which respond to a particular sound. 'Oh, she's fine,' he said, and then clamped his lips together as though he'd gone too far.

'Sit down, Pyle,' I said. 'Excuse me while I look at this. It's from my office.'

I opened it. How inopportunely the unexpected can occur. The editor wrote that he had considered my last letter and that in view of the confused situation in Indo-China, following the death of General de Lattre and the retreat from Hoa Binh, he was in agreement with my suggestion. He had appointed a temporary foreign editor and would like me to stay on in Indo-China for at least another year. 'We shall keep the chair warm for you,' he reassured me with complete incomprehension. He believed I cared about the job, and the paper.

I sat down opposite Pyle and re-read the letter which had come too late. For a moment I had felt elation as on the instant of waking before one remembers.

'Bad news?' Pyle asked.

'No.' I told myself that it wouldn't have made any difference anyway: a reprieve for one year couldn't stand up against a marriage settlement.

'Are you married yet?' I asked.

'No.' He blushed – he had a great facility in blushing. 'As a matter of fact I'm hoping to get special leave. Then we could get married at home – properly.'

'Is it more proper when it happens at home?'

'Well, I thought – it's difficult to say these things to you, you are so darned cynical, Thomas, but it's a mark of respect. My father and mother would be there – she'd kind of enter the family. It's important in view of the past.'

'The past?'

'You know what I mean. I wouldn't want to leave her behind there with any stigma . . .'

'Would you leave her behind?'

'I guess so. My mother's a wonderful woman – she'd take her around, introduce her, you know, kind of fit her in. She'd help her to get a home ready for me.'

I didn't know whether to feel sorry for Phuong or not – she had looked forward so to the skyscrapers and the Statue of Liberty but she had so little idea of all they would involve, Professor and Mrs Pyle, the women's lunch clubs; would they teach her Canasta? I thought of her that first night in the Grand Monde, in her white dress, moving so exquisitely on her eighteen-year-old feet, and I thought of her a month ago, bargaining over meat at the butcher's stores in the Boulevard de la Somme. Would she like those bright clean little New England grocery stores where even the celery was wrapped in cellophane? Perhaps she would. I couldn't tell. Strangely I found myself saying as Pyle might have done a month ago, 'Go easy with her, Pyle. Don't force things. She can be hurt like you or me.'

'Of course, of course, Thomas.'

'She looks so small and breakable and unlike our women, but don't think of her as – as an ornament.'

'It's funny, Thomas, how differently things work out. I'd been dreading this talk. I thought you'd be tough.'

'I've had time to think, up in the north. There was a woman there . . . Perhaps I saw what you saw at that whorehouse. It's a good thing she went away with you. I might one day have left her behind with someone like Granger. A piece of tail.'

'And we can remain friends, Thomas?'

'Yes, of course. Only I'd rather not see Phuong. There's quite enough of her around here as it is. I must find another flat – when I've got time.'

He unwound his legs and stood up. 'I'm so glad, Thomas. I can't tell you how glad I am. I've said it before, I know, but I do really wish it hadn't been you.'

'I'm glad it's you, Pyle.' The interview had not been the way I had foreseen: under the superficial angry schemes, at some deeper level, the genuine plan of action must have been formed. All the time that his innocence had angered me, some judge within myself had summed up in his favour, had compared his idealism, his half-baked ideas founded on the works of York Harding, with my cynicism. Oh, I was right about the facts, but wasn't he right too to be young and mistaken, and wasn't he perhaps a better man for a girl to spend her life with?

We shook hands perfunctorily, but some half-formulated fear made me follow him out to the head of the stairs and call after him. Perhaps there is a prophet as well as a judge in those interior courts where our true decisions are made. 'Pyle, don't trust too much in York Harding.'

'York!' He stared up at me from the first landing.

'We are the old colonial peoples, Pyle, but we've learnt a bit of reality, we've learned not to play with matches. This Third Force – it comes out of a book, that's all. General Thé's only a bandit with a few thousand men: he's not a national democracy.'

It was as if he had been staring at me through a letter-box to see who was there and now, letting the flap fall, had shut out the unwelcome intruder. His eyes were out of sight. 'I don't know what you mean, Thomas.'

'Those bicycle bombs. They were a good joke, even though one man did lose a foot. But, Pyle, you can't trust men like Thé. They aren't going to save the East from Communism. We know their kind.'

'We?'

'The old colonialists.'

'I thought you took no sides.'

'I don't, Pyle, but if someone has got to make a mess of things in your outfit, leave it to Joe. Go home with Phuong. Forget the Third Force.'

'Of course I always value your advice, Thomas,' he said formally. 'Well, I'll be seeing you.'

'I suppose so.'

2

The weeks moved on, but somehow I hadn't yet found myself a new flat. It wasn't that I hadn't time. The annual crisis of the war had passed again: the hot wet *crachin* had settled on the north: the French were out of Hoa Binh, the rice-campaign was over in Tonkin and the opium-campaign in Laos. Dominguez could cover easily all that was needed in the south. At last I did drag myself to see one apartment in a so-called modern building (Paris Exhibition 1934?) up at the other end of the rue Catinat beyond the Continental Hotel. It was the Saigon pied-à-terre of a rubber planter who was going home. He wanted to sell it lock, stock and barrel. I have always wondered what the barrels contain: as for the stock, there were a large number of engravings from the Paris

Salon between 1880 and 1900. Their highest common factor was a big-bosomed woman with an extraordinary hair-do and gauzy draperies which somehow always exposed the great cleft buttocks and hid the field of battle. In the bathroom the planter had been rather more daring with his reproductions of Rops.

'You like art?' I asked and he smirked back at me like a fellow conspirator. He was fat with a little black moustache and insufficient hair.

'My best pictures are in Paris,' he said.

There was an extraordinary tall ash-tray in the living-room made like a naked woman with a bowl in her hair, and there were china ornaments of naked girls embracing tigers, and one very odd one of a girl stripped to the waist riding a bicycle. In the bedroom facing his enormous bed was a great glazed oil painting of two girls sleeping together. I asked him the price of his apartment without his collection, but he would not agree to separate the two.

'You are not a collector?' he asked.

'Well, no.'

'I have some books also,' he said, 'which I would throw in, though I intended to take these back to France.' He unlocked a glass-fronted bookcase and showed me his library – there were expensive illustrated editions of *Aphrodite* and *Nana*, there was *La Garçonne*, and even several Paul de Kocks. I was tempted to ask him whether he would sell himself with his collection: he went with them: he was period too. He said, 'If you live alone in the tropics a collection is company.'

I thought of Phuong just because of her complete absence. So it always is: when you escape to a desert the silence shouts in your ear.

'I don't think my paper would allow me to buy an art-collection.'

He said, 'It would not, of course, appear on the receipt.'

I was glad Pyle had not seen him: the man might have lent his features to Pyle's imaginary 'old colonialist', who was repulsive enough without him. When I came out it was nearly half past eleven and I went down as far as the Pavillon for a glass of iced beer. The Pavillon was a coffee centre for European and American women and I was confident that I would not see Phuong there. Indeed I knew exactly where she would be at this time of day – she was not a girl to break her habits, and so, coming from the planter's apartment, I had crossed the road to avoid the milk-bar where at this time of day she had her chocolate malt. Two young American girls sat at the next table, neat and clean in the heat, scooping up ice-cream. They each had a bag slung on the left shoulder and the bags were identical, with brass eagle badges. Their legs were identical too, long and slender, and their noses, just a shade tilted, and they were eating their ice-cream with concentration as though they were making an experiment in the college laboratory. I wondered whether they were Pyle's colleagues: they were charming, and I wanted to send them home, too. They finished their ices and one looked at her watch. 'We'd better be going,' she said, 'to be on the safe side.' I wondered idly what appointment they had.

'Warren said we mustn't stay later than eleven twenty-five.'

'It's past that now.'

'It would be exciting to stay. I don't know what it's all about, do you?'

'Not exactly, but Warren said better not.'

'Do you think it's a demonstration?'

'I've seen so many demonstrations,' the other said wearily, like a tourist glutted with churches. She rose and laid on their table the money for the ices. Before going she looked around the café, and the mirrors caught her profile at every freckled angle. There was only myself left and a dowdy middle-aged Frenchwoman who was carefully and uselessly making up her face. Those two hardly needed make-up, the quick dash of lipstick, a comb through the hair. For a moment her glance had rested on me – it was not like a woman's glance, but a man's, very straightforward, speculating on some course of action. Then she turned quickly to her companion. 'We'd better be off.' I watched them idly as they went out side by side into the sun-splintered street. It was impossible to conceive either of them a prey to untidy passion: they did not belong to rumpled sheets and the sweat of sex. Did they take deodorants to bed with them? I found myself for a moment envying them their sterilized world, so different from this world that I inhabited – which suddenly inexplicably broke in pieces. Two of the mirrors on the wall flew at me and collapsed half-way. The dowdy Frenchwoman was on her knees in a wreckage of chairs and tables. Her compact lay open and unhurt in my lap and oddly enough I sat exactly where I had sat before, although my table had joined the wreckage around the Frenchwoman. A curious garden-sound filled the café: the regular drip of a fountain, and looking at the bar I saw rows of smashed bottles which let out their contents in a multi-coloured stream – the red of porto, the orange of cointreau, the green of chartreuse, the cloudy yellow of pastis, across the floor of the café. The Frenchwoman sat up and calmly looked around for her compact. I gave it her and she thanked me formally, sitting on the floor. I realized that

I didn't hear her very well. The explosion had been so close that my ear-drums had still to recover from the pressure.

I thought rather petulantly, 'Another joke with plastics: what does Mr Heng expect me to write now?' but when I got into the Place Garnier, I realized by the heavy clouds of smoke that this was no joke. The smoke came from the cars burning in the car-park in front of the national theatre, bits of cars were scattered over the square, and a man without his legs lay twitching at the edge of the ornamental gardens. People were crowding in from the rue Catinat, from the Boulevard Bonnard. The sirens of police-cars, the bells of the ambulances and fire-engines came at one remove to my shocked ear-drums. For one moment I had forgotten that Phuong must have been in the milk-bar on the other side of the square. The smoke lay between. I couldn't see through.

I stepped out into the square and a policeman stopped me. They had formed a cordon round the edge to prevent the crowd increasing, and already the stretchers were beginning to emerge. I implored the policeman in front of me, 'Let me across. I have a friend . . .'

'Stand back,' he said. 'Everybody here has friends.'

He stood on one side to let a priest through, and I tried to follow the priest, but he pulled me back. I said, 'I am the Press,' and searched in vain for the wallet in which I had my card, but I couldn't find it: had I come out that day without it? I said, 'At least tell me what happened to the milk-bar': the smoke was clearing and I tried to see, but the crowd between was too great. He said something I didn't catch.

'What did you say?'

He repeated, 'I don't know. Stand back. You are blocking the stretchers.'

Could I have dropped my wallet in the Pavillon? I turned to go back and there was Pyle. He exclaimed, 'Thomas.'

'Pyle,' I said, 'for Christ's sake, where's your Legation pass? We've got to get across. Phuong's in the milk-bar.'

'No, no,' he said.

'Pyle, she is. She always goes there. At eleven thirty. We've got to find her.'

'She isn't there, Thomas.'

'How do you know? Where's your card?'

'I warned her not to go.'

I turned back to the policeman, meaning to throw him to one side and make a run for it across the square: he might shoot: I didn't care

– and then the word 'warn' reached my consciousness. I took Pyle by the arm. 'Warn?' I said. 'What do you mean "warn"?'

'I told her to keep away this morning.'

The pieces fell together in my mind. 'And Warren?' I said. 'Who's Warren? He warned those girls too.'

'I don't understand.'

'There mustn't be any American casualties, must there?' An ambulance forced its way up the rue Catinat into the square and the policeman who had stopped me moved to one side to let it through. The policeman beside him was engaged in an argument. I pushed Pyle forward and ahead of me into the square before we could be stopped.

We were among a congregation of mourners. The police could prevent others entering the square; they were powerless to clear the square of the survivors and the first-comers. The doctors were too busy to attend to the dead, and so the dead were left to their owners, for one can own the dead as one owns a chair. A woman sat on the ground with what was left of her baby in her lap; with a kind of modesty she had covered it with her straw peasant hat. She was still and silent, and what struck me most in the square was the silence. It was like a church I had once visited during Mass – the only sounds came from those who served, except where here and there the Europeans wept and implored and fell silent again as though shamed by the modesty, patience and propriety of the East. The legless torso at the edge of the garden still twitched, like a chicken which has lost its head. From the man's shirt, he had probably been a trishaw driver.

Pyle said, 'It's awful.' He looked at the wet on his shoes and said in a sick voice, 'What's that?'

'Blood,' I said. 'Haven't you ever seen it before?'

He said, 'I must get them cleaned before I see the Minister.' I don't think he knew what he was saying. He was seeing a real war for the first time: he had punted down into Phat Diem in a kind of schoolboy dream, and anyway in his eyes soldiers didn't count.

I forced him, with my hand on his shoulder, to look around. I said, 'This is the hour when the place is always full of women and children – it's the shopping hour. Why choose that of all hours?'

He said weakly, 'There was to have been a parade.'

'And you hope to catch a few colonels. But the parade was cancelled yesterday, Pyle.'

'I didn't know.'

'Didn't know!' I pushed him into a patch of blood where a stretcher had lain. 'You ought to be better informed.'

'I was out of town,' he said, looking down at his shoes. 'They should have called it off.'

'And missed the fun?' I asked him. 'Do you expect General Thé to lose his demonstration? This is better than a parade. Women and children are news, and soldiers aren't, in a war. This will hit the world's Press. You've put General Thé on the map all right, Pyle. You've got the Third Force and National Democracy all over your right shoe. Go home to Phuong and tell her about your heroic dead – there are a few dozen less of her people to worry about.'

A small fat priest scampered by, carrying something on a dish under a napkin. Pyle had been silent a long while, and I had nothing more to say. Indeed I had said too much already. He looked white and beaten and ready to faint, and I thought, 'What's the good? he'll always be innocent, you can't blame the innocent, they are always guiltless. All you can do is control them or eliminate them. Innocence is a kind of insanity.'

He said, 'Thé wouldn't have done this. I'm sure he wouldn't. Somebody deceived him. The Communists . . .'

He was impregnably armoured by his good intentions and his ignorance. I left him standing in the square and went on up the rue Catinat to where the hideous pink Cathedral blocked the way. Already people were flocking in: it must have been a comfort to them to be able to pray for the dead to the dead.

Unlike them, I had reason for thankfulness, for wasn't Phuong alive? Hadn't Phuong been 'warned'? But what I remembered was the torso in the square, the baby on its mother's lap. They had not been warned: they had not been sufficiently important. And if the parade had taken place would they not have been there just the same, out of curiosity, to see the soldiers, and hear the speakers, and throw the flowers? A two-hundred-pound bomb does not discriminate. How many dead colonels justify a child's or a trishaw driver's death when you are building a national democratic front? I stopped a motor-trishaw and told the driver to take me to the Quai Mytho.

PART FOUR

Chapter 1

I HAD given Phuong money to take her sister to the cinema so that she would be safely out of the way. I went out to dinner myself with Dominguez and was back in my room waiting when Vigot called sharp on ten. He apologized for not taking a drink – he said he was too tired and a drink might send him to sleep. It had been a very long day.

'Murder and sudden death?'

'No. Petty thefts. And a few suicides. These people love to gamble and when they have lost everything they kill themselves. Perhaps I would not have become a policeman if I had known how much time I would have to spend in mortuaries. I do not like the smell of ammonia. Perhaps after all I will have a beer.'

'I haven't a refrigerator, I'm afraid.'

'Unlike the mortuary. A little English whisky, then?'

I remembered the night I had gone down to the mortuary with him and they had slid out Pyle's body like a tray of ice-cubes.

'So you are not going home?' he asked.

'You've been checking up?'

'Yes.'

I held the whisky out to him, so that he could see how calm my nerves were. 'Vigot, I wish you'd tell me why you think I was concerned in Pyle's death. Is it a question of motive? That I wanted Phuong back? Or do you imagine it was revenge for losing her?'

'No. I'm not so stupid. One doesn't take one's enemy's book as a souvenir. There it is on your shelf. *The Rôle of the West.* Who is this York Harding?'

'He's the man you are looking for, Vigot. He killed Pyle – at long range.'

'I don't understand.'

'He's a superior sort of journalist – they call them diplomatic correspondents. He gets hold of an idea and then alters every situation to fit the idea. Pyle came out here full of York Harding's idea. Harding had been here once for a week on his way from Bangkok to Tokyo. Pyle made the mistake of putting his idea into practice. Harding wrote about a Third Force. Pyle formed one – a shoddy little bandit with two thousand men and a couple of tame tigers. He got mixed up.'

'You never do, do you?'

'I've tried not to be.'

'But you failed, Fowler.' For some reason I thought of Captain Trouin and that night which seemed to have happened years ago in the Haiphong opium house. What was it he had said? something about all of us getting involved sooner or later in a moment of emotion. I said, 'You would have made a good priest, Vigot. What is it about you that would make it so easy to confess – if there were anything to confess?'

'I have never wanted any confessions.'

'But you've received them?'

'From time to time.'

'Is it because like a priest it's your job not to be shocked, but to be sympathetic? "M. Flic, I must tell you exactly why I battered in the old lady's skull." "Yes, Gustave, take your time and tell me why it was."'

'You have a whimsical imagination. Aren't you drinking, Fowler?'

'Surely it's unwise for a criminal to drink with a police officer?'

'I have never said you were a criminal.'

'But suppose the drink unlocked even in me the desire to confess? There are no secrets of the confessional in your profession.'

'Secrecy is seldom important to a man who confesses: even when it's to a priest. He has other motives.'

'To cleanse himself?'

'Not always. Sometimes he only wants to see himself clearly as he is. Sometimes he is just weary of deception. You are not a criminal, Fowler, but I would like to know why you lied to me. You saw Pyle the night he died.'

'What gives you that idea?'

'I don't for a moment think you killed him. You would hardly have used a rusty bayonet.'

'Rusty?'

'Those are the kind of details we get from an autopsy. I told you, though, that was not the cause of death. Dakow mud.' He held out his glass for another whisky. 'Let me see now. You had a drink at the Continental at six ten?'

'Yes.'

'And at six forty-five you were talking to another journalist at the door of the Majestic?'

'Yes, Wilkins. I told you all this, Vigot, before. That night.'

'Yes. I've checked up since then. It's wonderful how you carry such petty details in your head.'

'I'm a reporter, Vigot.'

'Perhaps the times are not quite accurate, but nobody could blame you, could they, if you were a quarter of an hour out here and ten minutes out there. You had no reason to think the times important. Indeed how suspicious it would be if you had been completely accurate.'

'Haven't I been?'

'Not quite. It was at five to seven that you talked to Wilkins.'

'Another ten minutes.'

'Of course. As I said. And it had only just struck six when you arrived at the Continental.'

'My watch is always a little fast,' I said. 'What time do you make it now?'

'Ten eight.'

'Ten eighteen by mine. You see.'

He didn't bother to look. He said, 'Then the time you said you talked to Wilkins was twenty-five minutes out – by your watch. That's quite a mistake, isn't it?'

'Perhaps I readjusted the time in my mind. Perhaps I'd corrected my watch that day. I sometimes do.'

'What interests me,' Vigot said, '(could I have a little more soda? – you have made this rather strong) is that you are not at all angry with me. It is not very nice to be questioned as I am questioning you.'

'I find it interesting, like a detective-story. And, after all, you know I didn't kill Pyle – you've said so.'

Vigot said, 'I know you were not present at his murder.'

'I don't know what you hope to prove by showing that I was ten minutes out here and five there.'

'It gives a little space,' Vigot said, 'a little gap in time.'

'Space for what?'

'For Pyle to come and see you.'

'Why do you want so much to prove that?'

'Because of the dog,' Vigot said.

'And the mud between its toes?'

'It wasn't mud. It was cement. You see, somewhere that night, when it was following Pyle, it stepped into wet cement. I remembered that on the ground-floor of the apartment there are builders at work – they are still at work. I passed them tonight as I came in. They work long hours in this country.'

'I wonder how many houses have builders in them – and wet cement. Did any of them remember the dog?'

'Of course I asked them that. But if they had they would not have told me. I am the police.' He stopped talking and leant back in his chair, staring at his glass. I had a sense that some analogy had struck him and he was miles away in thought. A fly crawled over the back of his hand and he did not brush it away – any more than Dominguez would have done. I had the feeling of some force immobile and profound. For all I knew, he might have been praying.

I rose and went through the curtains into the bedroom. There was nothing I wanted there, except to get away for a moment from that silence sitting in a chair. Phuong's picture-books were back on the shelf. She had stuck a telegram for me up among the cosmetics – some message or other from the London office. I wasn't in the mood to open it. Everything was as it had been before Pyle came. Rooms don't change, ornaments stand where you place them: only the heart decays.

I returned to the sitting-room and Vigot put the glass to his lips. I said, 'I've got nothing to tell you. Nothing at all.'

'Then I'll be going,' he said. 'I don't suppose I'll trouble you again.'

At the door he turned as though he were unwilling to abandon hope – his hope or mine. 'That was a strange picture for you to go and see that night. I wouldn't have thought you cared for costume drama. What was it? *Robin Hood*?'

'*Scaramouche*, I think. I had to kill time. And I needed distraction.'

'Distraction?'

'We all have our private worries, Vigot,' I carefully explained.

When Vigot was gone there was still an hour to wait for Phuong and living company. It was strange how disturbed I had been by Vigot's visit. It was as though a poet had brought me his work to criticize and through some careless action I had destroyed it. I was a man without a vocation – one cannot seriously consider journalism as a vocation, but I could recognize a vocation in another. Now that Vigot was gone to close his uncompleted file, I wished I had the courage to call him back and say, 'You are right. I did see Pyle the night he died.'

Chapter 2

On the way to the Quai Mytho I passed several ambulances driving out of Cholon heading for the Place Garnier. One could almost reckon the pace of rumour from the expression of the faces in the street, which at first turned on someone like myself coming from the direction of the Place with looks of expectancy and speculation. By the time I entered Cholon I had outstripped the news: life was busy, normal, uninterrupted: nobody knew.

I found Mr Chou's godown and mounted to Mr Chou's house. Nothing had changed since my last visit. The cat and the dog moved from floor to cardboard box to suitcase, like a couple of chess knights who cannot get to grips. The baby crawled on the floor, and the two old men were still playing mah jongg. Only the young people were absent. As soon as I appeared in the doorway one of the women began to pour out tea. The old lady sat on the bed and looked at her feet.

'Monsieur Heng,' I asked. I shook my head at the tea: I wasn't in the mood to begin another long course of that trivial bitter brew. 'Il faut absolument que je voie Monsieur Heng.' It seemed impossible to convey to them the urgency of my request, but perhaps the very abruptness of my refusal of tea caused some disquiet. Or perhaps like Pyle I had blood on my shoes. Anyway after a short delay one of the women led me out and down the stairs, along two bustling bannered streets and left me before what they would have called I suppose in Pyle's country a 'funeral parlour', full of stone jars in which the resurrected bones of the Chinese dead are eventually placed. 'Monsieur Heng,' I said to an old Chinese in the doorway, 'Monsieur Heng.' It seemed a suitable halting place on a day which had begun with the planter's erotic collection and continued with the murdered bodies in the square. Somebody called from an inner room and the Chinese stepped aside and let me in.

Mr Heng himself came cordially forward and ushered me into a little inner room lined with the black carved uncomfortable chairs you find in every Chinese ante-room, unused, unwelcoming. But I had the sense that on this occasion the chairs had been employed, for there were five little tea-cups on the table, and two were not empty. 'I have interrupted a meeting,' I said.

'A matter of business,' Mr Heng said evasively, 'of no importance. I am always glad to see you, Mr Fowler.'

'I've come from the Place Garnier,' I said.

'I thought that was it.'

'You've heard . . .'

'Someone telephoned to me. It was thought best that I keep away from Mr Chou's for a while. The police will be very active today.'

'But you had nothing to do with it.'

'It is the business of the police to find a culprit.'

'It was Pyle again,' I said.

'Yes.'

'It was a terrible thing to do.'

'General Thé is not a very controlled character.'

'And bombs aren't for boys from Boston. Who is Pyle's chief, Heng?'

'I have the impression that Mr Pyle is very much his own master.'

'What is he? OSS?'

'The initial letters are not very important. I think now they are different.'

'What can I do, Heng? He's got to be stopped.'

'You can publish the truth. Or perhaps you cannot?'

'My paper's not interested in General Thé. They are only interested in your people, Heng.'

'You really want Mr Pyle stopped, Mr Fowler?'

'If you'd seen him, Heng. He stood there and said it was all a sad mistake, there should have been a parade. He said he'd have to get his shoes cleaned before he saw the Minister.'

'Of course, you could tell what you know to the police.'

'They aren't interested in Thé either. And do you think they would dare to touch an American? He has diplomatic privileges. He's a graduate of Harvard. The Minister's very fond of Pyle. Heng, there was a woman there whose baby – she kept it covered under her straw hat. I can't get it out of my head. And there was another in Phat Diem.'

'You must try to be calm, Mr Fowler.'

'What'll he do next, Heng?'

'Would you be prepared to help us, Mr Fowler?'

'He comes blundering in and people have to die for his mistakes. I wish your people had got him on the river from Nam Dinh. It would have made a lot of difference to a lot of lives.'

'I agree with you, Mr Fowler. He has to be restrained. I have a suggestion to make.' Somebody coughed delicately behind the door, then noisily spat. He said, 'If you would invite him to dinner tonight at the Vieux Moulin. Between eight thirty and nine thirty.'

'What good . . . ?'

'We would talk to him on the way,' Heng said.

'He may be engaged.'

'Perhaps it would be better if you asked him to call on you – at six thirty. He will be free then: he will certainly come. If he is able to have dinner with you, take a book to your window as though you want to catch the light.'

'Why the Vieux Moulin?'

'It is by the bridge to Dakow – I think we shall be able to find a spot and talk undisturbed.'

'What will you do?'

'You do not want to know that, Mr Fowler. But I promise you we will act as gently as the situation allows.'

The unseen friends of Heng shifted like rats behind the wall. 'Will you do this for us, Mr Fowler?'

'I don't know,' I said, 'I don't know.'

'Sooner or later,' Heng said, and I was reminded of Captain Trouin speaking in the opium house, 'one has to take sides. If one is to remain human.'

2

I left a note at the Legation asking Pyle to come and then I went up the street to the Continental for a drink. The wreckage was all cleared away; the fire-brigade had hosed the square. I had no idea then how the time and the place would become important. I even thought of sitting there throughout the evening and breaking my appointment. Then I thought that perhaps I could frighten Pyle into inactivity by warning him of his danger – whatever his danger was, and so I finished my beer and went home, and when I reached home I began to hope that Pyle would not come. I tried to read, but there was nothing on my shelves to hold the attention. Perhaps I should have smoked, but there was no one to prepare my pipe. I listened unwillingly for footsteps and at last they came. Somebody knocked. I opened the door, but it was only Dominguez.

I said, 'What do you want, Dominguez?'

He looked at me with an air of surprise. 'Want?' He looked at his watch. 'This is the time I always come. Have you any cables?'

'I'm sorry – I'd forgotten. No.'

'But a follow-up on the bomb? Don't you want something filed?'

'Oh, work one out for me, Dominguez. I don't know how it is – being there on the spot, perhaps I got a bit shocked. I can't think of the thing in terms of a cable.' I hit out at a mosquito which came droning at my ear and saw Dominguez wince instinctively at my blow. 'It's all right, Dominguez, I missed it.' He grinned miserably. He could not justify this reluctance to take life: after all he was a Christian – one of those who had learnt from Nero how to make human bodies into candles.

'Is there anything I can do for you?' he asked. He didn't drink, he didn't eat meat, he didn't kill – I envied him the gentleness of his mind.

'No, Dominguez. Just leave me alone tonight.' I watched him from the window, going away across the rue Catinat. A trishaw driver had parked beside the pavement opposite my window; Dominguez tried to engage him, but the man shook his head. Presumably he was waiting for a client in one of the shops, for this was not a parking place for trishaws. When I looked at my watch it was strange to see that I had been waiting for little more than ten minutes, and, when Pyle knocked, I hadn't even heard his step.

'Come in.' But as usual it was the dog that came in first.

'I was glad to get your note, Thomas. This morning I thought you were mad at me.'

'Perhaps I was. It wasn't a pretty sight.'

'You know so much now, it won't hurt to tell you a bit more. I saw Thé this afternoon.'

'Saw him? Is he in Saigon? I suppose he came to see how his bomb worked.'

'That's in confidence, Thomas. I dealt with him very severely.' He spoke like the captain of a school-team who has found one of his boys breaking his training. All the same I asked him with a certain hope, 'Have you thrown him over?'

'I told him that if he made another uncontrolled demonstration we would have no more to do with him.'

'But haven't you finished with him already, Pyle?' I pushed impatiently at his dog which was nosing around my ankles.

'I can't. (Sit down, Duke.) In the long run he's the only hope we have. If he came to power with our help, we could rely on him . . .'

'How many people have to die before you realize . . . ?' But I could tell that it was a hopeless argument.

'Realize what, Thomas?'

'That there's no such thing as gratitude in politics.'

'At least they won't hate us like they hate the French.'

'Are you sure? Sometimes we have a kind of love for our enemies and sometimes we feel hate for our friends.'

'You talk like a European, Thomas. These people aren't complicated.'

'Is that what you've learned in a few months? You'll be calling them childlike next.'

'Well – in a way.'

'Find me an uncomplicated child, Pyle. When we are young we are a jungle of complications. We simplify as we get older.' But what good was it to talk to him? There was an unreality in both our arguments. I was becoming a leader-writer before my time. I got up and went to the bookshelf.

'What are you looking for, Thomas?'

'Oh, just a passage I used to be fond of. Can you have dinner with me, Pyle?'

'I'd love to, Thomas. I'm so glad you aren't mad any longer. I know you disagree with me, but we can disagree, can't we, and be friends?'

'I don't know. I don't think so.'

'After all, Phuong was much more important than this.'

'Do you really believe that, Pyle?'

'Why, she's the most important thing there is. To me. And to you, Thomas.'

'Not to me any longer.'

'It was a terrible shock today, Thomas, but in a week, you'll see, we'll have forgotten it. We are looking after the relatives too.'

'We?'

'We've wired to Washington. We'll get permission to use some of our funds.'

I interrupted him. 'The Vieux Moulin? Between nine and nine thirty?'

'Where you like, Thomas.' I went to the window. The sun had sunk below the roofs. The trishaw driver still waited for his fare. I looked down at him and he raised his face to me.

'Are you waiting for someone, Thomas?'

'No. There was just a piece I was looking for.' To cover my action I read, holding the book up to the last light:

'I drive through the streets and I care not a damn,
The people they stare, and they ask who I am;
And if I should chance to run over a cad,
I can pay for the damage, if ever so bad.
So pleasant it is to have money, heigh ho!
So pleasant it is to have money.'

'That's a funny kind of poem,' Pyle said with a note of disapproval.

'He was an adult poet in the nineteenth century. There weren't so many of them.' I looked down into the street again. The trishaw driver had moved away.

'Have you run out of drink?' Pyle asked.

'No, but I thought you didn't . . .'

'Perhaps I'm beginning to loosen up,' Pyle said. 'Your influence. I guess you're good for me, Thomas.'

I got the bottle and glasses – I forgot one of them the first journey and then I had to go back for water. Everything that I did that evening took a long time. He said, 'You know, I've got a wonderful family, but maybe they were a little on the strict side. We have one of those old houses in Chestnut Street, as you go up the hill on the right-hand side. My mother collects glass, and my father – when he's not eroding his old cliffs – picks up all the Darwin manuscripts and association-copies he can. You see, they live in the past. Maybe that's why York made such an impression on me. He seemed kind of open to modern conditions. My father's an isolationist.'

'Perhaps I would like your father,' I said. 'I'm an isolationist too.'

For a quiet man Pyle that night was in a talking mood. I didn't hear all that he said, for my mind was elsewhere. I tried to persuade myself that Mr Heng had other means at his disposal but the crude and obvious one. But in a war like this, I knew, there is no time to hesitate: one uses the weapon to hand – the French the napalm bomb, Mr Heng the bullet or the knife. I told myself too late that I wasn't made to be a judge – I would let Pyle talk awhile and then I would warn him. He could spend the night at my house. They would hardly break in there. I think he was speaking of the old nurse he had had – 'She really meant more to me than my mother, and the blueberry pies she used to make!' when I interrupted him. 'Do you carry a gun now – since that night?'

'No. We have orders in the Legation . . .'

'But you're on special duties?'

'It wouldn't do any good – if they wanted to get me, they always could. Anyway I'm as blind as a coot. At college they called me Bat – because I could see in the dark as well as they could. Once when we were fooling around . . .' He was off again. I returned to the window.

A trishaw driver waited opposite. I wasn't sure – they looked so much alike, but I thought he was a different one. Perhaps he really had a client. It occurred to me that Pyle would be safest at the Legation. They must have laid their plans, since my signal, for later in the evening: something that involved the Dakow bridge. I couldn't understand why or how: surely he would not be so foolish as to drive through Dakow after sunset and our side of the bridge was always guarded by armed police.

'I'm doing all the talking,' Pyle said. 'I don't know how it is, but somehow this evening . . .'

'Go on,' I said, 'I'm in a quiet mood, that's all. Perhaps we'd better cancel that dinner.'

'No, don't do that. I've felt cut off from you, since . . . well . . .'

'Since you saved my life,' I said and couldn't disguise the bitterness of my self-inflicted wound.

'No, I didn't mean that. All the same how we talked, didn't we, that night? As if it was going to be our last. I learned a lot about you, Thomas. I don't agree with you, mind, but for you maybe it's right – not being involved. You kept it up all right, even after your leg was smashed you stayed neutral.'

'There's always a point of change,' I said. 'Some moment of emotion . . .'

'You haven't reached it yet. I doubt if you ever will. And I'm not likely to change either – except with death,' he added merrily.

'Not even with this morning? Mightn't that change a man's views?'

'They were only war casualties,' he said. 'It was a pity, but you can't always hit your target. Anyway they died in the right cause.'

'Would you have said the same if it had been your old nurse with her blueberry pie?'

He ignored my facile point. 'In a way you could say they died for democracy,' he said.

'I wouldn't know how to translate that into Vietnamese.' I was suddenly very tired. I wanted him to go away quickly and die. Then I could start life again – at the point before he came in.

'You'll never take me seriously, will you, Thomas?' he complained, with that schoolboy gaiety which he seemed to have kept up his sleeve for this night of all nights. 'I tell you what – Phuong's at the cinema – what about you and me spending the whole evening together? I've nothing to do now.' It was as though someone from outside were directing him how to choose his words in order to rob me of any possible excuse. He went on. 'Why don't we go to the Chalet? I haven't been there since that night. The food is just as good as the Vieux Moulin, and there's music.'

I said, 'I'd rather not remember that night.'

'I'm sorry. I'm a dumb fool sometimes, Thomas. What about a Chinese dinner in Cholon?'

'To get a good one you have to order in advance. Are you scared of the Vieux Moulin, Pyle? It's well wired and there are always police on the bridge. And you wouldn't be such a fool, would you, as to drive through Dakow?'

'It wasn't that. I just thought it would be fun tonight to make a long evening of it.'

He made a movement and upset his glass, which smashed upon the floor. 'Good luck,' he said mechanically. 'I'm sorry, Thomas.' I began to pick up the pieces and pack them into the ash-tray. 'What about it, Thomas?' The smashed glass reminded me of the bottles in the Pavillon bar dripping their contents. 'I warned Phuong I might be out with you.' How badly chosen was the word 'warn'. I picked up the last piece of glass. 'I have got an engagement at the Majestic,' I said, 'and I can't manage before nine.'

'Well, I guess I'll have to go back to the office. Only I'm always afraid of getting caught.'

There was no harm in giving him that one chance. 'Don't mind being late,' I said. 'If you do get caught, look in here later. I'll come back at ten, if you can't make dinner, and wait for you.'

'I'll let you know . . .'

'Don't bother. Just come to the Vieux Moulin – or meet me here.' I handed back the decision to that Somebody in whom I didn't believe: You can intervene if You want to: a telegram on his desk: a message from the Minister. You cannot exist unless you have the power to alter the future. 'Go away now, Pyle. There are things I have to do.' I felt a strange exhaustion, hearing him go away and the pad of his dog's paws.

3

There were no trishaw drivers nearer than the rue d'Ormay when I went out. I walked down to the Majestic and stood awhile watching the unloading of the American bombers. The sun had gone and they worked by the light of arc-lamps. I had no idea of creating an alibi, but I told Pyle I was going to the Majestic and I felt an unreasoning dislike of telling more lies than were needed.

'Evening, Fowler.' It was Wilkins.

'Evening.'

'How's the leg?'

'No trouble now.'

'Got a good story filed?'

'I left it to Dominguez.'

'Oh, they told me you were there.'

'Yes, I was. But space is tight these days. They won't want much.'

'The spice has gone out of the dish, hasn't it?' Wilkins said. 'We ought to have lived in the days of Russell and the old *Times*. Dispatches by balloon. One had time to do some fancy writing then. Why, he'd even have made a column out of *this*. The luxury hotel, the bombers, night falling. Night never falls nowadays, does it, at so many piastres a word.' From far up in the sky you could faintly hear the noise of laughter: somebody broke a glass as Pyle had done. The sound fell on us like icicles. '"The lamps shone o'er fair women and brave men,"' Wilkins malevolently quoted. 'Doing anything tonight, Fowler? Care for a spot of dinner?'

'I'm dining as it is. At the Vieux Moulin.'

'I wish you joy. Granger will be there. They ought to advertise special Granger nights. For those who like background noise.'

I said good night to him and went into the cinema next door – Errol Flynn, or it may have been Tyrone Power (I don't know how to distinguish them in tights), swung on ropes and leapt from balconies and rode bare-back into technicolour dawns. He rescued a girl and killed his enemy and led a charmed life. It was what they call a film for boys, but the sight of Oedipus emerging with his bleeding eyeballs from the palace at Thebes would surely give a better training for life today. No life is charmed. Luck had been with Pyle at Phat Diem and on the road from Tanyin, but luck doesn't last, and they had two hours to see that no charm worked. A French soldier sat beside me with his hand in a girl's lap, and I envied the simplicity of his happiness or his misery, whichever it might be. I left before the film was over and took a trishaw to the Vieux Moulin.

The restaurant was wired in against grenades and two armed police-men were on duty at the end of the bridge. The *patron*, who had grown fat on his own rich Burgundian cooking, let me through the wire himself. The place smelt of capons and melting butter in the heavy evening heat.

'Are you joining the party of M. Granjair?' he asked me.

'No.'

'A table for one?' It was then for the first time that I thought of the future and the questions I might have to answer. 'For one,' I said, and it was almost as though I had said aloud that Pyle was dead.

There was only one room and Granger's party occupied a large table at the back; the *patron* gave me a small one closest to the wire. There were no window-panes, for fear of splintered glass. I recognized a few of the people Granger was entertaining, and I bowed to them before I sat down: Granger himself looked away. I hadn't seen him for months – only once since the night Pyle fell in love. Perhaps some offensive remark I had made that evening had penetrated the alcoholic fog, for he sat scowling at the head of the table while Madame Desprez, the wife of a public-relations officer, and Captain Duparc of the Press Liaison Service nodded and becked. There was a big man whom I think was an *hôtelier* from Pnom Penh and a French girl I'd never seen before and two or three other faces that I had only observed in bars. It seemed for once to be a quiet party.

I ordered a pastis because I wanted to give Pyle time to come – plans go awry and so long as I did not begin to eat my dinner it was as though I still had time to hope. And then I wondered what I hoped for. Good luck to the OSS or whatever his gang were called? Long life to plastic bombs and General Thé? Or did I – I of all people – hope for some kind of miracle: a method of discussion arranged by Mr Heng which wasn't simply death? How much easier it would have been if we had both been killed on the road from Tanyin. I sat for twenty minutes over my pastis and then I ordered dinner. It would soon be half past nine: he wouldn't come now.

Against my will I listened: for what? a scream? a shot? some movement by the police outside? but in any case I would probably hear nothing, for Granger's party was warming up. The *hôtelier*, who had a pleasant untrained voice, began to sing and as a new champagne cork popped others joined in, but not Granger. He sat there with raw eyes glaring across the room at me. I wondered if there would be a fight: I was no match for Granger.

They were singing a sentimental song, and as I sat hungerless over my apology for a *Chapon duc Charles* I thought, for almost the first time since I had known that she was safe, of Phuong. I remembered how Pyle, sitting on the floor waiting for the Viets, had said, 'She seems fresh like a flower,' and I had flippantly replied, 'Poor flower.' She would never see New England now or learn the secrets of Canasta. Perhaps she would never know security: what right had I to value her less than the dead bodies in the square? Suffering is not increased by numbers: one body can contain all the suffering the world can feel. I had judged like a journalist in terms of quantity and I had betrayed my own principles; I had become as *engagé* as Pyle, and it seemed to me that no decision would ever be simple again. I looked at my watch and it was nearly a quarter to ten. Perhaps, after all, he had been caught; perhaps that 'someone' in whom he believed had acted on his behalf and he sat now in his Legation room fretting at a telegram to decode, and soon he would come stamping up the stairs to my room in the rue Catinat. I thought, 'If he does I shall tell him everything.'

Granger suddenly got up from his table and came at me. He didn't even see the chair in his way and he stumbled and laid his hand on the edge of my table. 'Fowler,' he said, 'come outside.' I laid enough notes down and followed him. I was in no mood to fight with him, but at that moment I would not have minded if he had beaten me unconscious. We have so few ways in which to assuage the sense of guilt.

He leant on the parapet of the bridge and the two policemen watched him from a distance. He said, 'I've got to talk to you, Fowler.'

I came within striking distance and waited. He didn't move. He was like an emblematic statue of all I thought I hated in America – as ill-designed as the Statue of Liberty and as meaningless. He said without moving, 'You think I'm pissed. You're wrong.'

'What's up, Granger?'

'I got to talk to you, Fowler. I don't want to sit there with those Frogs tonight. I don't like you, Fowler, but you talk English. A kind of English.' He leant there, bulky and shapeless in the half-light, an unexplored continent.

'What do you want, Granger?'

'I don't like Limies,' Granger said. 'I don't know why Pyle stomachs you. Maybe it's because he's Boston. I'm Pittsburgh and proud of it.'

'Why not?'

'There you are again.' He made a feeble attempt to mock my accent. 'You all talk like poufs. You're so damned superior. You think you know everything.'

'Good night, Granger. I've got an appointment.'

'Don't go, Fowler. Haven't you got a heart? I can't talk to those Froggies.'

'You're drunk.'

'I've had two glasses of champagne, that's all, and wouldn't you be drunk in my place? I've got to go north.'

'What's wrong in that?'

'Oh, I didn't tell you, did I? I keep on thinking everyone knows. I got a cable this morning from my wife.'

'Yes?'

'My son's got polio. He's bad.'

'I'm sorry.'

'You needn't be. It's not your kid.'

'Can't you fly home?'

'I can't. They want a story about some damned mopping-up operations near Hanoi and Connolly's sick.' (Connolly was his assistant.)

'I'm sorry, Granger. I wish I could help.'

'It's his birthday tonight. He's eight at half past ten our time. That's why I laid on a party with champagne before I knew. I had to tell someone, Fowler, and I can't tell these Froggies.'

'They can do a lot for polio nowadays.'

'I don't mind if he's crippled, Fowler. Not if he lives. Me, I'd be no good crippled, but he's got brains. Do you know what I've been doing in there while that bastard was singing? I was praying. I thought maybe if God wanted a life he could take mine.'

'Do you believe in a God, then?'

'I wish I did,' Granger said. He passed his whole hand across his face as though his head ached, but the motion was meant to disguise the fact that he was wiping tears away.

'I'd get drunk if I were you,' I said.

'Oh, no, I've got to stay sober. I don't want to think afterwards I was stinking drunk the night my boy died. My wife can't drink, can she?'

'Can't you tell your paper . . . ?'

'Connolly's not really sick. He's off after a bit of tail in Singapore. I've got to cover for him. He'd be sacked if they knew.' He gathered his shapeless body together. 'Sorry I kept you, Fowler. I just had to tell someone. Got to go in now and start the toasts. Funny it happened to be you, and you hate my guts.'

'I'd do your story for you. I could pretend it was Connolly.'

'You wouldn't get the accent right.'

'I don't dislike you, Granger. I've been blind to a lot of things . . .'

'Oh, you and me, we're cat and dog. But thanks for the sympathy.'

Was I so different from Pyle, I wondered? Must I too have my foot thrust in the mess of life before I saw the pain? Granger went inside and I could hear the voices rising to greet him. I found a trishaw and was pedalled home. There was nobody there, and I sat and waited till midnight. Then I went down into the street without hope and found Phuong there.

Chapter 3

'HAS Monsieur Vigot been to see you?' Phuong asked.

'Yes. He left a quarter of an hour ago. Was the film good?' She had already laid out the tray in the bedroom and now she was lighting the lamp.

'It was very sad,' she said, 'but the colours were lovely. What did Monsieur Vigot want?'

'He wanted to ask me some questions.'

'What about?'

'This and that. I don't think he will bother me again.'

'I like films with happy endings best,' Phuong said. 'Are you ready to smoke?'

'Yes.' I lay down on the bed and Phuong set to work with her needle. She said, 'They cut off the girl's head.'

'What a strange thing to do.'

'It was in the French Revolution.'

'Oh. Historical. I see.'

'It was very sad all the same.'

'I can't worry much about people in history.'

'And her lover – he went back to his garret – and he was miserable and he wrote a song – you see, he was a poet, and soon all the people who had cut off the head of his girl were singing his song. It was the Marseillaise.'

'It doesn't sound very historical,' I said.

'He stood there at the edge of the crowd while they were singing, and he looked very bitter and when he smiled you knew he was even more bitter and that he was thinking of her. I cried a lot and so did my sister.'

'Your sister? I can't believe it.'

'She is very sensitive. That horrid man Granger was there. He was drunk and he kept on laughing. But it was not funny at all. It was sad.'

'I don't blame him,' I said. 'He has something to celebrate. His son's out of danger. I heard today at the Continental. I like happy endings too.'

After I had smoked two pipes I lay back with my neck on the leather pillow and rested my hand in Phuong's lap. 'Are you happy?'

'Of course,' she said carelessly. I hadn't deserved a more considered answer.

'It's like it used to be,' I lied, 'a year ago.'

'Yes.'

'You haven't bought a scarf for a long time. Why don't you go shopping tomorrow?'

'It is a feast day.'

'Oh yes, of course. I forgot.'

'You have not opened your telegram,' Phuong said.

'No, I'd forgotten that too. I don't want to think about work tonight. And it's too late to file anything now. Tell me more about the film.'

'Well, her lover tried to rescue her from prison. He smuggled in boy's clothes and a man's cap like the one the gaoler wore, but just as she was passing the gate all her hair fell down and they called out "*Une aristocrate, une aristocrate*". I think that was a mistake in the story. They ought to have let her escape. Then they would both have made a lot of money with his song and they would have gone abroad to

America – or England,' she added with what she thought was cunning.

'I'd better read the telegram,' I said. 'I hope to God I don't have to go north tomorrow. I want to be quiet with you.'

She loosed the envelope from among the pots of cream and gave it to me. I opened it and read: 'Have thought over your letter again stop am acting irrationally as you hoped stop have told my lawyer start divorce proceedings grounds desertion stop God bless you affectionately Helen.'

'Do you have to go?'

'No,' I said, 'I don't have to go. I'll read it to you. Here's your happy ending.'

She jumped from the bed. 'But it is wonderful. I must go and tell my sister. She will be so pleased. I will say to her, "Do you know who I am? I am the second Mrs Fowlair."'

Opposite me in the bookcase *The Rôle of the West* stood out like a cabinet portrait – of a young man with a crew-cut and a black dog at his heels. He could harm no one any more. I said to Phuong, 'Do you miss him much?'

'Who?'

'Pyle.' Strange how even now, even to her, it was impossible to use his first name.

'Can I go, please? My sister will be so excited.'

'You spoke his name once in your sleep.'

'I never remember my dreams.'

'There was so much you could have done together. He was young.'

'You are not old.'

'The skyscrapers. The Empire State Building.'

She said with a small hesitation, 'I want to see the Cheddar Gorge.'

'It isn't the Grand Canyon.' I pulled her down on to the bed. 'I'm sorry, Phuong.'

'What are you sorry for? It is a wonderful telegram. My sister . . .'

'Yes, go and tell your sister. Kiss me first.' Her excited mouth skated over my face, and she was gone.

I thought of the first day and Pyle sitting beside me at the Continental, with his eye on the soda-fountain across the way. Everything had gone right with me since he had died, but how I wished there existed someone to whom I could say that I was sorry.

March 1952– June 1955

TRAVELS WITH MY AUNT

For
H. H. K.
who helped me more
than I can tell

PART ONE

Chapter 1

I MET my Aunt Augusta for the first time in more than half a century at my mother's funeral. My mother was approaching eighty-six when she died, and my aunt was some eleven or twelve years younger. I had retired from the bank two years before with an adequate pension and a silver handshake. There had been a take-over by the Westminster and my branch was considered redundant. Everyone thought me lucky, but I found it difficult to occupy my time. I have never married, I have always lived quietly, and, apart from my interest in dahlias, I have no hobby. For those reasons I found myself agreeably excited by my mother's funeral.

My father had been dead for more than forty years. He was a building contractor of a lethargic disposition who used to take afternoon naps in all sorts of curious places. This irritated my mother, who was an energetic woman, and she used to seek him out to disturb him. As a child I remember going to the bathroom – we lived in Highgate then – and finding my father asleep in the bath in his clothes. I am rather short-sighted and I thought that my mother had been cleaning an overcoat, until I heard my father whisper, 'Bolt the door on the inside when you go out.' He was too lazy to get out of the bath and too sleepy, I suppose, to realize that his order was quite impossible to carry out. At another time, when he was responsible for a new block of flats in Lewisham, he would take his catnap in the cabin of the giant crane, and construction would be halted until he woke. My mother, who had a good head for heights, would climb ladders to the highest scaffolding in the hope of discovering him, when as like as not he would have found a corner in what was to be the underground garage. I had always thought of them as reasonably happy together: their twin roles of the hunter and the hunted probably suited them, for my mother by the time I first remembered her had developed an alert poise of the head and a wary trotting pace which reminded me of a gun-dog. I must be forgiven these memories of the past: at a funeral they are apt to come unbidden, there is so much waiting about.

Not many people attended the service, which took place at a famous crematorium, but there was that slight stirring of excited expectation which is never experienced at a graveside. Will the oven doors open? Will the coffin stick on the way to the flames? I heard a voice behind me saying in very clear old accents, 'I was present once at a premature cremation.'

It was, as I recognized with some difficulty from a photograph in the family album, my Aunt Augusta, who had arrived late, dressed rather as the late Queen Mary of beloved memory might have dressed if she had still been with us and had adapted herself a little bit towards the present mode. I was surprised by her brilliant red hair, monumentally piled, and her two big front teeth which gave her a vital Neanderthal air. Somebody said, 'Hush,' and a clergyman began a prayer which I believe he must have composed himself. I had never heard it at any other funeral service, and I have attended a great number in my time. A bank manager is expected to pay his last respects to every old client who is not as we say 'in the red', and in any case I have a weakness for funerals. People are generally seen at their best on these occasions, serious and sober, and optimistic on the subject of personal immortality.

The funeral of my mother went without a hitch. The flowers were removed economically from the coffin, which at the touch of a button slid away from us out of sight. Afterwards in the troubled sunlight I shook hands with a number of nephews and nieces and cousins whom I hadn't seen for years and could not identify. It was understood that I had to wait for the ashes and wait I did, while the chimney of the crematorium gently smoked overhead.

'You must be Henry,' Aunt Augusta said, gazing reflectively at me with her sea-deep blue eyes.

'Yes,' I said, 'and you must be Aunt Augusta.'

'It's a very long time since I saw anything of your mother,' Aunt Augusta told me. 'I hope that her death was an easy one.'

'Oh yes, you know, at her time of life – her heart just stopped. She died of old age.'

'Old age? She was only twelve years older than I am,' Aunt Augusta said accusingly.

We took a little walk together in the garden of the crematorium. A crematorium garden resembles a real garden about as much as a golf links resembles a genuine landscape. The lawns are too well cultivated and the trees too stiffly on parade: the urns resemble the little boxes containing sand where one tees up. 'Tell me,' Aunt Augusta said, 'are you still at the bank?'

'No, I retired two years ago.'

'Retired? A young man like you! For heaven's sake, what do you do with your time?'

'I cultivate dahlias, Aunt Augusta.' She gave a regal right-about swing of a phantom bustle.

'Dahlias! Whatever would your father have said!'

'He took no interest in flowers, I know that. He always thought a garden was a waste of good building space. He would calculate how many bedrooms one above the other he could have fitted in. He was a very sleepy man.'

'He needed bedrooms for more than sleep,' my aunt said with a coarseness which surprised me.

'He slept in the oddest places. I remember once in the bathroom . . .'

'In a bedroom he did other things than sleep,' she said. 'You are the proof.'

I began to understand why my parents had seen so little of Aunt Augusta. She had a temperament my mother would not have liked. My mother was far from being a puritan, but she wanted everything to be done or said at a suitable time. At meals we would talk about meals. Perhaps the price of food. If we went to the theatre we talked in the interval about the play – or other plays. At breakfast we spoke of the news. She was adept at guiding conversation back into the right channel if it strayed. She had a phrase, 'My dear, this isn't the moment . . .' Perhaps in the bedroom, I found myself thinking, with something of Aunt Augusta's directness, she talked about love. That was why she couldn't bear my father sleeping in odd places, and, when I developed an interest in dahlias, she often warned me to forget about them during banking hours.

By the time we had finished our walk the ashes were ready for me. I had chosen a very classical urn in black steel, and I would have liked to assure myself that there had been no error, but they presented me with a package very neatly done up in brown paper with red paper seals which reminded me of a Christmas gift. 'What are you going to do with it?' Aunt Augusta said.

'I thought of making a little throne for it among my dahlias.'

'It will look a little bleak in winter.'

'I hadn't considered that. I could always bring it indoors at that season.'

'Backwards and forwards. My sister seems hardly likely to rest in peace.'

'I'll think over it again.'

'You are not married, are you?'

'No.'

'Any children?'

'Of course not.'

'There is always the question to whom you will bequeath my sister. I am likely to predecease you.'

'One cannot think of everything at once.'

'You could have left it here,' Aunt Augusta said.

'I thought it would look well among the dahlias,' I replied obstinately, for I had spent all the previous evening designing a simple plinth in good taste.

'*À chacun son goût*,' my aunt said with a surprisingly good French accent. I had never considered our family very cosmopolitan.

'Well, Aunt Augusta,' I said at the gates of the crematorium (I was preparing to leave, for my garden called), 'it's been many years since we saw each other . . . I hope . . .' I had left the lawn-mower outside, uncovered, and there was a hint of rain in the quick grey clouds overhead. 'I would like it very much if one day you would take a cup of tea with me in Southwood.'

'At the moment I would prefer something stronger and more tranquillizing. It is not every day one sees a sister consigned to the flames. Like the Pucelle.'

'I don't quite . . .'

'Joan of Arc.'

'I have some sherry at home, but it's rather a long ride and perhaps . . .'

'My apartment is at any rate north of the river,' Aunt Augusta said firmly, 'and I have everything we require.' Without asking my assent she hailed a taxi. It was the first and perhaps, when I think back on it now, the most memorable of the journeys we were to take together.

Chapter 2

I WAS quite right in my weather forecast. The grey clouds began to rain and I found myself preoccupied with my private worries. All along the shiny streets people were putting up umbrellas and taking shelter in the doorways of Burton's, the United Dairies, Mac Fisheries or the ABC. For some reason rain in the suburbs reminds me of a Sunday.

'What's on your mind?' Aunt Augusta said.

'It was so stupid of me. I left my lawn-mower out, on the lawn, uncovered.'

My aunt showed me no sympathy. She said, 'Forget your lawn-mower. It's odd how we seem to meet only at religious ceremonies. The last time I saw you was at your baptism. I was not asked but I came.' She gave a croak of a laugh. 'Like the wicked fairy.'

'Why didn't they ask you?'

'I knew too much. About both of them. I remember you were far too quiet. You didn't yell the devil out. I wonder if he is still there?' She called to the driver, 'Don't confuse the Place with the Square, the Crescent or the Gardens. I am the Place.'

'I didn't know there was any breach. Your photograph was there in the family album.'

'For appearances only.' She gave a little sigh which drove out a puff of scented powder. 'Your mother was a very saintly woman. She should by rights have had a white funeral. La Pucelle,' she added again.

'I don't quite see . . . La Pucelle means – well, to put it bluntly, *I* am here, Aunt Augusta.'

'Yes. But you were your father's child. Not your mother's.'

That morning I had been very excited, even exhilarated, by the thought of the funeral. Indeed, if it had not been my mother's, I would have found it a wholly desirable break in the daily routine of retirement, and I was pleasurably reminded of the old banking days, when I had paid the final adieu to so many admirable clients. But I had never contemplated such a break as this one which my aunt announced so casually. Hiccups are said to be cured by a sudden shock and they can equally be caused by one. I hiccupped an incoherent question.

'I have said that your official mother was a saint. The girl, you see, refused to marry your father, who was anxious – if you can use such an energetic term in his case – to do the right thing. So my sister covered up for her by marrying him. (He was not very strong-willed.) Afterwards, she padded herself for months with progressive cushions. No one ever suspected. She even wore the cushions in bed, and she was so deeply shocked when your father tried once to make love to her – after the marriage but before your birth – that, even when you had been safely delivered, she refused him what the Church calls his rights. He was never a man in any case to stand on them.'

I leant back hiccupping in the taxi. I couldn't have spoken if I had tried. I remembered all those pursuits up the scaffolding. Had they been caused then by my mother's jealousy or was it the apprehension that she might be required to pass again so many more months padded with cushions of assorted sizes?

'No,' my aunt said to the taxi-driver, 'these are the Gardens. I told you – I am the Place.'

'Then I turn left, ma'm?'

'No. Right. On the left is the Crescent.

'This shouldn't come as a shock to you, Henry,' Aunt Augusta said. 'My sister – your stepmother – perhaps we should agree to call her that – was a very noble person indeed.'

'And my – hic – father?'

'A bit of a hound, but so are most men. Perhaps it's their best quality. I hope you have a little bit of the hound in you too, Henry.'

'I don't – huc – think so.'

'We may discover it in time. You *are* your father's son. That hiccup is best cured by drinking out of the opposite rim of a glass. You can imitate a glass with your hand. Liquid is not a necessary part of the cure.'

I drew a long free breath and asked, 'Who was my mother, Aunt Augusta?' But she was already far away from that subject, speaking to the driver. 'No, no, my man. This is the Crescent.'

'You said turn *right*, lady.'

'Then I apologize. It was my mistake. I am always a little uncertain about right and left. Port I can always remember because of the colour – red means left. You should have turned to port not starboard.'

'I'm no bloody navigator, lady.'

'Never mind. Just continue all the way round and start again. I take all the blame.'

We drew up outside a public house. The driver said, 'Ma'am, if you had only told me it was the Crown and Anchor . . .'

'Henry', my aunt said, 'if you could forget your hiccup for a moment.'

'Huc?' I asked.

'It's six and six on the clock,' the driver said.

'Then we will let it reach seven shillings,' Aunt Augusta retorted. 'Henry, I feel I ought perhaps to warn you before we go in that a white funeral in my case would have been quite out of place.'

'But-you've-never-married,' I said, very quickly to beat the hiccups.

'I have nearly always, during the last sixty or more years, had a friend,' Aunt Augusta said. She added, perhaps because I looked incredulous, 'Age, Henry, may a little modify our emotions – it does not destroy them.'

Even those words did not prepare me properly for what I found next. My life in the bank had taught me, of course, to be unsurprised, even by the demand for startling overdrafts, and I had always made it a point neither to ask for nor to listen to any explanation. The overdraft was given or refused simply on the previous credit of the client. If I seem to the reader a somewhat static character he should appreciate the long conditioning of my career before retirement. My aunt, I was to discover, had never been conditioned by anything at all, and she had no intention of explaining more than she had already done.

Chapter 3

THE Crown and Anchor was built like a bank in Georgian style. Through the windows I could see men with exaggerated moustaches in tweed coats, which were split horsily behind, gathered round a girl in jodhpurs. They were not the type to whom I would have extended much credit, and I doubted whether any of them, except the girl, had ever ridden a horse. They were all drinking bitter, and I had the impression that any spare cash they might have put aside went on tailors and hairdressers rather than equitation. A long experience with clients had made me prefer a shabby whisky-drinker to a well-dressed beer-drinker.

We went in by a side door. My aunt's apartment was on the second floor, and on the first floor there was a small sofa which I learnt later had been bought by my aunt so that she could take a little rest on the way up. It was typical of her generous nature that she had bought a sofa, which could barely be squeezed on to the landing, and not a chair for one. 'I always take a little rest at this point. Come and sit down, too, Henry. The stairs are steep, though perhaps they don't seem so at your age.' She looked at me critically. 'You have certainly changed a lot since I saw you last, though you haven't got much more hair.'

'I've had it, but I've lost it,' I explained.

'I have kept mine. I can still sit upon it.' She added surprisingly. 'Rapunzel, Rapunzel, let down your hair. Not that I could have ever let it down from a second-floor flat.'

'Aren't you disturbed by the noise from the bar?'

'Oh no. And the bar is very convenient if I suddenly run short. I just send Wordsworth down.'

'Who is Wordsworth?'

'I call him Wordsworth because I can't bring myself to call him Zachary. All the eldest sons in his family have been called Zachary for generations – after Zachary Macaulay who did so much for them on Clapham Common. The surname was adopted from the bishop not the poet.'

'He's your valet?'

'Let us say he attends to my wants. A very gentle sweet strong person. But don't let him ask you for a CTC. He receives quite enough from me.'

'What is a CTC?'

'That is what they called any tip or gift in Sierra Leone when he was a boy during the war. The initials belonged to Cape to Cairo Cigarettes which all the sailors handed out generously.'

My aunt's conversation went too quickly for my understanding, so that I was not really prepared for the very large middle-aged negro wearing a striped butcher's apron who opened the door when my aunt rang. 'Why, Wordsworth,' she said with a touch of coquetry, 'you've been washing up breakfast without waiting for me.' He stood there glaring at me, and I wondered whether he expected a CTC before he would let me pass.

'This is my nephew, Wordsworth,' my aunt said.

'You be telling me whole truth, woman?'

'Of course I am. Oh Wordsworth, Wordsworth!' she added with tender banter.

He let us in. The lights were on in the living-room, now that the day had darkened, and my eyes were dazzled for a moment by rays from the glass ornaments which flashed back from every open space. There were angels on the buffet wearing robes striped like peppermint rock; and in an alcove there was a Madonna with a gold face and a gold halo and a blue robe. On a sideboard on a gold stand stood a navy-blue goblet, large enough to hold at least four bottles of wine, with a gold trellis curled around the bowl on which pink roses grew and green ivy. There were mauve storks on the bookshelves and red swans and blue fish. Black girls in scarlet dresses held green candle sconces, and shining down on all this was a chandelier which might have been made out of sugar icing hung with pale blue, pink and yellow blossoms.

'Venice once meant a lot to me,' my aunt said rather unnecessarily.

I don't pretend to be a judge of these things, but I thought the effect exaggerated and not in the best of taste.

'Such wonderful craftsmanship,' my aunt said. 'Wordsworth, be a dear and fetch us two whiskies. Augusta feels a teeny bit sad after the sad sad ceremony.' She spoke to him as though he were a child – or a lover, but that relationship I was reluctant to accept.

'Everything go OK?' Wordsworth asked. 'No bad medicine?'

'There was no contretemps,' my aunt said. 'Oh gracious, Henry, you haven't forgotten your parcel?'

'No, no, I have it here.'

'I think perhaps Wordsworth had better put it in the refrigerator.'

'Quite unnecessary, Aunt Augusta. Ashes don't deteriorate.'

'No, I suppose not. How silly of me. But let Wordsworth put it in the kitchen just the same. We don't want to be reminded all the time of my poor sister. Now let me show you my room. I have more of my Venice treasures there.'

She had indeed. Her dressing-table gleamed with them: mirrors and powder-jars and ash-trays and bowls for safety pins. 'They brighten the darkest day,' she said. There was a very large double-bed as curlicued as the glass. 'I am especially attached to Venice,' she explained, 'because I began my real career there, and my travels. I have always been very fond of travel. It's a great grief to me that my travels now are curtailed.'

'Age strikes us all before we know it,' I said.

'Age? I was not referring to age. I hope I don't look all that decrepit, Henry, but I like having a companion and Wordsworth is very occupied now because he's studying to enter the London School of Economics. This is Wordsworth's snuggery,' and she opened the door of an adjoining room. It was crowded with glass Disney figures and worse – all the grinning mice and cats and hares from inferior American cartoon films, blown with as much care as the chandelier.

'From Venice too,' my aunt said, 'clever but not so pretty. I thought them suitable, however, for a man's room.'

'Does he like them?'

'He spends very little time there,' my aunt said, 'what with his studies and everything else . . .'

'I wouldn't like to wake up to them,' I said.

'He seldom does.'

My aunt led me back to the sitting-room where Wordsworth had laid out three more Venetian glasses with gold rims and a jug of water with colours mingled like marble. The bottle of Black Label looked normal and out of place, rather like the only man in a dinner-jacket at a fancy-dress party, a comparison which came at once to my mind because I have found myself several times in that uncomfortable situation, since I have a rooted objection to dressing up.

Wordsworth said, 'The telephone talk all the bloody time while you not here. Ar tell them you don gone to a very smart funeral.'

'It's so convenient when one can tell the truth,' my aunt said. 'Was there no message?'

'Oh, poor old Wordsworth not understand one bloody word. Ar say to them you no talk English. They go away double quick.'

My aunt poured out larger portions of whisky than I am accustomed to.

'A little more water please, Aunt Augusta.'

'I can say now to both of you how relieved I am that everything went without a hitch. I once attended a very important funeral – the wife of a famous man of letters who had not been the most faithful of husbands. It was soon after the first great war had ended, I was living in Brighton, and I was very interested at that time in the Fabians. I had learnt about them from your father when I was a girl. I arrived early as a spectator and I was leaning over the Communion rail – if you can call it that in a crematorium chapel – trying to make out the names on the wreaths. I was the first there, all alone with the flowers and the coffin. Wordsworth must forgive me for telling this story at such length – he has heard it before. Let me refresh your glass.'

'No, no, Aunt Augusta. I have more than enough.'

'Well, I suppose I was fumbling about a little too much and I must have accidentally touched a button. The coffin began to slide away, the doors opened, I could feel the hot air of the oven and hear the flap of the flames, the coffin went in and the doors closed, and at that very moment in walked the whole grand party, Mr and Mrs Bernard Shaw, Mr H. G. Wells, Miss E. Nesbit (to use her maiden name), Doctor Havelock Ellis, Mr Ramsay MacDonald, and the widower, while the clergyman (non-denominational of course) came through a door on the other side of the rail. Somebody began to play a humanist hymn by Edward Carpenter, "Cosmos, O Cosmos, Cosmos shall we call Thee?" But there was no coffin.'

'Whatever did you do, Aunt Augusta?'

'I buried my face in my handkerchief and simulated grief, but you know I don't think anyone (except, I suppose, the clergyman and he kept dumb about it) noticed that the coffin wasn't there. The widower certainly didn't, but then he hadn't noticed his wife for some years. Doctor Havelock Ellis made a very moving address (or so it seemed to me then: I hadn't finally plumped for Catholicism, though I was on the brink) about the dignity of a funeral service conducted without illusions or rhetoric. He could truthfully have said without a corpse too. Everybody was quite satisfied. You can understand why I was very careful this morning not to fumble.'

I looked at my aunt surreptitiously over the whisky. I didn't know what to say. 'How sad' seemed inappropriate. I wondered whether the funeral had ever really taken place, though in the months that followed I was to realize that my aunt's stories were always basically true – only minor details might sometimes be added to compose a picture. Wordsworth found the right words for me. He said, 'We must allays go careful careful at a funeral.' He added, 'In Mendeland – ma first wife she was Mende – they go open deceased person's back an they go take out the spleen. If spleen be too big, then deceased person was a witch an everyone mock the whole family and lef the funeral double quick. That happen to ma wife's pa. He dead of malaria, but these ignorant people they don know malaria make the spleen big. So ma wife and her ma they go right away from Mendeland and come to Freetown. They don wan to be mocked by the neighbours.'

'There must be a great many witches in Mendeland,' my aunt said.

'Ya'as, sure thing there are. Plenty too many.'

I said, 'I really think I must be going now, Aunt Augusta. I can't keep my mind off the mowing-machine. It will be quite rusted in this rain.'

'Will you miss your mother, Henry?'

'Oh yes . . . yes,' I said. I hadn't really thought about it, so occupied had I been with all the arrangements for the funeral, the interviews with her solictor, with her bank manager with an estate agent arranging for the sale of her little house in North London. It is difficult too for a single man to know how to dispose of all the female trappings. Furniture can be auctioned, but what can one do with all the unfashionable underclothes of an old lady, the half-empty pots of old-fashioned cream? I asked my aunt.

'I am afraid I didn't share your mother's taste in clothes, or even in cold cream. I would give them to her daily maid on condition she takes everything – everything.'

'It has made me so happy meeting you, Aunt Augusta. You are my only close relative now.'

'As far as you know,' she said. 'Your father had spells of activity.'

'My poor stepmother . . . I shall never be able to think of anyone else as my mother.'

'Better so.'

'In a new block under construction my father was always very careful about furnishing the specimen flat. I used to think that sometimes he went to sleep in it in the afternoon. I suppose it might have been in one of those I was . . .' I checked the word 'conceived' in deference to my aunt.

'Better not to speculate,' she said.

'You will come one day and see my dahlias, won't you? They are in full bloom.'

'Of course, Henry, now that I have found you again I shan't easily let you go. Do you enjoy travel?'

'I've never had the opportunity.'

'With Wordsworth so occupied we might make a little trip or two together.'

'Gladly, Aunt Augusta.' It never occurred to me that she meant further than the seaside.

'I will telephone you,' my aunt said.

Wordsworth showed me to the door, and it was only outside, when I passed the Crown and Anchor, that I remembered I had left behind my little package. I wouldn't have remembered at all if the girl in the jodhpurs had not said angrily as I pushed past the open window, 'Peter can talk about nothing but cricket. All the summer it went on. Nothing but the fucking Ashes.'

I don't like to hear such adjectives on the lips of an attractive young girl, but her words reminded me sharply that I had left all that remained of my mother in Aunt Augusta's kitchen. I went back to the street door. There was a row of bells with a kind of microphone above each of them. I touched the right one and heard Wordsworth's voice. 'Who be there?'

I said, 'It's Henry Pulling.'

'Don know anyone called that name.'

'I've only just left you. I'm Aunt Augusta's nephew.'

'Oh, that guy,' the voice said.

'I left a parcel with you in the kitchen.'

'You wan it back?'

'Please, if it's not too much trouble . . .'

Human communication, it sometimes seems to me, involves an exaggerated amount of time. How briefly and to the point people always seem to speak on the stage or on the screen, while in real life we stumble from phrase to phrase with endless repetition.

'A brown-paper parcel?' Wordsworth's voice asked.

'Yes.'

'You wan me bring it down right away?'

'Yes, if it's not too much . . .'

'It's a bloody lot of trouble,' Wordsworth said. 'Stay there.'

I was prepared to be very cold to him when he brought the parcel, but he opened the street door wearing a friendly grin.

'Thank you,' I said, with as much coldness as I could muster, 'for the great trouble you have taken.'

I noticed that the parcel was no longer sealed. 'Has somebody opened this?'

'Ar jus wan to see what you got there.'

'You might have asked me.'

'Why, man,' he said, 'you not offended at Wordsworth?'

'I didn't like the way you spoke just now.'

'Man, it's jus that little mike there. Ar wan to make it say all kind of rude things. There ar am up there, and down there ma voice is, popping out into the street where no one see it's only old Wordsworth. It's a sort of power, man. Like the burning bush when he spoke to old Moses. One day it was the parson come from St George's in the square. An he says in a dear brethren sort of voice, "I wonder, Miss Bertram, if I could come up and have a little chat about our bazaar." "Sure, man," ar say, "you wearing your dog collar?" "Why, yes," he say, "of course, who is that?" "Man," ar say, "you better put on a muzzle too before you go come up here."'

'What did he say?'

'He wen away and never come back. Your auntie laugh like hell when ar told her. But ar didn't mean him harm. It was just old Wordsworth tempted by that little old mike.'

'Are you really studying for the London School of Economics?' I asked.

'Oh, tha's a joke your auntie makes. Ar was workin at the Grenada Palace. Ar had a uniform. Jus lak a general. She lak ma uniform. She stop an say, "Are you the Emperor Jones?" "No, ma'm," I say, "arm only old Wordsworth." "Oh," she say, "thou child of joy, shout round me, let me hear thy shouts, thou happy shepherd boy." "You write that down for me," ar say. "It sound good. Ar like it." Ar say it over and over. Ar know it now good lak a hymn.'

I was a little confused by his garrulity. 'Well, Wordsworth,' I said, 'thank you for all your trouble and I hope one day I shall see you again.'

'This here mighty important parcel?'

'Yes. I suppose it is.'

'Then ar think you owe a dash to old Wordsworth,' he said.

'A dash?'

'A CTC.'

Remembering what my aunt had told me, I went quickly away.

Just as I had expected my new lawn-mower was wet all over: I dried it carefully and oiled the blades before I did anything else. Then I boiled myself two eggs and made a cup of tea for lunch. I had much to think about. Could I accept my aunt's story and in that case who was my mother? I tried to remember the friends my mother had of her own age, but what was the good of that? The friendship would have been broken before my birth. If indeed she had been only a stepmother to me, did I still want to place her ashes among my dahlias? While I washed up my lunch I was sorely tempted to wash out the urn as well into the sink. It would serve very well for the home-made jam which I was promising myself to make next year – a man in retirement must have his hobbies if he is not to age too fast – and the urn would have looked quite handsome on the tea table. It was a little sombre, but a sombre jar was well suited for damson jelly or for blackberry-and-apple jam. I was seriously tempted, but I remembered how kind my stepmother had been to me in her rather stern way when I was a child, and how could I tell that my aunt was speaking the truth? So I went out into the garden and chose a spot among the dahlias where the plinth could be built.

Chapter 4

I WAS weeding the dahlias, the Polar Beauties and the Golden Leaders and the Requiems, when my telephone began to ring. Being unused to the sound which shattered all the peace of my little garden, I assumed that it was a wrong number. I had very few friends, although before my retirement I boasted a great many acquaintances. There were clients who had stayed with me for twenty years, who had known me in the same branch as clerk, cashier and manager, and yet they remained acquaintances. It is rare for a manager to be promoted from the staff of a branch in which he will have to exercise authority, but there were special circumstances in my case. I had been acting manager for nearly a year owing to my predecessor's illness, and one of my clients was a very important depositor who had taken a fancy to me. He threatened to remove his custom if I did not remain in charge. His name was Sir Alfred Keene: he had made a fortune in cement and my father, having been a builder, gave us an interest in common. He would invite me to dinner at least three times a year and he always consulted me on his investments, though he never took my advice. He said it helped him to make up his mind. He had an unmarried daughter called Barbara who was interested in tatting, which I think she must have given to the church bazaar. She was always very kind to me, and my mother suggested I might pay her attentions, for she would certainly inherit Sir Alfred's money, but the motive seemed to me a dishonest one and in my case I have never been greatly interested in women. The bank was then my whole life, and now there were my dahlias.

Unfortunately Sir Alfred died a little before my retirement, and Miss Keene went to South Africa to live. I was intimately concerned, of course, with all her currency difficulties: it was I who wrote to the Bank of England for this permit or that and reminded them constantly that I had received no reply to my letters of the 9th ult.; and on her last night in England, before she caught her boat at Southampton, she asked me to dinner. It was a sad occasion without Sir Alfred, who had been a very jovial man, laughing immoderately even at his own jokes. Miss Keene asked me to look after the drinks and I chose an Amontillado, and for dinner Sir Alfred's favourite Chambertin. The house was one of those big Southwood mansions surrounded by rhododendron bushes which dripped that night with the steady slow November rain. There was an oil painting of a fishing boat in a storm after Van de Velde over Sir Alfred's place at the dining-room table, and I expressed the hope that Miss Keene's voyage would be less turbulent.

'I have sold the house as it stands with all the furniture,' she told me. 'I shall live with second cousins.'

'Do you know them well?' I asked.

'I have never seen them,' she said. 'They are once removed. We have only exchanged letters. The stamps are like foreign stamps. With no portrait of the Queen.'

'You will have the sun,' I encouraged her.

'Do you know South Africa?'

'I have seldom been out of England,' I said. 'Once when I was a young man I went with a school friend to Spain, but my stomach was upset by the shell-fish – or perhaps it was the oil.'

'My father was a very overpowering personality,' she said. 'I never had friends – except you, of course, Mr Pulling.'

It is astonishing to me now how nearly I came to proposing marriage that night and yet I refrained. Our interests were different, of course – tatting and dahlias have nothing in common, unless perhaps they are both the interests of rather lonely people. Rumours of the great bank merger had already reached me. My retirement was imminent, and I was well aware that the friendships I had made with my other clients would not long survive it. If I had spoken would she have accepted me? – it was quite possible. Our ages were suitable, she was approaching forty and I would soon be half-way through the fifth decade, and I knew my mother would have approved. How different everything might have been if I had spoken then. I would never have heard the disturbing story of my birth, for she would have accompanied me to the funeral and my aunt would not have spoken in her presence. I would never have travelled with my aunt. I would have been saved from much, though I suppose I would have missed much too. Miss Keene said, 'I shall be living near Koffiefontein.'

'Where is that?'

'I don't really know. Listen. It's raining cats and dogs.'

We got up and moved into the drawing-room for coffee. There was a Venetian scene copied from Canaletto on the wall. All the pictures in the house seemed to represent foreign parts, and she was leaving for Koffiefontein. I would never travel so far, I thought then, and I wished that she was staying here, in Southwood.

'It seems a very long way to go,' I said.

'If there was anything to keep me here . . . Will you take one lump or two?'

'No sugar, thank you.' Was it an invitation for me to speak? I have always asked myself since. I didn't love her, and she certainly didn't love me, but perhaps in a way we could have made a life together. I heard from her a year later; she wrote, 'Dear Mr Pulling, I wonder how Southwood is and whether it's raining. We are having a beautiful sunny winter. My cousins have a small (!) farm of ten thousand acres and they think nothing of driving seven hundred miles to buy a ram. I am not quite used to things yet and I think often of Southwood. How are the dahlias? I have given up tatting. We lead a very open air existence.'

I replied and gave her what news I could, but I had retired by then and was no longer at the centre of Southwood life. I told her of my mother's failing health and how the dahlias were doing. There was a rather gloomy variety in royal purple called Deuil du Roy Albert which had not been a success. I was not sorry. It was an odd name to give a flower. My Ben Hurs were flourishing.

I had neglected the telephone, feeling so sure that it was a wrong number, but when the ringing persisted, I left my dahlias and went in.

The telephone stood on the filing cabinet where I keep my accounts and all the correspondence which my mother's death caused. I had not received as many letters as I was receiving now since I ceased to be manager: the solicitor's letters, letters from the undertaker, from the Inland Revenue, the crematorium fees, the doctor's bills, National Health forms, even a few letters of condolence. I could almost believe myself a businessman again.

My aunt's voice said, 'You are very slow to answer.'

'I was busy in the garden.'

'How was the mowing-machine by the way?'

'Very wet, but no irreparable damage.'

'I have an extraordinary story to tell you,' my aunt said. 'I have been raided by the police.'

'*Raided* . . . by the police?'

'Yes, you must listen carefully for they may call on *you*.'

'What on earth for?'

'You still have your mother's ashes?'

'Of course.'

'Because they want to see them. They may even want to analyse them.'

'But Aunt Augusta . . . you must tell me exactly what happened.'

'I am trying to, but you continually interrupt with unhelpful exclamations. It was midnight and Wordsworth and I had gone to bed. Luckily I was wearing my best nightdress. They rang the bell down below and told us through the microphone that they were police officers and had a warrant to search the flat. "What for?" I asked. Do you know, for a moment I thought it might be something racial. There are so many rules now for races and against races that you don't know where you stand.'

'Are you sure they were police officers?'

'Of course I asked to see their warrant, but do you know what a warrant looks like? For all I know it might have been a reader's ticket to the British Museum library. I let them in, though, because they were polite, and one of them, the one in uniform, was tall and good-looking. They were rather surprised by Wordsworth – or perhaps it was the colour of his pyjamas. They said, "Is this your husband, ma'm?" I said, "No, this is Wordsworth." The name seemed to ring a bell with one of them – the young man in uniform – who kept on glancing at him surreptitiously, as though he were trying to remember.'

'But what were they looking for?'

'They said they had reliable information that drugs were kept on the premises.'

'Oh, Aunt Augusta, you don't think Wordsworth . . .'

'Of course not. They took away all the fluff from the seams of his pockets, and then the truth came out. They asked him what was in the brown-paper package which he was seen handing to a man who had been loitering in the street. Poor Wordsworth said he didn't know, so I chipped in and said it was my sister's ashes. I don't know why, but they became suspicious of me at once. The elder, who was in plain clothes, said, "Please don't be flippant, ma'am. It doesn't exactly help." I said, "As far as my sense of humour goes, there is nothing whatever flippant in my dead sister's ashes." "A sort of powder, ma'am?" the younger policeman asked – he was the sharper of the two, the one who thought he knew the name of Wordsworth. "You can call it that if you like," I said, "grey powder, human powder," and they looked as though they had won a point. "And who was the man who received this powder?" the man in plain clothes asked. "My nephew," I said. "My sister's son." I saw no reason to go into that old story which I told you yesterday with members of the Metropolitan Police. Then they asked for your address and I gave it to them. The sharp one said, "Was the powder for his private use?" "He wants to put it amongst his dahlias," I said. They made a very thorough search, especially in Wordsworth's room, and they took away samples of all the cigarettes they could find, and some aspirins I had left in a cachet box. Then they said, "Good night, ma'am," very politely and left. Wordsworth had to go downstairs and open the door for them, and just before he left the sharp one said to him, "What's your first name?" "Zachary," Wordsworth told him and he went out looking puzzled.'

'What a very strange thing to have happened,' I said.

'They even read some letters and asked who Abdul was.'

'Who was he?'

'Someone I knew a very long time ago. Luckily I had kept the envelope and it was marked Tunis, February 1924. Otherwise they would have read all sorts of things into it about the present.'

'I am sorry, Aunt Augusta. It must have been a terrifying experience.'

'It was amusing in a way. But it did give me a guilty feeling . . .'

There was a ring from the front door and I said, 'Hold on a moment, Aunt Augusta.' I looked through the dining-room window and saw a policeman's helmet. I returned and said, 'Your friends are here.'

'Already?'

'I'll ring you back when they've gone.'

It was the first time I had ever been called on by the police. There was a short middle-aged man in a soft hat with a rough but kindly face and a broken nose and the tall good-looking young man in uniform. 'Mr Pulling?' the detective asked.

'Yes.'

'May we come in for a few moments?'

'Have you a warrant?' I asked.

'Oh no, no, it hasn't come to that. We just want to have a word or two with you.' I wanted to say something about the Gestapo, but I thought it wiser not. I led them into the dining-room, but I didn't ask them to sit down. The detective showed me an identity card and I read on it that he was Detective-Sergeant Sparrow, John.

'You know a man called Wordsworth, Mr Pulling?'

'Yes, he's a friend of my aunt's.'

'Did you receive a package from him in the street yesterday?'

'I certainly did.'

'Would you have any objection to our examining the package, Mr Pulling?'

'I most certainly would.'

'You know, sir, we could easily have obtained a search-warrant, but we wanted to do things delicately. Have you known this man Wordsworth a long time?'

'I met him for the first time yesterday.'

'Perhaps, sir, he asked you as a favour to deliver that package and you seeing no harm at all in that and him being an employee of your aunt . . .'

'I don't know what you are talking about. The package is mine. I had accidentally left it in the kitchen.'

'The package is yours, sir? You admit that.'

'You know very well what's in the package. My aunt told you. It's an urn with my mother's ashes.'

'Your aunt has been in communication with you, has she?'

'Yes, she has. What do you expect? Waking up an old lady in the middle of the night.'

'It had only just gone twelve, sir. And so those ashes . . . They are Mrs Pulling's?'

'There they are. You can see for yourself. On the bookcase.'

I had put the urn there temporarily, until I was ready to bed it, above a complete set of Sir Walter Scott which I had inherited from my father. In his lazy way my father was a great reader, though not an adventurous one. He was satisfied with possessing a very few favourite authors. By the time he had read the set of Scott through he had forgotten the earlier volumes and was content to begin again with *Guy Mannering*. He had a complete set too of Marion Crawford, and he had a love of nineteenth-century poetry which I have inherited – Tennyson and Wordsworth and Browning and Palgrave's *Golden Treasury*.

'Do you mind if I take a look?' the detective asked, but naturally he couldn't open the urn. 'It's sealed,' he said. 'With Scotch tape.'

'Naturally. Even a tin of biscuits . . .'

'I would like to take a sample for analysis.'

I was becoming rather cross by this time. I said, 'If you think I am going to let you play around with my poor mother in a police laboratory . . .'

'I can understand how you feel, sir,' he said, 'but we have rather serious evidence to go on. We took some fluff from the man Wordsworth's pockets and when analysed it contained pot.'

'Pot?'

'Marijuana to you, sir. Likewise cannabis.'

'Wordsworth's fluff has got nothing to do with my mother.'

'We could get a warrant. sir, easily enough, but seeing how you may be an innocent dupe, I would rather take the urn away temporarily with your permission. It would sound much better that way in court.'

'You can check with the crematorium. The funeral was only yesterday.'

'We have already sir, but you see it's quite possible – don't think I'm presuming to suggest your line of defence, that's a matter entirely for your counsel – that the man Wordsworth took out the ashes and substituted pot. He may have known he was being watched. Now wouldn't it be much better, sir, from all points of view to know for certain that these are your mother's ashes? Your aunt told us you planned to keep it in your garden – you wouldn't want to see that urn every day and wonder, are those really the ashes of the dear departed or are they an illegal supply of marijuana?'

He had a very sympathetic manner, and I really began to see his point.

'We'd only take out a tiny pinch, sir, less than a teaspoonful. We'd treat the rest with all due reverence.'

'All right,' I said, 'take your pinch. I suppose you are only doing your duty.' The young policeman had been making notes all the time. The detective said, 'Take a note that Mr Pulling behaved most helpfully and that he voluntarily surrendered the urn. That will sound well in court, sir, if the worst happens.

'When will I get the urn back?'

'Not later than tomorrow – if all is as it should be.' He shook hands quite cordially as if he believed in my innocence, but perhaps that was just his professional manner.

Of course I hastened to telephone to my aunt. 'They've taken away the urn,' I said. 'They think my mother's ashes are marijuana. Where's Wordsworth?'

'He went out after breakfast and hasn't come back.'

'They found marijuana dust in the fluff of his suit.'

'Oh dear, how careless of the poor boy. I thought he was a little disturbed. And he asked for a CTC before he went out.'

'Did you give him one?'

'Well, you know, I'm really fond of him, and he said it was his birthday. He never had a birthday last year, so I gave him twenty pounds.'

'Twenty pounds! I never keep as much as that in the house.'

'It will get him as far as Paris. He left in time for the Golden Arrow, now I come to think of it, and he always carries his passport to prove he's not an illegal immigrant. Do you know, Henry, I've a great desire for a little sea air myself.'

'You'll never find him in Paris.'

'I wasn't thinking of Paris. I was thinking of Istanbul.'

'Istanbul is not on the sea.'

'I think you are wrong. There's something called the Sea of Marmara.'

'Why Istanbul?'

'I was reminded of it by that letter from Abdul the police found. A strange coincidence. First that letter and then this morning in the post another – the first for a very long time.'

'From Abdul?'

'Yes.'

It was weak of me, but I did not then realize the depth of my aunt's passion for travel. If I had I would have hesitated before I made the first fatal proposal: 'I have nothing particular to do today. If you would like to go to Brighton . . .'

Chapter 5

BRIGHTON was the first real journey I undertook in my aunt's company and proved a bizarre foretaste of much that was to follow.

We arrived in the early evening, for we had decided to spend the night. I was surprised by the smallness of her luggage which consisted only of a little white leather cosmetics case which she called her *baise en ville*. I find it difficult myself to go away for a night without a rather heavy suitcase, for I am uneasy if I have not at least one change of suit and that entails also a change of shoes. A change of shirt, a change of underclothes and of socks are almost an essential to me, and taking into consideration the vagaries of the English climate I like to take some woollens just in case. My aunt looked askance at my suitcase and said, 'We must take a cab. I had hoped we could walk.'

I had booked our rooms at the Royal Albion because my aunt wished to be near the Palace Pier and the Old Steine. She told me, incorrectly I think, that this was named after the wicked marquess of *Vanity Fair*. 'I like to be at the centre of all the devilry,' she said, 'with the buses going off to all those places.' She spoke as though their destinations were Sodom and Gomorrah rather than Lewes and Patcham and Littlehampton and Shoreham. Apparently she had come first to Brighton when she was quite a young woman, full of expectations which I am afraid were partly fulfilled.

I thought I would have a bath and a glass of sherry, a quiet dinner in the grill, and an early bedtime, so that we would both be rested for a strenuous morning on the front and in the Lanes, but my aunt disagreed. 'We don't want dinner for another two hours,' she said, 'and first I want you to meet Hatty if Hatty's still alive.'

'Who is Hatty?'

'We worked together once with a gentleman called Mr Curran.'

'How long ago was that?'

'Forty years or more.'

'Then it seems unlikely . . .'

'*I* am here.' Aunt Augusta said firmly, 'and I got a card from her the Christmas before last.'

It was a grey leaden evening with an east wind blowing on our backs from Kemp Town. The sea was rising and the pebbles turned and ground under the receding waves. Ex-President Nkrumah looked out at us from the window of the waxworks, wearing a grey suit with a Chinese collar. My aunt paused and regarded him, I thought, a little sadly. 'I wonder where Wordsworth is now,' she said.

'I expect you'll hear from him soon.'

'I very much doubt it,' she said. 'My dear Henry,' she added, 'at my age one has ceased to expect a relationship to last. Think how complicated life would be if I had kept in touch with all the men I have known intimately. Some died, some I left, a few have left me. If they were all with me now we would have to take over a whole wing of the Royal Albion. I was very fond of Wordsworth while he lasted, but my emotions are not as strong as they once were. I can support his absence, though I may regret him for a while tonight. His knackers were superb.' The wind took my hat and tossed it against a lamp-post. I was too surprised by her vulgarity to catch it, and my aunt laughed like a young woman. I returned, brushing it down, but Aunt Augusta still lingered at the waxworks.

'It's a kind of immortality,' she said.

'What is?'

'I don't mean the waxworks here in Brighton, they are rather a job lot, but in Madame Tussaud's. With Crippin and the Queen.'

'I'd rather have my portrait painted.'

'But you can't see all round a portrait, and at Tussaud's they take some of your own clothes to dress you in, or so I've read. There's a blue dress of mine I could easily spare . . . Oh well,' she said with a sigh, 'it's unlikely I'll ever be famous like that. Idle dreams . . .' She walked on, I thought a little cast down. 'Criminals,' she said, 'and queens and politicians. Love is not highly regarded, except for Nell Gwynn and the Brides in the Bath.'

We came to the saloon doors of the Star and Garter and my aunt suggested that we take a drink. The walls were covered with inscriptions of a philosophic character: 'Life is a one-way street and there's no coming back'; 'Marriage is a great Institution for those who like Institutions'; 'You will never persuade a mouse that a black cat is lucky'. There were old programmes too and photographs. I ordered a sherry and my aunt said she would like a port and brandy. When I turned round from the bar I saw her examining a yellowed photograph. There was an elephant and two performing dogs drawn up in front of the Palace Pier behind a stout man in a tail-coat wearing a top hat and a watch chain, and a shapely young woman in tights stood beside him carrying a carriage whip. 'There's Curran,' my aunt said. 'That's how it all began.' She pointed at the young woman. 'And there's Hatty. Those were the days.'

'Surely you never worked in a circus, Aunt Augusta?'

'Oh no, but I happened to be there when the elephant trod on Curran's toe, and we became very close friends. Poor man, he had to go to hospital, and when he came out, the circus had gone on without him to Weymouth. Hatty too, though she came back later when we were established.'

'Established at what?'

'I'll tell you one day, but now we have to find Hatty.' She drained her port and brandy, and out we went into the cold blow of the wind. Just opposite was a stationer's which sold comic postcards and she stopped there to inquire: the metal stands for the cards rattled and strained and turned like a windmill. I noticed a card with a bottle of Guinness on it, and a fat woman in a snorkel floating face down. The legend read 'Bottoms Up!' I was looking at another of a man in hospital saying to a surgeon, 'But I said circumcision, doctor', when my aunt came out. 'It's just here,' she said. 'I knew I wasn't far wrong,' and in the window of the very next house a card in front of some net curtains read 'Hatty's Teapot. By Appointment Only'. There were photographs by the door of Marilyn Monroe and Frank Sinatra and the Duke of Edinburgh which seemed to have been signed by their subjects, although it seemed unlikely in the case of the Duke.

We rang the bell and an old lady answered it. She was wearing a black evening dress and a lot of jet objects jangled when she moved. 'You're too late,' she said sharply.

'Hatty,' said my aunt.

'I close at six-thirty sharp except by special appointment.'

'Hatty, it's Augusta.'

'Augusta!'

'Hatty! You haven't changed a bit.'

But remembering the young girl in tights carrying the whip and looking sideways at Curran I thought there had been greater changes than my aunt made out.

'This is my nephew Henry, Hatty. You remember about *him*.' They exchanged a look which I found disturbing. Why should I have been discussed all those years ago? Had she let Hatty into the secret of my birth?

'Come on in, the two of you. I was just going to have a cup of tea – an unprofessional cup of tea,' Hatty added and giggled.

'In here?' my aunt asked, opening a door.

'No dear, that's the waiting-room.' I just had time to see an engraving by Sir Alma Tadema of a lot of tall naked ladies in a Roman bathhouse.

'Here's my den, dear,' Hatty said, opening another door. It was a small over-crowded room, and everything seemed to be covered with fringed mauve shawls, the table, the backs of chairs, the mantel – there was even a shawl dangling from a studio portrait of a stout man whom I recognized as Mr Curran.

'The Revered,' Aunt Augusta said, looking at it.

'The Revered,' Hatty repeated, and then they both laughed at some secret joke of their own.

'The Rev. for short,' Aunt Augusta said, 'but that, of course, was only a coincidence. You remember how we explained it to the police. They've still got a photo of him, Hatty, stuck up in the Star and Garter.'

'I haven't been there for years,' Hatty said. 'I'm off the hard liquor.'

'You are there and the elephant too,' Aunt Augusta said. 'Can you remember the elephant's name?'

Hatty was putting out two more cups from a china cabinet. There was a fringed shawl over that too. She said, 'It wasn't a common name like Jumbo. Something classical. How one forgets things, Augusta, at our age.'

'Was it Caesar?'

'No, it wasn't Caesar. Do you take sugar, Mr–?'

'Call him Henry, Hatty.'

'One lump,' I said.

'Oh dear, oh dear, I had such a good memory once.'

'The water's boiling, dear.'

The kettle was on a spirit ring close to a big brown teapot. She began to pour out.

'Oh, I quite forgot the strainer,' she said.

'Never mind, Hatty.'

'It's because of my clients. I never strain theirs, so I forget when I'm alone.'

There was a plate of ginger-snaps and I accepted one for politeness' sake. 'From the Old Steine,' Aunt Augusta told me. 'Ye Olde Bunne

Shoppe. You don't get ginger-snaps like that anywhere else in the world.'

'And now they have turned it into a betting shop,' Hatty said. 'Pluto, dear? Was it Pluto?'

'No, I'm sure it wasn't Pluto. I think it began with a T.'

'I can't think of anything classical beginning with T.'

'There was a point to his name.'

'There certainly was.'

'Historical.'

'Yes.'

'You remember the dogs, dear. They are in the photo, too.'

'It was them gave Curran the idea.'

'The Revered,' Aunt Augusta repeated again, and they laughed in unison at their private memory. I felt very much alone, so I took another ginger-snap.

'The boy has a sweet tooth,' Hatty remarked.

'To think that little shop in the Old Steine survived two great wars.'

'We've survived,' Hatty replied, 'but they aren't turning us into betting shops.'

'Oh, it will need an atom bomb to destroy *us*,' Aunt Augusta said.

I thought it was time to speak. 'The situation in the Middle East is pretty serious,' I said, 'judging from today's *Guardian*.'

'You can never tell,' Hatty said, and they were both for a while buried in thought. Then my aunt picked out a tealeaf, put it on the back of her hand and slapped it with the other; it clung obstinately to a vein which was surrounded by what my mother used to call grave-marks.

'Can't get rid of the fellow,' Aunt Augusta said. 'I hope he's tall and handsome.'

'That isn't a stranger,' Hatty corrected her. 'That's the thought of a departed you can't get out of your mind.'

'Living or dead?'

'It could be either. How stiff does he feel?'

'If he's living I suppose it could be poor Wordsworth.'

'Wordsworth is dead, dear,' Hatty said, 'a very long time ago.'

'Not my Wordsworth. It's stiff as wood. I wonder who a dead one could be.'

'Poor Curran perhaps.'

'I have thought a lot about him since I came to Brighton.'

'Would you like me to do a professional cup, dear, for you and your friend?'

'Nephew,' Aunt Augusta corrected Hatty in her turn. 'It would be fun, dear.'

'I'll make another pot. The leaves have to be fresh and I use Lapsang Souchong professionally, though I drink Ceylon – Lapsang gives big leaves and good results.'

When she came back after washing the pot and our cups my aunt said, 'You must let us pay.'

'I wouldn't dream of it, dear, not after all we've been through together.'

'With the Revered.' They giggled again.

Hatty poured in the boiling water. She said, 'I don't let the pot draw. The leaves speak better fresh.' She filled our cups. 'Now toss the tea away, dear, in this basin.'

'I've got it,' my aunt said. 'Hannibal.'

'Who's Hannibal?'

'The elephant that trod on Curran's toe.'

'I do believe you're right, dear.'

'I was watching the tea and it came to me suddenly in a flash.'

'I often notice that with the leaves. Things come back. You are watching the leaves and things come back.'

'I suppose Hannibal's dead too.'

'You can't tell, dear, with elephants.'

She picked up my aunt's cup and studied it closely. 'It's interesting,' she said, 'very interesting.'

'Bad or good?'

'A bit of both.'

'Just tell me the good.'

'You are going to do a lot of travelling. With another person. You are going to cross the ocean. You are going to have many adventures.'

'With men?'

'That the leaves don't say, dear, but knowing you as I do, it wouldn't surprise me. You will be in danger of your life and liberty on more than one occasion.'

'But I'll come through?'

'I see a knife – or it might be a syringe.'

'Or it could be something else, Hatty – you know what I mean?'

'There is some mystery in your life.'

'That's nothing new.'

'I see a lot of confusion – a lot of running about this way and that. I'm sorry, Augusta, but I can't see any peace at the close. There's a cross. Perhaps you find religion. Or it could be a double-cross.'

'I've always been interested in religion,' my aunt said, 'ever since Curran.'

'Or it could be a bird, of course – a vulture perhaps. Keep away from deserts.' Hatty gave a sigh. 'Things don't come to me so easily as they once did. I exhaust myself with strangers.'

'But you'll take one look at Henry's cup too, dear, won't you? Just one look.'

She poured my tea away and looked in the cup. 'Men are difficult,' she said. 'They have so many occupations beyond a woman's knowledge and that affects the interpretation. I had a client once who said he was a bevel-edger. I don't know what he meant. Are you an undertaker?'

'No.'

'There's something that looks like an urn. Do you see it there? On the left of the handle. That's the recent past.'

'It might be an urn,' I said, looking.

'You will do a lot of travelling.'

'That's not very likely. I've always been rather stay-at-home. It's quite an adventure for me coming as far as Brighton.'

'It's in the future you're going to travel. Across the ocean. With a lady friend.'

'Perhaps he's coming with me,' Aunt Augusta said.

'It's possible. The leaves don't lie. There's a round thing like a target. There's a mystery in your life too.'

'I've only just discovered that,' I said.

'I see a lot of confusion too and running about. Just like in Augusta's cup.'

'That's most unlikely,' I said. 'I lead a very regular life. A game of bridge once a week at the Conservative Club. And my garden, of course. My dahlias.'

'The target might be a flower,' Hatty admitted. 'Forgive me. I'm tired. I'm afraid it was not a very good reading.'

'It was most interesting,' I told her for politeness' sake. 'But of course, I'm no believer.'

'Have another ginger-snap,' Hatty said.

Chapter 6

WE had dinner that night at the Cricketers', a small public house nearly opposite a second-hand bookseller, where I saw a complete set of Thackeray for sale at a very reasonable price. I thought it would go well on my shelves below my father's edition of the Waverley novels. Perhaps tomorrow I would come back and buy it. The thought gave me a warm feeling towards my father, a sense of something in common. I too would start at Volume I and continue to the end, and by the time that last volume was finished it would be time to begin again. Too many books by too many authors can be confusing, like too many shirts and suits. I like to change my clothes as little as possible. I suppose some people would say the same of my ideas, but the bank had taught me to be wary of whims. Whims so often end in bankruptcy.

When I wrote that we had dinner at the Cricketers', it would have been more correct to say we ate a substantial snack. There were baskets of warm sausages on the bar, and we helped ourselves and washed the sausages down with draught Guinness. I was surprised by the number of glasses my aunt could put down and feared a little for her blood pressure.

After her second pint she said, 'It was odd about that cross. In the leaves I mean. I've always been interested in religion – ever since I knew Curran.'

'What church do you attend?' I asked. 'Didn't you tell me you were a Roman Catholic?'

'I call myself that for convenience,' she said. 'It belongs to my French and Italian periods. After I left Curran. I suppose he had influenced me, and then all the girls I knew were Catholic and I didn't like to look superior. I expect you'd be surprised to hear that we ran a church once ourselves – me and Curran, here in Brighton.'

'"Ran"? I don't understand.'

'It was the performing dogs that gave us the idea. Two of them came to see Curran in hospital before the circus moved on. It was visiting day and there were a lot of women around to see their husbands. At first the dogs weren't allowed into the ward. There was quite a fuss, but Curran got round matron, telling her they weren't ordinary dogs, they were human dogs. Bathed in disinfectant they were, he told her, every dog, before they were allowed to give a performance. It wasn't true, of course, but he was very convincing. They came up to the bed, wearing their pointed hats and pierrot collars, and each gave Curran a paw to shake and touched his face with its nose like an eskimo. Then they were taken quickly away in case the doctor might appear. You should have heard those women. "The darlings, the sweet little doggies." It was lucky neither of them had raised a leg. "Just like humans." One woman said, "You can't tell me that dogs haven't got souls." Another one asked, "Are they gentlemen doggies or lady doggies?" as though she had been too refined to look. "One of each," Curran said, and just out of devilry he added, "They are married as a matter of fact." "Oh, isn't that too sweet? Oh, the darlings. And have any little doggies come yet?" "Not yet," Curran said. "You see, they have only been married a month. At the doggies' church in Potters Bar." "Married in church?" they squealed and I really thought he'd gone too far, but how they swallowed it down! They all gathered round Curran's bed and left their husbands abandoned. Not that the husbands minded. Visiting day is always a horrible reminder of home to a man.'

My aunt took another sausage and ordered another Guinness. 'They all wanted to know about the church in Potters Bar. "And to think," one said, "we have to leave our doggies at home when we go to St Ethelburga's. My dog is as good a Christian as the vicar is with his raffles and his tea-fights." "Once a year," Curran said, "they have a collection of dog biscuits. To help the poor strays." When at last they left us alone and went back to their husbands I said, "You've started something," and "Why not?" Curran said.'

My aunt put down her glass and asked the woman behind the bar, 'Did you ever hear of the doggies' church?'

'I seem to remember hearing something, but it was donkey's years ago, wasn't it? Long before my time. Somewhere in Hove, wasn't it?'

'No, dear. Not a hundred yards from where you are standing now. We used to come to the Cricketers' after the service. The Rev. Curran and me.'

'Didn't the police interfere or something?'

'They tried to make out that he had no right to the title of Rev. But we pointed out that it stood for Revered and not Reverend in *our* church, and we didn't belong to the established. They couldn't touch us, we were breakaways like Wesley, and we had all the dog-owners of Brighton and Hove behind us – they even came over from as far as Hastings. The police tried to get us once under the Blasphemy Act, but nobody could find any blasphemy in our services. They were very very solemn. Curran wanted to start the churching of bitches after the puppies came, but I said that was going too far – even the Church of England had abandoned churching. Then there was the question of marrying divorced couples – I thought it would treble our income, but there it was Curran who stood firm. "We don't recognize divorce," he said, and he was quite right – it would have sullied the sentiment.'

'Did the police win in the end?' I asked.

'They always do. They had him up for speaking to girls on the front, and a lot was said in court that wasn't apropos. I was young and angry and uncomprehending, and I wouldn't help him any more. No wonder he abandoned me and went to look for Hannibal. No one can stand not being forgiven. That's God's privilege.'

We left the Cricketers' and my aunt took a turning this way and a turning that until we came to a shuttered hall and a sign which read: 'Text for the Week. "If thou hast run with the footmen, and they have wearied thee, Then how canst thou contend with horses? Jeremiah 12"' I can't say that I understood the meaning very well, unless it was a warning against Brighton races, but perhaps the ambiguity was the attraction. The sect, I noticed, was called The Children of Jeremiah.

'This was where we held our services,' Aunt Augusta said. 'Sometimes you could hardly hear the words for the barking. "It's their form of prayer," Curran would say, "let each pray after his own fashion," and sometimes they lay quite peacefully licking their parts. "Cleansing themselves for the House of the Lord," Curran would say. It makes me a little sad to see strangers here now. And I never much cared for the prophet Jeremiah.'

'I know little about Jeremiah.'

'They sank him in the mud,' Aunt Augusta said. 'I studied the Bible very carefully in those days, but there was little that was favourable to dogs in the Old Testament. Tobias took his dog with him on his journey with the angel, but it played no part in the story at all, not even when a fish tried to eat Tobias. A dog was an unclean beast, of course, in those times. He only came into his own with Christianity. It was the Christians who began to carve dogs in stone in the cathedrals, and even while they were still doubtful about women's souls they were beginning to think that maybe a dog had one, though they couldn't get the Pope to pronounce one way or the other, not even the Archbishop of Canterbury. It was left to Curran.'

'A big responsibility,' I said. I couldn't make out whether she was serious about Curran or not.

'It was Curran who set me reading theology,' Aunt Augusta said. 'He wanted references to dogs. It wasn't easy to find any – even in St Francis de Sales. I found lots about fleas and butterflies and stags and elephants and spiders and crocodiles in St Francis but a strange neglect of dogs. Once I had a terrible shock. I said to Curran, "It's no good. We can't go on. Look what I've just found in the Apocalypse. Jesus is saying who can enter the city of God. Just listen to this – 'Without are dogs and sorcerers and whoremongers and murderers and idolaters, and whosoever loveth or maketh a lie.' You see the company dogs are supposed to keep?"

'"It proves our point", Curran said. "Whoremongers and murderers and the rest – they all have souls, don't they? They only have to repent, and it's the same with dogs. The dogs who come to our church have repented. They don't consort any more with whoremongers and sorcerers. They live with respectable people in Brunswick Square or Royal Crescent." Do you know that Curran was so little put off by the Apocalypse he actually preached a sermon on that very text, telling people that it was their responsibility to see that their dogs didn't back-slide? "Loose the lead and spoil the dog," he said. "There are only too many murderers in Brighton and whoremongers at the Metropole all ready to pick up what you loose. And as for sorcerers –" Luckily Hatty, who was with us by that time, had not yet become a fortune-teller. It would have spoilt the image.'

'He was a good preacher?'

'It was music to hear him,' she said with happy regret, and we began to walk back towards the front; we could hear the shingle turning over from a long way away. 'He was not exclusive,' my aunt said. 'For him dogs were like the House of Israel, but he was an apostle also to the Gentiles – and the Gentiles, to Curran, included sparrows and parrots and white mice – not cats, cats he always regarded as Pharisees. Of course no cat dared to come into the church with all those dogs around, but there was one who used to sit in the window of a house opposite and sneer when the congregation came out. Curran excluded fish too – it would be too shocking to eat something with a soul, he said. Elephants he had a great feeling for, which was generous of him considering Hannibal had trodden on his toe. Let's sit down here, Henry. I always find Guinness a little tiring.'

We sat down in a shelter. The lights ran out to sea along the Palace

Pier and the edge of the water was white with phosphorescence. The waves were continually pulled up along the beach and pulled back as though someone were making a bed and couldn't get the sheet to lie properly. A bit of pop music came from the dance hall standing there like a blockade ship a hundred yards out. This trip was quite an adventure, I thought to myself, little knowing how small a one it would seem in retrospect.

'I found a lovely piece about elephants once in St Francis de Sales,' Aunt Augusta said, 'and Curran used it in his last sermon – after all that business with the girls had upset me. I really think what he wanted was to tell me it was me he loved, but I was a hard young woman in those days and I wouldn't listen. I've always kept the piece though in my purse and, when I read it, it's not the elephant that I see now, it's Curran. He was a fine fellow – not as big as Wordsworth but a good deal more sensitive.'

She fumbled in her bag and found her purse. 'You read it to me, dear, I can't see properly in this light.'

I held the rather yellowed creased paper at an angle to catch one of the lights of the front. It wasn't easy to read though my aunt's handwriting was young and bold, because of the creases. '"The elephant",' I read, '"is only a huge animal, but he is the most worthy of beasts that lives on the earth, and the most intelligent. I will give you an example of his excellence; he . . ."' The writing ran along a crease and I couldn't read it, but my aunt chimed gently in. '"He never changes his mate and he tenderly loves the one of his choice." Go on, dear.'

'"With whom",' I read, '"nevertheless he mates but every third year, and then for five days only and so secretly that he has never been seen to do so."'

'He was trying to explain,' my aunt said, 'I am sure of it now, that if he had been a little slack in his attentions, it was only because of the girls – he didn't love me less.'

'"But he is to be seen again on the sixth day, on which day, before doing anything else, he goes straight to some river and he bathes his whole body, for he has no desire to return to the herd until he has purified himself."'

'Curran was always a clean man,' my aunt said. 'Thank you, dear, you read it very well.'

'It doesn't seem very applicable to dogs,' I said.

'He turned it so beautifully that no one noticed, and it was really directed at me. I remember he had a special dogs' shampoo which had been blessed at the altar on sale outside the church door that Sunday.'

'What became of Curran?'

'I've no idea,' Aunt Augusta said. 'He must have left his church, for he couldn't have carried on without me. Hatty hadn't the right touch for a deaconess. I dream of him sometimes – but he would be ninety years old now, and I find it hard to picture him as an old man. Well, Henry, I think it is time for us both to sleep.'

All the same I found sleep difficult to attain, even in my comfortable bed at the Royal Albion. The lights of the Palace Pier sparkled on the ceiling, and round and round, in my head, went the figures of Wordsworth and Curran, the elephant and the dogs of Hove, the mystery of my birth, the ashes of my mother who was not my mother, and my father asleep in the bath. This was not the simple life which I had known at the bank, where I could judge a client's character by his credits and debits. I had a sense of fear and exhilaration too, as the music pounded from the Pier and the phosphorescence rolled up the beach.

Chapter 7

THE affair of my mother's ashes was not settled so easily as I had anticipated (I call her my mother still, because at this period I had no real evidence that my aunt was telling me the truth). No urn was awaiting me in the house when I returned from Brighton, and so I rang up Scotland Yard and asked for Detective-Sergeant Sparrow. I was put on without delay to a voice which was distinctly not Sparrow's. It sounded very similar to that of a rear-admiral whom I had once had as a client. (I was very glad when he changed his account to the National Provincial Bank, for he treated my clerks like ordinary seamen and myself like a sub-lieutenant who had been court-martialled for keeping the mess books improperly.)

'Can I speak to Detective-Sergeant Sparrow?' I asked.

'On what business?' whoever it was rapped back.

'I have not yet received my mother's ashes,' I said.

'This is Scotland Yard, Assistant Commissioner's Office, and not a crematorium,' the voice replied and rang off.

It took me a long while (because of engaged lines) to get the same gritty voice on the line again.

'I want Detective-Sergeant Sparrow,' I said.

'On what business?'

I was ready this time and prepared to be ruder than the voice could be.

'Police business of course,' I said. 'What other business do you deal in?' It was almost as though my aunt were speaking through me.

'Detective-Sergeant Sparrow is out. You had better leave a message.'

'Ask him to ring Mr Pulling, Mr Henry Pulling.'

'What address? What telephone number?' he snapped as though he suspected me to be some unsavoury police informer.

'He knows them both. I am not going to repeat them unnecessarily. Tell him I am disappointed at his failure to keep a solemn promise.' I rang off before the other had time for a word in reply. Going out to the dahlias I gave myself the rare award of a satisfied smile. I had never spoken to the rear-admiral like that.

My new cactus dahlias were doing well, and after my trip to Brighton their names gave me some of the pleasure of travel: Rotterdam, a deeper red than a pillar-box, and Dentelle de Venise with spikes sparkling like hoar-frost. I thought that next year I would plant some Pride of Berlin to make a trio of cities. The telephone disturbed my happy ruminations. It was Sparrow.

I said to him firmly, 'I hope you have a good excuse for failing to return the ashes.'

'I certainly have, sir. There's more cannabis than ashes in your urn.'

'I don't believe you. How could my mother possibly . . . ?'

'We can hardly suspect your mother, sir, can we? As I told you, I think the man Wordsworth took advantage of your call. Luckily for your story there *are* some human ashes in the urn, though Wordsworth must have dumped most of them down the sink to make room. Did you hear any sound of running water?'

'We were drinking whisky. He certainly filled a jug of water.'

'That must have been the moment, sir.'

'In any case I would like to have back the ashes that remain.'

'It isn't practicable, sir. Human ashes have a kind of sticky quality. They adhere very closely to any substance, which in this case is pot. I am sending you back the urn by registered post. I suggest, sir, that you place it just where you intended and forget the unfortunate circumstances.'

'But the urn will be empty.'

'Memorials are often detached from the remains of the deceased. War memorials are an example.'

'Well,' I said, 'I suppose there's nothing to be done. It won't feel the same at all. I hope you don't suspect my aunt had any hand in this?'

'An old lady like that? Oh no, sir. She was obviously deceived by her valet.'

'What valet?'

'Why, Wordsworth, sir – who else?' I thought it best not to enlighten him about their relationship.

'My aunt thinks Wordsworth may be in Paris.'

'Very likely, sir.'

'What will you do about it?'

'There's nothing we *can* do. He hasn't committed an extraditable offence. Of course, if he ever returns . . . He has a British passport.' There was a note of malicious longing in Detective-Sergeant Sparrow's voice that made me feel, for a moment, a partisan of Wordsworth. I said, 'I sincerely hope he won't.'

'You surprise and disappoint me, sir.'

'Why?'

'I hadn't taken you for one of that kind.'

'What kind?'

'People who talk about there being no harm in pot.'

'Is there?'

'From our experience, sir, nearly all the cases hooked on hard drugs begin with pot.'

'And from my experience, Sparrow, all or nearly all the alcoholics I know have started with a small whisky or a glass of wine. I even had a client who was first hooked, as you call it, on mild and bitter. In the end because of his frequent absences on a cure he had to give his wife a power of attorney.' I rang off. It occurred to me with a certain pleasure that I had sowed a little confusion in Detective-Sergeant Sparrow's mind – not so much confusion on the subject of cannabis but confusion about my character, the character of a retired bank manager. I discovered for the first time in myself a streak of anarchy. Had it been perhaps the result of my visit to Brighton or was it possibly my aunt's influence (and yet I was not a man easily influenced), or some bacteria in the Pulling blood? I found a buried affection for my father reviving in me. He had been a very patient as well as a very sleepy man, and yet there was about his patience something unaccountable: it might well have been absence of mind rather than patience – or even indifference. He might have been all the time, without our knowing it, elsewhere. I remembered the ambiguous reproaches launched against him by my mother. They seemed to confirm my aunt's story, for they possessed the nagging qualities of an unsatisfied woman. Imprisoned by ambitions which she had never realized, my mother had never known freedom. Freedom, I thought, comes only to the successful and in his trade my father was a success. If a client didn't like my father's manner or his estimates, he could go elsewhere. My father wouldn't have cared. Perhaps it is freedom, of speech and conduct, which is really envied by the unsuccessful, not money or even power.

It was with these muddled and unaccustomed ideas in my mind that I awaited the arrival of my aunt for dinner. We had arranged the rendezvous before leaving the Brighton Belle at Victoria the day before. As soon as she arrived I told her about Sergeant Sparrow, but she treated my story with surprising indifference, saying only that Wordsworth should have been 'more careful'. Then I took her out and showed her my dahlias.

'I have always preferred cut flowers,' she said, and I had a sudden vision of strange continental gentlemen offering her bouquets of roses and maidenhair fern bound up in tissue paper.

I pointed out to her the site where I had thought to put the urn in memory of my mother.

'Poor Angelica,' she said, 'she never understood men,' and that was all. It was as though she had read my thoughts and commented on them.

I had dialled CHICKEN and the dinner arrived exactly as ordered, the main course only needing to be put into the oven for a few minutes, while we ate the smoked salmon. Living alone I had been a regular customer whenever there was a client to entertain or my mother on her weekly visit. Now for months I had neglected Chicken, for there were no longer any clients and my mother, during her last illness, had been too ill to make the journey from Golders Green.

We drank sherry with the smoked salmon, and as some small return for my aunt's generosity to me in Brighton I had bought a bottle of Burgandy, Chambertin 1959, Sir Alfred Keene's favourite, to go with the Chicken à la King. When the wine had spread a pleasant glow through both our minds my aunt reverted to my conversation with Sergeant Sparrow.

'He is determined,' she said, 'that Wordsworth is the guilty party, yet it might equally well be one of us. I don't think the sergeant is a racialist, but he is class-conscious, and though the smoking of pot depends on no class-barrier, he prefers to think otherwise and to put the blame on poor Wordsworth.'

'You and I can give each other an alibi,' I said, 'and Wordsworth did run away.'

'We could have been in collusion, and Wordsworth might be taking his annual holiday. No,' she went on, 'the mind of a policeman is set firmly in a groove. I remember once when I was in Tunis a travelling company was there who were playing *Hamlet* in Arabic. Someone saw to it that in the Interlude the Play King was really killed – or rather not quite killed but severely damaged in the right ear – by molten lead. And who do you suppose the police at once suspected? Not the man who poured the lead in, although he must have been aware that the ladle wasn't empty and was hot to the touch. Oh no, they knew Shakespeare's play too well for that, and so they arrested Hamlet's uncle.'

'What a lot of travelling you have done in your day, Aunt Augusta.'

'I haven't reached nightfall yet,' she said. 'If I had a companion I would be off tomorrow, but I can no longer lift a heavy suitcase, and there is a distressing lack of porters nowadays. As you noticed at Victoria.'

'We might one day,' I said, 'continue our seaside excursions. I remember many years ago visiting Weymouth. There was a very pleasant green statue of George III on the front.'

'I have booked two couchettes a week from today on the Orient Express.'

I looked at her in amazement. 'Where to?' I asked.

'Istanbul, of course.'

'But it takes days . . .'

'Three nights to be exact.'

'If you want to go to Istanbul surely it would be easier and less expensive to fly?'

'I only take a plane,' my aunt said, 'when there is no alternative means of travel.'

'It's really quite safe.'

'It is a matter of choice, not nerves,' Aunt Augusta said. 'I knew Wilbur Wright very well indeed at one time. He took me for several trips. I always felt quite secure in his contraptions. But I cannot bear being spoken to all the time by irrelevant loud-speakers. One is not badgered at a railway station. An airport always reminds me of a Butlin's Camp.'

'If you are thinking of me as a companion . . .'

'Of course I am, Henry.'

'I'm sorry, Aunt Augusta, but a bank manager's pension is not a generous one.'

'I shall naturally pay all expenses. Give me another glass of wine, Henry. It's excellent.'

'I'm not really accustomed to foreign travel. You'd find me . . .'

'You will take to it quickly enough in my company. The Pullings have all been great travellers. I think I must have caught the infection through your father.'

'Surely not my father . . . He never travelled further than Central London.'

'He travelled from one woman to another, Henry, all through his life. That comes to much the same thing. New landscapes, new customs. The accumulation of memories. A long life is not a question of years. A man without memories might reach the age of a hundred and feel that his life had been a very brief one. Your father once said to me, "The first girl I ever slept with was called Rose. Oddly enough she worked in a flower shop. It really seems a century ago." And then there was your uncle . . .'

'I didn't know I had an uncle.'

'He was fifteen years older than your father and he died when you were very young.'

'He was a great traveller?'

'It took an odd form,' my aunt said, 'in the end.' I wish I could reproduce more clearly the tones of her voice. She enjoyed talking, she enjoyed telling a story. She formed her sentences carefully like a slow writer who foresees ahead of him the next sentence and guides his pen towards it. Not for her the broken phrase, the lapse of continuity. There was something classically precise, or perhaps it would be more accurate to say old-world, in her diction. The bizarre phrase, and occasionally, it must be agreed, a shocking one, gleamed all the more brightly from the old setting. As I grew to know her better, I began to regard her as bronze rather than brazen, a bronze which has been smoothed and polished by touch, like the horse's knee in the lounge of the Hotel de Paris in Monte Carlo, which she once described to me, caressed by generations of gamblers.

'Your uncle was a bookmaker known as Jo,' Aunt Augusta said. 'A very fat man. I don't know why I say that, but I have always liked fat men. They have given up all unnecessary effort, for they have had the sense to realize that women do not, as men do, fall in love with physical beauty. Curran was stout and so was your father. It's easier to feel at home with a fat man. Perhaps travelling with me you will put on a little weight yourself. You had the misfortune to choose a nervous profession.'

'I have certainly never banted for the sake of a woman,' I said jokingly.

'You must tell me all about your women one day. In the Orient Express we shall have plenty of time for talk. But now I am speaking to you of your Uncle Jo. His was a very curious case. He made a substantial fortune as a bookmaker, yet more and more his only real desire was to travel. Perhaps the horses continually running by, while he had to remain stationary on a little platform with a signboard Honest Jo Pulling, made him restless. He used to say that one race meeting merged into another and life went by as rapidly as a yearling out of Indian Queen. He wanted to slow life up and he quite rightly felt that by travelling he would make time move with less rapidity. You have noticed it yourself, I expect, on a holiday. If you stay in one place, the holiday passes like a flash, but if you go to three places, the holiday seems to last at least three times as long.'

'Is that why you have travelled so much, Aunt Augusta?'

'At first I travelled for my living,' Aunt Augusta replied. 'That was in Italy. After Paris, after Brighton. I had left home before you were born. Your father and mother wished to be alone, and in my case I never got on very well with Angelica. The two A's we were always called. People used to say my name fitted me because I seemed proud as a young girl, but no one said my sister's name fitted her. A saint she may well have been, but a very severe saint. She was certainly not angelic.'

One of the few remarks of age which I noticed in my aunt was her readiness to abandon one anecdote while it was yet unfinished for another. Her conversation was rather like an American magazine where you have to pursue a story, skipping from page twenty to page ninety-eight and turning over all kinds of subjects in between: childhood delinquency, some novel cocktail recipes, the love life of a film star, and even quite a different fiction to the one so abruptly interrupted.

'The question of names,' my aunt said, 'is an interesting one. Your own Christian name is safe and colourless. It is better than being given a name like Ernest, which has to be lived up to. I once knew a girl called Comfort and her life was a very sad one. Unhappy men were constantly attracted to her simply by reason of her name, when all the time, poor dear, it was really she who needed the comfort from them. She fell unhappily in love with a man called Courage, who was desperately afraid of mice, but in the end she married a man called Payne and killed herself in what Americans call a comfort station. I would have thought it a funny story if I hadn't known her.'

'You were telling me about my Uncle Jo,' I said.

'I know that. I was saying that he wanted to make life last longer. So he decided on a tour round the world (there were no currency restrictions in those days), and he began his tour curiously enough with the Simplon Orient, the train we are travelling by next week. From Turkey he planned to go to Persia, Russia, India, Malaya, Hong Kong, China, Japan, Hawaii, Tahiti, U.S.A., South America, Australia, New Zealand perhaps – somewhere he intended to take a boat home. Unfortunately he was carried off the train at Venice right at the start on a stretcher, after a stroke.'

'How very sad.'

'It didn't alter at all his desire for a long life. I was working in Venice at the time, and I went to see him. He had decided that if he couldn't travel physically, he would travel mentally. He asked me if I could find him a house of three hundred and sixty-five rooms so that he could live for a day and a night in each. In that way he thought life would seem almost interminable. The fact that he had probably not long to live had only heightened his passion to extend what was left of it. I told him that, short of the Royal Palace at Naples, I doubted whether such a house existed. Even the Palace in Rome probably contained fewer rooms.'

'He could have changed rooms less frequently in a smaller house.'

'He said that then he would notice the pattern. It would be no more than he was already accustomed to, travelling between Newmarket, Epsom, Goodwood and Brighton. He wanted time to forget the room which he had left before he returned to it again, and there must be opportunity too to redecorate it in a few essentials. You know there was a brothel in Paris in the Rue de Provence between the last two wars (oh, I forgot. There have been many wars since, haven't there, but they don't seem to belong to us like those two do). This brothel had rooms decorated in various styles – the far West, China, India, that kind of thing. My uncle had much the same idea for his house.'

'But surely he never found one,' I exclaimed.

'In the end he was forced to compromise. I was afraid for a time that the best we could do would be twelve bedrooms – one room a month – but a short while afterwards, through one of my clients in Milan . . .'

'I thought you were working in Venice,' I interrupted with some suspicion.

'The business I was in,' my aunt said, 'was peripatetic. We moved around – a fortnight's season in Venice, the same in Milan, Florence and Rome, then back to Venice. It was known as *la quindicina*.'

'You were in a theatre company?' I asked.

'The description will serve,' my aunt said with that recurring ambiguity of hers. 'You must remember I was very young in those days.'

'Acting needs no excuse.'

'I wasn't excusing myself,' Aunt Augusta said sharply, 'I was explaining. In a profession like that, age is a handicap. I was lucky enough to leave in good time. Thanks to Mr Visconti.'

'Who was Visconti?'

'We were talking about your Uncle Jo. I found an old house in the country which had once been a *palazzo* or a *castello* or something of the kind. It was almost in ruins and there were gypsies camping in some of the lower rooms and in the cellar – an enormous cellar which ran under the whole ground floor. It had been used for wine, and there was a great empty tun abandoned there because it had cracked with age. Once there had been vineyards around the house, but an autostrada had been built right across the estate not a hundred yards from the house, and the cars ran by all day between Milan and Rome and at night the big lorries passed. A few knotted worn-out roots of old vines were all that remained. There was only one bathroom in the whole house (the water had been cut off long ago by the failure of the electric pump), and only one lavatory, on the top floor in a sort of tower, but of course there was no water there either. You can imagine it wasn't the sort of house anyone could sell easily – it had been on the market for twenty years and the owner was a monogoloid orphan in an asylum. The lawyers talked about historic values, but Mr Visconti knew all about history as you could guess from his name. Of course he advised strongly against the purchase, but after all poor Jo was unlikely to live long and he might as well be made happy. I had counted up the rooms, and if you divided the cellar into four with partitions and included the lavatory and bathroom and kitchen, you could bring the total up to fifty-two. When I told Jo he was delighted. A room for every week of the year, he said. I had to put a bed in every one, even in the bathroom and kitchen. There wasn't room for a bed in the lavatory, but I bought a particularly comfortable chair with a footstool and I thought we could always leave that room to the last – I didn't think Jo would survive long enough to reach it. He had a nurse who was to follow him from room to room, sleeping one week behind him, as it were. I was afraid he would insist on a different nurse at every stopping place, but he liked her well enough to keep her as a travelling companion.'

'What an extraordinary arrangement.'

'It worked very well. When Jo was in his fifteenth room he told me – I was back that week in Milan on my tour and I came out to see him with Mr Visconti on my day off – that it really seemed at least a year since he had moved in. He was going on next day to the sixteenth room on the floor above with a different view and his suitcases were all packed and ready (he insisted on everything being moved by suitcase, and I had found a second-hand one which was already decorated with labels from all kinds of famous hotels – the George V in Paris, the Quisisana in Capri, the Excelsior in Rome, Raffles in Singapore, Shepheard's in Cairo, the Pera Palace in Istanbul).

'Poor Jo! I've seldom seen a happier man. He was certain that death would not catch him before he reached the fifty-second room, and if fifteen rooms had seemed like a year, then he had several years of travel still before him. The nurse told me that about the fourth day in each room he would get a little restless with the wanderlust, and the first day in the new room he would spend more than his usual time in sleep, tired after the journey. He began in the cellar and worked his way upwards until at last he reached the top floor, and he was already beginning to talk of revisiting his old haunts. "We'll take them in a different order this time," he said, "and come at them from a different direction." He was content to leave the lavatory to the last. "After all these luxury rooms," he said, "it would be fun to rough it a bit. Roughing it keeps one young. I don't want to be like one of those old codgers one sees in the Cunard travelling first-class and complaining of the caviar." Then it was that in the fifty-first room that he had his second stroke. It paralysed him down one side and made speech difficult. I was in Venice at the time, but I got permission to leave the company for a couple of days and Mr Visconti drove me to Jo's *palazzo*. They were having a lot of difficulty with him. He had spent seven days in the fifty-first room before the stroke knocked him out, but the doctor was insisting that he remain in the same bed without a move for at least another ten days. "Any ordinary man," the doctor said to me, "would be content to lie still for a while."

'"He wants to live as long as possible," I told him.

'"In that case he should stay where he is till the end. With any luck he'll have two or three more years."

'I told Jo what the doctor said, and he mouthed a reply. I thought I made out, "Not enough."

'He stayed quiet that night and all the next morning, and the nurse believed that he had resigned himself to staying where he was. She left him sleeping and came down to my room for a cup of tea. Mr Visconti had bought some cream cakes in Milan at the good pastry-cook's near the cathedral. Suddenly from up the stairs there came a strange grating noise. "*Mamma mia*," the nurse said, "what's that?" It sounded as though someone were shifting the furniture. We ran upstairs and what do you think? Jo Pulling was out of bed. He had fixed an old club tie of his, the Froth-blowers or the Mustard Club or something of the kind, to the handle of the suitcase because he had no strength in his legs, and he was crawling down the passage towards the lavatory tower pulling the suitcase after him. I shouted for him to stop, but he paid no attention. It was painful to look at him, he was going so slowly, with such an effort. It was a tiled passage and every tile he crossed cost him enormous exertion. He collapsed before we reached him and lay there panting, and the saddest thing of all to me was that he made a little pool of wee-wee on the tiles. We were afraid to move him before the doctor came. We brought a pillow and put it under his head and the nurse gave him one of his pills. "*Cattivo*," she said in Italian, which means, "You bad old man," and he grinned at the two of us and brought out the last sentence which he ever spoke, deformed a bit but I could understand it very well. "Seemed like a whole lifetime," he said and he died before the doctor came. He was right in his way to make that last trip against the doctor's orders. The doctor had only promised him a few years.'

'He died in the passage?' I asked.

'He died on his travels,' my aunt said in a tone of reproof. 'As he would have wished.'

'"Here he lies where he longed to be,"' I quoted in order to please my aunt, though I couldn't help remembering that Uncle Jo had not succeeded in reaching the lavatory door.

'Home is the hunter, home from the sea,' my aunt finished the quotation in her own fashion, 'And the sailor home from the hill.'

We were silent for quite a while after that as we finished the Chicken à la King. It was a little like the two minutes' silence on Armistice Day. I remembered that, when I was a boy, I used to wonder whether there was really a corpse buried there at the Cenotaph, for governments are usually economical with sentiment and try to arouse it in the cheapest possible way. A brilliant advertising slogan doesn't need a body, a box of earth would do just as well, and now I began to wonder too about

Uncle Jo. Was my aunt a little imaginative? Perhaps the stories of Jo, of my father and of my mother were not entirely true.

Without breaking the silence I took a reverent glass of Chambertin to Uncle Jo's memory, whether he existed or not. The unaccustomed wine sang irresponsibly in my head. What did the truth matter? All characters once dead, if they continue to exist in memory at all, tend to become fictions. Hamlet is no less real now than Winston Churchill, and Jo Pulling no less historical than Don Quixote. I betrayed myself with a hiccup while I changed our plates, and with the blue cheese the sense of material problems returned.

'Uncle Jo,' I said, 'was lucky to have no currency restrictions. He couldn't have afforded to die like that on a tourist allowance.'

'They were great days,' Aunt Augusta said.

'How are we going to manage on ours?' I asked. 'With fifty pounds each we shall not be able to stay very long in Istanbul.'

'Currency restrictions have never seriously bothered me,' my aunt said. 'There are ways and means.'

'I hope you don't plan anything illegal.'

'I have never planned anything illegal in my life,' Aunt Augusta said. 'How could I plan anything of the kind when I have never read any of the laws and have no idea what they are?'

Chapter 8

It was my aunt who suggested that we should fly as far as Paris. I was a little surprised after what she had just said, for there was certainly in this case an alternative means of travel. I pointed out the inconsistency. 'There are reasons,' Aunt Augusta said. 'Cogent reasons. I know the ropes at Heathrow.'

I was puzzled too at her insistence that we must go to the Kensington air terminal and take the airport bus. 'It's so easy for me,' I said, 'to pick you up by car and drive you to Heathrow. You would find it much less tiring, Aunt Augusta.'

'You would have to pay an exorbitant garage fee,' she replied, and I found her sudden sense of economy unconvincing.

I arranged next day for the dahlias to be watered by my next-door neighbour, a brusque man called Major Charge. He had seen Detective-Sergeant Sparrow come to the door with the policeman, and he was bitten by curiosity. I told him it was about a motoring offence and he became sympathetic immediately. 'A child murdered every week,' he said, 'and all they can do is prosecute motorists.' I don't like lies and I felt in my conscience that I ought to defend Sergeant Sparrow who had been as good as his word and posted back the urn, registered and express.

'Sergeant Sparrow is not in homicide,' I replied, 'and motorists kill more people in a year than murderers.'

'Only a lot of jaywalkers,' Major Charge said. 'Cannon fodder.' However, he agreed to water the dahlias.

I picked my aunt up in the bar of the Crown and Anchor where she was having a stirrup-cup and we drove by taxi to the Kensington terminal. I noticed that she had brought two suitcases, one very large, although, when I asked her how long we were to stay in Istanbul, she had replied, 'Twenty-four hours.'

'It seems a short stay after such a long journey.'

'The point is the journey,' my aunt had replied. 'I enjoy the travelling not the sitting still.'

Even Uncle Jo, I argued, had put up with each room in his house for a whole week.

'Jo was a sick man,' she said, 'while I am in the best of health.'

Since we were travelling first-class (which seemed again an unnecessary luxury between London and Paris) we had no over-weight, although the larger of her suitcases was unusually heavy. While we were sitting in the bus I suggested to my aunt that the garage fee for my car would probably have been cheaper than the difference between first and tourist fares. 'The difference,' she said, 'is nearly wiped out by the caviar and the smoked salmon, and surely between us we can probably put away half a bottle of vodka. Not to speak of the champagne and cognac. In any case I have more important reasons for travelling by bus.'

As we approached Heathrow she put her mouth close to my ear. 'The luggage,' she said, 'is in a trailer behind.'

'I know.'

'I have a green suitcase and a red suitcase. Here are the tickets.'

I took them, not understanding.

'When the bus stops please get out quickly and see whether the trailer is still attached. If it is still there let me know at once and I'll give you further instructions.'

Something in my aunt's manner made me nervous. I said, 'Of course it will be there.'

'I sincerely hope not,' she said. 'Otherwise we shall not leave today.'

I jumped out as soon as we arrived and sure enough the trailer wasn't there. 'What do I do now?' I asked her.

'Nothing at all. Everything is quite in order. You may give me back the tickets and relax.'

As we sat over two gins and tonics in the departure lounge a loud-speaker announced, 'Passengers on Flight 378 to Nice will proceed to customs for customs inspection.'

We were alone at our table and my aunt did not bother to lower her voice amid the din of passengers, glasses and loud-speakers. 'That is what I wished to avoid,' she said. 'They have now taken to spot-checks on passengers leaving the country. They whittle away our liberties one by one. When I was a girl you could travel anywhere on the continent except Russia without a passport and you took what you liked in the way of money. Until recently they only *asked* what money you had, or at the very worst they wanted to see your wallet. If there's one thing I hate in any human being it is mistrust.'

'The way you speak,' I said jokingly, 'I suspect we are lucky that it is not your bags which are being searched.'

I could well imagine my aunt stuffing a dozen five-pound notes into the toe of her bedroom slippers. Having been a bank manager, I am perhaps over-scrupulous, though I must confess that I had an extra five-pound note folded up in my ticket pocket, but that was something I might genuinely have overlooked.

'Luck doesn't enter into my calculations,' my aunt said. 'Only a fool would trust to luck, and there is probably a fool now on the Nice flight who is regretting his folly. Whenever new restrictions are made, I make a very careful study of the arrangements for carrying them out.' She gave a little sigh. 'In the case of Heathrow I owe a great deal to Wordsworth. For a time he acted as a loader there. He left when there was some trouble about a gold consignment. Nothing was ever proved against him, but the whole affair had been too impromptu and disgusted him. He told me the story. A very large ingot was abstracted by a loader, and the loss was discovered too soon, before the men went off duty. They knew as a result that they would be searched by the police on leaving, all taxis too, and they had no idea what to do with the thing until Wordsworth suggested rolling it in tar and using it as a doorstop in the customs shed. So there it stayed for months. Every time they brought crates along to the shed, they could see their ingot propping open the door. Wordsworth said he got so maddened by the sight of it that he threw up the job. That was when he became a doorman at the Grenada Palace.'

'What happened to the ingot?'

'I suppose the authorities lost interest when the diamond robberies started. Diamonds are money for jam, Henry. You see, they have special sealed sacks for valuable freight and these sacks are put into ordinary sacks, the idea being that the loaders can't spot them. The official mind is remarkably innocent. By the time you've been loading sacks a week or two, you can feel which sack contains another inside it. Then all you've got to do is to slit both coverings open and take pot luck. Like a children's bran tub at Christmas. Nobody is going to discover the slit until the plane arrives at the other end. Wordsworth knew a man who struck lucky the first time and pulled out a box with fifty gem stones.'

'Surely somebody's watching?'

'Only the other loaders and they take a share. Of course occasionally a man has bad luck. Once a friend of Wordsworth's fished out a fat packet of notes, but they proved to be Pakistani. Worth about a thousand pounds if you happened to live in Karachi, but who was going to change them for him here? The poor fellow used to haunt the tarmac whenever a plane was taking off to Karachi, but he never found a safe customer. Wordsworth said he got quite embittered.'

'I had no idea such things went on at Heathrow.'

'My dear Henry,' Aunt Augusta said, 'if you had been a young man I would have advised you to become a loader. A loader's life is one of adventure with far more chance of a fortune than you ever have in a branch bank. I can imagine nothing better for a young man with ambition except perhaps illicit diamond digging. That is best practised in Sierra Leone where Wordsworth comes from. The security guards are less sophisticated and less ruthless than in South Africa.'

'Sometimes you shock me, Aunt Augusta,' I said, but the statement had already almost ceased to be true. 'I have never had anything stolen from my suitcase and I don't even lock it.'

'That is probably your safeguard. No one is going to bother about an unlocked suitcase. Wordsworth knew a loader who had keys to every kind of suitcase. There are not many varieties, though he was baffled once by a Russian one.'

The loud-speaker announced our flight and we were told to proceed at once to Gate 14 for immediate embarkation.

'For someone who doesn't like airports,' I said, 'you seem to know a great deal about Heathrow.'

'I've always been interested in human nature,' Aunt Augusta said. 'Especially the more imaginative sides of it.'

She ordered another two gins and tonics immediately we arrived on the plane. 'There goes ten shillings towards the first-class fare,' she said. 'A friend of mine calculated once that on a long flight to Tahiti – it took in those days more than sixty-four hours – he recuperated nearly twenty pounds, but of course he was a hard drinker.'

Again I had the impression that I was turning the pages in an American magazine in search of a contribution which I had temporarily lost. 'I still don't understand,' I said, 'about the luggage-trailer and the suitcase. Why were you so anxious that the trailer should disappear?'

'I have an impression,' my aunt said, 'that you are really a little shocked by trivial illegalities. When you reach my age you will be more tolerant. Years ago Paris was regarded as the vice-centre of the world, as Buenos Aires was before that, but Madame de Gaulle altered things there. Rome, Milan, Venice and Naples survived a decade longer, but then the only two cities left were Macao and Havana. Macao has been cleaned up by the Chinese Chamber of Commerce and Havana by Fidel Castro. For the moment Heathrow is the Havana of the West. It won't last very long, of course, but one must admit that at the present time London Airport has a glamour which certainly puts Britain first. Have you got a little vodka for the caviar?' she asked the hostess who brought our trays. 'I prefer it to champagne.'

'But, Aunt Augusta, you have still not told me about the trailer.'

'It's very simple,' my aunt said. 'If the luggage is to be loaded direct on to the aircraft, the trailer is detached outside the Queen Elizabeth building – there are always traffic hold-ups at this point and nothing is noticed by the passengers. If when the bus arrives at the B.E.A. or Air France entrance you find the trailer is still attached, this means that the luggage is going to be sent to the customs. Personally I have a rooted objection to unknown hands, which have fiddled about in all kinds of strange luggage, some not over-clean, fiddling about in mine.'

'What do you do then?'

'I reclaim my bags, saying that after all I don't require them on the voyage and wish to leave them in the cloakroom. Or I cancel my flight and try again another day.' She finished her smoked salmon and went on to the caviar. 'There is no such convenient system as that at Dover, or I would prefer to go by boat.'

'Aunt Augusta,' I said, 'what are you carrying in your suitcases?'

'Only one is a little dangerous,' she said, 'the red. I always use thc red for that purpose. Rcd for danger,' she added with a smile.

'But what have you got in the red one?'

'A trifle,' Aunt Augusta said, 'something to help us in our travels. I can't really endure any longer these absurd travel allowances. Allowances! For grown people! When I was a child I received a shilling a week pocket money. If you consider the value of the pound today, that is rather more than what we are allowed to travel with annually. You haven't eaten your portion of foie gras.'

'It doesn't agree with me,' I said.

'Then I will take it. Steward, another glass of champagne and another vodka.'

'We are just descending ma'am.'

'The more reason for you to hurry, young man.' She fastened her seat-belt. 'I'm glad that Wordsworth left Heathrow before I came to know him. He was in danger of being corrupted. Oh, I don't mean thieving. A little honest thieving hurts no one, especially when it is a question of gold. Gold needs free circulation. The Spanish Empire would have decayed far more quickly if Sir Francis Drake had not kept a proportion of the Spanish gold in circulation. But there are other things. I have mentioned Havana, and you mustn't think me strait-laced. I am all for a little professional sex. You have probably read about the activities of Superman. And I am sure that the sight of him cured many a frigidity. Thank you, steward.' She drained her vodka. 'We have not done badly. I would say we have almost covered the difference between first-class and tourist, if you take into account a little over-weight with my red suitcase. There was a brothel in Havana where the Emperor's Crown was admirably performed by three nice girls. These establishments saved many a marriage from boredom. And then there was the Shanghai Theatre in the Chinese Quarter of Havana with three blue films which were shown in the intervals of a nude review, all for the price of one dollar with a pornographic bookshop in the foyer thrown in. I was there once with a Mr Fernandez who had a cattle farm in Camaguey. (I met him in Rome after Mr Visconti had temporarily disappeared and he invited me to Cuba for a month's holiday.) The place was ruined, though, long before the revolution. I am told that to compete with television they put in a large screen. The films, of course, had all been shot on sixteen millimetre, and when they were enlarged practically to cinerama size, it really needed an act of faith to distinguish any feature of the human body.'

The plane banked steeply over Le Bourget.

'It was all very harmless,' my aunt said, 'and gave employment to a great many people. But the things which go on around Heathrow . . .'

The steward brought another vodka and my aunt tossed it down. She had a strong head – I had noticed that already – but her mind under the influence of alcohol ranged to and fro.

'We were talking of Heathrow,' I reminded her, for my curiosity had been aroused. In my aunt's company I found myself oddly ignorant about my own country.

'There are a number of big firms around Heathrow,' my aunt said. 'Electronics, engineering, film manufacturers. Glaxo, as one would expect, is quite untouched by the Heathrow influence. After office hours some of the technicians give private parties; air crews are always welcome, so long as stewardesses are included in the party. Even loaders. Wordsworth was always invited, but only on condition he brought a girl and was willing to exchange her at the party for another. Pornographic films are shown first as an encouragement. Wordsworth was genuinely attached to his girl, but he had to surrender her in exchange for a technician's wife who was a homely woman of fifty called Ada. It seems to me that the old professional brothel system was far healthier than those exaggerated amateur distractions. But then an amateur always goes too far. An amateur is never in proper control of his art. There was a discipline in the old-time brothels. The madame in many ways played a role similar to that of the headmistress of Roedean. A brothel after all is a kind of school, and not least a school of manners. I have known several madames of real distinction who would have been just as at home in Roedean and have lent distinction to any school.'

'How on earth did you get to know them?' I asked, but the plane was bumping on the Le Bourget field, and my aunt began to fuss about her luggage. 'I think it better,' she said, 'if we pass through customs and immigration separately. My red case is rather a heavy one and I would be glad if you would take that with you. Employ a porter. It is always easier to obtain a taxi with a porter's help. And show in your manner that the tip will be a good one before you arrive at the customs. There is often an understanding between a porter and a *douanier*. I will meet you outside. Here is the ticket for the red case.'

Chapter 9

I HAD no clear idea what my aunt intended by her elaborate precautions. There was obviously little danger from the *douanier* who waved me through with the careless courtesy which I find so lacking in the supercilious young men in England. My aunt had booked rooms in the St James and Albany, an old-fashioned double hotel, of which one half, the Albany, faces the Rue de Rivoli and the other, the St James, the Rue Saint-Honoré. Between the two hotels lies the shared territory of a small garden, and on the garden front of the St James I noticed a plaque which tells a visitor that here La Fayette signed some treaty or celebrated his return from the American revolution, I forget which.

Our rooms in the Albany looked out on the Tuileries gardens and my aunt had taken a whole suite, which seemed rather unnecessary as we were only spending one night before we caught the Orient Express. When I mentioned this, however, she rebuked me quite sharply. 'This is the second time today,' she said, 'that you have mentioned the subject of economy. You retain the spirit of a bank manager, even in retirement. Understand once and for all that I am not interested in economy. I am over seventy-five, so that it is unlikely I will live longer than another twenty-five years. My money is my own and I do not intend to save for the sake of an heir. I made many economies in my youth and they were fairly painless because the young do not particularly care for luxury. They have other interests than spending and can make love satisfactorily on a Coca-Cola, a drink which is nauseating in age. They have little idea of real pleasure: even their love-making is apt to be hurried and incomplete. Luckily in middle age pleasure begins, pleasure in love, in wine, in food. Only the taste for poetry flags a little, but I would have always gladly lost my taste for the sonnets of Wordsworth (the other Wordsworth I mean of course) if I could have bettered my palate for wine. Love-making too provides as a rule a more prolonged and varied pleasure after forty-five. Aretino is not a writer for the young.'

'Perhaps it's not too late for me to begin,' I said facetiously in an effort to close that page of her conversation, which I found a little embarrassing.

'You must surrender yourself first to extravagance,' my aunt replied. 'Poverty is apt to strike suddenly like influenza, it is well to have a few memories of extravagance in store for bad times. In any case this suite is not wasted. I have to receive some visitors in private, and I don't suppose you would want me to receive them in my bedroom. One of them, by the way, is a bank manager. Did *you* visit lady clients in their bedrooms?'

'Of course not. Nor in their drawing-rooms either. I did all business at the bank.'

'Perhaps in Southwood you didn't have any very distinguished clients.'

'You are quite wrong,' I said and I told her about the unbearable rear-admiral and my friend, Sir Alfred Keene.

'Or any really confidential business.'

'Nothing certainly which could not be discussed in my office at the bank.'

'You were not bugged, I suppose, in the suburbs.'

The man who came to see her was not my idea of a banker at all. He was tall and elegant with black side-burns and he would have fitted very well into a matador's uniform. My aunt asked me to bring her the red suitcase, and I then left them alone, but looking back from the doorway I saw that the lid was already open and the case seemed to be stacked with ten-pound notes.

I sat down in my bedroom and read a copy of *Punch* to reassure myself. The sight of all the smuggled money had been a shock, and the suitcase was one of those fibre ones which are as vulnerable as cardboard. It is true that no experienced loader at Heathrow would have expected it to contain a small fortune, but surely it was the height of rashness to trust in a bluff which depended for its success on the experience of a thief. She might easily have tumbled on a novice.

My aunt had obviously spent many years abroad and this had affected her character as well as her morality. I couldn't really judge her as I would an ordinary Englishwoman, and I comforted myself, as I read *Punch*, that the English character was unchangeable. True, *Punch* once passed through a distressing period, when even Winston Churchill was a subject of mockery, but the good sense of the proprietors and of the advertisers drew it safely back into the old paths. Even the admiral had begun to subscribe again, and the editor had, quite correctly in my opinion, been relegated to television, which is at its best a vulgar medium. If the ten-pound notes, I thought, were tied in bundles of twenty, there could easily be as much as three thousand pounds in the suitcase, or even six, for surely bundles of forty would not be too thick . . . Then I remembered the case was a Revelation. Twelve thousand was not an impossible total. I felt a little comforted by that idea. Smuggling on such a large scale seemed more like a business coup than a crime.

The telephone rang. It was my aunt. 'Which would you advise?' she asked. 'Union Carbide, Genesco, Deutsche Texaco? Or even General Electric?'

'I wouldn't like to advise you at all,' I said. 'I am not competent. My clients never went in for American bonds. The dollar premium is too high.'

'There's no question of a dollar premium in France,' Aunt Augusta said with impatience. 'Your customers seem to have been singularly unimaginative.' The line went dead. Did she expect the admiral to smuggle notes?

I went restlessly out and crossed the little garden where an American couple (from the St James or the Albany) were having tea. One of them was raising a little bag, like a drowned animal, from his cup at the end of a cord. At that distressing sight I felt very far away from England, and it was with a pang that I realized how much I was likely to miss Southwood and the dahlias in the company of Aunt Augusta. I walked up to the Place Vendôme and then by the Rue Daunou to the Boulevard des Capucines. Outside a bar on the corner two women spoke to me, and suddenly I saw, bearing down on me with a happy grin of welcome, a man whom I recognized with apprehension.

'Mr Pullen?' he exclaimed. 'Praise to the Holiest in the height.'

'Wordsworth!'

'In all His works most wonderful. You wan those two gels?'

'I was just taking a stroll,' I said.

'Women lak that they humbug you,' Wordsworth said. 'They just short-timers. They do jig-jig, one two three, out you go. If you wan a gel you come along with Wordsworth.'

'But I don't want a girl, Wordsworth. I am here with my aunt. I am taking a little walk because she has business to transact.'

'Your auntie here?'

'Yes.'

'Where you live?'

I didn't want to give our address without my aunt's permission. I had a vision of Wordsworth moving in, to the room next door. Suppose Wordsworth began to smoke marijuana in the St James and Albany . . . I was uncertain of French laws on the subject.

'We are staying with friends,' I said vaguely.

'With a man?' Wordsworth asked with instant savagery. It seemed incredible that anyone could be jealous of a woman of seventy-five, but jealous Wordsworth undoubtedly was, and now I saw the banker with side-burns in a different light.

'My dear Wordsworth,' I said, 'you are imagining things,' and I allowed myself a white lie. 'We are staying with an elderly married couple.' I felt it was hardly suitable to discuss my aunt like this at a street corner, and I began to move down the boulevard, but Wordsworth kept pace with me. 'You got CTC for Wordsworth?' he asked. 'Ar find you lovely gel, school-teacher.'

'I don't *want* a girl, Wordsworth,' I repeated, but I gave him a ten-franc note to keep him quiet.

'Then you have one drink with old Wordsworth. Ar know. A.1 first-class joint right here.'

I agreed to a drink, and he led the way into the entrance of what seemed to be a theatre, the Comédie des Capucines. A gramophone was howling below, as we descended under the theatre.

'I'd rather go somewhere more quiet,' I said.

'You jus wait. This A.1 racket.' It was very hot in the cellar. A number of unaccompanied young women were sitting at the bar, and turning towards the music I saw an almost naked woman passing between the tables where a number of men, wearing shabby mac-intoshes like uniforms, sat before untasted drinks.

'Wordsworth,' I said crossly, 'if this is what you call jig-jig I don't want it.'

'No jig-jig here,' Wordsworth said. 'If you wan jig-jig you take her to hotel.'

'Take who?'

'These gels – you wan one?'

Two of the girls at the bar came and sat down, one on either side of me. I felt imprisoned. Wordsworth, I noticed, had already ordered four whiskies which he obviously couldn't pay for with the ten francs I had given him.

'Zak, *chéri*', one of the girls said, 'present your friend please.'

'Mr Pullen, you meet Rita. Lovely gel. School-teacher.'

'Where does she teach?'

Wordsworth laughed. I realized I had made a fool of myself, and I watched Wordsworth with dismay as he entered into what seemed a long business negotiation with the girls.

'Wordsworth,' I said, 'what are you doing?'

'They wan two hundred francs. I say no. I tell em we got British passports.'

'What on earth has that got to do with it?'

'They know British people very poor, can't afford good dash.' He began to talk to them again in a kind of French which I couldn't follow at all, though they seemed to understand him well enough.

'What are you talking, Wordsworth?'

'French.'

'I don't understand a word.'

'Good Coast French. This lady she know Dakar well. Ar tell her ar work in Conakry one time. They say hundred and fifty francs.'

'You can thank them very much, Wordsworth, but say I'm not interested. I have to return to my aunt.'

One of the women laughed. I suppose she recognized the word 'aunt', though I couldn't for the life of me see why a rendezvous with an aunt should be funnier than a rendezvous with a cousin, an uncle, or even one's mother. The girl repeated '*tante*' and both laughed.

'Tomorrow?' Wordsworth asked.

'I am going with my aunt to Versailles and in the evening we take the Orient Express to Istanbul.'

'Istanbul,' Wordsworth exclaimed. 'What she do there? Who she go for see?'

'I imagine we shall see the Blue Mosque, Santa Sophia, the Golden Horn, the Topkapi Museum.'

'You be careful, Mr Pullen.'

'Please call me by my right name, Pulling.' I tried to temper my rebuke with humour. 'You would not like it if I continually called you Coleridge.'

'Coleridge?'

'Coleridge was a poet and a friend of Wordsworth.'

'Ar never met that man. If he say ar did he humbug you.'

I said firmly, 'Now I really must be off, Wordsworth. Get the bill or I shall leave you to pay.'

'You waste good White Horse?'

'You can drink it yourself or share it with these ladies.' I paid the bill – it seemed an exorbitant one, but I suppose the floor show was thrown in. A naked black girl was dancing with a white feather boa. I wondered what all the men here did for a living. It seemed extraordinary that one could watch such a scene during banking hours.

Wordsworth said, 'You give three hunded francs to these ladies for private show.'

'The price seems to be going up.'

'Maybe ar make them say two hunded francs. You lef it to Wordsworth, O.K.?'

It was no use appealing to Wordsworth's sense of morality. I said, 'As you have a British passport, you should know that an Englishman is only allowed to take fifteen pounds in currency out of the country. Two hundred francs would exhaust the whole amount.'

This was a reason Wordsworth could understand. He looked down at me from his great height with melancholy and commiseration. 'Governments all the same no good,' he said.

'One must make sacrifices. The cost of defence and the social services is very high.'

'Travellers' cheques,' Wordsworth suggested quickly.

'They can only be exchanged at a bank, an official exchange or a registered hotel. In any case I shall need them in Istanbul.'

'Your auntie got plenty.'

'She has only a travel allowance too,' I said.

I felt the weakness of this last argument, for Wordsworth cannot have lived for very long with my aunt before learning that she resorted to ways and means. I changed the subject by attacking him. 'What on earth did you mean, Wordsworth, by sending me away with cannabis in my mother's urn?'

His mind was elsewhere, brooding perhaps on the travel allowance. 'No cannibals,' he said, 'in England. No cannibals in Sierra Leone.'

'I'm talking about the ashes.'

'Cannibals in Liberia, not Sierra Leone.'

'I didn't say cannibals.'

'Leopard Society in Sierra Leone. They kill plenty people but not chop them.'

'Pot, Wordsworth, pot.' I hated the vulgar word which reminded me of childhood. 'You mixed pot with my mother's ashes.'

At last I had embarrassed him. He drank the whisky quickly. 'You come away,' he said, 'ar show you much better damned place. Rue de Douai.'

I harried him all the way up the stairs. 'You had no business to do such a thing, Wordsworth. The police came and took the urn.'

'They give it you back?' he asked.

'Only the urn. The ashes were inextricably mixed with the pot.'

'Old Wordsworth meant no harm, man,' he said, halting on the pavement. 'Those bloody police.'

I was glad to see there was a taxi rank close by. I was afraid he might try to follow me and discover the whereabouts of Aunt Augusta.

'In Mendeland,' he said, 'you bury food with your ma. You bury pot. All the same thing.'

'My mother didn't even smoke cigarettes.'

'With your pa you bury best hatchet.'

'Why not food with him too?'

'He go hunt food with hatchet. He kill bush chicken.'

I got into the taxi and drove away. Looking through the rear window, I could see Wordsworth standing bewildered on the pavement edge, like a man on a river bank waiting for a ferry. He raised his hand tentatively, as though he were uncertain of my response, whether I had left him in friendship or anger, as the traffic swept between us. I wished then that I had given him a bigger CTC. After all he meant no harm. Even in his size he exhibited a clumsy innocence.

Chapter 10

I FOUND Aunt Augusta sitting alone in the centre of the large and shabby salon, filled with green velvet chairs and marble mantelpieces. She had not bothered to remove the suitcase, which lay open and empty on the floor. There were traces of tears in her eyes. I turned on the dim lights of the dusty chandelier, and my aunt gave me an uncertain smile.

'Has something happened, Aunt Augusta?' I asked. It occurred to me that she might have been robbed by the man with side-burns and I regretted having left her alone with such a large amount of cash.

'Nothing, Henry,' she said in a voice surprisingly gentle and wavery. 'I decided after all on a deposit account in Berne. What banalities they drive us to with their rules and regulations.' At this moment she had all the weary manner I would have expected of an old lady of seventy-five.

'You are upset.'

'Only by memories,' Aunt Augusta said. 'For me this hotel has many memories, and very old ones at that. You would have been only a boy . . .'

Suddenly I felt a real affection for my aunt. Perhaps a hint of weakness is required to waken our affections, and I remembered Miss Keene's fingers faltering over her tatting as she spoke of unknown South Africa – it had been then that I came nearest to a proposal.

'What kind of memories, Aunt Augusta?'

'Of a love affair, Henry. A very happy one while it lasted.'

'Tell me.'

I was moved, as I had sometimes been at the theatre, at the sight of old age remembering. The faded luxury of the room seemed like a stage set at the Haymarket. It brought to my mind photographs of Doris Keene in *Romance* and who was it in *Milestones*? Having very few memories of my own to linger over, I appreciate sentiment all the more in others.

She dabbed at her eyes. 'You'd be bored, Henry. An unfinished bottle of champagne found in an old cupboard with all the sparkle gone . . .' The jaded phrase was worthy of a Haymarket author.

I drew up a chair and took her small hand in mine: it was creamy to the touch and I was much moved by a small brown grave-mark which she had failed to cover with powder. 'Tell me,' I repeated. We were both silent thinking of very different things. I felt as though I were on the stage taking part in a revival of *The Second Mrs Tanqueray*. My aunt had led a very mixed-up life – that was certain – but she had loved deeply in her time, in the hotel St James and Albany, and who knew what excuses in her past there might be for her relations with poor Wordsworth? This sitting-room of the hotel reminded me of that other Albany in London where Captain Tanqueray had lived.

'Dear Aunt Augusta,' I said and put my arm around her shoulders. 'It helps sometimes to speak to another person. I know I belong to a different generation – perhaps a more conventional generation . . .'

'It's a rather disgraceful story,' my aunt said and she looked down in her lap with an air of modesty which I had never seen before.

I found myself kneeling uncomfortably beside her, one knee in the empty suitcase, holding her hand. 'Trust me,' I said.

'It's your sense of humour, Henry, that I don't fully trust. I don't think we find the same things funny.'

'I was expecting a sad story,' I said rather sharply, climbing out of the suitcase.

'It *is* a very sad story in its special way,' my aunt said, 'but it's rather funny too.' I had let go her hand and now she turned it this way and that like a glove in a bargain basement. 'I must really have a manicure tomorrow,' she said.

I felt some irritation at her quick change of mood. I had been betrayed into a feeling of sentiment which was not natural to me. I said, 'I saw Wordsworth just now,' thinking to embarrass her.

'What? Here?' she exclaimed.

'I am sorry to disappoint you, no. Not here in the hotel. In the street.'

'Where is he living?'

'I didn't ask. Nor did I give him your address. I hadn't realized that you would be so anxious to see him again.'

'You are a hard man, Henry.'

'Not hard, Aunt Augusta. Prudent.'

'I don't know from which side of the family you inherited prudence. Your father was lazy but never, never prudent.'

'And my mother?' I asked in the hope of trapping her.

'If she had been prudent you would not be here now.' She went to the window and looked across the Rue de Rivoli into the Tuileries gardens. 'So many nursemaids and perambulators,' she said and sighed. Against the hard afternoon light she looked old and vulnerable.

'Would you have liked a child, Aunt Augusta?'

'At most times it would have been inconvenient,' she said. 'Curran was not to be trusted as a father and by the time I knew Mr Visconti the hour was really getting late – not too late of course, but a child belongs to the dawn hours, and with Mr Visconti one was already past the blaze of noon. In any case I would have made a very unsatisfactory mother. God knows where I would have dragged the poor child after me, and suppose he had turned out completely respectable . . .'

'Like myself,' I said.

'I don't yet despair of you,' my aunt said. 'You were reasonably kind about poor Wordsworth. And you were quite right not to give him my address. He wouldn't fit in with the St James and Albany. What a pity that the days of slavery are passed, for then I could have pretended that he served some utilitarian purpose. I might have lodged him in the St James across the garden.' She gave a reminiscent smile. 'I really think I ought to tell you about Monsieur Dambreuse. I loved him a lot, and if we didn't have a child together, it was purely owing to the fact that it was a late love. I took no precautions, none at all.'

'Were you thinking about him when I came in?'

'I was. They were six of the happiest months of my life, those which we shared, and they were all spent here in the Albany. I met him first one Monday evening outside Fouquet's. He asked me to join him in a coffee, and by Thursday we were installed here, a genuine couple on good terms with the porter and the maid. The fact that he was a married man didn't worry me at all, for I am not in the least a jealous woman, and anyway I had far the larger slice of him, or so I thought. He told me he had a house in the country where his wife lived with his six children, happy and occupied and requiring very little attention, somewhere near Toulouse. He would leave me on a Saturday morning after *petit déjeuner* and return in time for bed on Monday evening. Perhaps as a sign of his fidelity, he was always very loving on a Monday night, so much so that the middle of the week would often pass very quietly. That suited my temperament well – I have always preferred an occasional orgy to a nightly routine. I really loved Monsieur Dambreuse – perhaps not with the tenderness I felt for Curran but with more freedom from care than I had ever experienced with Mr Visconti. The deepest love is not the most carefree. How Monsieur Dambreuse and I used to laugh. Of course I realized later that he had a very good reason for laughter.'

Why should I have been haunted at that moment by the thought of Miss Keene? 'Have you ever been to Koffiefontein?' I asked.

'No,' my aunt said. 'Why? Where is it?'

'A very long way away,' I said.

'The really awful thing that I discovered,' my aunt said, 'was that Monsieur Dambreuse never went very far away. Not even as far as Toulouse. He was in fact a real Parisian. The truth, when it came out, was that he had a wife and *four* children (one was already employed in the PTT) no further away than the Rue de Miromesnil – ten minutes' walk, taking the back way by the Hotel St James into the Rue Saint-Honoré, and he had another mistress installed in a first-floor suite exactly the same as ours (he was a very just man) in the St James. The weekends he spent with his wife and family in the Rue de Miromesnil and the afternoons of Tuesday, Wednesday, Thursday, Friday, when I thought he was at work, he spent with this girl, who was called Louise Dupont, in the St James across the garden. I must say it was an achievement for a man who was well over fifty and had retired from full-time work (he was a director of a metallurgical company) for reasons of ill-health.'

'Was he older than I am?' I remarked before I realized what I was saying.

'Certainly he was. He had told the other woman exactly what he had told me. She knew about the wife in Toulouse, but she had no idea at all that there was another woman more or less in the same hotel. He was a man of great fantasy and he liked women of a certain age. It was a very happy time, and sometimes he reminded me a little of your father – there were periods of lethargy punctuated by bursts of energy. He told me later, when everything was known, that he thought of me always as his lady of the night. I looked so well, he said by full electric light. The other woman he knew as the afternoon girl – although she was only a year or two younger than me. He was a very lecherous man, quite out of place, I would have thought, in a metallurgical company.'

'How did you discover?'

'He traded too much on his luck. Everything had gone so easily for six months. When I went shopping I always went out by the Rue de Rivoli. When I had shopped enough I would take tea at W. H. Smith's bookshop. And Louise was, of course, usually occupied in the afternoons. She shopped in the morning when I was engaged, for Monsieur Dambreuse never rose before eleven, and she always left the hotel by the Rue Saint-Honoré. Then one day the spirit of devilry took him. It was a weekend and he had led his wife and two younger children to the Louvre to look at the Poussins. Afterwards his family wanted tea and his wife suggested the Ritz. "It's too noisy," he told her, "it's like a parrot cage of dowagers. Now I know a quiet little garden where nobody ever comes . . ." The trouble that afternoon was that both of us came – I and Louise.

'I had never had tea in the garden between the St James and Albany before, nor had Louise, but some impulse – I sometimes believe in a Higher Power, even though I am a Catholic – led the two of us that afternoon into the garden. We were the only people there, and you know how sociable French women are. A polite bow and '*Bonjour madame*', and exchange of words between our tables about the balmy weather, and within a few minutes we were seated together, offering each other the sugar and the sandwiches, and only too glad perhaps of a little female conversation after six months in a hotel-room with one man.

'We introduced ourselves, and both of us spoke of our so-called husbands. It seemed no more than a curious coincidence when we found that the two of them worked for the same metallurgical firm. One of the things about Monsieur Dambreuse that I particularly like in memory is the fact that he always preferred to tell the truth when it was practicable – indeed he was more trustworthy than most men, who often lie uselessly from vanity. "I wonder whether they know each other," Louise was saying when into the garden walked Mousieur Dambreuse followed by his rather stout wife and two over-grown children, the female one squinting a little and suffering from hay-fever. Louise cried, "Achille," and when I think of his expression as he turned and saw the two of us sitting at tea together, I cannot help smiling even today.' My aunt dabbed her eyes with her handkerchief. 'And crying a little too,' she added, 'for it was the end of an idyll. A man cannot forgive being made to look foolish.'

I said with some indignation, 'Surely it was for you to forgive?'

'Oh no, dear. I was quite ready to continue as we were. Louise too would have agreed to share him, and I don't think Madame Dambreuse ever quite realized the situation. His name really was Achille and he introduced us to her as the wives of two fellow directors of the metallurgical firm. But Monsieur Dambreuse never quite recovered his self-esteem. Now when he was rather tranquil in mid-week he knew I realized the cause and it embarrassed him. He was not a promiscuous man. He had loved his little secret. He felt naked, poor man, and exposed to ridicule.'

'But surely, Aunt Augusta,' I exclaimed, 'you couldn't bear the man after you had discovered how he had deceived you all those months?'

She got up and strode towards me with her small hands clenched. I thought she was going to hit me. 'You young fool,' she said as if I were no more than a schoolboy. 'Monsieur Dambreuse was a *man*, and I only wish you had been given a chance of growing up like him.'

Suddenly she smiled and put her hand comfortingly against my cheek. 'I am sorry, Henry, it is not your fault. You were brought up by Angelica. Sometimes I have an awful feeling that I am the only one left anywhere who finds any fun in life. That was why I was crying a little when you came in. I said to Monsieur Dambreuse, "Achille, I love the things we do just as much as before. I don't mind knowing where you go in the afternoons. It doesn't make any difference." But of course it did to him, because he had no secret any more. His fun had been in the secret, and he left us both only so that somewhere he could find a new secret. Not love. Just a secret. The saddest thing he ever said to me was, "There's no other St James and Albany in all Paris." I said, "Couldn't you take two rooms at the Ritz on different floors?" He said, "The lift man would know. It wouldn't be really secret."'

I had listened to her with amazement and some perturbation. I realized for the first time the perils that lay ahead of me. I felt as though I were being dragged at her heels on an absurd knight-errantry, like

Sancho Panza at the heels of Don Quixote, but in the cause of what she called fun instead of chivalry. 'Why are you going to Istanbul, Aunt Augusta?' I asked.

'Time will show,' she said.

A far-fetched idea came to me. 'You are not looking for Monsieur Dambreuse?'

'No, no, Henry. Achille is probably dead just like Curran – he would be nearly ninety years old by now anyway. And Mr Visconti – poor foolish Mr Visconti. He too will be getting on – eighty-five at least, an age when you need a woman's company. There was a story that he came back to Venice after the war and was drowned in the Grand Canal after a fight with a gondolier about a woman, but I never really believed that. He wasn't the kind who fought about a woman, he was up to so many tricks, he always survived. What a long life I have had – just like your Uncle Jo.'

She was touched again by melancholy, and for the first time I thought that perhaps dahlias were not a sufficient occupation for a man's retirement. 'I'm glad to have found you, Aunt Augusta,' I said on an impulse.

She replied in a slang expression quite out of character, 'Oh, there's life in the old girl yet,' with a smile so speculative, so carefree and youthful, that I was no longer surprised by Wordsworth's jealousy.

Chapter 11

THE Orient Express left the Gare de Lyon just after midnight. The two of us had spent an exhausting day – first at Versailles, which my aunt curiously enough was seeing for the first time (she found the palace a little vulgar). 'I didn't get very far afield,' she told me, 'in the days of Monsieur Dambreuse, and in earlier times when I lived in Paris I was much too occupied.'

I had become very curious about my aunt's history, and I was interested to arrange her various periods in some kind of chronological sequence. 'Would that earlier time have been before or after you went on the stage?' I asked her. We were standing on the terrace looking down towards the lake, and I had been thinking how much more pretty and homely Hampton Court was than Versailles. But then Henry VIII was a more homely man than Louis XIV; an Englishman could identify more easily with a man of his married respectability than with the luxurious lover of Madame de Montespan. I remembered the old music-hall song, ''Enery the Eighth I am'.

> I married the widder next door,
> She 'ad 'ad seven 'Eneries before.
> 'Enery the Eighth I am.

Nobody could have written a music-hall song about the Sun King.

'On the stage, did you say?' my aunt asked rather absent-mindedly.

'Yes. In Italy.'

She seemed to be trying hard to recollect, and I was aware as never before of her great age. 'Oh,' she said, 'yes, yes, now I remember. You mean the touring company. That came after my Paris days. It was in Paris that I was spotted by Mr Visconti.'

'Was Mr Visconti a theatrical manager?'

'No, but he was a great amateur of what you insist on calling the stage. We met one afternoon in the Rue de Provence and he said I had a fine talent, and he persuaded me to leave the company I was with. And so we travelled together to Milan where my career really started. It was fortunate for me; if I had stayed in France I would never have been able to help your Uncle Jo, and Jo, having quarrelled with your father, left me most of his money. Poor dear man, I can see him still, crawling, crawling, down the corridor towards the lavatory. Let us go back to Paris and visit the Musée Grévin. I need to be cheered up.' And cheered up she certainly was by the waxworks. I remembered how at Brighton she had told me that her idea of fame was to be represented at Tussaud's, dressed in one of her own costumes, and I really believe she would have opted for the Chamber of Horrors rather than have had no image made of her at all. A bizarre thought, for my aunt was not of a criminal temperament, even though some of her activities were not strictly legal. I think that the childish saying, 'Finding's keeping', was one of her ten commandments.

I would myself have preferred to visit the Louvre and see the Venus of Melos and the Winged Victory, but my aunt would have none of it. 'All those naked women with bits missing,' she said. 'It's morbid. I once knew a girl who was chopped up that way between the Gare du Nord and Calais Maritime. She had met a man in the place where I worked who travelled in ladies' underwear – or so he said, and he certainly had an attaché case with him full of rather fanciful brassières which he persuaded her to try on. There was one shaped like two clutching black hands that greatly amused her. He invited her to go to England with him, and she broke her contract with our *patronne* and decamped. It was quite a *cause célèbre*. He was called the Monster of the Chemins de Fer by the newspapers, and he was guillotined, after making his confession and receiving the sacrament, in an odour of sanctity. It was said by his counsel that he had a misplaced devotion to virginity owing to his education by the Jesuits, and he therefore tried to remove all girls who led loose lives like poor Anne-Marie Callot. The brassières were a kind of test. You were condemned if you chose the wrong one like those poor men in *The Merchant of Venice*. He was certainly not an ordinary criminal, and a young woman who was praying for him in a chapel in the Rue du Bac had a vision of the Virgin, who said to her, "The crooked ways shall be made straight," which she took as proclaiming his salvation. There was a popular Dominican preacher on the other hand who believed it to be a critical reference to his Jesuit education. Anyway quite a cult started for what they called "the good murderer". Go and see your Venus if you want, but let me go to the waxworks. Our manager had to identify the body and he said it was just a torso, and that gave me a turn against all old statues.'

In the evening we had a quiet dinner at Maxim's, in the smaller room where Aunt Augusta thought to escape the tourists. There was one however whom we could not escape; she wore a suit and a tie, and she had a voice like a man's. She not only dominated her companion, a little mousy blonde woman of uncertain age, she dominated the whole room. Like so many English abroad she seemed to ignore the presence of foreigners around her and spoke in a loud voice as though she were alone with her companion. Her voice had a peculiar ventriloquial quality, and when I first became aware of it I thought it came from the mouth of an old gentleman with a rosette of the Legion of Honour in his buttonhole who sat at the table opposite ours, and who had obviously been taught to chew every morsel of his meat thirty-two times. 'Four-legged animals, my dear, always remind me of tables. So much more solid and sensible than two legs. One could sleep standing up.' Everyone who could understand English turned to look at him. His mouth closed with a startled snap when he saw himself the centre of attention. 'One could even serve dinner on a man with a broad enough back,' the voice said, and the mousy woman giggled and said, 'O, Edith,' and so identified the speaker. I am sure the woman had no idea of what she was doing – she was an unconscious ventriloquist, and surrounded as she believed by ignorant foreigners and perhaps excited a little by unaccustomed wine, she really let herself go.

It was a deep cultured professorial voice. I could imagine it lecturing on English literature at one of the older universities, and for the first time my attention strayed from Aunt Augusta. 'Darwin – the other Darwin – wrote a poem on the Loves of the Plants. I can well imagine a poem on the Loves of the Tables. Cramping it might be, but how deliciously so, when you think of a nest of tables, each fitting so blissfully, my dear, into one another.'

'Why is everyone staring at you?' Aunt Augusta asked. It was an embarrassing moment, all the more so as the woman had suddenly stopped speaking and had plunged into her *carré d'agneau*. The trouble is that I have an unconscious habit of moving my lips when I am thinking, so that to all except my immediate neighbours I seemed to be the author of her ambiguous remark.

'I have no idea, Aunt Augusta,' I said.

'You must have been doing *something* very odd, Henry.'

'I was only thinking.'

How I wish I could conquer the habit. It must have been established first when I was a cashier and silently counted bundles of notes. The habit betrayed me very badly once with a woman called Mrs Blennerhasset who was stone-deaf and a lip-reader. She was a very beautiful woman who was married to the mayor of Southwood. She came to my private office once about some question of investments, and while I turned over her file my thoughts couldn't help dwelling a little wistfully on her loveliness. One is more free in thought than in speech and when I looked up I saw that she was blushing. She finished her business very quickly and left. Later to my surprise she dropped in to see me again. She made some small alteration to the decision we had reached about her War Loan and then said, 'Did you really mean what you told me?' I thought she was referring to my advice about National Savings Certificates.

'Of course,' I said. 'That is my honest opinion.'

'Thank you,' she said. 'You mustn't think I am at all offended. No woman could be when you put it so poetically, but, Mr Pulling, I must tell you that I truly love my husband.' The awful thing, of course, was that she couldn't in her deafness distinguish between the lip movements made by spoken words and the movements which expressed my unspoken thoughts. She was always kind to me after that day, but she never came to my private office again.

That night at the Gare de Lyon I saw my aunt into her couchette and ordered her *petit déjeuner* from the conductor for 8 a.m. Then I waited on the platform for the train from London to come in from the Gare du Nord. It was five minutes late, but the Orient Express had to wait for it.

As the train moved slowly in, drowning the platform with steam, I saw Wordsworth come striding through the smoke. He recognized me at the same moment and cried, 'Hi, fellah.' He must have learnt the Americanism during the war when the convoys for the Middle East gathered in Freetown Harbour. I went reluctantly towards him. 'What are you doing here?' I asked. I have always disliked the unexpected, whether an event or an encounter, but I was growing accustomed to it in my aunt's company.

'Mr Pullen. Mr Pullen,' Wordsworth said, 'you an honest man, Mr Pullen.' He reached my side and grasped my hand. 'Ar allays was your friend, Mr Pullen.' He spoke as if he had known me for years and that I had been a long time in his debt. 'You no humbug me, Mr Pullen?' He gazed wildly up and down the train. 'Where's that gel?'

'My aunt,' I said, 'if that's whom you mean, is fast asleep by now in her couchette.'

'Then please go double quick tell her Wordsworth here.'

'I have no intention of waking her up. She's an old lady and has a long journey ahead of her. If it's money you want, you can take this.' I held out to him a fifty-franc note.

'I no wan CTC,' Wordsworth said waving one hand hard for emphasis, while at the same time he took the note with the other. 'I wan my bebi gel.'

Such an expression used in connection with Aunt Augusta offended me and I turned away to climb the steep steps into the coach, but he put his hand on my arm and held me back on the platform. He was a very strong man. 'You jig-jig with my bebi gel,' he accused me.

'You're preposterous, Wordsworth. She is my aunt. My mother's sister.'

'No humbug?'

'No humbug,' I said, though I hated the expression. 'Even if she were not my aunt, can't you understand that she is a very old lady?'

'No one too old for jig-jig,' Wordsworth said. 'You tell her she come back here to Paris. Wordsworth wait long long time for her. You speak her sweet. You tell her she still my bebi gel. Wordsworth no slip good when she gone.'

The conductor asked me to get on to the train, for we were about to leave, and Wordsworth unwillingly released me. I stood on the top of the steps as the train began to move out from the Gare de Lyon in short jerks, and Wordsworth followed it down the platform, wading through the steam. He was crying, and I was reminded of a suicide walking out fully dressed into the surf. Suddenly, staring at a window beyond me, he began to sing:

> 'Slip gud-o, bebi gel:
> An luk me wan minit
> Befo yu slip.'

The train gathered momentum and with a final jerk and strain it had left him behind.

I squeezed down the corridor to my aunt's couchette which was number 72. The bed was made up, but there was a strange girl in a mini-skirt sitting on it, while my aunt leant out of the window waving and blowing kisses. The girl and I looked at each other with embarrassment. We could hardly speak and interrupt this ceremony of separation. She was very young, perhaps eighteen, and she was elaborately made up with a chalk-white face, dark shadowed eyes and long auburn hair falling over her shoulders. With the strokes of a pencil she had continued her eyelashes below and above the lids, so that the real eyelashes, standing out, had a false effect like a stereoscopic photograph. Her shirt had two buttons missing at the top as though they had popped off with the tension of her puppy fat and her eyes bulged like a pekinese dog's, but they were pretty nonetheless. They had in them what used to be called by my generation a sexy look, but this might have been caused by short sight or constipation. Her smile, when she realized that I was not a stranger intruding into my aunt's compartment, was oddly timid for someone who looked so flagrant. It was as though someone else had dolled her up to attract. She was like a kid tethered to a tree to draw a tiger out of the jungle.

My aunt pulled in her head; her face was smeared with smuts and tears. 'Dear man,' she said. 'I had to take a last look. At my age one never knows.'

I said with disapproval, 'I thought that chapter was closed,' and added for the sake of the girl, 'Aunt Augusta.'

'One can never be quite sure,' my aunt said. 'This is 71,' she added, indicating the girl.

'71?'

'The next-door couchette. What's your name, dear?'

'Tooley,' the girl replied. It might have been a pet name or a family name – one couldn't be sure.

'Tooley is going to Istanbul too. Aren't you, dear?'

'*En passant*,' she said with an American accent.

'She's going to Katmandu,' my aunt explained.

'I thought that was in Nepal.'

'I guess that's where it is,' the girl said. 'Something like that.'

'She and I got talking,' my aunt told me, 'because – what's your name again, dear?'

'Tooley,' the girl said.

'Tooley has brought a sack of provisions with her. Do you realize, Henry, that the Orient Express has no restaurant-car? How times have changed. No restaurant-car till after the Turkish frontier. We face two days of starvation.'

'I've got a lot of milk chocolate,' the girl said, 'and a little sliced ham.'

'And thirst,' Aunt Augusta said.

'I've got a dozen bottles of coke, but it's getting pretty warm now.'

'When I think of the party I once had on this very train,' Aunt Augusta said, 'with Mr Visconti and General Abdul. Caviar and champagne. We practically lived in the dining-car. One meal ran into another and night into day.'

'You are very welcome to share my coke,' Tooley said. 'And the milk chocolate. The ham too, of course, but there's not much of that.'

'At least the conductor has promised us coffee and *croissants*,' I said, 'in the morning.'

'I shall sleep as late as I can,' my aunt said, 'and we shall be able to get a bite at Milan station. With Mario,' she added.

'Who's Mario?' I asked.

'We stop at Lausanne and St Maurice,' said the well-informed girl.

'Switzerland is only bearable covered with snow,' Aunt Augusta said, 'like some people are only bearable under a sheet. Now I shall go to bed. You two young people are old enough to be left alone.'

Tooley looked at me askance as though after all I might be the tiger type. 'Oh, I'll sleep too,' she said, 'I love sleep.' She looked at a huge wrist-watch on a strap an inch wide with only four numerals, coloured scarlet, 'It's not one yet,' she said doubtfully, 'I'd better take a pill.'

'You'll sleep,' my aunt said in a tone not to be denied.

Chapter 12

We were just pulling out of Lausanne when I awoke. I could see the lake between two tall grey apartment buildings and there was a tasteful advertisement for chocolates and then another for watches. It was the conductor who had woken me, bringing me coffee and *brioches* (I had asked for *croissants*). 'Is the lady in 72 awake?' I asked.

'She did not wish to be disturbed before Milan,' he replied.

'Is it true that there's no restaurant-car?'

'Yes, monsieur.'

'At least you will give us breakfast tomorrow?'

'No, monsieur. I leave the train at Milan. There is another conductor.'

'Italian?'

'Yugoslav, monsieur.'

'Does he speak English or French?'

'It is not likely.' I felt hopelessly abroad.

I drank my coffee, and then from the corridor I watched the small Swiss towns roll smoothly by: the Montreux Palace in baroque Edwardian like the home of a Ruritanian king, and rising behind it, out of a bank of morning mist, pale mountains like an under-exposed negative: Aigle, Bex, Visp . . . We stopped at nearly every station, but it was seldom that anyone either got in or out. Like my aunt foreign passengers were not interested in Switzerland without snow, and yet it was here that I was seriously tempted to leave her. I had fifty pounds of travellers' cheques and I had no interest at all in Turkey. I caught glimpses of meadows running down to water, of old castles on hills spiked with vines and of girls on bicycles; everything seemed clean and arranged and safe, as my life had been before my mother's funeral. I thought of my garden. I missed my dahlias, and at some small station, where a postman was delivering letters from a bicycle, there was a bed of mauve and red flowers. I think I might really have got off if the girl called Tooley hadn't at that moment touched my arm. Was there anything so wrong with the love of peace that I had to be forcibly drawn away from it by Aunt Augusta?

'Did you sleep well?' Tooley asked.

'Oh yes, and you?'

'I hardly slept a wink.' Her pekinese eyes stared up at me, as though she were waiting for something from my plate. I offered her a *brioche*, but she refused it.

'Oh no, thanks a lot. I've had a chocolate bar.'

'Why couldn't you sleep?'

'I'm sort of worried.'

I remembered, from my cashier days, faces just as timid as hers, peering through a hygienic barrier where a notice directed them to speak through a slot placed inconveniently low. I almost asked her whether she had an overdraft.

'Anything I can do?'

'I just want to talk,' she said.

What could I do but invite her in? My bed had been made into a sofa while I stood in the corridor, and we sat down side by side. I offered her a cigarette. It was an ordinary Senior Service, but she turned it over as though it were something special she had never seen before.

'English?' she asked.

'Yes.'

'What does Senior Service mean?'

'The Navy.'

'You don't mind, do you, if I smoke one of my own?' She took a tin marked Eucalyptus-and-Menthol Lozenges out of her bag and picked from it an anonymous cigarette which looked as though it had been home-rolled. On second thoughts she offered me one, and I thought it would be a little unkind of me to refuse. It was a very small cigarette, and it looked rather grubby. It had an odd herbal flavour, not disagreeable.

'I've never smoked an American cigarette before,' I said.

'I got these in Paris – from a friend.'

'Or French ones.'

'He was a terribly nice man. Groovy.'

'Who was?'

'This man I met in Paris. I told him my trouble too.'

'What is your trouble?'

'I had a quarrel – with my boy-friend, I mean. He wanted to go third-class to Istanbul. I said it's crazy, we couldn't sleep together in the third-class, and I've got the money, haven't I? "Your stinking allowance," he said. "Sell all you have and give it to the poor" – that's a quotation, isn't it, from somewhere? I said, "It wouldn't be any use. Father would pay me back." "He need never know," he said. "He has sources of information," I said, "he's very high up, I mean, in the CIA."

He said, "You can stick your money up your arse" – that's an English expression, isn't it? He's English. We met when we were sitting down in Trafalgar Square.'

'Feeding the pigeons?' I asked.

She gave a bubble of a laugh and choked on the smoke. 'You are ironic,' she said. 'I like men who are ironic. My father's ironic too. You are a bit like him when I come to think of it. Irony is a very valuable literary quality too, isn't it, like passion?'

'You mustn't ask me about literature, Miss Tooley,' I said. 'I'm very ignorant.'

'Don't call me *Miss* Tooley. Tooley's what my friends call me.'

At St Maurice a gang of schoolgirls passed down the platform. They were nice-looking schoolgirls; not one of them wore a mini-skirt or visible make-up and they carried neat little satchels.

'How can such a beautiful country be so dull?' Tooley thought aloud.

'Why dull?'

'They aren't turned on here,' she said. 'None of them will ever be turned on. Would you like another cigarette?'

'Thank you. They are very mild. Agreeable flavour too. They don't rasp the throat.'

'I do like the expressions you use. They really are groovy.'

I felt more awake than I usually do at that hour of the morning, and I found Tooley's company something of a novelty. I was glad that my aunt was sleeping late and giving me an opportunity to get better acquainted. I felt protective. I would have liked a daughter, though I had never been able to imagine Miss Keene as a mother. A mother should not be in need of protection herself.

'This friend of yours in Paris,' I said, 'was a very good judge of cigarettes.'

'He was fabulous,' she said. 'I mean, he's really together.'

'French?'

'Oh no, he came from darkest Africa.'

'A negro?'

'We don't call them that,' she said reprovingly. 'We call them coloured or black – whichever they prefer.'

A sudden suspicion struck me. 'Was he called Wordsworth?'

'I only knew him as Zach.'

'That's the man. Was it you he came to see off at the station?'

'Sure. Who else? I never expected him, but there he was at the gate to say goodbye. I bought him a platform ticket, but I think he was scared. He wouldn't come any further.'

'He knows my aunt too,' I said. I didn't tell her that he had used her ticket for another purpose.

'Now isn't that the wildest sort of coincidence? Like something in Thomas Hardy.'

'You seem to know a lot about literature.'

'I'm majoring in English Literature,' she said. 'My father wanted me to take Social Science because he wanted me to serve a while in the Peace Corps, but I guess our ideas didn't coincide in that and other things.'

'What does your father do?'

'I told you – he has a very secret job in the CIA.'

'That must be interesting,' I said.

'He travels about a terrible lot. I haven't seen him more than once since Mum divorced him last fall. I tell him he sees the world horizontally, I mean that's superficial, isn't it? I want to see the world vertically.'

'In depth,' I said. I was rather proud of catching up with her ideas.

'These help,' she said, waving her cigarette. 'I feel a bit turned on already. It's your fabulous way of talking. I feel I sort of met you in the English Literature course. As a character. We did Dickens in depth.'

'Vertically,' I said, and we laughed together.

'What's your name?'

'Henry.' She laughed again and I followed suit though I was not sure why.

'They didn't even call you Harry?' she asked.

'Harry is the diminutive. One cannot be baptized Harry. There was never a Saint Harry.'

'Is that what they call Canon Law?'

'I believe so.'

'Because I knew a fabulous guy once who was baptized Knock-Me-Down.'

'I doubt if he was really baptized that.'

'Are you a Roman Catholic?'

'No, but I believe my aunt is one. I'm not quite sure though.'

'I nearly became a Roman Catholic once. Because of the Kennedys. But then when two of them got shot – I mean I'm superstitious. Was Macbeth a Catholic?'

'It's not a question that's ever occurred to me . . . I suppose . . . well, I mean I don't really know.' It seemed to me that I was picking up her phrases.

'Maybe we ought to lock the door and open the window,' she said. 'What country are we in now?'

'I think we must be coming near to the Italian frontier.'

'Then open the window quick.' I couldn't follow her reasoning, but I obeyed. I had already finished my cigarette, and she tossed away her stump and then emptied the ashtray on to the line. Then I remembered Wordsworth.

'What have we been smoking?' I said.

'Pot, of course. Why?'

'Do you realize we could be sent to prison? I don't know the Swiss law or the Italian, but . . .'

'I wouldn't be. I'm under age.'

'And me?'

'You could plead innocence,' she said and began to laugh: she was laughing when the door opened and the Italian police looked in.

'Passports,' they demanded, but they didn't even open them; the draught of the open window blew off one man's cap, and I could only hope the smell of cannabis had dispersed down the corridor. They were followed closely by the customs men who were equally considerate, except that one man wrinkled his nose. A few minutes later they were safely on the platform. The sign read Domodossola.

'We're in Italy,' I said.

'Then have another.'

'I'll do no such thing, Tooley. I had no idea . . . For goodness' sake get rid of them before night. Yugoslavia's a Communist country, and they won't hesitate to imprison someone under age.'

'I was always taught that Yugoslavs were *good* Communists. We sell them strategic material, don't we?'

'But not drugs,' I said.

'Now you're being ironical again. I mean I wanted to tell you my great trouble, but how can I do it if you're ironical?'

'You said just now that irony was a valuable literary quality.'

'But you aren't a novel,' she said and began to cry as Italy went by outside. The cannabis had caused the laughter and now I suppose it caused the tears. I felt a little unhappy myself watching her. My head swam. I shut the window and saw through the pane a hill-village all yellow and ochre, like something grown of itself out of rain and earth, and beside the line a factory and a red housing estate and an autostrada and an advertisement for Perugina and all the wires and grids of a smokeless age.

'What's your trouble, Tooley?' I asked.

'I forgot the damn pill and I haven't had the curse for six weeks. I nearly talked to your mother last night . . .'

'My aunt,' I corrected her. 'You ought to speak to her. I don't really know about these things.'

'But I want to talk to a man,' Tooley said. 'I mean I'm sort of shy of women. I don't get on terms with them fast the way I do with men. The trouble is men are so ignorant now. In the old days a girl never knew what to do, and now it's the men who don't know. Julian said it was my fault – he trusted me.'

'Julian is the boy-friend?' I asked.

'He was angry because I forgot the pill. He wanted to hitch-hike to Istanbul. He said it might do the trick.'

'I thought he wanted to go third-class.'

'That was before I told him. And before he met a man with a truck going to Vienna. Then he gave me an ultimatum. We were in this café in the Place St Michel and he said, "We've got to leave now or never," and I said, "No", and he said, "Find your own fucking way then."'

'Where is he now?'

'Somewhere between here and Istanbul.'

'How will you find him?'

'They'll know at the Gulhane.'

'What's that?'

'It's near the Blue Mosque. Everyone knows where everyone is at the Gulhane.' She began to remove carefully the traces of tears. Then she looked at her huge watch with the four numbers and said, 'It's nearly lunchtime. I'm as hungry as a dog. I hope I'm not feeding two. Want some chocolate?'

'I'll wait until Milan,' I said.

'Have another cigarette?'

'No thank you.'

'I will. It might do the trick.' She began to smile again. 'It's funny the ideas I get, I mean I think almost anything might do the trick. I drank brandy and ginger ale in Paris because at school they said ginger did the trick. And I had sauna baths too. It's funny when all you really need is a *curetage*. Wordsworth said he'd find me a doctor, but he said he'd need a few days to find him, and then I'd have to lay up a little, and it wouldn't be much good getting to the Gulhane and finding Julian gone. Gone where? I ask you. I met a boy in Paris who said they were turning us all out of Katmandu and Vientiane was the place now. Not for Americans of course because of the draft.'

There were moments when she gave the impression that all the world was travelling.

Tooley said, 'I slept with a boy in Paris when Julian walked out because I thought, well, it might stir things up a bit. I mean the curse comes that way sometimes right on top of the orgasm, but I didn't get any orgasm. I guess I was worrying about Julian because I don't often have difficulty that way.'

'I think you ought to go straight back home and tell your parents.'

'In the singular,' she said. 'I don't count Mum, and I don't exactly know where Father is. He travels an awful lot. Secret missions. He might be in Vientiane for all I know – they say it's lousy with CIA.'

'Haven't you anywhere you call home?' I asked her.

'Julian and me felt like home, but then he got angry about my forgetting the pill. He's very quick-tempered. "If I have to remind you all the time," he said, "it takes away my spontaneity, don't you understand that?" He's got a theory women want to castrate their men, and one way is to take away their spontaneity.'

'And you felt at home with him?'

'We could discuss just everything,' she said with a happy and reminiscent smile as the pot began to work again. 'Art and sex and James Joyce and psychology.'

'You oughtn't to smoke that stuff,' I protested.

'Pot? Why? There's no harm in pot. Acid's another thing. Julian wanted me to try acid, but I said not, I mean I don't want to warp my chromosomes.'

There were moments when I didn't understand a word she said, and yet it seemed to me that I could listen to her for a long while without wearying. There was something gentle and sweet about her which reminded me of Miss Keene. It was an absurd comparison to make, of course, and perhaps this was what she meant by being turned on.

Chapter 13

WHEN a train pulls into a great city I am reminded of the closing moments of an overture. All the rural and urban themes of our long journey were picked up again: a factory was followed by a meadow, a patch of autostrada by a country road, a gas-works by a modern church: the houses began to tread on each other's heels, advertisements for Fiat cars swarmed closer together, the conductor who had brought breakfast passed, working intensely down the corridor to rouse some important passenger, the last fields were squeezed out and at last there were only houses, houses, houses, and Milano, flashed the signs, Milano.

I said to Tooley, 'We've arrived. We'd better get lunch. It's our last chance to get a square meal . . .'

'Your mother . . .' Tooley began.

'Aunt Augusta – she's here.'

The conductor had preceded her down the corridor (I should have realized who the important passenger was) and now she stood in the doorway of our compartment wrinkling her nose. 'What have you two been up to?' she asked.

'Smoking and talking,' I said.

'You seem extraordinarily cheerful, Henry. It's not quite like you.' She sniffed again. 'I can almost believe that poor Wordsworth is with us still.'

'It's fabulous,' Tooley said, 'that you know Wordsworth, I mean.'

'*Il y a un monsieur qui vous demande, madame*,' the conductor interrupted, and I saw beyond my aunt, between a trolley of newspapers and a trolley of refreshments, a very tall thin man with exquisite white hair gesticulating with an umbrella.

'Oh, it's Mario,' my aunt said, without bothering to turn. 'I wrote to him that we should need lunch. He will have ordered it. Come, my dear, come, Henry, there's no time to be lost.' She preceded us down the steps and dropped straight into the arms of the white-haired man, who with steely strength held her for a moment suspended. '*Madre mia, madre mia*,' he said breathlessly and dropped his umbrella as he put her carefully down on to the platform as though she might break – the very idea connected with Aunt Augusta was ridiculous.

'What on earth is he calling you that for?' I whispered. Perhaps it was the effect of the cannabis, but I had taken an extreme dislike to the man who was now kissing Tooley's hand.

'I knew him since he was a baby,' Aunt Augusta said. 'He is Mr Visconti's son.'

He was very good-looking in a histrionic way; he had the appearance of an ageing actor and I didn't like the way he was trying to dazzle Tooley with pieces of his repertoire. After his burst of theatrical emotion with my aunt he was conducting Tooley ahead of us down the platform to the restaurant, holding his umbrella by the ferrule and pointing the crook up like a crozier. With his white hair and his head bent towards Tooley he looked like a hypnotic bishop instructing a neophyte on purity.

'What does he do, Aunt Augusta? Is he an actor?'

'He writes verse drama.'

'Can he live on that?'

'Mr Visconti settled a little money on him before the war. Luckily in Swiss francs. I suspect too that he gets money from women.'

'Rather disgusting at his age,' I said.

'He can make a woman laugh. Look how Tooley is laughing now. His father was the same. It's the best way, Henry, to win a woman. They are wiser than men. They think of the period that must elapse between one love-making and another. In my youth not many women smoked cigarettes. Look out for that trolley.'

I could feel in my head the cunning of cannabis. 'He must have been born when you knew Mr Visconti . . . Did you know his mother too?'

'Not very well.'

'She must have been a beautiful woman.'

'I am not a fair judge. I detested her and she detested me. Mario always thought of me as his real mother. Mr Visconti called her the blonde cow. She was German.'

Mario Visconti had ordered a *saltimbocca Romana* for each of us and a bottle of Frascati wine. My aunt began to speak to him in Italian. 'You must forgive me,' my aunt said, 'but Mario speaks no English, and it is many many years since we have seen each other.'

'Do you speak Italian?' I asked Tooley.

'Not a word.'

'You seemed to be having quite a conversation.'

'Oh, he was very expressive.'

'What was he expressing?'

'He sort of liked me. What does *cuore* mean?'

I looked at Mario Visconti with resentment and saw that he had begun to weep. He was talking a great deal and using his hands in explanation and once he picked up his umbrella and held it above his head. In the short intervals between paragraphs he put a lot of *saltimbocca Romana* into his mouth, leaning his handsome face forward over the plate, so that the fork only had a short distance to travel and the tears only a little way to fall. It was lucky that the dish was heavily salted already. My aunt lent him a wispy lace handkerchief which he applied to his eyes and afterwards adjusted becomingly in his breast pocket to show a frilly corner. Then he became dissatisfied with the wine, which seemed very good to me, and called to the waiter to change it. Only after he had tasted a new bottle did he resume his tears. I noticed the waiters were as indifferent to the scene as usherettes at a cinema are to a movie which has been running a week.

'I don't like a man who cries,' I said to Tooley.

'Have you never cried?'

'No,' I said and then added for the sake of accuracy, 'not in public.' The waiter brought us all ice-creams in three colours. They looked dangerous to me and I left mine untasted, but Mario's disappeared quickly and I noticed how his tears were quenched as though the ice had frozen the ducts. He gave my aunt a shy boyish smile which went strangely with his white hair, and she lent him surreptitiously her purse to pay with.

On the steps of the train I was afraid he would begin to cry again when he embraced her, but instead he gave her a small brown-paper parcel and walked silently away holding up his crook to hide his emotion or perhaps his lack of it. 'So that's that,' my aunt said with cool thoughtfulness. Tooley had disappeared – I suspected into the lavatory to smoke another cigarette – and I decided a tell Aunt Augusta about her trouble.

But I found when I sat down beside her that she wanted to do the talking herself. 'Mario seems rather an old man,' she said, 'or has he dyed his hair, I wonder? He cannot be more than forty-five. Or six. I am bad about dates.'

'He certainly looks a good deal older than that. Perhaps it is the poetry.'

'I have never much cared,' she said, 'for men with umbrellas, but he was charming as a child.' She looked out of the window and I looked too: a new housing estate in red brick straggled beside the line and on the hill beyond a medieval village crumbled away behind its ramparts.

'Why was he crying?' I asked.

'He wasn't crying. He was laughing,' she said. 'Something about Mr Visconti. I haven't seen Mario for more than thirty years,' she said. 'He was a sweet boy then – too sweet perhaps to last. The war came. We were separated.'

'And his father?'

'I never associated sweetness with Mr Visconti. Charm perhaps. He was a terrible twister. Very generous with cream buns, of course, but one can't live on cream buns. Perhaps I am being unfair. One is apt to be unfair to somebody one has loved a great deal. And after all he was kind to me from the very start – he found me my situation in Italy.'

'At the theatre?'

'I can't think why you persist in calling it a theatre. "All the world's a stage", of course, but a metaphor as general as that loses all its meaning. Only a second-rate actor could have written such a line out of pride in his second-rate calling. There were occasions when Shakespeare was a very bad writer indeed. You can see how often in books of quotations. People who like quotations love meaningless generalizations.'

I was a little shocked by her unexpected attack on Shakespeare. Perhaps it was because he wrote verse dramas like Mario. 'You were talking about Mr Visconti,' I reminded her.

'I must admit he was very kind to me in Paris. I was quite heart-broken when I left Curran. I couldn't appeal to your father because I had promised Angelica to stay away, and when Curran left, after our final quarrel, he took everything except the cash in the church collecting-boxes and twelve tins of sardines. He had an unnatural passion for sardines. He said they calmed his nerves, that eating them was like pouring oil on troubled waters. There was enough in the collecting-boxes to pay my passage across the Channel and I was lucky to get this job of mine in the Rue de Provence. But I wasn't really happy there, and I was grateful to Mr Visconti when he took me to Italy. The work, of course, was the same. but I enjoyed the travel from one city to another. And every eight weeks when I came back to Milan I enjoyed seeing Mr Visconti. Cream buns were a great improvement on sardines. Sometimes too he would pop up unexpectedly in Venice. He was a twister, no doubt of it, but there are many worse people than twisters.' She sighed, looking out at the dull scenery of the Po. 'I grew to be very very fond of him. Fonder than any other man I have ever known. Except the first, but the first is always a special case.'

'How did you come to retire?' I asked. I was going to say 'from the stage', but I remembered her inexplicable dislike of the term. I had not forgotten Tooley's trouble, but I thought it only fair to let my aunt finish first with the memories stirred up by the sight of Visconti's son.

'Your Uncle Jo left me all his money. It was quite a shock. The house, too, of course, but there was nothing to be done about that. It's still crumbling away near the autostrada. I settled the house on Mario when I had to leave Italy because of the war and I think he sometimes takes a woman there to spend a weekend in the ancient family *palazzo*. He even calls it the Palazzo Visconti (he's a bit of a snob: quite unlike his father). One day they'll want to build a connecting road to the autostrada and then the state will have to pay him compensation if he can show that the house was inhabited.'

'Why didn't you marry Mr Visconti, Aunt Augusta?'

'There's no divorce in Italy, and Mr Visconti was a Catholic, even though a non-practising one. He even insisted on my being received into the Church. It was his wife who had all the money and that hampered Mr Visconti badly until he managed to get his fingers on most of what Jo had left me. I was very careless in those days and Mr Visconti was very plausible. It was lucky for me that no one would buy the house – that at least was left me for a time. He had a scheme for selling fresh vegetables – tomatoes, particularly, of course – to Saudi Arabia. At the beginning I think he really believed he would make our fortune. Even his wife lent him money. I shall always remember the conferences at the Excelsior in Rome with Arab notables in long robes who arrived with a dozen wives and a food-taster. Mr Visconti would take a whole floor in the Excelsior – you can imagine that made quite a hole in Jo's money. But it was very romantic while it lasted. I had my fun. Mr Visconti was never for a moment dull. He even persuaded the Vatican to put in money, so we had cardinals for cocktails at the Grand Hotel. The Grand had once been a convent, and I suppose they felt more at home there. They were greeted at the door by flunkeys with tall candles, and it was a wonderful sight when the Arabs and the cardinals met, the desert robes and the scarlet skull-caps and all the bowings and embracings and the genuflections of the management and the kissing of rings and the blessings. The Arabs, of course, only drank orange juice, and the tasters stood at the bar sampling each jug and occasionally snatching a whisky and soda on the side. Everybody enjoyed these parties, but only the Arabs could really afford their fun, as it turned out.'

'Was Mr Visconti ruined?'

'He pulled out in time with what was left of my money and what was left of his wife's and to do him justice he had settled some of mine on Mario. Of course he disappeared for a while, but he came back after things had quietened down. The Vatican made a very profitable deal, you remember, with Mussolini, so that what they lost to Mr Visconti seemed very small beer indeed. He had left me enough to live on in a modest way, but I had never been very keen on modesty. Life was very monotonous after Mr Visconti disappeared. I even visited Havana, as I told you, and afterwards I went back to Paris for a while (Mario was with the Jesuits in Milan) – that was when I met Monsieur Dambreuse. But when the affair was over I came back to Rome. I always hoped that one day Mr Visconti would turn up again. I had a two-roomed apartment, and I did a little part-time work in an establishment behind the *Messaggero*. Life was very middle-class after all the Arabs and the cardinals. I had been spoilt by Curran and Mr Visconti. No men have ever given me more amusement than those two did. Poor Wordsworth!' my aunt added. 'He was not in the same league.' She gave a very young laugh and laid her hand on my knee. 'And then – Oh praise to the Holiest in the height, as Wordsworth is fond of saying – I was putting in a little part-time behind the *Messaggero* when who should walk into the reception room but Mr Visconti. A pure coincidence. He wasn't looking for me. But how happy we were. How happy. Just to see each other again. The girls didn't understand when we joined hands then and there and danced between the sofas. It was one o'clock in the morning. We didn't go upstairs. We went straight out into the lane outside. There was a drinking fountain shaped like an animal's head, and he splashed my face with water before he kissed me.'

'What was that half-time employment?' I suddenly broke out. 'Who were the girls? What were the sofas there for?'

'What does it matter now?' my aunt said. 'What did any of it matter? We were together again and he splashed me and splashed me and he kissed me and kissed me.'

'But surely you must have despised the man after all he had done to you?'

We were crossing the long aqueduct through the lagoons which leads to Venice-Mestre, but there were no signs of the beautiful city, only tall chimneys with pale gas flames hardly visible in the late afternoon sunlight. I was not expecting my aunt's outburst.

She turned on me with real fury as though I were a child who had carelessly broken some vase she had cherished over the years for its beauty and the memories it contained. 'I despise no one,' she said, 'no one. Regret your own actions, if you like that kind of wallowing in self-pity, but never, never despise. Never presume yours is a better morality. What do you *suppose* I was doing in the house behind the *Messaggero*? I was cheating, wasn't I? So why shouldn't Mr Visconti cheat me? But you, I suppose, never cheated in all your little provincial banker's life because there's not anything you wanted enough, not even money, not even a woman. You looked after people's money like a nanny who looks after other people's children. Can't I see you in your cage, stacking up the little fivers endlessly before you hand them over to their proper owner? Angelica certainly brought you up as she wanted you. Your poor father didn't have a chance. He was a cheat too, and I only wish you were. Then perhaps we'd have something in common.'

I was astonished. I could find nothing to say in reply. I thought of leaving the train at Venice, but then there was Tooley and I felt responsible for Tooley. The squalid station wrapped us round with its dirt and its noise. I said, 'I think I'd better find Tooley,' and I went away, leaving the old lady glaring on her couchette. Only as I closed the door of the compartment I thought I heard her laugh.

Chapter 14

I FELT glad that I had not lost my temper, but nonetheless I was shocked and needed a little time for reflection, so I climbed down on to the platform and began to look around me for food. It was the last chance before Belgrade next morning. I bought six ham rolls off a trolley and a bottle of Chianti and some sweet cakes – it was not so good a meal as Chicken would have provided, I thought sadly, and what a dreary station it was. Travel could be a waste of time. This was the hour of the early evening when the sun had lost its heat and the shadows fell across my small lawn, the hour when I would take my yellow watering-can and fill it from the garden tap . . .

Tooley's voice said, 'Would you mind getting me some more coke?'

'There's nowhere on the train to keep it cold.'

'I don't mind warm coke.'

Oh the absurdity of it all, I could have cried aloud, for now the man with the trolley wouldn't take a pound note, and I had to give him two of the dollars which I was carrying in my pocket-book against emergencies, and he refused any change, though I knew the exact rate and told him the lire required.

'Julian did a fabulous picture of a coke bottle once,' Tooley said.

'Who's Julian?' I asked absent-mindedly.

'The boy-friend, of course. I told you. He painted the coke bright yellow. *Fauve*,' she added in a defiant way.

'He paints, does he?'

'That's why he thinks the East's very important to him. You know like Tahiti was for Gauguin. He wants to experience the East before he starts on his big project. Let me take the coke.'

There was less than an hour's wait at Venice, but the dark was falling when we pulled out and I saw nothing at all – I might have been leaving Clapham for Victoria. Tooley sat with me and drank one of her cokes. I asked her what her boy-friend's project was.

'He wants to do a series of *enormous* pictures of Heinz soups in fabulous colours, so a rich man could have a different soup in each room in his apartment – say fish soup in the bedroom, potato soup in the dining-room, leek soup in the drawing-room, like they used to have family portraits. There would be these fabulous colours, all *fauve*. And the cans would give a sort of unity – do you see what I mean? It would be kind of intimate – you wouldn't break the mood every time you changed rooms. Like you do now if you have de Staël in one room and a Rouault in another.'

The memory of something I had seen in a Sunday supplement came back to me. I said, 'Surely somebody once *did* paint a Heinz soup tin?'

'Not Heinz, Campbell's,' Tooley said. 'That was Andy Warhol. I said the same thing to Julian when he first told me of the project. "Of course," I said, "Heinz and Campbell are not a bit the same shape. Heinz is sort of squat and Campbell's are long like English pillar-boxes." I love your pillar-boxes. They are fabulous. But Julian said that wasn't the point. He said that there are certain subjects which belong to a certain period and culture. Like the Annunciation did. Botticelli wasn't put off because Piero della Francesca had done the same thing. He wasn't an *imitator*. And think of all the Nativities. Well, Julian says, we sort of belong to the soup age – only he didn't call it that. He said it was the Art of Techno-Structure. In a way, you see, the more people who paint soups the better. It *creates* a culture. One Nativity wouldn't have been any use at all. It wouldn't have been noticed.'

I was badly out of my depth with Tooley in terms of culture and of human experience. She was closer to my aunt: she would never, I felt sure, have criticized Mr Visconti: she would have accepted him, as she accepted Julian's project, a voyage to Istanbul, my company, her baby.

'Where does your mother live?'

'I guess she's in Bonn at the moment. She married a man on *Time-Life* who covers West Germany and Eastern Europe, so they move around a lot. Like Father. Do you want a cigarette?'

'Not for me. And you'd better wait till we're past the next frontier.'

It was nearly nine-thirty in the evening when we arrived at Sezana. A surly passport man looked at us as though we were Imperialist spies. Old women heavily laden with small parcels came down the unplatformed track making for the third-class. They emerged from everywhere like a migration, even from between the goods trucks which stood uncoupled all along the line looking as though they would never be linked together. No one else joined the train: no one got off. There were no lights, no waiting-room in sight, it was cold and the heating had not been turned on. On the road beyond – if there was a road – no cars passed. No railway hotel offered a welcome.

'I'm cold,' Tooley said. 'I'm going to bed.' She offered to leave me a cigarette, but I refused. I didn't want to be compromised on this cold frontier. Another uniformed man looked in and regarded my new suitcase on the rack with hatred.

At moments during the night I woke – in Ljubljana, in Zagreb – but there was nothing to be seen except the lines of stationary rolling-stock which looked abandoned as though nothing was left anywhere to put in the trucks, no one had the energy any more to roll them, and it was only our train which steamed on impelled by a foolish driver who hadn't realized that the world had stopped and there was nowhere for us to go.

At Belgrade Tooley and I had breakfast in the station hotel – dry bread and jam and bad coffee, and we bought a bottle of sweet white wine for lunch, but they had no sandwiches. I let my aunt sleep on: it was not a meal worth waking her to share.

'Why are you two going to Istanbul?' Tooley asked, taking a spoonful of jam – she had given up trying to crumble the bread.

'She likes to travel,' I said.

'But why to Istanbul?'

'I haven't asked her.'

In the fields horses moved slowly along, dragging harrows. We were back in the pre-industrial age. Tooley and I were both depressed, yet it wasn't the lowest point of our journey; that came as evening fell in Sofia, and we tried to buy something to eat, but no one would take any money but Bulgarian except at an exorbitant rate, and even when I agreed to that, there were only tepid sausages on sale made of some coarse unrecognizable meat and chocolate cake made of a chocolate substitute and pink fizzy wine. I hadn't seen my aunt all day except once when she looked in on us and refused Tooley's last bar of chocolate and said sadly and unexpectedly, 'I loved chocolate once. I am growing old.'

'So this is the great Orient Express,' Tooley said.

'All that's left of it.'

'Istanbul can't be much worse, can it?'

'I've never been there, but I don't imagine so.'

'I guess you are going to tell me that I mustn't smoke because there'll soon be another frontier.'

'There will be three frontiers,' I said, looking at the timetable, 'in less than four hours. The Bulgarian frontier, the Greek-Macedonian frontier, the Turkish frontier.'

'Maybe it's real luxury travel,' Tooley said, 'for people not in a hurry. Do you think they have an abortionist on the train? It's lucky I'm not nine months gone, isn't it, or I wouldn't know whether my baby was going to be Bulgarian or Turkish or – what was the other?'

'Greek-Macedonian.'

'That sounds a bit special. I'd choose that. Not a Bulgar. If he was a boy there'd be dirty jokes.'

'But you wouldn't have a choice.'

'I'd hang on. When they said push I wouldn't push. Not till after the Greek-Macedonian frontier. How long are we in Greece-Macedonia?'

'Only forty minutes,' I said.

'My, it's complicated. I'd have to work quick.' She added, 'It's not funny at all. I'm scared. What's Julian going to say when the curse hasn't come? I really thought the train would do it, sort of shake it out of me, I mean.'

'It's Julian's fault as much as yours.'

'But it isn't any longer, not with the pill. It's all the girl's fault now. I really did forget. When I take a sleeping pill I wake up muzzy and I forget, and then, when I take a methedrine to wake up properly, I get so excited I don't remember all the dull things – like the pill and washing the dishes. But I guess Julian won't believe all that. He'll feel trapped. He often feels trapped. He was trapped first by his family, he says, and then he was nearly trapped by Oxford – so he went away fast without a degree. Then he very nearly got trapped by the Trotskyists, but he realized just in time. He sees traps a terribly long way ahead. But, Henry, I don't mean to be a trap. Really I don't. I can't call you Henry. It doesn't sound like a real name. Can I call you Smudge?'

'Why Smudge?'

'I had a dog once called Smudge. I used to talk to him a lot. When Father and Mother got divorced I told him all the horrid details. About the mental cruelty I mean.'

She leant against me in the carriage. I liked the smell of her hair. I suppose if I had known more about women I could have identified the shampoo she must have had in Paris. Her hand was on my knee, and the enormous wrist-watch stared up at me with its great blank white face and its four figures in scarlet, 12 3 6 9, as if those were the only important ones to remember – the hours when you had to take your medicine. I remembered Miss Keene's minute gold wrist-watch like a doll's which Sir Alfred had given her on her twenty-first birthday. In its tiny ring it contained all the figures of the hours as though none were unimportant or without its special duty. Most of the hours of my life had been eliminated from Tooley's watch. There were no hours marked for sitting quietly and watching a woman tat. I felt as though one night in Southwood I had turned my back on any possibility of home, so that here I was shaken up and down between two segments of Bulgarian darkness.

'What was the mental cruelty?' I had to ask her questions: it was the only way in which I could find my way about in this new world, but questioning was not a habit I had ever formed. For years people had asked me questions: 'What unit trust would you recommend? Do you think I should sell my hundred Imperial Tobacco shares before the next cancer report?' And when I retired most of the questions I might have wanted to ask were answered for me in *Everyman His Own Gardener*.

'The only mental cruelty I ever saw personally,' Tooley said, 'was when Father woke her up bringing her early morning tea in bed. I don't think that awful Bulgarian sausage was good for my metabolism. I've got a terrible stomach-ache. I'll go and lie down. You don't think it was horse, do you?'

'I've always understood that horse has a sweetish taste.'

'Oh God, Smudge,' she said, 'I didn't want a literal answer, not real information I mean.' She dabbed her lips against my cheek and was off.

I went down the corridor rather nervously to find Aunt Augusta. I'd hardly seen her all day and the problem of Tooley was one which I felt she ought to share. I found her with a Baedeker opened and a map of Istanbul spread over her knee. She looked like a general planning a campaign.

'I'm sorry about yesterday afternoon, Aunt Augusta,' I said. 'I really didn't mean to say anything against Mr Visconti. After all I don't know the circumstances. Tell me more about him.'

'He was a quite impossible man,' my aunt said, 'but I loved him and what he did with my money was the least of his faults. For example he was what they call a collaborator. During the German occupation he acted as adviser to the German authorities on questions of art, and he had to get out of Italy very quickly after the death of Mussolini. Goering had been making a big collection of pictures, but even he couldn't easily steal pictures from places like the Uffizi where the collection was properly registered, but Mr Visconti knew a lot about the unregistered – all sorts of treasures hidden away in *palazzos* almost as crumbling as your Uncle Jo's. Of course his part got to be known, and there'd be quite a panic in a country place when Mr Visconti appeared taking lunch in the local *taverna*. The trouble was he wouldn't play even a crooked game straight or the Germans might have helped him to escape. He began to take money from this marchese and that not to tip off the Germans – this gave him liquid cash or sometimes a picture he fancied for himself, but it didn't make him friends and the Germans soon suspected what was going on. Poor old devil,' she added, 'he hadn't a friend he could trust. Mario was still at school with the Jesuits and I had gone back to England when the war began.'

'What happened to him in the end?'

'I thought for a long time he'd been liquidated by the partisans, for I never believed that story about the gondolier. I suspect he got someone to spread it for him. Mr Visconti, as I told you, was not a man for fighting with knives or fists. A man who fights never survives long, and Mr Visconti was great at survival. Why, the old sod,' she said with tender delight, 'he survives to this moment. He must be eighty-four if he's a day. He wrote to Mario and Mario wrote to me, and that's why you and I have taken the train to Istanbul. I couldn't explain all that in London, it was too complicated, and anyway I hardly knew you. Thank goodness for the gold brick, that's all I can say.'

'The gold brick?'

'Never mind. That's quite another thing.'

'You told me about a gold brick at London Airport, Aunt Augusta, surely . . . ?'

'Of course not. It's not that one. That was quite a little one. Don't interrupt. I'm telling you now about poor Mr Visconti. It seems he's fallen on very lean times.'

'Where is he? In Istanbul?'

'It's better you shouldn't know, for there are people still after him. Oh dear, he's certainly escaped the hard way. Mr Visconti was a good Catholic, but he was very very anti-clerical, and yet in the end it was the priesthood which saved him. He went to a clerical store in Rome, when the Allies were coming close, and he paid a fortune to be fitted out like a monsignor even to the purple socks. He said that a friend of his had lost all his clothes in a bombing raid and they pretended to believe him. Then he went with a suitcase to the lavatory in the

Excelsior Hotel, where we had given all those cocktail parties to the cardinals, and changed. He kept away from the reception-desk, but he was unwise enough to look in at the bar – the barman, he knew, was very old and short-sighted. Well, you know, in those days a lot of girls used to come to the bar to pick up German officers. One of the girls – I suppose it was the approach of the Allied troops that did it – was having a *crise de conscience*. She wouldn't go to her friend's bedroom, she regretted her lost purity, she would never sin again. The officer plied her with more and more cocktails, but with every drink she became more religious. Then she spied Mr Visconti, who was having a quick whisky in a shady corner. "Father," she cried to him, "hear my confession." You can imagine the tension at the bar, the noise outside as the evacuation got under way, the crying children, people drinking up what there was in the bar, the Allied planes overhead . . .'

'How did you hear the story, Aunt Augusta?'

'Mr Visconti told Mario the essentials when he got to Milan, and I can imagine the rest. Especially I can picture poor Mr Visconti in his purple socks. "My child," he said, "this is no fit place for a confession."

'"Never mind the place. What does the place matter? We are all about to die, and I am in mortal sin. Please, please, Monsignor." (She had noticed his socks by this time.) What worried Mr Visconti most was the attention she was provoking.

'"My child," he told her, "in this state of emergency a simple act of contrition is enough," but oh no, she wasn't going to be fobbed off with something cheap like that – "Bargain sale owing to closing down of premises." She came and knelt at his knees. "Your Grace," she exclaimed. She was used to giving officers a superior rank – it nearly always pleased a captain to be called a major.

'"I am not a bishop," Mr Visconti said. "I am only a humble monsignor." Mario questioned his father closely about this episode, and I have invented nothing. If anyone invented a detail it is Mario. You have to remember that he writes verse plays.

'"Father," the girl implored, taking the hint, "help me."

'"The secrecy of the confessional," Mr Visconti pleaded back – they were now, you see, pleading to each other, and she pawed Mr Visconti's knee, while he pawed the top of her head in an ecclesiastical way. Perhaps it was the pawings which made the German officer interrupt with impatience.

'"For God's sake," he said, "if she wants to confess Monsignor, let her. Here's the key of my room, just down the passage, past the lavatory."

'So off went Mr Visconti with the hysterical girl – he remembered just in time to put down his whisky. He had no choice, though he hadn't been to confession himself for thirty years and he had never learnt the priest's part. Luckily there was an air-conditioner in the room breathing heavily, and that obscured his whispers, and the girl was too much concerned with her role to pay much attention to his. She began right away; Mr Visconti had hardly time to sit on the bed, pushing aside a steel helmet and a bottle of schnapps, before she was getting down to details. He had wanted the whole thing finished as quickly as possible, but he told Mario that he couldn't help becoming a little interested now she had got started and wanting to know a bit more. After all he was a novice – though not in the ecclesiastical sense.

'"How many times, my child?" That was a phrase he remembered very well from his adolescence.

'"How can you ask that, Father? I've been at it all the time ever since the occupation. After all they were our allies, Father."

'"Yes, yes, my child." I can just see him enjoying the chance he had of learning a thing or two, even though his life was in danger. Mr Visconti was a very lecherous man. He said, "Always the same thing, my child?"

'She regarded him with astonishment. "Of course not, Father. Who on earth do you think I am?"

'He looked at her kneeling in front of him and I am sure he longed to pinch her. Mr Visconti was always a great pincher. "Anything unnatural, my child?"

'"What do you mean unnatural, Father?"

'Mr Visconti explained.

'"Surely that's not unnatural, Father?"

'Then they had quite a discussion about what was natural and what wasn't, with Mr Visconti almost forgetting his danger in the excitement, until someone knocked on the door and Mr Visconti, vaguely sketching a cross in a lop-sided way, muttered what sounded through the noise of the air-conditioner like an absolution. The German officer came in in the middle of it and said, "Hurry up, Monsignor. I've got a more important customer for you."

'It was the general's wife who had come down to the bar for a last dry Martini before escaping north and heard what was going on. She drained her Martini in one gulp and commanded the officer to arrange her confession. So there was Mr Visconti caught again. There was an awful row now in the Via Veneto as the tanks drove out of Rome. The general's wife had positively to shout at Mr Visconti. She had a rather masculine voice and Mr Visconti said it was like being on the parade ground. He nearly clicked his feet together in his purple socks when she bellowed at him, "Adultery. Three times."

'"Are you married, my daughter?"

'"Of course I'm married. What on earth do you suppose? I'm Frau General" – I've forgotten what ugly Teutonic name she had.

'"Does your husband know of this?"

'"Of course he doesn't know. He's not a priest."

'"Then you have been guilty of lies too?"

'"Yes, yes, naturally, I suppose so, you must hurry, Father. Our car's being loaded. We are leaving for Florence in a few minutes."

'"Haven't you anything else to tell me?"

'"Nothing of importance."

'"You haven't missed Mass?"

'"Oh, occasionally, Father. This is war-time."

'"Meat on Fridays?"

'"You forget. It is permitted now, Father. Those are Allied planes overhead. We have to leave immediately."

'"God cannot be hurried, my child. Have you indulged in impure thoughts?"

'"Father, put down yes to anything you like, but give me absolution. I have to be off."

'"I cannot feel that you've properly examined your conscience."

'"Unless you give me absolution at once, I shall have you arrested. For sabotage."

'Mr Visconti said, "It would be better if you gave me a seat in your car. We could finish your confession tonight."

'"There isn't room in the car, Father. The driver, my husband, myself, my dog – there simply isn't space for another passenger."

'"A dog takes up no room. It can sit on your knee."

'"This is an Irish wolfhound, Father."

'"Then you must leave it behind," Mr Visconti said firmly, and at that moment a car back-fired and the Frau General took it for an explosion.

'"I need Wolf for my protection, Father. War is very dangerous for women."

'"You will be under the protection of our Holy Mother Church," Mr Visconti said, "as well as your husband's."

'"I cannot leave Wolf behind. He is all I have in the world to love."

'"I would have assumed that with three adulteries – and a husband . . ."

'"They mean nothing to me."

'"Then I suggest," Mr Visconti said, "that we leave the general behind." And so it came about. The general was dressing down the hall porter because of a mislaid spectacle-case when the Frau General seated herself beside the driver and Mr Visconti sat beside Wolf at the back. "Drive off ", the general's wife said.

'The driver hesitated, but he was more afraid of the wife than the husband. The general came out into the street and shouted to them as they drove off – a tank had stopped to give precedence to the staff car. Nobody paid any attention to the general's shouts except Wolf. He clambered all over Mr Visconti, thrusting his evil-smelling parts against Mr Visconti's face, knocking off Mr Visconti's clerical hat, barking furiously to get out. The Frau General may have loved Wolf, but it was the general whom Wolf loved. Probably the general concerned himself with his food and his exercise. Blindly Mr Visconti fumbled for the handle of the window. Before the window was properly open Wolf jumped right in the path of the following tank. It flattened him. Mr Visconti looking back thought that he resembled one of those biscuits they make for children in the shape of animals.

'So Mr Visconti was rid of both dog and general and was able to ride in reasonable comfort to Florence. Mental comfort was another matter and the general's wife was hysterical with grief. I think Curran would have dealt with the situation a great deal better than Mr Visconti. At Brighton Curran would offer the last sacrament in the form of a ritual bone, which the poor beast of course could not possibly chew, to a dying dog. A lot of dogs were killed by cars on Brighton front, and the police were quite annoyed by owners who refused to have bodies shifted until Curran had been summoned to give the corpse absolution. But Mr Visconti, as I have told you, was not a religious man, and the consolations he offered, I can well imagine, were insufficient and unconvincing. Perhaps he spoke of punishment for the Frau General's sins (for Mr Visconti had a sadistic streak), and of the purgatory which we suffer on earth. Poor Mr Visconti, he must have had a hard time of it all the way to Florence.'

'What happened to the general?'

'He was captured by the Allies, I believe, but I'm not sure whether or not he was hanged at Nuremberg.'

'Mr Visconti must have a great deal on his conscience.'

'Mr Visconti hasn't got a conscience,' my aunt said with pleasure.

Chapter 15

For some reason an old restaurant-car with a kind of faded elegance was attached to the express after the Turkish frontier, when it was already too late to be of much use. My aunt rose that day early, and the two of us sat down to excellent coffee, toast and jam: Aunt Augusta insisted on our drinking in addition a light red wine though I am not accustomed to wine so early in the morning. Outside the window an ocean of long undulating grass stretched to a pale green horizon. There was the talkative cheerfulness of journey's end in the air, and the car filled with passengers whom we had never seen before: a Vietnamese in blue dungarees spoke to a rumpled girl in shorts, and two young Americans, the man with hair as long as the girl's, joined them, holding hands. They refused a second cup of coffee after carefully counting their money.

'Where's Tooley?' my aunt asked.

'She wasn't feeling well last night. I'm worried about her, Aunt Augusta. Her young man's hitch-hiking to Istanbul. He may not have arrived. He may even have gone on without her.'

'Where to?'

'She's not sure. Katmandu or Vientiane.'

'Istanbul is a rather unpredictable place,' Aunt Augusta said. 'I'm not even sure what I expect to find there myself.'

'What do you think you'll find?'

'I have a little business to do with an old friend, General Abdul. I was expecting a telegram at the St James and Albany, but none came. I can only hope that there's a message waiting for us at the Pera Palace.'

'Who is the General?'

'I knew him in the days of poor Mr Visconti,' my aunt said. 'He was very useful to us in the negotiations with Saudi Arabia. He was Turkish Ambassador then in Tunis. What parties we had in those days at the Excelsior. A little different from the Crown and Anchor and a drink with poor Wordsworth.'

The scenery changed as we approached Istanbul. The grassy sea was left behind and the express slowed down to the speed of a little local commuters' train. When I leant from the window I could see over a wall into the yard of a cottage; I was in talking distance of a red-skirted girl who looked up at us as we crawled by; a man mounted a bicycle and for a while kept pace with us. Birds on a red tiled roof looked down their long beaks and spoke together like village gossips.

I said, 'I'm awfully afraid that Tooley's going to have a baby.'

'She ought to take precautions, Henry, but in any case it's far too early for you to worry.'

'Good heavens, Aunt Augusta, I didn't mean that . . . how can you possibly think . . . ?'

'It's a natural conclusion,' my aunt said, 'you have been much together. And the girl has a certain puppy charm.'

'I'm too old for that sort of thing.'

'You are a young man in your fifties,' Aunt Augusta replied.

The door of the restaurant-car clanged, and there was Tooley, but a Tooley transformed. Perhaps it was only that she had put on less shadow, but her eyes seemed to be sparkling as I had never known them do before. 'Hi,' she called down the length of the car. The four young people turned and looked at her and called back 'Hi,' as though they had been long acquainted. 'Hi', she greeted them in return, and I felt a small ache of jealousy, irrational as the irritations of early morning.

'Good morning, good morning,' she said to the two of us; she seemed to be speaking a different language to the old. 'Oh, Mr Pulling, it's happened.'

'What's happened?'

'The curse. I've got the curse. I was right, you see. The jolting of the train, I mean – it did do it. I've got a terrible belly-ache, but I feel fabulous. I can't wait to tell Julian. Oh, I hope he's at the Gulhane, when I get there.'

'You going to the Gulhane?' the American boy called across.

'Yes, are you?'

'Sure. We can all go together.'

'That's fabulous.'

'Come and have a coffee if you've got the money.'

'You don't mind, do you?' Tooley said to my aunt. 'They're going to the Gulhane too.'

'Of course we don't mind, Tooley.'

'You've been so kind, Mr Pulling,' she said. 'I don't know what I'd have done without you. I mean it was a bit like the dark night of the soul.'

I realized then that I preferred her to call me Smudge.

'Go gently on the cigarettes, Tooley,' I advised her.

'Oh,' she said, 'I don't need to economize now. They'll be easy to get, I mean at the Gulhane. You can get anything at the Gulhane. Even acid. I'll be seeing you both again before we go, won't I?'

But she didn't. She had become one of the young now, and I could only wave to her back as she went ahead of us through the customs. The two Americans still walked hand in hand, and the Vietnamese boy carried Tooley's sack and had his arm round her shoulder to protect her from the crowd which was squeezing to get through the barrier into the customs hall. My responsibility was over, but she stayed on in my memory like a small persistent pain which worries even in its insignificance; doesn't a sickness as serious as cancer start in just such a way?

I wondered whether Julian was waiting for her. Would they go on to Katmandu? Would she always remember to take her pill? When I shaved again more closely at the Pera Palace I found I had missed in the obscurity of my coach a small dab of lipstick upon the cheek. Perhaps that was why my aunt had jumped to so wrong a conclusion. I wiped it off and found myself wondering at once where she was now. I scowled at my own face in the glass, but I was really scowling at her mother in Bonn and her father somewhere in the CIA, and Julian afraid of castration, and at all those who ought to have been looking after her and yet felt no responsibility at all.

Aunt Augusta and I had lunch in a restaurant called Abdullah's and then she took me around the tourist sights – the Blue Mosque and Santa Sophia – but I could tell all the time that she was worried. There had been no message waiting for her at the hotel.

'Can't you telephone to the General?' I asked her.

'Even at the Tunis Embassy,' she said, 'he never trusted his own line.'

We stood dutifully in the centre of Santa Sophia – the shape, which had been beautiful once perhaps, was obscured by ugly Arabic signs in pale khaki, so that it looked like the huge drab waiting-hall of a railway station out of peak traffic hours. A few people stood about looking for the times of trains, and there was a man who carried a suitcase.

'I'd forgotten how hideous it was,' my aunt said. 'Let's go home.'

Home was an odd word to use for the Pera Palace which had the appearance of an eastern pavilion built for a world fair. My aunt ordered two rakis in the bar which was all fretwork and mirrors – there was still no message from General Abdul, and for the first time I saw my aunt nonplussed.

'When did you last hear from him?' I asked.

'I told you I heard from him in London, the day after those policemen came. And I had a message from him in Milan through Mario. Everything was in order, he said. If there had been any change Mario would have known.'

'It's nearly dinner-time.'

'I don't want any food. I'm sorry, Henry. I feel a little upset. Perhaps it is the result of the train's vibration. I shall go to bed and wait for the telephone. I cannot believe that he will let me down. Mr Visconti had a great belief in General Abdul, and there were very few people whom he trusted.'

I had dinner by myself in the hotel in a vast restaurant which reminded me of Santa Sophia – not a very good dinner. I had drunk several rakis, to which I was unaccustomed, and perhaps the absence of my aunt made me a little light-headed. I was not ready for bed, and I wished I had Tooley with me as a companion. I went outside the hotel and found a taxi-driver there who spoke a little English. He told me he was Greek, but that he knew Istanbul as well as if it were his own city. 'Safe,' he kept on saying, 'safe with me,' waving his hand as though to indicate that there were wolves lurking by the walls and alleys. I told him to show me the city. He drove down narrow street after narrow street with no vista anywhere and very little light, and then drew up at a dark and forbidding door with a bearded night watchman asleep on the step. 'Safe house,' he said, 'safe, clean. Very safe,' and I was reminded uncomfortably of something I would have gladly forgotten, the house with the sofas behind the *Messaggero*.

'No, no,' I said, 'drive on. I didn't mean that.' I tried to explain. 'Take me,' I said, 'somewhere quiet. Somewhere you would go yourself. With your friends. For a drink. With your friends.'

We drove several miles along the sea of Marmara and came to a stop outside a plain uninteresting building marked 'West Berlin Hotel'. Nothing could have belonged less to the Istanbul of my imagination. It was three square storeys high and might well have been built among the ruins of Berlin by a local contractor at low cost. The driver led the way into a hall which occupied the whole ground space of the hotel. A young woman stood by a small piano and sang what I supposed were sentimental songs to an audience of middle-aged men in their shirt-sleeves sitting at big tables drinking beer. Most of them, like my own driver, had big grey moustaches, and they applauded heavily and dutifully when the song was over. Glasses of beer were placed in front of us, and the driver and I drank to each other. It was good beer, I noticed, and when I poured it on top of all the raki and the wine I had already drunk, my spirits rose. In the young girl I saw a resemblance to Tooley, and in the heavy men around me I imagined – 'Do you know General Abdul?' I asked the driver. He hushed me quickly. I looked around again and realized that there was not a single woman in the big hall except the young singer, and at this moment the piano stopped and with a glance at the clock, which marked midnight, the girl seized her handbag and went out through a door at the back. Then, after the glasses had been refilled, the pianist struck up a more virile tune, and all the middle-aged men rose and put their arms around each other's shoulders and began to dance, forming circles which they enlarged, broke and formed again.

They charged, they retreated, they stamped the ground in unison. No one spoke to his neighbour, there was no drunken jollity, I was like an outsider at some religious ceremony of which he couldn't interpret the symbols. Even my driver left me to put his arm round another man's shoulder, and I drank more beer to drown my sense of being excluded. I was drunk, I knew that, for drunken tears stood in my eyes, and I wanted to throw my beer glass on the floor and join the dancing. But I was excluded, as I had always been excluded. Tooley had joined her young friends and Miss Keene had departed to cousins in Koffiefontein, leaving her tatting on a chair under the Van de Velde. I would always be protected, as I had been when a cashier, by a hygienic plastic screen. Even the breath of the dancers didn't reach me as they circled my table. My aunt was probably talking about things which mattered to her with General Abdul. She had greeted her adopted son in Milan more freely than she had ever greeted me. She had said goodbye to Wordsworth in Paris with blown kisses and tears in her eyes. She had a world of her own to which I would never be admitted, and I would have done better, I told myself, if I had stayed with my dahlias and the ashes of my mother who was not – if my aunt were to be believed – my real one. So I sat in the West Berlin Hotel shedding beery tears of self-pity and envying the men who danced with their arms round strangers' shoulders. 'Take me away,' I said to the driver when he returned, 'finish your beer but take me away.'

'You are not pleased?' he asked as we drove uphill towards the Pera Palace.

'I'm tired, that's all. I want to go to bed.'

Two police cars blocked our way outside the Pera Palace. An elderly man who carried a walking stick crooked over his left arm was reaching with a stiff right leg towards the ground as we drew up. My driver told me in a tone of awe, 'That is Colonel Hakim.' The colonel wore a very English suit of grey flannel with chalk stripes, and he had a small grey moustache. He looked like any veteran member of the Army and Navy alighting at his club.

'Very important man,' my driver told me. 'Very fair to Greeks.'

I went past the colonel into the hotel. The receptionist was standing in the entrance presumably to welcome him; I was of so little importance that he wouldn't shift to let me by. I had to walk round him and he didn't answer my goodnight. A lift took me up to the fifth floor. When I saw a light under my aunt's door, I tapped and went in. She was sitting upright in bed wearing a bed-jacket and she was reading a paperback with a lurid cover.

'I've been seeing Istanbul,' I told her.

'So have I.' The curtains were drawn back and the lights of the city lay below us. She put her book down. The jacket showed a naked young woman lying in bed with a knife in her back, regarded by a man with a cruel face in a red fez. The title was Turkish Delight. 'I have been absorbing local atmosphere,' she said.

'Is the man in the fez the murderer?'

'No, he's the policeman. A very unpleasant type called Colonel Hakim.'

'How very odd because . . .'

'The murder takes place in this very Pera Palace, but there are a good many details wrong, as you might expect from a novelist. The girl is loved by a British secret agent, a tough sentimental man called Amis, and they have dinner together on her last night at Abdullah's – you remember we had lunch there ourselves. They have a love scene too in Santa Sophia, and there is an attempt on Amis's life at the Blue Mosque. We might almost have been doing a literary pilgrimage.'

'Hardly literary,' I said.

'Oh, you're your father's son. He tried to make me read Walter Scott, especially *Rob Roy*, but I much prefer this. It moves a great deal quicker and there are fewer descriptions.'

'Did Amis murder her?'

'Of course not, but he is suspected by Colonel Hakim who has very cruel methods of interrogation,' my aunt said with relish.

The telephone rang. I answered it.

'Perhaps it's General Abdul at last,' she said, 'though it seems a little late for him to ring.'

'This is the reception speaking. Is Miss Bertram there?'

'Yes, what is it?'

'I am sorry to disturb her, but Colonel Hakim wishes to see her.'

'At this hour? Quite impossible. Why?'

'He is on the way up now.' He rang off.

'Colonel Hakim is on the way to see you,' I said.

'Colonel Hakim?'

'The real Colonel Hakim. He's a police officer too.'

'A police officer?' Aunt Augusta said. 'Again? I begin to think I am back in the old days. With Mr Visconti. Henry, will you open my suitcase? The green one. You'll find a light coat there. Fawn with a fur collar.'

'Yes, Aunt Augusta, I have it here.'

'Under the coat in a cardboard box you will find a candle – a decorated candle.'

'Yes, I see the box.'

'Take out the candle, but be careful because it's rather heavy. Put it on my bedside table and light it. Candlelight is better for my complexion.'

It was extraordinarily heavy, and I nearly dropped it. It probably had some kind of lead weight at the bottom, I thought, to hold it steady. A big brick of scarlet wax which stood a foot high, it was decorated on all four sides with scrolls and coats of arms. A great deal of artistry had gone into moulding the wax which would melt away only too quickly. I lit the wick. 'Now turn out the light,' my aunt said, adjusting her bed-jacket and puffing up her pillow. There was a knock on the door and Colonel Hakim came in.

He stood in the doorway and bowed. 'Miss Bertram?' he asked.

'Yes. You are Colonel Hakim?'

'Yes. I am sorry to call on you so late without warning.' He spoke English with only the faintest intonation. 'I think we have a mutual acquaintance, General Abdul. May I sit down?'

'Of course. You'll find that chair by the dressing-table the most comfortable. This is my nephew, Henry Pulling.'

'Good evening, Mr Pulling. I hope you enjoyed the dancing at the West Berlin Hotel. A convivial spot unknown to most tourists. May I turn on the light, Miss Bertram?'

'I would rather not. I have weak eyes, and I always prefer to read by candlelight.'

'A very beautiful candle.'

'They make them in Venice. The coats of arms belong to their four greatest doges. Don't ask me their names. How is General Abdul? I had been hoping to meet him again.'

'I am afraid General Abdul is a very sick man.' Colonel Hakim hooked his walking stick over the mirror before he sat down. He leant his head forward to my aunt at a slight angle, which gave him an air of deference, but I noticed that the real reason was a small hearing-aid that he carried in his right ear. 'He was a great friend of you and Mr Visconti, was he not?'

'The amount you know,' my aunt said with an endearing smile.

'Oh, it's my disagreeable business,' the colonel said, 'to be a Nosey Harker.'

'Parker.'

'My English is rusty.'

'You had me followed to the West Berlin Hotel?' I asked.

'Oh no, I suggested to the driver that he should take you there,' Colonel Hakim said. 'I thought it might interest you and hold your attention longer than it did. The fashionable night clubs here are very banal and international. You might just as well be in Paris or London except that in those cities you would see a better show. Of course I told the driver to take you somewhere else first. One never knows.'

'Tell me about General Abdul,' my aunt said impatiently. 'What is wrong with him?'

Colonel Hakim leant forward a little more in his chair and lowered his voice as though he were confiding a secret. 'He was shot,' he said, 'while trying to escape.'

'Escape?' my aunt exclaimed. 'Escape from whom?'

'From me,' Colonel Hakim said with shy modesty and he fiddled at his hearing-aid. A long silence followed his words. There seemed nothing to say. Even my aunt was at a loss. She sat back against the cushions with her mouth a little open. Colonel Hakim took a tin out of his pocket and opened it. 'Excuse me,' he said, 'eucalyptus and menthol. I suffer from asthma.' He put a lozenge into his mouth and sucked. There was silence again until my aunt spoke.

'Those lozenges can't do you much good,' she said.

'I think it is only the suggestion. Asthma is a nervous disease. The lozenges *seem* to alleviate it, but only perhaps because I believe they alleviate it.' He panted a little when he spoke. 'I am always apt to get an attack when I am at the climax of a case.'

'Mr Visconti suffered from asthma too,' Aunt Augusta said. 'He was cured by hypnotism.'

'I would not like to put myself so completely in someone else's hands.'

'Of course Mr Visconti had a hold on the hypnotist.'

'Yes, that makes a difference,' Colonel Hakim said with approval. 'And where is Mr Visconti now?'

'I've no idea.'

'Nor had General Abdul. We only want the information for the Interpol files. The affair is more than thirty years old. I just ask you in passing. I have no personal interest. It is not the real subject of my interrogation.'

'Am I being interrogated, colonel?'

'Yes. In a way. I hope an agreeable way. We have found a letter from you to General Abdul which speaks about an investment he had recommended. You wrote to him that you found it essential to make the investment while in Europe and anonymously, and this presented certain difficulties.'

'Surely you are not working for the Bank of England, colonel?'

'I am not so fortunate, but General Abdul was planning a little trouble here; he was very short of funds. Certain friends with whom he had speculated in the old days came back to his mind. So he got in touch with you (perhaps he hoped through you to contact Visconti again), with a German called Weissmann of whom you probably haven't heard, and with a man called Harvey Crowder, who is a meat packer in Chicago. The CIA have had him under observation for a long while and they reported to us. Of course I mention these names only because all the men are under arrest and have talked.'

'If you really have to know,' my aunt said, 'for the sake of your files, General Abdul recommended me to buy Deutsche Texaco Convertible Bonds – out of the question in England because of the dollar premium, and away from England, for an English resident, quite illegal. So I had to remain anonymous.'

'Yes,' Colonel Hakim said, 'that is not bad at all as a cover story.' He began to pant again and took another lozenge. 'I only mentioned those names to show you that General Abdul is now a little senile. One doesn't finance an operation in Turkey with foreign money of that kind. A wise woman like yourself must have realized that if his operation had any chance of success, he could have found local support. He would not have had to offer a Chicago meat packer twenty-five per cent interest and a share of the profits.'

'Mr Visconti would certainly have seen through that,' my aunt said.

'But now you are a lady living alone. You haven't the benefit of

Visconti's advice. You might be tempted a little by the quick profits . . .'

'Why? I have no children to leave them to, colonel.'

'Or perhaps by the sense of adventure.'

'At my age?' My aunt beamed with pleasure.

There was a knock on the door and a policeman entered. He spoke to the colonel and the colonel translated for our benefit. 'Nothing,' he said, 'has been found in Mr Pulling's baggage, but if you wouldn't mind . . . My man is very careful, he will wear clean gloves, and I assure you he will leave not the smallest wrinkle . . . Would you mind if I put on the electric light while he works?'

'I would mind a great deal,' my aunt said. 'I left my dark glasses on the train. Unless you wish to give me a splitting headache . . .'

'Of course not, Miss Bertram. He will do without. You will forgive us if the search takes a little longer.'

The policeman first went through my aunt's handbag and handed certain papers to Colonel Hakim. 'Forty pounds in travellers' cheques,' he noted.

'I have cashed ten,' my aunt said.

'I see from your air ticket you plan to leave tomorrow – I mean today. A very short visit. Why did you come by train, Miss Bertram?'

'I wanted to see my stepson in Milan.'

The colonel gave her a quizzical look. 'May one ask? According to your passport you are unmarried.'

'Mr Visconti's son.'

'Ah, always that Mr Visconti.'

The policeman was busy now with my aunt's suitcase. He looked in the cardboard box which had contained the candle, shook it and smelt it.

'That is the box for my candle,' my aunt said. 'As I told you, I think, they make these candles in Venice. One candle does for a whole journey – I believe it is guaranteed for twenty-four hours continuously. Perhaps forty-eight.'

'You are burning a real work of art,' the colonel said.

'Henry, hold the candle for the policeman to see better.'

Again I was astonished by the weight of the candle when I lifted it.

'Don't bother, Mr Pulling, he has finished.'

I was glad to put it down again.

'Well,' Colonel Hakim said with a smile, 'we have found nothing compromising in your luggage.' The policeman was repacking the case. 'Now just as a formality we must go through the room. And the bed, Miss Bertram, if you will consent to sit in a chair.'

He took part in this search himself, limping from one piece of furniture to another, sometimes feeling with his stick, under the bed and at the back of a drawer. 'And now Mr Pulling's pockets,' he said. I emptied them rather angrily on the dressing-table. He looked carefully through my notebook and drew out a cutting from the *Daily Telegraph*. He read it aloud with a puzzled frown: '"Those that took my fancy were the ruby-red Maître Roger, light red, white-tipped Cheerio, deep crimson Arabian Night and Black Flash, and scarlet Bacchus . . ."'

'Please explain, Mr Pulling.'

'It is self-explanatory,' I said stiffly.

'Then you must forgive my ignorance.'

'The report of a dahlia show. In Chelsea. I am very interested in dahlias.'

'Flowers?'

'Of course they are flowers.'

'The names sounded so oddly like those of horses. I was puzzled by the deep crimson.' He put the cutting down and limped to my aunt's side. 'I will say goodnight now, Miss Bertram. You have made my duty tonight a most agreeable one. You cannot think how bored I get with exhibitions of injured innocence. I will send a police car to take you to your plane tomorrow.'

'Please don't bother. We can take a taxi.'

'We should be sorry to see you miss your plane.'

'I think perhaps I ought to stop over one more day and see poor General Abdul.'

'I am afraid he is not allowed visitors. What is this book you are reading? What a very ugly fellow with a red fez. Has he stabbed the girl?'

'No. He is the policeman. He is called Colonel Hakim,' my aunt said with a look of satisfaction.

After the door had closed I turned with some anger on my aunt. 'Aunt Augusta,' I said, 'what did all that mean?'

'Some little political trouble, I would imagine. Politics in Turkey are taken more seriously than they are at home. It was only quite recently that they executed a Prime Minister. We dream of it, but they act. I hadn't realized, I admit, what General Abdul was up to. Foolish of him at his age. He must be eighty if a day, but I believe in Turkey there are more centenarians than in any other European country. Yet I doubt whether poor Abdul is likely to make his century.'

'Do you realize that they're deporting us? I think we should call the British Embassy.'

'You exaggerate, dear. They are just lending us a police car.'

'And if we refuse to take it?'

'I have no intention of refusing. We were already booked on the plane. After making my investment here I had no intention of lingering around. I didn't expect quick profits, and twenty-five per cent always involves a risk.'

'What investment, Aunt Augusta? Forty pounds in travellers' cheques?'

'Oh no, dear. I bought quite a large gold ingot in Paris. You remember the man from the bank . . .'

'So that was what they were looking for. Where on earth had you hidden it, Aunt Augusta?'

I looked at the candle, and I remembered its weight.

'Yes, dear,' my aunt said, 'how clever of you to guess. Colonel Hakim didn't. You can blow it out now.' I lifted it up again – it must have weighed nearly twenty pounds.

'What do you propose to do with this now?'

'I shall have to take it back to England with me. It may be of use another time. It was most fortunate, when you come to think of it, that they shot poor General Abdul before I gave him the candle and not after. I wonder if he is really still alive. They would be likely to glide over any grisly detail like that with a woman. I shall have a Mass said for him in any case because a man of that age is unlikely to survive a bullet long. The shock alone, even if it were not in a vital part . . .'

I interrupted her speculations. 'You're not going to take that ingot back into England?' Ingot – England. I was irritated by the absurd jangle which sounded like a comic song. 'Have you no respect at all for the law?'

'It depends, dear, to which law you refer. Like the ten commandments. I can't take very seriously the one about the ox and the ass.'

'The English customs are not so easily fooled as the Turkish police.'

'A used candle is remarkably convincing. I've tried it before.'

'Not if they lift it up.'

'But they won't, dear. Perhaps if the wick and the wax were intact they might think they could charge me purchase tax. Or some suspicious officer might think it a phoney candle containing drugs. But a *used* candle. Oh no, I think the danger is very small. And there's always my age to protect me.'

'I refuse to go back into England with that ingot.' The jangle irritated me again.

'But you have no choice, dear. The colonel will certainly see us on to the plane and there is no stop before London. The great advantage of being deported is that we shall not have to pass the Turkish customs again.'

'Why on earth did you do it, Aunt Augusta? Such a risk . . .'

'Mr Visconti is in need of money.'

'He stole yours.'

'That was a long time ago. It will all be finished by now.'

Chapter 16

IT seemed at first another and a happier world which I had re-entered: I was back home, in the late afternoon, as the long shadows were falling; a boy whistled a Beatle tune and a motor-bicycle revved far away up Norman Lane. With what relief I dialled Chicken and ordered myself cream of spinach soup, lamb cutlets and Cheddar cheese: a better meal than I had eaten in Istanbul. Then I went into the garden. Major Charge had neglected the dahlias; it was a pleasure to give them water, which the dry soil drank like a thirsty man, and I could almost imagine that the flowers were responding with a lift of the petals. The Deuil du Roy Albert was too far gone to benefit, but the colour of the Ben Hurs took on a new sheen, as though the long dry chariot race were now a memory only. Major Charge looked over the fence and asked, 'Good journey?'

'Interesting, thank you,' I said drily, pouring the water in a thick stream on to the roots. I had removed the absurd nozzle which serves no useful purpose.

'I was very careful,' Major Charge said, 'not to give them too much water.'

'The ground certainly seems very dry.'

'I keep goldfish,' Major Charge said. 'If I go away, my damned daily always gives them too much food. When I return I find half the little buggers dead.'

'Flowers are not the same as goldfish, Major. In a dry autumn like this they can do with a great deal of water.'

'I hate excess,' Major Charge said. 'It's the same in politics. I've no use for Communist or Fascist.'

'You are a Liberal?'

'Good God, man,' he said, 'what makes you think that?' and disappeared from sight.

The afternoon post arrived punctually at five: a circular from Littlewood's, although I never gamble, a bill from the garage, a pamphlet from the British Empire Loyalists which I threw at once into the waste-paper basket, and a letter with a South African stamp. The envelope was typewritten, so that I did not at once conclude that it had been sent by Miss Keene. I was distracted too by a package of Omo propped against the scraper. I had certainly not ordered any detergent. I looked closer and saw that it was a gift package. What a lot of money manufacturers waste by not employing the local stores to do their distribution. There they would have known that I am already a regular purchaser of Omo. I took the packet into the kitchen and noticed with pleasure that mine was almost exhausted, so I had been saved from buying another.

It was getting chilly by this time, and I turned on the electric fire before opening the letter. I saw at once that it came from Miss Keene. She had bought herself a typewriter, but it was obvious that as yet she had not had much practice. Lines were unevenly placed, and her fingers had often gone astray to the wrong keys or missed a letter altogether. She had driven in, she wrote, to Koffiefontein – three hours by road – to a matinée of *Gone with the Qind* which had been revived at a cinema there. She wrote that Clark Fable was not as good as she remembered him. How typical it was of her gentleness, and perhaps even of her sense of defeat, that she had not troubled to correct her errors. Perhaps it would have seemed to her like disguising a fault. 'Once a week,' she wrote, 'my cousin drives into the bak. She's on very good terms with the manager, but he is not a real friend as you always were to my father and me. I miss very much St John's Church and the vicar's sermons. The only church near here is Dutch Deformed, and I don't like it at all.' She had corrected Deformed. She may have thought that otherwise I might take it for an unkindness.

I wondered how I was to reply. I knew that the letter she would like best would contain news of Southwood: the small details of every day, even to the condition of my dahlias. How was I to deal with my bizarre journey to Istanbul? To mention it only in passing would seem both unnatural and pretentious, but to describe the affair of Colonel Hakim and the gold brick and General Abdul would cause her to feel that my mode of life had entirely changed, and this might increase her sense of separation and of loneliness near Koffiefontein. I asked myself whether it would not be better to refrain from writing at all, but then on the last page – her paper had slipped in the machine and the print ran diagonally up into the previous line – she had typed, 'I look forward so to your letters because they bring Southwood close to me.' I put her letter away with others of hers that I kept in a drawer of my desk.

It was quite dark now, and yet more than an hour would have to pass before Chicken arrived, so I went to choose a book from my shelves. Like my father I rarely buy new books though I don't confine my reading, as he did, to almost a single author. Modern literature has never appealed to me; to my mind it was in the Victorian age that English poetry and fiction reached the highest level. If I had been able to write myself – and in my boyhood before my mother found me the position at the bank I sometimes had that dream – I would have modelled myself on one of the minor Victorians (for the giants are inimitable): perhaps R. L. Stevenson or even Charles Reade. I have quite a collection too of Wilkie Collins, though I prefer him when he is not writing a detective story, for I don't share my aunt's taste in that direction. If I could have been a poet I would have been happy in a quite humble station, to be recognized, if at all, as an English Mahony and to have celebrated Southwood as he celebrated Shandon (it is one of my favourite poems in Palgrave's *Golden Treasury*). Perhaps it was Miss Keene's mention of St John's Church, the bells of which I can hear on a Sunday morning while I am working in the garden, that made me think of him and take down the volume.

There's a bell in Moscow,
While on tower and kiosk O
In Santa Sophia
  The Turkman gets;
And loud in air
Calls men to prayer
From the tapering summit
  Of tall minarets.
Such empty phantom
I freely grant them;
But there is an anthem
  More dear to me, –
'Tis the bells of Shandon,
That sound so grand on
The pleasant waters
  Of the River Lee.

The lines on Santa Sophia had never before rung so true: that dingy mausoleum could not compare with our St John's and the mention of it would remind me always of Colonel Hakim.

One book leads to another, and I found myself, for the first time in many years, taking down a volume of Walter Scott. I remembered how my father had used the volumes for playing the *Sortes Virgilianae* – a game my mother considered a little blasphemous unless it was played with the Bible, in all seriousness. I sometimes suspected my father had dog-eared various pages so that he could hit on a suitable quotation to tease and astound my mother. Once, when he was suffering severely from constipation, he opened *Rob Roy* apparently at random and read out, 'Mr Owen entered. So regular were the motions and habits of this worthy man . . .' I tried the *Sortes* myself now and was astonished at the apposite nature of the quotation which I picked: 'I had need of all the spirits a good dinner could give, to resist the dejection which crept insensibly on my mind.'

It was only too true that I was depressed: whether it was due to Miss Keene's letter or to the fact that I missed my aunt's company more than I had anticipated, or even that Tooley had left a blank behind her, I could not tell. Now that I had no responsibility to anyone but myself, the pleasure of finding again my house and garden had begun to fade. Hoping to discover a more encouraging quotation, I opened *Rob Roy* again and found a snapshot lying between the leaves: the square yellowing snapshot of a pretty girl in an old-fashioned bathing-dress taken with an old-fashioned Brownie. The girl was bending a little towards the camera; she had just slipped one shoulder out of its strap, and she was laughing, as though she had been surprised at the moment of changing. It was some moments before I recognized Aunt Augusta and my first thought was how attractive she had been in those days. Was it a photograph taken by her sister, I wondered? But it was hardly the kind of photograph my mother would have given my father. I had to admit that it was more likely he had taken it himself and hidden it there in a volume of Scott which my mother would never read. This then was how she had looked – she could have hardly been more than eighteen – in the long ago days before she knew Curran or Monsieur Dambreuse or Mr Visconti. She had an air of being ready for anything. A phrase about Die Vernon printed on one of the two pages between which the photograph lay caught my eye: 'Be patient and quiet, and let me take my own way; for when I take the bit between my teeth, there is no bridle will stop me.' Had my father deliberately chosen that page with that particular passage for concealing the picture? I felt the melancholy I sometimes used to experience at the bank when it was my duty to turn over old documents deposited there, the title-deeds of a passion long spent. I thought of my father with an added tenderness – of that lazy man lying in his overcoat in the empty bath. I have never seen his grave, for he had died on the only trip which he had ever taken out of England, and I was not even sure of where it lay.

I rang up my aunt, 'Just to say goodnight and make sure that all is well.'

'The apartment,' she told me, 'seems a little solitary without Wordsworth.'

'I am feeling lonely too – without you and Tooley.'

'No news when you came home?'

'Only a letter from a friend. She seems lonely too.'

I hesitated before I spoke again. 'Aunt Augusta, I have been thinking, I don't know why, of my father. It's strange how little one knows of one's own family. Do you realize I don't even know where he is buried?'

'No?'

'Do you?'

'Of course.'

'I would have liked, if only once, to visit his grave.'

'Cemeteries to me are rather a morbid taste. They have a sour smell like jungles. I suppose it comes from all that wet greenery.'

'As one grows old I think one becomes more attached to family things – to houses and graves. I feel very badly that my mother had to finish like that in a police laboratory.'

'Your stepmother,' my aunt corrected me.

'Where *is* my father?'

'As a half-believing Catholic,' Aunt Augusta said, 'I cannot answer that question with any certainty, but his body, what is left of it, lies in Boulogne.'

'So near? Why wasn't it brought back?'

'My sister had a very practical and unsentimental side. Your father had gone to Boulogne without her knowledge on a day excursion. He was taken ill after dinner and died almost immediately. Food poisoning. It was before the days of antibiotics. There had to be an autopsy and my sister didn't like the idea of transporting home a mutilated corpse. So she had him buried in the cemetery there.'

'Were you present?'

'I was on tour in Italy. I only heard about it much later. My sister and I didn't correspond.'

'So you've never seen the grave either?'

'I once suggested to Mr Visconti that we make a trip, but his favourite Biblical quotation was, "Let the dead bury their dead."'

'Perhaps one day we might go together.'

'I am strongly of Mr Visconti's opinion, but I am always ready for a little travel,' my aunt added with unsentimental glee.

'This time you must be my guest.'

'The anniversary of his death,' my aunt said, 'falls on 2 October. I remember the date because it is the feast day of the Guardian Angel. The Angel seems to have slipped up badly on that occasion, unless of course he was saving your father from a worse fate. That is quite a possibility, for what on earth was your father doing in Boulogne out of season?'

Chapter 17

STRANGELY enough I felt almost immediately at home in Boulogne.

As the direct boat from Folkestone no longer sailed, we took the Golden Arrow from Victoria and I was relieved to notice that my aunt had not brought with her the red suitcase. The English side of the channel lay bathed in a golden autumn sunlight. By the time we reached Petts Wood the buses had all turned green, and at Orpington the oast-houses began to appear with their white cowls like plumes in a medieval helmet. The hops climbing their poles were more decorative than vines, and I would gladly have given all the landscape between Milan and Venice for these twenty miles of Kent. There were comfortable skies and unspectacular streams; there were ponds with rushes and cows which seemed contentedly asleep. This was the pleasant land of which Blake wrote, and I found myself regretting that we were going abroad again. Why had my father not died in Dover or Folkestone, both equally convenient for a day's excursion?

And yet when at last we came to Boulogne, stepping out of the one coach from Calais reserved for that port on the Flèche d'Or, I felt that I was at home. The skies had turned grey and the air was cold and there were flurries of rain along the quays, but there was a photograph of the Queen over the reception desk in our hotel, and on the windows of a *brasserie* I could read 'Good Cup Of Tea. East Kent Coach Parties Welcome Here.' The leaden gulls which hovered over the fishing boats in the leaden evening had an East Anglian air. A scarlet sign flashed over the Gare Maritime saying 'Car Ferry' and 'British Railways'.

It was too late that evening to search for my father's grave (in any case the next day was his true anniversary), and so my aunt and I walked up together to the Ville Haute and strolled around the ramparts and through the small twisted streets which reminded me of Rye. In the great crypt of the cathedral an English king had been married, there were cannon balls lying there shot by the artillery of Henry VIII, and in a little square below the walls was a statue of Edward Jenner in a brown tailed-coat and brown tasselled boots. An old film of *Treasure Island* with Robert Newton was showing at a small cinema in a side-street not far from a club called Le Lucky where you could listen to the music of the Hearthmen. No, my father had not been buried on foreign soil. Boulogne was like a colonial town which had only recently ceased to be part of the Empire, and British Railways lingered on at the end of the quay as though it had been granted permission to stay until the evacuation was complete. Locked bathing-huts below the casino were like the last relics of the occupying troops, and the mounted statue of General San Martín on the quay might have been that of Wellington.

We had dinner in the restaurant of the Gare Maritime, after walking over the cobble-stones and across the railway lines with no one about. The pillars of the station resembled the pillars in a cathedral deserted after dark: only a train from Lyon was announced like a hymn number which no one had bothered to take down. No porter or passenger stirred on the long platforms. The British Railways office stood empty and unlighted. There was a smell everywhere of oil and weed and sea and a memory of the morning's fish. In the restaurant we proved to be the sole diners: only two men and a dog stood at the bar and they were preparing to go. My aunt ordered soles *à la Boulonnaise* for both of us.

'Perhaps my father came here the night before he died,' I considered aloud. Ever since I had picked *Rob Roy* from the shelf I had thought frequently of my father, and remembering the photograph and the expression of the young girl, I believed that my aunt must have loved him too in her way. But if I were looking for sentimental memories I had come to the wrong character – a man dead was a man dead, so far as my aunt was concerned.

'Order the wine, Henry,' she said. 'You know you have a morbid streak. This whole expedition is a sign of it – and the urn which you so carefully preserve. If your father had been buried at Highgate I would never have come with you. I don't believe in pilgrimages to graves unless they serve another purpose.'

'What other purpose does this serve?' I asked rather snappily.

'I have never before been to Boulogne,' Aunt Augusta said. 'I am always ready to visit a new place.'

'Like Uncle Jo,' I said, 'you want to prolong life.'

'Certainly I do,' my aunt replied, 'because I enjoy it.'

'And how many rooms have you occupied so far?'

'A great many,' my aunt said cheerfully, 'but I don't think I have yet reached the lavatory floor.'

'I got to go home.' One of the men at the bar spoke in piercing English. He was a little tight and when he stooped to pat his dog he missed it completely.

'One more for the ferry,' his companion said. From the phrase I took it that he belonged to British Railways.

'The bloody Maid of Kent. My wife was a maid of Kent once.'

'But no longer, billyo, no longer.'

'No longer. Tha's why I have to be home at twenty-one fucking hours.'

'She's jealous, billyo.'

'She's hungry.'

'I've never loved a weak man,' my aunt said. 'Your father wasn't weak – he was lazy. Nothing in his opinion was really worth a fight. He wouldn't have fought for Cleopatra herself – but he would have found a way round. Unlike Antony. It astonishes me that he ever came as far as Boulogne.'

'Perhaps it was on business.'

'He would have sent his partner. Now his partner – his name was William Curlew – was a weak man if ever there was one. He envied your father his little adventures – he found it hard enough to satisfy one woman. It weighed on his mind terribly, for his wife was really without fault. She was sweet, efficient, good-tempered – the fact that she was a little demanding might have been taken by another man as a virtue. Your father, who was a much more imaginative man than people usually thought or your mother realized, suggested a plan to him, for, as William had pointed out, one can't leave a perfect woman – one has to be left. He was to write his wife anonymous letters accusing himself of infidelity. The letters would serve a fourfold purpose. They would protect his vanity, offer a reasonable explanation of his flagging attentions, crack his wife's perfection, and might even lead eventually to divorce with his honour as a man saved (for he was determined to deny nothing). Your father composed the first letter himself; William typed it badly on his own typewriter, and put it in the kind of yellow envelope he used for bills (that was a mistake). The letter read. "Your husband, madam, is a shameful liar and an ignoble lecher. Ask him how he spends his evenings when you are at the Women's Institute, and how he gets through all the money he spends. What you save on the housekeeping enriches another woman's placket." Your father liked obsolete words – that was the influence of Walter Scott.

'There was to be a party at the Curlews' the evening the letter arrived. Mrs Curlew was very busy plumping cushions; she took the yellow envelope for a bill, and so she put it down on a table without looking at it. You can imagine poor William's anxiety. I knew him well in those days, indeed your parents and I were both present at the party. Your father hoped to be in at the death, but when the time came to go, and your father couldn't linger any longer, even on the excuse of talking a little business, the letter still remained unopened. He had to learn the details of what happened later from William.

'Melany – that was her silly name and it sounded even sillier when attached to Curlew – was tidying up the glasses when William found the yellow envelope under an occasional table. "Is this yours, dear?" he asked and she said it was only a bill.

'"Even a bill has to be opened," William said and handed her the envelope. Then he went upstairs to shave. She never insisted on his shaving before dinner, but very early in their marriage she had indicated unmistakably that she preferred him at night with a smooth cheek – her skin was very delicate. (Foreigners always said that her complexion was typically English.) The bathroom door was open and William saw her put the yellow envelope down on the dressing-table still sealed. He nicked himself in three places under the strain of waiting and had to stick on little dabs of cotton wool to stop the bleeding.'

The man trailed past our table with the dog. 'Come on, you bugger,' he said, hauling dispiritedly on the lead.

'Back to the maid of Kent,' his friend teased him from the bar.

I had begun to recognize the gleam in my aunt's eyes. She had had it in Brighton, when she recounted the history of the dog's church, and in Paris, when she told me of the affair with Monsieur Dambreuse, and in the Orient Express when she described Mr Visconti's escape . . . She was deeply absorbed in her story. I am sure my father – the admirer of Walter Scott – would not have told the story of the Curlews nearly so dramatically; there would have been less dialogue and more description.

'William,' my aunt went on, 'came in from the bathroom and climbed into the enormous double bed which Melany had chosen herself at Maples. In his anxiety William had not taken a book with him. He wanted the crisis to arrive. "I won't be long, dear," Melany said, busy with Pond's cold cream which she preferred to any newer brand for the sake of her old-world complexion.

'"Was it a bad bill?" William asked.

'"Bill?"

'"The one you dropped."

'"Oh that. I haven't opened it yet."

'"You'll lose it again if you're not careful."

'"That would be a good thing to do, wouldn't it, with a bill?" Melany said good-humouredly, but the words belied her nature – she never kept a tradesman waiting and never allowed one to extend her credit beyond a month. Now she wiped her fingers on the Kleenex and opened the yellow envelope. The first words she read, unevenly typed, were "Your husband, madam . . ."

'"No," she said, "not bad. Just tiresome." And she read the letter carefully to the end – it was signed "A neighbour and well-wisher". Then she tore it in little pieces and dropped them in her waste-paper basket.

'"You shouldn't destroy a bill," William said.

'"A few shillings at the newspaper shop. I paid it this morning." She looked at William and said, "What a good husband you've always been, William." She came to the bed and kissed him and William could detect her intention. "How tired a party makes me," he said, excusing himself weakly, with a faint yawn.

'"Of course, dear," Melany said, lying down beside him without any complaint. "Happy dreams," and then she noticed all those dabs of cotton wool. "Oh you poor dear," she said, "you've cut yourself. Let your Melany make them clean," and then and there she busied herself, for ten minutes at least, washing the wounds in chemists' alcohol and fixing bits of Elastoplast, as though nothing important had happened. "How funny you look now," she said, quite gay and carefree, and William told your father there was no longer any hint of danger in the kiss she planted on the end of his nose. "Dear funny William. I could forgive you anything." It was then William gave up all hope – she was a perfect wife, uncrackably perfect, and your father used to say that the word "forgive" tolled on in William's ears like the bell at Newgate signalling an execution.'

'So he never escaped?' I asked.

'He died many years later in Melany's arms,' Aunt Augusta said, and we finished our apple tart in silence.

Chapter 18

NEXT morning, which was just as grey as the last had been, Aunt Augusta and I climbed the long hill towards the cemetery. A shop advertised '*Deuil en 24 heures*', and a wild boar, hung outside a butcher's shop, dripped blood, and a notice pinned on the muzzle read, '*Retenez vos morceaux pour jeudi*,' but Thursday meant nothing to me, and not very much to Aunt Augusta. 'The feast of the Little Flower,' she said, looking the date up in her missal which she had brought with her because it was a suitable occasion, 'but a boar seems hardly suitable. Also apparently the feast of St Thomas of Hereford who died in exile in Orvieto, but I doubt if even the English have heard of him.'

Outside the gates of the Ville Haute there was a plaque commemorating the death of a 'Hero of the Resistance'. 'The dead of an army,' my aunt said, 'become automatically heroes like the dead of the Church become Martyrs. I wonder about this man St Thomas. I would have thought he was very lucky to die in Orvieto rather than in Hereford. A small civilized place even today with a far, far better climate and an excellent restaurant in the Via Garibaldi.'

'Are you really a Roman Catholic?' I asked my aunt with interest. She replied promptly and seriously, 'Yes, my dear, only I just don't believe in all the things they believe in.'

To find my father's grave in the enormous grey cemetery would have been like finding an individual house without a street number in Camden Town. The noise of trains came up from below the hill and the smoke of coal fires from the high town blew across the maze of graves. A man from a little square house, which was like a tomb itself, offered to conduct us. I had brought a wreath of flowers, though my aunt thought my gesture a little exaggerated. 'They will be very conspicuous,' she said. 'The French believe in remembering the dead once a year on the Feast of All Souls. It is tidy and convenient like Communion at Easter,' and it is true that I saw few flowers, even *immortelles*, among the angels, the cherubs, the bust of a bold man like a lycée professor, and the huge tomb, which apparently contained La Famille Flageollet. An English inscription on one monument caught my eye: 'In loving memory of my devoted son Edward Rhodes Robinson who died in Bombay where he is buried', but there was nothing English about his pyramid. Surely my father would have preferred an English graveyard of lichened stones with worn-out inscriptions and tags of pious verse to these shiny black made-to-last slabs which no Boulogne weather could ever erode, all with the same headlines, like copies of the same newspaper: 'À la mémoire', 'Ici repose le corps . . .' Except for a small elderly woman in black who stood with bowed head at the end of a long aisle like the solitary visitor in a provincial museum there seemed no one but ourselves in the whole heartless place.

'*Je me suis trompé*,' our conductor said, turning sharply on his heel, and he led us back towards the grave where the old woman stood, apparently in prayer.

'How odd! There seems to be another mourner,' Aunt Augusta said, and sure enough, on the slab of marble lay a wreath twice as large as mine made of flowers twice as expensive from the hot-houses of the south. I laid my own beside it. The headlines were hidden: there was only part of my father's name sticking out like an exclamation: '. . . chard Pulling', and a date, 2 October 1923.

The little woman looked at us with astonishment. '*Qui êtes-vous?*' she asked us.

Her accent was not quite French and my aunt replied as bluntly in English, 'Who are you?'

'Miss Paterson,' the little woman replied with a hint of frightened defiance.

'And what has this grave to do with you?' my aunt demanded.

'I have come here on this day for more than forty years, and I have never seen either of you here before.'

'Have you any rights over this grave?' my aunt asked.

Something in the woman's manner had riled her – perhaps it was her air of timid belligerence, for my aunt had little patience with weakness even when it was concealed.

The woman was cornered and showed fight. 'I've never heard there are rights in a grave,' she said.

'A grave – like a house – has been paid for by someone.'

'And if a house is left abandoned for forty years, hasn't even a stranger the right . . . ?'

'Who are you?' my aunt repeated.

'I told you. I am Miss Paterson.'

'Did you know my brother-in-law?'

'Your brother-in-law!' the old lady exclaimed. She looked at my wreath, she looked at me, she looked at my aunt.

'And this, my good woman, is Richard Pulling's son.'

She said with dismay, 'The family', as though the word meant 'the enemy'.

'So you see,' my aunt said, 'we at any rate do have certain rights.'

I couldn't understand my aunt's harshness and I intervened. 'I think it is very kind of you,' I said, 'to lay flowers on my father's grave. It may seem strange to you that I have never been here before . . .'

'It is quite typical of you all,' Miss Paterson said, 'of you all. Your mother never even came to the funeral. I was the only one. I and the concierge of the hotel. A kind man.' She added with tears in her eyes, 'It was a wet wet day, and he brought his big umbrella . . .'

'Then you knew my father . . . You were here . . . ?'

'He died gently gently in my arms,' Miss Paterson said. She had a way of repeating words as though she were used to reading children's books aloud.

'It is very cold,' my aunt interrupted. 'Henry, you have laid your wreath, I shall go back to the hotel, this is not a place for prolonged conversation.' She began to walk away: it was almost like an admission of defeat, and she tried to carry it off with disdain, like a great dane which turns its back on some small defenceless dog defiant in a corner and pretends it unworthy of its teeth.

I said to Miss Paterson, 'I must see my aunt home. Couldn't you come and take a cup of tea with us this evening? I was only a small boy when my father died. I hardly knew him. I should have come here before, but, you know, I thought nobody cared any more about such things . . .'

'I know I am old-fashioned,' Miss Paterson said, 'so very old-fashioned.'

'But you will at least have tea with us? At the Meurice?'

'I will come,' Miss Paterson said with frightened dignity. 'You must tell your aunt however – she is your aunt? – that she mustn't take offence at me. He has been dead a long time. It is unfair of her to be jealous of me because I care so much, so much still.'

I repeated the message to my aunt exactly, and she was astonished.

'Did she really believe me to be jealous? The only time I can remember being jealous was over Curran, and that experience taught me better. You know how little jealous I was even of Monsieur Dambreuse . . .'

'You don't have to defend yourself to me, Aunt Augusta,' I said.

'Defend myself? I certainly have not fallen as low as that. I am trying to explain my feelings, that is all. The woman seemed to me totally inadequate to her grief. You can't pour a glass of wine into an after-dinner cup of coffee. She irritated me. To think that she was with your father when he died.'

'Presumably there was a doctor too.'

'He wouldn't have died if she had not been so feeble. I am convinced of that. Your father had to be shaken into action. The trouble with Richard was his appearance. He was strikingly good-looking. He never had to make an effort with a woman. And finally he was too lazy to struggle. If I had been with him I would have seen that he was alive today.'

'Today?'

'He would not have been much older than Mr Visconti.'

'Be kind to her all the same, Aunt Augusta.'

'I shall be as sweet as sugar,' my aunt promised.

And that afternoon I could tell that she was really trying to hide her irritation at Miss Paterson's mannerisms, of which there were many besides her habit of repeating words. She had for example a twitch in her right foot (the first time it happened I really thought that Aunt Augusta had kicked her), and, when she had been silent a little while and her mind wandered, her teeth began to click as though she were manipulating a pair of false dentures. We had tea in my aunt's room, for there was no proper lounge in the square miniature skyscraper which sat between two identical others on the quay.

'You must forgive us,' my aunt said, 'they have only Lipton's Indian.'

'Oh, but I like Lipton's,' Miss Paterson said, 'with one little little lump.'

'Did you come via Calais?' my aunt asked, making polite conversation. 'We came that way yesterday. Or by the ferry?'

'Oh no,' Miss Paterson said, 'you see, I live here. I have always lived here, that is to say since Richard died.' She gave a scared glance at me and said, 'Mr Pulling, I mean.'

'Even during the war?' my aunt asked with a touch of suspicion. She would have been glad, I think, to have found a chink in Miss Paterson's integrity, if only a small error of fact.

'It was a time of some privation,' Miss Paterson said. 'Perhaps the bombardments seemed less terrible to me because I had my children to think of.'

'Your children?' my aunt exclaimed. 'Surely Richard . . .'

'Oh no, no, no,' Miss Paterson said, 'I refer only to the children whom I taught. I taught English in the Lycée.'

'Didn't the Germans intern you?'

'The people here were very good to me. I was protected. The mayor provided me with an identity card.' Miss Paterson's leg jumped. 'After the war they even gave me a medal.'

'A medal for teaching English?' my aunt asked incredulously.

'And other things,' Miss Paterson said. She leant back in her chair and her teeth began to click. Her thoughts were far away.

'Tell me about my father,' I told her. 'What brought him to Boulogne?'

'He wanted to give me a holiday,' Miss Paterson said. 'He was worried about my health. He said I needed sea air.' My aunt rattled her spoon and I feared for her patience. 'Just a day trip you know. We took the boat like you to Calais, for he wanted to show me where the burghers came from, and then we took a bus here to see the Napoleon column – he had just read his biography by Sir Walter Scott – and we found there was no boat back from Boulogne.'

'That came as a surprise to him, I suppose?' my aunt asked with an irony which was obvious to me but not to Miss Paterson.

'Yes,' Miss Paterson said. 'He was very apologetic for his lack of forethought. However we found two clean rooms in a little little inn up in the high town in the square by the *mairie*.'

'Adjoining rooms, I assume,' my aunt said. I couldn't understand why she was so severe.

'Yes,' Miss Paterson said, 'because I was frightened.'

'Of what?'

'I had never been abroad before, nor had Mr Pulling. I had to translate for both of us.'

'You knew French?'

'I had taken a course at the Berlitz.'

'You mustn't mind our interest, Miss Paterson,' I said. 'You see, I have never heard any details of my father's death – my mother never spoke of it. She always shut me up when I asked questions. She told me he had died on a business trip, and somehow I always assumed that he had died at Wolverhampton – he often went to Wolverhampton.'

'When did you meet my brother-in-law?' Aunt Augusta asked. 'May I pour you another cup of tea?'

'Yes, please. A little bit weaker if it would not be a trouble to you. We met on the top of a 49 bus.'

My aunt paused with a lump of sugar in mid air, 'A 49 bus?' she repeated.

'Yes, you see, I had heard him ask for his ticket and when his destination came he was fast asleep, so I woke him up, but it was too late. It was a request stop. He was very grateful and came all the way to Chelsea Town Hall with me. I had a basement room then in Oakley Street and he walked back to the house with me. I remember it all so clearly, so clearly,' Miss Paterson said, 'as though it were only yesterday. We found many things in common.' Her foot gave a kick again.

'That surprises me,' my aunt said.

'Oh how we talked that day!'

'What about?'

'Mainly I think about Sir Walter Scott. I knew *Marmion* and little else, but he knew everything that Sir Walter had ever written. He could quote . . . He had a wonderful memory for poetry.' She whispered as though to herself:

> 'Where shall the traitor rest,
>   He the deceiver,
> Who could win maiden's breast
>   Ruin and leave her?
> In the last battle . . .'

'And so it all began,' my aunt interrupted in a tone of impatience. 'And the traitor rests in Boulogne.'

Miss Paterson coiled up in her chair and kicked her foot vigorously.

'Nothing began – in the way you mean,' she said. 'In the night I heard him knock on the door and call "Dolly?"'

'Dolly!' my aunt repeated with distaste as though Dolly were an unmentionable word.

'Yes. That was what he called me. My name is Dorothy.'

'You had locked your door, of course.'

'I had done no such thing. He was a man I trusted absolutely. I told him to come in. I knew he wouldn't have woken me for any trivial reason.'

'Certainly I would not describe his reason as trivial,' my aunt said, 'go on,' but Miss Paterson was far away again and her teeth clicked and clicked. She was gazing at something we could not see, and there were the beginnings of tears in her eyes. I put my hand on her arm and said, 'Miss Paterson, don't talk about it any more if it hurts you.' I was angry with my aunt: her face looked as hard as a face stamped on a coin.

Miss Paterson looked at me and I could watch her beginning to return from that long time ago. 'He came in,' she said, 'and he whispered, "Dolly, my darling," and he fell down on the floor. I got down beside him and put his poor poor head in my lap and he never spoke again. I never knew why he came or what he meant to say to me.'

'I can guess,' Aunt Augusta said.

Again Miss Paterson coiled herself back in her chair and struck back. It was a sad sight to see these two old women at loggerheads over something that had happened so many years ago. 'I hope you are right,' Miss Paterson said. 'I know well what you are thinking and I hope you are right. I would have done anything that he asked me without hesitation or regret. And I have never loved another man.'

'You didn't have the time to love him, it seems,' my aunt said.

'There you are quite wrong. Perhaps because you don't know what love is. I loved him from the moment he got off the bus at Chelsea Town Hall, and I love him today. When he was dead I did everything for him – everything – there was no one else to help my poor dear – his wife wouldn't come. There had to be a post-mortem, and she wrote to the authorities to bury him in Boulogne – she didn't want his poor poor mutilated body. So there was only myself and the concierge . . .'

'You have certainly been very constant,' my aunt said, but the remark did not sound like a compliment.

'No one else has ever again used that name he called me, Dolly,' Miss Paterson said, 'but in the war, when I had to use an alias, I let them call me Poupée.'

'Why on earth did you have an alias?'

'They were troubled times,' Miss Paterson said and she began to look for her gloves.

I resented the way my aunt had behaved to Miss Paterson, and a slow flame of anger still burned in me when we went out to dinner for the second and last time in the deserted station. The gay wave-worn fishing boats lay against the jetty, each with a painted pious phrase across the bridge: '*Dieu bénit la famille*' and '*Dieu a bien fait*', and I wondered what comfort the mottoes brought in a strong Channel gale. There was the same smell of oil and fish, the same train from Lyon was awaited by no one, and in the restaurant there was the same disgruntled Englishman with the same companion and the same dog – he made the restaurant seem all the emptier with his presence as though there had never been a different customer.

My aunt said, 'You are very silent, Henry.'

'I have a lot to think about,' I said.

'You were quite taken by that miserable little woman,' Aunt Augusta accused me.

'I was touched to meet someone who loved my father.'

'A lot of women loved him.'

'I mean a woman who *really* loved him.'

'That little sentimental creature? She doesn't know what love is.'

'Do you?' I asked, letting my anger out.

'I think I have had rather more experience of it than you,' Aunt Augusta replied with calm and careful cruelty. It was true – I hadn't even answered Miss Keene's last letter. My aunt sat opposite me over her sole with an air of perfect satisfaction. She ate the shrimps that went with it one by one before she tackled the sole; she enjoyed the separate taste and she was in no hurry.

Perhaps she did have reason to despise Miss Paterson. I thought of Curran and Monsieur Dambreuse and Mr Visconti – they lived in my imagination as though she had actually created them: even poor Uncle Jo struggling towards the lavatory. She was one of the life-givers. Even Miss Paterson had come to life, stung by the cruelty of her question. Perhaps if she ever talked about me to another – I could well imagine what a story she could make out of my dahlias and my silly tenderness for Tooley and my stainless past – even I would come to some sort of life, and the character she drew, I felt sure, would be much more vivid than the real I. It was useless to complain of her cruelty. I had once read, in a book on Charles Dickens, that an author must not be attached to his characters, he must treat them without mercy. In the act of creation there is always, it seems, an awful selfishness. So Dickens's wife and mistress had to suffer so that Dickens could make his novels and his fortune. At least a bank manager's money is not so tainted by egotism. Mine was not a destructive profession. A bank manager doesn't leave a trail of the martyred behind him. Where was Curran now? Did even Wordsworth still survive?

'Have I ever told you,' my aunt asked, 'of a man called Charles Pottifer? In his way he clung to a dead man as fervently as your Miss Paterson. But in his case the dead man was himself.'

'Not tonight, Aunt Augusta,' I pleaded. 'My father's death is enough of a story for one day.'

'And she told it reasonably well,' my aunt admitted, 'though I think that given her opportunity I would have told it a great deal better. But I warn you – you will be sorry one day that you refused to let me tell you the story I proposed.'

'What story?' I asked, thinking of my father.

'The story of Charles Pottifer, of course,' my aunt said.

'Another time, Aunt Augusta.'

'You are wrong to be so confident in the existence of another time,' my aunt replied and called for the bill so loudly that the dog barked back at her from the bar.

Chapter 19

MY aunt did not return with me to England by the car-ferry as I thought she intended. She told me at breakfast that she was taking a train to Paris. 'There are things which I must settle,' she said, and I remembered her warning of the night before and wondered – quite wrongly as it turned out – if she had a premonition of death.

'Would you like me to go with you?' I asked.

'No,' she said, 'from the way you spoke to me last night I think you have had enough of my company for a while.'

Obviously I had hurt her deeply by refusing to listen to the story of the man called Charles Pottifer.

I saw her off at the station and received the coldest of cold pecks upon the cheek.

'I didn't mean to offend you, Aunt Augusta,' I said.

'You resemble your father more than your mother. He believed no story was of interest outside the pages of Walter Scott.'

'And my mother?' I asked quickly. Perhaps at last I was to be given a clue.

'She tried in vain to read *Rob Roy*. She loved your father very dearly and was anxious to please, but *Rob Roy* was going too far.'

'Why didn't she marry him?'

'She hadn't the right disposition for a life in Highgate. Will you buy me a *Figaro* before you go?'

When I came back from the bookstall she gave me the keys to her apartment. 'If I am away a long time,' she said, 'I may want you to send me something or just to look in to see that all is well. I will write to the landlord and tell him you have the keys.'

I returned to London on the car-ferry. Two days before, from the window of the train, I had watched a golden England spread beside the line – now the picture was very different: England lay damp and cold, as grey as the graveyard, while the train lagged slowly from Dover Town towards Charing Cross under the drenching rain. One window could not be closed properly and a little pool of water collected at the side of the compartment; the heating had not been turned on. In the opposite corner a woman sneezed continuously while I tried to read the *Daily Telegraph*. There was a threatened engineering strike, and the car industry was menaced by a stoppage of cleaners in some key factory which turned out windscreen-wipers. Cars in all the BMC factories waited without wipers on the production line. Export figures were down and so was the pound.

I came at last beyond the Court News to the Obituaries, but there was little of interest to read in that column. Somebody called Sir Oswald Newman had died at the age of seventy-two, he was the star death in a poor programme. He had been chief arbitrator in a building dispute in the 1950s after retiring as Permanent Secretary in the Ministry of Works. He had married Rosa Urquhart in 1928, by whom he had three sons, and she survived him. His eldest was now secretary of the International Federation of Thermofactors and an OBE. I thought of my father whispering, 'Dolly, my darling,' before he died on the floor of the *auberge* in the Haute Ville, too soon to meet Sir Oswald Newman during the building dispute, which would probably not have concerned him anyway. He always kept on good terms with his men – so my mother had told me. Laziness and good nature often go together. There were always Christmas bonuses, and he was never in the mood to fight over the rise of a penny an hour. When I looked out of the window it was not Sir Oswald Newman's England I saw, but my father's grave in the smoky rain and Miss Paterson standing before it in prayer, and I envied him his inexplicable quality of drawing women's love. Had Rosa Newman so loved Sir Oswald and her son, the OBE?

I let myself into the house. I had been away two nights, but like a possessive woman it had the histrionic air of being abandoned. Dust collected quickly in autumn even with the windows closed. I knew the routine that I would certainly follow: a telephone call to Chicken, a visit to the dahlias if the rain stopped. Perhaps Major Charge might address a remark to me over the hedge. 'Dolly, my darling,' my father whispered, dying in the small hotel, as I lay in the Highgate nursery with a night-light beside the bed to drive away the fears which always gathered after my mother – or was it my stepmother? – had pecked me good night. I was afraid of burglars and Indian thugs and snakes and fires and Jack the Ripper, when I should have been afraid of thirty years in a bank and a take-over bid and a premature retirement and the Deuil du Roy Albert.

A month passed, and no news came to me from my aunt. I rang several times, but there was never any reply. I tried to interest myself in a novel of Thackeray's, but it lacked the immediacy of my aunt's stories. As she had foreseen I even regretted having prevented her telling me the story of Charles Pottifer. I found myself living now, when I lay awake or waited in the kitchen for the kettle to boil, or when I let *The Newcomes* fall shut on my lap, with memories of Curran, Monsieur Dambreuse and Mr Visconti. They peopled my loneliness. When six weeks went by without news I became anxious, in case, like my father, she had died in a foreign land. I even telephoned to the St James and Albany – it was the first time since I left the bank that I had telephoned abroad. I was nervous of my poor French when I spoke into a receiver, as though the errors might be magnified by the microphone. The receptionist told me that my aunt was no longer there – she had left three weeks before for Cherbourg.

'Cherbourg?'

'The boat-train,' the receptionist said and the line was cut before I could ask him what boat.

I feared then that my aunt had left me for good. She had come into my life only to disturb it. I had lost the taste for dahlias. When weeds swarmed up I was tempted to let them grow. Once I even consented, as a possible relief to my tedium, to attend, on Major Charge's invitation, a political meeting: it turned out to be a meeting of British Empire Loyalists, and I supposed then that it was Major Charge who had given the organization my address for their pamphlets. I saw several of my old clients there, including the admiral, and I was glad for the first time that I was in retirement. A bank manager is not expected to have strong political preferences, particularly eccentric ones, and how quickly the gossip of my presence would have gone around Southwood. Now, if my old clients looked at me at all, it was with a puzzled expression as though they were uncertain when it was we had met and on what occasion. Like a waiter on his day-off I passed virtually unrecognized. It was an odd feeling for one who had been so much in the centre of Southwood life. As I went upstairs to bed I felt myself to be a ghost returning home, transparent as water. Curran was more alive than I was. I was almost surprised to see that my image was visible in the glass.

Perhaps it was to prove the reality of my existence that I began a letter to Miss Keene. I made several drafts before I was satisfied with what I wrote, and the letter I am copying now differs in many small details from the one I dispatched. 'My dear Miss Keene,' I can read in the draft, but I cut out the 'My' in the final version, for it seemed to presume an intimacy which she had never acknowledged and which I had never claimed. 'Dear Miss Keene, I am truly distressed that you don't feel properly settled yet in your new home at Koffiefontein, though of course I cannot help feeling a little glad' (I altered the 'I' to a 'we' in later drafts) 'that your thoughts still rest sometimes on our quiet life here in Southwood. I have never known so good a friend as your father, and my thoughts often go back to those pleasant evenings when Sir Alfred sat under the Van de Velde dispensing hospitality, and you sat sewing while he and I finished the wine.' (That last phrase I cut from the next draft – there was too much emotion in it barely concealed.) 'I have been leading a rather unusual life the last month, much of it in the company of my aunt of whom I wrote to you. We have even gone as far afield together as Istanbul where I was a good deal disappointed with the famed Santa Sophia. I can say to you – as I couldn't say to my aunt – that I much prefer our own St John's Church for a religious atmosphere, and I am glad that the vicar doesn't feel it necessary to summon the faithful to prayer by a gramophone record in a minaret. At the beginning of October we paid a visit together to my father's grave. I don't think I ever told you (indeed I only learnt of it recently myself) that he died and was buried in Boulogne by a strange concatenation of circumstances too long to write here. How I wish you were in Southwood that I might tell you of them.' That sentence too I thought it prudent to eliminate. 'I am reading *The Newcomes* at the moment, but I don't enjoy it as I enjoyed *Esmond*. Perhaps that is the romantic in me. I open Palgrave too from time to time and read over my old favourites.' I went on with a sense of hypocrisy: 'My books are a good antidote to foreign travel and reinforce the sense of the England I love, but sometimes I wonder whether that England exists still beyond my garden hedge or further than Church Road. Then I think how much harder it must be for you in Koffiefontein to keep the taste of the past. The future here seems to me to have no taste at all: it is like a meal on a menu, which serves only to kill the appetite. If you ever come back to England –' but that was a sentence I never finished, and I can't remember now what I intended to write.

Christmas approached with no news of my aunt, not even by the medium of a Christmas card. A card, of course, arrived from Koffiefontein, a rather unlikely card with an old church seen across an acre of snow, and a comic one from Major Charge which showed goldfish in a bowl being fed by Father Christmas; it was delivered by hand to save the stamp. The local store sent me a tear-off calendar with a different treasure of British art for each month, the colours bright and shiny as though they had been washed in Omo, and on 23 December the postman brought a large envelope which when I opened it at breakfast shed a lot of silvery tinsel into my plate, so that I couldn't finish my marmalade. The tinsel came from an Eiffel Tower which Father Christmas was climbing with his sack over his shoulder. Under the printed *Meilleurs Vœux* was only one name, written in block capitals: 'Wordsworth'. He must have seen my aunt in Paris, for how else could he have obtained my address? At the bank I had always used the official Christmas cards to send to my best clients, with the bank's coat of arms stamped on the cover and inside a picture of the main office in Cheapside or a photograph of the board of directors. Now that I had retired there were few people to whom I posted cards: Miss Keene, of course, Major Charge perforce. I sent one also to my doctor, my dentist, to the vicar of St John's and my former chief cashier who had become manager of a branch in Nottingham.

A year before my mother had come to me for Christmas dinner, and without the aid of Chicken I had cooked a turkey quite successfully under her directions, then we had sat almost silent, like strangers in a restaurant-car, both of us feeling that we had eaten too much, until she left at ten. Afterwards I had, as was my habit, attended the midnight service with carols at St John's. This year, since I had no wish to cook a meal for myself alone, I booked a table for dinner at the Abbey Restaurant off Latimer Road. It proved a mistake. I had not realized they were mounting a special menu with turkey and plum pudding to attract the lonely and the nostalgic from all over Southwood. Before I left home I had rung my aunt's number in the vain hope that she might have returned just in time for Christmas, but the bell tolled and tolled in the empty flat, and I could imagine the noise setting all the Venetian glasses atinkle.

The first person I saw when I came into the restaurant, which was a very small one with heavy beams and stained-glass windows and a piece of mistletoe in an undangerous position over the toilet, was the admiral sitting all alone. He had obviously dined early and he wore a scarlet paper crown – a torn cracker lay on his plate with the remains of plum pudding. I bowed to him and he said angrily, 'Who are you?' At a table beyond him I could see Major Charge, who was frowning over what looked like a political pamphlet.

'I am Pulling,' I said.

'Pulling?'

'Late of the bank.'

There was an angry flush below the red paper hat, and an empty bottle of Chianti stood on the table. I added, 'Happy Christmas, Admiral.'

'Good God, man,' he said, 'haven't you read the news?'

I managed to get by, though the channel between the tables was very narrow, and found to my distress that my table had been reserved next to Major Charge's.

'Good evening, Major,' I said. I began to wonder whether I was the only civilian in the place.

'I have a favour to ask of you,' Major Charge said.

'Of course . . . any help . . . I am afraid I no longer keep up with the stock market . . .'

'Who's talking about the stock market? You don't suppose I'd have anything to do with the City? They've sold this country down the river. I'm talking about my fish.'

Miss Truman interrupted us to take my order. Perhaps to encourage her customers she was wearing a paper cap, vaguely military in shape but yellow in colour. She was a large boisterous woman who liked to be called Peter; the little restaurant had always seemed too small to contain her and her partner as well – a woman named Nancy who was timid and retiring and perhaps for that reason showed herself only occasionally framed at the service hatch.

Unable to look elsewhere, I made some complimentary reference to her cap.

'Like the old days,' she said, looking pleased, and I remembered that she had been an officer in the women's navy.

How ambiguous my feelings were. I realized in those moments how deep was the disturbance my aunt had caused. This was my familiar world – the little local world of ageing people to which Miss Keene longed to return, where one read of danger only in the newspapers and the deepest change to be expected was a change of government and the biggest scandal I could remember one defecting clerk who had lost too much money at the Earl's Court greyhound track. It was more my country than England could be, for I had never seen the satanic mills or visited the northern wastes, and in my way I had been happy here; yet I was looking at Peter (Miss Truman) with an ironic eye, as though I had borrowed my aunt's vision and saw with her eyes. Beyond Latimer Road there stretched another world – the world of Wordsworth and Curran and Monsieur Dambreuse and Colonel Hakim and the mysterious Mr Visconti who had dressed up as a monsignor to escape the Allied troops, yes, and of my father too, saying 'Dolly darling' to Miss Paterson with his last breath on the *auberge* floor and gaining a life-long devotion by dying in her arms. To whom now could I apply for a visa to that land with my aunt gone?

'Will you take the set meal, Mr Pulling?'

'I don't think I can manage the plum pudding.'

'Nancy has made some smashing mince pies.'

'Perhaps one,' I said, 'because it's Christmas.'

Miss Truman rolled away with a Tom Bowling stride and I turned to Major Charge. 'You were saying?'

'I'm going away for the New Year. To a study group at Chesham. I've got to board my fish. Can't trust them with the daily. I thought of Peter – but she's a woman too, in a way. You can see how she feeds us. Any excuse to pile it on. She would probably do the same with the little buggers.'

'You want me to look after your fish?'

'I looked after your dahlias.'

And starved them of water, I thought, but I had to say, 'Yes, of course, I will.'

'I'll bring you the food. Just one teaspoonful once a day. Don't pay any attention if they come guzzling at the glass. They don't know what's good for them.'

'I'll harden my heart,' I said. I waved away the turtle soup – it was over-familiar. Too often I had opened a bottle of it when I had no appetite even for eggs. I asked, 'What kind of a study group?'

'The problems of empire,' he replied, staring at me with eyes enlarged and angry as though I had already made some foolish or unsympathetic reply.

'I thought we had got rid of all those.'

'A temporary failure of nerve,' he snapped and bayoneted his turkey.

I would certainly have preferred him as a client to Curran. He would never have bothered me about overdrafts: he lived carefully within the limits of his pension: he was an honest man even if I found his ideas repulsive, and then I thought of Mr Visconti dancing with my aunt in the reception room of the brothel behind the *Messaggero* after swindling the Vatican and the King of Saudi Arabia and leaving a wide trail of damage behind him in the banks of Italy. Was the secret of lasting youth known only to the criminal mind?

'A man's been looking for you,' Major Charge said after a long silence. The admiral got up from his table and made unsteadily for the door. He was still wearing his paper crown, but when his fingers were already on the handle, he remembered it and scrunched it into a ball.

'What man?'

'You'd gone to the post office – or so I imagine. At any rate you turned right not left at the bottom of Southwood Road.'

'What did he want?'

'He didn't tell me. He rang and knocked and rang and knocked, making the hell of a din. Even the fish were scared, poor little buggers. There were two of them. I thought I ought to speak to them before they disturbed the whole street.'

I don't know why, but I thought at that moment of Wordsworth, a possible message from my aunt . . .

'Was he black?' I asked.

'Black? What an extraordinary question. Of course he wasn't.'

'He didn't give a name?'

'Neither of them did. He asked where he could find you, but I had no idea you were planning to come here. You weren't here last year or the year before. I don't think I've ever seen you here before. All I could tell him was that I knew you went to the carol service at St John's.'

'I wonder who it could be,' I said.

I had a deep conviction that I was about to find myself again in Aunt Augusta's world, and my pulse beat with an irrational sense of pleasure. When Miss Truman brought me two mince pies I accepted them both as though I needed them to sustain me for a long voyage. I even helped myself liberally to brandy butter.

'I used real Rémy Martin,' Miss Truman said. 'You haven't pulled your cracker.'

'Pull it with me, Peter,' I said with daring. She had a strong wrist, but I got the winning end, and a small plastic object rolled on to the floor. I was glad to see that it was not a hat. Major Charge leapt at it and gave a snort of laughter as merciless as a nose-blowing. He put it to his mouth and breathed hard, making a sound like a raspberry. Then I saw that it was shaped like a tiny po with a whistle in the handle.

'Lower-deck humour,' Miss Truman said in a kindly way.

'It's the festive season,' Major Charge said. He blew another raspberry. 'Hark! the herald-angels sing,' he said in a tone of savagery, as though he were taking some kind of revenge on Christmas Eve and all its impedimenta of holy families and mangers and wise men, a revenge on love, a revenge for some deep disappointment.

I arrived at St John's Church by a quarter past eleven. The service always began at half past eleven so as to distinguish it from the Roman Catholic Midnight Mass. I had begun to attend when I first became the bank manager, for it gave me a stable family air if I were seen at the service, and though, unlike Aunt Augusta, I have no religious convictions, I could be there without hypocrisy since I have always enjoyed the more poetic aspects of Christianity. Christmas, it seems to me, is a necessary festival; we require a season when we can regret all the flaws in our human relationships: it is the feast of failure, sad but consoling.

For years now I have always sat in the same pew below a stained-glass window which was dedicated in 1887 to the memory of Councillor Trumbull. It shows Christ surrounded by children as he sits in the shade of a very green tree – the text, of course, is 'Suffer little children'. Councillor Trumbull was responsible for building the square redbrick block with barred windows in Cranmer Road, which, once an orphanage, is now a detention centre for juvenile delinquents.

The carol service began with a gentler version than Major Charge's of 'Hark! the Herald-Angels sing', and then we proceeded to the old favourite, 'Good King Wenceslas'.

'Deep and crisp and even' the high female voices sang from the gallery – it has always seemed to me a very beautiful line, conveying the landscape of a small country England with no crowds, no traffic, to soil the snow, when even the royal palace stood among the silent and untrodden fields.

'No white Christmas, sir, this year,' a voice whispered in my ear from the pew behind, and turning I saw Detective-Sergeant Sparrow.

'What on earth are you doing here?'

'If you can spare me a moment after the service, sir,' he replied, and raising his prayer-book he sang in a very fine baritone voice:

> 'Though the frost was cru-el,
> When a poor man hove in sight

(perhaps Detective-Sergeant Sparrow like Miss Truman had once been in the Navy)

> Gathering winter fu-u-el.'

I looked back at his companion. He was smartly dressed with a lean legal face. He wore a dark grey overcoat and carried an umbrella crooked for safety over his arm – I wondered what he would do with it or with the sharp crease to his trousers when the time came for him to kneel. He didn't seem as much at home in the church as Detective-Sergeant Sparrow. He was not singing and I doubt whether he was praying.

'Mark my footsteps, good my page,'

the sergeant sang lustily,

'Tread thou in them boldly,'

and the voices in the gallery rose ardently to the unexpected competition from below.

At last the proper service began, and I was glad when the Athanasian Creed, which they invariably inflict on us at Christmas, was safely over. 'As also there are not three incomprehensibles, nor three uncreated: but one uncreated, and one incomprehensible.' (Sergeant Sparrow coughed several times in the course of it.)

I intended – it is always my custom at Christmas – to go to Communion. The Anglican Church is not exclusive: Communion is a commemoration service, and I had as much right to commemorate a beautiful legend as any true believer has. The vicar was saying clearly, while the congregation buzzed ambiguously to disguise the fact that they had forgotten the words: 'We acknowledge and bewail our manifold sins and wickedness, which we, from time to time, have committed . . .' I noticed that the detective-sergeant, perhaps from professional prudence, did not join in this plea of guilty. 'We do earnestly repent, and are heartily sorry for these our misdoings . . .' I had never before noticed how the prayer sounded like the words of an old lag addressing the Bench with a plea for mercy. The presence of Detective-Sergeant Sparrow seemed to alter the whole tone of the service. When I stepped into the nave to go up to the altar I heard an outburst of argumentative whispers in the pew behind me and the words, 'You, Sparrow,' spoken very forcibly, so that I was not surprised when I saw that it was Detective-Sergeant Sparrow who knelt as my neighbour at the communion rail. Perhaps they had been uncertain whether I might not take advantage of the Communion to escape through a side-door.

When his turn with the chalice came Detective-Sergeant Sparrow took a very long swig, and I noticed afterwards that more wine had to be fetched before the Communion was finished. When I returned to my seat, the detective-sergeant trod on my heels, and in the pew behind me the whispers broke out again. 'My throat's like a grater,' I heard the sergeant say. I suppose he was apologizing for his performance with the chalice.

At the end of the service they stood and waited for me at the church door, and Sergeant Sparrow introduced his companion. 'Detective-Inspector Woodrow,' he said, 'Mr Pulling.' He added with awe in a lower voice, 'Inspector Woodrow belongs to the Special Branch.'

I shook hands after a little hesitation on both sides.

'We were wondering, sir, if you would mind assisting us again,' Sergeant Sparrow said. 'I told Inspector Woodrow how helpful you had been once before over the jar of pot.'

'I suppose you are referring to my mother's urn,' I replied with as much coldness as I could muster on Christmas morning.

The congregation poured out on either side. I saw the admiral go by. In his breast-pocket he had a patch of scarlet, which I suppose was the paper cap serving as a handkerchief.

'They told us at the Crown and Anchor,' Inspector Woodrow said to me in a stiff unfriendly tone, 'that you have your aunt's keys.'

'We like to do things nicely,' Sergeant Sparrow explained, 'with the free consent of all parties concerned. It goes down so much better in court.'

'What exactly do you want?' I asked.

'A happy Christmas, Mr Pulling.' The vicar put his hand on my shoulder. 'Have I the pleasure of meeting two new parishioners?'

'Mr Sparrow, Mr Woodrow, the vicar,' I said.

'I hope you all enjoyed our carol service.'

'Indeed I did,' Sergeant Sparrow said heartily. 'If there's one thing I like it's a good tune with words I can understand.'

'Just a moment while I find copies of our parish magazine. Quite a bumper Christmas number.' The vicar dived back into the dark church looking like a ghost in his surplice.

'You understand, sir,' Sergeant Sparrow said, 'we could have easily got a search-warrant and made a forcible entry, but besides ruining a good lock – it's a Chubb, very prudent of Miss Bertram – it looks bad in evidence, you understand what I mean, for the good lady. If it comes to evidence. Which we hope will not be the case.'

'But what on earth are you looking for? Not pot again surely?'

Inspector Woodrow said in a grave hangman's tone, 'We are pursuing an inquiry at the request of Interpol.'

The vicar came hurrying back to us waving copies of the parish magazine. He said, 'If you would both just turn to the last page you will find a tear-out subscription form for the coming year. Mr Pulling already subscribes.'

'Thank you, thank you, I am sure,' Detective-Sergeant Sparrow said. 'I haven't a pen with me at the moment, but just leave it with me. A very tasteful and original design – all that holly and the birds and gravestones.'

Inspector Woodrow took his copy with evident reluctance. He held it in front of him as a witness holds a Bible in court, not quite certain what to do with it.

'It's a very *swinging* number,' the vicar said. 'Oh, forgive me. Poor lady. I'll be back in one sec.' He pursued an elderly lady down the path to Latimer Road calling, 'Mrs Brewster, Mrs Brewster.'

'I think before he returns,' Inspector Woodrow said, 'we had better go somewhere and discuss things.'

Sergeant Sparrow had already opened the parish magazine and was reading it with absorption.

'You can come home with me,' I said.

'I would prefer to go to Miss Bertram's with no further delay. We can explain matters in the car.'

'Why do you want to go to my aunt's flat?'

'I've told you. There has been an inquiry from Interpol. We don't want to disturb a magistrate on Christmas night. You are next of kin. Your aunt by giving you her keys has left the flat in your care . . .'

'Has something happened to my aunt?'

'It is not impossible.' He was never satisfied unless he made four words serve for one. He said sharply, 'The vicar is coming back . . . For God's sake, Sparrow, pay attention.'

'Now I hope you won't either of you forget your subscription,' the vicar said. 'It will go to a good cause. We are furnishing a Children's Corner in time for Easter. I would have preferred to call it a chapel, but we have some old Protestant battle-axes in Southwood. I'll let you into a very deep secret. I haven't even told my committee. The other day I obtained in Portobello Road an *original* drawing of Mabel Lucy Atwell's. We shall unveil it at Easter, and I am wondering if we couldn't persuade Prince Andrew . . .'

'I'm afraid, Vicar, we shall have to go,' Inspector Woodrow said, 'but I hope your Corner will be a great success.' It was beginning to rain. He looked at his umbrella, but he didn't open it. Perhaps he was not confident that the neat folds could ever be properly reproduced.

'I will be calling on you both one day very soon,' the vicar said, 'when I have your addresses on the subscription form.'

'Sparrow!' Inspector Woodrow spoke quite sharply.

Sparrow closed the parish magazine with reluctance and followed us at the run because of the rain. As he sat down beside Woodrow in the driver's seat, he explained apologetically, 'There's a story called *Who's Guilty?* I thought it might be a murder story – I like a good murder story – but it was only about an old lady who was unkind to a pop singer. You can't tell anything from titles nowadays.'

'Now, Mr Pulling,' Inspector Woodrow said, 'when did you last see your aunt?' The phrase sounded vaguely familiar.

'Some weeks – months – ago. In Boulogne. Why?'

'You travel about a great deal with her, don't you?'

'Well . . .'

'When did you last hear from her?'

'I've told you – Boulogne. Do I have to answer these questions?'

'You have your constitutional rights,' Sergeant Sparrow began, 'like any citizen. Duties too of course. A voluntary statement always has a better sound in court. The court takes into account . . .'

'For God's sake hold your tongue, Sparrow,' Inspector Woodrow said. 'Aren't you surprised, Mr Pulling, that you've heard nothing from your aunt since Boulogne?'

'There is nothing about my aunt which surprises me.'

'You aren't anxious – in case something might have happened to her?'

'Should I be?'

'She has kept some very queer company. Have you ever heard of a Mr Visconti?'

'The name,' I said, 'is somehow familiar.'

'A war criminal,' Detective-Sergeant Sparrow added unwisely.

'Please keep your eye on the road, Sparrow,' the inspector said. 'General Abdul – you've heard of General Abdul, I presume?'

'. . . Perhaps, yes, I seem to know the name.'

'You were with your aunt in Istanbul some time ago. You arrived by train and you were expelled after a few hours. You saw a Colonel Hakim.'

'I saw some police officer or other certainly. An absurd mistake.'

'General Abdul made a statement before he died.'

'Died? Poor fellow. I didn't know. I can't see how his statement can concern me.'

'Or your aunt?'

'I'm not my aunt's keeper.'

'The statement concerned Mr Visconti. Interpol has circulated the details. Until now we had always assumed that Mr Visconti was dead. We had written him off.'

'By the way,' I said, 'before we go any further, I must tell you that I haven't got my aunt's keys with me.'

'I had hardly expected that. I wanted only your permission to enter. I assure you that we'll do no damage.'

'I'm afraid I can't allow it. The flat is in my charge.'

'It would look so much better if it ever came to a jury, Mr Pulling,' Sparrow began, but the inspector interrupted him. 'Sparrow. Take the next turning on the left. We will take Mr Pulling home.'

'You can call on me after Christmas,' I said, 'that is, if you have a search-warrant.'

Chapter 20

I HAD expected the inspector and Detective-Sergeant Sparrow to come and see me, but they didn't even telephone. A picture postcard turned up unexpectedly from Tooley. It was the view of a rather ugly temple in Katmandu and she had written on it, 'I am on a marvellous trip. Love Tooley.' I had quite forgotten that I had given her my address. There was no reference to Christmas (the season, I suppose, had passed unnoticed in Nepal), and I felt the more proud of her casual remembrance.

When Boxing Day was over I drove to the Crown and Anchor a little before closing time in the afternoon. I wanted to see the flat in case the inspector turned up with his search-warrant. If there were any discreditable remnants of Wordsworth still lying about the place I wanted to remove them, and I carried a small weekend case with me for the purpose. All my working life I had been strictly loyal to one establishment, the bank, but my loyalty now was drawn in quite another direction. Loyalty to a person inevitably entails loyalty to all the imperfections of a human being, even to the chicanery and immorality from which my aunt was not entirely free. I wondered whether she had ever forged a cheque or robbed a bank, and I smiled at the thought with the tenderness I might have shown in the past to a small eccentricity.

When I reached the Crown and Anchor I looked cautiously in at the window of the saloon bar. Why cautiously? I had every right to be there – it was still opening time. The day was grey with a threat of snow and the customers were all pressing against the bar to get their last refill before three o'clock. I could see the back of the girl, who was still in jodhpurs, and a large hairy hand laid against it. 'Another double', 'Pint of best bitter', 'Double pink'. The clock stood at two minutes to three. It was as though they were whipping up their horses on the last straight before the winning post, and there was a great deal of irregular crowding. I found the right key to open the side-door and climbed the stairs. On the second landing I sat down for a moment on my aunt's sofa. I felt as illicit as a burglar and I listened for footsteps, but of course there was only the buzz and murmur of the bar.

When I opened the door of the flat I found everything in deep darkness. I set an occasional table rocking in the hall and something Venetian tinkled into fragments on the floor. When I drew the curtains the Venetian glasses had no glitter – they had gone dead like unused pearls. There was a scurf of correspondence on the floor among the broken glass, but it consisted mainly of circulars and I didn't bother to examine them for the moment. I went into my aunt's bedroom with a sense of shame – yet hadn't she asked me to see that all was in order? I remembered how meticulously Colonel Hakim had explored the hotel room and how easily he had been outwitted, but I could see no candles anywhere, except in the kitchen where they were of a normal size and weight – presumably a genuine precaution against an electric failure.

In Wordsworth's room the bed had been stripped and the hideous Walt Disney figures had all been put into drawers. The only decoration left was a framed photograph of Freetown harbour which showed market women in bright dresses descending some old steps with baskets on their heads towards the waterfront. I hadn't noticed it when I came before – perhaps my aunt had hung it there in memory of Wordsworth.

I returned to the sitting-room and began to go through the post. One day my aunt might send me a forwarding address, but in any case I wanted to save anything remotely personal from the scrutiny of Woodrow and Sparrow if they came. My old acquaintance Omo had written, and there were various bills from a laundry, a wine-merchant's, a grocer's. I was surprised not to find a bank statement, but remembering the gold brick and the suitcase stuffed with notes, I thought that perhaps my aunt preferred to keep her resources liquid. In that case it seemed to me wise to take a closer look among the dresses she had left behind, for it would be dangerous to leave cash about in the empty flat.

Then among the bills I came on something which interested me – a picture postcard from Panama showing a French liner on a very blue sea. The card was written in French, in a tiny economic script to take full advantage of the small space. The writer signed himself with the initials AD and he wrote, so far as I could make out, what a *concours de circonstances miraculeux* it had been to find my aunt on the ship after all these years of a *triste séparation* and what a calamity it was that she had left the boat before the end of the cruise and not given him a longer chance to live over again the memories they shared. After her departure AD's lumbago had taken a turn for the worse and the gout had revived in his right toe.

Could this possibly, I wondered, be Monsieur Dambreuse, the gallant lover who had kept two mistresses in the same hotel? If he were alive, then perhaps Curran was alive too. It was as though my aunt's crooked world were destined to a kind of immortality – only my poor father lay certainly dead in the smoke and rain of Boulogne. I admit that a pang of jealousy struck me because on this voyage I had not been my aunt's companion. It was to others that she now recounted her stories.

'Forgive us coming in without ringing, Mr Pulling,' said Detective-Sergeant Sparrow. He stood back to allow Inspector Woodrow to precede him according to protocol into the sitting-room. The inspector was carrying his umbrella which looked as if it hadn't been opened since I had seen him last.

'Good afternoon,' Inspector Woodrow said stiffly. 'It is just as well we have found you here.'

'The door being open . . .' Sergeant Sparrow said.

'I have a search-warrant,' Inspector Woodrow told me before I could ask him, and he held it out for my inspection. 'All the same we prefer a member of the family to be present at a search.'

'Not wishing to make a commotion,' Sergeant Sparrow said, 'which would be disagreeable to all, we were waiting in our car across the street till the manager closed the bar, but then seeing you come in, we thought we could do things on the quiet without even the manager knowing. Much nicer for your aunt because there would have been a lot of gossip in the bar tonight, you can be sure of that. You can't trust a barman not to talk to his locals. It's like husband and wife.'

While he spoke the inspector was busy examining the room.

'Looking at her mail, eh?' the sergeant asked me. He took the card out of my hand and said, 'Panama. Signed AD. Now you wouldn't have an idea who AD is?'

'No.'

'You see, it might be an alias. Interpol doesn't get much cooperation in Panama,' the sergeant said, 'except in the American zone.'

'Keep the card, Sparrow,' the inspector said, 'nonetheless.'

'What have you got against my aunt?'

'You know, sir, we err on the side of kindness,' Sergeant Sparrow said. 'We could have charged her over that cannabis affair, but seeing what an old lady she was and the coloured man taking off to Paris like that, we let her be. The case wouldn't have stood up in court anyway. Of course we didn't know a thing about this undesirable connection of hers.'

'What connection?'

I wondered if they had arranged their two parts beforehand: the sergeant being told to keep me occupied while the inspector searched the flat, as he was now doing.

'This man Visconti, sir. An Italian as you might surmise with a name like that. He's a viper.'

'All this glass,' the inspector said. 'Curious stuff. It's like a museum.'

'Venetian glass. My aunt worked once in Venice. I expect a lot were gifts – from her clients.'

'Very valuable? Collectors' pieces?'

'I wouldn't have thought so.'

'Works of art?'

'It's a matter of taste,' I said.

'Miss Bertram knew a lot about art, I daresay. Any pictures?'

'I don't think so. Only a photo of Freetown in the spare room.'

'Why Freetown?'

'Wordsworth came from there.'

'Who's Wordsworth?'

'The black valet,' Sergeant Sparrow said. 'The one who took off to France when we found the pot.'

They trailed from room to room and I followed them. I thought that Woodrow was less thorough in his search than Colonel Hakim. I had the impression that he expected nothing and was only anxious to make a formal report to Interpol that every effort had been made. Every now and then he tossed me a question without looking round. 'Has your aunt ever mentioned this fellow Visconti?'

'Oh yes, many times.'

'Is he alive, would you say?'

'I don't know.'

'Any idea if they are still in contact?'

'I wouldn't think so.'

'The old viper would be over eighty by now,' Sergeant Sparrow said. 'Nearer ninety, I'd guess.'

'It seems a bit late to be chasing him even if he *is* alive,' I said. We had left my aunt's room and entered Wordsworth's.

'That's one of the troubles of Interpol,' Sergeant Sparrow said. 'Too many files. It's not real police work they do. Not one of them has ever been on the beat. It's a Civil Service. Like Somerset House.'

'They do their duty, Sparrow,' Woodrow said. He took down the photo of Freetown harbour and turned it over. Then he hung it up again. 'It's a good-looking frame,' he said. 'Cost more than the photograph.'

'Italian too from the look of it,' I said, 'like the glass.'

'Perhaps given her by the man Visconti?' Sergeant Sparrow asked.

'There's no indication on the back,' the inspector said. 'I had hoped for an inscription. Interpol haven't even a specimen of his signature – leave alone finger-prints.' He consulted a piece of paper.

'Have you ever heard your aunt mention any of these names – Tiberio Titi?'

'No.'

'Stradano? Passerati? Cossa?'

'She's never spoken to me very much about her Italian friends.'

'These weren't friends,' Inspector Woodrow said.

'Leonardo da Vinci?'

'No.'

He began to go through the rooms all over again, but I could tell that it was only for form's sake. At the door he gave me a telephone number. 'If you hear from your aunt,' he said, 'if you ever do, please ring us at once.'

'I promise nothing.'

'We only want to ask her a few questions,' Sergeant Sparrow said. 'There's no charge against her.'

'I'm glad to hear it.'

'It is even possible,' Inspector Woodrow said, 'that she might be in serious personal danger. From her unfortunate associations.'

'Particularly from that viper Visconti,' Sergeant Sparrow chimed in.

'Why do you keep calling him a viper?'

Sergeant Sparrow said, 'It's the only description Interpol has given us. They haven't so much as a passport photo. But he was once described as a viper by the Chief of Police in Rome in 1945. All their war records were destroyed, the chief's dead, and we don't know now whether viper was a physical description or what you might call a moral judgement.'

'At least,' the inspector said, 'we now have a postcard from Panama.'

'It's something for the files,' Detective-Sergeant Sparrow explained to me.

When I double-locked the door and followed them, I was left with the sad impression that my aunt might be dead and the most interesting part of my life might be over. I had waited a long while for it to arrive, and it had not lasted very long.

PART TWO

Chapter 1

WHILE the ship was tugged out into the yellow tidal rush and the untidy skyscrapers and the castellated customs house jerked away, as though they rather than the ship were at the end of the rope, I thought of that distant day's depression and of how wrong my fears had proved. It was eight on a July morning and the sea-birds wailed like the cats in Latimer Road and the clouds were heavy with coming rain. There was one break of sunlight over La Plata which gave the dull river a single silver streak, but the brightest spot in the sombre scape of water and shore was the flames from gas pipes flapping against the black sky. There were four days ahead of me, up the Plata, the Paraná and the Paraguay, before I joined my aunt, and I left the Argentine winter for my over-heated cabin and began to hang up my clothes and arrange my books and papers into a semblance of home.

More than half a year passed after my encounter with the detectives before I received any news of my aunt. I had become convinced of her death by that time, and once in a dream I was badly frightened by a creature crawling across the floor towards me with broken legs which swung like a snake's tail. It was going to pull me down within reach of its teeth, and I was paralysed with terror like a bird before a snake. When I awoke I remembered Mr Visconti, though I believe it is a cobra and not a viper which is supposed to paralyse birds.

During that empty time I received one more letter from Miss Keene. She wrote in her own hand, for a clumsy servant had broken the keyboard of her typewriter. 'I was just going to write,' she said, 'how stupid and clumsy these blacks are, and then I remembered how you and my father had discussed racialism one night at dinner and I felt as though I were betraying our old house in Southwood and the companionship of those days. Sometimes I fear that I am going to be quite assimilated. In Koffiefontein the Prime Minister no longer seems the monster we thought him at home: indeed he's criticized here sometimes as an old-fashioned liberal. I find myself when I meet a tourist from England explaining apartheid so convincingly. I don't want to be assimilated, and yet if I am to make my life here . . .' The broken sentence sounded like an appeal which she was too shy to make clear. There followed the gossip of the farm: a dinner party to neighbours who lived more than a hundred miles away, and then one paragraph which I found a little disturbing: 'I have met a Mr Hughes, a land surveyor, and he wants to marry me (please don't laugh at me). He is a kind man in his late fifties, a widower with a teenage daughter whom I like well enough. I don't know what to do. It would be the final assimilation, wouldn't it? I've always had a silly dream of one day coming back to Southwood and finding the old house empty (how I miss that dark rhododendron walk) and beginning my life all over again. I am afraid of talking to anyone here about Mr Hughes – they would all be too encouraging. I wish you were not so far away, for I know you would counsel me wisely.'

Was I wrong to read an appeal in the last sentence, a desperate appeal in spite of its calm wording, an appeal for some decisive telegram 'come back to Southwood and marry me'? Who knows whether I might not have sent one in my loneliness if a letter had not arrived which drove poor Miss Keene right out of my mind?

It was from my aunt, written on stiff aristocratic note-paper bearing simply a scarlet rose and the name Lancaster with no address, like the title of a noble family. Only when I read a little way into the letter did I realize that Lancaster was the name of an hotel. My aunt made no appeal; she simply issued a command, and there was no explanation of her long silence. 'I have decided,' she wrote, 'not to return to Europe and I am giving up my apartment over the Crown and Anchor at the end of the next quarter. I would be glad if you would pack what clothes there may be there and dispose of all the furniture. On second thoughts however keep the photograph of Freetown harbour for me as a memento of dear Wordsworth and bring it with you.' (She had not even told me where to come at that point of the letter or asked me if it were possible.) 'Preserve it in its frame which has great sentimental value because it was given me by Mr V. I enclose a cheque on my account at the Crédit Suisse, Berne, which will be sufficient for a first-class ticket to Buenos Aires. Come as soon as you can, for I get no younger. I do not suffer from gout like an old friend whom I met the other day on a packet boat, but I feel nonetheless a certain stiffness in the joints.

I want very much to have with me a member of my family whom I can trust in this rather bizarre country, not the less bizarre for having a shop called Harrods round the corner from the hotel, though it is less well stocked, I fear, than in the Brompton Road.'

I telegraphed to Miss Keene, 'Joining my aunt in Buenos Aires shortly. Will write,' and set about selling the furniture. The Venetian glass, I am afraid, went for a song. When all was sold at Harrods' auction rooms (I had some dispute with the landlord of the Crown and Anchor over the sofa on the landing) I received enough for my return ticket and fifty pounds in travellers' cheques, so I did not cash my aunt's draft on the Swiss bank and I paid the little that was over into my own account, for I thought it better for her to have no assets in England if she planned not to return.

But as for joining my aunt in Buenos Aires, my forecast had been too optimistic. There was no one to meet me at the airport, and when I arrived at the Lancaster Hotel I found only my room reserved and a letter. 'I am sorry not to be here to greet you,' she wrote, 'but I have had to move on urgently to Paraguay where an old friend of mine is in some distress. I have left you a ticket for the river-boat. For reasons too complicated to explain now I do not wish you to take a plane to Asunción. I cannot give you an address, but I will see that you are met.'

It was a highly unsatisfactory arrangement, but what could I do? I hadn't sufficient funds to stay in Buenos Aires until I heard from her again, and I felt it impossible to return to England, when I had travelled so far on her money, but I took the precaution of changing her single ticket to Asunción into a return.

I propped the photograph of Freetown harbour in its expensive frame at the back of my dressing-table and supported it with books on either side. I had brought with me among more ephemeral literature Palgrave's *Golden Treasury*, the collected poems of Tennyson and Browning, and at the last minute I had added *Rob Roy*, perhaps because it contained the only photograph I possessed of my aunt. When I opened the book now the pages naturally divided at the photograph, and I found myself thinking not for the first time that the happy smile, the young breasts, the curve of her body in the old-fashioned bathing costume were like the suggestion of a budding maternity. The memory of Visconti's son as he took her in his arms on Milan platform hurt me a little, and I looked out of my porthole, to escape my thoughts, into the winter day, and saw a tall lean sad grey man gazing back at me. My window gave on to the bows and he turned quickly away to watch the ship's wake, embarrassed at having been noticed. I finished my unpacking and went down to the bar.

There was the restlessness of departure about the ship. Lunch, as I learnt, was to be served at the curious hour of eleven-thirty, but until that time the passengers could no more settle than can the passengers on a Channel crossing. They came up and down the stairs, they looked at the bar and inspected the bottles and went away again without ordering a drink. They streamed into the dining-room and out again, they sat down for a moment at a table in the lounge, then rose to look through a porthole at the monotonous river scene which was to be with us for the next four days. I was the only one to take a drink. There was no sherry, so I took a gin and tonic, but the gin was Argentinian, though the name was English, and had a foreign flavour. The low wooded shore of what I took to be Uruguay unrolled in the misty rain which now began to clear the decks. The water of the river was the colour of coffee with too much milk.

An old man who must have been well into his eighties reached a decision and sat down beside me. He asked me a question in Spanish which I couldn't answer. '*No hablo Español, señor,*' I said, but this scrap of Spanish which I had learnt from a phrase-book he took as an encouragement and at once began to deliver a small lecture, removing from his pocket a large magnifying glass and laying it down between us. I tried to escape by paying my bill, but he grabbed it from my hand and stuck it under his own glass, at the same time ordering the barman to refill mine. I have never been in the habit of taking two drinks before lunch, and I definitely did not like the taste of gin, but for lack of Spanish I had to submit.

He was making some demand on me, but I could not guess what. The words *el favor* were repeated several times, and when he saw I didn't understand, he held out his own hand as a demonstration and began to examine it through the magnifying glass. A voice said, 'Can I be of any help?' and turning I saw the sad lean man who had watched me through my porthole.

I said, 'I don't understand what this gentleman wants.'

'His hobby is reading hands. He says he's never had the opportunity to read an American's.'

'Tell him I'm English.'

'He says the same applies. I don't think he sees much difference. We are both Anglo-Saxon.'

There was nothing I could do but hold out my hand. The old man examined it with extreme care through the magnifying glass. 'He asks me to translate, but maybe you'd rather I didn't. It's kind of personal, a fortune.'

'I don't mind,' I said, and I thought of Hatty and her tea-leaves and how she had foreseen my travels in her best Lapsang Souchong.

'He says you have come from a long way off.'

'That's a bit obvious, isn't it?'

'But your travels are nearly over.'

'That can hardly be true. I have to go back home.'

'He sees a reunion of someone very close to you. Your wife perhaps.'

'I have no wife.'

'He says it could be your mother.'

'She's dead. At least . . .'

'You have had a great deal of money in your care. But no longer.'

'At any rate he's scored there. I was in a bank.'

'He sees a death – but it's far away from your heart-line and your life-line. It's not an important death. Perhaps a stranger's.'

'Do you believe in this nonsense?' I asked the American.

'No, I guess not, but I try to keep an open mind. My name's O'Toole. James O'Toole.'

'Mine's Pulling – Henry,' I said. In the background the old man continued his report in Spanish. He seemed not to care whether it was translated or not. He had pulled out a notebook and was writing things down.

'You a Londoner?'

'Yes.'

'I come from Philadelphia. He wants me to tell you that yours is the nine hundred and seventy-second hand he's studied. Sorry, nine hundred and seventy-fifth.' The old man closed his notebook with an air of satisfaction. Then he shook hands with me and thanked me, paid for the drinks, bowed and departed. The magnifying glass bulged in his pocket like a gun.

'Mind if I join you?' the American asked. He wore an English tweed coat and a pair of old grey flannel trousers: thin and melancholy, he looked as English as I did; there were small lines bitten by care around the eyes and mouth, and like a man who has lost his way he had a habit of looking this way and that with anxiety. He had nothing in common with the Americans whom I had met in England, noisy and self-confident, with the young unlined faces of children romping and shouting to one another across the nursery floor.

He said, 'You going to Asunción too?'

'Yes.'

'There's nowhere else on this trip worth a visit. Corrientes isn't too bad – if you don't spend a night. Formosa – that's a dump. Only smugglers get off there, though they do talk of the fishing. I guess you're not a smuggler?'

'No. You seem to know these parts well.'

'Too well,' he said. 'You on vacation?'

'I suppose so. Yes.'

'Going to see the Iguazú Falls? Lots of people go there. If you do, better stay on the Brazilian side. Only good hotel.'

'Are they worth a visit?'

'Maybe. If you like that kind of thing. Just a lot of water if you ask me.'

The barman obviously knew the American well, for he had made him a dry Martini without a word said, and he drank it now morosely and without pleasure. 'It's not like Gordon's,' he said. He took a slow look at me, almost as if he were memorizing my features. 'I took you for a businessman, Henry,' he said. 'Vacationing all by yourself? Not much fun. Strange country. And you don't speak the language – not that Spanish is any good outside the city. In the country they all speak Guaraní.'

'Do you?'

'A smattering.' I noticed he asked questions more than he answered them, and when he gave me information it was the kind of information which I could have obtained from any guide-book. 'Picturesque ruins,' he said, 'old Jesuit settlements. They appeal to you, Henry?'

I felt he wouldn't be satisfied until I had told him more. What was the harm? I wasn't carrying a gold brick or a suitcase stuffed with notes. As he said, I was no smuggler. 'I am visiting an old relation of mine,' I said and added, 'James.' I could see he wanted that too.

'My friends call me Tooley,' he said automatically, and it was quite a while before in my mind the coin fell.

'Are you in business here?'

'Not exactly,' he said. 'I do research work. Social research. You know the sort of thing, Henry. Cost of living. Malnutrition. Degree of illiteracy. Have a drink.'

'Two is all I can take, Tooley,' I said, and it was only at the repetition of the name that I remembered, remembered Tooley. He pushed his own glass forward for another.

'Do you find things easy in Paraguay? I've read in the papers you Americans have a lot of trouble in South America.'

'Not in Paraguay,' he said. 'We and the General are like that.' He raised his thumb and forefinger and then transferred them to his refilled glass.

'He's quite a tough dictator, so they tell me.'

'It's what the country needs, Henry. A strong hand. Don't mistake me though. I keep out of politics. Simple research. That's my line.'

'Have you published anything?'

'Oh,' he replied vaguely, 'reports. Technical. They wouldn't interest you, Henry.'

It was inevitable that when the bell rang we should go into lunch together. We shared the table with two other men. One was a grey-faced man in a blue city suit who was on a diet (the steward, who knew him well, brought him a special dish of boiled vegetables which he looked at carefully before eating, twitching the end of his nose and his upper lip like a rabbit). The other was a fat old priest with rogue eyes who looked rather like Winston Churchill. I was amused to watch O'Toole set about the two of them. Before we had finished our bad liver paté, he had found that the priest had a parish in a village near Corrientes, on the Argentine side of the border, and before we had eaten our equally bad pasta he had broken a little way into the taciturnity of the man with the nose like a rabbit's. He was apparently a businessman returning to Formosa. When he mentioned Formosa O'Toole looked at me and gave a little nod of confirmation: he had placed him.

'Now I'd guess you to be a pharmacist?' he said, leading him on.

The man had little English, but he understood that. He looked at O'Toole and twitched his nose. I thought he was not going to reply, but out the phrase came with all its international ambiguity, 'Import-export.'

The priest for some reason began to speak of flying saucers. They swarmed over Argentina, so it seemed - perhaps if we had clear nights we would observe one from the boat.

'You really believe in them?' I asked, and the old priest in his excitement abandoned his little English altogether.

'He says,' O'Toole explained, 'that you must have seen yesterday's *Nación*. Twelve cars were stopped coming from Mar del Plata to Buenos Aires on Monday night. When a flying saucer passes overhead a car-engine stops. The reverend father believes they have a divine origin.' He translated almost as rapidly as the other talked. 'Recently a couple who were driving to Mar del Plata for the weekend were surrounded by a cloud. The car stopped and when the cloud dispersed they found they were in Mexico near Acapulco.'

'And he believed even that?'

'Sure. They all do. Once a week on the radio at Buenos Aires you can hear a programme all about flying saucers. Who's seen them that week, and where. Our friend here says it may be the explanation of the flying house of Loretto. It was just picked up in Palestine, like those people on the road to Mar del Plata, and dumped down in Italy.'

They served us a tough steak and afterwards oranges. The priest lapsed into silence and ate with a slight frown. Perhaps he felt in the presence of unbelievers. The businessman pushed back his plate of boiled vegetables and excused himself. I asked my neighbour what I had been longing to ask all through the meal: 'Are you married, Tooley?'

'Yeah. Sort of.'

'You've got a daughter?'

'Sure. Why? She's studying in London.'

'She's in Katmandu,' I said.

'Katmandu! Why, that's Nepal.'

The lines of anxiety deepened. 'That's a hell of a thing to tell me,' he said. 'How do you know?' I told him about the Orient Express, but I left out any references to the young man. I said she was with a group of students, which was true when I last saw her. He said, 'What can I do, Henry? I've got my work. I can't go chasing round the world. Lucinda doesn't know the worry she gives.'

'Lucinda?'

'Her mother chose the name,' he said with bitterness.

'She calls herself Tooley now like you.'

'She does? That's new.'

'She seemed to have a great admiration for you.'

'I let her go to England,' he said. 'I thought she'd be safe there. But Katmandu!' He pushed away the orange which he had so carefully sliced. 'Where's she living? I doubt if there's a good hotel in the place. If there's a Hilton at least you know where you are. What shall I do, Henry?'

'She'll be all right,' I said without conviction.

'I could send a cable to the embassy – I suppose there's an embassy.' He got up abruptly and said, 'I've got to take a leak.'

I followed him out of the dining-room and down a corridor to the lavatory. There we stood side by side in silence. I noticed his lips moving – perhaps, I thought, he was having an imaginary dialogue with his daughter. We left the lavatory together and without a word he sat down on a bench on the port side of the deck. It was no longer raining, but it was grey and cold. There was nothing to see but some small trees growing at the edge of the dirty river, an occasional hut, and through the trees an expanse of brown scrub stretching to the horizon without a hill in sight.

'Argentina?' I asked to break the silence.

'It's all Argentina,' he said, 'till we reach the Paraguay river our last day.' He took out a pocket-book and made some notes. They seemed to be figures. When he had finished he said, 'Excuse me. It's a record I keep.

'Kind of a study I'm making.'

'Your daughter told me you were in the CIA.'

He turned on me his sad and anxious eyes. 'She's a romantic,' he said. 'She imagines things.'

'Is the CIA romantic?'

'A kid thinks so. I guess she saw some report of mine marked Secret. Anything's Secret that goes to a government department. Even malnutrition in Asunción.'

I wasn't sure which of them I believed.

He asked me with an air of helplessness, 'What would you do, Henry?'

I said, 'If you were really in the CIA you could probably find out how she was from one of your men there. You must have a man in Katmandu.'

'If I were really in the CIA,' he said, 'I wouldn't want to get them mixed up in my private affairs. Have you any children Henry?'

'No.'

'You are a lucky man. People talk about the age of reason. There's no such thing. When you have a child you are condemned to be a father for life. They go away from you. You can't go away from them.'

'How would I know?'

He brooded awhile, staring out over the scrub which never changed. The boat moved slowly against the strong flow to the sea. He said. 'My dad was all against the divorce – for the sake of the child. But there are limits to what a man can take – she began to bring her boy-friends home. She was corrupting Lucinda.'

'She didn't succeed,' I said.

Chapter 2

NEXT morning I missed O'Toole: he didn't appear at breakfast, and I looked for him in vain upon the deck. There was a heavy mist over the river which the sun took a long time to disperse. I felt a little lonely without my only contact. Everyone else was settling into a shipboard relation: even a few flirtations had begun. Two old men paced the deck fiercely, showing off their physical fitness. There was something obscene to me about their rapid regular walk – they seemed to be indicating to all the women they passed that they were still in full possession of their powers. They wore slit jackets in imitation of the English – they had probably bought them at Harrods – and they reminded me of Major Charge.

We had pulled up at a town called Rosario during the night (the voices, the shouts, the noise of chains had entered my dreams and made them dreams of violence some while before I woke), and now the river, when the mist rose, had changed its character. The water was sprinkled with islands, and there were cliffs and sand bars and strange birds piping and whispering beside us. I experienced far more the sensation of travel than when I passed all the crowded frontiers in the Orient Express. The river was low, and a rumour spread that we might not be able to get beyond Corrientes because the expected rains of winter had not come. A sailor on the bridge was continually heaving the lead. We were within half a metre, the priest told me, of the ship's draught, and he moved on to spread despondency further.

I began for the first time seriously to read *Rob Roy*, but the moving scenery was a distraction. I would begin a page while the shore was half a mile away, and when I lifted my eyes after a few paragraphs, it had approached within a stone's throw – or was it an island? At the beginning of the next page I looked again, and the water was now nearly a mile wide. A Czech sat down beside me. He spoke English and I was content to close *Rob Roy* and listen to him. He was a man who having once known prison enjoyed freedom to the full. His mother had died under the Nazis, his father under the Communists, he had escaped to Austria and married an Austrian girl. His training had been scientific, and when he decided to settle in the Argentine he had borrowed the money to start a plastics factory. He said, 'I looked around first in Brazil and Uruguay and Venezuela. One thing I noticed. Everywhere but in the Argentine they used straw for cold drinks. Not in the Argentine. I thought I'd make my fortune. I made two million plastic straws and I couldn't sell a hundred. You want a straw? You can have two million for free. There they are stacked in my factory today. The Argentines are so conservative they won't drink through a straw. I was very nearly bankrupt, I can tell you,' he said happily.

'So what do you do now?'

He gave me a cheerful grin. He seemed one of the happiest men I had ever met. He had shed his past fears and failures and sorrows more completely than most of us can do. He said, 'I manufacture plastic material and let other fools risk their money on what they make with it.'

The man with the rabbit nose went twitching by, grey as the grey morning. 'He gets off at Formosa,' I said.

'Ah, a smuggler,' the Czech said and laughed and went on his way.

I began to read *Rob Roy* again while the leadsman called the sounding. 'You must remember my father well; for as your own was a member of the mercantile house, you knew him from infancy. Yet you hardly saw him in his best days, before age and infirmity had quenched his ardent spirit of enterprise and speculation.' I thought of my father lying in his bath in his clothes, just as later he lay in his Boulogne coffin, and giving me his impossible instructions, and I wondered why I felt an affection for him, while I felt none for my faultless mother who had brought me up with rigid care and found me my first situation in a bank. I had never built the plinth among the dahlias and before I left home I had thrown away the empty urn. Suddenly a memory came back to me of an angry voice. I had woken up, as I sometimes did, afraid that the house was on fire and that I had been abandoned. I had climbed out of bed and sat down at the top of the stairs, reassured by the voice below. It didn't matter how angry it was: it was there: I was not alone and there was no smell of burning. 'Go away,' the voice said, 'if you want to, but I'll keep the child.'

A low reasonable voice, which I recognized as my father's, said, 'I *am* his father,' and the woman I knew as my mother slammed back like a closing door, 'And who's to say that I'm not his mother?'

'Good morning,' O'Toole said, sitting down beside me. 'Did you sleep well?'

'Yes. And you?'

He shook his head. 'I kept on thinking of Lucinda,' he said. He took out his notebook and again began to write down his mysterious columns of numerals.

'Research?' I asked.

'Oh,' he said, 'this is not official.'

'Making a bet on the ship's run?'

'No, no. I'm not a betting man.' He gave me one of his habitual looks of melancholy and anxiety. 'I've never told anyone about this, Henry,' he said. 'It would seem kind of funny to most people, I guess. The fact is I count while I'm pissing and then I write down how long I've taken and what time it is. Do you realize we spend more than one whole day a year pissing?'

'Good heavens,' I said.

'I can prove it, Henry. Look here.' He opened his note-book and showed me a page. His writing went something like this:

July 28		
7.15	0·17	
10.45	0·37	
12.30	0·50	
13.15	0·32	
13.40	0·50	
14.05	0·20	
15.45	0·37	
18.40	0·28	
10.30	?	Forgot to time
	4 m. 31 sec	

He said, 'You've only got to multiply by seven. That makes half an hour a week. Twenty-six hours a year. Of course shipboard life isn't quite average. There's more drinking between meals. And beer keeps on repeating. Look at this time here – 1 m. 55 sec. That's more than the average, but then I've noted down two gins. There's a lot of variations too I haven't accounted for, and from now on I'm going to make a note of the temperature too. Here's July 25 – 6 m. 9 sec n.c. – that stands for not complete. I went out to dinner in BA and left my notebook at home. And here's July 27 – only 3 minutes 12 seconds in all, but, if you remember, there was a very cold north wind on July 25 and I went out to dinner without an overcoat.'

'Are you drawing any conclusions?' I asked.

'That's not my job,' he said. 'I'm no expert. I just report the facts and any data – like the gins and the weather – that seem to have a bearing. It's for others to draw the conclusions.'

'Who are the others?'

'Well, I thought when I had completed six months' research I'd get in touch with a urinary specialist. You don't know what he mightn't be able to read into these figures. Those guys deal all the time with the sick. It's important to them to know what happens in the case of an average fellow.'

'And you are the average fellow?'

'Yes. I'm hundred per cent healthy, Henry. I have to be in my job. They give me the works every so often.'

'The CIA!' I asked.

'You're kidding, Henry. You can't believe that crazy girl.'

He fell into a sad silence as he thought of her, leaning forward with his chin in his hand. An island with the appearance of a gigantic alligator floated downstream with its snout extending along the water. Pale green fishing boats drifted downstream faster than our engines could drive us against the current – they passed rapidly like little racing cars. Each fisherman was surrounded by floating blocks of wood to which his lines were attached. Rivers branched off into the grey misty interior, wider than the Thames at Westminster but going nowhere at all.

He asked, 'And she really called herself Tooley?'

'Yes, Tooley.'

'I guess she must think of me sometimes?' he said with a sort of questioning hope.

Chapter 3

IT was two days later that we came to Formosa on a day which was as humid as all the others had been. The heat broke on the cheek like little bubbles of water. We had turned off the great Paraná river the night before near Corrientes, and now we were on the Paraguay. Fifty yards across the water from the Argentinian Formosa the other country lay, sodden and empty. The import-export man went ashore in his dark city suit carrying a new suitcase. He went with rapid steps, looking at his watch like the rabbit in *Alice in Wonderland*. It certainly seemed an ideal town for smugglers with only a river to cross. In Paraguay I could see only a crumbling hut, a pig and a small girl.

I was tired of walking the deck, so I went ashore too. It was a Sunday and quite a crowd had collected to see the boat come in. There was a pervading smell of orange petals, but it was the only sweet thing about Formosa. One long avenue was lined with oranges and trees bearing rose-coloured flowers, which I learnt later to be *lapachos*. The side-streets petered out a few yards away into a niggardly wild nature of mud and scrub. Everything to do with government business, justice or amusement lay in the one avenue: a tourist hotel of grey cement on the water's edge had been half-built, for what tourists? little shops selling Coca-Cola: a cinema which advertised an Italian Western: two hairdressers: a garage with one wrecked car: a *cantina*. The only house of more than one storey was the hotel, and the only old and beautiful building in the long avenue proved, as I came closer to it, to be the prison. There were fountains all down the avenue but they didn't play.

The avenue must lead me somewhere, I thought, but I was wrong. I passed the bust of a bearded man called Urquiza who, judging from the carved inscription, must have had something to do with Liberation – from what? – and ahead of me I saw rise up above the orange trees and the *lapachos* a marble man upon a marble horse who was certainly General San Martín – Buenos Aires had made me familiar with his features and I had seen him upon the sea-front at Boulogne too. The statue closed the avenue as the Arc de Triomphe closes the Champs Élysées; I expected some further avenue beyond, but when I reached the statue I found the hero sat on his horse in a waste of mud at the furthest limit of the town. No strollers came so far, and the road went no further. Only a starving dog, like a skeleton from the Natural History Museum, picked his way timorously across the dirt and the rain pools towards me and San Martín. I began to walk back.

If I describe this ignoble little town in such detail, it is because it was the scene of a long dialogue I held with myself which was only interrupted by a surprising encounter. I had begun, as I passed the first hairdresser, to think of Miss Keene and her letter of shy appeal which surely deserved a better response than my brief telegram, and then in this humid place, where the only serious business or entertainment was certainly crime, and even the national bank had to be defended on a Sunday afternoon by a guard with an automatic rifle, I thought of my home in Southwood, of my garden, of Major Charge trumpeting across the fence, and of the sweet sound of the bells from

Church Road. But I remembered Southwood now with a kind of friendly tolerance – as the place which Miss Keene should never have left, the place where Miss Keene was happy, the place where I myself no longer belonged. It was as though I had escaped from an open prison, had been snatched away, provided with a rope ladder and a waiting car, into my aunt's world, the world of the unexpected character and the unforeseen event. There the rabbit-faced smuggler was at home, the Czech with his two million plastic straws, and poor O'Toole busy making a record of his urine.

I passed the end of a street called Rua Dean Furnes which petered away like all the others into no-man's-land, and I stayed a moment outside the governor's house, which was painted with a pink wash. On the verandah were two unoccupied *chaises-longues* and the windows were wide open on an empty room with a portrait of a military man, the President I suppose, and a row of empty chairs lined up against the wall like a firing squad. The sentry made a small movement with his automatic rifle and I moved on towards the national bank where another sentry made the same warning movement when I paused.

That morning in my bunk I had read Wordsworth's great Ode in Palgrave's *Golden Treasury*. Palgrave like Scott carried signs of my father's reading in the form of dog-eared pages and knowing so little about him I had followed every clue and so learned to enjoy what he had enjoyed. Thus when I first entered the bank as junior clerk I had thought of it in Wordsworth's terms as a 'prison-house' – what was it my father had found a prison, so that he double-marked the passage? Perhaps our home, and my stepmother and I had been the warders.

One's life is more formed, I sometimes think, by books than by human beings: it is out of books one learns about love and pain at second hand. Even if we have the happy chance to fall in love, it is because we have been conditioned by what we have read, and if I had never known love at all, perhaps it was because my father's library had not contained the right books. (I don't think there was much passionate love in Marion Crawford, and only a shadow of it in Walter Scott.)

I can remember very little of the vision preceding the prison-house: it must have faded very early 'into the light of common day', but it seemed to me, as I put Palgrave down beside my bunk and thought of my aunt, that she for one had never allowed the vision to fade. Perhaps a sense of morality is the sad compensation we learn to enjoy, like a remission for good conduct. In the vision there is no morality. I had been born as a result of what my stepmother would have called an immoral act, an act of darkness. I had begun in immoral freedom. Why then should I have found myself in a prison-house? My real mother had certainly not been imprisoned anywhere.

It's too late now, I said to Miss Keene, signalling to me desperately from Koffiefontein, I'm no longer there, where you think I am. Perhaps we might have comforted ourselves once and been content in our prison cell, but I'm not the same man you regarded with a touch of tenderness over the tatting. I have escaped. I don't resemble whatever identikit portrait you have of me. I walked back towards the landing stage, and looking behind me I saw the canine skeleton on my tracks. I suppose to that dog any stranger represented hope.

'Hi, man,' a voice called. 'You in number one hurry?' and Wordsworth was suddenly there a few yards away. He had risen from a bench beside the bust of the liberator Urquiza and advanced towards me with both hands out and his face slashed open with the wide wound of his grin. 'Man, you not forget old Wordsworth?' he asked, wringing both my hands, and laughing so loudly aad deeply that he sprayed my face with his happiness.

'Why, Wordsworth,' I said with equal pleasure, 'what on earth are you doing here?'

'My lil bebi gel,' he said, 'she tell me go off Formosa and wait for Mr Pullen come.'

I noticed that he was every bit as smartly dressed now as the rabbit-nosed importer and he too carried a very new suitcase.

'How is my aunt, Wordsworth?'

'She pretty OK,' he said, but there was a look of distress in his eyes and he added, 'She dance one hell too much. Ar tell her she no bebi gel no more. Ef she no go stop . . . Man, she got me real worried.'

'Are you coming on the boat with me?'

'Ar sure am, Mr Pullen. You lef everyting to old Wordsworth. Ar know the customs fellows in Asunción. Some good guys. Some bad like hell. You lef me talk. We don wan no humbug.'

'I'm not *smuggling* anything, Wordsworth.' The noise of the ship's siren summoned us, wailing up from the river.

'Man, you lef everyting to old Wordsworth. Ar just gone tak a look at that boat and ar see a real bad guy there. We gotta be careful.'

'Careful of what, Wordsworth?'

'You in good hands, Mr Pullen. You lef old Wordsworth be now.'

He suddenly took my fingers and pressed them. 'You got that picture, Mr Pullen?'

'You mean of Freetown harbour? Yes, I've got that.'

He gave a sigh of satisfaction. 'Ar lak you, Mr Pullen. You allays straight with old Wordsworth. Now you go for boat.' I was just leaving him when he added. 'You got CTC for Wordsworth?' and I gave him what coins I had in my pocket. Whatever trouble he might have caused me in that dead old world of mine, I was overjoyed to see him now.

They were carrying the last cargo on to the ship through the black iron doors open in the side. I made my way through the steerage quarters where women with Indian faces sat around suckling their children and climbed the rusting stairs to the first-class. I never noticed Wordsworth come on board, and at dinner he was nowhere to be seen. I supposed that he was travelling in the steerage and saving for other purposes the difference in the fare, for I was quite certain that my aunt would have given him a first-class ticket.

After dinner O'Toole suggested a drink in his cabin. 'I've got some good bourbon,' he said, and though I have never been a spirit-drinker, preferring a glass of sherry before a meal or a glass of port after it, I accepted his invitation gladly, for it was our last night together on board. Again the spirit of restlessness had taken over all the passengers in the ship, and they seemed touched with a kind of mania. In the saloon an amateur band had begun to play, and a sailor with hairy legs and arms, dressed inadequately as a woman, had whirled in a dance between the tables, demanding a partner. Now in the captain's cabin, which was close to O'Toole's, someone was playing the guitar and a woman squealed. It wasn't what you expected to hear from a captain's quarters.

'No one will sleep tonight,' O'Toole remarked, pouring out the bourbon.

'If you don't mind,' I said, 'a lot more soda.'

'We've made it. I thought we were going to be stuck fast at Corrientes. The rain is damn late this year,' and as though to soften his rebuke of the weather there came a long peal of thunder which almost drowned the music of the guitar.

'What did you think of Formosa?' O'Toole asked.

'There wasn't much to see. Except the prison. A fine colonial building.'

'Not so good inside,' O'Toole said. A splash of lightning was flung over the wall and made the cabin lights flicker. 'Met a friend, didn't you?'

'A friend?'

'I saw you talking to a coloured guy.'

What was it that made me cautious, for I liked O'Toole? I said, 'Oh, he wanted money. I didn't see you on shore.'

'I was up on the bridge,' O'Toole said, 'looking through the captain's glasses.' He changed course abruptly. 'I can't get over you knowing my daughter, Henry. You can't imagine how I miss that girl. You never told me how she looked.'

'She looked fine. She's a very pretty girl.'

'Yeah,' he said, 'so was her mother. If I ever married again I'd marry a plain girl.' He brooded a long time over the bourbon, and I looked around his cabin. He had made no attempt, as I had made the first day, to make it a temporary home. His suitcases lay on the floor filled with clothes; he had not bothered to hang them. A razor beside the wash-basin and a Bantam book beside his bed seemed to be the extent of his unpacking. Suddenly the rain hit the deck outside like a cloud-burst.

'I guess winter's here all right,' he said.

'Winter in July.'

'I've got used to it,' he said. 'I haven't seen the snow for six years.'

'You've been out here for six years?'

'No, but I was in Thailand before this.'

'Doing research?'

'Yeah. Sort of . . .' If he was usually as tongue-tied as this it must have taken him a long time to unearth every fact he required.

'How are the urine statistics?'

'More than four minutes thirty seconds today,' he said. He added glumly. 'And I haven't reached the end,' lifting the bourbon. When the next peal of thunder had trembled out he went on, obviously straining after any subject to fill the pause, 'So you didn't like Formosa?'

'No. Of course it may be all right for fishing,' I said.

'Fishing!' he exclaimed with scorn. 'Smuggling is what you mean.'

'I keep on hearing all the time about smuggling. Smuggling what?'

'It's the national industry of Paraguay,' he said. 'It brings in nearly as much as the maté and a lot more than hiding war criminals with Swiss bank accounts. And a darn sight more than my research.'

'What have they got to smuggle?'

'Scotch whisky and American cigarettes. You get yourself an agent in Panama who buys wholesale and he flies the stuff down to Asunción. They are marked "goods in transit", see. You pay only a small duty at the international airport and you transfer the crates to a private plane. You'd be surprised to see how many private Dakotas there are now in Asunción. Then your pilot takes off to Argentina just across the river. At some *estancia* a few hundred kilometres from BA you touch down – they nearly all have private landing grounds. Not built for Dakotas perhaps but that's the pilot's risk. You unload into trucks and there you are. You've got your distributors waiting with their tongues hanging out. The government makes them thirsty with duties of a hundred and twenty per cent.'

'And Formosa?'

'Oh, Formosa's for the small guy working himself up on the river traffic. All the goods that arrive from Panama don't go on in the Dakota. What do the police care if some of the crates stay behind? You'll buy Scotch cheaper in the stores at Asunción than you will in London and the street boys will sell you good American cigarettes at cut-rate. All you need's a rowboat and a contact. One day though you'll get tired of that game – perhaps a bullet's come too close – and you'll buy a share in a Dakota and then you're in the big money. You tempted, Henry?'

'I didn't have the right training at the bank,' I said, but I thought of my aunt and her suitcases stuffed with notes and her gold brick – perhaps there was something in my blood to which a career like that might once have appealed. 'You know a lot about it,' I said.

'It's part of my sociological research.'

'Did you never think of researching a bit deeper? The frontier spirit, Tooley.' I teased him only because I liked him. I could never have teased Major Charge or the admiral in that way.

He gave me a long sad look, as though he wanted to answer me quite truthfully. 'You don't save enough money in a job like mine to buy a Dakota. And the risks are big too, Henry, for a foreigner. These guys fall out sometimes and then there's hijacking. Or the police get greedy. It's easy to disappear in Paraguay – not necessarily disappear either. Who's going to make a fuss about an odd body or two? The General keeps the peace – that's what people want after the civil war they had – and a dead man makes no trouble for anyone. They don't have coroners in Paraguay.'

'So you prefer life to the frontier spirit, Tooley.'

'I know I'm not much good for my girl three thousand miles away, Henry, but at least she gets her monthly check. A dead man can't write a check.'

'And I suppose the CIA aren't interested?'

'You shouldn't believe that nonsense, Henry. I told you – Lucinda's romantic. She wants an exciting father, and what's she got? She's saddled with me. So she has to invent things. A report on malnutrition's not romantic.'

'I think you ought to bring her home, Tooley.'

'Where's home?' he said and I looked around the cabin and wondered too. I don't know why I wasn't quite convinced. He was a great deal more reliable than she was.

I left him with his Old Forester and returned to my cabin on the opposite deck. O'Toole was port and I was starboard. I looked out at Paraguay and he looked at Argentina. The guitar was still playing in the captain's cabin and someone was singing in a language I couldn't recognize – perhaps it was Guaraní. I hadn't locked my door, and yet it wouldn't open when I pushed. I had to put my shoulder to it to make it give. Through the crack I saw Wordsworth. He faced the door and he had a knife in his hand. When he saw who it was he held the knife down.

'Come in, boss,' he said in a whisper.

'How can I come in?'

He had wedged the door with a chair. He removed it now and let me in.

'Ar got to be careful, Mr Pullen,' he said.

'Careful of what?'

'Too much bad people on this boat, too much humbug.'

His knife was a boy's knife with three blades and a corkscrew and a tin-opener and something for taking stones out of horses' hoofs – cutlers are conservative and so are schoolboys. Wordsworth closed it and put it in his pocket.

'Well,' I said, 'what do you want, you happy shepherd boy?'

He shook his head. 'Oh, she's a wonder, your auntie. No one ever talk to Wordsworth like that befo. Why, she come right up to me in the street outside the movie palace an she say, clear the day, "Thou child of joy." Ar love your auntie, Mr Pullen. Ar ready to die for her any time she raise a finger an say, "Wordsworth, you go die."'

'Yes, yes,' I said, 'that's fine, but what are you doing barricaded in my cabin?'

'Ar come for the picture,' he said.

'Couldn't you wait till we get ashore?'

'Your auntie say bring that picture safe, Wordsworth, double quick or you no come here no more.'

A suspicion returned to me. Could the frame like the candle be made of gold? Or did the photograph cover some notes of a very high denomination? Neither seemed likely, but neither was impossible with my aunt.

'Ar got friends in customs,' Wordsworth said, 'they no humbug me, but, Mr Pullen, you a stranger here.'

'It's only a photograph of Freetown harbour.'

'Ya'as, Mr Pullen. But your auntie say . . .'

'All right. Take it then. Where are you sleeping?'

Wordsworth jerked his thumb at the floor. 'Ar more comfortable down below there, Mr Pullen. The folks thar they sing and dance an have good time. They don wear no carats an they no don go wash befo meals. Ar don like soap with my chop.'

'Have a cigarette, Wordsworth.'

'If you don mine, Mr Pullen, I smoke this here.'

He pulled a ragged reconstructed cigarette out of a crumpled pocket.

'Still on pot, Wordsworth?'

'Well, it's a sort of medicine, Mr Pullen. Arm not too well these days. Ar got a lot o' worry.'

'Worry about what?'

'Your auntie, Mr Pullen. She allays safe with old Wordsworth. Ar no cost her nothing. But she got a fellah now – he cost her plenty plenty. And he too old for her, Mr Pullen. Your auntie no chicken. She need a young fellah.'

'You aren't exactly young yourself, Wordsworth.'

'Ar no got ma big feet in no tomb, Mr Pullen, lak that one. Ar no trust that fellah. When we come here he plenty sick. He say, "Please Wordsworth, please Wordsworth," and he mak all the sugar in the world melt in his mouth. He live in low-class hotel, but he aint got no money. They go to turn him out an, man, he were plenty scared to go. When your auntie came he cry like a lil bebi. He no man, sure he no man, but he plenty plenty mean. He say sweet things alright alright, but he allays act mean. What wan she leave Wordsworth for a mean man like him? Tell me that, man, tell me that.' He let his great bulk down on my bed and he began to weep. It was like a spring forcing its hard way to the surface, spilling out of the crevices of a rock.

'Wordsworth,' I said, 'are you jealous of Aunt Augusta?'

'Man,' he said, 'she war my bebi gel. Now she gon bust ma heart in bits.'

'Poor Wordsworth.' There was nothing more I could say.

'She wan me quit,' Wordsworth said. 'She wan me for come bring you, and then she wan me quit. She say, "I give you biggest CTC you ever saw, you go back Freetown and find a gel," but I no wan her money, Mr Pullen, I no wan Freetown no more, and I no wan any gel. I love your auntie. I wan for to stay with her like the song say: "Abide with me; fast falls the eventide; the darkness deepens: oh with me abide . . . Tears have not bitterness," but man, these tears are bitter, tha's for sure.'

'Wherever did you learn that hymn, Wordsworth?'

'We allays sang that in St George's cathedral in Freetown. "Fast falls the eventide." Plenty sad songs like that we sang there, an they all mak me think now of my bebi gel. "Here lingrin still we ask for nought but simply worship thee." Man, it's true. But now she wan me to quit, an go right away an never see her no more.'

'Who is this man she's with, Wordsworth?'

'I won spik his name. My tongue turn up if I spik his name. Oh, man, I bin faithful to your auntie long time now.'

It was to distract him from his misery and not to reproach him that I said, 'You remember that girl in Paris?'

'That one who wan do jig-jig?'

'No, no, not that one. The young girl on the train.'

'Oh ya'as. Sure, I member her.'

'You gave her pot,' I said.

'Sure. Why not? Very good medicine. You don think I do anytin bad with her? Why, man, she was the ship that gone by one day. She too young for old Wordsworth.'

'Her father's on the boat now.'

He looked at me with astonishment. 'You don say! '

'He was asking me about you. He saw us on shore.'

'What he look lak?'

'He's as tall as you but very thin. He looks unhappy and worried and he wears a tweed sportscoat.'

'Oh, God Almighty! I know *him*. I seen him plenty in Asunción. You got to be bloody careful of *him*.'

'He says he's doing social research work.'

'What that mean?'

'He investigates things.'

'Oh, man, you're right there. I tell you sometin. Your auntie's fellah – he don like that man around.'

I had meant to distract him, and I had certainly succeeded. He pressed my hand hard when he left me, carrying the picture concealed under his shirt. He said, 'Man, you know what you are to Wordsworth. You help of the helpless, Mr Pullen. O abide with me.'

Chapter 4

WHEN I went up on deck after breakfast we were already approaching Asunción. Red cliffs were honeycombed with caves. Half-ruined huts stood at the very edge of the cliff and naked children with the pot-bellies of malnutrition stared down on us as the boat passed, moving like an overfed man who picks his slow way home after a heavy meal, giving little belches on the siren. Above the huts, like a medieval castle dominating some wretched village of mud and wattle, stood the great white bastions of Shell.

O'Toole came and stood beside me as the immigration officers arrived on board. He asked, 'Can I be of any help? Give you a lift or anything?'

'Thank you very much, but I think I shall be met.'

The steerage passengers were going ashore. He said, 'If you want any help at any time . . . I know most of the ropes. You'll find me at the embassy. They call me a second secretary. It's convenient.'

'You're very kind.'

'You are a friend of Lucinda . . .' he said. 'Katmandu seems the hell of a long way off. Maybe some mail will have come in.'

'Is she a good correspondent?'

'She writes me picture postcards,' he said. He leant forward on the rail. 'Isn't that your friend?' he asked.

'What friend?'

I looked at the steerage queue on the gangway and saw Wordsworth.

'The man who spoke to you onshore.'

I said, 'All coloured men look very much alike to me at that distance.'

'It's not often you see an African here,' he said. 'I guess it's your friend.'

When at last the formalities were over and I stood beside my luggage on the corner of a street named after Benjamin Constant, I looked around awhile in vain for Wordsworth. Families exchanged greetings and drove away in cars. The Czech plastics manufacturer offered me a lift in his taxi. A small boy wanted to clean my shoes and another tried to sell me American cigarettes. A long colonnaded street, which sloped uphill in front of me, was full of liquor shops, and old women sat against the wall with baskets of bread and fruit. In spite of the dirt and fumes of old cars the air was sweet with orange blossom.

Somebody whistled and I turned to see Wordsworth getting out of a taxi. He lifted my two heavy suitcases as though they were empty cardboard boxes. 'Ar look for friend,' he said, 'too plenty humbug here.' I had never before been driven in quite such a decrepit taxi. The lining was torn and the stuffing leaked out of the seat. Wordsworth punched at it to make it more comfortable. Then he made motions to the driver which the man seemed to understand. 'We drive around a bit,' Wordsworth said. 'Ar wan to see if they lef us alone.' He looked out of the window, while the taxi ground and shook. All the other taxis which passed us were smart enough, and sometimes the drivers shouted what I took to be insults to our old man who had a white moustache and a hat without a crown.

'Suppose we're *not* left alone,' I said, 'what do we do?'

'We tak bloody good care,' Wordsworth said vaguely.

'You seem to have chosen the oldest taxi.'

Soldiers were goose-stepping in front of the cathedral, and a very early tank stood on a plinth up on the green sward. The orange trees were everywhere, some in fruit and some in blossom.

'He good friend of mine.'

'You talk Spanish?' I asked.

'No. He don know no Spanish.'

'What does he talk?'

'He talk Indian lingo.'

'How do you make him understand?'

'I give him smokes,' Wordsworth said. 'He lak pot.'

Except for the skyscraper of a new hotel it was a very Victorian town. One soon ceased to notice the cars – they were an anachronism; there were mule carts and sometimes men on horses, there was a little white castellated Baptist church, a college built like a neo-Gothic abbey, and when we reached the residential quarter I saw big stone houses with bosky gardens and pillared porticos above stone steps which reminded me of the oldest part of Southwood, but in Southwood the houses would have been split into flats and the grey stone would have been whitewashed and the roofs would have bristled with television masts. In place of the orange and banana trees, I would have seen neglected rhododendrons and threadbare lawns.

'What is the name of my aunt's friend, Wordsworth?' I asked.

'I don remember,' Wordsworth said. 'I don wanta remember. Ar wanta forget.'

A little crumbling house with corinthian pillars and broken windows was called School of Architecture on a board which had been split by the seasons, but, however tumbledown the houses, the flowers were everywhere. A bush of jasmine blossomed with white and blue flowers on the same bush.

'We stop here,' Wordsworth said and he shook the driver's shoulder.

It was an enormous house with a great untidy lawn which ended in a dark green fuzz of trees, a small wood of banana, orange, lemon, grapefruit, *lapacho*. On the two sides visible to me through the gates wide stone steps led up to separate entrances. The walls were blotched with lichen and were four storeys high.

'It's a millionaire's house,' I said.

'You jus wait,' Wordsworth replied.

The iron gates were rusty and padlocked. Worn pineapples were carved on the gateposts, but the gates, draped with barbed wire, had lost their dignity. A millionaire may once have lived there, I thought, but no longer.

Wordsworth led me round the corner of the street and we approached the house from the back through a little door which he locked behind him and through the grove of sweet-smelling trees and bushes. 'Hi!' he called to the great square block of stone, 'hi!' and got no response. The house in its solidity and its silence reminded me of the great family tombs in the cemetery at Boulogne. This was a journey's end too.

'Your auntie she got a bit deaf,' Wordsworth said, 'she no young no more, no more.' He spoke regretfully, as though he had known her as a girl, and yet she had been over seventy when she picked him up outside the Grenada Palacc. We went up one flight of stone steps and into the hall of the house.

Paved with cracked marble, the big hall was unfurnished. The windows had been shuttered and the only light came from a bare globe in the ceiling. There was no chair, no table, no sofa, no pictures. The one sign of human occupation was a mop which leant against one wall, but it might have been left there a generation ago by someone hired to tidy up after the furniture-removers had departed.

'Hi!' Wordsworth shouted. 'Hi! Mr Pullen be here,' and I heard the click of high heels along a passage overhead. A flight of pink marble stairs rose to the first floor, and at the head of them my aunt appeared. The light was too dim to see her clearly, and it may have been my imagination which read into her voice an older, more tremulous tone than I had remembered. 'Why, Henry,' she said, 'you are welcome home.' She came slowly down the stairs, and perhaps it was the bad light which caused her to clutch the banister. 'I am so sorry', she said. 'that Mr Visconti is not here to greet you. I had expected him yesterday.'

'Mr Visconti?'

'Yes,' my aunt said, 'Mr Visconti. We are happily reunited. Did you bring the picture safely?'

'Ar got it,' Wordsworth said, holding up his new suitcase.

'Mr Visconti will be relieved. He was afraid of the customs. You look well, Henry,' she said, kissing my cheek and leaving on the air a smell of lavender. 'Come, let me show you your room.' She led me up to the first landing which was as bare as the hall and opened a door. This room at least contained a bed and a chair and a cupboard, though nothing else. My aunt may have thought some explanation was needed, for she said, 'The furniture will be arriving any day now.' I opened another door and saw a room which was empty except for two mattresses laid together on the floor and a dressing-table and stool that looked new. 'I have given you the bed,' my aunt said, 'but I couldn't do without my dressing-table.'

'Is this your room?'

'Sometimes I miss my Venetian glass, but when the curtains go up and the furniture arrives . . . You must be hungry, Henry. Wordsworth will bring your bags. I have a little meal prepared.'

I could no longer be surprised by the furnishing of the dining-room – an immense room which had been lit once by three chandeliers; the wires sprouted like weeds out of holes in the ceiling. There was a table but no cloth, and the chairs were packing-cases. 'It's all a little rough,' my aunt said, 'but when Mr Visconti returns you will see how soon we shall get things in order.' The meal came out of tins, and there was a sweet red wine of local origin which tasted like an evil medicine of childhood. I thought of my first-class ticket on the boat with shame.

'When Mr Visconti is back,' Aunt Augusta said, 'we plan to give you a party. A house like this is made for parties. We shall have a barbecue with an ox roasted whole in the garden, and there will be coloured lights in the trees, and music, of course, for dancing. A harp and a guitar – that is the fashion here. The polka and the gallop are the national dances. I shall invite the Chief of Police, the Jesuit Provincial (for his conversation of course), the British Ambassador and his wife. The Italian Ambassador, no – it would not be tactful. We must find some pretty girls for you, Henry.' A splinter from the packing-case scratched my thigh.

I said, 'You will need a little furniture first, Aunt Augusta.'

'That goes without saying. I regret that I cannot ask the Italian Ambassadaor – he is such a handsome man, but under the circumstances . . . I shall have to tell you something, Henry, that only Wordsworth knows . . .'

'Where is Wordsworth now?'

'In the kitchen. Mr Visconti prefers us to eat alone. As I was going to say, Henry, when you interrupted me, Mr Visconti has taken to an Argentine passport and he is known here as Mr Izquierdo.'

'I am not altogether surprised, Aunt Augusta.' I told her how the two detectives had searched her flat.

'General Abdul is dead by the way.'

'I rather expected that. Did they take anything away?'

'Nothing except a picture postcard from Panama.'

'Why did they want that?'

'They thought it might have something to do with Mr Visconti.'

'How absurd the police always seem to be. The card must have been sent by Monsieur Dambreuse. I met him on the boat going out to Buenos Aires. Poor man, he had aged a great deal. I didn't even recognize him until he began to tell me about his metallurgical company and his family in Toulouse.'

'And he hadn't recognized you?'

'That is not so surprising. In those days, when we were living at the St James and Albany, I had black hair, not red. Red was Mr Visconti's favourite colour. I kept red especially for him.'

'The police were acting for Interpol,' I said.

'It's absurd of them to treat Mr Visconti like a common war criminal. There are lots of such men hidden around here. Martin Bormann is just across the border in Brazil and the unspeakable Dr Mengele of Auschwitz is said to be with the army near the Bolivian border. Why doesn't Interpol do anything about *them*? Mr Visconti was always very kind to Jews. Even when he had those dealings with Saudi Arabia. Why should he be chased out of the Argentine where he was doing quite well in the antique business? There was an American in Buenos Aires who made the most impertinent inquiries, Mr Visconti told me. Mr Visconti had sold a picture to a private purchaser in the States, and this American, who claimed to be a representative of the Metropolitan Museum, said the picture had been looted . . .'

'Was the man's name O'Toole by any chance?'

'It was.'

'He's here in Asunción now.'

'Yes, I know that. But he is not finding people so cooperative here. After all the General has German blood.'

'He was with me on the boat and he told me he was doing social research.'

'That's quite untrue. Like the Metropolitan Museum. He's in the CIA.'

'He's Tooley's father.'

'Tooley?'

'The girl on the Orient Express.'

'How very interesting. I wonder if that could be of any use to us,' my aunt reflected. 'You say he was on the boat with you?'

'Yes.'

'He may have been following you. Such a fuss about a few pictures. I seem to remember that you and his daughter became great friends on the train. And there was all that business of the pregnancy . . .'

'Aunt Augusta, that had nothing to do with me.'

'Rather a pity,' Aunt Augusta said, 'under the circumstances.'

Wordsworth came into the room wearing the butcher's apron in which I had first seen him in the flat above the Crown and Anchor. Then his services in washing up had been recognized and praised, but I could tell they were taken for granted now.

'Chop finished?'

'We will have our coffee in the garden,' my aunt said grandly.

We sat down in the meagre shade of a banana tree. The air was sweet with orange and jasmine, and the moon swam palely in the pale blue daylight sky. It looked as worn and thin as an old coin, and the craters were the same colour as the sky, so that one seemed to be looking through holes at the universe behind. There was no sound of traffic. The clip-clop of a horse belonged to the same ancient world of silence.

'Yes, it's very peaceful,' my aunt said, 'only an occasional gun-shot after dark. The police are sometimes trigger-happy. I forget whether it's one lump or two.'

'I wish you would tell me a little more, Aunt Augusta. I can't help being puzzled. This big house and no furniture . . . and Wordsworth here with you.'

'I brought him from Paris,' Aunt Augusta said. 'I was travelling with rather a lot of ready money – nearly everything I had left, though I kept enough in Berne to pay for your ticket. A frail old lady like myself needed a bodyguard.' It was the first time I had ever heard her admit to being old.

'You could have taken me with you.'

'I wasn't sure about your attitude to certain things. You were rather shocked, you remember, about that gold bar in Istanbul. What a pity General Abdul made a mess of the affair. We could have done now with the twenty-five per cent.'

'Where has all your money gone, Aunt Augusta? You haven't even a bed to sleep in.'

'The mattresses are perfectly comfortable, and I have always found a soft bed enervating. When I arrived here poor Mr Visconti was in a very low state. He was living on credit in a really horrible little hotel. All his money had gone on his new passport and bribes to the police. God knows how Dr Mengele manages, but I expect he has a numbered account in Switzerland. I only arrived just in time. He was sick too, poor fellow, from living mainly on *mandioca*.'

'So you gave him your money a second time, Aunt Augusta?'

'Of course, what do you expect? He needed it. We bought this house for a song (someone was murdered here twenty years ago and people are very superstitious) and what was left has been well invested now. We have a half share in a very promising enterprise.'

'A Dakota by any chance?'

My aunt gave a little excited giggle. 'Mr Visconti will tell you all about it himself.'

'Where is he?'

'He meant to be back yesterday, but there has been a lot of rain and the roads are very bad.' She looked with pride at the empty shell of her house. She said, 'You won't know this place in a week's time. When the chandeliers are hung in the hall, and the furniture arrives. I so wanted it to be ready before you came, but there were delays in Panama. A lot always depends on Panama.'

'And what about the police?'

'Oh, they won't interfere with an established business,' my aunt said.

All the same another day passed and Mr Visconti had not returned from wherever he was. My aunt slept late on her mattresses, Wordsworth was busy cleaning, and I walked around the town. Preparations were in progress for some festival. There were decorated cars of pretty girls parked at street corners. Outside the cathedral and the military academy, which faced each other over the little memorial tank, squads of soldiers goose-stepped. There were pictures of the General everywhere – sometimes in uniform and sometimes in civilian clothes looking like the amiable well-fed host of a Bavarian *bierstube*. There had been unpleasant stories in Buenos Aires about his early rule – enemies tossed out of aeroplanes into the jungle, bodies washed up on the Argentine shore of the two great rivers with their hands and feet bound with wire, but there were cheap cigarettes on the street and cheap whisky in the stores and no income tax to pay (so my aunt had told me) and even the bribes were not unreasonable if one were doing well and could pay regularly, and the oranges lay under the trees hardly worth the bother of gathering when they were threepence a dozen in the market, and everywhere there was the smell of flowers. I hoped that Mr Visconti's investment would prove a success. There were worse places than this to end one's days.

But when I returned home the second evening Mr Visconti was not there, and my aunt was having a bitter argument with Wordsworth. As I crossed the lawn I could hear her voice sounding hollowly from the empty hall at the head of the garden steps. 'I am not your bebi gel, Wordsworth, any more. Understand that. I have kept enough money for you to return to Europe . . .'

'Ar no wan yo money,' Wordsworth's voice replied.

'You've taken plenty of my money in the past. The CTCs you've had from me and all my friends . . .'

'Ar tak yo money them times because you lov me, you slip with me, you lak jig-jig with Wordsworth. Now you no slip with me, you no lov me, I no wan your damn money. You give it *him*. He tak everytin you got. When you got noting at all, you come to Wordsworth, and ar work for you and ar slip with you an you lov me and you lak jig-jig all same last time.'

I stood at the bottom of the steps. I couldn't turn my back and walk away. They would have seen me.

'Don't you understand, Wordsworth, all that's finished now I have Mr Visconti back. Mr Visconti wants you to go, and I want what he wants.'

'He be feared of Wordsworth.'

'Dear, dear Wordsworth, it's you who should be afraid. I want you to leave me now – today – don't you understand that.'

'Okay,' Wordsworth said, 'ar go. You ask me an ar go. Ar no feared of *that* man. But you no slip with me no more an ar go.' My aunt made a movement as though she wished to embrace him, but Wordsworth turned away from her and came down the steps. He didn't even see me, though I was only a step away. 'Goodbye, Wordsworth,' I said and held out my hand. I had a fifty-dollar note, concealed in it. Wordsworth looked at the note but he didn't take it. He said, 'Goodbye, Mr Pullen. Man, darkness deepens, sure thing, sure thing, she no abide with me.' He pressed my left hand which was moneyless and went off down the garden.

My aunt came out on to the steps to see the last of him.

'How will you do without him in this big house?' I asked.

'Staff are easy to come by and much cheaper than Wordsworth with all his CTCs. Oh, I'm sorry for poor Wordsworth,' she added, 'but he was only a stop-gap. Everything has been a stop-gap since Mr Visconti and I were separated.'

'You must love Mr Visconti a great deal. Is he worth it?'

'To me he is. I like men who are untouchable. I've never wanted a man who needed me, Henry. A need is a claim. I thought that Wordsworth wanted my money and the comfort I gave him at the Crown and Anchor, but there's not much comfort for anyone here and you saw how he wouldn't even take a CTC. I'm disappointed in Wordsworth.' She added as though it were relevant, 'Your father was pretty untouchable too.'

'All the same I found your photograph in *Rob Roy*.'

'Perhaps he wasn't untouchable enough,' she said, and she added with venom in her voice, 'Think of the little school-teacher and "Dolly, darling" and dying in *her* arms.'

The house was twice as empty now that Wordsworth had gone and we were alone. We ate our evening meal almost in silence, and I drank too much of the heavy sweet medicinal wine. Once we heard the distant sound of a car and my aunt went at once to the big windows which gave on to the garden. The single globe on the enormous ceiling hardly stretched that far, so that she looked slim and young in her dark dress, and in the obscurity I would never have taken her for an old woman. She quoted at me with a scared smile.

> 'She only said, "The night is dreary,
> He cometh not," she said.'

She added, 'Your father taught me that.'

'Yes, I learnt it from him too – in a way. He turned down that page in Palgrave.'

'And no doubt he taught it to Dolly darling,' she said. 'Can't you imagine her reciting it over the grave in Boulogne like a prayer?'

'*You* are not untouchable, Aunt Augusta.'

'That's why I need a man who is. Two touchables together, what a terrible life they always make of it, two people suffering, afraid to speak, afraid to act, afraid of hurting. Life can be bearable when it's only one who suffers. It's easy to put up with your own suffering, but not someone else's. I'm not afraid of making Mr Visconti suffer. I wouldn't know how. I have a wonderful feeling of freedom. I can say what I like, and it will never get under that thick dago skin of his.'

'And if he makes you suffer?'

'It's only for a little time, Henry. Like now. When he doesn't come and I don't know what's keeping him, and I fear . . .'

'There can't be anything seriously wrong. If there had been an accident you would have heard from the police.'

'My dear, this is Paraguay. I am afraid of the police.'

'Then why do you stay here?'

'Mr Visconti hasn't all that much choice. I daresay he might be safe in Brazil if he had enough money. Perhaps when he's made a fortune, we can move there. Mr Visconti has always wanted to make a fortune, and he believes he can at last make one here. He has come close to making a fortune so many times. There was Saudi Arabia and then there were the Germans . . .'

'If he makes one now he won't have very long to enjoy it.'

'That's not the point. He'll die happy if it's there. Stacked gold bars. (He has always had a fancy for gold bars.) He'll have done what he set out to do.'

'Why did you want me to come, Aunt Augusta?'

'You are the only family I have, Henry – and you can be of great use to Mr Visconti.'

It was not an idea which appealed to me greatly.

'I can't speak a word of Spanish,' I said.

'Mr Visconti wants somebody he can trust to keep the books. Accounts have always been his weak point.'

I looked around at the empty room. The bare globe flickered with an approaching storm. The packing-case scratched hard against my thigh. I thought of the two mattresses and the dressing-table upstairs. The books didn't seem to need very much accounting. I said, 'I planned to leave after I had seen you.'

'Leave? Why?'

'I was thinking that perhaps it's almost time I settled down.'

'What else have you been doing? For far too long.'

'And married I was going to say.'

'At your age?'

'I'm not nearly as old as Mr Visconti.'

A gust of rain splashed against the windows. I began to tell my aunt about Miss Keene and of the evening when I had nearly proposed to her.

'You are suffering from loneliness,' my aunt said. 'That's all. You won't be lonely here.'

'I really think Miss Keene loves me a little. I get a bit of pleasure from the thought that perhaps I could make her happy.' I was arguing without conviction, waiting for my aunt's denial, and even hoping for it.

'In a year,' my aunt said, 'what would you two have to talk about? She would sit over her tatting – I didn't realize that anyone still tatted – and you would read gardening catalogues, and then when the silence was almost unbearable she would begin to tell you a story of Koffiefontein which you had heard a dozen times before. Do you know what you'll think about when you can't sleep in your double bed? Not of women. You don't care enough about them, or you wouldn't even consider marrying Miss Keene. You will think how every day you are getting a little closer to death. It will stand there as close as the bedroom wall. And you'll become more and more afraid of the wall because nothing can prevent you coming nearer and nearer to it every night while you try to sleep and Miss Keene reads. What does Miss Keene read?'

'You may be right, Aunt Augusta, but isn't it the same everywhere at our age?'

'Not here it isn't. Tomorrow you may be shot in the street by a policeman because you haven't understood Guaraní, or a man may knife you in a *cantina* because you can't speak Spanish and he thinks you are acting in a superior way. Next week, when we have our Dakota, perhaps it will crash with you over Argentina. (Mr Visconti is too old to fly with the pilot.) My dear Henry, if you live with us, you won't be edging day by day across to any last wall. The wall will find you of its own accord without your help, and every day you live will seem to you a kind of victory. "I was too sharp for it that time," you will say, when night comes, and afterwards you'll sleep well.' She said, 'I only hope the wall hasn't found Mr Visconti. If it has I will have to go out and look for it myself.'

Chapter 5

THE far-off murmur of great crowds woke me next morning; I thought at first that I was back in Brighton and that the sea was turning the shingle. My aunt was already up and had prepared breakfast with grapefruit picked in the garden. From the town came snatches of music.

'What's happening?'

'It's the National Day. Wordsworth warned me, but I had forgotten. If you go into town carry something red.'

'Why?'

'It's the colour of the governing party. The Liberal party is blue, but it's unhealthy to carry blue. No one does.'

'I haven't got anything red.'

'I've got a red scarf.'

'I can hardly wear a woman's scarf.'

'Stuff it in your breast pocket. It will look like a handkerchief.'

'Won't you come into town with me, Aunt Augusta?'

'No. I must wait for Mr Visconti. He will come today for sure. Or at least he'll send a message.'

I needn't have been shy of wearing the scarf. Most men in the street wore red scarves round their necks, and many scarves were printed with a picture of the General. Only the bourgeois confined themselves to a handkerchief, and some to a handkerchief barely on display at all but pressed in the hand and showing only through the knuckles – perhaps they would rather have carried blue. There were red flags everywhere: you would have thought the town had been taken over by the Communists, but red here was the colour of conservatism. I was held up continually at street crossings by processions of women in red scarves carrying portraits of the General and slogans about the great Colorado party. Groups of gauchos came riding into town with scarlet reins. A drunk man fell out of a tavern door and lay face down in the road with the General's genial face spread over his back as the horses picked their way across him. Decorated cars carrying pretty girls with scarlet camellia blossoms in their hair went by. Even the sun looked red through the morning mist.

The movement of the crowd edged me towards the Avenue of Mariscal Lopez where the processions were passing. Across the road were stands reserved for the government and the diplomats. I could recognize the General taking the salute, and the stand next door must have been that of the American Embassy, for in the back row I could see my friend O'Toole pressed into a corner by a stout military attaché. I waved to him and I think he must have seen me because he gave a shy smile and spoke to the fat man at his side. Then a procession passed and I lost sight of him.

It was a procession of elderly men in shabby suits – a few were on crutches and some had lost an arm. They carried banners representing their old units. They had fought in the Chaco war, and once a year, I suppose, they had this moment of pride. They looked more human than the colonels who followed them, standing upright in their cars, in dress uniforms with gold tassels and epaulettes, all with black moustaches and all quite indistinguishable; the colonels looked like painted skittles waiting for a ball to bowl them over.

After an hour I had had enough of watching and walked into the centre of town, to the new skyscraper hotel, to buy an English-language newspaper, but there was only a five-day-old *New York Times*. A man spoke to me in a confidential voice before I went into the hotel; he had a distinguished intellectual air; he might have been a diplomat or a university professor. 'I beg your pardon,' I said.

'Any US dollars?' he asked me rapidly, and when I shook my head (for I had no desire to break any local currency laws) he walked away. Unfortunately when I emerged again from the hotel with my newspaper he was back on the opposite pavement and failed to recognize me. 'Any US dollars?' he whispered. I said 'No' again and he glared at me with an air of disgust and disdain, as though I had been playing a childish practical joke.

I walked back towards the edge of town and my aunt's house, interrupted at street corners by the tag end of processions. A palatial house covered in banners bore a number of scarlet placards; it was probably the headquarters of the Colorado party. Stout men in city suits who sweated in the morning sun climbed up and down the wide steps wearing red scarves. One of them stopped and demanded, or so I supposed, what I wanted. 'Colorado?' I asked.

'Yes. Are you American?'

I was glad to find someone who spoke English. He had the face of an amiable bulldog, but he needed a shave.

'No,' I said, 'I'm English.'

He gave a short bark which did not sound amiable at all, and at that moment, perhaps because of the heat, the sun and the scent of flowers, I was overcome by a fit of sneezing. Without thinking I drew my aunt's red scarf from my breast pocket and blew my nose. It was most unfortunate. I found myself sitting on the pavement without knowing how I got there, and my nose streamed with blood. Fat men surrounded me, all of them in dark suits and all with faces of bulldogs. Others like them appeared on the balcony of the Colorado house and looked down at me with curiosity and disapproval. I heard the word '*Ingles*' repeated often, and then a policeman yanked me to my feet. Afterwards I was to think how lucky I had been; if I had blown my nose near a group of gauchos I might well have received a knife in the ribs.

Several fat men accompanied me to the police station, including the one who had struck me. He carried my aunt's scarf, the evidence of a crime. 'It's all a mistake,' I assured him.

'Mistake?' His English was very limited.

At the police station – a very imposing building, built to withstand a siege – everyone began to speak at once with noise and fury. I felt at a loss how to behave. I kept on repeating '*Ingles*' without any effect. Once I tried 'Ambassador', but it wasn't in their vocabulary. The police officer was young and worried – I imagine his superior officers were all at the parade. When I said '*Ingles*' for the third time and 'Ambassador' for the second he hit me but without conviction – a blow which hardly hurt me at all. I was discovering something new. Physical violence, like the dentist's drill, is seldom as bad as one fears.

I tried 'Mistake' again, but no one could translate that word. The scarf was handed from one to another, and a patch of snot was pointed out to the officer. He picked up what looked like an identity card and waved it at me. I suppose he was demanding my passport. I said, 'I left it at home,' and three or four people began to argue. Perhaps they were disagreeing on the meaning of what I said.

Oddly enough it was the man who had struck me who proved most sympathetic. My nose was still bleeding and he gave me his handkerchief. It was not very clean and I feared blood poisoning, but I didn't want to reject his help, so I dabbed rather tentatively at my nose and then offered him his handkerchief back again. He waved it away with a gesture of generosity. Then he wrote something on a piece of paper and showed it me. I read the name of a street and a number. He pointed at the floor and then pointed at me and held out the pencil. Everyone pressed nearer with great curiosity. I shook my head. I knew how to walk to my aunt's house, but I had no idea of the street. My friend – I was beginning to think of him as that – wrote down the name of three hotels. I shook my head.

Then I spoilt everything. For some unknown reason, standing beside the officer's desk in the hot and crowded room, with an armed sentry at the door, my mind went suddenly back to the morning of my stepmother's funeral, the chapel full of distant relatives, and the voice of my aunt breaking the reverent whispers: 'I was present once at a premature cremation.' I had looked forward to the funeral as a break in the orderly routine of my retirement and what a break it had proved. I had been worried, I remembered, about the rain falling on my lawn-mower. I began to laugh, and when I laughed all the enmity returned. I was again the insolent foreigner who had blown his nose on the flag of the Colorado party. My first assailant snatched away his handkerchief, and the officer, pushing aside those who stood in his way, strode to my side and gave me a severe cuff on my right ear which began to bleed in its turn. Desperately trying to find the name of anyone they might know, I let out Mr Visconti's alias. 'Señor Izquierdo,' I said with no effect at all, and then, 'Señor O'Toole.' The officer paused with his hand raised to strike again and I tried, 'Embassy – Americano.'

Something about those words worked, though I was not sure whether the working was in my favour. Two policemen were summoned and I was pushed down a corridor and locked into a cell. I could hear the officer telephoning and I could only hope that Tooley's father really knew the ropes. There was nothing to sit on in the cell – only a piece of sacking under a barred window too high for me to see anything but a patch of monotonous sky. Somebody had written on the wall in Spanish – perhaps a prayer, perhaps an obscenity, I couldn't tell. I sat down on the sacking and prepared for a long wait. The wall opposite me reminded me of what my aunt had said: I trained myself to be thankful that the wall seemed to keep its distance.

To pass the time I took out my pen and began to doodle on the whitewash. I put down my initials and was irritated, as often before, because they represented a famous sauce; then I wrote the date of my birth, 1913, with a dash against it where someone else could fill in the date of my death. It occurred to me to record a family history – it would help to pass the time if I were to have a long stay – so I wrote down my father's death in 1923 and my stepmother's less than a year ago. I knew nothing of my grandparents, so the only relative left me was my aunt. She had been born somewhere around 1895, and I put a question mark after the year. It occurred to me to try to work out my aunt's history on the wall which had already begun to take on a more friendly family air, I didn't entirely believe all her stories and perhaps I might discover a chronological flaw. She had seen me at my baptism and never again, so she must have left my father's house somewhere around 1913, when she was eighteen – it could not have been long after the snapshot had been taken. There had been the period with Curran in Brighton – that must surely have been after the first world war, so I put Dogs' Church 1919 with another question mark. Curran had left her, she had gone to Paris, and there in the establishment in the Rue de Provence she had met Mr Visconti – perhaps about the same time as my father died in Boulogne. She would have been in her twenties then. I began to work on the Italian period, her travels between Milan and Venice, Uncle Jo's death, her life with Mr Visconti, which had been interrupted by the failure of his Saudi Arabia scheme. I put tentatively the date 1937 against Paris and Monsieur Dambreuse, for she had returned to Italy and been reunited with Mr Visconti at the house behind the *Messaggero* before the outbreak of the second war. Of the last twenty years of her life I knew nothing before the arrival of Wordsworth. I had to admit that I had found nothing intrinsically false in the chronology. There was ample time for all she had told me to happen and a great deal more besides. I began to speculate on the nature of the quarrel with my so-called mother. It must have occurred round about the time of the pretended pregnancy – if that story were true . . . The door of the cell was thrown open and a policeman brought in a chair. It seemed a kindly action and I got up from the sacking to take advantage of it, but the policeman pushed me roughly away. O'Toole came in. He looked embarrassed. 'You seem to be in trouble, Henry,' he said.

'It's all a mistake. I sneezed and then I happened to blow my nose . . .'

'On the Colorado colours outside the Colorado HQ.'

'Yes. But I thought it was my handkerchief.'

'You are in an awful spot.'

'I suppose I am.'

'You could easily have a ten-year sentence. Do you mind if I sit down? I've been standing for hours at that damn parade.'

'Of course. Please.'

'I could ask for another chair.'

'Don't bother. I'm getting used to this sack.'

'I guess what makes it worse,' O'Toole said, 'is that you did it on their National Day. It seems kind of provocative. Otherwise they might have been content to expel you. What made you ask for me?'

'You said you knew the ropes and they didn't seem to understand "English Embassy".'

'Your people don't count for very much here, I'm afraid. We provide their arms – and then there's the new hydro-electric station we are helping them to build . . . not too far from the Iguazú Falls. It will serve Brazil too – but Brazil will have to pay them royalties. Great thing for the country.'

'Very interesting,' I said with some bitterness.

'Of course I'd like to help you,' O'Toole said. 'You are a friend of Lucinda. I've had a postcard from her by the way. She's not in Katmandu. She's in Vientiane. I don't know why.'

'Look, O'Toole,' I said, 'if you can't do anything else, you might at least ring up the British Embassy. If I'm to have ten years in prison I'd like a bed and a chair.'

'Sure,' O'Toole said, 'I can arrange all that. I guess I could arrange your release too – the Chief of Police is a good friend of mine . . .'

'I think my aunt knows him too,' I said.

'Don't bank on that. You see, we've had some fresh information about your relative. The police don't want to act, I guess some money has passed, but we're bringing pressure on them. You seem to be mixed up with some pretty shady characters, Henry.'

'My aunt's an old lady of seventy-five.' I glanced at the notes I had made on the wall: Rue de Provence, Milan, *Messaggero*. I would have certainly called her career shady myself nine months ago, and yet now there seemed nothing so very wrong in her *curriculum vitae*, nothing so wrong as thirty years in a bank. 'I don't see what you can have against her,' I said.

'Your friend, that black fellow, came to see us.'

'I'm certain he told you nothing against my aunt.'

'That's right, he didn't, but he had plenty to say about Mr Izquierdo. So I persuaded the police to keep him out of circulation for a while.'

'Is that part of your social research?' I asked. 'Perhaps he suffered from malnutrition.'

'I guess I sort of lied to you, Henry,' he said, looking ashamed again.

'Are you in the CIA like Tooley told me?'

'Well . . . kind of . . . not exactly,' he said, clinging to his torn rag of deception like a blown-out umbrella in a high wind.

'What did Wordsworth tell you?'

'He was in a pretty bitter mood. If your aunt hadn't been so old I'd have said it was love. He seemed jealous of this guy Izquierdo.'

'Where's Wordsworth now?'

'He's sticking around. He wants to see your aunt again when things blow over.'

'Are they likely to blow over?'

'Well, Henry, they could. If everyone were reasonable.'

'Even my sneeze?'

'I guess so. As for Mr Izquierdo's smuggling racket – no one cares a devalued dime about that if only he'd be reasonable. Now *you* know Mr I.'

'I've never met him.'

'Maybe you know him under another name?'

'No,' I said.

O'Toole sighed. 'Henry,' he said, 'I want to help you. Any friend of Lucinda can count on me. We can have this whole thing tied up in a few hours. Visconti's not important, not like Mengele or Bormann.'

'I thought we were talking about Izquierdo.'

'You and I and your friend Wordsworth know it's the same man. So do the police, but they protect these guys – anyway till they run out of cash. Visconti nearly ran out of cash, but then Miss Bertram arrived and paid up.'

'I don't know a thing,' I said. 'I'm simply here on a visit.'

'I guess there was a good reason why Wordsworth met you in Formosa, Henry. Anyway I'd like to have a word with your aunt and a word from you might make it easier for me. If I persuaded the police to let you go, you and I could see her together . . .'

'What exactly are you after?'

'She must be anxious about Visconti by this time. I can reassure her. They'll only hold him in jail a few days till I give the word.'

'Are you offering her some kind of bargain? I warn you she won't do anything to hurt Mr Visconti.'

'I just want to talk to her, Henry. With you there. She mightn't trust me alone.'

I was feeling very cramped on the sacking, and I saw no reason why not to agree.

He said, 'It may take an hour or two to get you released. Everything is disorganized today.' He stood up.

'How are the statistics, O'Toole?'

'This parade's put everything out. I was afraid to drink any coffee for breakfast. All these hours of standing without taking a leak. I ought to cancel today altogether. It's not what you'd call a normal day.'

It took him more than an hour or two to persuade them to let me go, but they forgot to take the chair from the cell after he'd gone and they brought me some thin gruel, and these I took for favourable signs. To my own surprise I wasn't bored, though there was nothing I could usefully add to the history on the wall, except two problematical dates for Tunis and Havana. I began in my head to compose a letter to Miss Keene describing my present circumstances: 'I have insulted the ruling party of Paraguay and I'm mixed up with a war criminal wanted by Interpol. For the first offence the maximum penalty is ten years. I am in a small cell ten feet by six, and I have nothing to sleep on but a piece of sacking. I have no idea what is going to happen next, but I confess I am not altogether unhappy, I am too deeply interested.' I would never really write the letter, for she would be quite unable to reconcile the writer with the man she had known.

It was quite dark outside when at last they came to release me. I was led back down the corridor and through the office, and there they solemnly returned me my aunt's red scarf, and the young officer slapped my back in a friendly way, urging me through into the street where O'Toole waited for me in an ancient Cadillac. He said, 'I'm sorry. It took longer than I thought. I'm afraid Miss Bertram will be nervous about you too.'

'I don't think I count much beside Mr Visconti.'

'Blood's thicker than water, Henry.'

'Water's not the term to use for Mr Visconti.'

There were only two lights on in the house. As we came through the trees at the bottom of the garden someone flashed a light in our faces, but the light went out before I could see who held the torch. I looked back from the lawn and could see nothing.

'Are you having the place watched?' I asked.

'Not me, Henry.'

I could tell that he was uneasy. He put his hand inside his jacket.

'Are you armed?' I said.

'One has to take precautions.'

'Against an old lady? My aunt's the only one here.'

'You can never be sure.'

We went forward across the lawn and climbed the steps. The globe in the dining-room shone down on two empty glasses and an empty bottle of champagne. It was still cold to the touch when I picked it up. When I put it down I knocked over one of the glasses and the sound rang through the house. My aunt must have been in the kitchen, for she came at once to the door.

'Where on earth have you been, Henry?'

'In prison. Mr O'Toole helped me to get out.'

'I never expected to see Mr O'Toole in my house. Not after what he did to Mr Izquierdo in Argentina. So you are Mr O'Toole.'

'Yes, Miss Bertram. I thought it would be a good thing if we could have a friendly talk. I know how anxious you must be about Mr Visconti.'

'I'm not in the least anxious about Mr Visconti.'

'I thought perhaps . . . that not knowing where he was . . . all this long delay . . .'

'I know perfectly well where he is,' my aunt said. 'He's in the lavatory.' The flush of water could not have come more exactly on cue.

Chapter 6

I WAITED with excited curiosity to see Mr Visconti. Not many men can have been so loved or have been forgiven so much, and I had an image in my mind's eye to fit the part, of an Italian tall and dark and lean, as aristocratic as his name. But the man who came through the door to meet us was short and fat and bald; when he held his hand out to me I saw that his little finger had been broken and this made his hand resemble a bird's claw. He had soft brown eyes quite without expression. One could read into them whatever one liked. If my aunt read love, I felt sure that O'Toole read dishonesty.

'So here you are at last, Henry,' Mr Visconti said. 'Your aunt has been anxous.' He spoke English very well with practically no accent.

O'Toole said, 'You are Mr Visconti?'

'My name is Izquierdo. To whom have I the pleasure . . . ?'

'My name's O'Toole.'

'In that case,' Mr Visconti said with a smile which was rendered phoney by a large gap in his front teeth, 'pleasure is not the word I ought to use.'

'I thought you were safe in jail.'

'The police and I came to an understanding.'

O'Toole said, 'That's what I've come here for – an understanding.'

'An understanding is always possible,' Mr Visconti said, as though he were quoting from a well-known source – perhaps from Machiavelli, 'if there are equal advantages on either side.'

'I guess there are in this case.'

'I think,' Mr Visconti said to my aunt, 'there are still two bottles of champagne left in the kitchen.'

'*Two* bottles?' my aunt asked.

'There are four of us, my dear.' He turned to me and said, 'It is not the best champagne. It has travelled a long way and rather roughly by way of Panama.'

'Then I suppose,' O'Toole said, 'your arrangements with Panama are now okay.'

'Exactly,' Mr Visconti said. 'When the police arrested me at your suggestion they thought they were once again arresting a poor man. I was able to convince them that I am now again potentially a man of means.'

My aunt came in from the kitchen carrying the champagne. 'And glasses,' Mr Visconti said, 'you have forgotten the glasses.'

I watched Aunt Augusta with fascination. I had never seen her taking orders from anyone before.

'Sit down, sit down, my friends,' Mr Visconti said. 'You must forgive the rough nature of our chairs. We have passed through a period of some privation, but all our difficulties, I hope, are over. Soon we shall be able to entertain our friends in proper fashion. Mr O'Toole, I raise my glass to the United States. I have no ill feelings towards you or your great country.'

'That's big of you,' O'Toole said. 'But tell me, who's the man in the garden?'

'In my position I have to take precautions.'

'He didn't stop us.'

'Only against my enemies.'

'Which do you prefer to be called, Izquierdo or Visconti?' O'Toole asked.

'By this time I have grown quite accustomed to both. Let us finish this bottle and open another. Champagne, if you are seeking the truth, is better than a lie-detector. It encourages a man to be expansive, even reckless, while lie-detectors are only a challenge to tell lies successfully.'

'You've had experience of them?' O'Toole asked.

'I had a session with one before I left BA. The results, I suspect, were not very useful to the police – or to you. You received them, I imagine? I had prepared myself beforehand very carefully. They strapped two rubber belts around my arms and I thought at first they were taking my blood pressure. Perhaps they were doing that among other things. They warned me that however much I lied the machine would always tell the truth. You can imagine my reaction to that. Scepticism is inbred in a Catholic. First they asked me a number of innocent questions, such as what was my favourite food, and did I become breathless going upstairs? As I answered those innocent questions I thought very hard of what a joy it would one day be for me to see again my dear friend here and my heart beat and my pulses jumped, and they couldn't understand what was making me so excited about walking upstairs or eating cannelloni. Then they allowed me to calm down and afterwards they shot the name Visconti at me. "Are you Visconti?" "You're Visconti, the war criminal," but that had no effect on me at all because I had trained my old daily woman to call me Visconti in the morning when she drew the curtains. "Visconti, you war criminal, wake up." It had become a homely phrase to me meaning "Your coffee is ready". After that they went back to the question about going upstairs and this time I was very calm, but when they asked me why I liked cannelloni, I thought of my darling and I got excited again, so that at the next question which was a serious one, the cardiogram – if that's what it was called – became much calmer because I stopped thinking of my dear. In the end they were in quite a rage – both with the machine and with me. You notice how champagne makes me talk. I am in the mood to tell you everything.'

'I've come here to propose an arrangement, Mr Visconti. I'd hoped to have you out of circulation for a while so that I could convince Miss Bertram in your absence.'

'I would have agreed to nothing,' my aunt said, 'until I had talked to Mr Visconti.'

'We could still make a pack of trouble for you here. Every time we put pressure on the police it would cost you money in bribes. Now suppose we persuaded Interpol to close the files on you and we told the police we were not interested any more, that you were free to come and go . . .'

'I wouldn't entirely trust you,' Mr Visconti said, 'I would prefer to stop here. Besides I am making friends.'

'Sure, stay, if you want to. The police wouldn't be able to blackmail you any more.'

'It's an interesting proposal,' Mr Visconti said. 'You obviously imagine I have something to offer you in return? Let me fill your glass again.'

'We are prepared to do a deal,' O'Toole said.

'I'm a businessman,' Mr Visconti replied. 'In my time I've had dealings with many governments. Saudi Arabia, Turkey, the Vatican.'

'And the Gestapo.'

'They were not gentlemen,' Mr Visconti said. 'Force of circumstances alone impelled me.' His way of speaking reminded me of Aunt Augusta's. They must have grown together with the years. 'You realize, of course, I've had other offers of a private nature.'

'A man in your position can't afford private offers. Unless you deal with us you'll never be able to live in this house of yours. I wouldn't bother about buying the furniture.'

'The furniture,' Mr Visconti said, 'is no longer a problem. My Dakota did not return empty yesterday from Argentina. Miss Bertram had already arranged with Harrods at Buenos Aires to deliver the furniture to a friend's estancia. So many chandeliers for so many cigarettes. The bed was an expensive item. How many cases of whisky did we pay, my dear? To my friend of course, not to Harrods. An honourable firm. It takes a lot of whisky or cigarettes in these days to furnish a few essential rooms, and I admit frankly that I could do with a little ready cash. A beefsteak is sometimes more necessary than a chandelier. Panama cannot deliver again for two weeks. I'm in the position of a sound business with good prospects, but short of petty cash.'

'I'm offering you security,' O'Toole said, 'not money.'

'I'm used to being insecure. It doesn't worry me. In my situation cash alone has a tongue.'

I was wondering what kind of an overdraft I would have granted Mr Visconti on his say-so alone, when my aunt took my hand. 'I think.' she whispered to me, 'that we should leave Mr Visconti alone with Mr O'Toole.' Aloud she said to me, 'Henry, come with me a moment. I've got something to show you.'

'Has Mr Visconti any Jewish blood?' I asked when we were outside the room.

'No,' Aunt Augusta said, 'Saracen perhaps. He always got on well with the Saudi Arabians. Do you like him, Henry?' she asked with an appeal which touched me under the circumstances. She was not a woman who found it easy to make an appeal.

'It's early for me to judge,' I said. 'He doesn't seem to me very trustworthy.'

'If he were, would I have loved him, Henry?'

She led me through the kitchen – one chair, a drying rack, an ancient gas stove, tins of food stacked upon the floor – to the back of the house. The yard was full of wooden crates. My aunt said with pride. 'You see our furniture. Enough for two bedrooms and a dining-room. A little garden furniture too for our celebration.'

'And for the food and drink?'

'That is what Mr Visconti is discussing now.'

'Does he really expect the CIA to pay for your party? What happened to all the money you had in Paris, Aunt Augusta?'

'It was very expensive settling with the police, and then I had to find a house worthy of Mr Visconti's position.'

'Has he got one?'

'He has walked in his time with cardinals and Arabian princes,' Aunt Augusta said. 'You don't imagine that a little country like Paraguay will hold him down for long.'

A light went on at the bottom of the garden and then was extinguished. 'Who is it prowling there?' I asked.

'Mr Visconti doesn't altogether trust his partner. He has been betrayed too often.' I couldn't help wondering how many he had himself betrayed; my aunt, his wife, those cardinals and princes, even the Gestapo.

My aunt sat down on one of the smaller crates. She said, 'I am so happy, Henry, that you are here and Mr Visconti is safely returned. Perhaps I am getting a little old, for I shall be quite content with a spell of family life. You and me and Mr Visconti working together . . .'

'Smuggling cigarettes and whisky?'

'Yes.'

'And the bodyguard in the garden.'

'I wouldn't want my days to *peter* out, Henry, with no interest in them at all.'

Mr Visconti's voice called from somewhere in the vast house. 'My dear, my dear. Can you hear me?'

'Yes.'

'Fetch me the picture, dear.'

My aunt rose. 'The deal, I think, must have been concluded,' she said. 'Come, Henry.' But I let her go without me. I walked away from the house towards the trees. The stars were so brilliant in the low sky that I must have been easily visible to anyone watching from the trees. A small warm breeze blew around me the scent of orange and jasmine. It was as though I had plunged my head into a box of cut flowers. As I entered the shade a light flashed on my face and went out again, but this time I was ready for it and I knew exactly where the man stood. I had kept a match ready and I struck it. I saw leaning against a *lapacho* a little old man with long moustaches; his mouth had fallen open with surprise and perplexity so that I could see the toothless gums before the match burnt down. '*Buenas noches*,' I said, which was one of the few expressions I had picked up from my phrase-book, and he mumbled something in reply. I turned to go back and stumbled on the uneven ground and he flashed on his torch to aid me. I thought to myself that Mr Visconti could not as yet afford much in the way of a bodyguard. Perhaps with the second load from Panama he would be able to afford something better.

In the dining-room I found all three of them, gathered round the picture. I recognized it from the frame, for it had been propped up in my cabin for four days.

'I don't understand,' O'Toole said.

'Nor do I,' said Mr Visconti. 'I expected a photograph of the Venus of Milo.'

'You know that I can't stand torsos, dear,' Aunt Augusta said. 'I told you about that murder on the *chemin de fer*. I found this photograph in Wordsworth's room.'

O'Toole said, 'I don't understand what in hell all this is about. What murder on the *chemin de fer*?'

'It's too long a story to tell you now,' Aunt Augusta said. 'Besides Henry knows it, and he doesn't care for my stories.'

'That's not true,' I said. 'I was simply tired that night in Boulogne . . .'

'Look,' O'Toole said, 'I'm not interested in what happened in Boulogne. I made an offer for a picture which Mr Visconti here stole . . .'

'I did not steal it,' Mr Visconti said. 'The prince gave it me quite voluntarily to present to Field-Marshal Goering in recognition . . .'

'Oh sure, sure, we know all that. The prince didn't give you a photo of a lot of African women . . .'

'It should have been the Venus of Milo,' Mr Visconti said, shaking his head in perplexity. 'You had no need to change it, dear. It was a very fine photograph.'

'It should have been a drawing of Leonardo da Vinci's,' O'Toole replied.

'What did you do with the photograph?' Mr Visconti asked.

'I threw it away. I won't have any torsos to remind me . . .'

'I'll have you pulled in again in the morning,' O'Toole threatened, 'whatever bribes you pay. The Ambassador himself . . .'

'Ten thousand dollars was the agreed price, but I'll accept payment in the local currency if it's more convenient.'

'For a photograph of a lot of black women,' O'Toole said.

'If you really want the photograph I would throw it in with the other.'

'What other?'

'The prince's picture.'

Mr Visconti turned the frame over and began to tear away the backing. My aunt said, 'Would anyone like some whisky?'

'Not after champagne, dear.'

Mr Visconti removed a small drawing which had been hidden behind the photograph of Freetown. It could not have been more than eight inches by six. O'Toole looked at it with wonder. Mr Visconti said, 'There you are. Is anything wrong?'

'I guess I thought it would be a madonna.'

'Leonardo was not primarily interested in madonnas. He was the chief engineer of the Pope's army. Alexander VI. You know about Alexander?'

'I'm not a Roman Catholic,' O'Toole said.

'He was the Borgia Pope.'

'A bad guy?'

'In some respects,' Mr Visconti said, 'he resembled my patron, the late Marshal Goering. Now this, as you can see, is an ingenious device for attacking the walls of a city. A sort of dredge, very much the same as they use on building sites today, though motivated by human power. It grabs out the foundations of a wall and throws the stones up to this catapult which projects them into the city. In fact you bombard the city with its own walls. Ingenious, isn't it?'

'Ten thousand dollars for this . . . Would it work?'

'I'm no engineer,' Mr Visconti said. 'I cannot judge it practically, but I challenge anyone today to make so beautiful a drawing of a dredge.'

'I guess you're right,' O'Toole said and added with reverence, 'So this is the real McCoy. We've been looking for this and for you for nearly twenty years.'

'And where does it go now?'

'The prince died in prison, so I guess we hand it over to the Italian government.' He gave a sigh. I don't know whether it was of disillusion or satisfaction.

'You may keep the frame,' Mr Visconti said kindly.

I went with O'Toole down through the garden to the gate. There was no sign now of the old bodyguard. O'Toole said, 'It goes against the grain to see the US government pay ten thousand dollars for a stolen picture.'

'It would be difficult to prove,' I said. 'Perhaps it was a sort of present to Goering. I wonder why they shut the prince up.'

We stood together by his car. He said, 'I got a letter today from

Lucinda. The first in nine months. She writes about a boy-friend of hers. She says they are hitch-hiking to Goa because Vientiane wasn't right for him.'

'He's a painter,' I explained.

'A painter?' He put the Leonardo carefully on the back seat.

'He paints pictures of Heinz soup tins.'

'You are joking.'

'Leonardo drew a dredge and you paid ten thousand dollars for it.'

'I guess I'll never understand art,' O'Toole said. 'Where's Goa?'

'On the coast of India.'

'That girl's one hell of an anxiety,' he said, but if she hadn't existed, I thought, he'd have been anxious just the same. Anxieties in his case would always settle on him like flies on an open wound.

'Thanks for getting me out of the jail,' I said.

'Any friend of Lucinda's . . .'

'Give my love to Tooley when you write.'

'I'm putting your friend Wordsworth on the next boat. Why don't you go with him?'

'My family . . .'

'Visconti's no relation of yours. He's not your type, Henry.'

'My aunt . . .'

'An aunt's not all that close. An aunt's not a mother.' He couldn't get his starter to work. He said, 'It's time they gave me a newer car. Think about it, Henry.'

'I will.'

I found Mr Visconti laughing when I returned, my aunt watching him with disapproval.

'What's up?'

'I told him ten thousand dollars was too little for a Leonardo.'

'It didn't belong to him,' I said. 'And he's got security as well. The file's closed.'

'Mr Visconti,' my aunt said, 'has never cared about security.'

'The boat goes back the day after tomorrow. O'Toole is putting Wordsworth on board. He wants me to go with him.'

'She said I ought to have asked double,' Mr Visconti said, 'for a Leonardo.'

'So you should have.'

'But it's not a Leonardo at all. It's only a copy,' Mr Visconti said. 'That's why they shut the prince up.' He was a little breathless with laughter. He said, 'It was nearly a perfect copy. The prince was afraid of thieves and he kept the original in a bank. Unfortunately the bank was obliterated by the American air force. No one knew, except the prince, that the Leonardo was obliterated too.'

'If it was so good a copy how could the Gestapo tell?' I asked.

'The prince was a very old man,' Mr Visconti said with all the pride of his mere eighty years. 'When I came to see him – on behalf of the Marshal – he pleaded for his picture. He told me it was only a copy and I wouldn't believe him. Then he showed me. If you look through a magnifying glass at the cog-wheel of the dredge you can see the forger's initials in looking-glass writing. I kept the drawing in memory of the prince, because I thought it might prove useful one day.'

'You told the Gestapo?'

'I couldn't trust them not to have it examined by an expert,' Mr Visconti said. 'He hadn't long to live. He was very old.'

'As you are now.'

'He had nothing to live for,' Mr Visconti said, 'and I have your aunt.'

I looked at Aunt Augusta. The corner of her mouth twitched. 'It was very wrong of you,' was all she said, 'very, very wrong.'

Mr Visconti rose and picking up the photograph of Freetown he tore it in small pieces. 'And now to our well-earned rest,' he said.

'I wanted to send that back to Wordsworth,' my aunt protested, but Mr Visconti put his arm around her and they went up the marble staircase side by side, like any old couple who have continued to love each other through a long and difficult life.

Chapter 7

'THEY described you as a viper,' I said to Mr Visconti.

'They?'

'Well, in fact, it was not the detectives: it was the Chief of Police in Rome.'

'A Fascist,' Mr Visconti said.

'In 1945?'

'Ah, a collaborator then.'

'The war was over.'

'A collaborator nonetheless. One collaborates always with the victorious side. One supports the losing.' It sounded again like a quotation from Machiavelli.

We were drinking champagne together in the garden, for the house at the moment was impossible. Men were carrying furniture. Other men were up ladders. Electricians were repairing lights and hanging chandeliers. My aunt was very much in charge.

'I preferred flight to a new form of collaboration,' Mr Visconti said. 'One can never tell who will win in the end. Collaboration is always a temporary measure. It's not that I care much for security, but I like to survive. Now if the *Questore* had described me as a rat, I would have had no objection. Indeed I have a great fellow feeling for rats. The future of the world lies with the rat. God, at least as I imagine him, created a number of possibilities in case some of his prototypes failed – that is the meaning of evolution. One species would die out. I have never understood why Protestants object so much to the ideas of Darwin. Perhaps if he had concentrated on the evolution of sheep and goats he would have appealed to the religious sense.'

'But rats . . .' I objected.

'Rats are highly intelligent creatures. If we want to find out anything new about the human body we experiment on rats. Rats indeed are ahead of us indisputably in one respect – they live underground. We only began to live underground during the last war. Rats have understood the danger of surface life for thousands of years. When the atom bomb falls the rats will survive. What a wonderful empty world it will be for them, though I hope they will be wise enough to stay below. I can imagine them evolving very quickly. I hope they don't repeat our mistake and invent the wheel.'

'It's odd all the same how much we hate them,' I said. I had drunk three glasses of champagne and I found that I could talk to Mr Visconti as freely as I had talked to Tooley. 'We call a coward a rat, and yet it is we who are the cowards. We are afraid of them.'

'The *Questore* may not have been afraid of me, but perhaps he had an uneasy sense that I would outlive him. It is an uncomfortable form of envy which is experienced only by those in a really secure position. I don't feel it about you, although you are much younger than I am, because we live here in an equally blessed state of insecurity. You go first? I go first? Mr O'Toole goes first? It all depends on who is the best rat. That is why in a modern war old men read the casualty lists with a certain smug satisfaction. They may survive longer than their grand-children.'

'I met a rat once in my garden,' I said and allowed Mr Visconti to refill my glass. 'He was standing motionless so as not to be seen in the flower-bed. His fur looked fluffy like a bird who has blown out its feathers against the cold. He wasn't repulsive like a smooth rat. Without thinking I threw a stone at him. I missed him and I expected him to run, but instead he only limped away. One of his legs must have been broken. There was a hole in the hedge and he made for it very slowly. Once he stopped exhausted and peered over his shoulder at me. He looked rejected, and I was sorry for him. I couldn't throw another stone. He limped on to the hole and went through it. There was a cat in the next garden and I knew he didn't stand a chance. He had such dignity, going to his death. I felt ashamed of myself all that morning.'

'It does you credit,' Mr Visconti said. 'Speaking as an honorary rat on behalf of other rats, I forgive the stone. Have another glass.'

'I'm not used to champagne in the morning.'

'There is nothing more useful that we can do at the moment than put ourselves in a good humour. My wife is quite happy in the house preparing for her party.'

'Your wife?'

'Yes, I speak prematurely, but last night we decided to marry. Now that the sexual urge is behind us, marriage presents no danger of infidelity or boredom.'

'You lived a long time without marriage.'

'Our life has been what the French call *mouvementé*. Now I can leave a great deal of the burden of work to you. My partner needs watching, but you can leave him to me. And I will look after relations with the police. The Chief of Police is coming tomorrow night. He has a charming daughter by the way. It's a pity you are not a Catholic, he would make a valuable father-in-law, but perhaps we could remedy that.'

'You talk as if I were settling here for life.'

'I know that "for life" has a rather lugubrious sound, as in the term "imprisonment for life", but here you know "for life" can so easily mean for a day, for a week, for a month. And you won't die in a traffic accident.'

'You speak as though I were a young man looking for adventure. O'Toole wants me to take the boat tomorrow.'

'But you are one of the family now,' Mr Visconti replied, putting his hand like a bird's claw on my knee and digging a little with his fingers to retain a grip. 'I feel towards you very like a father.' His smile, which he must have meant to be a tender one, was not of the kind which one associates with paternity: the missing teeth ruined it. He must have seen me looking at his mouth, for he explained, 'I had very good dentures once. Some magnificent gold work. It's the only form of jewellery a man can wear that women fully appreciate. Dear things, they like to put their lips on gold. Unfortunately the Nazis were acquisitive that way, and although I tried to remain on friendly terms, I thought it safer to have the teeth removed. There was an officer of the Gestapo who had a drawer full of teeth. I noticed that he always looked me in the mouth, not the eyes.'

'How did you explain their absence?'

'I told them I had exchanged them for cigarettes. I cannot think what I would have done without those teeth when I had to run away. Before I reached Milan and Mario's Jesuits I was down to my last tooth.'

Aunt Augusta joined us from the house. 'I could do with a glass myself,' she said. 'I hope it's not going to rain tomorrow. I'm keeping the dining-room empty for dancing in case. Your room is looking quite furnished, Henry. Everything is a little slow because there are misunderstandings. I keep on using Italian words, and they don't understand. I find myself looking round for Wordsworth to explain. He had a way of explaining . . .'

'I thought we had agreed, dear, that his name was not to be spoken.'

'I know, but it's so absurd to inconvenience ourselves with jealousies at our age. Do you know, Henry, Mr Visconti was quite disturbed when I told him that I met Achille on the boat? Poor Achille. He couldn't move for gout.'

'I like the dead to stay dead,' Mr Visconti said.

'Unlike Pottifer,' my aunt replied and laughed.

'Who was Pottifer?' I asked.

'I was going to tell you at Boulogne, but you wouldn't listen.'

'Tell me now.'

'There are too many things to see about.'

I could see that the only way to atone for my conduct in the restaurant of the Gare Maritime was to beg her to tell me. 'Please, Aunt Augusta, I want to know . . .' I felt like a child pretending interest in a story to delay bedtime. What was it that I was delaying? Perhaps the moment when I had finally to decide to catch the boat home, to find again my dahlias and Major Charge, to reply to Miss Keene's letter, or to pass the border into my aunt's world where I had lived till now as a tourist only. It seemed to me, watching the champagne from Panama shooting up its bubbles like balls dancing on water at a fair, inconceivable that I could abandon forever the region of Colonel Hakim and Curran and O'Toole . . .

'What are you smiling at?' Aunt Augusta asked.

'I was thinking of O'Toole flying off today to Washington with the fake Leonardo.'

'Not today. There are no planes to the north. He will be at the party tomorrow night. I asked him before he left. When once he had got what he wanted he was quite a charming man. Good-looking in a sad way.'

'But perhaps today when he has time to examine the drawing . . .'

'Mr O'Toole is no art expert,' Mr Visconti said. 'The man who did that forgery was a genius. He was quite illiterate. A peasant on the prince's estate, but with a wonderful hand and eye. The prince never knew what a treasure he had living there until the police descended – that was in the early days of Mussolini – and arrested the man. He was making counterfeit notes. He had rigged up a little printing works at the back of the estate forge. They were extraordinarily good, his forgeries, but he didn't know his own value, he gave them away to his fellow labourers. The prince could never understand how it was his people had become so prosperous – there wasn't a labourer without a radio set. In socialist circles the prince gained a high reputation as an enlightened employer – they even wanted him to stand as a deputy. Then all the peasants began buying refrigerators and even motor-cycles. And of course they went too far . . . somebody bought a Fiat. And the paper the forger used wasn't up to the mark. When the man came out of prison the prince welcomed him back, and he was very careful to give him the correct materials for copying the Leonardo.'

'Extraordinary. And you say he was illiterate?'

'It really helped him with the forging. He had no preconceived idea for example of how a letter was written. A letter was simply an abstract shape. It's easier to copy something with no meaning.'

The heat of the morning deepened, and the smell of flowers. We had nearly finished the bottle of champagne. The lotos land, I thought.

> To hear each other's whispered speech,
> Eating the lotos day by day.

What were the lines about 'the long-leaved flowers weep'? It was the trees which wept here, golden tears. I heard an orange strike the ground. It rolled a few inches and lay among a dozen others.

'What are you thinking, dear?'

'Tennyson has always been my favourite poet. I used to believe there was something Tennysonian in Southwood. The old church perhaps, the rhododendrons, Miss Keene sewing. I always liked his lines:

> Then take the broidery frame, and add
> A crimson to the quaint Macaw

although of course it wasn't embroidery she did.'

'Are you missing Southwood even here?'

'No,' I said, 'there was another Tennyson and I find him here more than there.

> Death is the end of life; ah, why should life all labour be?

'Mr Pottifer didn't believe that – that death was the end of life.'

'A lot of people don't.'

'Yes, but he took positive action.'

I realized that Aunt Augusta passionately wanted to tell me about Pottifer. I caught Mr Visconti's eye and he gave a very slight shrug. 'Who was Pottifer?' I asked my aunt.

'He was an income tax consultant,' Aunt Augusta said and fell silent.

'Is that all?'

'He was a very proud man.'

I could tell that my remark in Boulogne still rankled and that I would have to drag the story out of her piecemeal.

'Yes?'

'He had formerly been employed by the inland revenue – a tax inspector.'

The sun shone down on the orange trees, the lemon and the grapefruit. Under the rosy *lapachos* grew the blue and white flowers on the same bush of jasmine. Mr Visconti poured what was left of the champagne into our three glasses. The transparent moon was dropping over the horizon. Somerset House, income tax . . . They were as distant as the Mare Crisium or the Mare Humorum on the pale globe in the sky.

'Please tell me about him, Aunt Augusta,' I said reluctantly.

'He had the idea,' my aunt said, 'of prolonging his life after death by means of the answering service of the general post office. Not very convenient for his clients, of whom I was one. It was when I was separated for the second time from Mr Visconti by war. In Italy I had never been accustomed to pay taxes. They came as a rude shock to me. Especially as the little income I had was regarded as unearned. When I think of those endless tours, Rome, Milan, Florence, Venice before Jo died, and I joined forces with Mr Visconti . . .'

'A happy day for me, dear,' Mr Visconti said, 'but you were telling Henry about the man Pottifer.'

'I have to give a little background or Henry wouldn't understand about the company.'

'What company?' I asked.

'It was invented by Mr Pottifer to take care of my case and that of a few other ladies in my position. It was called Meerkat Products Ltd. We were appointed directors and our incomes (unearned indeed!) were put down as directors' fees. The fees appeared on the books and helped the company to show what Mr Pottifer always called a healthy little loss. In those days, the bigger the loss, the more valuable the company when the time came to sell it. I never understood why.'

'Your aunt is not a business-woman,' Mr Visconti said with tenderness.

'I trusted Mr Pottifer and I was right to trust him. During his years as an inspector he had developed quite a hatred for the office he served. He would do anything to help anyone about tax. He was very proud of his ability to circumvent a new law. He always went into purdah for three weeks after a new Finance Act.'

'What was Meerkat and what did it produce?'

'It produced nothing or we might have shown a profit. When Mr Pottifer died I did look up Meerkat in the dictionary. It said a small South African mammal like an ichneumon. As I didn't know what an ichneumon was I looked that up too. Apparently it was something which destroyed crocodile's eggs – I would have thought an unproductive occupation. I think the tax inspectors probably thought that it was a province in India.'

Two men came down into the garden carrying a black metal frame.

'What's that, dear?'

'The barbecue.'

'It looks enormous.'

'It has to be if it's to roast an ox whole.'

I said, 'You haven't told me about the answering service.'

'It was most awkward,' my aunt said, 'income tax demands came in – exorbitant as usual – and every time I tried to telephone to Mr Pottifer I heard the answering service, "Mr Pottifer is at a meeting of the Commissioners. He will call you back." This went on for nearly a fortnight, and then it occurred to me to ring him up at one in the morning. The answer was just the same: "Mr Pottifer is at a meeting of the Commissioners . . ." Then I knew something was wrong. It all came out in the end. He had been dead for three weeks, but in his will he had insisted that his brother should keep on the telephone and make an arrangement with the answering service.'

'But why?'

'I think the reason lay partly in his idea of immortality, but I think too it belonged to his war against the Inland Revenue. He was a great believer in delaying tactics. "Never answer all their questions," he would say. "Make them write again. And be ambiguous. You can always decide what you mean later according to circumstances. The bigger the file the bigger the work. Personnel frequently change. A newcomer has to start looking at the file from the beginning. Office space is limited. In the end it's easier for them to give in." Sometimes, if the inspector was pressing very hard, he told me that it was time to fling in a reference to a non-existing letter. He would write sharply, "You seem to have paid no attention to my letter of April 6, 1963." A whole month might pass before the inspector admitted he could find no trace of it. Mr Pottifer would send in a carbon copy of the letter containing a reference which again the inspector would be unable to trace. If he was a newcomer to the district, of course he blamed his predecessor; otherwise, after a few years of Mr Pottifer, he was quite liable to have a nervous breakdown. I think when Mr Pottifer planned to carry on after death (of course there was no notice in the papers and the funeral was very quiet) he had these delaying tactics in mind. He didn't think of the inconvenience to his clients, only of the inconvenience to the inspector.'

Aunt Augusta gave a deep sigh, as ambiguous as one of Pottifer's letters. I couldn't tell whether it was of melancholy for Pottifer's death or of satisfaction in having at last told the story she had begun in the Gare Maritime at Boulogne.

'In this blessed land of Paraguay,' Mr Visconti spoke as though he were adding a moral to the story, 'there is no income tax and no evasions are necessary.'

'Mr Pottifer would not have been happy here,' Aunt Augusta said.

That night, as I was preparing to undress, she came to my room. She sat down on the bed. 'It's quite comfortable here now, isn't it?' she asked me.

'Very comfortable.'

She noticed at once the photograph of herself which I had taken from *Rob Roy* and stuck into a corner of a looking-glass. A bedroom without a photograph always seems to indicate a heartless occupant, for one needs the presence of others when one falls asleep, standing around as Matthew, Mark, Luke and John used to in childhood. 'Where did that come from?' Aunt Augusta asked.

'I found it in a book.'

'Your father took it.'

'I thought so.'

'It was a very happy day,' she said. 'There weren't many arguments about *your* future.'

'Mine?'

'And you weren't even born. Now again I wish that I could know your future. Are you going to stay with us? You are so evasive.'

'It's too late for the boat now.'

'There's sure to be an empty cabin.'

'I don't think I want three days with poor Wordsworth.'

'There are planes . . .'

'Exactly,' I said, 'so you see I needn't make up my mind. I can go next week, or the week after. We can wait and see how things go.'

'I have always thought that one day we might be together.'

'Always, Aunt Augusta? We've known each other for less than a year.'

'Why do you suppose I came to the funeral?'

'It was your sister's funeral.'

'Yes, of course, I had forgotten that.'

'There's plenty of time to make plans,' I said. 'You may not even want to settle here yourself. After all you are a great traveller, Aunt Augusta.'

'This is my journey's end,' Aunt Augusta said. 'Perhaps travel for me was always a substitute. I never wanted to travel as long as Mr Visconti was there. What is there in Southwood which draws you back?'

The question had been in my mind for several days and now I did my best to answer it. I spoke of my dahlias, I even talked of Major Charge and his goldfish. The rain began to fall, rustling through the trees in the garden: a grapefruit tumbled heavily to earth. I spoke of the last evening with Miss Keene and her sad undecided letter from Koffiefontein. Even the admiral stalked through my memories, flushed with Chianti and wearing a scarlet paper cap. Packages of Omo were left on the doorstep. I felt a sense of relief as a patient must feel under pentothal, and I let my random thoughts dictate my words. I spoke of Chicken and of Peter and Nancy in the Abbey Restaurant in Latimer Road, of the bells of St John's Church and the tablet to Councillor Trumbull, the patron of the grim orphanage. I sat on the bed beside my aunt and she put her arm round me while I went over the uneventful story of my life. 'I've been very happy,' I concluded as though it needed an excuse.

'Yes, dear, yes, I know,' she said.

I told her how very kind to me Sir Alfred Keene had been, and I told her of the bank and of how Sir Alfred threatened to remove his account if I did not remain as manager.

'My darling boy,' she said, 'all that is over now,' and she stroked my forehead with her old hand as though I were a schoolboy who had run away from school and she was promising me that I would never have to return, that all my difficulties were over, that I could stay at home.

I was sunk deep in my middle age. All the same I laid my head against her breast. 'I have been happy,' I said, 'but I have been so bored for so long.'

Chapter 8

THE party was larger than I had conceived possible after seeing my aunt alone in the empty unfurnished house, and I could only explain it by the fact that not one real friend was present among all the hundred guests, unless one could call O'Toole a friend. As more and more guests assembled I wondered from what highways and hedges Mr Visconti had drummed them up. The street was lined with cars, among them two armoured ones, for the Chief of Police had arrived as promised bringing with him a very fat and ugly wife and a beautiful daughter called Camilla. Even the young officer who had arrested me was there, and he gave me a hearty slap on the back to show that there was no ill feeling on his part. (I had still a piece of plaster on my ear where he had struck me on the earlier occasion.) I think Mr Visconti must have visited every hotel bar in town, and the most passing acquaintances had been invited to bring their friends. The party was to be his apotheosis. After it no one would ever care to remember the former Mr Visconti who had lain sick and impoverished in a mean hotel by the yellow Victorian station.

The great gates had been cleaned of rust and flung open; the chandeliers sparkled in the *sala*, lights were turned on in even the empty rooms, while coloured globes had been strung from tree to tree and over the boards of the dance-floor laid on the grass. On the terrace two musicians tuned a guitar and a harp. O'Toole was there, the Czech who had failed to sell two million plastic straws had brought his wife from the Hotel Guaraní, and suddenly I saw moving inconspicuously through the crowd and disappearing again as though into some warren in the garden the export-import merchant who had shared our table on the boat, grey and thin, twitching his rabbit nose. On the lawn the ox steamed and crackled on its iron frame, and the smell of roasting meat chased away the perfume of orange and jasmine.

My memories of the party are very confused, perhaps because I helped myself rather liberally to champagne before dinner. There were more women than men, as so often happens in Paraguay, where the male population has been reduced by two terrible wars, and I found myself on more than one occasion dancing or speaking with the beautiful Camilla. The musicians played mainly polkas and gallops, the steps of which were unknown to me, and I was astonished to see how my aunt and Mr Visconti picked them up on the spot by a kind of second nature. Whenever I looked among the dancers, on the lawn or in the *sala*, they were there. Camilla who could speak very little English tried in vain to teach me: it was too much a matter of duty on her part for me to respond. I said, 'I am glad I am not in prison tonight.'

'How?'

'That young man over there put me in a cell.'

'How?'

'Do you see this plaster? That's where he hit me.'

I was trying to make light conversation, but when there was a pause in the music she hastened away.

O'Toole was suddenly at my side. He said, 'It's a great party. Great. I wish Lucinda could have been here. She'd have found it great too. There's the Dutch Ambassador talking to your aunt. I saw your British Ambassador just now. And the Nicaraguan. I wonder how Mr Visconti corralled the diplomatic corps. I guess it's his name – if it is his real name. There's not much to do in Asunción, and I suppose if you get an invitation from a guy called Visconti . . .'

'Have you seen Wordsworth?' I asked. 'I half-expected him to turn up as well.'

'He'll be on the boat by now. They sail at six, as soon as it's light. I guess he wouldn't be very welcome here as things are.'

'No.'

The guests were crowding to the steps of the terrace, clapping and crying '*Brava*'. I saw Camilla up there dancing with a bottle balanced on her head. Mr Visconti pulled at my arm and said, 'Henry, I want you to meet our representative in Formosa.' I turned and held out my hand to the man with the grey rabbit face.

'We were on the boat together coming from Buenos Aires,' I reminded him, but of course he spoke no English.

'He handles our river-borne traffic,' Mr Visconti said, as though he were talking about some great legal enterprise. 'You will be seeing a lot of each other. Now come and meet the Chief of Police.'

The Chief of Police spoke English with an American accent. He told me he had studied in Chicago. I said, 'You have a beautiful daughter.'

He made a bow and said, 'She has a beautiful mother.'

'She tried to teach me to dance, but I have no ear for music and your dances are new to me.'

'The polka and the gallop. They are our national dances.'

'The names sound very Victorian,' I said. I had meant it as a compliment, but he moved abruptly away.

The charcoal under the ox was turning black, and there was little left of the ox but a skeleton. It had been a good dinner. We had sat on benches in the garden before trestle tables and carried our plates to the barbecue. I had noticed how a stout man who sat beside me refilled his plate four times with huge steaks. 'You have a good appetite,' I said.

He ate like a good trencherman in a Victorian illustration, with the elbows stuck out and the head well down and a napkin tucked in his collar. He said, 'This is nothing. At home I eat eight kilos of beef a day. A man needs strength.'

'What do you do?' I asked.

'I am the chief customs officer,' he said. He pointed with his fork down the table to a slim pale girl who looked scarcely eighteen. 'My daughter,' he said. 'I tell her to eat more meat, but she is obstinate like her mother.'

'Which is her mother?'

'She died. In the Civil War. She had no resistance. She did not eat meat.'

Now in the small hours I found him again beside me. He put his arm around my shoulders and squeezed me as if we were old friends. He said, 'Here is Maria. My daughter. She speaks English good. You must dance with her. Tell her she must eat more meat.'

We walked away together. I said, 'Your father says he eats eight kilos of meat a day.'

'Yes. That is true,' she said.

'I don't know your dances, I'm afraid.'

'It does not matter. I have danced enough.'

We walked towards the trees and I found two chairs. A photographer stopped beside us and held up his flash. Her face was startlingly white and her eyes looked frightened in the glare. Then everything faded out and I could hardly see her. 'How old are you?' I asked.

'Fourteen,' she said.

'Your father thinks you should eat more meat.'

'I do not care for meat,' she said.

'What do you like?'

'Poetry. English poetry. I like English poetry very much.' She recited very seriously, '"Hearts of oak are our ships, Hearts of oak are our men."' She added, 'And *Lord Ullin's Daughter*.' She said, 'I cry often when I read *Lord Ullin's Daughter*.'

'And Tennyson?'

'Yes, I know Lord Tennyson too.' She was gaining confidence, finding an interest we shared. 'He is sad also. I like very much sad things.'

The guests crowded the floor as the harpist and the guitarist played another polka: we could see beyond the terrace through the windows of the *sala* the ebb and flow of the dancers. I quoted *Maud* in my turn to the customs officer's daughter: '"The brief night goes in babble and revel and wine".'

'I do not know that poem. Is it sad?'

'It's a very long poem, and it ends very sadly.' I tried to remember some of the sad lines, but the only one that came to my mind was: 'I hate the dreadful hollow behind the little wood', which had little meaning out of context. I said, 'If you like I will lend it to you. I have the collected poems of Tennyson here with me.'

O'Toole came towards us and I saw a chance of escaping, for I was feeling very tired and my ear hurt. I said, 'This is Maria. She is studying English literature like your daughter.' He was a sad and serious man. They would get on well together. It was nearly two in the morning. I wanted to find some unobtrusive corner where I could sleep a while, but halfway across the lawn I found the Czech in conversation with Mr Visconti. Mr Visconti said, 'Henry, we have an offer.'

'An offer?'

'This gentleman has two million plastic straws which he would let us have at half the cost price.'

'That's nearly the whole population of Paraguay,' I said.

'I am not thinking of Paraguay.'

The Czech said with a smile, 'If you could persuade them to drink maté through a plastic straw . . .' He wasn't taking the business discussion very seriously, but I could see that Mr Visconti's imagination had taken wing – I was reminded of Aunt Augusta when she began to embroider one of her anecdotes. It was probably the sound of that very round de luxe number – two million – that had excited Mr Visconti.

He said, 'I was thinking of Panama. If our agent there could get them into the Canal Zone. Think of all those American sailors and tourists . . .'

'Do American sailors take soft drinks?' the Czech asked.

'Have you never heard,' Mr Visconti said, 'that beer is much more intoxicating drunk through a straw?'

'Surely that is only a legend.'

'There speaks a Protestant,' Mr Visconti said. 'Any Catholic knows that a legend which is believed has the same value and effect as the truth. Look at the cult of the saints.'

'But the Americans may be Protestants.'

'Then we produce medical evidence. That is the modern form of the legend. The toxic effect of imbibing alcohol through a straw. There is a Doctor Rodriguez here who would help me. The statistics of cancer of the liver. Suppose we could persuade the Panama government to prohibit the sale of straws with alcoholic drink. The straws would be sold illicitly from under the counter. The demand would be tremendous. Remote danger is a great attraction. From the profits I would found the Visconti Research Institute . . .'

'But these are *plastic* straws.'

'We can call them *cured* straws; there will be articles showing that the cure is quite useless like filters on cigarettes.'

I left the two of them to their discussion. As I skirted the dance-floor I saw my aunt dancing the gallop with the Chief of Police: nothing seemed to tire her. The Chief's daughter Camilla was in the arms of the customs officer, but the dancers had thinned out and a car with a CD plate was driving away.

I found a chair in the yard behind the kitchen where a few crates of furniture still remained unopened, and almost immediately I fell asleep. I dreamt that the rabbit-nosed man was feeling my pulse and telling Mr Visconti that I was dead of the fluke – whatever that might mean. I tried to speak out to prove that I was alive, but Mr Visconti commanded some shadowy figures in the background, in a jumbled phrase from *Maud*, to bury me deeper, only a little deeper. I tried to cry out to my aunt who stood there pregnant in a bathing dress, holding Mr Visconti's hand, and I woke gasping for breath and for words and heard the sound of the harp and the guitar playing on.

I looked at my watch and saw that it was nearly four. Sunrise was not far off, the lights had been turned out in the garden, and the flowers seemed to breathe their scent more deeply in the small chill of the dawn. I felt oddly elated to be alive, and I knew in a moment of decision that I would never see Major Charge again, nor the dahlias, the empty urn, the packet of Omo on the doorstep or a letter from Miss Keenc. I walked down towards the little wood of fruit trees nursing my decision close to my heart – I think even then I knew there would be a price to pay for it. The dancers who remained must all be in the *sala* now, for the lawn was empty, and there were no cars left outside the gates so far as I could see, though I heard the sound of one receding down the road towards the city. Again lines from Maud came to mind in the early sweet-scented morning: 'Low on the sand and loud on the stone the last wheel echoes away.' It was as though I were safely back in the Victorian world where I had been taught by my father's books to feel more at home than in our modern day. The wood sloped down towards the road and up again to the back gate, and as I entered the little hollow I trod on something hard. I stooped down and picked the object up. It was Wordsworth's knife. The tool for taking stones out of horses' hoofs was open – perhaps he had meant to open the blade and in his hurry he had made an error. I struck a match and before the flame went out I saw the body on the ground and the black face starred with white orange petals, which had been blown from the trees in the small breeze of early morning.

I knelt down and felt for the pulse in the heart. There was no life in the black body and my hand was wet from the wound I couldn't see. 'Poor Wordsworth,' I said aloud with some idea of showing to his murderer if he were anywhere nearby that Wordsworth had a friend. I thought how his bizarre love for an old woman had taken him from the doors of the Grenada cinema, where he used to stand so proudly in his uniform, to die on the wet grass near the Paraguay river, but I knew that if this was the price he had to pay, he would have paid it gladly. He was a romantic, and in the only form of poetry he knew, the poetry which he had learnt at St George's Cathedral, Freetown, he would have found the right words to express his love and his death. I could imagine him at the last, refusing to admit that she had dismissed him forever, reciting a hymn to keep his courage up as he walked towards the house through the hollow in the little wood:

'If I ask Her to receive me,
Will she say me nay?
Not till earth and not till heav'n
Pass away.'

The sentiment had always been sincere even if the changes in the words were unliturgical.

There was no sound except my own breathing. I closed the knife and put it in my pocket. Had he drawn it when he first entered the grounds with the intention of attacking Visconti? I preferred to think otherwise – that he had come with the simple purpose of appealing to his love once more before abandoning hope and that when he heard someone move among the trees he had drawn the knife hurriedly in self-defence, pointing at his unseen enemy the useless tool for horses' hoofs.

I went slowly back towards the house to break the news as gently as I might to Aunt Augusta. The musicians were still playing on the terrace, they were tired out and almost falling asleep over their instruments, but when I entered the *sala* there remained only one couple – my aunt and Mr Visconti. I was reminded of the house behind the *Messaggero* where they had met after a long separation and danced together between the sofas while the prostitutes watched with amazement. They were dancing a slow waltz now and they never saw me enter, two old people bound in the deep incurable egotism of passion. They had turned off the lights, and in the big room illumined only from the terrace there rested pools of darkness between the windows. As they moved I lost their faces and found them again. At one moment the shadows gave my aunt a deceptive air of youth: she looked like the young woman in my father's photograph pregnant with happiness, and at another I recognized the old woman who had faced Miss Paterson with such merciless cruelty and jealousy.

I called out to her as she went by, 'Aunt Augusta,' but she didn't answer to the name; there was no sign that she even heard me. They danced on in their tireless passion into the shadows.

I took a few steps further into the room as they returned towards me, calling to her a second time, 'Mother, Wordsworth's dead.' She only looked over her partner's shoulder and said, 'Yes, dear, all in good time, but can't you see that now I am dancing with Mr Visconti?'

A flash-bulb broke the shadows up. I have the photograph still – all three of us are petrified by the lightning flash into a family group: you can see the great gap in Visconti's teeth as he smiles towards me like an accomplice. I have my hand thrown out in frozen appeal, and my mother is regarding me with an expression of tenderness and reproof. I have cut from the print another face which I hadn't realized was in the room with us, the face of a little old man with long moustaches. He had been first with the news, and Mr Visconti sacked him later at my insistence (my mother took no part in the dispute which she said was a matter to be settled between men), so Wordsworth did not go entirely unavenged.

Not that I have time to think of the poor fellow very much. Mr Visconti has not yet made a fortune, and our import-export business takes more and more of my time. We have had our ups and downs, and the photographs of what we call the great party and of our distinguished guests have proved useful more than once. We own a complete Dakota now, for our partner was accidentally shot dead by a policeman because he couldn't make himself understood in Guaraní, and most of my spare time is spent in learning that language. Next year, when she is sixteen, I am to marry the daughter of the Chief of Customs, a union which has the approval of Mr Visconti and her parents. There is, of course, a considerable difference in our ages, but she is a gentle and obedient child, and often in the warm scented evenings we read Browning together.

> God's in his heaven –
> All's right with the world!

THE HONORARY CONSUL

'All things merge in one another –
good into evil, generosity into
justice, religion into politics . . .'

THOMAS HARDY

For Victoria Ocampo with love,
and in memory of the many happy weeks
I have passed at San Isidro
and Mar del Plata.

Not one of the characters in this book is based on a living character, from the British Ambassador to the old man José. The province and the city in Argentina where the scene is principally set bear, of course, resemblances to a real city and a real province. I have left them nameless because I wished to take certain liberties and not to be tied down to the street plan of a particular city or the map of a particular province.

PART ONE

Chapter 1

DOCTOR EDUARDO PLARR stood in the small port on the Paraná, among the rails and yellow cranes, watching where a horizontal plume of smoke stretched over the Chaco. It lay between the red bars of sunset like a stripe on a national flag. Doctor Plarr found himself alone at that hour except for the one sailor who was on guard outside the maritime building. It was an evening which, by some mysterious combination of failing light and the smell of an unrecognized plant, brings back to some men the sense of childhood and of future hope and to others the sense of something which has been lost and nearly forgotten.

The rails, the cranes, the maritime building – these had been what Doctor Plarr first saw of his adopted country. The years had changed nothing except by adding the line of smoke which when he arrived here first had not yet been hung out along the horizon on the far side of the Paraná. The factory that produced it had been built when he came down from the northern republic with his mother more than twenty years before on the weekly service from Paraguay. He remembered his father as he stood on the quay at Asunción beside the short gangway of the small river boat, tall and grey and hollow-chested, and promised with a mechanical optimism that he would join them soon. In a month – or perhaps three – hope creaked in his throat like a piece of rusty machinery.

It seemed in no way strange to the fourteen-year-old boy, though perhaps a little foreign, that his father kissed his wife on her forehead with a sort of reverence, as though she were a mother more than a bed-mate. Doctor Plarr had considered himself in those days quite as Spanish as his mother, while his father was very noticeably English-born. His father belonged by right, and not simply by a passport, to the legendary island of snow and fog, the country of Dickens and of

Conan Doyle, even though he had probably retained few genuine memories of the land he had left at the age of ten. A picture book, which had been bought for him at the last moment before embarkation by *his* parents, had survived – *London Panorama* – and Henry Plarr used often to turn over for his small son Eduardo the pages of flat grey photographs showing Buckingham Palace, the Tower of London, and a vista of Oxford Street, filled with hansoms and horse-drawn cabs and ladies who clutched long skirts. His father, as Doctor Plarr realized much later, was an exile, and this was a continent of exiles – of Italians, of Czechs, of Poles, of Welsh, of English. When Doctor Plarr as a boy read a novel of Dickens he read it as a foreigner might do, taking it all for contemporary truth for want of any other evidence, like a Russian who believes that the bailiff and the coffin-maker still follow their unchanged vocations in a world where Oliver Twist is somewhere imprisoned in a London cellar asking for more.

At fourteen he could not understand the motives which had made his father stay behind on the quay of the old capital on the river. It took him more than a few years of life in Buenos Aires before he began to realize that the existence of an exile did not make for simplicity – so many documents, so many visits to government offices. Simplicity belonged by right to those who were native-born, those who could take the conditions of life, however bizarre, for granted. The Spanish language was Roman by origin, and the Romans were a simple people. *Machismo* – the sense of masculine pride – was the Spanish equivalent of *virtus*. It had little to do with English courage or a stiff upper lip. Perhaps his father in his foreign way was trying to imitate *machismo* when he chose to face alone the daily increasing dangers on the other side of the Paraguayan border, but it was only the stiff lip which showed upon the quay.

The young Plarr and his mother reached the river port at almost this hour of the evening on their way to the great noisy capital of the republic in the south (their departure having been delayed some hours by a political demonstration), and something in the scene – the old colonial houses, a crumble of stucco in the street behind the waterfront – two lovers embracing on a bench – a moonstruck statue of a naked woman and the bust of an admiral with a homely Irish name – the electric light globes like great ripe fruit above a soft-drink stand – became lodged in the young Plarr's mind as a symbol of unaccustomed peace, so that, at long last, when he felt an urgent need to escape somewhere from the skyscrapers, the traffic blocks, the sirens of police-cars and ambulances, the heroic statues of liberators on horseback, he chose to come back to this small northern city to work, with all the prestige of a qualified doctor from Buenos Aires. Not one of his friends in the capital or his coffee-house acquaintances came near to understanding his motive: he would find a hot humid unhealthy climate in the north, they all assured him of that, and a town where nothing ever happened, not even violence.

'Perhaps it's unhealthy enough for me to build a better practice,' he would reply with a smile which was quite as unmeaning – or false – as his father's expression of hope.

In Buenos Aires, during the long years of separation, they had received one letter only from his father. It was addressed on the envelope to both of them, *Señora e hijo*. The letter had not come through the post. They found it stuck under the door of the apartment on a Sunday evening about four years after their arrival when they returned from the cinema where they had watched *Gone with the Wind* for the third time. His mother never missed a revival, perhaps because the old film and the old stars made civil war seem for a few hours something static and undangerous. Clark Gable and Vivien Leigh bobbed up again through the years in spite of all the bullets.

The envelope was very dirty and scrumpled and it was marked 'By Hand', but they were never to learn by whose hand. It was not written on their old notepaper, which had been elegantly stamped in Gothic type with the name of the *estancia*, but on the lined leaves of a cheap notebook. The letter was full, like the voice on the quay had been, of pretended hope – 'things', his father wrote, were bound to settle down soon; it was undated, so perhaps the 'hope' had been exhausted for a long time before the letter arrived. They never heard from his father again; not even a report or a rumour reached them either of his imprisonment or of his death. He had concluded the letter with Spanish formality, 'It is my great comfort that the two whom I love best in the world are both in safety, your affectionate husband and father, Henry Plarr.'

Doctor Plarr could not measure himself exactly how much he had been influenced to return to the small river port by the sense that here he would be living near the border of the country where he had been born and where his father was buried – whether in a prison or a patch of ground he would probably never know. He had only to drive a few kilometres north-east and look across the curve of the river. He had only like the smugglers to take a canoe . . . He felt some times like a watchman waiting for a signal. There was of course a more immediate motive. Once to a mistress he had said, 'I left Buenos Aires to get away as far as possible from my mother.' It was true she had mislaid her beauty and become querulous over her lost *estancia* as she lived on into middle age in the great sprawling muddled capital with its *fantástica arquitectura* of skyscrapers in mean streets rising haphazardly and covered for twenty floors by Pepsi-Cola advertisements.

Doctor Plarr turned his back on the port and continued his evening promenade along the bank of the river. The sky was dark by now so that he could no longer distinguish the plume of smoke or see the line of the opposite bank. The lamps of the ferry which linked the city to the Chaco approached like an illuminated pencil at a slow-drawn wavering diagonal as it fought through the current moving heavily south. The Three Marys hung in the sky like all that was left of a broken rosary chain – the cross lay where it had fallen elsewhere. Doctor Plarr, who every ten years, without quite knowing why, renewed his English passport, felt a sudden desire for company which was not Spanish.

There were only two other Englishmen, so far as he was aware, in the city, an old English teacher who had adopted the title of doctor without ever having seen the inside of a university, and Charley Fortnum, the Honorary Consul. Since the morning months ago when he had begun sleeping with Charley Fortnum's wife, Doctor Plarr found he was ill at ease in the Consul's company; perhaps he was plagued by primitive sensations of guilt; perhaps he was irritated by the complacency of Charley Fortnum who appeared so modestly confident of his wife's fidelity. He talked with pride rather than anxiety of his wife's troubles in her early pregnancy as though they were a kind of compliment to his prowess until Doctor Plarr was almost ready to exclaim, 'But who do you suppose is the father?'

There remained Doctor Humphries . . . though it was still too early to go and find the old man where he lived at the Hotel Bolívar.

Doctor Plarr found a seat under one of the white globes which lit the river-front and took a book out of his pocket. From where he sat he could keep his eye on his car parked by the Coca-Cola stall. The book Doctor Plarr carried with him was a novel written by one of his patients, Jorge Jullo Saavedra. Saavedra too bore the title of doctor, but it was an authentic title, for twenty years ago he had been awarded an honorary degree in the capital. The novel, which had been Doctor Saavedra's first and most successful, was called *The Taciturn Heart*, and it was written in a heavily loaded melancholy style, full of the spirit of *machismo*.

Doctor Plarr found it hard to read more than a few pages at a time. These noble and uncommunicative characters in Latin-American literature seemed to him too simple and too heroic ever to have had living models. Rousseau and Chateaubriand were a greater influence in South America than Freud – there was even a city in Brazil named after Benjamin Constant. He read: 'Julio Moreno would sit for hours in silence, on those days when the wind blew continuously from the sea and salted their few hectares of dry earth, shrivelling the rare plants which had survived the last wind, his chin in his hands, his eyes closed as though he wished to live only in some hidden corridor of his nature from which his wife was excluded. He never complained. She would stand beside him for long minutes, holding the maté gourd in her left hand, and when he opened his eyes Julio Moreno would take it from her without a word spoken. Only a relaxation of the muscles around the stern and unbeaten mouth appeared to her like an expression of thanks.'

Doctor Plarr, who had been brought up by his father on the works of Dickens and Conan Doyle, found the novels of Doctor Jorge Julio Saavedra hard to read, but he regarded the effort as part of his medical duties. In a few days he would have to take one of his regular dinners with Doctor Saavedra at the Hotel Nacional and he must be ready to make some comment on the book which Doctor Saavedra had so warmly inscribed 'To my friend and counsellor Doctor Eduardo Plarr, this my first book to show him I have not always been a political novelist and to disclose, as I can only do to a close friend, the first fruit of my inspiration.' Doctor Saavedra was in fact far from taciturn, but Doctor Plarr suspected he regarded himself as a Moreno *manqué*. Perhaps it was significant that he had given Moreno one of his own Christian names . . .

Doctor Plarr had never caught anyone else reading in the whole city. When he dined out he saw only books imprisoned behind glass to guard them from humidity. He never met anyone unawares reading by the river or even in one of the city squares – except occasionally *El Litoral*, the local paper. There were sometimes lovers on the benches or tired women with shopping baskets, or tramps, but never readers. A tramp would proudly occupy a whole bench. No one cared to share the bench with a tramp, so unlike the rest of the world he could stretch at full length.

Perhaps reading in the open air was a habit he had acquired from his father who always took a book with him when he went farming, and in the orange scented air of his abandoned country Doctor Plarr had got through all the works of Dickens except *Christmas Tales*.

People when they first saw him sitting on a bench with an open book had looked at him with keen curiosity. Perhaps they thought it was a custom peculiar to foreign doctors. It was not exactly unmanly, but it was certainly foreign. The men here preferred to stand at street corners and talk, or sit drinking cups of coffee and talk, or lean out of a window and talk. And all the time, while they talked, they touched each other to emphasize a point or just from friendship. In public Doctor Plarr touched nobody, only his book. It was a sign, like his English passport, that he would always remain a stranger; he would never be properly assimilated.

He began to read again. 'She herself worked in an unbroken silence, accepting the hard toil, like the bad seasons, as a law of nature.'

Doctor Saavedra had enjoyed a period of critical and popular success in the capital. When he began to feel himself neglected by the reviewers – and still worse by the hostesses and the newspaper-reporters – he had come to the north where his great-grandfather had been governor and where he was shown the proper respect due to a famous novelist from the capital, even though there were probably few people who actually read his books. Strangely enough the mental geography of his novels remained unaltered. Wherever he might choose to live now, he had found his mythical region once and forever as a young man, the result of a holiday which he had taken in a small town by the sea, in the far south near Trelew. He had never encountered a Moreno, but he had imagined him very clearly one evening in the bar of a small hotel, where a man sat in melancholy silence over a drink.

Doctor Plarr had learnt all this in the capital from an old friend and jealous enemy of the novelist, and he found the knowledge of Saavedra's background of some value when he came to treat his patients, who suffered from bouts of voluble manic-depression. The same character appeared again and again in all his books, his history changed a little, but never his strong sad silence. The friend and enemy, who had accompanied the young Saavedra on that voyage of discovery, had exclaimed scornfully, 'And do you know who the man was? He was a Welshman, a Welshman. Who has ever heard of a Welshman with *machismo*? There are a lot of Welshmen in those parts. He was drunk, that was all. His weekly drunk when he came in from the country.'

A ferry left for the invisible shore of scrub and swamp, and later the same ferry returned. Doctor Plarr found it difficult to concentrate on the taciturnity of Julio Moreno's heart. Moreno's wife left him at last with a casual labourer on his land who had youth and good looks and some facility in talking, but she was unhappy in the city by the sea where her lover remained unemployed. He soon became habitually drunk in bars and garrulous in bed, and she felt a nostalgia for the long silences and the dry salt ruined earth. So back she came to Moreno, who made room for her without a word at the table where he had prepared a meagre dinner, and afterwards he sat mutely in his customary chair with his chin in his hands while she stood beside him holding his maté gourd. There were still another hundred pages to come, though the story, it seemed to Doctor Plarr, might well have ended there. However Julio Moreno's *machismo* had not yet found full expression, and when he indicated to his wife, in the fewest possible words, his decision to visit the city of Trelew, Doctor Plarr felt quite certain of what would happen there. Julio Moreno would encounter the labourer in a bar of the city and then there would be a fight with knives, won of course by the younger man. Hadn't his wife, when he left, seen in Moreno's eyes 'the expression of an exhausted swimmer who surrenders to the dark tide of his ineluctable destiny'?

It could not be said that Doctor Saavedra wrote badly. There was a heavy music in his style, the drum-beats of destiny were never very far away, but Doctor Plarr sometimes had a longing to exclaim to his melancholy patient, 'Life isn't like that. Life isn't noble or dignified. Even Latin-American life. Nothing is ineluctable. Life has surprises. Life is absurd. Because it's absurd there is always hope. Why, one day we may even discover a cure for cancer and the common cold.' He turned to the last page. Sure enough Julio Moreno's life blood was draining away between the broken tiles on the floor of the Trelew bar and his wife (how had she got there so quickly?) stood by his side, though for once she was not holding a maté gourd. 'A relaxation of the muscles around the hard unbeaten mouth told her, before the eyes closed on the immense weariness of existence, that he found her presence welcome.'

Doctor Plarr closed the book with a bang of irritation. The Southern Cross lay on its cross-piece in a night which was full of stars. No towns or television masts or lighted windows broke the flat black horizon. If he went home might there still be the danger of a telephone call?

When the time had come to leave his last patient, the finance secretary's wife who was suffering from a touch of fever, he was determined not to go home before the early morning. He wanted to keep away from the telephone until it was too late for any unprofessional call. There was one particular possibility, at this hour on this day, of being troubled. Charley Fortnum, he knew, was dining with the

Governor, who needed an interpreter for his guest of honour, the American Ambassador. Clara, now she had overcome her fear of using the telephone, might easily call him and demand his company, with her husband out of the way, and he had no wish to see her on this Tuesday night of all nights. His sexual feeling was anaesthetized by anxiety. He knew how likely it was that Charley would return unexpectedly early; for the dinner would certainly, sooner or later, be cancelled for a reason he had no right to know in advance.

Doctor Plarr decided that it was better to keep out of the way until midnight. The Governor's party would have surely dispersed by that time, and Charley Fortnum would be well on his way home. I am not a man with *machismo*, Doctor Plarr reflected ruefully, though he could hardly imagine Charley Fortnum coming at him with a knife. He got up from the bench. The hour was late enough for the professor of English.

He did not find Doctor Humphries, as he expected, at the Hotel Bolívar. Doctor Humphries had a small room with a douche on the ground floor with a window opening on the patio which contained one dusty palm and a dead fountain. He had left his door unlocked and this perhaps showed his confidence in stability. Doctor Plarr remembered how at night his father in Paraguay would lock even the internal doors of his house, the bedrooms, the lavatories, the unused guest rooms, not against robbers but against the police, the military and the official assassins, though they would certainly not have been deterred long by locked doors.

In Doctor Humphries' room there was hardly space for a bed, a dressing-table, two chairs, a basin and the douche. You had to fight your way between them as though they were passengers in a crowded subway. Doctor Plarr saw that Doctor Humphries had pasted a new picture on the wall, from the Spanish edition of *Life*, showing the Queen perched on a horse at Trooping the Colour. The choice was not necessarily a mark of patriotism or nostalgia: patches of damp were continually appearing on the plaster of the room and Doctor Humphries covered them with the nearest picture which came to hand. Perhaps however his choice did show a certain preference for wakening with the Queen's face rather than Mr Nixon's on the wall (Mr Nixon's face would surely have appeared somewhere in the same number of *Life*). Inside the small room it was cool, but even the coolness was humid. The douche behind the plastic curtain had a faulty washer and dripped upon the tiles. The narrow bed was pulled together rather than made – the bumpy sheet might have been hastily drawn over a corpse, and a mosquito net hung bundled above it like a grey cloud threatening rain. Doctor Plarr was sorry for the self-styled doctor of letters: it was not the kind of surroundings in which any one with free will – if such a man existed – would have chosen to await death. My father, he thought with disquiet, must be about the same age as Humphries now, and perhaps he survives in even worse surroundings.

A scrap of paper was inserted in the frame of Humphries' looking-glass – 'Gone to the Italian Club.' Perhaps he had been expecting a pupil and that was the reason why he had left his door unlocked. The Italian Club was in a once impressive colonial building across the road. There was a bust of somebody, perhaps of Cavour or Mazzini, but the stone was pock-marked and the inscription no longer readable; it stood between the house, which had a stone garland of flowers over every tall window, and the street. Once there had been a great number of Italians living in the city, but now all that was left of the club was the name, the bust, the imposing façade which bore a nineteenth-century date in Roman numerals. There were a few tables where you could eat cheaply without paying a subscription, and only one Italian was left, the solitary waiter who had been born in Naples. The cook was of Hungarian origin and served little else but goulash, a dish in which he could easily disguise the quality of the ingredients, a wise thing to do since the best beef went down the river to the capital, more than eight hundred kilometres away.

Doctor Humphries was seated at a table close to an open window with a napkin tucked into his frayed collar. However hot the day he was always dressed in a suit with a tie and a waistcoat like a Victorian man of letters living in Florence. He wore steel-rimmed spectacles; probably the prescription had not been revised for years, for he bent very low over the goulash to see what he was eating. His white hair was streaked the colour of youth by nicotine, and there were smears of nearly the same colour on his napkin from the goulash. Doctor Plarr said, 'Good evening, Doctor Humphries.'

'Ah, you found my note?'

'I'd have looked in here anyway. How did you know I was coming to your room?'

'I didn't, Doctor Plarr. But I thought somebody might look in, somebody . . .'

'I had been going to suggest we had dinner at the Nacional,' Doctor Plarr explained. He looked around the restaurant for the waiter without any anticipation of pleasure. They were the only clients.

'Very kind of you,' Doctor Humphries said. 'Another day, if you'll let me have what I believe the Yankees call a rain-check. The goulash here is not so bad, one grows a little tired of it, but at least it's filling.' He was a very thin old man. He gave the impression of someone who had worked a long while at eating in the hopeless hope of filling an inexhaustible cavity.

For want of anything better Doctor Plarr too ordered goulash. Doctor Humphries said,'I am surprised to see you. I would have thought the Governor might have invited you . . . he must need someone who speaks English for his dinner tonight.'

Doctor Plarr realized why the message had been stuck into the looking-glass. There could have been a last minute slip in the Governor's arrangements. It had happened once, and Doctor Humphries had been summoned . . . After all there were only three Englishmen who were available. He said, 'He has invited Charley Fortnum.'

'Oh yes, of course,' Doctor Humphries said, 'our Honorary Consul.' He underlined the adjective in a tone of embittered denigration. 'This is a diplomatic dinner. I suppose the Honorary Consul's wife could not appear for reasons of health?'

'The American Ambassador is unmarried, Doctor Humphries. It's informal – a stag-party.'

'A very suitable occasion one might have thought for inviting Mrs Fortnum to entertain the guests. She must be accustomed to stag-parties. But why does the Governor not invite you or me?'

'Be fair, doctor. You and I have no official position here.'

'But we know a lot more about Jesuit ruins than Charley Fortnum does. According to *El Litoral* the Ambassador has come here to see the ruins, not the tea or the maté crop, though that hardly seems likely. American Ambassadors are usually men of business.'

'The new Ambassador wants to create a good impression,' Doctor Plarr said. 'Art and history. He can't be suspected of a take-over bid there. He wants to show a scholarly interest in our province, not a commercial one. The secretary of finance has not been invited, even though he speaks a little English. Otherwise a loan might have been suspected.'

'And the Ambassador – doesn't he speak enough Spanish for a polite toast and a few platitudes?'

'They say he is making rapid progress.'

'What a lot you always seem to know about everything, Plarr. I only know what we read in *El Litoral*. He's off to the ruins tomorrow, isn't he?'

'No, he went there today. Tonight he returns to BA by air.'

'The paper's wrong then?'

'The official programme was a little inaccurate. I suppose the Governor didn't want any incidents.'

'Incidents here? What an idea! I haven't seen an incident in this province in twenty years. Incidents only happen in Córdoba. The goulash isn't so very bad, is it?' he asked hopefully.

'I've eaten worse,' Doctor Plarr said without trying to remember on what occasion.

'I see you've been reading one of Saavedra's books. What do you think of it?'

'Very talented,' Doctor Plarr said. Like the Governor he didn't want any incidents, and he recognized the malice which remained alive and kicking in the old man long after discretion had died from a lifetime's neglect.

'You can really read that stuff? You believe in all that *machismo*?'

'While I read it,' Doctor Plarr said with care, 'I can suspend my disbelief.'

'These Argentinians – they all believe their grandfathers rode with the gauchos. Saavedra has about as much *machismo* as Charley Fortnum. Is it true Charley's having a baby?'

'Yes.'

'Who's the lucky father?'

'Why not Charley?'

'An old man and a drunk? You're her doctor, Plarr. Tell me a little bit of the truth. I don't ask for a very big bit.'

'Why do you always want the truth?'

'Contrary to common belief the truth is nearly always funny. It's only tragedy which people bother to imagine or invent. If you really knew what went into this goulash you'd laugh.'

'Do you know?'

'No. People always conspire to keep the truth from me. Even you lie to me, Plarr.'

'Me?'

'You lie to me about Saavedra's novel and Charley Fortnum's baby. Let's hope, for his sake, it's a girl.'

'Why?'

'It's so much more difficult to detect the father from the features.' Doctor Humphries began to wipe his plate clean with a piece of bread. 'Can you tell me why I'm always hungry, doctor? I don't eat *well*, and yet I eat an awful lot of what they call nourishing food.'

'If you really wanted the truth I would have to examine you, take an X-ray . . .'

'Oh no, no. I only want the truth about other people. It's always other people who are funny.'

'Then why ask me?'

'A conversational gambit,' the old man said, 'to hide my embarrassment while I help myself to that last piece of bread.'

'Do they grudge us bread here?' Doctor Plarr called across a waste of empty tables, 'Waiter, some more bread.'

The only Italian came shuffling towards them. He carried a bread basket with three pieces of bread and he watched with black anxiety when the number was reduced to one. He might have been a junior member of the Mafia who had disobeyed the order of his chief.

'Did you see the sign he made?' Doctor Humphries asked.

'No.'

'He put out two of his fingers. Against the evil eye. He thinks I have the evil eye.'

'Why?'

'I once made a disrespectful remark about the Madonna of Pompeii.'

'What about a game of chess when you have finished?' Doctor Plarr asked. He had to pass the time somehow, away from his apartment and the telephone by the bed.

'I've finished now.'

They went back to the little over-lived-in room in the Hotel Bolívar. The manager was reading *El Litoral* in the patio with his flies open for coolness. He said, 'Someone was asking for you on the telephone, doctor.'

'For me?' Humphries exclaimed with excitement. 'Who was it? What did you tell them?'

'No, it was for Doctor Plarr, professor. A woman. She thought the doctor might be with you.'

'If she rings again,' Plarr said, 'don't say that I am here.'

'Have you no curiosity?' Doctor Humphries asked.

'Oh, I can guess who it is.'

'Not a patient, eh?'

'Yes, a patient. There's no urgency. Nothing to worry about.'

Doctor Plarr found himself checkmated in under twenty moves, and he began impatiently to set the pieces out again.

'Whatever you may say you are worried about something,' the old man said.

'It's that damn douche. Drip drip drip. Why don't you have it mended?'

'What harm does it do? It's soothing. It sings me to sleep.'

Doctor Humphries began with a king's pawn opening. 'K P4,' he said. 'Even the great Capablanca would sometimes begin as simply as that. Charley Fortnum,' he added, 'has got his new Cadillac.'

'Yes.'

'How's your home-grown Fiat?'

'Four – five years old.'

'It pays to be a consul, doesn't it? Permission to import a car every two years. I suppose he's got a general lined up in the capital to buy it as soon as he's run it in.'

'Probably. It's your move.'

'If he got his wife made a consul too they could import a car a year between them. A fortune. Is there any sexual discrimination in the consular service?'

'I don't know the rules.'

'How much did he pay to get appointed, do you suppose?'

'That's a canard, Humphries. He paid nothing. It's not the way our Foreign Office works. Some very important visitors wanted to see the ruins. They had no Spanish. Charley Fortnum gave them a good time. It was as simple as that. And lucky for him. He wasn't doing very well with his maté crop, but a Cadillac every two years makes a lot of difference.'

'Yes, you could say he married on his Cadillac. But I'm surprised that woman of his needed the price of a Cadillac. Surely a Morris Minor would have done.'

'I'm being unfair,' Doctor Plarr said. 'It wasn't only because he looked after royalty. There were quite a number of Englishmen in the province in those days – you know that better than I do. And there was one who got into a mess over the border – the time when the guerrillas went across – and Fortnum knew the local ropes. He saved the Ambassador a lot of trouble. All the same he was lucky – some Ambassadors are more grateful than others.'

'So now if we are in a spot of trouble we have to depend on Charley Fortnum. Check.'

Doctor Plarr had to exchange his queen for a bishop. He said, 'There are worse people than Charley Fortnum.'

'You are in bad trouble now and he can't save you.'

Doctor Plarr looked quickly up from the board, but the old man was only referring to the game. 'Check again,' he said. 'And mate.' He added, 'That douche has been out of order for six months. You don't always lose to me as easily as that.'

'Your game's improved.'

Chapter 2

DOCTOR PLARR refused a third game and drove home. He lived on the top floor of a block of yellow flats which faced the Paraná. The block was one of the eyesores of the old colonial city, but the yellow was fading a little year by year, and anyway he couldn't afford a house while his mother was alive. It was extraordinary how much a woman could spend on sweet cakes in the capital.

As Doctor Plarr closed his shutters the last ferry was approaching across the river, and after he got into bed he heard the heavy thunder of a plane which was making a slow turn overhead: it sounded very low as though it had lifted off the ground only a few minutes before. It was certainly not a long-distance jet over-flying the city on the way to Buenos Aires or Asunción – in any case the hour was too late for a commercial flight. It might, Plarr thought, be the American Ambassador's plane, but he had never expected to hear that. He turned off the light and lay in the dark thinking of all the things which could so easily have gone wrong as the noise of the engine faded, beating south, carrying whom? He wanted to lift the receiver and dial Charley Fortnum, but there was no excuse he could think of for disturbing him at that hour. He could hardly ask: did the Ambassador enjoy the ruins? Did the dinner pass off well? I suppose at the Governor's you must have had some decent steaks? It wasn't his habit to gossip with Charley Fortnum at that hour – Charley was an uxorious man.

He turned his light on again – better to read than worry, and as he knew now what the ending would be without any possibility of mistake, Doctor Saavedra's book proved a good sedative. There was little traffic along the river-front; once a police-car went by with the sirens screaming, but Plarr soon fell asleep with the light still burning.

He was woken by the telephone. His watch stood at exactly two in the morning. He knew of no patient likely to ring him at that hour.

'Yes,' he asked, 'who are you?'

A voice he didn't recognize replied, with elaborate caution, 'Our entertainment was a success.'

Plarr said, 'Who are you? Why tell me that? What entertainment? I'm not interested.' He spoke with the irritation of fear.

'We are worried about one of the cast. He was taken ill.'

'I don't know what you are talking about.'

'We are afraid the strain of his part may have been too great.'

Never before had they telephoned him so openly and at such a suspect hour. There was no reason to believe that his line was tapped, but they had no right to take the smallest risk. Refugees from the north were often kept under a certain loose surveillance in the border region since the days of the guerrilla fighting, if only for their own protection: there were cases of men who had been dragged home to Paraguay across the Paraná to die. There had been an exlled doctor in Posados . . . Because he was a man of the same profession the doctor's example had been present often in Plarr's mind since the plans for the entertainment were first disclosed to him. This telephone call to his apartment could not be justified except in a case of great urgency. One death among the entertainers – by the rules they had set themselves – was to be expected and justified nothing.

He said, 'I don't know what you are talking about. You have the wrong number.' He replaced the receiver and lay looking at the telephone as though it were a black and venomous object which would certainly strike again. It did two minutes later, and he had to listen – it might be an ordinary patient's call.

'Yes – who are you?'

The same voice said, 'You have to come. He may be dying.'

Doctor Plarr asked with resignation, 'What do you want me to do?'

'We'll pick you up in the street in exactly five minutes. If we are not there, then in ten minutes. After that be ready every five minutes.'

'What does your watch say?'

'Six minutes past two.'

The doctor put on a pair of trousers and a shirt; then he packed a briefcase with what might be required (a bullet wound seemed the most likely trouble) and ran lightly down the stairs in his socks. He knew the noise of the elevator was audible through the thin walls of every flat. By two ten he was standing outside the block and at two twelve he went in again and shut the door. At two sixteen he was watching a second time in the street and at two eighteen he was back inside. Fear made him furious. His liberty, perhaps his life, seemed to lie in hopelessly incompetent hands. He knew only two members of the group – they had been at school with him in Asunción – and those who share one's childhood never seem to grow up. He had no more belief in their efficiency than he had when they were students; the organization they had once belonged to in Paraguay, the Juventud Febrerista, had effected little except the death of most of the other members in an ill-advised and ill-led guerrilla action.

Indeed it was that very sense of amateurism which had persuaded him to become involved. He hadn't believed in their plans, and to listen to them was only a mark of friendship. When he questioned them about what they would do in certain eventualities the ruthlessness of their replies seemed to him a form of play-acting. (They had all three taken minor parts in a school performance of *Macbeth* – the prose translation did not make the play more plausible.)

Now, as he stood in the dark hall, watching intently the luminous dial of his watch, he realized he had never for a moment believed they would reach the point of action. Even when he had given them the precise information they required of the American Ambassador's movements (he had learnt the details from Charley Fortnum over a Long John) and supplied them with the drug they needed, he still didn't believe that anything would really happen. Only when he woke that morning and heard León's voice, 'The show goes on', did it occur to him that perhaps these amateurs might after all be dangerous. Was it León Rivas who was dying now? Or Aquino?

It was two twenty-two when he went outside for the third time. A car swerved round the block and stopped, the engine running. A hand waved to him.

As far as he could tell in the light of the dashboard, he didn't know the man at the wheel, but his companion he was able to guess at in the dark by the line of the thin beard which outlined the jaw. It was in a police station cell that Aquino had grown his beard and had begun to write his poetry, and it was in the cell too that he had developed a hungry passion for *chipá*, those doughy rolls made out of mandioca, that can only be properly appreciated after semi-starvation.

'What went wrong, Aquino?'

'The car would not start. Dust in the carburettor. That was it, Diego? And then there was a police patrol.'

'I meant who is dying?'

'Nobody, we hope.'

'León?'

'He is all right.'

'Why did you telephone? You promised not to involve me. León promised.'

He would never have consented to help them if it had not been for León Rivas. It had been León whom he had missed almost as much as his father when he and his mother left on the river boat. León was someone whose word he believed that he could always trust, even though his word seemed later to have been broken when Plarr heard that León had become a priest instead of the fearless *abogado* who would defend the poor and the innocent, like Perry Mason. In his school days León had possessed an enormous collection of Perry Masons stiffly translated into classical Spanish prose. He lent them carefully, one at a time, to selected friends. Perry Mason's secretary Della was the first woman to arouse Plarr's sexual appetite.

'Father Rivas told us to fetch you,' the man called Diego said.

He continued to call León Father, Doctor Plarr noticed, though he had broken a second vow when he left the Church and married, but that particular broken promise was not one which worried Plarr, who never went to Mass except when he accompanied his mother on one of his rare visits to the capital. León, it seemed to him, was struggling back from a succession of failures towards the primal promise to the poor he had never intended to break. He would end as an *abogado* yet.

They turned into Tucumán and then into San Martín, but Doctor Plarr after that tried to avoid looking out. It was as well not to know where they were going. If the worst happened he wanted to betray as little as possible under interrogation.

They were driving fast enough to attract attention. He asked, 'You are not afraid of the police patrols?'

'León has them all mapped out. He has studied them for a month.'

'But tonight – surely it's a little bit special.'

'The Ambassador's car will have been found in the upper Paraná. They will be searching every house on the border, and they will have warned them in Encarnación across the river. There will be road blocks on the road to Rosario. The patrols here must have been cut. They need the men elsewhere. And this is the last place they will look for him with the Governor waiting at his house to take him to the airport.'

'I hope you are right.'

For a moment, without meaning to, Doctor Plarr raised his eyes as the car lurched round a turning, and he saw on the pavement a deck-chair containing a stout elderly woman whom he knew, as he knew the small open doorway behind her – her name was Señora Sanchez and she never slept before her last customer had gone home. She was the richest woman in town or so it was believed.

Doctor Plarr said, 'What happened about the Governor's dinner? How long did they wait?' He could imagine the confusion. One couldn't telephone to a lot of ruins.

'I do not know.'

'Surely you had somebody on the watch?'

'We had enough on our hands.'

He was back with the amateurs; it seemed to Doctor Plarr that the plot would have been better written by Saavedra. Ingenuity, if not *machismo*, was distinctly lacking.

'I heard a plane. Was it the Ambassador's?'

'If it was, it must have gone back empty.'

'You seem to know very little,' Doctor Plarr said. 'Who is hurt?'

The car drew suddenly and roughly up on the margin of a dirt track. 'We get out here,' Aquino said. After Doctor Plarr had left the car he heard it being backed a few yards. He stood still, letting his eyes grow accustomed to the dark, until he was able to see by starlight the kind of place they had brought him to. It was part of the *bidonville* which lay between the city and the bend of the river. The track was almost as wide as a city street, and he could just see a shack made out of dried mud and old petrol cans hidden among the avocados. As his sight cleared he began to make out other huts standing concealed among the trees, like men in ambush. Aquino led him on. The doctor's feet sank more than ankle deep in mud. Even a jeep would have to pass slowly here. There would be plenty of warning if the police made a raid. Perhaps after all they were amateurs of some intelligence.

'Is *he* here?' he asked Aquino.

'Who?'

'Oh, for God's sake, there are no microphones in the trees. The Ambassador, of course.'

'Yes, he is here all right. But he has not come round after the injection.'

They moved as quickly as they could along the mud track, passing several dark huts. The silence seemed unnatural – not even a child crying. Doctor Plarr paused to recover breath. 'These people,' he whispered, 'they must have heard your car.'

'They will not talk. They think we are smugglers. Anyway you can imagine – they are no friends to the police.'

Diego led the way down a side turning where the mud was even deeper. It had not rained for two days, but in this *barrio* of the poor the mud lay permanently until the dry season was well advanced. There was nowhere for the water to drain, and yet, as Doctor Plarr knew well, the inhabitants had to walk as much as a mile in order to find a tap which gave water fit for drinking. The children – he had treated many of them – were big-bellied from protein deficiency. Perhaps he had been many times down this very track – it was indistinguishable from all the others; he had always needed a guide when he visited a patient here. For some reason *The Taciturn Heart* came back to his mind. To fight for one's honour with knives over a woman, that belonged to another, an absurdly outdated, world which had ceased to exist except in the romantic imagination of writers like Saavedra. Honour meant nothing to the starving. To them belonged the more serious fight for survival.

'Is that you, Eduardo?' a voice asked.

'Yes, is that you, León?'

Somebody held a candle up long enough for him to reach the threshold. Then the door was closed quickly behind him.

In the light of the candle he saw the man whom they still called Father Rivas; León looked as thin and immature in his T-shirt and jeans as the boy he had known in the country across the border. His brown eyes were too big for his face, the large ears set almost at right angles to his skull made him resemble one of the small mongrel dogs which haunted the *barrio* of the poor. There was the same soft fidelity in the eyes and a vulnerability in the protruding ears. He could have been taken in spite of his age for a shy seminarist.

'You have been a long time, Eduardo,' he complained softly.

'Ask your driver Diego about that.'

'The Ambassador is still in a coma. We had to give him a second injection. He was thrashing around too much.'

'I told you a second shot would be dangerous.'

'Everything is dangerous,' Father Rivas said gently, as though he were in the confessional warning someone against the temptation of proximity.

While Doctor Plarr unpacked his briefcase Father Rivas went on, 'He is breathlng very heavily.'

'What will you do if he stops breathing altogether?'

'We shall have to change our tactics.'

'How?'

'We shall have to announce he was executed. Revolutionary justice,' he added with an unhappy grin. 'Please, I beg you, do all you can.'

'Of course.'

'We do not want him to die,' Father Rivas said. 'Our job is to save lives.'

They went into the only other room, in which a bed had been improvised out of a long wooden box – he couldn't see clearly what kind of a box – with a few blankets spread over it. Doctor Plarr heard the deep uneven breathing of the drugged man, like someone struggling awake from a nightmare. He said, 'Bring the light closer.' He bent down and looked closely at the flushed face. For a long moment he couldn't believe his eyes. Then he laughed from the shock of what he had seen. 'Oh León,' he said, 'you have taken up the wrong profession.'

'What do you mean?'

'You would do better to go back to the Church. You are not made to be a kidnapper.'

'I do not understand. Is he dying?'

Doctor Plarr said, 'You needn't worry, León, he's not going to die, but this isn't the American Ambassador.'

'Not . . .'

'This is Charley Fortnum.'

'Who is Charley Fortnum?'

'Our Honorary Consul,' Doctor Plarr said in the same tone of mockery which Doctor Humphries had employed.

'But that is impossible,' Father Rivas exclaimed.

'Charley Fortnum's veins run with alcohol, not blood. The morphine I gave you would have acted more gently on the Ambassador. The Ambassador is afraid of alcohol. They had to provide Coca-Cola for the dinner tonight. So Charley told me. He will be all right in a little while. Leave him to sleep it off,' but before he had time to leave the room the man on the wooden box opened his eyes. He stared at Doctor Plarr and Doctor Plarr stared back at him. It was as well to know for certain whether he were recognized.

'Take me home,' Fortnum said, 'home,' and then his body lurched sideways into a deeper sleep.

'Did he recognize you?' Father Rivas asked.

'How would I know?'

'If he recognized you it would complicate matters.'

Somebody lit a second candle in the outer room, but no one spoke; it was as though they all waited to catch a suggestion in another man's eyes as to what should be done now. At last Aquino said, 'This will not please El Tigre.'

'It's really rather comic,' Doctor Plarr said, 'when you think of it. That must have been the Ambassador's plane I heard, and he was in it. On the way back to Buenos Aires. I wonder how the Governor's dinner went without an interpreter.' He looked from one face to another, but no one smiled in return.

There were two men in the room who were unknown to him, and for the first time he noticed a woman who lay asleep on the floor in a dark corner – he had mistaken her for a *poncho* which someone had dropped. One of them was a negro with a pock-marked face, the other an Indian who spoke up now. He couldn't understand the words – they were not Spanish. 'What is he saying, León?'

'Miguel thinks we ought to put him into the river to drown.'

'And what did you say?'

'I said the police would be interested in a body found three hundred kilometres away from the car.'

'The idea's absurd,' Doctor Plarr said. 'You can't murder Charley Fortnum.'

'I try not to think in those terms, Eduardo.'

'Is killing a matter of semantics to you now, León? I remember you were always good at semantics. You used to explain the Trinity to me in the old days, but your explanation was more complicated than the catechism.'

'We do not want to kill him,' Father Rivas said, 'but what can we do? He saw you.'

'He won't remember when he wakes. He always forgets things completely when he's drunk.' Doctor Plarr added, 'How on earth did you make such a mistake?'

'That I must find out,' Father Rivas replied, and he began to talk again in Guaraní.

Doctor Plarr took one of the candles and went back to the doorway of the other room. Charley Fortnum looked quite peacefully asleep on the box, just as though he were in his own great brass bedstead at home, where he lay always on the right side near the window. A sense of fastidiousness made the doctor choose the left side, near the door, when he slept in it himself with Clara.

Charley Fortnum's face as long as he had known him had always been a little flushed. His blood pressure was high and he was too fond of whisky. He had passed sixty, but his thin hair retained a soft and mouse-like tint like a boy's, and his colouring to the unprofessional eye gave a false impression of health. He looked like an out-of-doors man, a farmer. Indeed he had a camp about fifty kilometres from the city, where he grew a little grain and maté. He liked trundling from field to field in an old Land Rover which he called Fortnum's Pride. 'Off for a gallop,' he would say, grinding at the gears, 'hi-yup.'

Now he suddenly raised his hand and waved it. His eyes were closed. He was dreaming. Perhaps he thought he was waving to his wife and the doctor, as he left them on the verandah to deal with dull medical business. 'Women's insides,' Charley Fortnum had said once. 'Never understood them. One day you must draw me a diagram.'

Doctor Plarr went quickly back into the outer room. 'He's all right, León. You can dump him safely by the road somewhere for the police to find.'

'We cannot do that. He may have recognized you.'

'He's fast asleep. Anyway he would say nothing to hurt me. We are old friends.'

'I think I know what must have happened,' Father Rivas said. 'The information you gave us – it was quite correct up to a point. The Ambassador came from Buenos Aires by car, he spent three nights on the road because he wanted to see the country, and the Embassy sent a plane from Buenos Aires to bring him back after his dinner with the Governor. All those details were correct enough, but you never told us your Consul was going with him to the ruins.'

'I didn't know. He told me about the dinner – that was all.'

'He did not even go in the Ambassador's car. At least we would have grabbed both of them then. He must have taken his own car and then left while the Ambassador was still lingering around. Our men were only expecting one car to pass. Our outpost flashed the signal when it went by. He had seen the flag.'

'The Union Jack not the Stars and Stripes. He hadn't even the right to fly that.'

'In the dark you cannot see clearly and he had been told about the diplomatic number plate.'

'It was CC not CD.'

'The letters look much the same in the dark on a moving car. You cannot blame him. Alone in the dark – frightened probably. It could have happened to me or you. A fatality.'

'The police may not know what has happened to Fortnum yet. If you release him quickly . . .'

Doctor Plarr, in the face of their attentive silence, felt as though he were pleading before a tribunal. He said, 'Charley Fortnum's no good to you as a hostage.'

'He is a member of the diplomatic corps,' Aquino said.

'No, he isn't. An Honorary Consul is not a proper Consul.'

'The British Ambassador would have to intervene.'

'Of course. He would report the affair home. Just as he would for anyone British. If you kidnapped me or old Humphries it would be much the same.'

'The British will ask the Americans to bring pressure on the General in Asunción.'

'You can be sure the Americans will do nothing of the kind. Why should they? They don't want to anger their friend the General for the sake of Charley Fortnum.'

'But he is a British *Consul*.'

Doctor Plarr began to despair of ever convincing them of how unimportant Charley Fortnum was. He said, 'He had not even the right to put CC on his car. He was in trouble for that.'

'You knew him well, I think?' Father Rivas said.

'Yes.'

'And you liked him?'

'Yes. In a way.' It wasn't a good sign that León already spoke of Fortnum in the past tense.

'I am sorry. I can understand how you feel. It is always much easier to deal with strangers. Like in the confessional box. I used to hate it if I recognized a voice. One can be harsh so much more easily to a stranger.'

'What can you gain by holding him, León?'

'We came over the border to do a job. There are a lot of our people who would be discouraged if nothing happened. In our situation something must always happen. Even the kidnapping of a Consul is something.'

'An Honorary Consul,' Doctor Plarr corrected.

'It will be a warning to people who are more important. Perhaps they will take our next threat seriously. That is a small tactical point gained in a long war.'

Doctor Plarr said, 'So I suppose you'll be prepared to hear the stranger's confession and give him absolution before you kill him? Charley Fortnum's Catholic, you know. He'll appreciate having a priest at his deathbed.'

Father Rivas said to the negro, 'Give me a cigarette, Pablo.'

'He will be even glad of a married priest like you, León,' Doctor Plarr said.

'You were willing enough to help us, Eduardo.'

'In the case of the Ambassador, yes. His life wouldn't have been in any danger. They would have given way. In any case an American . . . he's a combatant. The Americans have killed plenty of men in South America.'

'Your father is among those we are trying to help – if he is still alive.'

'I don't know whether he would have liked your method.'

'We have not chosen our method. *They* have reduced us to this.'

'What on earth can you ask in return for Charley Fortnum? Perhaps a case of real Scotch?'

'For the American Ambassador we would have demanded the release of twenty prisoners. For a British Consul I think we shall have to halve the bill. That is up to El Tigre.'

'Where the hell is your El Tigre?'

'Only those in Rosario are in touch with him until the operation is finished.'

'I suppose his schedule did not allow for mistakes. Or for human nature. The General can kill the men you name and say they died years ago.'

'We have been through that argument many times. If they kill them our demands will be greater next time.'

'León, listen to me. If you can be sure that Charley Fortnum will remember nothing, surely . . . ?'

'How could we ever be certain? You have no drugs to wipe out memory. Does he mean so much to you, Eduardo?'

'He's a voice in the confessional box which I have recognized.'

'Ted,' a familiar voice called to him from the inner room. 'Ted.'

'You see,' Father Rivas said, 'he knows you.'

Doctor Plarr turned his back on the tribunal and went through the doorway. 'Yes, Charley,' he said, 'here I am. How do you feel?'

'God awful, Ted. What happened? Where am I?'

'You had an accident with your car. Nothing serious.'

'Are you going to take me home?'

'Not yet. You must lie quiet for a while. In the dark. You've got a bit of concussion.'

'Clara's going to be anxious.'

'Don't worry. I'll deal with Clara.'

'You mustn't upset her, Ted. The child . . .'

'I *am* her doctor, Charley.'

'Of course, old man, I'm a bloody fool. Will she be able to see me?'

'In a few days you'll be going home.'

'A few *days*! Have you a drink with you, Ted?'

'No. I'm going to give you something better – to make you sleep.'

'You are a good friend, Ted. Who are those men out there? Why do you have to use a torch?'

'There's a power cut. When you wake up it will be daylight.'

'You'll look in and see me?'

'Of course.'

Charley Fortnum lay still for a moment and then asked in a voice which must have carried clearly into the other room, 'It wasn't really an accident, Ted, was it?'

'Of course it was an accident.'

'The sunglasses . . . what happened to the sunglasses?'

'What sunglasses?'

'They were Clara's,' Charley Fortnum said. 'She liked those sunglasses. I shouldn't have borrowed them. Couldn't find my own.' He raised his knees towards his chest and settled on his side with a long sigh. 'It's the measure that counts,' he said and lay still like an aged embryo which had failed to get born.

In the other room Father Rivas sat with his chin on his crossed fingers and his eyes closed. He might be praying, Doctor Plarr thought as he came back into the room, or perhaps he was only listening carefully to the words of Charley Fortnum as he once used to listen in the confessional to the voice of a stranger in order to decide what penance . . .

'What blunderers you are,' Doctor Plarr accused him. 'What amateurs!'

'On our side we are all amateurs. The police and the soldiers are the professionals.'

'An Honorary Consul, alcoholic at that, in place of an Ambassador.'

'Yes. And Che took photographs like a tourist and left them around. At least no one here has a camera. Or keeps a journal. We learn from our mistakes.'

'Your driver will have to take me home,' Doctor Plarr said.

'Yes.'

'I will come back tomorrow . . .'

'You will not be needed any more, Eduardo.'

'Perhaps not by you, but . . .'

'It is better if he does not see you again before we decide . . .'

'León,' Doctor Plarr said, 'you can't be serious about this. Old Charley Fortnum . . .'

Father Rivas said, 'He is not in our hands, Eduardo. He is in the hands of the governments. In the hands of God too, of course. I do not forget my old claptrap, you notice, but I have never yet seen any sign that He interferes in our wars or our politics.'

[illegible]

[illegible] and read them. [illegible] hear the [illegible]

[illegible]

[illegible]

They [illegible] Clara [illegible]

In the other room, Father (S) [illegible]

[illegible]

On our side we are all [illegible] the police and the soldiers are [illegible]

[illegible]

[illegible]

It's [illegible]

[illegible]

Father [illegible] in the hands of [illegible]

PART TWO

Chapter 1

IT was easy for Doctor Plarr to remember the first time he met Charley Fortnum. The meeting occurred a few weeks after he had arrived in the city from Buenos Aires. The Honorary Consul was exceedingly drunk, and he had lost the use of both legs. Doctor Plarr was making his way up Bolívar when an elderly gentleman leant from the window of the Italian Club and called to him for help. 'The bloody waiter's gone home,' he explained, speaking in English.

When Doctor Plarr entered the club he found a drunk man who seemed perfectly content – the only trouble was he couldn't stand up, but this didn't worry him at all. He said he was quite comfortable on the floor. 'I've sat on worse things,' he said, 'including horses.'

'If you'll take one arm,' the old man said, 'I'll take the other.'

'Who is he?'

'The gentleman you see sitting here on the floor and refusing to get up is Mr Charles Fortnum, our Honorary Consul. You are Doctor Plarr, aren't you? Glad to meet you. I'm Doctor Humphries. Doctor of Letters, not medicine. We three, you may say, are the pillars of the English colony, but one pillar has fallen.'

Fortnum said, 'The measure was wrong.' He added something about the wrong kind of glass. 'You have to have the right sort of glass or you get confused.'

'Is he celebrating something?' Doctor Plarr asked.

'His new Cadillac arrived safely last week, and today he's found a purchaser.'

'You've been eating here?'

'He wanted to take me to the Nacional, but he's much too drunk for the Nacional – or even my hotel. Now we've got to get him home somehow, but he insists on going to see Señora Sanchez.'

'A friend of his?'

'Of half the men in this town. She runs the only good brothel here – or so they say. I'm not a good judge of that kind of thing myself.'

'Surely they are illegal,' said Doctor Plarr.

'Not in this city. We are a military headquarters – don't forget that. The military don't allow anyone in B A to dictate to them here.'

'Why not let him go?'

'You can see why – he can't stand up.'

'Surely the point of a brothel is that one can lie down?'

'Something has to stand up,' Doctor Humphries said with unexpected coarseness and an expression of distaste.

In the end they lugged Charley Fortnum between them across the street to the little room which Doctor Humphries occupied in the Hotel Bolívar. There were fewer pictures on the walls in those days because there were fewer damp stains, and the shower had not yet begun to drip.

Inanimate objects change at a faster rate than human beings. Doctor Humphries and Charley Fortnum were not noticeably different men that night than they were now; a crack in the plaster of a neglected house grows more quickly than a line on a human face, paint changes colour more rapidly than hair, and a room's decay is continuous: it never comes to a temporary halt on that high plateau of old age where a man may live a long time without apparent change. Doctor Humphries had been established on the plateau for many years, and Charley Fortnum, though he was still on one of the lower slopes, had found a reliable weapon in the fight against senility – he had pickled in alcohol some of the high spirits and the naïvety of earlier days. As the years passed, Doctor Plarr could discern little alteration in either of his early acquaintances – perhaps Humphries moved more slowly between the Bolívar and the Italian Club, and sometimes he believed he could detect in Charley Fortnum increasing spots of melancholy, like mould, in his well-bottled bonhomie.

Doctor Plarr left Fortnum with Humphries at the Hotel Bolívar and went to fetch his car. He was living in the same flat in the same block that he inhabited now. Lights were still burning in the port, where labourers worked through the whole night. On a flat barge in the Paraná they had mounted a metal tower from which an iron rod pounded the bottom of the river. Thud, thud, thud, the noise reverberated like tribal drums. From a second barge lengths of pipe were extended, attached to some underwater engine which sucked the gravel out of the river-bed and sent it scuttling and rattling down the waterfront to an inlet half a mile away. The Governor, who had been appointed by the newest President after that year's *coup d'état*, was planning to deepen the port so that it might take ferries of greater draught from the Chaco shore and receive larger passenger boats from the capital. When, after a second military coup, this time in Córdoba, he was dismissed from office, the idea was abandoned, to the benefit of Doctor Plarr's sleep. The Governor of the Chaco, it was said, had not been prepared to spend the necessary money to deepen his side of the river, and the passenger boats from the capital were already too large in the dry season to mount beyond the city where passengers had to be transferred anyway to smaller boats for the voyage to the Paraguayan republic in the north. It was difficult to judge who had made the initial mistake, if it was a mistake. The question *Cui bono*? pointed at no individual, since all the contractors had benefited and all undoubtedly had shared their benefits with others. The harbour works before they were abandoned had done a lot of good; they were responsible for a grand piano in one house, a new refrigerator in somebody's kitchen, and perhaps in some small unimportant sub-contractor's cellar, where spirits had hitherto been little known, lay a dozen or two cases of the national Scotch.

When Doctor Plarr returned to the Hotel Bolívar he found Charley Fortnum drinking strong black coffee made on a spirit-ring which was installed on a marble-topped washhandstand, beside the soap-dish and Doctor Humphries' tooth-glass. He had become a good deal more coherent, and it was all the more difficult to dissuade him from visiting Señora Sanchez. 'There's a girl there,' he said. 'A real girl. Not what you think at all. I've got to see her again. Last time I wasn't in a fit condition . . .'

'You aren't in a fit condition now,' Humphries said.

'You don't understand me at all, do you? I only want to talk to her. We aren't all bloody lechers, Humphries. There's a quality about María. She doesn't belong . . .'

'She's a whore like all the rest, I suppose,' Doctor Humphries said, clearing his throat. Doctor Plarr was soon to learn that, whenever Humphries disapproved of a subject, his throat clogged with phlegm.

'And that's where you're both of you so bloody wrong,' Charley Fortnum said, although Doctor Plarr had not expressed an opinion. 'She *is* different from all the others. She's got a sort of refinement. Her family comes from Córdoba. There's good blood in her or else I'm not Charley Fortnum. I know you think I'm a fool, but there's something well . . . almost virginal about that girl.'

'And you're the Consul here, honorary or not. You've no business to be seen in a low dive like that.'

'I respect the girl,' Charley Fortnum said, 'I respect her even when I sleep with her.'

'It's all you are capable of doing tonight.'

After a little more harsh persuasion, Fortnum allowed himself to be assisted to Doctor Plarr's car.

There he brooded in silence for a time, while his chin shook to the movement of the engine. 'One grows old I suppose,' he said suddenly. 'You are young. You don't suffer from memories, regrets . . . Are you married?' he asked abruptly as they drove up San Martín.

'No.'

'I was married once,' Fortnum said, 'twenty-five years ago – it seems a century now. It didn't work out. She was an intellectual if you understand what I mean. She didn't understand human nature.' He switched – by an association of ideas Doctor Plarr found impossible to follow – to his present condition. 'I always feel a great deal more human,' he said, 'when I've drunk just over half a bottle. A little less than half – that's no use at all, but a little more . . . Of course the effect doesn't last, but half an hour of feeling really good is worth some sadness afterwards.'

'Are you talking of wine?' Doctor Plarr asked with incredulity. He couldn't believe that Fortnum had been so moderate.

'Wine, whisky, gin it's all the same. It's the measure that counts. There's something psychological in the measure. Less than half a bottle and Charley Fortnum's a poor lonely bastard with only Fortnum's Pride for company.'

'Fortnum's Pride?'

'My proud and well-groomed steed. But one glass over the half-bottle – any glass, even a liqueur glass, it's just the measure that counts – and Charley Fortnum's quite himself again. Fit for royalty. You know I went on a picnic with some royals once among the ruins. We had two bottles between the three of us, and it was quite a day, I can tell you, but that's another story. Like Captain Izquierdo. Remind me to tell you one day about Captain Izquierdo.' It was very hard for a stranger to follow Charley Fortnum's associations.

'Where's the Consulate? Is it the next turning on the left?'

'Yes, but we could take the second or third just as well and make a little turn. I enjoy your company, doctor. What did you say your name was?'

'Plarr.'

'Do you know what my name is?'

'Yes.'

'Mason.'

'I thought . . .'

'That's what they called me at school. Mason. Fortnum and Mason, the inseparable twins. It was the best English school in B A. My career though was less than distinguished. A good word to get out so distinct . . . so well. The right measure you see. Not too much and not too little. I was never a prefect, and the marbles team was the only one I made. Not recognized officially. We were a snobbish school. All the same the headmaster, not the one I knew, that was Arden – we called him Smells – well, this new man wrote me a letter of congratulation when I became Honorary Consul. I wrote to him first, of course, and told him the glad news, so I suppose he couldn't very well ignore me altogether.'

'Will you tell me when we get to the Consulate?'

'We've passed it, old man, but never you mind. I've got a clear head. You just take another turn. First to the right and then left again. I'm in the sort of mood when I could drive like this all night. In sympathetic company. No need to pay attention to the one-way signs. Diplomatic privilege. The CC on the car. I can talk to you, doctor, as I can talk to no other man in this city. Spaniards. A proud people but they have no sentiment. Not as we English know it. No sense of Home. Soft slippers, the feet on the table, the friendly glass, the ever-open door. Humphries is not a bad chap – he's as English as you or me, or is he Scotch? – but he has the soul of a – pedagogue. Another good word that. He always tries to correct my morals, and yet I don't do much that's wrong, not really wrong. Tonight, if I'm a little pissed, it was the fault of the glasses. What's your other name, doctor?'

'Eduardo.'

'But I thought you were English?'

'My mother's Paraguayan.'

'Call me Charley. Would you mind if I called you Ted?'

'Call me what you like, but for God's sake tell me where the Consulate is.'

'The next corner. But don't go expecting too much. No marble halls, no chandeliers and potted palms. It's only a bachelor's digs – a bureau, a bedroom – all the usual offices of course. The best the buggers at home are ready to provide. No sense of national pride. Penny wise, pound foolish. You must come out to my camp – that's where my real home is. Nearly a thousand acres. Eight hundred anyway. Some of the best maté in the country. We could drive there now – it's only three quarters of an hour from here. A good night's sleep afterwards – a hair of the dog. I can give you real Scotch.'

'Not tonight. I have patients to see in the morning.'

They stopped outside an old colonial house with Corinthian pillars; the white plaster gleamed in the moonlight. On the first floor a flagstaff projccted and a shield bore the Royal arms. Charley Fortnum swayed a little on the pavement, gazing up. 'Is it true?' he asked.

'Is what true?'

'The flagstaff. Isn't it leaning over a bit too much?'

'It looks all right to me.'

'I wish we had a simpler flag than the Union Jack. I hung it upside down once on the Queen's birthday. I could see nothing wrong with the bloody thing, but Humphries was angry – he said he was going to write to the Ambassador. Come up and have a glass.'

'I must be getting home – if you can manage by yourself.'

'I promise you it's real Scotch. I get Long John from the Embassy. They all prefer Haig there. But Long John gives you a free glass with every bottle. Very nice glasses too with the measures marked. Women, Men, and Shipmaster. I count myself, of course, a Shipmaster. I've got dozens of Long John glasses out at the camp. I like that name Shipmaster. Better than Captain which could be a mere military term.'

He had the classical difficulty with his key, but succeeded in his third attempt. Swaying on the doorstep he made a speech from under the Corinthian columns to Doctor Plarr who waited impatiently on the pavement for him to finish.

'It's been a very agreeable evening, Ted, even if the goulash was damned awful. Good to speak occasionally the native tongue – gets rusty from unuse – the tongue that Shakespeare spoke. You mustn't think I'm always as happy as this, but it's the measure that counts. Moments of melancholy too when I'm glad of a friend's company. And remember any time you need a Consul, Charley Fortnum's only too happy to be of service. To an Englishman. Or Scotsman or Welshman for that matter. We all have something in common. All belong to the once United bloody Kingdom. Nationality's thicker than water, though that's a nasty term, when you think of it, thicker. Reminds you of things better forgotten and forgiven. Did they give you syrup of figs as a boy? Just walk straight up. Middle door on the first floor, but you can't miss the big brass plate. Wants so much polishing you wouldn't believe the hours of labour a brass plate needs. Grooming Fortnum's

Pride is nothing to it.' He slipped back into the dark hall behind, disappearing from sight.

Doctor Plarr drove home to the new yellow block and the noise of gravel grating up the pipes and the whine of the rusty cranes. It seemed to him, as he lay in bed and tried to sleep, that in the years to come he was unlikely to find much in common with the Honorary Consul.

Though Doctor Plarr was in no hurry to resume his acquaintance with Charles Fortnum, a month or two after their first encounter he received certain documents which had to be witnessed by a British Consul.

His first attempt to see the Consul was not successful. He arrived at the Consulate about eleven in the morning. The Union Jack fluttered from the dubious pole in the hot dry wind from the Chaco. He wondered why it was flying at all, until he remembered that the day was the anniversary of the armistice of one world war before the last. He rang the bell and soon he felt sure that an eye was watching him through a spyhole in the door. He stood well back in the sunlight to be inspected, and immediately a small dark woman with a big nose snatched the door open. She stared at him with the intense preoccupied gaze of a bird of prey which was accustomed to watch a point from far off for indications of carrion; perhaps she was surprised to find the carrion so close and still alive. No, she said, the Consul was not in. No, she was not expecting him. Tomorrow? . . . Perhaps. She couldn't be sure about that. It hardly seemed to Doctor Plarr the proper way to run a Consulate.

Doctor Plarr took an hour's siesta after lunch and then he returned to the Consulate on his way to some bedridden patients in the *barrio popular* – if you could call what they lay on beds. He was agreeably surprised when the door was opened by Charles Fortnum himself. The Consul had spoken at their first meeting of having moments of melancholy. Perhaps he was suffering from such a moment now. He looked at the doctor with a frown which was defensive and puzzled as though an unpleasant memory stirred somewhere in his unconscious.

'Yes?'

'I'm Doctor Plarr.'

'Plarr?'

'We met one night with Humphries.'

'Oh yes, did we? Of course. Come in.'

Three doors opened off a dark passage. From behind one of them there seeped the smell of unwashed dishes. Perhaps another indicated a bedroom. The third stood open and Fortnum led him in. A desk, two chairs, a filing cabinet, a safe, a coloured reproduction of Annigoni's portrait of the Queen with a crack in the glass – that was about all. And the desk was quite bare except for a stand-up calendar which advertised an Argentinian tea.

'I'm sorry to disturb you,' Doctor Plarr said. 'I looked in this morning . . .'

'I can't always be here. I have no assistant. There are a lot of official duties. This morning . . . yes, I was with the Governor. What can I do for you?'

'I've brought some documents I want witnessed.'

'Show them to me.'

Fortnum sat heavily down and began to open a number of drawers. From one he pulled a blotting-pad, from another paper and envelopes, from a third a seal, a ballpoint pen. He began to arrange them on the desk as though they were chessmen. He reversed the position of the seal and the pen – perhaps inadvertently he had put the queen on the wrong side of the king. He read the documents with apparent care, but his eyes betrayed him – the words obviously meant nothing to him – then he waited for Doctor Plarr to sign. Afterwards he stamped the papers and added his own signature. Charles Q. Fortnum. 'A thousand pesos,' he said. 'Don't ask about the Q. I keep it dark.' He offered no receipt, but Doctor Plarr paid without question.

The Consul said, 'I've got a splitting headache. You know how it is – the heat, the humidity. This is a damnable climate. God knows why my father chose to live in it and die in it. Why didn't he settle in the south? Anywhere but here.'

'If you feel that way, why don't you sell up and go?'

'Too late,' the Consul said, 'I'm sixty-one next year. What's the good of doing anything at sixty-one? Have you any aspirin in that case of yours, Plarr?'

'Yes. Have you some water?'

'Just give it me as it is. I eat the things. They work quicker that way.' He chewed up the aspirin and asked for another.

'Don't you find the taste disagreeable?'

'You get accustomed. I don't like the taste of water here either if it comes to that. My God, I do feel like hell today.'

'Perhaps I ought to take your blood pressure.'

'Why? Do you think there's something wrong?'

'No, but a check is always good at your age.'

'It's not my blood pressure that's wrong. It's life.'

'Overworked?'

'I wouldn't exactly say that. But there's a new Ambassador – he bothers me.'

'What about?'

'He wants a report on the maté industry in this province. Why? Nobody drinks maté in the old country. Never heard of it probably, but I'll have to work for a week, driving around on bad roads, and then those fellows at the Embassy wonder why I have to import a new car every two years. It's my right to have one. My diplomatic right. I pay for it myself and if I choose to sell it again it's my concern not the Ambassador's. Fortnum's Pride is more reliable on these roads. I charge nothing for her, and yet I'm wearing her out in their service. What a lot of mean bastards they are, Plarr, at the Embassy. They even question the rent I pay for this office.'

Doctor Plarr unpacked his briefcase.

'What's all that nonsense?'

'I thought we agreed to take your blood pressure.'

'Then we'd better go into the bedroom,' the Consul said. 'It wouldn't look good if my maid came in. The news would be all over the city in no time that I was a dying man. And then the bills would pour in.'

The bedroom was almost as bare as the bureau. The bed had been disturbed during the siesta hour, and a pillow lay on the floor beside an empty glass. A photograph of a man with a heavy moustache in riding kit hung above the bed like a substitute for the Queen. The Consul sat on the rumpled coverlet and bared his arm. Doctor Plarr began to inflate the rubber band.

'Do you really think there's something wrong about these headaches?'

Doctor Plarr watched the dial. He said, 'I think there's something wrong in drinking so much at your age.' He let the air run out.

'Headaches run in the family. My father had terrible headaches. He died suddenly. A stroke. That's him up there. He was a great horseman. He tried to make me one too, but I couldn't bear the stupid brutes.'

'I thought you told me you had a horse. Fortnum's Pride, wasn't it?'

'Oh, that's not a horse, that's my Land Rover. You'll never catch me on a horse's back. Tell me the worst, Plarr.'

'These contraptions never tell the worst – or the best. All the same your pressure's a bit high. I'll give you some tablets, but couldn't you cut down the drink a little?'

'That's what the doctors were always saying to my father. He told me once he might have been paying a lot of parrots for squawking the same thing. I suppose I must take after the old bastard – except for the horses. They scare me stiff. He used to be angry about that. He said, "You've got to conquer fear, Charley, or it will conquer you." What's your other name, Plarr?'

'Eduardo.'

'I'm Charley to my friends. Mind if I call you Ted?'

'If you must.'

Charley Fortnum sober had arrived at the same stage of intimacy which he had reached on the last occasion, though by a longer route. Doctor Plarr wondered how often, if their acquaintance continued, they would have to tread the same path before they arrived on the last lap as Charley and Ted.

'You know there's only one other Englishman in this city. A fellow called Humphries, an English teacher. Met him?'

'We were all together one night Don't you remember? I saw you home.'

The Honorary Consul looked at him with an expression of near-fear. 'No, I don't. Not a thing. Is that a bad sign?'

'Oh, it happens to all of us sometimes if we are drunk enough.'

'When I saw you outside the door, I did think for a moment I remembered your face. That's why I asked your name. I thought I might have bought something from you and forgotten to pay. I'll have to go a bit steadier, won't I? For a while I mean.'

'It wouldn't do you any harm.'

'I remember some things very well, but I'm like the old man – he used to forget a lot too. Do you know once – I'd fallen off my horse, it got up suddenly on its hind legs – just to test me, the beast I mean. I was only six, it knew I was only a kid, it was right by the house, and my father was sitting there on the verandah. I was scared in case he might be angry, but what scared me worse was I could see when he looked down at me, where I lay on the ground, that he didn't even remember who I was. He wasn't angry at all, he was puzzled and worried, and he went back to his chair and took up his glass again. So I went round the back to the kitchen (the cook was always a good friend of mine), and I left the bloody horse. Of course I understand now. We had that much in common. He forgot things when he was drunk. Are you married, Ted?'

'No.'

'I was once.'

'Yes, so you told me.'

'I was glad when we split up, but all the same I wish we'd had a child first. When there's no child it's generally the man's fault, isn't it?'

'No. I think the chances are about even.'

'I'd be sterile anyway, wouldn't I, by now?'

'Of course not. Age doesn't make you sterile.'

'If I had a child I wouldn't try to make him conquer fear like my father did. It's part of human nature, isn't it, fear? If you conquer fear, you conquer your human nature, too. It's a bit like the balance of nature. I read in a book once that, if we killed all the spiders in the world, we would all of us be suffocated under the weight of flies. Have you got a child, Ted?'

The name Ted had an irritating effect on Doctor Eduardo Plarr. He said, 'No. If you want to call me by a Christian name I wish you'd call me Eduardo.'

'But you are as English as I am.'

'I'm only half English and that half is in prison or dead.'

'Your father?'

'Yes.'

'And your mother?'

'She's living in BA.'

'You're lucky. You have somebody to save for. My mother died when I was born.'

'It's not a good reason to kill yourself with drink.'

'That's not the reason, Ted. I only mentioned my mother in passing, that's all. What's the good of a friend if one can't talk to him?'

'A friend doesn't make a good psychiatrist.'

'You sound a hard man, Ted. Haven't you ever loved anyone?'

'That depends on what you call love.'

'You analyse too much,' Charley Fortnum said. 'It's a young man's fault. Don't turn up too many stones is what I always say. You never know what you'll find underneath.'

Doctor Plarr said, 'My job is to turn up stones. Guesswork is not much good when you make a diagnosis.'

'And what's your diagnosis?'

'I'm going to give you a prescription, but it won't do you any good unless you cut down on your drinking.'

He went back into the Consul's office. He was irritated by the sense of time wasted. He could have seen three or four patients in the poor quarter of the city during the time he had spent listening to the self-pity of the Honorary Consul. He walked out of the bedroom and sat down at the desk and wrote his prescription. He felt the same sense of wasted time as when he visited his mother and she complained of headaches and loneliness while she sat before a plate heaped up with éclairs in the best teashop of Buenos Aires. She always implied that she had been deserted by her husband – because a husband's first duty was to his wife and child and he should have fled with them.

Charley Fortnum put on his jacket in the next room. 'You aren't going, are you?' he called.

'Yes. I've left the prescription on the desk.'

'What's thc hurry? Stay and have a drink.'

'I have patients to see.'

'Well, I'm your patient too, aren't I?'

'You are not the most important of them,' Doctor Plarr said. 'The prescription isn't renewable. You'll have enough tablets for a month, and then we'll see.'

Doctor Plarr closed the door of the Consulate with a sense of relief, the relief he always felt when he finally left his mother's apartment after a visit to the capital. He hadn't enough time available to waste any of it on the incurable.

Chapter 2

NEARLY two years passed before Doctor Plarr visited for the first time the establishment which was so ably run by Señora Sanchez, and then it was not in the company of the Honorary Consul. He went there with his friend and patient, the novelist, Doctor Jorge Julio Saavedra. Saavedra, as he himself explained over a plate of tough beef at the Nacional, was a man who believed in following a very strict discipline. An observer might have guessed so much from his appearance, which was neat, of a uniform grey, grey hair, grey suit, grey tie. Even in the northern heat he wore the same well-cut double-breasted waistcoat that he used to wear in the coffee-houses of the capital. His tailor there, he told Doctor Plarr, was English. 'You wouldn't believe it, but I haven't had to buy a new suit in ten years.' As for the discipline of work, 'I write five hundred words a day after my breakfast. No more no less,' he said, not for the first time.

Doctor Plarr was a good listener. He had been trained to listen. Most of his middle-class patients were accustomed to spend at least ten minutes explaining a simple attack of 'flu. It was only in the *barrio* of the poor that he ever encountered suffering in silence, suffering which had no vocabulary to explain a degree of pain, its position or its nature. In those huts of mud or tin where the patient often lay without covering on the dirt floor he had to make his own interpretation from a shiver of the skin or a nervous shift of the eyes.

'Discipline,' Jorge Julio Saavedra was repeating, 'is more necessary to me than to other more facile writers. You see I have a daemon where others have a talent. Mind you I envy them their talent. A talent is friendly. A daemon is destructive. You cannot conceive how much I suffer when I write. I have to force myself day after day to sit down pen in hand and I struggle for expression . . . You will remember in my last book, that character, Castillo, the fisherman, who wages an endless war with the sea for a small reward. In a way you might say that Castillo is a portrait of the artist. Such daily agony and the result – five hundred words. A very small catch.'

'I seem to remember Castillo died from a revolver shot in a bar defending his one-eyed daughter from rape.'

'Ah yes, I am glad you notice the Cyclops symbol,' Doctor Saavedra said. 'A symbol of the novelist's art. A one-eyed art because one eye concentrates the vision. The diffuse writer is always two-eyed. He includes too much – like a cinema screen. And the violator? Perhaps he represents this melancholy of mine which descends for weeks at a time, when I struggle for hours to do my daily stint.'

'I hope you find my tablets give you some help.'

'Yes, yes, they help a little, of course, but sometimes I think it is only the daily discipline which saves me from suicide.' Doctor Saavedra, with his fork suspended on the way to the mouth, repeated, 'Suicide.'

'Oh come, surely your faith wouldn't allow you . . . ?'

'In those black moments, doctor, I have no faith, no faith at all. *En una noche oscura*. Shall we open another bottle? This wine from Mendoza is not wholly bad.'

After the second bottle the novelist revealed another rule of his self-imposed discipline, his weekly visit to the house of Señora Sanchez. He explained that it was not merely a question of keeping his body calm so as to prevent importunate desires coming between him and his work; from his weekly visit he learned a great deal about human nature. In the social life of the city there was no contact between the classes. How could dinner with Señora Escobar or Señora Vallejo provide him with any insight into the life of the poor? The character of Carlota, the daughter of Castillo, the heroic fisherman, was based on a girl he had met in the establishment of Señora Sanchez. Of course she had two eyes. She was indeed remarkably pretty, but when he came to write his novel he found her beauty gave her story a false and banal turn; it fitted ill with the bleak severity of the fisherman's life. Even the violator became a conventional character. Pretty girls were being violated all the time everywhere, especially in the books of his contemporaries, those facile writers of undoubted talent.

At the end of dinner Doctor Plarr was easily persuaded to accompany the novelist on his disciplinary visit, though he was tempted more by curiosity than sexual desire. They left their table at midnight and set out on foot. Though Señora Sanchez was protected by the authorities it was better not to leave a car outside in case an inquisitive policeman noted the number. Such an addition to one's police file might one day prove undesirable. Doctor Saavedra wore pointed highly polished shoes and gave the impression of hopping when he walked because he was a little pigeon-toed. One half expected to see bird-marks left behind on the dusty pavement.

Señora Sanchez sat in a deck-chair outside her house knitting. She was a very stout lady with a dimpled face and a welcoming smile from which kindliness was oddly lacking, as though it had been mislaid accidentally a moment before like a pair of spectacles. The novelist introduced Doctor Plarr.

'I am always glad to welcome a medical gentleman,' Señora Sanchez said. 'You will appreciate how well my girls are looked after. I employ your colleague Doctor Benevento, a most sympathetic man.'

'So I have heard. I have not met him,' Doctor Plarr said.

'He comes here on Thursday afternoons and all my girls are very fond of him.'

They passed through the narrow lighted doorway. Except for Señora Sanchez in her deck-chair there were no exterior signs to differentiate her establishment from the other houses in the respectable street. A good wine, Doctor Plarr thought, needs no bush.

It was a house very different in character from the clandestine brothels he had occasionally visited in the capital where small rooms were darkened by closed shutters and crammed with bourgeois furniture. There was a pleasant country air about this house. An airy patio about the size of a tennis court was surrounded by small cells. Two open doors faced him when he had taken a seat, and he thought the cells looked gayer, cleaner, and in better taste than Doctor Humphries' bedroom at the Hotel Bolívar. Each possessed a little shrine with a lighted candle which gave the tidy interiors the atmosphere of a home rather than of a place of business. A group of girls sat at a table apart, while two talked with young men, leaning against the pillars of the verandah which surrounded the patio. There was no sign of hustling – it was obvious Señora Sanchez was strict about that; here a man might take his time. One man sat alone over a glass, and another, dressed like a *peôn*, stood by a pillar, watching the girls with an unhappy, envious expression (perhaps he hadn't the means to buy even a drink).

A girl called Teresa came immediately to take the novelist's order ('Whisky,' he advised, 'the brandy is not to be trusted'), and afterwards sat down with them unasked. 'Teresa comes from Salta,' Doctor Saavedra explained, leaving his hand in her care like a glove in a cloak-room. She turned it this way and that and examined the fingers as though she were looking for holes. 'I am thinking of setting my next novel in Salta.'

Doctor Plarr said, 'I hope your daemon won't insist on giving her one eye.'

'You laugh at me,' the novelist said, 'because you have so little idea of how a writer's imagination works. He has to transform reality. Look at her – those big brown eyes, those plump little breasts, she's pretty isn't she' – the girl gave a gratified smile and scratched his palm with her nail – 'but what does she represent? I am not planning a love story for a woman's magazine. My characters must symbolize more than themselves. Now it *has* occurred to me that with perhaps one leg . . .'

'A girl with one leg could be more easily violated.'

'There is no violation in my story. But a beauty with one leg – don't you see the significance of that? Think of her halting walk, her moments of despair, the lovers who feel they do her a favour if they stay with her one night. Her stubborn faith in a future which somehow will be better than today's. For the first time,' Doctor Saavedra said, 'I am proposing to write a political novel.'

'Political?' Doctor Plarr asked with some surprise.

A cell door opened and a man came out. He lit a cigarette, went to a table and drank from an unfinished glass. In the glow of light, below the saint's shrine, Doctor Plarr could see a thin girl who was straightening the bed. She arranged the coverlet with care before she came out and joined her companions at their communal table. An unfinished glass of orange juice awaited her. The *peón* by the pillar watched her with his hungry envy.

'Don't you resent that man?' Doctor Plarr asked Teresa.

'What man?'

'The one over there who stands staring, doing nothing.'

'Let him stare, he does no harm, poor man. And he has no money.'

'I was telling you about my political novel.' Doctor Saavedra spoke with irritation. He removed his hand from Teresa's grasp.

'But I don't understand the point of one leg.'

'A symbol,' Doctor Saavedra said, 'of this poor crippled country, where we still hope . . .'

'Will your readers understand? I would have thought something more direct. Those students last year in Rosario . . .'

'If one is to write a political novel of lasting value it must be free from all the petty details that date it. Assassinations, kidnapping, the torture of prisoners – these things belong to our decade. But I do not want to write merely for the seventies.'

'The Spaniards tortured their prisoners three hundred years ago,' Doctor Plarr murmured, and he looked again for some reason towards the girl at the communal table.

'Are you not coming with me tonight?' Teresa asked Doctor Saavedra.

'Yes, yes, all in good time. I am talking to my friend here on a subject of great importance.'

Doctor Plarr noticed on the other girl's forehead, a little below the hairline, a small grey birth-mark, in the spot where a Hindu girl wears the scarlet sign of her caste.

Jorge Julio Saavedra said, 'A poet – the true novelist must always be in his way a poet – a poet deals in absolutes. Shakespeare avoided the politics of his time, the minutiae of politics. He wasn't concerned with Philip of Spain, with pirates like Drake. He used the history of the past to express what I call the abstraction of politics. A novelist today who wants to represent tyranny should not describe the activities of General Stroessner in Paraguay – that is journalism not literature. Tiberius is a better example for a poet.'

Doctor Plarr thought how agreeable it would be to take the girl to her room. He had not slept with a woman for more than a month, and how easily sexual attention can be caught by something superficial, like a birth-mark in an unusual position.

'Surely you understand what I mean?' the novelist asked him severely.

'Yes. Yes. Of course.'

Doctor Plarr was prevented by a certain fastidiousness from treading quickly in another man's tracks. What interval, he wondered, would he be prepared to accept? Half an hour, an hour – or merely the physical absence of his predecessor, who had already ordered himself another drink?

'I can see the subject has no interest at all for you,' Doctor Saavedra said with disappointment.

'The subject . . . forgive me . . . I've drunk rather heavily tonight.'

'I was talking of politics.'

'But of course politics interest me. I'm a kind of political refugee myself. And my father . . . I don't even know whether my father is alive. Perhaps he died. Perhaps he was murdered. Perhaps he is shut up in a police station somewhere across the border. The General doesn't believe in prisons for political offenders – he leaves them to rot alone in police stations all over the country.'

'That is exactly my point, doctor. Of course I sympathize with you, but how can I make art out of a man shut up in a police station?'

'Why not?'

'Because it is a special case. It is a situation which belongs to the nineteen seventies. I hope my books will be read, if only by discriminating readers, in the twenty-first century. My fisherman Castillo I have tried to make timeless.'

Doctor Plarr remembered how seldom he had thought of his father, and perhaps it was a sense of guilt because of his own safety and comfort which made him a little angry now. He said, 'Your fisherman is timeless because he never existed.' He regretted his words immediately. 'I am sorry,' he said. 'Don't you think we ought to have another drink? And your charming companion – we are neglecting her.'

'There are more important subjects than Teresa,' Saavedra said, but he surrendered his hand again into her keeping. 'Isn't there a girl here who pleases you?'

'Yes, there is one, but she has found another customer.'

The girl with the birth-mark had joined the solitary drinker and they were proceeding together to her cell. She passed her former companion without a glance and he hadn't enough curiosity to look at his successor. There was something clinical in a brothel which appealed to Doctor Plarr. It was as though he were watching a surgeon accompanying a new patient to the operating theatre – the previous operation had been successful and was already out of mind. Only in television dramas did emotions of love, anxiety or fear infiltrate into the wards. His first years in Buenos Aires, while his mother complained, dramatized and wept over his missing father's fate, and the later years when she became volubly content with sweet cakes and chocolate ices had given Doctor Plarr a suspicion of any emotion which was curable by means as simple as an orgasm or an éclair. The memory of a conversation – if you could call it that – with Charley Fortnum came back to him. He asked Teresa, 'Do you know a girl here called María?'

'There are several Marías,' Teresa said.

'She comes from Córdoba.'

'Oh, that one. She died a year ago. She was really bad, that one. Somebody killed her with a knife. He went to prison, poor man.'

'I suppose I had better go with the girl,' Saavedra said. 'I am sorry. It is not often I have an opportunity to discuss problems of literature with a cultivated man. In a way I would really much prefer to have another drink and continue our talk.' He looked at his captive hand as though it belonged to someone else and he hadn't the right to pick it up.

'There will be other opportunities,' Doctor Plarr encouraged him, and the novelist surrendered. 'Come, *chica*,' he said and rose. 'You will wait for me, doctor? I shall not be long tonight.'

'Perhaps you will learn a lot about Salta.'

'Yes, but there is always a moment when a writer has to say "Enough". One mustn't know too much.' Doctor Plarr had the impression that Jorge Julio Saavedra under the influence of drink was beginning to repeat a lecture he had once delivered to some woman's club in the capital.

Teresa pulled him by the hand. He rose reluctantly and followed her to where the candle burnt below her statue of the Avila saint. The door closed on them. A novelist's work, he had once said sadly to Doctor Plarr, is never finished.

It was a quiet evening at the establishment of Señora Sanchez. All the doors were open except the two which hid Teresa and the girl with the birth-mark. Doctor Plarr finished his drink and left the patio. He was sure the novelist, in spite of his promise, would take his time. After all he had a decision to make – whether the girl should lose her leg at the femur or the knee.

Señora Sanchez was still plying her needles. A friend had joined her. She sat and knitted in a second deck-chair. 'You found a girl?' Señora Sanchez asked.

'My friend did.'

'There was no one who pleased you?'

'Oh, it wasn't that, but I drank too much at dinner.'

'You can ask your colleague Doctor Benevento about my girls. They are very clean.'

'I am sure they are. I shall certainly return, Señora Sanchez.'

But in fact more than a year passed before he did come back. He looked in vain then for the girl with the birth-mark on her forehead. He was neither surprised nor disappointed. Perhaps it was the time of her period, but in any case girls in such establishments change frequently. Teresa was the only one he recognized. He stayed with her for an hour, and they talked about Salta.

Chapter 3

DOCTOR PLARR's practice prospered. He never regretted leaving the harsh competition of the capital, where there were too many doctors with German, French and English degrees, and he had grown fond of the small city by the great Paraná river. There was a local legend that those who once visited the city always returned, and it had certainly proved true in his case. One glimpse of the little port with its background of colonial houses, seen for an hour one dark night, had drawn him back. Even the climate did not displease him – the heat was less humid than he remembered it in the land of his childhood, and when the summer broke up at last with an enormous eruption of thunder, he liked watching from the window of his apartment the forked flashes dig into the Chaco shore. Nearly every month he gave a dinner to Doctor Humphries, and sometimes now he would take a meal with Charley Fortnum who was always either sober, laconic and melancholy, or drunk, talkative, and what he liked to term 'elevated'. Once he went out to Charley Fortnum's camp, but he was no judge of a maté crop and he found the heaving motion of Fortnum's Pride as he was driven around hectare by hectare – Charley called it 'farming' – so disagreeable that he refused the next invitation. He preferred a night at the Nacional when Charley would talk unconvincingly of a girl he had found.

Every three months Doctor Plarr flew down to Buenos Aires and spent a weekend with his mother who was growing more and more stout on her daily diet of cream-cakes and *alfajores* stuffed with *dulce de leche*. He could not remember the features of the beautiful woman in her early thirties who had said goodbye to his father on the river-front and who wept continuously for lost love throughout the three days' voyage to the capital. Since he had no old photograph of her to remind him of the past he always pictured her as the woman she had become with three chins and heavy dewlaps and a stomach which, outlined in black silk, imitated pregnancy. On the shelves of his apartment the works of Doctor Jorge Julio Saavedra annually increased by one volume, and of all his books Doctor Plarr thought he preferred the story of the one-legged girl of Salta. After that first visit, he had lain with Teresa several times at the Sanchez house and he was amused to observe how far fiction deviated from reality. It was almost a lesson in the higher criticism. He possessed no close friends, though he remained on good terms with two former mistresses whom he had first met as patients; he was also on friendly terms with the latest Governor, and enjoyed his visits to the Governor's big maté plantation in the east, flying there in the Governor's private plane and descending on the lawn between two flower-beds in time for an excellent lunch. At Bergman's orange-canning factory closer to the city he was an occasional guest, and sometimes he went fishing in a tributary of the Paraná with the director of the airport.

Twice there were attempted revolutions in the capital which made big headlines in *El Litoral*, but on both occasions when he telephoned to his mother he found she knew nothing of the disturbances; she read no newspaper and never listened to the radio, and Harrods and her favourite teashop remained open through all the troubles. She told him once that she had been satiated forever with politics during their life in Paraguay. 'Your father could talk of nothing else. Such undesirable people used to come to the house, sometimes in the middle of the night, dressed in any old clothes. And you know what became of your father.' The last was an odd turn of phrase since neither of them knew anything at all – whether he had been killed in the civil war or died of disease or become a political prisoner under the dictatorship of the General. His body was never identified among the corpses which were sometimes washed up on the Argentine side of the river with hands and legs tied with wire, but his might well have been one of those skeletons which remained for years undiscovered after they had been tossed from planes into the Chaco wastes.

Nearly three years after his first meeting with Charley Fortnum Doctor Plarr was drawn into a conversation about him by Sir Henry Belfrage, the British Ambassador – a successor to the man who had given the Honorary Consul so much trouble with the maté report. It was one of the periodic cocktail parties for the British colony, and Doctor Plarr, who happened to be in the capital on a visit to his mother, attended it with her. He knew nobody there by more than sight – at best a nodding acquaintance. There was Buller, the manager of the

Bank of London and South America, Fisher, the Secretary of The Anglo-Argentinian Society, and an old gentleman called Forage who spent all his days at the Hurlingham Club. The Representative of the British Council was, of course, there too – his name for some Freudian reason Plarr always forgot – a pale frightened little man with a bald head who came to the party in charge of a visiting poet. The poet had a high-pitched voice and an air of being consciously out of place under the chandeliers. 'How soon can we get away?' he was heard to shriek. And again, 'Too much water with the whisky.' It was the only voice in the room which carried any distance above the low continuous din like that of an aeroplane engine, and one naturally expected it to cry something more relevant, like 'Fasten your seat-belts.'

Doctor Plarr thought Belfrage was only interested in making polite conversation when they found themselves alone together between a gilt-edged sofa and a Louis Quinze chair. They were far enough away from the hubbub around the buffet to hear themselves speak. He could see his mother firmly wedged in and gesticulating at a priest with a canapé. She was always happy with priests, and so he felt relieved of responsibility.

'I think you know our Consul up there?' Sir Henry Belfrage said. He always referred to the northern province as 'up there' as though he wanted to emphasize the vast length of the Paraná river winding its slow way down from those distant frontiers so far from the southern civilization of the Rio de la Plata.

'Charley Fortnum? Oh yes, I do see him occasionally. But I haven't for some months. I've been busy – a lot of sickness.'

'You know – in a job like this – one always inherits a few *difficulties* with a new post. Strictly between ourselves the Consul up there is one of them.'

'Really?' Doctor Plarr replied with caution, 'I would have thought . . .', though he had no idea how he would finish the sentence if it were required of him.

'There's nothing for him to do up there. I mean as far as we are concerned. Now and then I ask him to make a report on something – for the sake of appearances. I don't want him to think he's forgotten. He *was* useful once to one of my predecessors. Some young fool who got mixed up with the guerrillas and tried to do a Castro against the General in Paraguay. As far as I can see from the files we've paid for half his telephone bills and most of his stationery ever since.'

'Didn't he once help with some royals too? Guiding them round the ruins?'

'There was something of that sort,' Sir Henry Belfrage said. 'Very minor royals as far as I remember. I oughtn't to say it, of course, but royalty can cause us an awful lot of trouble. Once we had to ship a polo pony . . . you have no idea of the complications *that* involved, and it was during the meat embargo too.' He meditated a while. 'At least Fortnum could try a little harder to get on with the English colony up there.'

'As far as I know there are only three of us within fifty miles. The fellows with camps seldom come to the city.'

'Then it shouldn't be difficult for him. You know this chap Jeffries?'

'Do you mean Humphries? If you are thinking about the Union Jack episode – flying it upside down – do *you* know the right way up?'

'No, but thank God I've got chaps who do. I wasn't thinking of that – that happened in Callow's time. The trouble now is that Fortnum seems to have made a most unsuitable marriage – according to this man Humphries. I wish he'd stop writing to us. Who is he?'

'I hadn't heard about Fortnum's marriage. He's a bit old for it. Who's the woman?'

'Humphries didn't say. In fact he was a bit ambiguous all round. Fortnum seems to have kept it a great secret. I don't take the story seriously, of course. There's no security involved. He's only an Honorary Consul. We don't have to *investigate* her. I just thought – if you happened to have heard anything . . . In a way an Honorary Consul is more difficult to get rid of than a career man. He can't be transferred. That word honorary . . ., it's a bit bogus when you come to think of it. Fortnum imports a new car every two years and sells it. He's not entitled to – he's not in the service – but I suppose he's pulled a fast one with the local authorities there. I wouldn't be surprised if he doesn't make more than my Consul does here. Poor old Martin has to toe the line. He can't go buying cars on his salary, nor can I. Unlike the Ambassador of Panama. My God, my poor wife's tied up with that poet. What's his name?'

'I don't know.'

'I just wanted to say – Plarr isn't it? . . . As you live up there . . . I've never met this man Humphries . . . oh well, they send them here in droves.'

'Humphries?'

'No, no. Poets. If they are poets. The British Council always say they are, but I've never heard of any of them. When you are back up there, Plarr, do what you can. You're someone I can trust to drop the right word . . . no scandal, you understand what I'm getting at . . .

This fellow Humphries, he strikes me as the sort of man who might write home. To the FO. After all it's no concern of ours whom Fortnum marries. If you could somehow tactfully tell this chap Humphries to mind his own business and not bother us. Thank God he's getting old. Fortnum, I mean. We'll retire him the first chance we have. Oh dear, look at my poor wife. She's trapped.'

'I'll go and save her if you like.'

'My dear chap, will you? I daren't. These poets are touchy brutes. And I always get their names mixed up. They are like this fellow Humphries – they write home – to the Arts Council. I won't forget this, Plarr. Anything I can ever do for you . . . up there . . .'

The doctor found himself with more work than usual on his hands when he returned to the north. He had no time for Humphries, that old trouble-maker, and he was not interested in Charley Fortnum's marriage – whether fortunate or unfortunate. Once, when some remark recalled the Ambassador's words to him, he wondered whether Charley might possibly have married his housekeeper, that hawk-like woman who had opened the door when he visited the Consulate for the first time. A marriage like that seemed not improbable. Old men, like dissident priests, were frequently known to marry their housekeepers, sometimes as a measure of false economy, sometimes from fear of a lonely death. Death to Doctor Plarr, who was still in his early thirties, appeared in the guise of a fortuitous accident on the road or an unforeseen cancer, but in the mind of an old man it was the inevitable end of a long and incurable sickness. Perhaps Charley Fortnum's alcoholism was a symptom of his fear.

One afternoon, while the doctor was taking an hour's siesta, his bell rang. He opened the door and there was the hawk-like woman, bristling yet again in the hope of carrion. He nearly took a chance and addressed her as Señora Fortnum.

The guess would have proved mistaken. Señor Fortnum, she said, had telephoned to her from the camp. His wife was ill. He wanted Doctor Plarr to drive out to the camp and visit her.

'Did he say what was wrong?'

'Señora Fortnum has a pain in the stomach,' the woman replied with contempt. The marriage had obviously pleased her no more than it had pleased Doctor Humphries.

Doctor Plarr drove to the camp in the cool of the evening. The small ponds on either side of the highway looked like patches of molten lead in the last lingering light. Fortnum's Pride was standing at the end of a mud road under a grove of avocados, the heavy brown pears the size and shape of cannonballs. On the verandah of the rambling bungalow Charley Fortnum sat before a bottle of whisky, a syphon and, astonishingly, two clean glasses. 'I've been waiting for you,' he said reproachfully.

'I couldn't come earlier. What's the trouble?'

'Clara's been in a lot of pain.'

'I'll go and see her.'

'Have a whisky first. I looked in at her just now and she was asleep.'

'Thank you then, I will. I'm thirsty. There's a lot of dust on the road.'

'Soda? Say when.'

'Right to the top.'

'I wanted to have a word with you anyway – before you went in. You've heard about my marriage I suppose?'

'The Ambassador told me.'

'Had he anything to say?'

'No. Why?'

'There's been a lot of talk. And Humphries cuts me.'

'That's lucky for you.'

'You see –' Charley Fortnum hesitated. 'Well, she is very young,' he said. It was not clear whether he was excusing his critics or apologizing for himself.

Doctor Plarr said, 'Lucky again.'

'She's not twenty, and, you know, I won't see sixty again.'

Doctor Plarr wondered if he had been summoned to advise the Consul on a less soluble problem than his wife's stomach-ache. He drank to fill what he thought might be an awkward silence.

'That's not the trouble,' Charley Fortnum said. (Doctor Plarr was surprised by his insight.) 'I can manage things well enough so far . . . and afterwards . . . there's always the bottle, isn't there? An old family friend. The bottle I mean. Helped my father too, the old bastard. I just wanted to explain about her. Otherwise you might be a bit surprised when you see her. She's so very young. And shy too. She's not used to this sort of life. A house like this and servants. And the country. The country's awfully quiet after dark.'

'Where does she come from?'

'Tucumán. Real Indian blood. A long way back of course. I ought to warn you – she doesn't much care for doctors. She's had a bad experience of them.'

'I'll try to win her confidence,' Doctor Plarr said.

'This pain,' Charley Fortnum said, 'it did occur to me it might be, you know, a child. Or something of the kind.'

'She doesn't take the pill?'

'You know what these Spanish Catholics are like. Superstition, of course. Like walking under a ladder. Clara doesn't know who Shakespeare is, but she's heard all about the Pope's what-do-you-call-it. Anyway I'd have to get the pills somehow through the Embassy. Can you imagine what they'd say? You can't even buy them under the counter here. Of course I always wore a thing until we were really together.'

'So you bore the sin for her?' Doctor Plarr teased him.

'Oh well, my conscience has got pretty tough with age. Another little thing won't do any harm. And if she's happier that way . . . When you've finished your whisky . . .'

He led Doctor Plarr down a corridor hung with Victorian sporting prints: riders falling into a stream, checked at a bullfinch, rebuked by the master. He walked softly on tiptoe. At the end of the corridor he opened a door just a crack and looked in. 'I think she's awake,' he said. 'You'll find me on the verandah, Ted, with the whisky. Don't be long.'

One electric candle was alight below the statuette of a saint, a saint whom Doctor Plarr didn't recognize, and he was reminded for a moment of the small cells that stood around the patio at the house of Señora Sanchez, each with a votive candle. 'Good evening,' he said to the head on the pillow. The face was so covered in dark hair that only the eyes were visible; they peered back at him, like a cat's from a shrubbery.

'I don't want to be examined,' the girl told him. 'I won't be examined.'

'I don't want to examine you. I want to hear about your stomach-ache, that's all.'

'It's better now.'

'Good. Then I won't stay long. May I turn up the light?'

'If you have to,' she said and brushed the hair away from her face. Below the hairline Doctor Plarr saw a small grey birthmark in the spot where a Hindu girl . . .

He said, 'Whereabouts do you feel the pain? Show me.'

She turned the sheet down and indicated a place on her naked body. He put his hand out to touch her, but she moved her body away from him. He said, 'Don't be afraid. I'm not going to examine you in Doctor Benevento's way,' and he heard her catch her breath. Nonetheless she allowed him to press his fingers on her stomach.

'There?'

'Yes.'

'Nothing to worry about,' he said. 'A little inflammation of the intestine, that's all.'

'Intestine?' He could see the word was strange to her and frightening.

'I'll leave some bismuth powder for you with your husband. Take it in water. If you mix some sugar with it, it doesn't taste too bad. I wouldn't drink whisky if I were you. You are more used to orange juice, aren't you?'

She looked at him with a startled expression and whispered, 'What's your name?'

'Plarr,' he said, and added, 'Eduardo Plarr.' He doubted whether she knew the surname of any man apart from Charley Fortnum.

'Eduardo,' she repeated, and this time took a bolder look at him. She asked, 'I don't know you, do I?'

'No.'

'But you know Doctor Benevento?'

'I've met him once or twice.' He stood up. 'I don't suppose those Thursday visits were very agreeable.' He added, before she could speak, 'You aren't ill. You don't have to stay in bed.'

'Charley' (she pronounced the name as 'Charlee' with an accent on the last syllable) 'said I must stay in bed until the doctor came.'

'Well, the doctor's come, hasn't he? So there's no longer any need . . .'

When he looked back from the door he saw she was watching him. She had forgotten to draw up the sheet. He said, 'I never asked you your name.'

'Clara.'

He said, 'Teresa was the only girl I ever knew there.'

Returning down the passage he thought of the statuette of Saint Teresa of Avila which had presided over his own exercises and the more literary ones of Doctor Saavedra. Presumably it was the friend of Saint Francis who now looked down on the bed of Charley Fortnum. He remembered the way he had seen the girl first as she straightened the sheets in her cell, bent like a negress directly from the waist. He was accustomed by now to too many women's bodies. When he first became the lover of one of his patients it was not her body which excited him but a slight stammer and a scent he didn't recognize. There was nothing distinctive about Clara's body except for her unfashionable thinness, the smallness of her breasts, the immature thighs, the almost imperceptible mount of Venus. She might be nearly twenty, but she didn't look more than sixteen – Mother Sanchez recruited them early.

He stopped before the print of a man in a scarlet coat on a runaway horse which had overridden the hounds; the master, purple in the face, was shaking a fist at the culprit, and beyond the hounds lay a vista of fields and hedgerows and a small stream lined by what he took to be willows, an unfamiliar foreign countryside. He thought with a sense of surprise: I have never seen a little stream like that. In this continent even the smallest tributaries of the great rivers were wider than the Thames in his father's picture book. He tried the word 'stream' again on his tongue: a stream must have a strange poetic charm. You couldn't call a stream the shallow inlet where he sometimes went to fish and where you couldn't bathe for fear of stingrays. A stream had to be peaceful, gently running, shaded by willows, without danger. This land, he thought, is really too vast for human beings.

Charley Fortnum was waiting for him with the glasses refilled. He asked with uneasy jocularity, 'Well, what's the verdict?'

'Nothing. A little inflammation. There's no reason for her to lie in bed. I'll give you something she can take in water. Before meals. I wouldn't let her drink whisky.'

'I didn't want to run any risks, Ted. I don't know much about women. Their insides and all that. My first wife was never ill. She was a Christian Scientist.'

'Before you bring me all the way out here another time, do have a word first on the telephone. I'm pretty busy at this time of year.'

'I suppose you think me foolish, but she needs an awful lot of protection.'

Plarr said, 'I should have thought – in that sort of life – she would have learnt to look after herself.'

'What do you mean?'

'She worked with Mother Sanchez, didn't she?'

Charley Fortnum clenched a fist. A bubble of whisky hung on the corner of his lip. Doctor Plarr thought that he could almost see the blood pressure rise. 'What do you know about her?'

'I never went with her if that's what you are afraid of.'

'I thought you might be one of those bastards . . .'

'Surely you were "one of those" yourself. I seem to remember your telling me about a girl called María from Córdoba.'

'That was different. That was physical. Do you know I never touched Clara for months? Not until I was sure she loved me a little. We used to talk, that's all. I went to her room, of course, because otherwise she would have been in trouble with Señora Sanchez. Ted, you won't believe me, but I've never talked to any one about so many things as I have to that girl. She's interested in everything I tell her. Fortnum's Pride. The maté crop. The movies. She knows a lot about the movies. I was never much interested in them myself, but she always knows the latest dope about a woman called Elizabeth Taylor. Have you heard of her – and a fellow called Burton? I always thought Burton was a kind of beer. We even talked about Evelyn – that was my first wife. I can tell you I was pretty lonely before I met Clara. You'll think it nonsense, but I loved her the first moment I saw her. Somehow from the first I didn't want to do anything, not till she wanted it too. She couldn't understand that. She thought there was something wrong with me. But it was real love, not brothel love I wanted. I don't suppose you can understand that either.

'I'm not quite sure what the word love means. My mother loves *dulce de leche*. So she tells me.'

'Has no woman ever loved you, Ted?' Fortnum inquired. A kind of paternal anxiety in his voice irritated Doctor Plarr.

'Two or three have told me so, but they had no difficulty in finding someone else after I said good-bye. Only my mother's love of sweet cakes isn't likely to change. She will love them in sickness and in health till death do them part. Perhaps that's the real true love.'

'You're too young to be a cynic.'

'I'm not a cynic. I'm curious, that's all. I like to know the meaning which people put on the words they use. So much is a question of semantics. That's why in medicine we often prefer to use a dead language. There's no room for misunderstanding with a dead language. How did you get the girl away from Mother Sanchez?'

'I paid.'

'And she was happy to leave?'

'She was a bit bewildered at first and frightened too. Señora Sanchez was angry. She didn't like losing her. She told her she wouldn't have her back when I got tired of her. As if that would ever happen.'

'Life's a long time.'

'Mine isn't. Be frank, Ted, you wouldn't give me ten more years would you? Even though I've knocked down a bit on the drink since I knew Clara.'

'What will happen to her afterwards?'

'This isn't a bad little property. She could sell it and go to Buenos Aires. You can get fifteen per cent interest now without risk. Even eighteen if you take a chance. And you know I can import a car every two years . . . Perhaps five more cars to sell before I kick the bucket. I calculate that would mean another five hundred pounds a year.'

'She could eat sweet cakes with my mother at the Richmond.'

'No joking, would your mother consent to meet Clara one day?'

'Why not?'

'You don't know what a difference Clara's made to me.'

'You must have made quite a difference to her too,' Doctor Plarr said.

'When you get to my age you accumulate a lot of regrets. It's not a bad thing to feel you've made at least one person a little happier.'

It was the kind of simple, sentimental and self-confident statement which Doctor Plarr found embarrassing. No reply was possible. It was a statement which it would be rude to question and impossible to confirm. He made his excuses and drove home.

All down the dark country road he thought of the young woman in the great Victorian bed which had belonged, with the sporting prints, to the Honorary Consul's father. She was like a bird which had been bought in the market in a makeshift cage and transferred to one at home more roomy and luxurious, equipped with perches and feeding bowls and a swing to play on.

He was surprised by the amount of thought he was giving the girl, who was only a young prostitute he had noticed once in the establishment of Señora Sanchez because of her odd birth-mark. Had Charley really married her? Perhaps Doctor Humphries had misled the Ambassador when he spoke of a marriage. Probably Charley Fortnum had taken a new housekeeper – that was all. If that were the case he would be able to reassure the Ambassador. A wife provided worse material for a scandal than a mistress.

But his thoughts were like the deliberately banal words of a clandestine letter in which the important phrases have been added between the lines in secret ink to be developed in privacy. Those hidden phrases described a girl in a cell leaning down to make her bed, a girl who returned to her table and picked up her glass of orange juice, as though she had been momentarily interrupted by a tradesman at the door, a thin body stretched out on Charley Fortnum's double bed, with immature breasts which had never suckled a child. All three of Doctor Plarr's mistresses had been married women, mature women proud of their lush figures which smelt of expensive bath oils. She must have been a good whore, he thought, to have been taken out by two men in succession with a figure like hers, but that was no reason why he should think of her all the way home. He tried to change the direction of his thoughts. There were two hopeless cases of malnutrition in the *barrio* of the poor, there was a police officer he was attending who would soon be dead of throat cancer, there was Saavedra's melancholy and Doctor Humphries' dripping shower, and yet try as he would his mind returned continually to that small hill of Venus – mount was misnomer.

He wondered how many men she had known. Doctor Plarr's last mistress, who was married to a banker called Lopez, had told him with some pride of his four predecessors – perhaps she was trying to arouse a sense of competition. (One of her lovers, he knew from another source, had been her chauffeur.) The fragile body on Charley Fortnum's bed must have known hundreds. Her stomach was like the site of an old country battlefield where pale grass grew which had abolished the scars of war, and a small stream flowed peacefully between the willows: he was back in the passage, outside the bedroom, staring at the sporting prints and resisting the desire to return.

He braked sharply as he approached the road which led to Bergman's orange-canning factory, and for a moment he contemplated reversing the car and driving back to the camp. Instead he lit a cigarette. I will not be the victim of an obsession, he thought. The attraction of a whore-house is the attraction I sometimes find in trivial shopping – I may see a tie which momentarily attracts me, I wear it once or twice, then I leave it in the drawer and it becomes overlaid with newer ties. Why didn't I try her out when I had the chance? If I had bought her that night at Señora Sanchez's she would be lying safely forgotten at the bottom of the drawer. Is it possible, he wondered, if a man is too rational to fall in love, that he may be reserved for a worse fate, to fall into an obsession? He drove angrily in the direction of the city where the reflection of the light lay flat along the horizon and the Three Marys hung on their broken chain in the sky overhead.

Some weeks later Doctor Plarr woke early. It was a Saturday and he had a few hours free. He decided to spend them in the open air with a book while the morning was still fresh; he preferred somewhere out of sight of his secretary who read only what she called serious books – those of Doctor Saavedra among them.

He chose a collection of stories by Jorge Luis Borges. Borges shared the tastes he had himself inherited from his father – Conan Doyle, Stevenson, Chesterton. *Ficciones* would prove a welcome change from Doctor Saavedra's last novel which he had not been able to finish. He was tired of South American heroics. Now Doctor Plarr, sitting under the statue of an heroic sergeant – *machismo* again – who had saved the life of San Martín – was it a hundred and fifty years ago? – read with a sense of immense relaxation of the Countess de Bagno Regio, of Pittsburgh and Monaco. After a time he grew thirsty. To appreciate Borges properly he had to be taken, like a cheese biscuit, with an apéritif, but in this heat Doctor Plarr wanted a longer drink. He decided to call on his friend Gruber and demand a German beer.

Gruber was one of Doctor Plarr's earliest friends in the city. As a boy he had escaped from Germany in 1936 when the persecution of the Jews was intensified. He was an only child, but his parents had insisted that he escape abroad, if only to save the name of Gruber from becoming extinct, and his mother baked a special cake for his journey in which to hide the few small valuables they were able to send with him – his mother's engagement ring set with inconsiderable diamonds and his father's gold wedding ring. They told him they were too old to make a new life in a strange continent and they pretended to believe that they were too old to be regarded as a danger by the Nazi state. Of course he never heard from them again: they had made their withered little plus two sign to that mathematical formula – the Final Solution. So Gruber like Doctor Plarr was a man without a father. He didn't even possess a family grave. Now he kept a photographic store in the main shopping street of the city, which, with its overlapping signs and slogans stuck out over the sidewalks, had a Chinese look. He was an optician as well. 'Germans,' he once said to Doctor Plarr, 'always inspire confidence as chemists, opticians and photographic specialists. More people have heard of Zeiss and Bayer than of Goebbels and Goering, and even more people here have heard of Gruber.'

Gruber left his customer installed in the private section of his shop, where he worked on his lenses. There the doctor could see all that went on without being noticed himself, for Gruber (he had a passion for gadgets) had fitted a small internal television screen on which he was able to watch in miniature, as in a candid camera programme, the customers outside in the shop. For some reason, which Gruber had never been able to explain, his shop attracted the prettiest girls in the city (no *boutique* could compete with Gruber), as though pulchritude and the practice of photography were linked. They came in flocks to receive their colour-prints and they examined them with cries of excitement, chattering like birds. Doctor Plarr watched them while he drank his beer and listened to Gruber's gossip of the province.

'Have you met Charley Fortnum's woman?' Doctor Plarr asked.

'You mean his wife?'

'She can't be his wife, surely? Charley Fortnum's a divorced man.

And there's no remarriage here – it's convenient for single men like me.'

'Didn't you hear that his wife died?'

'No. I've been away. And when I saw him the other day he didn't mention it.'

'He went off with this new girl to Rosario and got married there. So people say. Nobody really knows, of course.'

'That was an odd thing for him to do. It couldn't have been necessary. You know where he found her?'

'Yes, but she's a very pretty girl,' Gruber said.

'Oh yes, one of the best of Mother Sanchez's lot. But one doesn't necessarily have to marry a pretty girl.'

'Girls of that kind often make good wives, especially for old men.'

'Why old men?'

'Old men are not very demanding and girls like that are glad of a rest.'

The phrase 'like that' irritated Doctor Plarr. After seven days he was still obsessed by the unremarkable body which Gruber had classified so easily. Now on the television screen he saw a girl who leant across the counter to buy a roll of Kodachrome in the same way Clara had leant across her bed at Señora Sanchez's. She was more beautiful than Charley Fortnum's wife, and he felt no desire for her at all.

'Girls like that are very content to be left alone,' Gruber repeated. 'You know they count it good luck when they find a caller who is impotent or too drunk to perform. They have a native word for it here – I have forgotten the Spanish, but it means a Lenten visitor.'

'Have you been often to the Sanchez place?'

'Why should I? Look at the temptations I have to resist nearer home with all these charming customers of mine. Some of the films they bring me to develop are quite intimate, and when I hand the packet back to one, I can see the amusement in her eyes. He has observed that moment when the bikini slipped, she is thinking – and so I have. By the way, there were two men in here the other day who asked about you. They wanted to know if you could possibly be the same Eduardo Plarr they knew years ago in Asunción. They saw your name on those films I sent round to you on Thursday. Of course I said I had no idea.'

'Were they police agents?'

'They didn't look like police agents, but of course it doesn't do to take chances. I heard one of them call the other father. He didn't look old enough to be his father and he wasn't dressed like a priest, and that made me suspicious.'

'I'm on good terms with the Chief of Police here. Sometimes he calls me in when Doctor Benevento's on holiday. Do you think those men came from across the border? The General's agents perhaps? But why should he be interested in me? I was only a boy when I left . . .'

'Talk of the devil,' Gruber said.

Doctor Plarr looked quickly at the television screen expecting to see two strangers reflected there, but all he saw was a thin girl in sunglasses of an exaggerated size – they might have been made for a skin-diver. 'She buys sunglasses,' Gruber said, 'as other women buy costume jewellery. I've sold her at least four pairs.'

'Who is she?'

'You ought to know. You were talking about her just now. Charley Fortnum's wife. Or girl if you prefer it.'

Doctor Plarr put down his beer and went into the shop. The girl was examining a pair of sunglasses and she was too absorbed to notice him. The lenses were coloured bright mauve, the rims were of incandescent yellow, and the side-pieces were encrusted with chips of what looked like amethyst. She took her own glasses off and tried the new ones on, and immediately added ten years to her age. Her eyes were quite invisible: all he could see was his own mauve face mirrored back at him.

The assistant said, 'We have only just received these from Mar del Plata. They are all the fashion there.'

Doctor Plarr knew that Gruber was probably watching him on the television screen, but why should he care? He asked, 'Do you like them, Señora Fortnum?'

She said, 'Who . . . ? Oh, it is you, Doctor, Doctor . . . ?'

'Plarr. They make you look a lot older, but of course you can afford to add a few years.'

'They cost too much. I was only trying them on for fun.'

'Wrap them up,' he told the assistant. 'And a case . . .'

'They have their own case, doctor,' she said, beginning to polish the glasses.

'No,' Clara said, 'I cannot . . .'

'You can with me. I am your husband's friend.'

'That makes it all right?'

'Yes.'

She gave a jump which he was to learn later was her expression of joy at any present, even a sweet cake. He had never known a woman accept a present so frankly, with less fuss. She said to the assistant. 'Please, I will wear them. Put the old ones in the case.' In these glasses, he thought, as they left Gruber's shop together, she looks more like my mistress and less like my younger sister.

'It is very kind of you,' she said, speaking like a well-brought up schoolgirl.

'Come and sit by the river where we can talk.' When she hesitated he added, 'Nobody can recognize you in those glasses. Not even your husband.'

'You do not like them?'

'No. I don't like them at all.'

'I thought they looked very rich and very smart,' she said with disappointment.

'They are a good disguise. That was why I wanted you to have them. No one would recognize the young Señora Fortnum with me now.'

She said, 'Who *would* recognize me? I know no one and Charley is at home. He sent me with the foreman. I said I wanted to buy something.'

'What?'

'Oh, just something. I did not know what.'

She walked contentedly beside him, following whatever direction he chose to take. He felt disturbed by the easy way that things were happening. He remembered the stupid conflict in his mind when he wanted to turn his car back towards the camp, and the number of occasions, during the last week, when he had lain awake, wondering what was the right move to make in order to see her again. He ought to have known it would be no more difficult than leading her to her cell at Señora Sanchez's house.

She said, 'I am not frightened of you today.'

'Perhaps because I have given you a present.'

She said, 'Yes, it could be that. A man would never bother to give a present to someone he did not like, would he? And the other day I thought you did not like me. I thought you were my enemy.'

They came to the bank of the Paraná. A small bastion jutted into the river, fringed with white pillars, making a tiny temple for a naked statue of classical innocence which faced the water. The ugly yellow block of flats where he lived was hidden by the trees. The leaves were like the lightest of feathers; they gave an illusion of coolness because they seemed to be always in motion – a breath of air undetectable on the skin was enough to set them waving. A heavy barge moved past them up the river, coughing against the current, and the usual black plume of smoke lay across the Chaco.

She sat and stared at the Paraná; when he looked at her all he could see was his own face reflected in the mirror-glass. He said, 'For God's sake take off those spectacles. I don't want to shave.'

'Shave?'

'I look at myself like that twice a day – that's quite enough.'

She took them off obediently and he saw her eyes, which were brown and expressionless and indistinguishable from all the Spanish women's eyes he had ever known. She said, 'I do not understand.'

'Oh, forget what I said. Is it true that you are married?'

'Yes.'

'What does it feel like?'

'I think it's like wearing another girl's dress,' she said, 'which doesn't fit.'

'Why did you do it?'

'He wanted to marry. Something to do with his money when he dies. And if there's a child . . .'

'Have you started one?'

'No.'

'Well it must be better than life at Mother Sanchez's.'

'It is different,' she said. 'I miss the girls.'

'And the men?'

'Oh, I am not bothered about them.'

They were alone on the long parade beside the Paraná: for men it was the hour of work, for women of shopping. Everything here had its proper hour – the hour for the Paraná was evening, and then it was the time for young true lovers, who held hands and didn't speak. He said, 'When do you have to be home?'

'The *capataz* is picking me up at Charley's office at eleven.'

'It is nine o'clock now. How will you fill in the time?'

'I will look at the shops and then I will have a coffee.'

'Do you never see any of your old friends?'

'The girls are all asleep now.'

'You see those flats there beyond the trees?' Doctor Plarr asked. 'I live there.'

'Yes?'

'If you want coffee I can give you coffee.'

'Yes?'

'Or orange juice,' he said.

'Oh, I do not really like orange juice. Señora Sanchez said we must keep sober, that was all.'

He asked, 'Will you come with me?'

'It would not be right, would it?' she asked, as though she were seeking information from someone whom she knew and trusted.

'It was right at Mother Sanchez . . .'

'But I had my living to earn there. I sent money home to Tucumán.'

'What happens now?'

'Oh, I send money to Tucumán just the same. Charley gives it me.'

He stood up and put out his hand. 'Come along.' He was prepared to be angry if she hesitated, but she took his hand with the same shallow obedience and followed him across the road, as though the distance were no greater than across the little patio at Mother Sanchez's. The lift, however, made her hesitate. She told him she had never been in a lift before – there were few houses in the city which stood more than two storeys high. She tightened her hand in excitement or fear, and when they reached the top floor she asked, 'Can we do that again, please?'

'When you go.'

He led her straight to his bedroom and began to undress her. A catch of her dress stuck, and she took the work out of his hands. All she said, while she lay naked on the bed waiting for him to join her, was, 'Those sunglasses cost you much more than a visit to Señora Sanchez,' and he wondered whether she thought of them as a payment in advance. He remembered how Teresa would count the peso notes and afterwards lay them on a ledge below her saint's statue as though they were the result of a collection in church. They would be divided later in the correct proportion with Señora Sanchez: the personal gift always came later.

As he joined her he thought with relief: this is the end of my obsession, and when she cried out, he thought: I'm a free man again, I can say goodnight to Señora Sanchez as she knits in her deck-chair and I can walk back along the river with a sense of lightness which wasn't mine when I left home. The last number of the *British Medical Journal* lay on his desk – it had remained a whole week in its wrapping, and he was in the mood for reading something in a style even more precise than a story by Borges, and of greater practical value than a novel by Jorge Julio Saavedra. He began to read an article of startling originality – or so it seemed to him – on the treatment of calcium deficiency by a doctor called Caesar Borgia.

'Are you asleep?' the girl asked.

'No,' but all the same he was surprised when he opened his eyes and saw the sunlight between the slats of the blind. He had thought it was night and that he was alone.

The girl caressed the inside of his thigh and ran her lips down his body. He felt no more than a mild interest, a curiosity to see if she were capable of arousing him a second time. Perhaps that was the secret of her success at Mother Sanchez's – she gave a man double his money's worth. She climbed on to his body and cried out an obscenity, taking his ear between her teeth, but the obsession had died with his desire, and he felt depressed at the void it left behind. For a week he had lived with one idea and now he missed the idea as a mother might miss the crying of an unwanted child. I never really desired her, he thought, I only desired my idea of her. He would have liked to get up and go, leaving her alone to make the bed and afterwards find another customer.

'Where is the bathroom?' she asked. There was nothing to distinguish her from the others he had known except that she played her comedy with more spirit and invention.

He had dressed when she returned, and he watched impatiently while she put on her clothes. He was afraid she would ask him for the coffee he had promised and linger a long time over it. It was his hour for visiting the *barrio popular*. The women by now would have finished their first chores and the children would have returned from carrying water. He asked, 'Do you want me to drop you at the Consulate?'

'No,' she said. 'I had better walk. The *capataz* may be there waiting.'

'You have not done much shopping.'

'I will show Charley the sunglasses. He will never know how much they cost.'

He took a ten thousand peso note from his pocket and held it out to her. She turned it over as if to make sure of the amount. She said, 'Nobody ever gave me more than five thousand afterwards. Generally it was two. Mother Sanchez did not like us taking more. She was afraid it meant we had been hustling. She was wrong. Men are odd that way. If they can do nothing they always give you more.'

'As if any of you cared,' he said.

'As if we cared.'

'A Lenten visitor.'

The girl laughed. She said, 'It is good to be able to talk free again. I cannot talk free to Charley. I think he wants to forget all about Señora Sanchez.' She handed him back the note. 'It would not be right,' she said, 'now I am married. And I do not need it. Charley is generous. And the sunglasses cost a lot.' She put them on, so that again he saw his own face staring back at him, in miniature, as though he were a doll looking out of a doll's house window. She asked. 'Shall I see you again?'

He wanted to say, 'No. It's all finished now,' but common politeness – and the relief he felt because she had forgotten the coffee – made him reply formally, like a host to a guest whom he doesn't really want to encourage to call again. 'Of course. One day when you come into town . . . I'll give you my telephone number.'

'You need not give me a present every time,' she assured him.

'And you needn't play a comedy,' he said.

'Comedy?'

He said, 'I know there are always men who want to believe you are finding the same pleasure that they do. Naturally at Mother Sanchez's you had to play a part to earn your present, but here you see – you need not act any longer. Perhaps you have to act with Charley, but not with me. You don't have to pretend anything at all with me.'

'I am sorry,' she said. 'I did something wrong?'

'It always used to annoy me,' Doctor Plarr went on, 'in that house of yours. A man is not nearly so stupid as he seems to you. He knows he has come to get a pleasure and not to give it.'

She said, 'All the same I think I pretended very well because I got bigger presents than the other girls.' She wasn't annoyed. He could tell that she was accustomed to this sadness after coition. He didn't differ, even in that, from the other men she had known. And this void, he thought – is she right? is it no more than the temporary *tristitia* most men feel when they leave a brothel behind?

'How long were you there?'

'Two years. I was nearly sixteen,' she said, 'when I arrived. The girls gave me a cake with candles on my birthday. I had never seen one before. It was very pretty.'

'Does Charley Fortnum like you to pretend like that?'

'He likes me to be very quiet,' she said, 'and very tender. Is that what you would have liked too? I am sorry . . . I thought . . . You are so much younger than Charley, so I thought . . .'

'I would like you to be yourself,' he said. 'Be as indifferent as you like. How many men have you known?'

'How could I remember that?'

He showed her the way to work the lift, and she asked him to come down with her – she was still a little afraid of it, even though it excited her. When she pressed the button and it began to descend she gave the same jump she had given in Gruber's shop. At the door she admitted to him that she was afraid of the telephone too. 'And your name – I have forgotten your name.'

'Plarr. Eduardo Plarr.' He tried her name for the first time aloud. 'You are Clara, aren't you?' He added, 'If you are afraid to use the telephone, *I* shall have to telephone to you. But perhaps Charley will answer.'

'He usually drives around the camp before nine. And Wednesdays he is nearly always in town – though he likes me to come with him.'

'Oh well,' Doctor Plarr said, 'we shall find a way.' He didn't bother to see her into the street or watch her go. He was a free man.

And yet, inexplicably, the same night, while he was trying to sleep, he thought with regret that he had a clearer memory of her stretched out in Charley Fortnum's bed than he had of her in his own. An obsession may sleep awhile, but it doesn't necessarily die, and in less than a week he wanted to see her again. He would have liked to hear her voice, however indifferent it might sound on the telephone, but the telephone never rang with any message of importance.

PART THREE

Chapter 1

Doctor Plarr did not arrive home from the hut until nearly three in the morning. Because of police patrols Diego took a circuitous route and dropped him near the house of Señora Sanchez, thus giving him an excuse, if one were needed, for being out on foot in the early morning. There was one awkward moment when he climbed the stairs and a door on the floor below him opened and a voice demanded, 'Who is that?' He called down, 'Doctor Plarr. Why are children born at unconscionable hours?'

Although he lay down on his bed he hardly slept at all. Nevertheless he got through his morning's work with more than usual expedition and drove out to Charley Fortnum's camp. He had no idea of the kind of situation with which he might have to cope, and he was in a tired, nervous and angry mood, expecting to find an hysterical woman awaiting him. While he lay sleepless in bed he had considered the possibility of disclosing all to the police, but that would be to condemn León and Aquino to almost certain death, probably Fortnum as well.

It was a heavy sun-drenched midday when he arrived at the camp and a police jeep stood beside Fortnum's Pride in the shade of the avocados. He walked into the house without ringing, and in the living-room he found the Chief of Police talking to Clara. She was not the hysterical woman he had anticipated but a young girl sitting stiffly on the sofa as though she were receiving orders from a superior. '. . . all we can,' Colonel Perez was saying.

'What are you doing here?' Doctor Plarr asked.

'I have come to see Señora Fortnum, doctor, and you?'

'I have come to see the Consul on business.'

'The Consul is not here,' Colonel Perez said.

Clara gave him no greeting. She seemed to be waiting without a will of her own, as she had often waited in the patio of the establishment, for one of many men to lead her away – hustling being forbidden by Mother Sanchez.

'He is not in town,' Doctor Plarr said.

'You have been to his office?'

'No. I telephoned.'

He regretted immediately what he had said, for Colonel Perez was no fool. One ought never to volunteer information to a policeman. Doctor Plarr had watched more than once the cool and efficient way Perez went to work. On one occasion a man had been found stabbed on a raft of logs which had been floated down the Paraná from two thousand kilometres away. In Doctor Benevento's absence Doctor Plarr was summoned to a bend of the river near the airport where the logs were waiting for trans-shipment. At the bottom of a little slippery country path, where snakes rustled in the undergrowth, he reached a small wooden jetty – the so-called port for timber.

A family had been living on the raft for a month. Doctor Plarr, stumbling across the logs behind Perez, admired the easy way in which the police officer balanced: he felt himself in constant danger of slipping when the logs sank underfoot and leapt up again. It must, he thought, be a little like standing on a horse as it cantered round a circus ring.

'You spoke to his housekeeper?' Colonel Perez asked.

Doctor Plarr was again annoyed at himself for his rash lies. He was Clara's doctor. Why had he not simply said that this was a routine medical visit to a pregnant wife? One lie in the presence of a policeman seemed to multiply like bacilli. He said, 'No. There was no answer.'

Colonel Perez considered his reply through a long silence.

He remembered how rapidly and easily Perez had walked over the heaving trunks as though he were treading a firm city pavement. The logs covered half the width of the river. A group of people, diminished by distance, stood in the very centre of the wide horizontal forest. Perez and he had to jump from one raft to another to reach them, and every time he jumped the doctor feared he would fall into the gap between the rafts, though the gap was usually less than a metre. His shoes became water-logged as the trunks sank beneath his weight and rose again. 'I warn you,' Perez said, 'it's not going to be very pretty. The family have been travelling on the raft for weeks with the body. It would have been much better if they had just pushed it into the water. We would never have known.'

'Why didn't they?' Doctor Plarr asked, with his arms stretched out as though he were walking a tightrope.

'The murderer,' Perez said, 'wanted him to have a Christian burial.'

'He has admitted killing him then?' the doctor asked.

'Oh, he admitted it to me,' Perez replied. 'You see – these are all my own people.'

When they reached the group – two men, a woman and a child with two officers – Doctor Plarr noticed that the police had not even bothered to take away the assassin's knife. He sat cross-legged beside the disagreeable corpse as though it were his job to guard it. He had an expression of sadness more than of guilt.

Colonel Perez said, 'I came to tell the señora that her husband's car has been found in the Paraná not far from Posadas. There is no sign of a body, so we hope he may have escaped.'

'An accident? Of course you know – the señora won't mind my saying it – Fortnum is rather a heavy drinker.'

'Yes. But there are other possibilities,' Colonel Perez said.

The doctor would have found it easier to play his part to the police officer or to Clara if he had been alone with either of them. He was afraid when he spoke that one or the other would detect something false in his tone. He asked, 'What do you think may have happened?'

'Any incident which occurs so close to the border may be political. We always have to remember that. You remember the doctor who was kidnapped in Posadas?'

'Of course. But why on earth Fortnum? There's nothing political about him.'

'He is a Consul.'

'Only an Honorary Consul.' Even the Chief of Police seemed unable to understand that distinction.

Colonel Perez spoke to Clara, 'We shall let you know, señora, as soon as there is any news.' He put his hand on the doctor's elbow. 'There is something I would like to ask you, doctor.' The colonel led Doctor Plarr across the verandah, where the dumb-waiter with its Long John glasses seemed to emphasize the remarkable absence of Charley Fortnum (he would certainly have invited them to take 'a spot' before they left), and on into the deep shade of the avocado trees. He picked up one of the fallen fruit, examined it for ripeness with an expert's eye and put it in the back of the police car, laying it down carefully where the sun wouldn't strike. 'A beauty,' he said. 'I like to eat them mashed in a little whisky.'

'What is it you want?' the doctor asked.

'There is one thing which worries me a little.'

'You don't really believe that Fortnum has been kidnapped?'

'It is one of the possibilities. It has even occurred to me that he might have been the victim of a silly mistake. He was with the American

Ambassador, you see, in the ruins. The Ambassador obviously would be a more likely target. If that is the case the men must be strangers – perhaps from Paraguay. You and I would never make a mistake like that, doctor. I only say "you" because you are nearly one of us. Of course there is always the possibility you might be indirectly concerned.'

'I'm not quite the kidnapping type, colonel.'

'I was thinking about your father across the border. You told me once that he was either dead or in prison. You might have a motive. Forgive the way I think aloud, doctor, but I always feel a little at sea when it comes to political crime. In politics crime is often the occupation of a *caballero*. I am more used to crimes which are committed by criminals – or at least by violent or poor men. For money or lust.'

'Or *machismo*,' the doctor said, venturing to tease him.

'Oh, everything here is *machismo*,' Perez said, and he smiled at the doctor's remark in so friendly a way that Plarr felt a little reassured. 'Here *machismo* is only another word for living. A word for the air we breathe. When there is no *machismo* a man is dead. Are you coming back to the city, doctor?'

'No. Now that I am here I may as well take a look at Señora Fortnum. She is expecting a baby.'

'Yes. She told me that.' The Chief of Police had his hand on the door of the car, but at the last moment he turned and said in a low voice as though they were sharing a friendly confidence, 'Doctor, why did you tell me you rang up the Consul's office and that there was no reply? I have had a man stationed there all the morning in case a call came.'

'You know what the telephone service is like in this city.'

'When a telephone is out of order one usually hears an engaged tone, not a ringing tone.'

'Not always, colonel. Anyway it may have been the engaged tone. I did not listen very carefully.'

'And yet you came all the way out to the camp?'

'It was about time anyway that I visited Señora Fortnum. Why should I lie to you?'

'I have to think of all the possibilities, doctor. Even a crime of passion is possible.'

'Passion?' the doctor smiled. 'I am an Englishman.'

'Yes, it is unlikely – I know that. And in the case of Señora Fortnum . . . one would not suppose a man like you with all your chances would find it necessary . . . yet I have known crimes of passion even in a brothel.'

'Charley Fortnum is a friend of mine.'

'Oh, a friend . . . It is usually a friend one betrays, isn't it, in these cases?' Colonel Perez put a hand on the doctor's shoulder. 'You must forgive me. I know you well enough, doctor, to allow myself a little speculation when I feel myself at a loss. As I do now. I have heard it said your relations with Señora Fortnum have been very close. All the same – I agree – I would not have thought they would require the elimination of her husband. And yet I still keep wondering why you lied to me.'

He climbed into the car. His revolver holster creaked as he eased himself down in his seat. He leant back to make sure that the avocado was not in a position where it could bounce and bruise.

Doctor Plarr said, 'I was not thinking, colonel, when I spoke, that was all. Lying to the police is almost an automatic reflex. And I was unaware you knew so much about me.'

'This is a small city,' Colonel Perez said. 'It is always safer to assume common knowledge when you sleep with a married woman.'

Doctor Plarr watched the police car out of sight and then went reluctantly back into the house. Secrecy, he thought, is part of the attraction in a sexual affair. An open affair has always a touch of absurdity.

Clara sat exactly where he had left her. He thought: this is the first time we have been together with no sense of hurry, no rendezvous for her to keep at the Consulate, no fear that Charley will return accidentally from farming. She asked, 'Do you think he is dead?'

'No.'

'Perhaps it would be good for everybody if he were.'

'Not for Charley.'

'Yes. Even for Charley. He is so afraid,' she said, 'of getting old.'

'All the samc I don't suppose he wants to die just yet.'

'The baby was kicking hard this morning.'

'Yes?'

'Do you want to go to the bedroom?'

'Of course.' He waited for her to get up and lead the way.

They never kissed on the mouth (that was part of the brothel training), and he followed her with a slow renewal of excitement. In a real love affair, he thought, you are interested in a woman because she is someone distinct from yourself; then bit by bit she adapts herself to you, she picks up your habits, your ideas, even your turns of phrase, she becomes part of you, and then what interest remains? One cannot love oneself, one cannot live for long close to oneself – everyone has need of a stranger in the bed, and a whore remains a stranger. Her body has been scrawled over by so many men you can never decipher your own signature there.

When they were quiet and her head was lying against his shoulder in the same attitude taken by a peaceful love, she began a sentence which he mistook for one he had too often heard, 'Eduardo, is it true? Do you really . . . '

'No,' he said firmly.

He thought she was demanding the same answer to a banal question that his mother had constantly forced out of him after they left his father, the answer which each of his mistresses sooner or later had always insisted on – 'Do you really love me, Eduardo?' One merit of a brothel is that the word love is seldom if ever employed. He repeated, 'No.'

'How can you be sure?' she asked. 'Just now you sounded so certain he was alive, but even that policeman thinks he is dead.'

Doctor Plarr realized he had been mistaken and in his relief he kissed her close to the mouth.

The news came over the radio from the local station while they were at lunch. It was the first meal they had ever taken together, and they were both of them ill at ease. Eating food side by side seemed more intimate to Doctor Plarr than the sexual act. The maid served them and disappeared between each course into the vast untidy regions of the ramshackle house, regions which he had never penetrated. First she served them an omelette, then an excellent steak (which was far better than the goulash at the Italian Club or the tough beef at the Nacional). There was a bottle of Charley's Chilean wine which had more body than the cooperative wine from Mendoza. It was odd eating so formally and so well with one of Señora Sanchez's girls. It opened an unexpected vista into quite another sort of life, a domestic life equally strange to both of them. It was as though he had taken a boat down one of the small tributaries of the Paraná and suddenly found himself in some great delta like that of the Amazon, where all sense of direction can be lost. He felt an unaccustomed tenderness towards Clara who had made this strange voyage possible. They picked their words carefully, it was the first time there were words to pick; they had a subject of conversation – Charley Fortnum's disappearance.

Doctor Plarr began to speak of him as though he were, after all, certainly dead – it seemed to him safer that way, for otherwise she might begin to wonder what was the source of his hope. Only when Clara spoke of the future did he change his tack in order to evade a dubious topic. Charley, he assured her, might yet prove to be alive. To navigate in this new Amazonian waste of deeps and shoals proved difficult – it made for a confusion of tenses. 'It's quite possible he escaped from the car, and then if he was exhausted he might have been carried a long way by the current . . . He may have landed far from any village . . .'

'But why was his car in the river there?' She added with regret, 'It was the new Cadillac. He was going to sell it next week in Buenos Aires.'

'Perhaps he had some errand in Posadas. He was a man who might well . . .'

'Oh no, I know he was not going to Posadas. He was coming to see me. He did not want to go to those ruins. He did not even want to go to the Governor's dinner. He was anxious about me and the baby.'

'Why? He had no reason. You are a strong girl, Clara.'

'I pretended sometimes to be sick so he would ask you to come and see me. It was easier for you that way.'

'What a little bitch you are,' he exclaimed with pleasure.

'And he took my best sunglasses, the ones you gave me. I shall never see them again now. They were my favourite sunglasses. They were so smart. And they came from Mar del Plata.'

'I will go to Gruber's tomorrow,' he said, 'and get you another pair.'

'It was the only one they had.'

'They can order another pair.'

'He borrowed them once before and nearly broke them.'

'He must have looked a bit odd in them,' Doctor Plarr said.

'He never cares what he looks like. And he saw very badly when he had been drinking.' The tenses, present and past, swung to and fro like the arrow of a barometer moving irregularly between settled and unsettled weather.

'Did he love you, Clara?' It was not a question which had ever troubled him. Charley Fortnum, as Clara's husband, had never meant more to him than a slight inconvenience when he felt the need to have her quickly, but Charley Fortnum, lying drugged on a box in a dirty back room, took on the appearance of a serious rival.

'He was always kind to me.'

After the avocado ice had been served he felt desire for her beginning to return. He had no patients to see before the evening; he could take a siesta at the camp without keeping his ear pricked for the rumbling approach of Fortnum's Pride. After the morning climax he would be able to prolong his pleasure through the whole afternoon. She had never, since that first occasion in his flat, attempted to play the comedy of passion, and her indifference had begun to represent a challenge. Sometimes when he was alone he dreamed of surprising her into a genuine cry of excitement.

'Did Charley ever say why he married you?' he asked.

'I told you. It was a question of money when he died. And now he's dead.'

'Perhaps.'

'Would you like to have more ice? I can call María. There is a bell, but Charley always rings it.'

'Why?'

'I am not used to bells. All these electric things – they frighten me.'

It amused him to watch her sitting upright at the end of the table like a hostess. He thought of his mother in the old days on the *estancia* when he had been brought in by his nurse for the dessert – she too had often served an avocado ice. She had been far more beautiful than Clara – they were not to be compared – but he remembered all the aids which she had bought for beauty in those days; they stood two deep on the long dressing-table that stretched from wall to wall. He wondered sometimes whether even in those days his father had not taken second place to Guerlain or Elizabeth Arden.

'What was Charley like as a lover?'

Clara did not bother to answer. She said, 'The radio . . . we ought to listen. There may be news.'

'News?'

'News of Charley, of course. What are you thinking about?'

'I was thinking of the long afternoon we can spend together.'

'He might turn up.'

Taken off his guard he said, 'He won't turn up.'

'Why are you so sure that he is dead?'

'I'm not sure, but if he is alive he will go to a telephone before he does anything else. He will not want to surprise you – and the baby.'

'We ought to listen all the same.'

After getting Asunción first he found a local station. There was no news. Only a sad Guaraní song came over the air and the music of a harp. She said, 'Do you like champagne?'

'Yes.'

'Charley has some champagne. He was given it once in exchange for Long John Whisky – real French champagne, he said.'

The music stopped. A voice announced the station and the news bulletin, and news of Charley Fortnum took first place. A British

Consul – the speaker left out the qualifying and diminishing adjective – had been kidnapped. There was no mention of the American Ambassador. Somehow León must have communicated with his contacts. The omission lent Charley a certain importance. It made him sound worth kidnapping. The authorities, so the speaker said, believed the kidnappers were Paraguayan. It was thought that the Consul might have been taken across the river and the kidnappers were making their demands through the Argentine government in order to confuse the trail. Apparently they had demanded the release of ten political prisoners who were held in Paraguay. Any police action in Paraguay or Argentina would endanger the life of the Consul. A plane to Havana or Mexico City must be arranged for the prisoners . . . There were the usual detailed conditions. The announcement had been made only an hour ago by a telephone call from Rosario to the *Nación* in Buenos Aires. The announcer said there was no possibility that the Consul was held in the capital, for his car had been found near Posadas more than a thousand kilometres away.

'I do not understand,' Clara said.

'Keep quiet and listen.' The announcer went on to explain that the kidnappers had chosen their time with some skill, for General Stroessner at the moment was on an unofficial holiday in the south of Argentina. He had been informed of the kidnapping and he was reported to have said, 'That is no concern of mine. I am here for the fishing.' The kidnappers had given the Paraguayan government until Sunday midnight to agree to their terms by an announcement on the radio. When that time expired they would be forced to execute their prisoner.

'But why Charley?'

'It must have been a mistake. There's no other explanation. You mustn't worry. He will be back home in a few days. Tell your maid you wish to see no one – I expect there will be journalists coming out here.'

'You will stay?'

'I'll stay for a while.'

'I do not think I want to make love.'

'No. Of course. I understand.'

They moved together down the long passage hung with sporting prints, and Doctor Plarr paused to look again at the narrow stream shaded by willows situated in that small northern island where his father had been born. No general went fishing with his colonels in streams like those. He carried the thought of his father's abandoned home into the bedroom. He asked, 'Do you ever want to go back to Tucumán?'

'No,' she said, 'of course not. Why do you ask me that?'

She lay on the bed without taking off her clothes. It was cool as a sea cave in the shuttered air-conditioned room.

'What does your father do?'

'He cuts cane,' she said, 'in the season, but he is getting old.'

'And out of season?'

'They live on the money I send them. They would starve if I died. I will not die, will I? with the baby?'

'No, of course not. Have you no brother or sister?'

'I had a brother, but he went away – no one knows where.' He sat on the edge of the bed and her hand touched his for a moment and withdrew. Perhaps she was afraid he would take her gesture for a comedy of tenderness and resent it. 'He went away,' she said, 'to cut cane one morning at four o'clock and then he never came back. Perhaps he died. Perhaps he just went away.'

He was reminded of his father's disappearance. Here they lived on a continent, not in an island. What a vast area of land, with ill-defined frontiers of mountain, river, jungle and swamp, there was to lose oneself in – all the way from Panama to Tierra del Fuego. 'Your brother never wrote?'

'How could he? He did not know how to read or write.'

'But you can.'

'A little. Señora Sanchez taught me. She liked her girls to be educated. And Charley has helped me too.'

'You had no sister?' he asked.

'Yes. She had a baby in the fields and strangled it and then she died.'

He had never asked about her family before. He could think of no reason for questioning her now, unless perhaps he was seeking to discover what lay behind his obsession. Was there some characteristic in which she differed from the other girls he had seen at Señora Sanchez's house? Perhaps if he discovered the nature of the difference, the obsession would be killed like a trauma at the end of analysis. He would have strangled the obsession as her sister had strangled her child. He said, 'I am tired. Let me lie down beside you for a bit. I need to sleep. I was up until three this morning.'

'What were you doing?'

'I was seeing a patient,' he said. 'Will you wake me when it begins to get dark?'

The air-conditioner humming by the window sounded like a natural summer sound, and once through his sleep he seemed to hear a bell ringing – the big ship's bell which hung on a rope from the eaves of the verandah. He was half aware that she had got up and left him. He heard distant voices, the sound of a car starting, and then she was back, lying beside him, and he slept again. He dreamt, as he hadn't dreamt for some years, of the *estancia* in Paraguay. He was lying in his child's bunk at the top of a ladder, he listened to the noise of keys which were turned and bolts which were pushed to – his father was making the house secure, but he was afraid all the same. Perhaps someone had been locked in who should have been locked out.

Doctor Plarr opened his eyes. The raised edge of the bunk became Clara's body set against his own. It was dark. He could see nothing. He put his hand out and touched her and he felt the baby move. He put his fingers up to her face. Her eyes were open. He said, 'Are you awake?' but she didn't answer. He asked, 'Is something wrong?'

She said, 'I do not want Charley back, but I do not want him to die either.'

He was astonished by this expression of emotion. She had shown none at all, as she sat and listened to Colonel Perez, and, when she had spoken to him after Perez left, it was of the Cadillac and of the lost sunglasses from Gruber's.

She said, 'He was good to me. He is a kind man. I do not want him to be hurt. I only want him not to be here.'

He began to comfort her with his hand as he would have comforted a frightened dog, and gently, without intention, they came together. He felt no lust, and when she moaned and tightened, he felt no sense of triumph.

He wondered with sadness, why did I ever want this to happen? Why did I think it would be a victory? There seemed to be no point in playing the game since now he knew what moves he had to make to win. The moves were sympathy, tenderness, quiet, the counterfeiting of love. He had been drawn to her by her indifference, even her enmity. She said, 'Stay with me tonight.'

'How can I? Your maid would know. You can't trust her not to tell Charley.'

'I could leave Charley.'

'It's too soon to think of that. First we have to save him – somehow.'

'Yes, of course, but afterwards . . .'

'You were anxious about him just now.'

'Not about him,' she said. 'About me. When he is here I can talk about nothing – only the baby. He wants to forget that Señora Sanchez ever existed, so I can never see my friends because they all work there. What good am I to him? He does not want to make love to me any more because he is afraid it will do something to the baby. Do what?

Sometimes I long to tell him – it is not yours anyway, so why do you bother about it?'

'Are you sure it isn't his?'

'Yes. I am sure. Perhaps if he knew about you he would let me go.'

'Who were those people who came to the house just now?'

'Two journalists.'

'Did you speak to them?'

'They wanted me to make an appeal to the kidnappers – for Charley. I did not know what to say. I knew one of them – he used to have me sometimes when I was with Señora Sanchez. I think he was angry about the baby. Colonel Perez must have told him about the baby. He said the baby was news. He always thought I liked him more than the other men. So I think his *machismo* was hurt. These men always believe you when you pretend. It suits their pride. He wanted to show his friend, the photographer, that there was something special between us, but there was nothing. Nothing. I was angry and I began to cry, and they took a picture. He said "Fine. OK. Fine. That's what we want. The sorrowing wife and mother-to-be", he said, and they drove away.'

It was not easy to interpret her tears correctly. Were they tears for Charley, tears of anger, tears for herself?

'What a funny beast you are, Clara,' he said.

'Is something wrong?'

'You were acting again just now, weren't you?'

'What do you mean? Acting?'

'When we made love.'

'Yes,' she said. 'Of course I was acting. I always try to do what you like. I always try to say what you like. Yes. Just like at Señora Sanchez. Why not? You have your *machismo* too.'

He half believed her. He wanted to believe her. If she were speaking the truth there might be something still to discover, the game was not over yet.

'Where are you going?' she asked.

'I have been wasting a lot of time here, Clara. There must be something I can do to help Charley.'

'And me? What about me?'

'You had better take a bath,' he said, 'or your maid might smell sex.'

Chapter 2

DOCTOR PLARR drove back to the city. He told himself it was necessary to do something about Charley Fortnum immediately, but he had no idea what. Perhaps if he stayed quiet everything might be put in order in the accustomed way – the British and American Ambassadors would bring the right diplomatic pressure to bear, Charley Fortnum would be found deposited some early morning in a church and go home – home? – and ten prisoners in Paraguay would be given their liberty – it was even possible his father might be among them. What else could he do but leave things to sort themselves out? He had already lied to Colonel Perez, he was implicated.

Of course, to salve his conscience, he might make an emotional appeal to León Rivas to let Charley Fortnum go – 'in the name of our old friendship'. But León was a man under orders and in any case Doctor Plarr had no clear idea of where to find him. In the *barrio* of the poor all the marshy tracks resembled one another, there were the same avocado trees everywhere, the same huts of mud or tin, and the same pot-bellied children carrying petrol tins of water. They would look at him with their blank eyes which were already infected by trachoma and reply nothing to any question. It might take him hours, even days, to find the hut where Charley Fortnum was hidden, and what good would his appeal do in any case? He tried unsuccessfully to reassure himself that León was not a man to commit murder nor was Aquino, but they were only instruments – there remained El Tigre, whoever he might be.

He had heard of El Tigre for the first time one evening when he had passed León and Aquino sitting side by side in his waiting-room. They were just two strangers among the other patients and he hadn't given them a second look. All who waited there were the responsibility of his secretary.

His secretary was a pretty young woman called Ana. She was dauntingly efficient and the daughter of an influential official in the public health department. Doctor Plarr sometimes wondered why he had never been tempted to make love to her. Perhaps he hesitated because of the white starched uniform which she had adopted of her own wish – it would creak or crackle if one touched her: she might have been connected to a burglar-alarm. Or perhaps it was the importance of her father, or her piety, real or apparent, which deterred him. She always wore a small gold cross round her neck, and once, when he had been driving through the square by the cathedral, he had seen her emerge with her family from Sunday Mass carrying a missal bound in white vellum – it might have been a first Communion present, for it closely resembled the sugar almonds which are distributed on such occasions.

The evening when León and Aquino came to see him, he had dealt with all the other patients before it became the turn of the two strangers. He had not remembered them because there were always new faces waiting his attention. Patience and patients were words closely allied. His secretary came with a crackle to his side and put a slip of paper on the desk. 'They want to see you together,' she said. He put back on the shelf a medical book he had been consulting in front of a patient – for some reason patients gained confidence if they could see a coloured picture, an aspect of human psychology which American publishers knew well. When he looked back the two men were standing side by side in front of his desk. The smaller, who had protruding ears, said, 'It *is* Eduardo surely?'

'León,' Plarr exclaimed, 'it is León, León Rivas?' They embraced with a certain shyness. Plarr asked, 'How many years . . . ? I haven't heard from you since you sent me that Ordination card. I was sorry I could not come to the ceremony – it would have been unsafe for me.'

'That is all over anyway.'

'Why? Have they thrown you out?'

'I am married for one thing. The archbishop did not like that.'

Doctor Plarr hesitated.

León Rivas said, 'I am very lucky. She is a fine woman.'

'Congratulations. Who in Paraguay did you find willing to celebrate the marriage?'

'We made our vows to each other. You know a priest at a marriage is never more than a witness. In an emergency . . . this was an emergency.'

'I had forgotten things were so easy.'

'Oh, I can assure you not so easy. It needs a lot of thought. That sort of marriage is more irrevocable than in a church. Don't you recognize my friend?'

'No . . . I don't think so . . . no . . .' Doctor Plarr tried to strip away the thin beard and identify some schoolboy face which he might have known years ago in Asunción.

'Aquino.'

'Aquino? Why of course it's Aquino.' Another embrace: it was like a military ceremony, a kiss on the cheek and a decoration awarded for a dead past in a devastated land. He asked, 'What are you doing now? You were going to be a writer, weren't you? Are you a writer?'

'There are no writers left in Paraguay.'

'We saw your name on a parcel in Gruber's shop,' León said.

'So he told me, but I thought you were police agents from over there.'

'Why? Are you watched?'

'I don't think so.'

'We have come from over there.'

'Are you in trouble?'

'Aquino has been in prison,' León said.

'They let you out?'

'The authorities did not exactly invite me to go,' Aquino said.

'We were lucky,' León explained. 'They were transferring him from one police station to another, there was a little shooting, but the only man who was killed was the policeman we were going to pay. He was shot by his own side, by accident. We had given him only half the money in advance, so we got Aquino cheap.'

'Are you going to settle here?'

'Not settle,' León said. 'We are here to do a job. Afterwards we shall go back.'

'You are not patients then?'

'No, we are not patients.'

Doctor Plarr appreciated the dangers of a frontier. He got up and opened the door. His secretary was standing beside the filing cabinet in the outer office. She inserted a card here, a card there. Her cross swung to and fro as she moved, like a priest's censer. He closed the door. He said, 'You know, León, I'm not interested in politics. Only medicine. I am not like my father.'

'Why are you here and not in Buenos Aires?'

'I was not doing very well in Buenos Aires.'

'We thought you might want to know what happened to your father.'

'Do *you* know?'

'I think we may soon be in a position to find out.'

Doctor Plarr said, 'I had better make notes about your condition. I'll put down low blood pressure for you, León, a suspicion of anaemia . . . Aquino – perhaps your gall-bladder . . . I will put you down for x-rays. You understand my secretary will expect to see what diagnosis I make.'

'We believe your father may be alive still,' León said. 'So naturally we thought of you . . .'

There was a knock on the door and the secretary came in. She said, 'I have finished all the cards. If you would let me go now . . .'

'A lover waiting?'

She said, 'Today is Saturday,' as though that ought to explain everything.

'I know that.'

'I want to go to Confession.'

'Oh,' Doctor Plarr said, 'of course. I am sorry, Ana. I forgot. Of course you must go.' His lack of desire for her irritated him, so he deliberately found an occasion to vex her. 'Pray for me,' he said.

She ignored his flippancy. 'If you will leave those two cards on my desk when you have finished . . .' Her dress crepitated, as she went out, like a nocturnal insect.

Doctor Plarr said, 'I doubt if her Confession will take very long.'

'Those who have nothing to confess always take the longest,' León Rivas said. 'They want to please the priest and give him something to do. A murderer has only one thing on his mind, so he forgets all the rest – perhaps worse things. One can deal with him very quickly.'

'You still talk like a priest, León. What made you marry?'

'I married when I lost faith. A man must have something to guard.'

'I can't imagine you without your faith.'

'I only mean my faith in the Church. Or in what they have made of it. Of course I know one day things may be better. But I was ordained when John was Pope. I am not patient enough to wait for another John.'

'You were going to be an *abogado* before you became a priest. What are you now?'

'A criminal,' León said.

'You are joking.'

'No. That is why I have come to you. We need your help.'

'To rob a bank?' Doctor Plarr asked. He couldn't take León seriously, when he looked at those familiar protruding ears and remembered so much . . .

'To rob an Embassy – you might call it that.'

'But I'm no criminal, León.' He added deliberately, 'Except for an abortion or two,' to see if the priestly eyes would flinch a little, but they stared back at him with indifference.

'In a wrong society,' León Rivas said, 'the criminals are honest men.' The phrase came a bit too glibly. It was probably a well-known quotation. Doctor Plarr remembered how first there had been the law books León studied – he had once explained to him the meaning of tort. Then there had been all the works of theology – León was able to make even the Trinity seem plausible by a sort of higher mathematics.

He supposed there must be other primers to read in the new life. Perhaps he was quoting Marx.

'The new American Ambassador,' León said, 'is planning to visit the north in November. You have contacts here, Eduardo. All we need are the exact details of his programme.'

'I'm not going to be an accomplice in murder, León.'

'There will be no murder. A murder would be of very little use to us. Aquino, tell him about the treatment they gave you.'

'It was simple,' Aquino said. 'Not at all up to date. Nothing electric. Like the *conquistadores* they managed with a knife . . . '

Doctor Plarr listened with nausea. He had been present at many unpleasant deaths which had affected him less. In those cases there had been something to do, some means of helping in however small a degree. He felt sickness at this narrative in the past tense, just as years ago, when he was a young student, he had been upset by the dissection of a cadaver for educational purposes. When it came to a living body there was always curiosity and hope. He asked, 'And you didn't talk?'

'Of course I talked,' Aquino said. 'They have it all in the files now. The counter-insurgency section of the CIA were pleased with me. Two of their agents were there, and they gave me three packets of Lucky Strike. A packet for each man I had betrayed.'

'Show him your hand, Aquino,' León said.

Aquino laid his right hand on the desk like a patient seeking advice. Three fingers were missing: the hand without them looked like something drawn up in a fish-net from the river where eels were active. Aquino said, 'That was why I began to write poetry. Verse was less tiring than prose with only a left hand. I could learn it by heart. I was allowed a visitor every three months (that was another reward they gave me) and I would recite her the verses I had made.'

'They were good verses,' León said, 'for a beginner. A kind of Purgatorio in *villancico*.'

'How many of you are there?' Doctor Plarr asked.

'A dozen of us crossed the border, not counting El Tigre. He was already in Argentina.'

'Who is El Tigre?'

'The one who gives the orders. We call him that, but it is a term of affection. He likes to wear striped shirts.'

'The scheme sounds mad, León.'

'It has been done before.'

'Why kidnap the American Ambassador here instead of the one you have in Asunción?'

'That was our first plan. But the General takes great precautions. Here, you must know it yourself, they have much less fear of guerrillas since the failure in Salta.'

'All the same you are in a foreign country.'

'South America is our country, Eduardo. Not Paraguay. Not Argentina. You know what Che said, "The whole continent is my country". What are you? English or South American?'

Doctor Plarr remembered the question, but he still could not answer it as he drove into the city past the white Gothic prison which always reminded him of a sugar decoration for a wedding cake. He told himself that León Rivas was a priest, and not a murderer. And Aquino? Aquino was a poet. It would have been easier to discount the danger to Charley Fortnum if he had never seen him lying unconscious on a box, a box so oddly shaped that it might have been a coffin.

Chapter 3

CHARLEY FORTNUM woke with the worst head he could ever remember having. His eyes were aching and his vision was blurred. He whispered, 'Clara,' putting out his hand to touch her side, but all he touched was a mud wall. Then an image came to his mind of Doctor Plarr standing over him during the night with an electric torch. The doctor had told him some implausible story of an accident.

It was daylight now. The sunlight seeped across the floor under the door of the next room, and he could tell, even through his bruised eyes, that this was no hospital. Nor was the hard box on which he lay a hospital bed. He swung his legs over the side and tried to stand up. He was giddy and nearly fell. Clutching the side of the box, he saw that he had been lying all night upon a coffin. It gave him, as he would have put it, a nasty turn.

'Ted?' he called. He didn't associate Doctor Plarr with practical jokes, but there had to be some sort of explanation, and he was anxious to be back with Clara. Clara would be frightened, Clara wouldn't know what to do. Why, she was afraid even to use the telephone. 'Ted?' he called again in a dry croak. Whisky had never treated him like this before, not even the local brand. Whom the bloody hell had he been drinking with and where? Mason, he told himself, you've got to pull yourself together. It was always to Mason he attributed his worst errors and his worst failings. In his boyhood when he still practised confession it was always Mason who knelt in the box and muttered abstract phrases concerning sins against purity, though it was Charley Fortnum who would leave the box, his face ashine with beneficence after Mason's absolution. 'Mason, Mason,' he whispered now, 'you snotty little beast, Mason, what were you up to last night?' He knew that when he exceeded the proper measure he was apt to forget things, but never before had he forgotten to quite this extent . . . He took a stumbling step towards the door and for the third time called out to Doctor Plarr.

The door was pushed open and a stranger stood there waving a sub-machine gun at him. He had the narrow eyes and jet black hair of an Indian and he shouted at Fortnum in Guaraní. Fortnum, in spite of his father's angry insistence, had never learnt more than a few words of Guaraní, but it was clear enough that the man was telling him to get back on to the so-called bed. 'All right, all right,' Fortnum said, speaking English so that the man would no more understand him than he understood Guaraní. 'Keep your shirt on, old man.' He sat down on the coffin and said, 'Piss off,' with a sense of relief.

Another stranger in blue jeans, naked to the waist, came in and ordered the Indian away. He carried a cup of coffee. The coffee smelt like home, and Charley Fortnum was a little comforted. The man had protruding ears and for a moment Charley was reminded of a boy at school whom Mason had unmercifully teased, though Fortnum repented afterwards and shared a bar of chocolate with the victim. This memory gave him a sense of reassurance. He asked, 'Where am I?'

'You do not need to worry,' the man replied. He held out the coffee.

'I have to go home. My wife will be anxious.'

'Tomorrow. I hope you will be able to go tomorrow.'

'Who was that man with a gun?'

'Miguel. A good man. Drink your coffee, please. You will feel much better then.'

'What's your name?' Charley Fortnum asked.

'León,' the man said.

'I mean your family name?'

'None of us here have families,' the mad said, 'so we are nameless.'

Charley Fortnum turned this statement over in his mind like a difficult phrase in a book; it made no more sense to him at the second reading.

'Doctor Plarr was here last night,' he said.

'Plarr? Plarr? I do not think I know anyone called Plarr.'

'He told me I had been in an accident.'

'It was I who told you that,' the man said.

'It was not you. I saw him. He carried an electric torch.'

'You dreamt him. You have had a shock . . . Your car was badly damaged. Please drink your coffee. You will remember things better perhaps afterwards.'

Charley Fortnum obeyed. It was very strong coffee, and it was true that his head began to clear. He askcd, 'Where is the Ambassador?'

'I do not know of any Ambassador.'

'I left him in the ruins. I wanted to see my wife before dinner. I wanted to see that she was all right. I don't like leaving her for long. She is expecting a baby.'

'Yes? That must make you very happy. It is a fine thing to be the father of a child.'

'I remember now. There was a car across the road. I had to stop. There was no accident. I'm quite sure there was no accident. And why the gun?' His hand shook a little as he drank his coffee. He said, 'I want to go home now.'

'It is much too far to walk from here,' the man said. 'You are not fit yet. And the way – you do not know the way.'

'I will find a road. I can stop a car.'

'Better to rest today. After the shock. Tomorrow perhaps we can find you some transport. Today is not possible.'

Fortnum threw what was left of his coffee in the man's face and charged into the other room. Then he stopped. The Indian stood twelve feet away in front of the outer door, pointing his gun at Charley Fortnum's stomach. His dark eyes shone with pleasure, as he moved the gun a little this way, a little that, as though he were deciding his target, between the navel and the appendix. He said something which amused him in Guaraní.

The man called León came from the inner room. He said, 'You see I told you. You cannot go today.' One cheek was flushed red from the hot coffee, but he spoke gently, without anger. He had the patience of someone who was more used to enduring pain than inflicting it. He said, 'You must be hungry, Señor Fortnum. If you would like some eggs . . .'

'You know who I am?'

'Yes, yes, of course. You are the British Consul.'

'What are you going to do with me?'

'You will have to stay with us for a little while. Believe me, we are not your enemies, Señor Fortnum. You will be helping us to save innocent men from imprisonment and torture. By this time our man in

Rosario will have telephoned to the *Nacion* to tell them you are in our care.'

Charley Fortnum began to understand. 'You got the wrong man, is that it? You were after the American Ambassador?'

'Yes, it was an unfortunate mistake.'

'A very bad mistake. No one is going to bother about Charley Fortnum. What will you do then?'

The man said, 'I am sure you are wrong. You will see. Everything will be arranged. The British Ambassador will talk to the President. The President will speak to the General. He is here in Argentina on a holiday. The American Ambassador will intervene too. We are only asking the General to release a few men. Everything would have been quite easy if one of our men had not made a mistake.'

'You were not very well informed, were you? The Ambassador had two police officers with him. And his secretary. That was why there was no room for me in his car.'

'We could have dealt with them.'

'All right. Give me your eggs,' Charley Fortnum said, 'but tell that man Miguel to put away his gun. It spoils my appetite.'

The man called León knelt before a small spirit stove on the earth floor and busied himself with matches, a frying pan, a bit of lard.

'I could do with some whisky if you have it.'

'I am sorry. We have no spirits.'

The lard began to bubble in the pan.

'Your name is León, eh?'

'Yes.' The man broke two eggs one after the other on the edge of the pan. As he held two half shells over the pan there was something in the position of the fingers which reminded Fortnum of that moment at the altar when a priest breaks the Host over the chalice.

'What will you do if they refuse?'

'I pray they will accept,' the kneeling man said, 'I am sure they will accept.'

'Then I hope to God God hears you,' Charley Fortnum said. 'Don't fry the eggs too hard.'

It was not until the afternoon that Charley Fortnum heard the official news about himself. The man León turned on a pocket radio at noon, but the battery failed in the middle of some Guaraní music and he had no spares. The young man with a beard whom León called Aquino went into town to buy more batteries. He was a long time gone. A woman came in from the market with food and cooked their lunch, a vegetable soup with a few scraps of meat. She made a great show too of cleaning the hut, raising the dust in one part so that it settled in another. She had a lot of untidy black hair and a wart on her face and she treated León with a mixture of possessiveness and servility. He called her Marta.

Once Charley Fortnum, with embarrassment because of the woman's presence, said he wanted to use a lavatory. León gave an order to the Indian who led him to a cabin in the yard at the back of the hut. The door had lost one of its hinges and wouldn't close, and inside there was only a deep hole dug in the earth with a couple of boards across it. When he came out the Guaraní was sitting a few feet away playing with his gun, sighting it on a tree, a bird flying past, at a stray mongrel dog. Through the trees Charley Fortnum could see another hut, even poorer than the one to which he was returning. He thought of running to it for help, but he felt sure the Indian would welcome the chance to try his gun. When he got back he said to León, 'If you can get a couple of bottles of whisky I'll pay you for them.' No one had stolen his wallet, he had noticed that, and he took out the necessary notes.

León gave the money to Marta. He said, 'You will have to be patient, Señor Fortnum. Aquino is not back. No one can go till he returns. And it is a long walk into the town.'

'I will pay for a taxi.'

'I am afraid that is not possible. There are no taxis here.'

The Indian squatted down again by the door. Charley Fortnum said, 'I'm going off to sleep a bit. That drug you gave me was pretty strong.' He went back into the inner room and stretched out on the coffin. He tried to sleep, but he was kept awake by his thoughts. He wondered how Clara was managing in his absence. He had never left her alone for a whole night before. He knew nothing about childbirth, but he had an idea that shock or anxiety could affect the unborn child. He had even tried to cut down his drinking after he married Clara – except for the first married night of whisky and champagne when for the first time they made love properly, without impediment, in the Hotel Italia in Rosario – an old-fashioned hotel which smelt agreeably of undisturbed dust like an ancient library.

They had gone there because he thought she would be a little scared of the Riviera Hotel which was new, expensive and air-conditioned. There were papers he had to collect at the Consulate at Santa Fe 939 (he remembered the number because it represented the month and year of his first marriage), the papers which if inquiries were made would show that there was no impediment to his second marriage – it had taken weeks to get a copy of Evelyn's death certificate from a small town in Idaho. He was able at the same time to leave his will in a sealed envelope in the Consulate safe. The Consul was a pleasant middle-aged man. He and Charley Fortnum had hit it off right away when for some reason the subject of horses came up. He invited them back after the civil and religious ceremonies and opened a bottle of genuine French champagne. That little drinking ceremony among the file boxes compared very favourably with the reception in Idaho after his first marriage. He remembered with horror the white cake and the relations-in-law who wore dark suits and even hard collars, although it was a civil marriage which was not acceptable in Argentina. They had been prudent and not spoken of it when they returned. His wife had refused a Catholic marriage – it was against her conscience as she had become a Christian Scientist. Of course the civil marriage made her inheritance unsafe – which was also an indignity. He wanted very much to arrange things more safely for Clara; to ensure there were no cracks in the walls of this second marriage. He intended to leave her, when he came to die, in a security which was impregnable.

After a while he slid into a deep dreamless sleep; he was only woken when the radio in the next room began to repeat his own name – Señor Carlos Fortnum. The police – the announcer said – believed he might have been brought to Rosario because the telephone call to the *Nación* had been traced to that city. A city of more than half a million inhabitants couldn't be searched very thoroughly, and the authorities had been given only four days in which to agree to the kidnappers' terms. One of these four days had already passed. Charley Fortnum thought: Clara will be listening to the broadcast, and he thanked God Ted would be around to reassure her. Ted would know what had happened. Ted would go to see her. Ted would do something to keep her calm. Ted would tell her that, even if they killed him, she would be all right. She had so much fear of the past – he could tell that from the way she never spoke of it. It was one of his reasons for marrying her, to prove she would never under any circumstances have to return to Mother Sanchez. He took exaggerated care of her happiness like a clumsy man entrusted with something of great fragility which didn't belong to him. He was always afraid of dropping her happiness. Someone was talking now about the Argentine football team which was touring Europe. He called, 'León!'

The small head with the bat-ears and the attentive eyes of a good servant peered round the door. León said, 'You have slept a long time, Señor Fortnum. That is good.'

'I heard the radio, León.'

'Ah, yes.' León was carrying a glass in one hand and a bottle of whisky was tucked under each arm. He said, 'My wife has brought two bottles from the town.' He showed the whisky proudly (it was an Argentine brand) and counted out the change with care. 'You must not worry. Everything will be over in a few days.'

'Everything will be over with me, you mean? Give me that whisky.' He poured out a third of a glass and drank it down.

'I am sure tonight we shall hear them announce that they have accepted our terms. And then by tomorrow evening you can go home.'

Charley Fortnum poured out another dose.

'You are drinking too much,' the man called León said with friendly anxiety.

'No, no. I know the right measure. And it's the measure that counts. What's your other name, León?'

'I told you I have no other name.'

'But you have a title, haven't you? Tell me what you are doing in this set-up, Father León.'

He could almost believe the ears twitched, like a dog's, at a familiar intonation – 'Father' taking the place of 'walk' or perhaps 'cat'.

'You are mistaken. You saw my wife just now. Marta. She brought you the whisky.'

'But once a priest always a priest, Father. I spotted you when you broke those eggs over the dish. I could see you at the altar, Father.'

'You are imagining things, Señor Fortnum.'

'And what are *you* imagining? You might have made a good bargain for the Ambassador, but you can't get anything in return for me. I'm not worth a peso to a human soul – except my wife. It seems an odd thing for a priest to become a murderer, but I suppose you'll get someone else to do the thing.'

'No,' the other said with great seriousness, 'if it should ever come to that, which God forbid, I will be the one. I do not want to shift the guilt.'

'Then I'd better leave you some of this whisky. You'll need a swig of it – in how many days did they say – three was it?'

The other man's eyes shifted. He had a frightened air. He shuffled two steps towards the door as though he were leaving the altar and was afraid of treading on the skirt of a soutane which was too long for him.

'You might stay and talk a bit,' Charley Fortnum said. 'I feel more scared when I'm alone. I don't mind telling *you* that. If one can't talk to a priest who can one talk to? That Indian now . . . he sits there and stares at me and smiles. He *wants* to kill.'

'You are wrong, Señor Fortnum. Miguel is a good man. He has no

Spanish, that is all, and so he smiles just to show he is a friend. Try to sleep again.'

'I've had enough sleep. I want to talk to you.'

The man made a gesture with his hands, and Charley Fortnum could imagine him in church, making his formal passes. 'I have so many things to do.'

'I can always keep you here if I try.'

'No, no. I *must* go.'

'I can keep you here easily. I know the way.'

'I will come back presently, I promise.'

'All I have to say to keep you is – Father, please hear my confession.'

The man stayed stuck in the doorway with his back turned. His protruding ears stood out like little hands raised over an offering.

'Since my last confession, Father . . .'

The man swung round and said angrily, 'You must not joke about things like that. I will not listen to you if you joke . . .'

'But that's no joke, Father. I'm not in a position to joke about anything at all. Surely every man has a lot to confess when it comes to dying.'

'My faculties have been taken away,' the other said in a stubborn voice. 'You must know what that means if you are really a Catholic.'

'I seem to know the rules better than you, Father. You do not need faculties, not in an emergency – if there is no other priest available . . . there isn't, is there? Your men would never let you bring one here . . .'

'There is no emergency – not yet.'

'All the same time is short . . . if I ask . . .'

The man reminded him again of a dog, a dog who has been reproved for a fault which he does not clearly understand. He began to plead, 'Señor Fortnum, I assure you there never will be an emergency . . . it will never be necessary . . .'

'"I am sorry and beg pardon" – that's how I begin, isn't it? It's been the hell of a long time . . . I've been once to church in the last forty years . . . a while ago when I got married. I was damned if I'd go to confession though. It would have taken too long and I couldn't keep the lady waiting.'

'Please Señor Fortnum, do not mock me.'

'I'm not mocking *you*, Father. Perhaps I'm mocking myself a bit. I can do that as long as the whisky lasts.' He added, 'It really is a funny thing when you come to think of it. "I ask forgiveness of God through you, Father." That *is* the formula, isn't it – and all the time you'll have the gun ready. Don't you think we ought to begin now? Before the gun is loaded. There are plenty of things I have on my mind.'

'I will not listen to you.' He made the gesture of putting his hands against the protruding ears. They flattened and sprang back.

Charley Fortnum said, 'Oh, don't worry, forget it. I was only half serious. What difference does it make anyway?'

'What do you mean?'

'I don't believe a thing, Father. I would never have bothered to marry in a church if the law hadn't forced me to. There was the question of money. For my wife, I mean. What was your intention, Father, when *you* married?' He added quickly, 'Forgive me. I had no business to ask that.'

But the little man, it seemed, was not angry. The question even appeared to have an attraction for him. He came slowly across the floor with his mouth ajar, as though he were a starving man drawn irresistibly by the offer of bread. A little saliva hung at the corner of his mouth. He came and crouched down on the floor beside the coffin. He said in a low voice (he might have been kneeling in the confessional box himself), 'I think it was anger and loneliness, Señor Fortnum. I never meant any harm to her, poor woman.'

'I can understand the loneliness,' Charley Fortnum said, 'I've suffered from that too. But why the anger? Who were you angry with?'

'The Church,' the man said and added with irony, 'my Mother the Church.'

'I used to be angry with my father. He didn't understand me, I thought, or care a nickel about me. I hated him. All the same I was bloody lonely when he died. And now –' he lifted his glass – 'I even imitate him. Though he drank more than I do. All the same a father's a father – I don't see how you can be angry with Mother Church. I could never get angry with a fucking institution.'

'She is a sort of person too,' the man said, 'they claim she is Christ on earth – I still half believe it even now. Someone like you – *un Inglés* – you are not able to understand how ashamed I felt of the things they made me read to people. I was a priest in the poor part of Asunción near the river. Have you noticed how the poor always cling close to the river? They do it here too, as though they plan one day to swim away, but they have no idea how to swim and there is nowhere to swim to for any of them. On Sunday I had to read to them out of the Gospels.'

Charley Fortnum listened with a little sympathy and a good deal of cunning. His life depended on this man, and it was vitally important for him to know what moved him. There might be some chord he could touch of fellow feeling. The man was speaking immoderately as a thirsty man drinks. Perhaps he had been unable to speak freely for a long time: perhaps this was the only way he could unburden himself to a man who was safely dying and would remember no more what he said than a priest in the confessional. Charley Fortnum asked, 'What's wrong with the Gospels, Father?'

'They make no sense,' the ex-priest said, 'anyway not in Paraguay. "Sell all and give to the poor" – I had to read that out to them while the old Archbishop we had in those days was eating a fine fish from Iguazú and drinking a French wine with the General. Of course the people were not actually starving – you can keep them from starving on mandioca, and malnutrition is much safer for the rich than starvation. Starvation makes a man desperate. Malnutrition makes him too tired to raise a fist. The Americans understand that well – the aid they give us makes just that amount of difference. Our people do not starve – they wilt. The words used to stick on my lips – "Suffer little children", and there the children sat in the front rows with their pot bellies and their navels sticking out like door knobs. "It were better that a millstone were hung around his neck". "He who gives to one of the least of these". Gives what? gives mandioca? and then I distributed the Host – it's not so nourishing as a good *chipá* – and then I drank the wine. Wine! Which of these poor souls had ever tasted wine? Why could we not use water in the sacrament? He used it at Cana. Wasn't there a beaker of water at the Last Supper He could have used instead?' To Charley Fortnum's astonishment the dog-like eyes were swollen with unshed tears.

The man said, 'Oh, you must not think we are all of us bad Christians as I am. The Jesuits do what they can. But they are watched by the police. Their telephones are tapped. If anyone seems dangerous he is quickly pushed across the river. They do not kill him. The Yankees would not like a priest to be killed, and anyway we are not dangerous enough. I spoke in a sermon once about Father Torres who was shot with the guerrillas in Colombia. I only said that unlike Sodom the Church did sometimes produce one just man, so perhaps she would not be destroyed like Sodom. The police reported me to the Archbishop and the Archbishop forbade me to preach any more. Oh well, poor man, he was very old and the General liked him, and he thought he was doing right, rendering to Caesar . . .'

'These things are a bit above my head, Father,' Charley Fortnum said, lying propped on his elbow on the coffin and looking down at the dark head which still showed the faint trace of a tonsure through the hair, like a prehistoric camp in a field seen from a plane. He interjected 'Father' as often as he could: it was somehow reassuring. A father didn't usually kill his son, although of course it had been a near miss in the case of Abraham. 'I am not to blame, Father.'

'I am not blaming you, Señor Fortnum, God forbid.'

'I can see how the American Ambassador from your point of view – well, he was a legitimate objective. But me – I'm not even a proper Consul and the English are not in *this* fight, Father.'

The priest muttered a cliché absent-mindedly, 'They say one man has to die for the people.'

'But that was what the crucifiers said, not the Christians.'

The priest looked up. 'Yes, you are right,' he said, 'I was not thinking when I spoke. You know your Testament.'

'I have not read it since I was a boy. But that's the kind of scene which sticks in the mind. Like Struwelpeter.'

'Struwelpeter?'

'He had his thumbs cut off.'

'I never heard of him. Is he one of your martyrs?'

'No, no, it's a nursery story, Father.'

'Have you children?' the priest asked sharply.

'No, but I told you. In a few months there should be one around. He kicks hard already.'

'Yes, I remember now.' He added, 'Don't worry, you will be home soon.' It was as though the sentence were framed in question marks, and he wanted the prisoner to reassure him by agreeing, 'Yes, of course. It goes without saying, but Charley Fortnum refused to play that game.

'Why this coffin, Father? It seems a bit morbid to me.'

'The earth is too damp for sleeping on, even with a cloth under you. We did not want you to catch rheumatism.'

'Well, that was a kindly thought, Father.'

'We are not barbarians. There is a man near here in the *barrio* who makes coffins. We bought one from him. It was much safer than buying a bed . . . There is a greater demand in the *barrio* for coffins than beds. Nobody asks questions about a coffin.'

'And I suppose you thought it might be handy later on for stowing away a body.'

'That was not in our minds, I swear. To ask for a bed would have been dangerous.'

'Oh well, I think I *will* have another whisky, Father. Have one with me.'

'No. You see – I am on duty. I have to guard you.' He gave a timid smile.

'You would not be difficult to overpower, would you? Even for an old man like me.'

'There are always two of us on duty,' the priest said. 'Miguel is out there now with his gun. Those are El Tigre's orders. There is another reason for that too. One man might be talked around. Or even bribed. We are all of us human beings. This is not the sort of life any of us would have chosen.'

'The Indian does not speak Spanish?'

'Yes, that too is a good thing.'

'Do you mind if I stretch my legs a little?'

'Of course you may.'

Charley Fortnum went to the doorway and checked the truth of what the priest had said. The Indian was squatting by the door with the gun on his lap. He smiled at Fortnum confidentially, as though they shared a secret joke. Almost imperceptibly he moved the position of his gun.

'You speak Guaraní, Father?'

'Yes. I used to preach in Guaraní once.'

A few minutes ago there had been a moment of closeness, of sympathy, even of friendship between them, but that moment had passed. When a Confession is finished, the priest and the penitent are each alone. They pretend not to recognize each other if they pass in the church. It was as though it were the penitent who stood now by the coffin looking at his watch. Charley Fortnum thought: he is checking to see how many hours are left.

'Change your mind and have a whisky with me, Father.'

'No. No thank you. One day perhaps when all this is over.' He added, 'He is late. I should have been gone long before now.'

'Who is late?'

The priest answered angrily, 'I have told you before that people like us have no names.'

The darkness was falling and in the shuttered outer room onc of them had lit a candle. They had left his door open and he could see the Indian sitting close beside the door nursing his gun. Charley Fortnum wondered when his turn would come to sleep. The man called León had been gone a long while. There was a negro he had not noticed before . . . If I had a knife, he wondered, could I make a hole to escape by?

The man called Aquino brought in a candle, carrying it in his left hand. Charley Fortnum noticed that he kept his right hand always concealed in his jeans. Perhaps it held a gun – or a knife – and his thoughts went back to the rather hopeless idea of cutting a hole through the dried mud of the wall. In an impossible situation one had to try the impossible. He asked, 'Where is the Father?'

'He has things to do in the town, Señor Fortnum.'

They always treated him with great courtesy, he noticed, as though they were trying to reassure him, 'There is nothing personal in this affair. Once it is over we can meet as friends'. Or was it perhaps the habitual courtesy which a prison warder is said to show even the most brutal murderer before his execution? People have the same awed respect for death as they have for a distinguished stranger, however unwelcome he may be, who visits their town.

He said, 'I'm hungry. I could eat an ox.' It wasn't true, but perhaps they would be foolish enough to let him have a knife with his food. He had an impression he was in the hands of amateurs, not professionals.

'Soon,' Aquino said, 'be a little patient, Señor Fortnum. We are waiting for Marta. She has promised to make us a stew. She is not a very good cook, but if you had been in prison like me . . .'

He thought: stew. That means I'll be given only a spoon again. 'There is still some whisky left,' he said. 'Will you have a drink with me?'

Aquino said, 'We are none of us supposed to drink.'

'A small one – to keep me company.'

'A very small one then. I will eat one of the onions Marta has brought for the stew. It will take away the smell. I do not want to disappoint León. For him it comes naturally to be strict, but we are not all priests, thank God. That is a very large whisky,' he protested.

'Large? Why, it is only half as big as mine. *Salud*.'

'*Salud*.'

He noticed Aquino still kept his right hand in his pocket. 'What are you, Aquino?'

'What do you mean, what am I?'

'Are you a worker?'

'I am a criminal,' Aquino said with pride. 'We are all criminals.'

'Is that a full-time occupation?' Fortnum raised his glass and Aquino followed suit. 'You must have begun somewhere.'

'Oh, I went to school like all the world. It was run by priests. They were good men, and it was a good school. León was there too – he wanted to be an *abogado*. As for me, I wanted to be a writer, but even a writer has to live, so I went into the tobacco business. I made money selling American cigarettes in the street. Smuggled cigarettes from Panama. Good money too . . . I mean I was able to share a room with three others and we had enough to buy *chipás*. You get quite fat on *chipás*. They are better than mandioca.'

'I have a camp outside the city,' Charley Fortnum said. 'I could do with a new *capataz*. You are an educated man. You could easily learn the job.'

'Oh, I have another job now.' Aquino said with pride, 'I told you – I am a criminal. I am also a poet.'

'A poet?'

'At school León helped me to write. He said I had talent, but once I sent an article to the paper in Asunción criticizing the Yankees. In our country it is forbidden by the General to publish anything against the Yankees, and afterwards they would not even read any of the articles I sent in. They thought I was writing something between the lines which would get them into trouble. They thought I was a *político*, and so naturally – what else could I do? I became a *político*. So then they sent me to prison. It happens always that way, if you are a *político* and you are not a Colorado, one of the General's party.'

'Was it bad in prison?'

'Pretty bad,' Aquino said. He pulled out his right hand and showed it to Charley Fortnum. 'That is when I started to make poetry. It takes a long time to learn to write anything with the left hand, and it is very slow work. I hate things which are slow. I would rather be a mouse than a tortoise, even though the tortoise lives a longer time.' He had become voluble after his second gulp of whisky. 'I admire the eagle which drops on its victims like a rock out of the sky, but not the vulture which flaps slowly down, looking as it goes to see if the carrion moves. That is why I took to poetry. Prose moves too slowly, poetry drops like an eagle and stabs before you know. Of course in prison they would not give me paper or pen, but I did not have to write the poetry. I could learn it by heart.'

'Was it good poetry?' Charley Fortnum asked. 'Not that I'd know the difference.'

Aquino said 'I think some of it was good.' He finished his whisky. 'León said some of it was good. He told me it was like a man called Villon. He was a criminal like me.'

'Never heard of him,' Charley Fortnum said.

'The first poem I wrote in prison,' Aquino said, 'was about the first prison of all – the one we all of us know. Do you know what Trotsky said when they showed him his new home in Mexico? They had made it secure from assassins, or so they thought. He said, "This reminds me of my first prison. The doors make the same sound." My poem had a refrain, "I see my father only through the bars." I was thinking, you see, of the pens in which they put children in bourgeois houses. In my poem the father went on following the child all through his life – he was the schoolmaster, and then he was the priest, the police officer, the prison warder, and last he was General Stroessner himself. I saw the General once when he was touring the countryside. He came to the police station I was in and I saw him through the bars.'

'I have a child on the way,' Charley Fortnum said. 'I would like to see the little bastard if only for a short time. But not through bars, you know. I would like to live long enough to know if it's a boy or a girl.'

'When will it be born?'

'In five months I think or thereabouts. I'm not quite sure. I'm a bit hazy about all that sort of thing.'

'Don't worry. You will be home, señor, long before then.'

'Not if you kill me,' Charley Fortnum replied, hoping against hope to receive the usual reassuring response, however false it might sound. He was not surprised when none was forthcoming. He was beginning to live in the region of truth.

'I have written a good many poems about death,' Aquino said cheerfully, with satisfaction, as he held the last drop of his whisky up to catch the light of the candle. 'The one I like best has the refrain, "Death is a common weed: requires no rain." León disagrees with me – he says I am writing there like a farmer – I wanted to be a farmer once. He likes better the one that goes, "Whatever the crime, the same meal's served to all." And there is another I am pleased with, though I do not really know what exactly I mean by it, but it sounds fine, when you recite it properly, "When death is on the tongue, the live man speaks."'

'You seem to have written the hell of a lot about death.'

'Yes. I think about half my poems are about death,' Aquino said. 'It is one of the two proper subjects of a man – love and death.'

'I don't want to die before my child is born.'

'I wish you all the luck in the world, Señor Fortnum. But none of us has a choice. Perhaps tomorrow I will be killed by a car or a fever. And a bullet is one of the quickest and most honourable of deaths.'

'I suppose that's the way you are going to kill me.'

'Naturally . . . What other way is there? We are not cruel men, Señor Fortnum. We shall not cut off your fingers.'

'And yet one can go on living without a few fingers. You haven't found them so important, have you?'

'Oh, I understand your fear of pain – I know what pain can do to a man – what it did to me – but I cannot understand why you are so afraid of death. Death will come in any case, and there is a long afterwards if the priests are right and nothing to fear if they are wrong.'

'Did you believe in that "afterwards" when they tortured you?'

'No,' Aquino admitted. 'But I did not think of death either. There was only the pain.'

'We have an expression in English – A bird in the hand is worth two in the bush. I don't know anything about that "afterwards". I only know I would like to live another ten years, at my camp, watching the little bastard grow.'

'But, Señor Fortnum, think what might happen in those ten years. Your child might die, children die so easily here, your wife might betray you, you might be tortured by a long cancer. A bullet is simple and quick.'

'Are you sure of that?'

'Perhaps a little more whisky would do me no harm,' Aquino said.

'I'm thirsty myself. You know the old saying – An Englishman is always two whiskies below par.'

He poured it out very carefully: there was hardly more than a quarter of a bottle left, and he thought with sadness of his camp, of the dumb-waiter on the verandah and the fresh bottle which had always stood ready at hand. He asked, 'Are you married?'

'Not exactly,' Aquino replied.

'I have been married twice. The first time it didn't take. The second time – I don't know why – I felt different. Would you like to see a photograph?'

He found one in his pocket book – a square Kodachrome print. Clara was sitting at the wheel of Fortnum's Pride, staring sideways at the camera with an expression of fear as though it might go off like a revolver.

'A pretty girl,' Aquino commented politely.

'Of course you know she can't really drive,' Fortnum said, 'and there's a lot too much blue in the print. You can see that from the colour of the avocados. It wasn't one of Gruber's best efforts.' He looked at the photograph with an expression of regret. 'It's a bit out of focus too,' he said, 'it doesn't do her proper justice, but I had taken one over the measure and I suppose my hand must have shaken a bit.' He looked anxiously at what remained in the bottle.

'As a rule,' he said, 'there is nothing better to steady the hand. What about finishing the bottle?'

'A very little for me,' Aquino said.

'Every man has his own proper measure. I'd never criticize anyone for not sharing mine. A measure's sort of built into a man's system, like a lift in a block of flats.' He was watching Aquino carefully. He had judged correctly that their measures were very different. He said, 'I liked that poem of yours about death.'

'Which one?'

'I have such a shocking memory. What will you do with the body?'

'Body?'

'My body.'

'Señor Fortnum, why talk about disagreeable subjects? I write about death, yes, but only death the great abstraction. I do not write about the death of friends.'

'Those people, you know, in London – they've never even heard of me. What do they care? I don't belong to the right club.'

'"Death is a common weed: requires no rain." Was that the poem you meant?'

'Yes, of course, that was the one. I remember now. All the same, Aquino, even if it's as common as all that, one ought to die with a bit of dignity. You will agree to that? *Salud*.'

'*Salud*, Señor Fortnum.'

'Call me Charley, Aquino.'

'*Salud*, Charley.'

'I wouldn't like people to find me like this – dirty, unshaven . . .'

'You can have a bowl of water if you like, Charley.'

'And a razor?'

'No.'

'Only a Gillette. I can't do much harm with a Gillette.'

It was the measure which counted all right. Everything seemed possible to him now. For instance, even with a pair of scissors – he could moisten the baked earth of the wall first.

'A pair of scissors then just for a trim?'

'I would have to ask León first, Charley.'

A pointed stick? – he searched for a suitable euphemism. He felt sure, now he had drunk the right measure and he had his wits about him, that it was possible to escape. He said, 'I want to write to Clara – she's my wife. The girl in the photo. You can keep the letter until it's all over and you are safe. I just want her to know that I thought of her at the end. A pencil – a sharp pencil,' he added incautiously, taking a look at the wall and wondering whether after all he was a bit overoptimistic. There was one point where the wall had crumbled a little: he could see wisps of straw which had been mixed with the mud.

'I have a ballpoint,' Aquino said, 'but I had better ask León, Charley.' He took it out of his pocket and looked at it carefully.

'What harm can there be, Aquino? I would ask your friend myself, but you know how it is, I never feel at ease with priests.'

Aquino said, 'You must give us anything you write. And we shall have to read it.'

'Of course. Shall we open the other bottle?'

'You are not trying to make me drunk? I can drink any man under the table.'

'No, no. It's only I haven't had the proper measure myself yet. It's one over the half that counts with me, and you've drunk half my measure yourself.'

'It may be a long time before we can buy you more.'

'Let tomorrow look after tomorrow. That sounds like something from the Bible. I'm getting the literary touch too. The whisky helps. You see I'm not much used to letter-writing. This is the first time I've been separated from Clara – since we were really together.'

'You will need some paper, Charley.'

'Yes, I'd forgotten that.'

Aquino brought him five sheets of paper pulled off a pad. 'I have counted them,' he said. 'You must return all the sheets to me, used or not.'

'And some water to wash in. I don't want to leave dirty marks all over my letter.'

Aquino obeyed, but he grumbled a little this time. 'This is not a hotel, Charley,' he said, plonking the basin down and splashing the water on the earth floor.

'If it was, I would be able to hang a notice "Not to be disturbed" on the door. Take a little more whisky with you, Aquino.'

'No. I have drunk enough.'

'Be a friend and shut the door. I can't bear that Indian staring at me.'

When he was alone Charley Fortnum chose the worn spot on the wall, rubbed water in, and attacked it with the ballpoint. After a quarter of an hour there was a little worm-cast of dirt on the floor, and a tiny indentation in the wall. If it had not been for the whisky he would have despaired. He propped himself on the floor to hide the mark, washed the ballpoint, and began a letter. He had to justify the time he had spent. 'My dear little Clara,' he began and hesitated a long while. For his official reports he used a typewriter which always seemed to find the right bureaucratic phrase, 'In reply to your letter of August 10,' 'I have received yours of December 22.' 'How I miss you,' he wrote now. It was the only important thing he had to write; anything he added would be only a repetition or a paraphrase of that. 'It seems years since I drove away from the camp. You had a headache that morning. Is it better now? Please do not take too many aspirins. They are bad for the stomach and they must be bad for the baby too. You will see, won't you, that a tarpaulin is kept over Fortnum's Pride in case the rains come.'

The letter, he thought, would not be delivered until he was home again or until he was dead, and the sense of an immense distance grew up between the mud hut and the camp, between the coffin and the jeep waiting under the avocados, Clara lying late in the double-bed, the dumb-waiter standing idle on the verandah. Tears pricked at his eyes, and he remembered how his father would rebuke him: 'Be a man, Charley, not a coward. You cry too easily. I can't bear self-pity. You should be ashamed. Ashamed. Ashamed.' The word rang like the knell of all hope. Sometimes, but not often. he would defend himself. 'But I'm not crying for me. I squashed a lizard this morning in the shutters. I didn't mean to. I was trying to let it out. I'm crying for the lizard, not for me.' He was not crying now for himself. The tears were for Clara and a few of them for Fortnum's Pride, both left alone and defenceless. All he was suffering was a little fear and a little discomfort. Loneliness, as he knew from experience, was a worse thing to suffer.

He abandoned the letter, took another swallow of whisky, and started to dig again with the ballpoint pen. The wall absorbed the water and was soon as dry again as a bone. After half an hour he gave up. He had made a hole as large as a mousehole, but not an inch deep. He took up his letter again and wrote defiantly. 'I can tell you Charley Fortnum's on his mettle. I'm not the poor chap they think I am. I'm your husband, and I love you far too much to let any bastards like these stand between you and me. I'm going to think up something and I'm going to put this letter in your hands myself, and we'll laugh at it together and we'll drink some of that good French champagne I've been saving for a special occasion. Champagne never did a baby any harm or so I'm told.' He stopped writing and laid the letter aside because an idea was really beginning to form in however hazy a way. He wiped the sweat off his forehead and for a moment he had the impression that he was wiping away the whisky too, leaving his mind clear.

'Aquino,' he called, 'Aquino.'

Aquino came reluctantly and suspiciously in. 'No more whisky,' he said.

'I want to use the lavatory, Aquino.'

'I will tell Miguel to go with you.'

'No, please, Aquino . . . I'll never get a proper shit with that Indian sitting outside waving his gun at me. He's longing to use it, Aquino.'

'Miguel means no harm. He is interested in the gun – that's all. He has never had one before.'

'He frightens me just the same. Why not take the gun yourself and guard me, Aquino? I know you wouldn't shoot unless you had to.'

'He would not like anyone else to hold his gun.'

'Then I'll damn well shit in here.'

'I will speak to him,' Aquino said.

It's difficult for most men to shoot a friendly man in cold blood – Charley Fortnum's plan was as simple as that.

When Aquino returned he was holding the sub-machine gun. 'All right,' he said, 'go ahead. I know I have only my left hand, but remember no one needs to be a marksman with one of these. One bullet will always go home.'

'Even a poet's bullet,' Charley Fortnum said, racking up a smile. 'I wish you would give me a copy of that poem. I'd like to keep it as a souvenir.'

'Which poem?'

'You know the one I mean. The one about death.'

He walked through the outer room. The Indian did not look at him. He was watching the gun with anxiety as though something very dear had been put in untrustworthy hands.

Charley Fortnum talked all the way to the shed among the avocados. His watch had stopped during his coma and he had no idea of the time, but he could see how long the shadows were. Under the trees heavy with dark brown fruit it was already night. He said, 'I've nearly finished that letter. It's a damned difficult one to write.' When he got to the door of the shed he turned and tried a smile out on Aquino. If Aquino smiled back it would be a good sign, but Aquino didn't smile. Perhaps he was only preoccupied. Perhaps he was composing a poem about death. Or perhaps he had drunk the wrong measure.

Charley Fortnum waited in the hut for a reasonable time, screwing his courage up. Then he came quickly out and turned sharp right to put the hut between them. It was only a matter of yards and under the trees the darkness waited. He heard a short burst of fire, a shout, an answering shout, he felt nothing. He cried out, 'Don't shoot, Aquino.' At the second burst he fell on the very edge of the dark.

PART FOUR

Chapter 1

THE day began badly for Sir Henry Belfrage at breakfast. For the third time running the cook had fried his egg on both sides. He said, 'Did you forget to tell Pedro, dear?'

'No,' Lady Belfrage said, 'I swear I didn't. I remember distinctly . . .'

'He must have picked the habit up from the Yankees. It's a Yankee custom. Don't you remember the trouble we had once at the Plaza in New York? They've got a name for "fried on one side". Can you remember it? Pedro might understand.'

'No, dear . . . I don't think I ever heard it.'

'Sometimes I sympathize with those chaps who write about Yankee imperialism. Why should we have to eat our fried eggs like this? Soon he'll be giving us maple syrup with our sausages. That was a terrible wine we had last night at the American Embassy, darling. Californian, I suppose.'

'No, dear. It was Argentine.'

'Ah, he was trying to curry favour with the Minister of the Interior. But the Minister would have preferred a good French table wine like we serve here.'

'Not a very good wine all the same.'

'The best we can afford with our miserable expense allowance. Did you notice that he served *Argentine* Scotch?'

'The trouble is, dear, he doesn't drink anything himself. Do you know he was quite shocked because Mr . . . poor Mr . . . you know our Consul, Mason isn't it?'

'No, no, the other chap. Fortnum.'

'Well, poor Mr Fortnum apparently brought two bottles of Scotch with him when they went to the ruins.'

'I don't blame him for that. Do you know the Ambassador travels with an ice-box full of Coca-Cola? I wouldn't have drunk so much of that bloody wine if he hadn't watched me with those New England eyes of his. I felt like that girl in the book who had a scarlet letter A on her dress. A for Alcoholism.'

'I think it was Adultery, dear.'

'I daresay. I only saw the film. Years ago. They didn't make it clear.'

The day which had begun miserably enough with the badly-fried eggs got steadily worse. Crichton, the Press Attaché, came to see him to protest that he was being driven up the wall by telephone calls from the press. He complained to Sir Henry, 'I keep telling them that Fortnum was only an Honorary Consul. The reporter on *La Prensa* can't understand the difference between Honorary and Honourable. I wouldn't be surprised if they make him the son of a peer.'

Sir Henry said soothingly, 'I doubt if they know enough about our titles for that.'

'They seem to think the whole affair is so very important.'

'Only because it's the silly season, Crichton. They have no Loch Ness monster here, and the flying saucers go on all through the year.'

'I wish we had some tranquillizing statement we could make, sir.'

'So do I, Crichton, so do I. Of course you can say I spent several hours last night with the American Ambassador – you needn't say I have a damn bad head as a consequence.'

'The *Nación* have had another anonymous telephone call – from Córdoba this time. Only four days left.'

'Thank God it's no longer,' the Ambassador said. 'Next week it will all be over. He'll be either dead or freed.'

'The police think that Córdoba is a blind and he may be in Rosario – or even here by this time.'

'We ought to have retired him six months ago and then none of this would have happened.'

'The police say the kidnapping was a mistake, sir. They wanted the American Ambassador. If that's right surely the Americans ought to be grateful to us and do something.'

'Wilbur,' Sir Henry Belfrage said, '– the Ambassador insists that I call him Wilbur – refuses to admit he was the intended victim. He says the USA is very popular in Paraguay – Nelson Rockefeller's tour proved that. No one threw stones in Paraguay or set fire to any offices. It was as quiet as it was in Haiti. He calls Rockefeller Nelson – it had me confused for a moment. Do you know I really thought for a moment he was going to invite me to call Rockefeller Nelson too?'

'I can't help feeling sorry for the poor devil.'

'I don't think Wilbur needs any of our sympathy, Crichton.'

'I didn't mean him – I meant –'

'Oh, Mason? Damnation, my wife has started calling him Mason and now I'm doing the same. If Mason gets into an official telegram, God knows where it will end up in London. They'll think it has something to do with the Mason-Dixon line. I shall have to say to myself Fortnum, Fortnum, Fortnum, like that raven which said Nevermore.'

'You don't think they will really kill him, sir?'

'Of course I don't, Crichton. They didn't even kill that Paraguayan consul they took a few years back. The General said he wasn't interested, and they let the fellow go. This isn't Uruguay or Colombia – or Brazil, for that matter. Or Bolivia. Or Venezuela. Or even Peru,' he added apprehensively as the field of hope narrowed.

'We are in South America, though, aren't we?' Crichton said with incontestable logic.

A few tiresome telegrams came in during the morning. Somebody had started another Falkland Islands scare: the islands cropped up, like Gibraltar, whenever there was nothing else to worry about. The Foreign Secretary wanted to know as a consequence how Argentina was likely to vote in the latest African issue before the United Nations. The Chief Clerk had issued a new directive about entertainment expenses, and Sir Henry Belfrage could see the time rapidly approaching when he too might have to serve Argentinian wine. There was also a question about the British entry at the Mar del Plata film festival – a Conservative member of Parliament had described the British entry by some man called Russell as pornographic. There had been no directive at all about Fortnum since the previous day when Belfrage had been ordered to see the Foreign Minister and afterwards to act in concert with the American Ambassador – the British Ambassador in Asunción had received the same instruction, and Sir Henry hoped he had an American to deal with who was a little more dynamic than Wilbur.

After lunch his secretary told him that a Doctor Plarr was asking to see him.

'Who's Plarr?'

'He comes from the north. I think he wants to see you about the Fortnum case.'

'Oh bring him in, bring him in,' Sir Henry Belfrage said, 'let them all come.' He was vexed at losing his siesta – it was the only time of day when he could feel a private person. There was a new Agatha Christie waiting by his bed, fresh from his bookshop in Curzon Street.

'We've met before somewhere,' he said to Doctor Plarr, and he looked at Plarr with suspicion – everyone in BA except the Army people seemed to have the title of Doctor. A thin lawyer's face, he thought; he never felt at ease with lawyers; he found himself shocked by the heartlessness of legal jokes – a convicted murderer was no more to them than a patient with incurable cancer to a surgeon.

'Yes – here at the Embassy,' Doctor Plarr reminded him. 'A cocktail party. I rescued your wife from a poet.'

'Of course, of course, I remember now, my dear chap. You live up there. We talked about Fortnum, didn't we?'

'That's right. I'm looking after his wife. She's having a baby, you know.'

'Oh, you *are* that kind of doctor, are you?'

'Yes.'

'Thank God! One never knows here, does one? And you really are British too. Not like the O'Briens and the Higginses. Well, well, it must be an awful anxiety for poor Mrs Fortnum. You must tell her we are doing everything in our power . . .'

'Yes,' Doctor Plarr said, 'of course, she realizes that, but I thought I'd like to know a little of how things are going. I flew down to B A this morning, because I felt I had to see you and learn a little, and I'm flying back tonight. If there were some definite news I could take back with me . . . to comfort Mrs Fortnum . . .'

'It's an awfully difficult situation, Plarr. You see, something which is everybody's responsibility is always nobody's responsibility. The General is down here in the south fishing and refuses to discuss the matter while he's on holiday. The Foreign Minister says it's a purely Paraguayan affair, and the President can't be expected to bring pressure on the General, when he's a guest of the nation. Of course the police are doing their best, but they've probably been told to act as discreetly as possible. For Fortnum's own sake.'

'But the Americans . . . Surely they can bring pressure on the General. He wouldn't exist twenty-four hours in Paraguay without their help.'

'I know all that, but it makes it the more awkward, Plarr. You see the Americans take the sensible view that these kidnappings have to be discouraged – even if it means, well, how shall I put it? a certain danger to life. Like that German ambassador they killed – where was it? Guatemala? In this case, to be quite frank . . . well, an Honorary Consul is not an Ambassador. They feel it would be a bad principle if they interfered. The English are not very popular with the General. Of course if Fortnum were an American he would probably take a different view.'

'The kidnappers thought he was. So the police say. They think the kidnappers were looking for a diplomatic car in the dark and CC is awfully like CD.'

'Yes, how often we've told the damned fool not to fly a flag or show CC plates. An Honorary Consul hasn't the right to use them.'

'Still a death sentence seems a bit severe.'

'What more can I do, Plarr? I've been twice to the Foreign Ministry. Last night I spoke unofficially to the Minister of the Interior. He was having dinner with Wilbur – I mean the American Ambassador. I can't do a thing more without instructions from London, and London has a remarkable sense of – well – unurgency. By the way how is your mother? It all comes back to me now. You are *that* Plarr. Your mother often has tea with my wife. They both like sweet cakes and those things with *dulce de leche*.'

'*Alfajores*.'

'That's the name. Can't stand them myself.'

Doctor Plarr said, 'I know what a nuisance I must seem to you, Sir Henry, but my father is in one of the General's gaols if he's still alive. Perhaps this kidnapping is his last chance. That makes me suspect to the police, so I feel personally concerned. And besides there's Fortnum. I can't help feeling responsible a bit for him. He's not a patient of mine, but Mrs Fortnum is.'

'Wasn't there something odd about that marriage? I got a letter from up there, from some old busybody called Jeffries.'

'Humphries.'

'Yes. That was the name. He wrote to me that Fortnum had married an "undesirable" woman. Lucky man! I've reached the age when I never meet anyone of that sort.'

'It did occur to me,' Doctor Plarr said, 'that I might be able to make contact with the kidnappers. They may telephone Mrs Fortnum if they find they are getting nowhere with the authorities.'

'A bit improbable, my dear chap.'

'But not impossible, sir. If something like that did happen and I had some hope to offer them . . . Perhaps I could persuade them to extend their time limit – say for a week. In that case surely there might be a chance to negotiate?'

'If you want my honest opinion you would only be extending the agony – for Fortnum and Mrs Fortnum. If I were Fortnum I'd prefer a quick death.'

'But surely something could be done?'

'I'm sure of this, Plarr. I've seen Wilbur twice and the Americans won't budge. If they can discourage kidnapping by letting an Honorary British Consul, in an obscure province, take the rap, they'll be very satisfied. Wilbur says Fortnum is an alcoholic – he brought two bottles of whisky to their picnic at the ruins and the Ambassador only drinks Coca-Cola. I looked up our file on him, but there wasn't anything very definite about alcoholism, though one or two of his reports . . . well, they did sort of ramble. There was a letter too from that man – Humphries? – saying he had flown the Union Jack upside down. But you don't need to be an alcoholic to do that.'

'All the same, Sir Henry, if the kidnappers could be persuaded to delay only a little . . .'

Sir Henry Belfrage knew the time for his siesta was irrevocably lost – the new Agatha Christie would have to wait. He was a kind man and a conscientious one, and he was modest into the bargain. He told himself that in Doctor Plarr's situation he would have been unlikely to fly in the November heat to Buenos Aires to help the husband of a patient. He said, 'There is something you might try to do. I very much doubt if you would be successful, but all the same . . .'

He hesitated. With a pen in his hand he was a master of compression: his reports were admirably short and lucid, and a telegram never presented him with the least difficulty. He was at home in his Embassy as he had been at home in his nursery. The chandeliers glittered like the glass fruit on a Christmas tree. In the nursery he could remember building neatly and quickly with his coloured bricks. 'Master Henry is a clever boy,' his nurse always said, but sometimes when he was let out on the vast green spaces of Kensington Gardens he strayed wildly. There were moments with strangers – just as there still were at his annual cocktail party – when he nearly panicked.

'Yes, Sir Henry?'

'I'm so sorry, my dear chap. My mind was wandering. I've got a terrible head this morning. That wine from Mendoza . . . Cooperatives! What can a Cooperative know about wine?'

'You were saying . . .'

'Yes, yes.' He put his hand into his breast-pocket and touched his ballpoint pen. It was like a talisman. He said, 'A delay would be only useful if we could get people sufficiently interested . . . I've been doing all I can, but nobody at home knows Fortnum. Nobody cares about an Honorary Consul. He doesn't belong to the Service. And to tell you the truth I advised getting rid of him six months ago. That letter will certainly be on the files. So everyone at home will be relieved when the dateline is passed and there are no more minutes to write – and he's released as I believe.'

'And if he's killed?'

'I'm afraid the FO will take the credit for that too. It will be a sign of firmness; it will show they won't treat with blackmailers. You know the kind of words they'll use in the Commons. Law and order. No Danegeld. They'll quote Kipling. Even the Opposition will applaud.'

'It's not only Charley Fortnum. There's his wife . . . she's having a baby. Suppose the Press took it up . . .'

'Yes. I see what you mean. The woman who waits etcetera. But from what that man Humphries wrote I don't think the kind of wife Fortnum has married will arouse the right sort of sentiment in the English press. Not family reading. The *Sun* might use the real story of course or the *News of the World*, but it would hardly have the effect we want.'

'What *do* you suggest, Sir Henry?'

'You must never, never quote me on this, Plarr. The FO would put me out to grass if they knew I had suggested anything of the kind. And I don't suppose for a moment my idea would do any good. Mason is not the right material.'

'Mason?'

'I'm sorry. I meant Fortnum.'

'You haven't suggested anything yet, Sir Henry.'

'Well, what I was getting at . . . There's nothing a civil servant hates more than a yelp in *respectable* papers. Sometimes the only way to get action is the right publicity. If you could organize some reaction in your city . . . Even a telegraphed appeal from the English Club to *The Times*. Tribute to his . . .' He touched his pen again as though he might draw from it the correct official jargon. '. . . his untiring pursuit of British interests.'

'But there is no English Club, sir. I don't think there are any other English in the city except Humphries and me.'

Sir Henry Belfrage took a quick look at his finger nails (he had mislaid his nailbrush). He said something so rapidly that Doctor Plarr couldn't catch a word.

'I'm sorry. I didn't hear . . .'

'My dear chap, I don't have to spell it out to *you*. Form an English Club immediately and telegraph your tribute to *The Times* and *Telegraph*.'

'Do you think it would do any good?'

'No, I don't, but there's no harm in trying. There's always some Opposition MP who will take it up whatever his leaders say. At least it might give the Parliamentary Secretary *un mauvais quart d'heure*. And then there are the American papers. It's just possible they might copy. The *New York Times* can be quite virulent. "Fighting Latin-American independence to the last Englishman." You know the kind of line the anti-war chaps might take. It's rather a forlorn hope, of course. If he'd been a business tycoon everybody would be a great deal more interested. The trouble is, Plarr, Fortnum is such pitiably small beer.'

There was no plane by which he could return north before the evening, and Doctor Plarr could think of no excuse with which to ease his conscience if he failed to meet his mother. He knew very well what would please her most, and he made a rendezvous by telephone for tea at the Richmond in the Calle Florida – she had no liking for inescapable family conversations in her apartment, which she kept almost as airless as the dome over the wax flowers she had bought at an antique shop near Harrods. He always had the impression in her flat that there were secrets from him lying about everywhere, on shelves and on tables, even pushed away under the sofa, secrets she didn't want him to see – perhaps only tiny extravagances on which she had spent the money he sent her. Cream-cakes were food, but a china parrot was an extravagance.

He had to move at a snail's pace through the crowd that filled the narrow *calle* every afternoon when it was closed to traffic. He was not displeased, for every minute he lost before meeting his mother was pure gain.

He saw her at the far end of the crowded tearoom, sitting in unrelieved black before a plate of sweet cakes. She said, 'You are ten minutes late, Eduardo.' From his early childhood they had always spoken Spanish together. Only with his father had he spoken English, and his father was a man of few words.

'I am sorry, mother. You should have begun.' When he bent to kiss her cheek he could smell the hot chocolate in her cup like a sweet breath from a tomb.

'Call the waiter, dear, if there is not a cake here that pleases you.'

'I don't really want to eat anything, mother. I'll just have a cup of coffee.'

She had heavy pouches below her eyes, but they were not, Doctor Plarr knew, the pouches of grief, but of constipation. He had an impression that if they were squeezed they would squirt cream like an éclair. It is terrible what time can do to a beautiful woman. A man's looks often improve with age, seldom a woman's. He thought: a man should never love a woman less than twenty years younger than himself. In that way he can die before the vision fades. Had Fortnum insured himself against disillusion when he married Clara, who was more than forty years younger than himself? Doctor Plarr thought, I'm not so wise, I shall outlive her attraction by many years.

'Why the mourning, mother?' he asked. 'I have never seen you in black before.'

'I am mourning for your father,' Señora Plarr said and wiped the chocolate off her fingers with a paper napkin.

'Have you had news then?'

'No, but Father Galvão has been speaking to me very seriously. He says that for the sake of my health I must give up vain hopes. Do you know what day it is, Eduardo?'

He searched his mind without success – he was even uncertain of the day of the month. 'The fourteenth?' he asked.

'It is the day we said good-bye to your father in the port of Asunción.'

He wondered whether his father, if he were to walk into the tearoom now, could possibly recognize the stout and pouchy woman who had a smear of cream at the corner of the mouth. In our memories people we no longer see age gracefully. Señora Plarr said, 'Father Galvão held a Mass this morning for the repose of his soul.' She scrutinized the plate of cakes and picked a particular éclair, not noticeably different from the others. Yet when he searched his memory he could still just remember a lovely woman who lay and wept in her cabin. Tears at the age she had been then enhanced the brilliance of her eyes. There were no pouches to mar them.

He said, 'I still have hope, mother. You know the kidnappers have named him on the list of prisoners they want released?'

'What kidnappers?' He had forgotten she never read the papers.

'Oh well,' he said, 'it's too long a story to tell you now.' He added politely, 'What a very nice black dress.'

'I am glad you like it. I had it made specially for the Mass this morning. The material was quite inexpensive, and I had it run up by a little woman . . . You must not think I am extravagant.'

'No, of course not, mother.'

'If only your father had been less obstinate . . . What was the use of staying on the *estancia* to be murdered? He could have sold it for a good price, and we could have been happy here together.'

'He was an idealist,' Doctor Plarr said.

'Ideals are all very well, but it was very wrong of him and very selfish of him not to put his family first.'

He wondered what kind of bitter and reproachful prayers she had muttered that morning at Father Galvão's Mass. Father Galvão was a Portuguese Jesuit who for some reason had been transferred from Rio de Janeiro. He was very popular with women – perhaps they were more ready to confide in him because he had come from a long way off.

All round him in the Richmond he heard the chatter of women's voices. He could hardly distinguish a single phrase. He might have been in an aviary, listening to a babel of birds from many different regions. There were those who twittered in English, others in German, he even heard a French phrase which his mother would appreciate, '*Georges est très coupable.*' He looked at her as she tipped her mouth towards the chocolate. Had she ever felt any love for his father or himself, or had she just played the comedy of love like Clara? He had grown up, during the years he spent alone with his mother in Buenos Aires, to despise comedy. There were no sentimental relics in his apartment – not even a photograph. It was as bare and truthful – almost – as a police station cell. Even during his affairs with women he had always tried to avoid that phrase of the theatre, 'I love you'. He had been accused often enough of cruelty, though he preferred to think of himself as a painstaking and accurate diagnostician. If for once he had been aware of a sickness he could describe in no other terms, he would have unhesitatingly used the phrase 'I love', but he had always been able to attribute the emotion he felt to a quite different malady – to loneliness, pride, physical desire, or even a simple sense of curiosity.

Señora Plarr said, 'He never loved either of us. He was a man who never knew what love meant.'

He wanted to ask her seriously, 'Do we?', but he knew she would take it as a reproach, and he had no desire to reproach her. With more justice he could reproach himself for equal ignorance. Perhaps, he thought, she is in the right and I resemble my father. He said, 'I do not remember him at all clearly, except that, when he said good-bye, I noticed how grey his hair had become. I remember too how he would go round locking all the doors at night. The noise always woke me up. I do not even know how old he would be if he were alive now.'

'He would have been seventy-one today.'

'Today? Then was it on his birthday . . . ?'

'He told me the best present he could receive from me was to watch the two of us go off down the river. It was very cruel of him to say that.'

'But mother, I don't think he could have meant it cruelly.'

'He had not even told me beforehand. I had no time to pack properly. I forgot some of my jewels. There was a little watch with diamonds which I used to wear with a black dress. You remember the black dress? But of course you would not remember. You were always such an unobservant boy. He said he was afraid I would tell my friends and they would gossip and the police would stop us. I had prepared a very nice birthday dinner for him, with a cheese savoury – he always liked savouries better than a dessert. That is what it is like to marry a foreigner. Our tastes were never the same. This morning I prayed very hard he might not be suffering too much.'

'I thought you believed he was dead.'

'Suffering in purgatory of course I mean. Father Galvão says that the worst pain in purgatory is when people see the consequence of their actions and the suffering they have caused to those they love.' She picked out another éclair.

'But you said he loved neither of us.'

'Oh, I suppose he did feel a certain affection. And duty. He was very English. He preferred the company of other men. I have no doubt he went to the Club after the boat left.'

'What club?' For years they had not spoken so much of his father.

'It was not a safe club for him to belong to. It was called the Constitutional, but the police closed it. Afterwards the members met in secret – once even at our *estancia*. He would not listen to me when I protested. I said, "You have a wife and child." He said, "Every member of the club has a wife and child." I said, "In that case they should have more important things to talk about than politics." Oh well,' she added with a little sigh, 'those are old quarrels. Of course I have forgiven him. Tell me a little about yourself, dear,' and her eyes glazed over with lack of interest.

'Oh,' he said, 'there is nothing really to tell.'

The evening plane to the north represented a hazard for a man like Doctor Plarr who liked to remain alone. Few strangers or tourists travelled by it. Among the passengers were usually local politicians returning from a visit to the capital, or expensive wives whom he had sometimes examined (they would have gone to Buenos Aires for a shopping expedition or a party, even for a hair-do because they didn't trust their local hairdresser). They would form a noisy group of familiars in the small two-engined plane.

There was only the smallest chance of an undisturbed flight, and his spirits sank when, from just across the gangway, Señora Escobar greeted him, before he even saw her, with a parrot cry of pleasure. 'Eduardo!'

'Margarita!'

He began resignedly to unbuckle his safety belt, so as to take the empty seat beside her.

'No,' she told him in a quick whisper, 'Gustavo is with me. He is at the back talking to Colonel Perez.'

'Colonel Perez is here too?'

'They are talking about the kidnapping. Do you know what I believe?'

'No?'

'I think the man Fortnum has run away from his wife.'

'Why would he do that?'

'You must know the story, Eduardo. She is a *putain*. She came from that horrible house in Calle . . . but you are a man. You know very well the one I mean.'

He remembered that Margarita had always, when she wished to be a little coarse, employed a French term. He could hear her crying, in the carefully measured shadows of her room, made by the *persianas* two-thirds closed, '*Baise-moi, baise-moi!*' Never would she have allowed herself to use the equivalent Spanish phrase. She said, 'I have not seen you for such a long time, Eduardo,' with a sigh as carefully adjusted for the occasion as the shutters of her bedroom. He wondered what had happened to her new lover – Gaspar Vallejo of the financial department. He hoped that there had been no quarrel.

The roar of the engines saved him from the need to reply, and by the time the overhead warnings had been switched off and they were high above the khaki-coloured Plata, which turned black as the evening darkened, he had a vague phrase ready on the tongue. 'You know what it is like to be a doctor, Margarita.'

'Yes,' she said, 'I know – who better? Do you still see Señora Vega?'

'No. I think she must have changed her doctor.'

'I would never do that, Eduardo – there are not so many good doctors as that. If I have not asked you to come to see me it is only that I have been disgustingly well. Why, here is my husband at last. Look whom we have here, Gustavo! Do not pretend you have forgotten Doctor Plarr.'

'How could I forget him? Where have you been all this long time, Eduardo?' Gustavo Escobar laid his hand heavily on Doctor Plarr's shoulder and kneaded it gently – he had the Latin-American desire to touch any man to whom he spoke. Even the knife-thrust in one of

Jorge Julio Saavedra's stories could be interpreted as a way of touching. 'We have missed you,' he went on in the loud voice of a deaf man. 'How often my wife has said "I wonder why Eduardo never calls on us now?"'

Gustavo Escobar had a large black moustache and abundant side-burns: his face, brick-red as laterite, resembled a clearing which has been hacked out of the bush, and his nose reared like the horse of a *conquistador*. Escobar said, 'I have missed you as much as my wife has. All those friendly little dinners we used to have . . .'

Doctor Plarr, during the whole time that he had been Margarita's lover, had never been able to distinguish with certainty between his rough playfulness and his irony. Margarita had always assured him that her husband was a man of the most passionate jealousy – it would have hurt her pride to feel he did not really care. Perhaps indeed he did care, for she was at least one of his women, even though he had a great many. Doctor Plarr on one occasion had encountered him at Mother Sanchez's house where he was entertaining four girls at once. The girls, against all the rules of the house, were drinking champagne, good French champagne which he must have brought with him. No rules of the house were likely to be enforced against Gustavo Escobar. Doctor Plarr sometimes wondered whether he had ever been a client of Clara's. What sort of comedy would she have played for him? Perhaps abasement?

'What have you been up to, my dear Eduardo, in Buenos Aires?'

'I have been to the Embassy,' Doctor Plarr shouted back at him, 'and I have seen my mother. And you?'

'My wife has been shopping. As for myself I had lunch at the Hurlingham.' He continued to finger Doctor Plarr's shoulder almost as though he were considering whether to buy him for breeding purposes (he had a big *estancia* on the Chaco side of the Paraná).

'Gustavo is deserting me again for a whole week,' Margarita said. 'He always allows me to go shopping just before he deserts me.'

Doctor Plarr would have liked to turn the conversation to his successor, Gaspar Vallejo, to whom the information she had given him ought more properly to have been addressed. It would have been reassuring to know that Vallejo was still a friend of the family.

'What about joining me on the *estancia*, Eduardo? I can give you some good shooting.'

'A doctor is tied to his patients,' Doctor Plarr said.

The plane dipped in an air pocket and Escobar had to grasp the back of Plarr's seat.

'Be careful, *caro*. You will hurt your precious self. Better sit down.'

Perhaps it was the mechanical expression of his wife's solicitude which irritated Escobar. Or perhaps he took the warning as a reflection on his *machismo*. He said with quite unmistakable irony, 'You are tied to a very favourite patient at the moment, I believe, Eduardo?'

'All my patients are favourite ones.'

'Señora Fortnum is having a baby, I believe?'

'Yes. And so, I expect you know, is Señora Vega, but she doesn't trust me with a childbirth. She goes to Doctor Benevento now.'

'A discreet man Eduardo,' Escobar said. He fumbled past his wife to the seat by the window and sat down. Almost as soon as he closed his eyes he appeared to be asleep, sitting bolt upright. He looked as one of his ancestors might have looked, asleep on the saddle, crossing the Andes; he rocked gently with the stride of the plane across the snowy summits of the clouds.

'What did he mean, Eduardo?' his wife asked in a whisper.

'How do I know?'

He remembered that Escobar had always been a very heavy sleeper. Once, very early in their relationship, Margarita had told him, 'Nothing ever wakes him except a sudden silence. Just go on talking.'

'What about?' he had asked.

'Anything. Why not tell me how much you love me?' They had been sitting together on a sofa and her husband was sleeping in an armchair at the opposite end of the room, the back of the chair turned to them. Doctor Plarr couldn't even tell whether his eyes were closed. He said cautiously, 'I want you.'

'Yes?'

'I want you.'

'Don't sound so staccato,' she said as she touched him. 'He needs to hear the steady murmur of conversation.'

It is difficult to keep a monologue going while a woman makes love to you. In desperation Doctor Plarr had begun to recount the story of the Three Bears, beginning it in the middle, while all the time he watched with anxiety the powerful statuesque head above the chair-back.

'And then the third bear said in his gruff voice "Who has been eating up my porridge?"'

Señora Escobar sat astride him as though she were a child playing ponies. 'And so all three bears went upstairs and the little bear said, "Who has been sleeping in my bed?"' He clutched Señora Escobar's shoulders, and lost the thread of the story, so that he had to continue with the first phrase which came into his head, 'This is the way the postboy rides. Gallopy, gallopy, gallopy.' When they were relaxed again on the sofa side by side Señora Escobar – he had not been given enough time to think of her yet as Margarita – said, 'You were speaking in English. What were you saying?'

'I was telling you how much I wanted you,' Doctor Plarr said warily. The postboy had been a game he had played with his father: his mother had no repertoire. Perhaps Spanish children had no games – or no childish ones.

'What did Gustavo mean about Señora Fortnum?' Margarita asked again, bringing him back to the present and the plane which lurched in the wind currents above the Paraná.

'I have no idea.'

'You would disappoint me terribly, Eduardo, if you really had anything to do with that little *putain*. I am still very fond of you.'

'Excuse me, Margarita,' he said. 'I want to have a word with Colonel Perez.' The lights of La Paz blinked below them – there was a white ruled line of lamps along the river with complete darkness on the other side, as though the lamps marked the edge of a flat world. Perez was sitting at the far end of the plane near the lavatory and the seat beside him was empty.

'Any news, Colonel?' Doctor Plarr asked.

'News of what?'

'Of Fortnum.'

'No. Why? Were you expecting any?'

'I thought perhaps the police might have some . . . Didn't the radio say you were looking for him in Rosario?'

'If he had been really in Rosario they could easily have brought him into Buenos Aires by this time.'

'And what about the call from Córdoba?'

'That was probably a stupid attempt to confuse us. Córdoba is out of the question. I doubt if they could have even reached Rosario by the time of the call. It would have taken fifteen hours in the fastest car.'

'Then where do you suppose he is?' Doctor Plarr asked.

'He is probably dead in the river or else he is hidden nearer home. What were you doing in Buenos Aires?'

It was a polite question, not a police question. He was no more interested than Escobar.

'I wanted to see the Ambassador about Fortnum.'

'Yes? What did he have to say?'

'I interrupted his siesta, poor man. He said the trouble is that no one's really interested.'

Colonel Perez said, 'I assure you I am. Yesterday I wanted to organize a thorough search of the *barrio popular*, but the Governor thought it too dangerous. He does not want shooting if possible. Ours has been a very quiet province up till now except for a little trouble from those third world priests. He sent me off to Buenos Aires today to talk to the Minister of the Interior. I think the Governor hopes to delay matters. If he can postpone action long enough and we are lucky Fortnum's body may be found outside the province. No one can complain then that we acted imprudently. The blackmail will have failed. Everyone will be happy. Except myself. Even your government will be happy. I hope they will pay a pension to the widow?'

'I doubt it. He was only an Honorary Consul. What did the Minister say?'

'He is not afraid of shooting, that man. We could do with more like him. He advises the Government to go ahead whatever happens and to use troops if necessary. The President wants everything settled before the General finishes his fishing. What else did your Ambassador say?'

'He said if the papers made enough fuss . . .'

'Why should they? Have you heard the afternoon radio? A BOAC plane has crashed. A hijacker let off his grenade this time. There are a hundred and sixty-seven deaths – a hundred and sixty-seven Fortnums, and one of them a film star. No, Doctor Plarr, we have to admit that ours is a very small affair.'

'Do you want to give up then?'

'Oh no – I have dealt all my life in small affairs, and I have always preferred to see them settled. Unfinished dossiers take up a lot of room. A smuggler was shot yesterday on the river, so we have been able to close his file. Somebody has stolen a hundred thousand pesos from a bedroom in the Nacional – but we have our eyes on the man. And early this morning there was a small bomb found in the church of La Cruz. A very small bomb – for we are a very quiet province – and it was set to go off at midnight when the church was empty. If it had exploded, though, it might have destroyed the miraculous cross – and that would have been real news in *El Litoral*, even if not in the *Nación*. Perhaps it may become news in any case. There are rumours already that Our Lady herself got down off her altar and defused the bomb with her own hands and the Archbishop has visited the scene. You know the cross was first saved – years before Buenos Aires even existed

– when lightning killed the Indians who were going to burn it.' The door of the lavatory opened. 'You know my colleague Captain Velardo, doctor? I was telling the doctor about our new miracle, Rubén.'

'You may laugh, colonel, but the bomb did not go off.'

'You see, doctor, Rubén half believes.'

'I keep an open mind. Like the Archbishop. The Archbishop is an educated man.'

'I think the fuse was badly set.'

'And why was the fuse badly set? One has to go back to the source, colonel. A miracle is very much like a crime. You say the fuse was badly set, but how can we be sure that it was not Our Lady who guided the hand which set the fuse?'

'All the same I prefer to believe we are kept in the air now by the engines – even though they are not Rolls Royce – rather than by divine intervention.'

The plane dropped again in a pocket of air and the warning lights went on, telling them to fasten seat-belts. Doctor Plarr thought that Colonel Perez looked a little uneasy. He went back to his seat.

Chapter 2

HAVING sent out invitations by telephone from the airport Doctor Plarr waited for his two guests on the terrace of the Nacional. On a sheet of hotel notepaper he drafted a careful letter which he believed the Ambassador would have found sober and convincing. The city was beginning to wake up for the evening hours after the long siesta of the afternoon. A chain of cars drove by along the riverside. The white naked statue in the belvedere shone under the lamplight, and the Coca-Cola sign glowed in scarlet letters like the shrine of a saint. Through the darkness the ferry boat was screaming a warning from the Chaco shore. It was a few minutes past nine – far too early for most people to dine – and Doctor Plarr was alone on the terrace except for Doctor Benevento and his wife. Doctor Benevento sat taking little sips at an apéritif, as though he were suspiciously testing the tonic of a rival, while his wife, a severe and middle-aged woman who wore a large gold cross like some order of distinction, ostentatiously took nothing and watched the disappearance of her husband's apéritif with a false air of patience. It was a Thursday, Doctor Plarr remembered, and perhaps Doctor Benevento had come straight to the hotel from his weekly inspection of Mother Sanchez's girls. The two doctors ignored each other: after all the years which had passed since he arrived from Buenos Aires Doctor Plarr was still in the eyes of Doctor Benevento a foreign interloper.

Humphries was the first of his guests to arrive. He was tightly buttoned in a dark suit and his forehead was wet in the humid night. His temper was not improved when a bold mosquito, immediately he sat down, attacked his ankle through a thick grey woollen sock. The professor of English struck angrily out and complained, 'I was just leaving for the Italian Club when I got your message,' as if he resented being deprived of his usual goulash. He looked at the third place at table and asked, 'Who's coming?'

'Doctor Saavedra.'

'In God's name why? I can't understand what you see in that fellow. A pompous ass.'

'I thought his advice might be useful. I want to draft a letter to the papers from the Anglo-Argentinian Club on behalf of Fortnum.'

'You are fooling me. What club? It doesn't exist.'

'You and I are going to found the club tonight. Saavedra, I hope, will be the president, I will be the chairman I thought you wouldn't mind taking on the job of honorary secretary. There won't be very much to do.'

'This is sheer madness,' Humphries said. 'As far as I know there's only one other Englishman in the city. Or there was. I'm convinced Fortnum's absconded. That woman of his must have been costing him a great deal of money. Sooner or later we shall hear that the accounts at the Consulate are in the red. Or more likely we shall hear nothing at all. Those Embassy fellows in BA are sure to hush things up. For the honour of their so-called service. One never gets at the truth of anything.' It was his perpetual and quite genuine complaint. Truth was like a difficult sentence which his pupils never succeeded in getting grammatically right.

Doctor Plarr said, 'At least there's no doubt about the kidnapping. That's true enough. I've talked to Perez.'

'Do you trust what a policeman says?'

'This policeman, yes. Look, Humphries, be reasonable. We have to do *something* for Fortnum. Even if he did fly the Union Jack upside down. The poor devil has only three days left to live. The Ambassador today – he doesn't want it known – suggested we ought to write some sort of tribute to the papers. Anything to stir up a little interest. From the English Club here. Oh, yes, yes, you've already said it. Of course there's no such club. Coming back on the plane I thought it would be better to call the club the Anglo-Argentinian. In that way we can use Saavedra's name and we have more chance of making the BA papers. We can talk about the good influence Fortnum has always had on our relations with Argentine. We can speak of his cultural activities.'

'Cultural activities! His father was a notorious drunkard and so is Charley Fortnum. Don't you remember the night we had to haul him back to the Bolívar? He couldn't even stand up. All he has done for our relations with Argentina is to marry a local whore.'

'All the same we can't just let him die.'

'I wouldn't raise my little finger,' Humphries said, 'for that man.'

Something was going on inside the Nacional. The *maître d'hotel*, who had come out on the terrace to breathe the air before the night's activities began, was hurrying back to the dining-room. A waiter, who was half way to Doctor Benevento's table, turned tail in response to a signal. Through the french window of the restaurant Doctor Plarr saw the pearl-grey gleam of Jorge Julio Saavedra's suit as the author paused to exchange a few words with the staff. A woman from the cloakroom took his hat, the waiter took his cane, the manager came hurrying from his office to join the *maître d'hotel*. Doctor Saavedra was explaining something, pointing here and there; when he came out on to the terrace, they escorted him in a phalanx towards Doctor Plarr's table. Even Doctor Benevento rose a few inches in his seat, as Doctor Saavedra pigeon-toed by in his gleaming pointed shoes.

'Here comes the great novelist,' Humphries sneered. 'I bet none of them has read a word he ever wrote.'

'You are probably right, but his great-grandfather was Governor here,' Doctor Plarr said. 'In Argentina they have a strong sense of history.'

The manager wanted to know whether the table was placed in a position satisfactory to Doctor Saavedra; the *maître d'hotel* whispered in Doctor Plarr's ear news of a second dish which was not marked on the menu – some salmon had arrived that day fresh from Iguazú; there was also a *dorado* if Doctor Plarr's guests would prefer that.

When the staff had departed one by one, Doctor Saavedra said, 'They make a ridiculous fuss of me. I was only telling them I was going to set a scene in my new novel in the restaurant of the Nacional. I wanted to explain where I wanted my character to be seated. I had to see exactly what would lie in his view at the moment when Fuerabbia, his assailant, enters armed from the terrace.'

'Is it a detective story?' Humphries asked with malice. 'I like a good detective story.'

'I trust I shall never write a detective story, Doctor Humphries, if by a detective story you mean one of those absurd puzzles, which are the literary equivalent of a jig-saw. In my new book I am concerned with the psychology of violence.'

'Gauchos again?'

'No, not gauchos. This is a contemporary novel – my second venture into politics. It is set in the time of the dictator Rosas.'

'I thought you said it was contemporary.'

'The ideas are contemporary. If you were a writer, Doctor Humphries, instead of a teacher of literature, you would know a novelist has to stand at a distance from his subject. Nothing dates more quickly than the immediately contemporary. You might as well expect me to write a story about the kidnapping of Señor Fortnum.' He turned to Doctor Plarr. 'I had some difficulty in getting away tonight, something unpleasant happened, but when my doctor calls I have to obey. What is it all about?'

Doctor Humphries and I have decided to found an Anglo-Argentinian Club.'

'An excellent idea. What activities . . . ?'

'Cultural of course. Literary, archaeological. We want you to be president.'

'I am honoured,' Doctor Saavedra said.

'One of the first things I would like the club to do is to make an appeal to the Press on the subject of Fortnum's kidnapping. If he had been here he would certainly have been a member.'

'How can I help you?' Doctor Saavedra asked. 'I have hardly spoken to Señor Fortnum. Just once at Señora Sanchez . . .'

'I have brought a rough draft – a very rough draft. I am no writer – except of prescriptions.'

Humphries said, 'The man has absconded. That is all there is to it. He probably arranged the whole affair himself. Personally I refuse to sign.'

'Then we shall have to do without you, Humphries. Only your friends – if you have any – may wonder, when the letter's published, why you are not a member of the Anglo-Argentinian Club. They may even think you were black-balled.'

'You know there's no such club.'

'Oh yes, there is, and Doctor Saavedra has agreed to be our president. This is the first club dinner. And we have a very good salmon from Iguazú. If you don't wish to be a member, go away and have some goulash at your Italian joint.'

'Are you trying to blackmail me?'

'In a good cause.'

'Morally you are no better than the kidnappers.'

'No better – all the same I would rather they didn't kill Charley Fortnum.'

'Charley Fortnum's a disgrace to his country.'

'No signature. No salmon.'

'You give me no alternative,' Doctor Humphries said, undoing his napkin.

Doctor Saavedra read the letter with care. He laid it down beside his plate. 'If I might take this home and work on it,' he said. 'It lacks – you must not mind my criticism, it comes from a professional conscience – it lacks the sense of urgency. It reads as coldly as a company report. If you would leave the letter in my hands I will write you something with colour and dramatic effect. Something the Press would have to print on its own merits.'

'I want to cable it tonight to *The Times* in London and get it into tomorrow's papers in Buenos Aires.'

'A letter like this cannot be hurried, Doctor Plarr, and I am a slow writer. Give me till tomorrow and I promise you the result will be worth waiting for.'

'The poor devil may have only about three days to live. I'd rather cable my rough draft tonight than wait till tomorrow. Over in England it's already tomorrow.'

'Then you will have to do without my signature. I'm sorry, doctor, it would be wrong for me to put my name to the letter as it stands now. No one in Buenos Aires would believe I had a hand in it. It contains – forgive me – some terrible clichés. Just listen to this . . .'

'That is why I wanted you to rewrite the letter. Surely you can do it now, at the table.'

'Do you believe writing is as easy as that? Would you do a delicate operation, on the spur of the moment, on this table? I will sit up all night if necessary. The quality of the letter I write you will more than make up for the delay, even in translation. By the way who is going to translate it – you or Doctor Humphries? I would like to check the translation before you send it abroad. I trust your accuracy, of course, but it is a question of style. In a letter like this we have to move the reader, to bring home to him the character of this poor man . . .'

'The less you bring home his character the better,' Humphries said.

'As I see it, Señor Fortnum is a simple man – not very wise or intelligent – and suddenly he finds himself close to violent death. Perhaps he has never even thought of death before. It is a situation in which such a man either succumbs to fear or he grows in stature. Consider the case of Señor Fortnum. He is married to a young wife, a child is on the way . . .'

'We have no time to write a novel on the subject,' Doctor Plarr said.

'When I met him, he had drunk a little too much. I found his company embarrassing until I saw, behind the superficial gaiety, a profound melancholy.'

'You are not far wrong there,' Doctor Plarr said with surprise.

'He was drinking, I think, for the same reason that I write – to escape the darkness of his own spirit. He confided to me that he was in love.'

'In love at sixty!' Humphries exclaimed. 'He ought to have got beyond all that nonsense.'

'I have not got beyond it,' Doctor Saavedra said. 'If I were beyond it, I would no longer be able to write. The sexual instinct and the creative instinct live and die together. Youth, Doctor Humphries, lasts longer in some men than you, from your personal experience, may suppose.'

'He just wanted to keep a whore handy. Do you call that love?'

'If we could get back to the letter . . .' Doctor Plarr said.

'And what do you call love, Doctor Humphries? An arranged marriage in the Spanish tradition? A large family of children? Let me tell you I have loved a whore myself. A whore can have more generosity of spirit than you will find in the bourgeoisie of Buenos Aires. As a poet I have been helped better by a whore than by any critic – or professor of literature.'

'I thought you were a novelist, not a poet.'

'In Spanish we do not confine the term poet to those who write metrically.'

'The letter,' Doctor Plarr interrupted. 'Let us try to finish the letter before we finish the salmon.'

'You must let me think quietly – the opening sentence is the key to the rest. One has to strike the right tone, even the right rhythm. The right rhythm in prose is every bit as important as the right metre in a poem. This is a very good salmon. May I have another glass of wine?'

'You can drink the whole bottle if you will write the letter.'

'What a fuss to make about Charley Fortnum,' Doctor Humphries said. He had finished his salmon, he had drained his glass, he had nothing to fear. 'You know there's another possible motive for his disappearance – he doesn't want to stand father to another man's child.'

'I want to begin the letter with a character study of the victim,' Doctor Saavedra said, ballpoint in hand, a little salmon shaking on his upper lip, 'but somehow Señor Fortnum refuses to come alive. I have had to cross out almost every other word. In a novel I could have created him in a few sentences. It is his reality which defeats me. I am hamstrung by his reality. When I write down a phrase it is as though Fortnum himself put a hand on my wrist and said, "But this is not how I am at all".'

'Let me pour you another glass.'

'There is another thing he says to me which makes me hesitate. "Why are you trying to send me back to the kind of life I used to lead, a life sad and without honour?"'

'Charley Fortnum never worried much about honour,' Doctor Humphries said, 'so long as there was enough whisky around.'

'If you could look deep enough into anyone's character, even perhaps your own, you would find the sense of *machismo*.'

It was past ten o'clock and guests were beginning to drift across the terrace for dinner. They moved along separate routes, passing on either side of Doctor Plarr's table, like migrating tribes passing a rock in the desert, and they carried their children with them. A baby, which might have been an idol of wax, sat upright in a pram: a pale-faced child of three staggered from fatigue across the marble desert dressed in a blue party dress, her little ears pierced for gold rings; a boy of six drummed his way, yawning at every step, along the terrace wall. One had the impression that they had crossed a whole continent to arrive here. No doubt at dawn, the grazing exhausted, they would pack up and move to another camping ground. Doctor Plarr said impatiently, 'Give me back my letter. I want to send it as it is.'

'In that case I cannot put my name to it.'

'And you, Humphries?'

'I won't sign. You can't threaten me now. I've finished my salmon.'

Doctor Plarr took the letter and tore it in two. He put some money on the table and rose.

'Doctor Plarr, I am sorry to anger you. Your style is not bad, it is workmanlike, but nobody would believe that I had written the letter.'

Doctor Plarr went to the lavatory. As he washed his hands he thought: I am like Pilate, a cliché of which Doctor Saavedra would not approve. He washed his hands scrupulously as though he were about to examine a patient. Raising them from the water he looked into the glass and threw a question at the worried image there – if they kill Fortnum will I marry Clara? It would not be a necessary consequence; she would never expect him to marry her. If she inherited the camp she could sell it and move elsewhere – home to Tucumán? Or perhaps she would take a flat in BA and eat sweet cakes like his mother? It would be more satisfactory for all of them if Fortnum lived. Fortnum would make a better father for the child than he would – a child needed love.

As he dried his hands he heard the voice of Doctor Saavedra behind him. 'You think I have failed you, doctor, but you are not aware of all the circumstances.'

The novelist was urinating. He had turned up the right sleeve of his pearl-grey jacket; he was a fastidious man.

Doctor Plarr said, 'I thought it was not too much to ask you to sign a letter, however badly written, and perhaps save a man's life.'

'I think I had better tell you the real reason. I need more than one of your pills tonight. Doctor, I have been deeply wounded.' Doctor Saavedra buttoned up his trousers and turned. 'I have spoken to you already about Montez?'

'Montez? No, I can't remember the name.'

'He is a young novelist in Buenos Aires – not so young now, I suppose, older than you, the years pass quickly. I helped him to get his first novel published. A very strange novel. Surrealist but excellently written. Emece turned it down, Sur would not accept it, and I only persuaded my own publisher to take it by promising that I would write a favourable criticism. In those days I was writing a weekly column in the *Nación* which had a lot of influence. I was fond of Montez. I felt myself to be a sort of father to him. Even though, during my last years in Buenos Aires, I saw very little of him. He had made his own friends after his success. All the same I never failed to praise his work when I had the chance. Now see what he has written about me.' He took from his pocket a folded page of print.

It was a long, and well-written article. The subject was the bad effect of the epic poem, *Martín Fierro*, on the Argentine novel. Borges the author excepted from his criticism. He had a few words of praise for Mallea and Sabato, but he made cruel fun of Jorge Julio Saavedra's novels. The word mediocre appeared frequently, the word *machismo* rang mockingly out from nearly every paragraph. Was he revenging the patronage which Saavedra had once shown him, all the boring counsel to which he had probably been forced to listen? Doctor Plarr said, 'Yes, it is a betrayal, Saavedra.'

'Not only of myself. Of his country. *Martín Fierro* is Argentina. Why, my own grandfather died in a duel. He fought with bare hands against a drunken gaucho who insulted him. Where would we be now' – his hands waved from basin to *urinoir* – 'if our fathers had not reverenced *machismo*? You see what he writes about the girl from Salta. He has not even understood the symbolism of her one leg. If I had signed your letter imagine how he would have sneered at the style. "Poor Jorge Julio – that is what happens to a writer who runs away from his peers and hides in the provinces. He writes like a clerk of the *intendente*.' I wish Montez were here now so that I could teach him the meaning of *machismo*. Here on these tiles.'

'Have you a knife handy?' Doctor Plarr asked, hoping in vain to raise a smile.

'I would fight him as my grandfather did with my bare hands.'

Doctor Plarr said, 'Your grandfather was killed.'

'I am not afraid of death,' Doctor Saavedra said.

'Charley Fortnum is. It's a very small thing to do – to sign a letter.'

'A small thing? To sign a piece of prose like that? It would be much easier to give my life. Oh, I know it's impossible for someone who is not a writer to understand.'

'I am trying to,' Doctor Plarr said.

'Your purpose is to draw attention to Señor Fortnum's case? Is that right?'

'Yes.'

'Then this is what I suggest. Inform the newspapers and your government that I have offered myself as a hostage in his place.'

'Are you serious?'

'I am quite serious.'

It might work, Doctor Plarr thought, there is just a faint possibility that in this crazy country it might work. He was moved to say, 'It's brave of you, Saavedra.'

'At least I will show young Montez that *machismo* is not an invention of the author of *Martín Fierro*.'

'You realize,' Doctor Plarr said, 'they might accept your offer? And then there would be no more novels by Jorge Julio Saavedra – unless perhaps the General reads you and you have a big public in Paraguay.'

'You will cable Buenos Aires and *The Times* of London too? You will not forget *The Times*? Two of my novels were published in England.

And *El Litoral*. You must telephone them. The kidnappers are sure to read *El Litoral*.'

They went together to the manager's office which was empty and Doctor Plarr wrote out the cables. When he turned he saw the eyes of Doctor Saavedra red with unshed tears. Saavedra said, 'Montez was like a son to me. I admired his books. They were so different from my own, and they had quality – I could see they had quality. Yet all the time he must have been despising me. I am an old man, Doctor Plarr, so death is not very far off from me in any case. That story I was describing to the hotel manager – the story of the intruder – I was going to call the novel *The Intruder* – it would probably never have been finished. Even while I was planning it I knew it belonged to *his* region of literature and not to mine. I used to give him advice and see me now – planning to imitate him. It is the privilege of the young to imitate. I would prefer to die in a way that even Montez would have to respect.'

'He will say that you were killed too in the end by *Martín Fierro*.'

'In Argentina we are most of us killed by *Martín Fierro*. But a man has the right to choose the moment of death.'

'Charley Fortnum has not been allowed to choose.'

'Señor Fortnum is caught up in a contingency. I agree that is not a dignified way to die. It is like a street accident or a case of *gripe*.'

Doctor Plarr offered to drive Saavedra home. He had never yet been invited to visit the novelist and he had imagined him in occupation of some old colonial house with barred windows looking out on a shady street, with a few orange trees and *lapachos* in the garden, a house as dignified and out of fashion as his clothes. Perhaps there would be portraits on the wall of the great-grandfather who had been Governor of the province and of the grandfather who had been killed by the gaucho.

'It is not far. I can easily walk,' Saavedra said.

'I think we ought to talk a little more about your offer and how it can be carried through.'

'All that is out of my hands now.'

'Not entirely.'

As he drove Doctor Plarr pointed out to the novelist that from the moment his offer was published in *El Litoral* he would be watched by the police. 'The kidnappers will have to communicate with you and suggest some way of making the exchange. It would be easier if you left the town tonight before the police know. You could stay out of sight with some friend in the country.'

'How would the kidnappers find me?'

'Perhaps through me. They probably know I am a friend of Señor Fortnum.'

'I cannot run away and hide like a criminal.'

'Then it will be difficult for them to take your offer up.'

'Besides,' Doctor Saavedra said, 'there is my work.'

'Surely you can take it with you.'

'That is easy for you to say. You can go and attend a patient anywhere, you carry your experience with you. But my work is tied to the room where I work. When I came here from Buenos Aires it was nearly a year before I could put a pen to paper. My room was like a hotel room. To write one must have a home.'

A home: Doctor Plarr was surprised to find the novelist lived in a block even more modern and shabby than his own in a quarter close by the prison wall. The grey apartment houses stood in squares as though they formed an extension of the prison. One expected them to be lettered A, B and C and to be reserved for different categories of criminal. Doctor Saavedra's apartment was on the third floor and there was no lift. Children played a kind of bowls with tin cans in front of the entrance, and the smell of cooking pursued them up the stairs. Perhaps Doctor Saavedra felt that an explanation was required. He spoke a little breathlessly after his climb as he paused on the second floor. 'You know a novelist does not pay visits like a doctor. He has to live with his subject. I could not live comfortably in a bourgeois setting because I write about the people. The good woman who cleans for me here is the wife of a warder at the prison. I feel myself in the right *milieu*. I put her in my last book. Do you remember? She was called Caterina and was the widow of a sergeant. I think I caught her way of thinking.' He opened his door and said with a note of defiance, 'Here you are at the head of what my critics call the world of Saavedra.'

It was indeed a very small world. Doctor Plarr had an impression that the long pursuit of literature had brought the novelist little material reward beyond his tidy suit and his polished shoes and the respect of the hotel manager. The living-room was narrow and long like a railway compartment. One shelf of books (most of them were Saavedra's own), a folding table which would have almost spanned the room if it had been opened, a nineteenth-century painting of a gaucho on a horse, one easy chair and two upright chairs – that was all the furnishing there was, apart from a huge antique mahogany cupboard which must have once belonged in more spacious quarters, for the baroque curlicues above the pediment had been cut to fit under the ceiling. Two open doors, which Doctor Saavedra quickly shut, gave Plarr glimpses of a monastic bedstead and the chipped enamel of a cooking stove. Through the window, which was veined by a rusty mesh against mosquitoes, came the clatter of tins from the children playing below.

'May I give you a whisky?'

'A small one, please.'

Doctor Saavedra opened the cupboard; it was like an enormous chest in which the possessions of a lifetime had been packed for an impending departure. Two suits hung there. Shirts and underwear and books had been stacked indiscriminately on the shelves: an umbrella leant among obscure shapes at the back: four ties dangled from a rod: a little pile of photographs in old-fashioned frames shared the floor with two pairs of shoes and some books for which there had been no room elsewhere. On a ledge over the suits stood a whisky bottle, a half-finished bottle of wine and a few glasses – one of them chipped – a pile of cutlery and a bowl of bread. Doctor Saavedra said defiantly, 'I am a little cramped for room, but I want the smallest possible space around me when I write. Space distracts.' He looked anxiously at Doctor Plarr and attempted a smile. 'This is the womb of my characters, doctor, and there is room for little else. You must forgive me if I cannot offer you any ice, but this morning my refrigerator failed and the electrician has not yet come.'

'I prefer my whisky neat after dinner,' Doctor Plarr said.

'Then I will get you a smaller glass.'

He had to stand on the points of his small gleaming shoes to reach the top of the wardrobe. A cheap plastic shade painted with pink flowers, which were beginning to brown from the heat, hardly dimmed the harshness of the central light. Watching Doctor Saavedra reach for the glass with his white hair, in his pearl-grey suit and his brightly polished shoes, Doctor Plarr felt much the same astonishment that he had felt in the *barrio* of the poor when he saw a young girl emerge in an immaculate white dress from a waterless hovel of mud and tin. He felt a new respect for Doctor Saavedra. His obsession with literature was not absurd whatever the quality of his books. He was willing to suffer poverty for its sake, and a disguised poverty was far worse to endure than an open one. The effort needed to polish his shoes, to press the suit . . . He couldn't, like the young, let things go. Even his hair must be cut regularly. A missing button would reveal too much. Perhaps he would be remembered in the history of Argentine literature only in a footnote, but he would have deserved his footnote. The bareness of the room could be compared to the inextinguishable hunger of his literary obsession.

Doctor Saavedra tripped towards him holding two glasses. He asked, 'How long do you think we shall have to wait for a response?'

'It may never come.'

'Your father's name, I believe, is on the list of those they want released?'

'Yes.'

'It would be strange for you, I imagine, to see your father again after all this time. How happy your mother will be if . . .'

'I think she would prefer him dead. He wouldn't fit in with her life now.'

'And perhaps if Señor Fortnum returned he would not be welcomed by his wife either?'

'How can I tell?'

'Oh come, Doctor Plarr, I have friends at the house of Señora Sanchez.'

'So she has been back there?' Doctor Plarr asked.

'I was there early this evening and so was she. They were making a great fuss of her – even Señora Sanchez. Perhaps she hopes to have her back. When Doctor Benevento came to see the other girls I took her to the Consulate.'

'She told you about me?'

He was a little irritated by her indiscretion, but nonetheless he felt a sense of relief. He was escaping from secrecy. There had not been one soul in the city to whom he could talk of Clara, and what better confidant could he hope to have than his own patient? There were secrets which Doctor Saavedra too would not want known.

'She told me how very kind you had been to her.'

'Is that all she said?'

'It was all that was necessary between old friends.'

'Was she one of your girls?' Doctor Plarr asked.

'I was with her only once, I think.'

Doctor Plarr felt no jealousy. To think of Clara waiting naked in her cell in the candlelight while Doctor Saavedra hung up his pearl-grey suit was like watching on the stage a scene, both sad and comic, from a remote seat at the back of the gallery. Distance removed the characters so far from him that he could be touched only by a formal compassion. He asked, 'Didn't you like her enough to try again?'

Doctor Saavedra said, 'It was not a question of liking. She was a good young woman, I am sure, quite attractive too, but she had nothing *special* for my purpose. She never struck me as a character – a character – forgive me if I speak like the critics – in the world of Jorge Julio Saavedra. Montez claims that the world has no real existence. What does he know in Buenos Aires? Doesn't Teresa exist – you remember the evening when you met her? Before we had been together five minutes Teresa was the girl from Salta. There was something she said – I can't remember the words now. I went with her four times and then I had to drop her, because she was saying too many things which were unsuitable. They confused my idea.'

'Clara comes from Tucumán. You got nothing from her?'

'Tucumán is not a suitable region for me. My region is the region of extremes. Montez does not understand that. Trelew . . . Salta. Tucumán is an elegant city, and it is surrounded by half a million hectares of sugar. What ennui! Her father was a cane-cutter, wasn't he? And her brother disappeared.'

'I would have thought that might have made a good subject for you, Saavedra.'

'Not for me. She never came alive. It was all dull poverty with no *machismo* in half a million hectares.' He added bravely as though the night were not noisy with the tins rolling back and forth in the cement yard below, 'You do not realize how quiet and dull bare poverty can be. Let me give you a little more whisky. It is a genuine Johnny Walker.'

'No, no thank you. I must go home.' All the same he lingered. Novelists were supposed to have acquired a certain wisdom . . . He asked, 'What do you suppose will become of Clara if Fortnum dies?'

'Perhaps you might marry her?'

'How can I? I would have to go away from here.'

'You could easily find a better living somewhere else. Rosario?'

Doctor Plarr said, 'This is my home too – or the nearest I have ever come to a home since I left Paraguay.'

'And you feel your father not so far away?'

'You *are* a perceptive man, Saavedra. Yes, it may have been my father's nearness which brought me here. In the *barrio* of the poor I am aware of doing something he would have liked to see me do, but when I am with my rich patients, I feel as though I had left his friends to help his enemies. I even sleep with them sometimes, and when I wake up I look at the face on the pillow through his eyes. I suppose that's one reason why my affairs never last long, and when I have tea with my mother in the Calle Florida among all the other ladies of B A . . . he sits there too and criticizes me with his blue English eyes. I think my father might have cared for Clara. She is one of his poor.'

'Do you love the girl?'

'Love, love, I wish I knew what you and all the others mean by the word. I want her, yes. From time to time. Sexual desire has its rhythms as you well know.' He added, 'She has lasted longer than I thought possible. Teresa was your one-legged girl from Salta. Perhaps Clara is – my poor. But I never want her to be my victim. Was that what Charley Fortnum felt when he married her?'

Doctor Saavedra said, 'I may not see you again. I have come to you for pills against melancholy, but at least I have my work. I wonder whether you do not need those pills more than I do.'

Doctor Plarr looked at him without understanding. His thoughts were elsewhere.

When he got into the lift to his flat Doctor Plarr remembered the excitement with which Clara had made her first ascent in it. Perhaps, he thought, I will telephone to the Consulate and tell her to join me. The bed at the Consulate was too narrow for both of them, and, if he joined her there, he would be forced to leave before the hawk-like woman came in the morning.

He let himself in and went first to his consulting room to see whether his secretary Ana had left a note on his desk, but there was nothing there. He drew the curtains and looked down on the port: three policemen were standing by the Coca-Cola stall, perhaps because the weekly boat to Asunción lay at the jetty. It was like the scene of his boyhood, but he looked at it in reverse from his fourth-floor window above the river.

He said, 'God help you, father, wherever you are,' speaking aloud. It was easier to believe in a god with a human sense of hearing than in some omniscient force which could read his unuttered thoughts. Strangely the face he conjured up when he spoke was not his father's but Charley Fortnum's. The Honorary Consul lay stretched out on the coffin and whispered, 'Ted.' Doctor Plarr's father had called him Eduardo as though in compliment to his wife. When he tried to substitute Henry Plarr's face for Charley Fortnum's he found his father's features had been almost eliminated by the years. As with an ancient coin that has been buried a long time in the ground he could only distinguish a faint unevenness of surface which might once have been the outline of a cheek or a lip. It was Charley Fortnum's voice which appealed to him again, 'Ted.'

He turned away – hadn't he done all in his power to help? – and opened the bedroom door. He saw by the light from the study the body of Fortnum's wife outlined under the sheets. 'Clara!' he said. She woke immediately and sat up. He noticed her clothes had been folded carefully on a chair, for she possessed the neatness of her former profession. For a woman who has to take off her clothes many times in a night it is essential to arrange them carefully or a dress would be hopelessly crumpled after two or three clients. She had told him once that Señora Sanchez insisted on each girl paying for her own laundry – it made for tidiness.

'How did you get in?'

'I asked the porter.'

'He opened the door for you?'

'He knows me.'

'He has seen you here?'

'Yes. And there too.'

So I have shared her with the porter as well, he thought. How many more of the unknown warriors of her battlefield would take form sooner or later? Nothing was more alien to the life of the Calle Florida and the tinkle of teacups and the cakes of *dulce de leche*, white as snow. He had shared Margarita for a while with Señor Vallejo – most affairs overlap at the beginning or the end – and he preferred the porter to Señor Vallejo, the smell of whose shaving lotion during those last dilatory months he had sometimes detected on Margarita's skin.

'I told him you would give him money. You will?'

'Of course. How much? Five hundred pesos?'

'A thousand would be better.'

He sat on the edge of the bed and pulled the sheet back. He was not yet tired of her thin body and the small breasts which barely yet, any more than her belly, indicated pregnancy. He said, 'I am very glad you are here. I was going to call you up, though it wouldn't have been very wise. The police think I had something to do with the kidnapping. They suspect my motive may be jealousy,' he added, smiling at the idea of it.

'They would not dare do anything to you. You look after the finance secretary's wife.'

'They might start watching me all the same.'

'What would that matter? They watch me.'

'Did they follow you here?'

'Oh, I know how to deal with men like that. It is not the police I worry about, but that swine of a journalist. He was back at the camp just after it got dark. He offered me money.'

'What for? A story?'

'He wanted to sleep with me.'

'What did you say?'

'I told him I did not need his money any more, and then he got angry. He really believed I liked him for himself when I was with Señora Sanchez. He thought he was a great lover. Oh, how I hurt his pride,' she went on with pleasure, 'when I told him that Charley was twice the man he was.'

'How did you get rid of him?'

'I called the policeman (they have left one at the camp – they say he is there to protect me, but he watches me all the time), and while the two of them were arguing I drove away.'

'But you don't know how to drive, Clara.'

'I watched Charley often enough. It is not so difficult. I knew the things to push and the things to pull. I got them mixed up at first, but all was right in the end. It went in jerks as far as the road, and then I found how to do things properly and I drove faster than Charley.'

'Poor Fortnum's Pride,' Plarr said.

'I think I drove a little too fast because I did not see the *camión* coming.

'What happened?'

'There was an accident.'

'Were you hurt?'

'The jeep was hurt but not me.'

Her eyes gleamed up at him from the pillows; they were bright with the excitement of strange events. Never before had he known her talk so much. She had for him still the attraction of a stranger – like some unknown girl at a cocktail party. He said, 'I like you,' lightly, without thought, as he might have said it over the cocktails, neither of them believing the words meant any more than 'Come and sleep with me'.

'The driver gave me a lift,' she said. 'Of course he wanted to make love, and I said I would when we got to the town at a house he goes to in San José, but I got out at the first traffic lights, before he could stop me, and I went to Señora Sanchez. Oh, she was glad to see me I can tell you, really glad, not angry with me at all, and she put on a bandage herself.'

'Then you *were* hurt?'

'I told her I knew a good doctor,' she said and smiled and pulled the sheet off to show the bandage round her left knee.

'Clara, I must take it off and see . . .'

'Oh, it can wait,' she said. 'You love me a little?' She corrected herself quickly, 'Do you want to make love to me?'

'Plenty of time for that. Lie still and let me take the bandage off.'

He tried to be as gentle as possible, but he knew he must be hurting her. She lay quiet without complaint, and he thought of some of his bourgeois patients who would have persuaded themselves that the pain was unbearable; they might even have fainted from fear or to win his attention. 'Good peasant stock,' he said with admiration.

'What do you mean?'

'You are a brave girl.'

'But that cut is nothing. You should see what men do to themselves in the fields when they cut cane. I have seen a boy with half his foot cut off.' She asked casually, as though she were making polite conversation about a relative whom they had in common, 'Is there any news yet of Charley?'

'No.'

'Do you still think he may be alive?'

'I am pretty sure of it,' he said.

'Then you *have* had news?'

'I have talked to Colonel Perez again. And I have been to Buenos Aires today to see the Ambassador.'

'But what shall we do if he comes back?'

'Do? I suppose what we are doing now. What else?' He finished retying the bandage. 'We shall go on just as we always did. I shall come to see you at the camp, and Charley will go farming.' It was as though he were describing some life which had been pleasant enough once, but in which he no longer quite believed.

'It was good seeing the girls again at Señora Sanchez. I told them I had a lover. Of course I did not tell them who.'

'I'm surprised they didn't know. Everybody in this town seems to know except poor Charley.'

'Why do you call him poor Charley? He was happy. I always did what he wanted me to do.'

'What did he want?'

'Not very much. Not very often. It was boring, Eduardo. I have not the words to tell you how boring it was. He was kind and careful of me. He never hurt me like you hurt me. Sometimes I say thank you to Our Lord and Our Blessed Lady that it is your child which is stuck in me here, not his. What sort of child would have come out if it had belonged to Charley? The child of an old man. I would have wanted to strangle it at birth.'

'Charley would make a better father than I could ever be.'

'He cannot do one thing better than you can.'

Oh, yes, he can, Doctor Plarr thought, he can die better, and that is quite something.

She put out a hand and touched him on the cheek – he could feel the nerves through her finger-tips. She had never caressed him like that before. A face was part of the forbidden territory of tenderness, and the purity of the gesture shocked him as much as though a young girl had touched his sex. He withdrew quickly. She said, 'Do you remember that time at the camp when I told you I was pretending? But, *caro*, I was not pretending. Now when you make love to me I pretend. I pretend I feel nothing. I bite my lip so as to pretend. Is it because I love you, Eduardo? Do you think I love you?' She added with a humility which put him on his guard as much as a demand, 'I am sorry. I did not really mean that . . . It makes no difference, does it?'

No difference? How could he begin to explain to her the vast extent of the difference? 'Love' was a claim which he wouldn't meet, a responsibility he would refuse to accept, a demand . . . So many times his mother had used the word when he was a child; it was like the threat of an armed robber, 'Put up your hands or else . . .' Something was always asked in return: obedience, an apology, a kiss which one had no desire to give. Perhaps he had loved his father all the more because he had never used the word or asked for anything. He could remember only a single kiss on the quay at Asunción and that was the kind of kiss one man can give to another. It was like the formal kiss he had seen French generals give in photographs after they have presented a decoration. It claimed nothing. His father would sometimes pull at his hair or tap him on his cheek. The English phrase 'Old fellow' was the nearest which he ever came to an endearment. He remembered his mother, as she wept in the cabin while the ship pulled into the current, telling him, 'I have only you to love me now', she had reached at him from her bunk, repeating 'Darling, my darling boy', as Margarita had reached at him years later from her bed, before Señor Vallejo had come to take his place, and he remembered how Margarita had called him 'the love of my life' as his mother had sometimes called him 'my only boy'. He felt no belief at all in sexual love, but lying awake in the overcrowded flat in Buenos Aires he had sometimes recalled, as his mother's footsteps creaked towards the privy, the illicit nocturnal sounds which he had heard on the *estancia* in Paraguay – the tiny reverberations of a muffled knock, strange tiptoes on the floor below, whispers from the cellar, a gunshot which rang out an urgent warning from far across the fields – those had been the signals of a genuine tenderness, a compassion deep enough for his father to be prepared to die for it. Was that love? Did León feel love? Even Aquino?

'Eduardo,' he came back from far away to hear her imploring him, 'I will say anything you want. I did not mean to make you angry. What do you want, Eduardo? Tell me. Please. What do you want? I want to know what you want, but how can I know if I do not understand?'

'Charley is simpler, isn't he?'

'Eduardo, will you always be angry if I love you? I swear it won't make any difference. I will stay with Charley. I will come only when you want me just like at the house.'

He was startled by the door bell which rang and stopped and rang again. He hesitated to go. Why hesitate? Hardly a week passed without a telephone call or a ring at the door during the night. 'Lie quiet,' he said, 'it is only a patient.' He went into the hall and looked through the spy-hole in the door, but no one was visible in the darkness of the stairhead. He felt he was back in the Paraguay of his childhood. How often his father must have called out before a bolted door as he called now, 'Who is it?' trying to make the intonation sound firm.

'The police.'

He unlocked the door and found himself face to face with Colonel Perez. 'May I come in?'

'When you say "Police" how can I refuse?' Doctor Plarr asked. 'If you said "Perez" I might have told you, since you are a friend, to call tomorrow morning, at a better time.'

'It was because we are good friends that I said "Police" to warn you this is an official call.'

'Too official for a drink?'

'No, it has not reached that point yet.'

Doctor Plarr led Colonel Perez to his consulting room and brought out two whiskies of the Argentinian mark. He said, 'I keep the little genuine Scotch I have for social visits.'

'Yes, I understand. And your meeting with Doctor Saavedra tonight, that I suppose was purely social?'

'Are you having me watched?'

'Not until now. Perhaps I ought to have done so earlier. Someone on the *El Litoral* told me of your telephone call tonight, and of course the cables you left at the hotel interested me when they showed them to me. There is no such thing in this city as an Anglo-Argentinian Club, is there?'

'No. Did the cables go off?'

'Why not? There was no harm in them. But then there was the lie you told me yesterday . . . You seem to be very mixed up in this affair, doctor.'

'You are right of course, if you mean I'm doing my best to have Fortnum released, but surely both of us are working for that.'

'There is quite a difference, doctor. I am not really interested in Fortnum, only in his kidnappers. I would prefer the blackmail to be unsuccessful, because it would discourage others. You on the other hand want the blackmail to succeed. Of course – it is only natural – I would like to win the game both ways, to save Señor Fortnum and capture or kill his kidnappers, but the second is much more important to me than the life of Señor Fortnum. Are you alone here?'

'Yes. Why?'

'I was looking out of the window and I thought I saw a light go off in the next room.'

'It was a car passing by the river road.'

'Yes. Perhaps.' He drank his whisky slowly. Doctor Plarr had an odd impression that he was at a loss for words. 'Do you really believe, doctor, these men can get your father released?'

'Well, prisoners have been released by the same method.'

'Not in return for a mere Honorary Consul.'

'Even an Honorary Consul is human – he has the right to live. The British Government would not want him murdered.'

'It does not depend on the British Government, it depends on the General, and I doubt if the General worries much about any human life. Except his own, of course.'

'He depends on American aid. If they insist . . .'

'Yes, but he already gives the Yankees something in return which they value a great deal more than an English Honorary Consul. The General has one great quality, like Papa Doc used to have in Haiti. He is anti communist. Are you quite sure you are alone, doctor?'

'Of course.'

'It was only . . . I thought I heard . . . well, never mind. Are *you* a Communist, doctor?'

'No. I have always found Marx unreadable. Like most economics. But you really believe these kidnappers are communist? It is not only communists who are against tyranny and torture.'

'Some of the men they want released are communist – or so the General claims.'

'My father is not.'

'Then you do really believe he is still alive?'

The telephone rang out at Doctor Plarr's elbow. He lifted the receiver unwillingly. A voice which he recognized as León's said, 'Something has happened. We need you urgently. We have been trying all day . . .'

'Is it so very urgent? I have a friend drinking with me.'

'Are you under arrest?' the voice whispered up the line.

'Not for the moment.'

Colonel Perez leant forward, watching him, trying to hear.

'It is too late to telephone me. Yes, yes, I know. A little fear is quite natural under the circumstances, but the temperature of a child always runs high. Give her two more aspirin.'

'I will call you again in fifteen minutes.'

'I hope you will not find it necessary. Ring me up tomorrow morning but not too early. I have had a long day, I have been to Buenos Aires.' He added with his eye on Colonel Perez, 'I want to get to bed.'

'In fifteen minutes,' the voice of León repeated. Doctor Plarr put down the receiver.

'Who was that?' Perez asked. 'Oh, forgive me, I get into the habit of asking questions. It is a police vice.'

'Only a worried parent,' Doctor Plarr said.

'I thought I heard a man's voice.'

'Yes. The father. Men are always much more worried about their children than women. The mother is in Buenos Aires shopping. What were we talking about, colonel?'

'Your father. It is strange that these men included his name in their list. There are so many others who would be much more useful to them. Younger men. Your father must be quite an old man now. It almost looks as though they were paying for some help you could give them . . .' He finished his sentence with a vague gesture.

'What could I do for them?'

'All this publicity you are trying to arrange – it's useful to them. It is something they cannot do for themselves. They do not want to kill the man. His death would be a sort of defeat. And then – it occurred to me only today, I am a slow thinker – they knew what the papers never printed – the real programme the Governor had made for the Ambassador's visit. It is funny how something so obvious escaped me for so long. They must have received information, confidential information.'

'Perhaps. But not from me. I am not in the Governor's confidence.'

'No, but Señor Fortnum knew and he might have told you. Or Señora Fortnum. It is not an unusual thing for a woman to mention to her lover when her husband is going to be away.'

'You make me out a Don Juan with my patients, colonel. I might be afraid of a husband in England, but here the General Medical Council does not operate. I hope you have not been bothering Señora Fortnum?'

'I wanted to have a word with her, but she was not at the camp. This evening she visited the Sanchez house. Then she went to the Consulate, but she is not there now. I was a little anxious at first because Señor Fortnum's Land Rover was found by the road damaged – poor man, he has had two cars smashed in two days. I was glad to hear she had been with Señora Sanchez and that her injuries were only small ones. You have been attending a patient, doctor, I think? Your right sleeve is turned up.'

Doctor Plarr pushed the telephone away from him. He was afraid it might speak to him again too soon. He said 'How observant you are, colonel. I did not trust Señora Sanchez as a doctor. Clara is with me here.'

'And I was right too about your lies yesterday.'

'An affair always involves a few lies.'

'I am sorry to have interrupted you, doctor, but it was the lies which bothered me. After all we are old friends. We have even shared a few adventures in our time. Señora Escobar, for example.'

'Yes, I remember. I told you I was leaving her and the coast was – nearly – clear. I never understood why in the end she preferred Vallejo to you.'

'She did not trust my motives. The common fate of a policeman. You see Señor Escobar has a landing strip on his *estancia* in the Chaco. Probably whisky and cigarettes come out of Paraguay by that route.'

'A public benefactor.'

'Yes, of course I would never have interfered with him. I hope those aspirins work. You will not want to be interrupted again.' Colonel Perez drained his whisky and stood up. 'You have relieved my mind a great deal. Of course I understand now why you would want Señor Fortnum released. A husband is of great importance in a love affair. He is a way of escape when an affair begins to get boring. No one would wish to leave a woman quite alone. Well, we shall have to try and save Señor Fortnum for you – and capture his kidnappers too. They will know what to do with them on the other side of the river.'

Doctor Plarr went with him to the door. 'I am glad you are feeling happier about me.'

'Secrets always smell bad to a policeman, even innocent secrets. We are trained, like a dog with cannabis, to scent them out. Take my advice, doctor, you have really done enough now, so please do not interfere any more. We have always been friendly, but if you meddle in this affair, you must look out for yourself. I will shoot first and send a wreath later.'

'You sound a bit like Al Capone.'

'Yes. Capone too supported order in his own way.' He opened the door and hesitated for a moment on the dark landing, as though something important had slipped his memory. 'There is one more thing I ought perhaps to have told you earlier. I *do* have news of your father. From the Chief of Police in Asunción. Naturally we checked with him all the names that the kidnappers put on their list. Your father was killed more than a year ago. He tried to escape with another man – a man called Aquino Ribera – but he was too old and too slow. He could not make it and he was abandoned. You see – it is no good thinking there is anything you can do to help him now. Goodnight, doctor. I am sorry to bring you bad news, but at any rate I leave you with a woman. A woman is the best comforter a man can have.'

The telephone began to sound again, almost as soon as the door closed.

Doctor Plarr thought: León cheated me. He has been lying to me all along in order to get my help. I won't answer the telephone. Let them get out of their own mess in their own way. Not for a moment did it occur to him that it might be Colonel Perez who had lied. The police were strong enough to speak the truth.

The bell rang and rang as he stood stubbornly in the hall, and then whoever was calling him gave it up. For all he knew this time it might have been one of his patients, and in the accusing silence he began to feel guilt for his egoism: it was like the silence after a suicide's cry for help. There was silence in the bedroom too. From Clara a little while ago had come an appeal. He had walked away from that too.

The small patch of marble floor on which he stood seemed like the edge of an abyss; he could not move one step in either direction without falling deeper into the darkness of involvement or guilt. He stood and listened to the silence – in the flat where Clara lay, in the midnight street outside where a police car would now be moving home, in the *barrio popular* where something must have happened among the huts of mud and tin. Silence, like a thin republic where his father was lying dead in the deepest silence of all – 'He was too old and slow. He couldn't make it and they abandoned him.' He felt giddy on his ledge of marble parquet. He couldn't stand motionless for ever. Again the telephone rang and he moved back into his office.

León's voice spoke. 'What has happened?'

'I had a visitor.'

'The police?'

'Yes.'

'You are alone now?'

'Yes. Alone.'

'Where have you been all day?'

'In Buenos Aires.'

'But we tried to get you last night.'

'I was called out.'

'And this morning at six.'

'I couldn't sleep. I took a walk by the river. You said you wouldn't need me any more.'

'Your patient needs you now. Go down to the river and stand near the Coca-Cola stall. We can see if anyone is watching. If the road is clear we will pick you up.'

'I have just had news of my father. From Colonel Perez. Is it true?'

'What news?'

'That he made a break, but he was too slow, and you abandoned him.'

He thought: if I detect one lie over the telephone – even a hesitation – I will put the receiver down, and I will never answer again.

León said, 'Yes. I am sorry. It is true. I could not tell you before. We needed your help.'

'And my father is dead?'

'Yes. They shot him at once. As he lay on the ground.'

'You could have told me.'

'Perhaps, but we could not take the risk.'

León's voice reached him as though across an immeasurable distance, 'Will you come?'

'Oh yes,' Doctor Plarr said, 'I'll come.' He put down the receiver and went into the bedroom. He turned on the light and saw Clara, her eyes wide open, watching him.

'Who was it came?'

'Colonel Perez.'

'Are you in trouble?'

'Not from him.'

'And the telephone?'

'A patient. I have to go out for a while, Clara.'

He remembered there was some question which had been left hanging unanswered between them, but he couldn't remember now what it was. He said, 'My father is dead.'

'Oh, Eduardo. I am sorry. Did you love him?' She couldn't take love for granted any more than he could, even between a father and son.

'Perhaps I did.'

He had once known a man in Buenos Aires who was illegitimate. The man's mother died without telling him the name of his father. He searched through his mother's letters, he asked questions of her friends. He even examined bank records – his mother had an income which must have come from somewhere. He was not angry, nor shocked, but the desire to know who his father was vexed him like an itch. He explained to Doctor Plarr, 'It is like one of those little picture puzzles with quicksilver. I cannot get the eyes in the right place, and yet I cannot put the puzzle down.' Then one day he learnt his father's name: that of an international banker who had been dead a long time. He said to Plarr, 'You cannot imagine how empty I feel now. What is there left to interest me?' It is that kind of emptiness, Doctor Plarr thought, which I am experiencing now.

'Come and lie down, Eduardo.'

'No. I must go out.'

'Where?'

'I am not sure. It is something to do with Charley.'

'Have they found his body?' she asked.

'No, no, nothing like that.' She had half thrown the sheet off and he tucked it around her. He said, 'You will catch cold from the air-conditioner.'

'I will go back to the Consulate.'

'No, stay here. I shall not be very long.'

In solitude, one welcomes any living thing – a mouse, a bird on the sill, Robert Bruce's spider. In complete loneliness even a certain tenderness can be born. He said, 'I am sorry, Clara. When I come back –' but he could not think of anything which was really worth while to promise her. He put his hand over her stomach and said, 'Look after it. Sleep well.' He turned the light out so that he could no longer see her eyes watching him – puzzled, as though his actions were too complicated for any girl from the establishment of Señora Sanchez to understand. On the stairs (the lift might have been heard by his neighbours) he tried to remember what that question of hers had been which he had never answered. It could not have been very important. The only questions of importance were those which a man asked himself.

PART FIVE

Chapter 1

DOCTOR PLARR came back from the inner room and said to Father Rivas, 'He will do well enough. Your man couldn't have aimed better if he had intended it. He hit the Achilles tendon. Of course, it will take time to mend. If you give him time. What happened?'

'He tried to escape. Aquino fired at the ground first and then at his legs.'

'It would be better if he could be taken to hospital.'

'You know that is impossible.'

'All I can do is to strap him up. His ankle ought to be put in plaster. Why don't you give up the whole affair, León? I can keep him in my car for three or four hours to give you the time to disappear, and I'll tell the police I found him by the road.'

Father Rivas did not trouble to reply. Doctor Plarr said, 'It is always the same when one thing goes wrong – it is like an error in an equation . . . Your first error was mistaking him for the Ambassador and now this follows. Your equation will never work out.'

'You may be right, but unless we receive orders from El Tigre . . .'

'Get your orders then.'

'Impossible. After we announced the kidnapping all contact was broken. We are on our own here. In that way if we are captured, we cannot talk.'

'I have to go. I must get some sleep.'

'You will stay here with us,' Father Rivas said.

'That's not possible. If I'm seen leaving in daylight . . .'

'If your telephone is tapped they will know you are an accomplice of ours already. If you go back they may arrest you and your friend Fortnum will be left without a doctor.'

'I have other patients to consider, León.'

'But *they* can find other doctors.'

'If you get your way . . . or you kill him . . . what happens to me?'

Father Rivas indicated the negro called Pablo in the doorway. 'You were abducted and kept here by force. It is the simple truth. We cannot allow you to leave now.'

'Suppose I just walk through that door?'

'I will tell him to shoot. Be reasonable, Eduardo. How can we trust you not to lead the police here?'

'I'm no police informer, León, in spite of the trick you played on me.'

'I wonder. A man's conscience is not a simple thing. I believe in your friendship. But how do I know you would not persuade yourself you had to return for the sake of your patient? The police would follow you, and your Hippocratic oath would condemn us all to die. And then there is that sense of guilt I think you feel. They say you sleep with Fortnum's wife. If it is true, trying to atone for that might demand all our deaths.'

'I am not a Christian any longer, León. I don't think in those terms. I have no conscience. I am a simple man.'

'I have never met a simple man. Not even in the confessional though I used to sit there for hours on end. Man was not created simple. When I was a young priest, I used to try to unravel what motives a man or woman had, what temptations and self-delusions. But I soon learned to give all that up, because there was never a straight answer. No one was simple enough for me to understand. In the end I would just say, "Three Our Fathers, Three Hail Marys. Go in peace."'

Doctor Plarr moved impatiently away. He looked once again at his patient. Charley Fortnum was sleeping quietly enough – a drugged contented sleep. They had collected some extra blankets from somewhere to make the coffin bed more comfortable. Doctor Plarr came back into the outer room and stretched on the floor. It seemed to him he had passed a very long day. It was difficult to believe he had taken tea only the afternoon before at the Richmond in the Calle Florida and watched his mother eat her éclairs.

The image of his mother remained with him when he fell asleep and she talked to him in her usual vein of complaint, telling him how his father would not rest like a respectable man of property in the interior of his coffin. They had constantly to shuffle him back inside, and that was no way for a *caballero* to enjoy his eternal peace. Father Galvão was on the way from Rio de Janeiro to see what he could do to persuade him to rest tranquil.

Doctor Plarr opened his eyes. The Indian Miguel lay asleep on the floor beside him, and Father Rivas had taken Pablo's place in the doorway with a gun across his lap. A candle stuck in a saucer cast a shadow of his ears on the wall behind. Doctor Plarr was reminded of the dogs his father would make for him on the nursery wall. For a while he lay awake looking at his old schoolmate. León, León dog-ears, Father dog-ears. He remembered León saying, in one of those long serious conversations which they used to have at fifteen, that there existed only half a dozen careers worth a man's while to follow: a man should be a doctor, a priest, a lawyer (always, of course, on the right side), a poet (if he wrote well enough), or a manual worker. He couldn't remember now what the sixth career was, but it certainly wasn't a kidnapper's or an assassin's.

He whispered across the floor, 'Where are Aquino and the others?'

'This is a military operation,' León said. 'We have been trained by El Tigre. We set our outposts, and we keep our watches at night.'

'And your wife?'

'She is in the town with Pablo. This hut belongs to him, and he is known there. It is safer that way. You need not whisper. An Indian falls asleep, at any moment, whenever he is not required. The only sound which can wake him is hearing his name – or a noise that may be dangerous. Look at him, lying quietly there while we talk. I envy him. That is real peace. Sleep is meant to be like that for all of us, but we have lost the animal touch.'

'Tell me about my father, León. I want the truth.' He had no sooner said it than he remembered how Doctor Humphries always demanded the real truth, even from the Neapolitan waiter, and got only a dusty answer.

'Your father and Aquino were in the same police station a hundred kilometres south-east of Asunción. Near Villarica. He had been there fifteen years, and Aquino only ten months. We did our best, but he was old and sick. El Tigre was against our trying to save your father, but we outvoted him. We were wrong. Perhaps your father would be alive now if we had listened to El Tigre.'

'Yes. Perhaps. In a police station. Dying slowly.'

'It was a question of seconds. A quick dash. He could have done it easily in the days when you knew him, but fifteen years in a police station – you decay there more quickly than in a prison. The General knows there is comradeship in a prison. And so he plants his victims out in separate pots with insufficient earth, and they wither with despair.'

'Did you see my father?'

'No, I was sitting in the escape car with a grenade ready in my lap. Praying.'

'Do you still believe in prayer?'

Father Rivas made no reply and Doctor Plarr fell asleep.

It was daylight when he woke and he went at once into the inner room to look at his patient. Charley Fortnum watched him come in. 'So you really *are* one of them,' he said.

'Yes.'

'I don't understand you, Ted. What has all this got to do with you?'

'I've told you often about my father. I thought these men might help him.'

'You were my friend – and Clara's.'

'I'm not responsible for their mistake. How does your ankle feel?'

'I've suffered much worse from toothache. You've got to get me out of here, Ted. For Clara's sake.'

Doctor Plarr told Fortnum of his visit to the Ambassador. He realized, as he spoke, that it was not an encouraging story. Charley Fortnum took the details slowly in. 'You really got to the old man himself?'

'Yes. He's doing his best.'

'Oh, they'll be relieved in BA when I'm dead. I know that well enough. They won't have to sack me then. An ungentlemanly act. They are all such bloody gentlemen there.'

'Colonel Perez too is doing all he can. It won't be long before they find this place.'

'It will come to the same thing if they do. Do you suppose these fellows will ever let me get out of here alive? Have you spoken to Clara?'

'Yes. She's all right.'

'And the baby?'

'Nothing to worry about.'

'I tried to write her a letter yesterday. I wanted her to have something she could look at afterwards, though I doubt if she would be able to make much out of it. She still finds reading pretty difficult. I thought that somebody might read it aloud to her – perhaps you, Ted. Of course that meant I couldn't say all I felt for her, but I thought if the worst happens you would let her know.'

'Know what?'

'How I feel. I know you are a cold fish, Ted. I've often called you that. I sound sentimental to you, but I've come to think about a lot of things lying here – I've had the hell of a time to fill in. It seems to me that all those years before I met Clara – what damned fools call the prime of life – well, they were pretty empty years, without any purpose, just growing that bloody weed maté to earn some cash – cash for what, for who? I wanted someone I could do something for – not just make a living for myself. There are people who fall back on cats and dogs, but I never cared much for them. Nor horses either. Horses! I could never stand the bloody brutes. All I had to fall back on was Fortnum's Pride. I used to pretend to myself she was alive. I'd give her gas and oil and listen to her innards, but I knew she was less real than one of those dolls which make wee-wee. Of course there was my wife for a while, only she was always so damned superior – there wasn't anything I could ever do for her which she couldn't do better for herself. I'm sorry. I'm talking too much, but you seem closer to me than anyone else because you've met Clara.'

'Talk all you want. There's nothing else we can do in the situation we are in. I'm as much a prisoner here as you are.'

'They won't let you go?'

'No.'

'Then Clara – she's got no one?'

Doctor Plarr said with irritation, 'She can look after herself for a day or two. It's a lot easier for her than for you or me.'

'They won't kill *you*.'

'No, they won't kill me if they can help it.'

'You know there was a time before I met Clara when I thought I'd found somebody I could love. She was a girl at Mother Sanchez's too. She was called María, but she was bad, that one.'

'Somebody knifed her.'

'Yes. Fancy you knowing. Well, it was a little while after that when I saw Clara. I don't know why I hadn't noticed her before. I'm not a good judge of women, I suppose, and María – well, she sort of dazzled me. Clara wasn't beautiful in that way, but she was honest. I could trust her. To make someone like Clara happy is a kind of success isn't it?'

'A modest sort of success.'

'Yes, *you* can say that, but I'm used to failing, and I can't set my sights very high. If things had gone better, who knows . . . I quit drinking for nearly a week when they made me an Honorary Consul, but of course that didn't last. I've still got the letter they sent me from the Embassy. I'd like you to give it to Clara if I don't get out of here. It's in the top left-hand drawer of my desk in the Consulate. You can pick it out easily because of the Royal Arms on the flap. She can keep it to show the child one day.' He tried to shift his position on the coffin and winced.

'Did that hurt?'

'Only a stab.' He gave a low laugh. 'When I think of my wife and Clara – my God, how different two women can be. My wife told me once she'd married me out of pity. Pity for what? She was like a man in the house – knew every damn thing about electricity. She could even fix a washer on a tap. And if I ever had a little one over the right measure she had no sympathy at all. Of course it wasn't reasonable to expect much from her. She was a Christian Scientist and even cancer didn't exist in her eyes, though her father died of it, so you could hardly expect her to believe in a hangover. All the same she needn't have talked so bloody loud when I had one. Her voice went through my head like a drill. Now Clara – Clara's a real woman, she knows when to be silent, God bless her. I'd like to keep her happy till the end.'

'That ought to be easy. She doesn't strike me as a difficult woman.'

'No. But I suppose sooner or later a test always comes. Like those bloody examinations we used to have at school. I'm not exactly insured against failing.'

They might have been talking, Doctor Plarr thought, about two different women – one was the woman whom Charley Fortnum loved – the other was a prostitute from Mother Sanchez's house who had waited in his bed the night before. She had asked him something. And then Colonel Perez had rung the bell. It was no use trying to remember now what it was she had asked him.

Towards the end of the morning Marta came back from the city with a copy of *El Litoral* – the Buenos Aires papers had not yet arrived. The editor had given headlines to Doctor Saavedra's offer – larger headlines, Doctor Plarr considered, than the story was likely to receive elsewhere. He waited to see León's reaction, but he made no comment when he passed the paper without a word to Aquino. Aquino said, 'Who is this Saavedra?'

'A novelist.'

'Why should he think we want a novelist in place of a Consul? What good is a novelist? Anyway he is an Argentinian. Who cares if an Argentinian dies? Not the General. Not even our own President. Nor the world either. One less of the underdeveloped to spend money on.'

At one o'clock Father Rivas turned on the radio and got a news-bulletin from Buenos Aires. Doctor Saavedra's offer was not even mentioned. Was he listening, Doctor Plarr wondered, in that little room near the prison, listening to a silence which must seem to him more humiliating than a rejection? The kidnapping had already ceased to interest the Argentinian public. There were other more exciting events which clamoured for attention. A man had killed the lover of his wife (in a fight with knives of course) – that was a story which never lost appeal to a Latin-American; the usual flying saucers had been reported from the south, there had been an army *coup* in Bolivia, and there was a detailed account of the activities of the Argentina football team in Europe (someone had cut up the referee). At the close of the broadcast the announcer said: 'There is still no news of the kidnapped British Consul. The time to fulfil the conditions set by the kidnappers expires on Sunday at midnight.'

Someone tapped on the outer door. The Indian who was back on guard stood flattened against the wall with his gun held out of sight. There were all six of them in the room at the moment – Father Rivas, Diego, the driver of the car, the pock-marked negro Pablo, Marta and Aquino. Two of them should have been on duty outside, but now in the broad daylight, when everything was quiet, León had allowed them to come in to listen to the news on the radio, a mistake which he was probably regretting. The knock came a second time, and Aquino turned off the radio.

'Pablo,' Father Rivas said.

Unwillingly Pablo approached the door. He pulled a revolver from his pocket, but the priest told him sharply, 'Put it back.'

Doctor Plarr wondered with a sense of resignation, even of relief, whether this was going to be the climax of the whole absurd affair. Would there be a burst of firing when the door opened?

Father Rivas may have had the same thought, for he moved to the centre of the room as though, if this were indeed the end, he wanted to be the first one to die. Pablo pulled the door back.

An old man stood outside. He wavered in the speckled sunlight and stared silently at them with what seemed an unnatural curiosity, until Doctor Plarr realized he was blind from cataract. The old man felt the edge of the door with a hand paper-thin, veined like an old leaf.

'José, what are you doing here?' the negro exclaimed.

'I came to find the father.'

'There is no Father here, José.'

'Oh yes, there is, Pablo. I was sitting by the water tap yesterday and I heard someone say, "The Father who lives with Pablo is a good Father."'

'What do you want a Father for? Anyway he has gone.'

The old man moved his head from one side to the other as though he were listening with each ear in turn, distinguishing the different breaths that sounded in the room, heavy breaths and muted breaths, one of them hurried, another – Diego's – with an asthmatic whistle.

'My wife has died,' he told them. 'When I woke this morning and put my hand out to wake her she was cold as a wet stone. She was all right last night. She made my soup, and it was very good soup. She never told me she was going to die.'

'You must get the priest of the *barrio*, José.'

'He is not a good priest,' the old man said. 'He is the Archbishop's priest. You know that very well, Pablo.'

'The Father who came here was only a visitor. A relation of my cousin in Rosario. He has gone away again.'

'Who are all the people in the room, Pablo?'

'My friends. What do you suppose? We were listening to the radio when you came.'

'My goodness, have you a radio, Pablo? How rich you have become all of a sudden.'

'It is not mine. It belongs to a friend.'

'What a rich friend you have. I need a coffin for my wife, Pablo, and I have no money.'

'You know that will all be arranged, José. We in the *barrio* will see to that.'

'Juan says you bought a coffin from him. You have no wife, Pablo. Let me have your coffin.'

'I need the coffin for myself, José. The doctor has told me I am a very sick man. Juan will make you a coffin and all of us in the *barrio* will pay him.'

'But there is the Mass. I want the Father to say the Mass. I do not want the Archbishop's priest.' The old man took a step into the room, feeling towards them with his hands, palms up.

'There is no Father here. I told you. He has gone back to Rosario.'

Pablo stood between the old man and Father Rivas as though he feared that even in his blindness he could pick a priest out.

'How did you find your way here, José?' Diego asked. 'Your wife was the only eyes you had.'

'Is that Diego? I can see well enough with my hands.' He held them out, fingers pointed first at Diego, then at where the doctor stood, and afterwards he turned them towards Father Rivas. They were like eyes on stalks, of some strange insect. He didn't even look at Pablo. Pablo he took for granted. It was the others, the strangers, whom his hands and ears sought. He gave the impression that he was numbering them like a prison warder, while they stood in silence for his inspection. 'There are four strangers here, Pablo.' He took a step towards Aquino and Aquino shuffled back.

'They are all friends of mine, José.'

'I never knew what a lot of friends you have, Pablo. They are not of this *barrio*.'

'No.'

'They will be welcome all the same to come and see my wife.'

'They will come later, but I must lead you home now, José.'

'Let me hear the radio speak, Pablo. I have never heard a radio speak.'

'Ted!' the voice of Charley Fortnum called from the next room. 'Ted!'

'Who is that calling, Pablo?'

'A sick man.'

'Ted! Where are you, Ted?'

'A gringo!' The old man added with awe, 'I have never known a gringo in the *barrio* before. And a radio. You have become a big man, Pablo.'

Aquino turned the sound of the radio full on to drown the voice of Charley Fortnum and a woman's voice spoke loudly of the outstanding merits of Kellogg's Rice Krispies. 'Popping with life and vigour,' the voice said. 'Golden and Honey Sweet.'

Doctor Plarr went quickly into the back room. He whispered, 'What do you want, Charley?'

'I dreamed someone was in the room. He was going to cut my throat. I was damn scared. I wanted to be sure you were still here.'

'Don't speak again. There's a stranger here. If you speak you will put all our lives in danger. I'll come back to you when he's gone.'

In the other room, as he returned, a woman's tinned voice was saying, 'She will love the scented smoothness of your cheek.'

The old man said, 'It is like a miracle. To think a box is able to say beautiful things like that.'

Then someone began to sing a romantic ballad of love and death.

'Here, José, touch the radio. Hold it in your hands.' They all felt easier when the old man's hands were occupied – not turning to look at them. He held the radio close to his ears as though he were afraid to miss a single one of the beautiful words it spoke.

Father Rivas took Pablo aside. He whispered, 'I will go with him if you think it will do any good.'

'No,' Pablo said, 'all the *barrio* will be gathered at his hut to see the body of his wife. They will know he has gone to fetch a priest. If the Archbishop's priest comes, he will want to know who you are. He will want to see your papers. He might send for the police.'

Aquino said, 'An accident should happen to the old one before he gets back.'

'No,' Pablo said, 'I will not agree to that. I have known him since I was a child.'

'Anyway,' the driver Diego gave his opinion in a sullen voice, 'to stop his mouth would be too late now. How did the woman at the water tap know a priest was here?'

Pablo said, 'I have told no one.'

'There are never any secrets for long in a *barrio*,' Father Rivas said.

'He knows of the radio and the gringo,' Diego said. 'That is the worst of all. We ought to move from here quickly.'

'You would have to carry Fortnum on a stretcher,' Doctor Plarr said.

The old man shook the radio. He complained, 'It does not rattle.'

'Why should it rattle?' Pablo asked.

'There is a voice in it.'

'Come, José,' Pablo said, 'it is time for you to go back to your poor wife.'

'But the Father,' José said, 'I want the Father to anoint her.'

'I tell you, José, there is no Father here. The Archbishop's priest will do that.'

'He never comes when we send for him. He is always busy at a meeting. It will be many hours before he comes, and where will the soul of my poor wife be wandering all that while?'

Father Rivas said, 'She will come to no harm, old man. God does not wait for the Archbishop's priest.'

The man's hands turned quickly towards him. He said, 'You – you there who spoke – you have a priest's voice.'

'No, no, I am not a priest. If you had your sight you would see my wife is here beside me. Speak to him, Marta.'

She said in a low voice, 'Yes. This is my husband, old one.'

Pablo said, 'Come. I will take you home.'

The old man clung obstinately to the radio. The music was loud, but not loud enough for him. He pressed it against his ear.

'He told us he came here alone,' Diego whispered. 'How could he? Suppose someone led him here on purpose and left him at the door . . .'

'He has been here twice before with his wife. The blind remember a path well. Anyway if I take him home I can tell if someone is waiting for him or watching.'

'If you do not return in two hours,' Aquino said, 'if they stop you . . . then we shall kill the Consul. You can tell them that.' He added, 'If only I had aimed at his back yesterday, we would be far away by now.'

'I have heard a radio,' the old man said with astonishment. He laid it down gently like a fragile thing. 'If only I could tell my wife . . .'

'She knows,' Marta said, 'she knows everything.'

'Come, José.' The negro took the old man's right hand and pulled him towards the door, but he was stubborn. He twisted round, and with his free hand he seemed to be counting them over again. He said, 'What a big party you have here, Pablo. Give me something to drink. Give me some *caña*.'

'We have nothing to drink here, José.' He pulled the blind man out and the Indian closed the door quickly behind them. For a moment they felt relief like a breath of wind cooling the thunder-heavy day.

'What do you think, León?' Doctor Plarr asked. 'Was he a spy?'

'How can I tell?'

'I think you should have gone with the poor man, Father,' Marta said. 'His wife is dead and there is no priest to help him.'

'If I had gone I would have endangered all of us.'

'You heard what he said. The Archbishop's priest cares nothing for the poor.'

'And do you think I care nothing for them? I am risking my life for them, Marta.'

'I know that, Father. I was not accusing you. You are a good man.'

'She has been dead for hours. What difference can a little oil make now? Ask the doctor.'

'Oh, I deal only with the living,' Doctor Plarr said.

The woman touched her husband's hand. 'I did not want to offend you, Father. I am your woman.'

'You are not my woman. You are my wife,' Father Rivas said with angry impatience.

'If you say so.'

'I have explained to you how it is over and over again.'

'I am a stupid woman, Father. I do not always understand. Does it matter so much? A woman, a wife . . .'

'It does matter. Human dignity matters, Marta. A man who feels lust takes a woman for the period of his desire, but I have taken you for life. That is marriage.'

'If you say so, Father.'

Father Rivas said in a voice which sounded tired with having eternally to teach the same thing, 'Not if I say so, Marta. It is the truth.'

'Yes, Father. I would feel better if sometimes I could hear you pray . . .'

'Perhaps I pray more often than you know.'

'Please do not be angry, Father. I am very proud that you chose me.' She turned on the others who were in the room. 'He could have slept with any woman he liked in our *barrio* in Asunción. He is a good man. If he did not go back with the old one, he must have had a good reason. Only, please Father . . .'

'I wish you would not call me Father all the time. I am your husband, Marta. Your husband.'

'Yes, but I would be so proud if just once I could see you as you used to be . . . all dressed at the altar . . . turning to bless us, Father.'

The word slipped out again; she put her hand to her mouth too late to stop it.

'You know I cannot do that.'

'If I could see you like I saw you in Asunción . . . in white for Easter . . .'

'You will never see me again like that.'

León Rivas turned away. 'Aquino,' he said, 'Diego, go back to your posts. We will relieve you in two hours. You, Marta, go back to the town and see if the newspapers have come yet from Buenos Aires.'

'You had better buy more whisky for Fortnum,' Doctor Plarr said. 'His sort of measure soon empties a bottle.'

'This time,' Father Rivas said, 'no one is to share it.'

'What are you hinting at?' Aquino asked.

'I am not hinting at anything. Do you think I could not smell your breath yesterday?'

At four it was Aquino who turned on the radio, but this time there was not a single reference to the kidnapping. It was as though they had been wiped off the world's memory. 'They do not even mention *your* disappearance,' Aquino said to Doctor Plarr.

'They may not know of it yet,' Doctor Plarr said. 'I am losing count of the days. Is it Thursday? I remember I gave my secretary a long weekend off. She will be busy somewhere gathering indulgences. For the souls in purgatory. I hope we shall not have the benefit of them.'

An hour later Pablo returned. No one had shown any suspicion, but he had stayed away longer than he intended because he was bound to join the queue which was waiting to pay the last respects to the dead woman. When he left, the Archbishop's priest had still not arrived. The only anxiety he had felt was when José chatted to everyone about the radio. The old man was immensely proud because he was the only one there who had ever listened to a radio and he had actually held one in his hands. For the time being he seemed to have forgotten about the gringo.

'He will remember soon enough,' Diego said. 'We ought to get away from here.'

Pablo said, 'How can we go? With a wounded man.'

'El Tigre would say "Kill him now",' Aquino argued.

'You had your chance,' Diego said.

'Where is Father Rivas?' Pablo asked.

'On guard.'

'There should be two of you out there.'

'A man must have a drink. My maté was finished. It was Marta's job to bring more, but Father Rivas sent her into the town to buy whisky for the gringo. He must never be left thirsty.'

'Aquino, you go.'

'I take no orders from you, Pablo.'

If this inaction goes on much longer, Doctor Plarr thought, they will be fighting each other.

It was evening by the time Marta returned. The papers from Buenos Aires had arrived and in the *Nación* a few lines were devoted to Doctor Saavedra, though the reporter found it necessary to remind his readers who Saavedra was. 'The novelist,' he wrote, 'who is best known by his first book, *The Silent Heart*,' getting the title wrong.

The evening seemed interminably drawn out. It was as though, sitting there for hours in silence, they formed part of a universal silence all around them, the silence of the radio, the silence of the authorities, even the silence of nature. No dogs barked. The birds had ceased to sing, and when rain began to fall it was in heavy spaced drops, as infrequent as their words – the silence seemed all the deeper between the drops. Somewhere far off there was a storm, but the storm was happening across the river in another country.

Whenever any of them spoke, the danger of a quarrel arose over even the most innocent remark. The Indian alone was unaffected. He sat and smiled with gentle content as he oiled his gun. He cleaned the crevices of the bolt with tenderness and with sensuous pleasure like a woman attending to her first baby. When Marta gave them soup, Aquino complained of a lack of salt, and Doctor Plarr thought for a moment she was going to throw a plate full of the despised soup in his face. He left them and went into the inner room.

Charley Fortnum said, 'If only I had something to read . . .'

Doctor Plarr said, 'There's not enough light to see by.' Only one candle lit the room.

'Surely they could give me a few more candles.'

'They don't want any light to show outside. Most people in this *barrio* sleep as soon as it's dark . . . or make love.'

'Thank God there's still plenty of whisky. Have a glass. It's an odd relationship, isn't it? They shoot me down like a dog and then they give me whisky. This time I didn't even pay for it. Is there any news? When they put the radio on they turn it so damn low I can't hear a thing.'

'There's no news at all. How are you feeling?'

'Pretty awful. Do you think I'll live to see the end of this bottle?'

'Of course.'

'Then be an optimist and give yourself a bigger dose.'

They drank together in the silence which they had only momentarily broken. Doctor Plarr wondered where Clara was. At the camp? At the Consulate? At last he said, 'What made you marry Clara, Charley?'

'I told you – I wanted to help her.'

'You needn't have married her to do that.'

'If I hadn't she'd have lost a lot in taxes when I died. Besides I wanted a child. I love her, Ted. I want her to feel secure. I wish you knew her a bit better. A doctor sees only the outside – oh, and the inside too, I suppose, but you know what I mean. To me she's like . . . like . . .' He couldn't find the word he wanted and Doctor Plarr was tempted to supply it. She's like a looking-glass, he thought, a looking-glass which has been manufactured by Mother Sanchez to reflect any man who looks at her – to reflect Charley's fumbling tenderness with her own imitation of it and my . . . my . . . but the right word failed him too. It certainly wasn't 'passion'. What was the question she had asked him just before he left her? She reflected even one's suspicion of her. He was angry with her as though in some obscure way she had done him an injury. One could use her to shave in, he thought, remembering Gruber's sunglasses.

'You'll laugh at me,' Charley Fortnum rambled on, 'but she reminds me a bit of Mary Pickford in those old silent movies . . . I don't mean her face, of course, but, well, a sort of . . . I suppose you might call it innocence.'

'Then I hope the child turns out to be a girl. A boy like Mary Pickford would hardly make his way in the world.'

'I don't mind which it is, but Clara seems to want a boy.' He added with self-mockery, 'Perhaps she wants him to take after me.'

Doctor Plarr had a savage desire to tell him the whole truth. It was only the wounded body which stopped him, stretched helplessly out on the coffin lid. To disturb a patient would be unprofessional. Charley Fortnum raised his glass of whisky and added, 'Not as I am now, of course. Cheers.'

Doctor Plarr heard the voices rise higher in the next room.

'What's happening out there?' Charley Fortnum asked.

'They are quarrelling among themselves.'

'What about?'

'Probably about you.'

Chapter 2

JUST after nine o'clock on Friday morning a helicopter came flying low down over the *barrio*. It went back and forth in regular lines, like a pencil along a ruler, up and down every muddy track, just above the trees, tireless and probing. Doctor Plarr was reminded of the way his own fingers had to make tracks sometimes along a patient's body, seeking the exact spot of pain.

Father Rivas told Pablo to join Diego and Marta who were on guard outside. 'The whole *barrio* will be watching,' he said. 'They will notice if in this one hut people show indifference.' He told Aquino to keep watch on Fortnum in the inner room. Though there was no possible way of Fortnum to signal his presence there, Father Rivas was taking no chances.

Doctor Plarr and the priest sat in silence and watched the roof of the room as though the machine at any moment might come crashing through on top of them. After the helicopter had passed, they could hear the rustle of the leaves falling like rain. When that sound ceased they stayed dumb, waiting for the chopper to return.

Pablo and Diego came in. Pablo reported, 'They were taking photographs.'

'Of this hut?'

'Of the whole *barrio*.'

'Then they have seen your car,' Doctor Plarr said. 'They will wonder what a car is doing here.'

'We have it well hidden,' Father Rivas said. 'We can only hope . . .'

'They were making a very careful search,' Pablo told them.

'It would be better to shoot Fortnum now,' Diego said.

'Our ultimatum does not expire till Sunday midnight.'

'They have rejected it already. The helicopter shows that.'

Doctor Plarr said, 'Extend your ultimatum a few days. You have to give time for my publicity to work. You are in no immediate danger. The police dare not attack you.'

'El Tigre set the time limit,' Father Rivas said.

'You *must* have some way of communicating with him, whatever you say.'

'We have none.'

'You sent news of Fortnum.'

'That line was cut immediately.'

'Then act yourself. Have someone telephone *El Litoral*. Give them another week.'

'Another week for the police to find us,' Diego said.

'Perez dare not search too closely. He does not want to find a dead man.'

The chopper became audible again. They heard it from a long way off, hardly louder than a man humming. The first time it had travelled from east to west. Now it tracked above the trees going from north to south and back again. Pablo and Diego returned into the yard, and their long wait was resumed to the sound of the dropping leaves. At last silence came back.

The two men returned. 'They were taking more photographs,' Diego said. 'They must have taken a picture of every path and hut in the *barrio*.'

'More than the city council ever did,' the negro said. 'Perhaps after this they will realize we need more water taps.'

Father Rivas called Marta in from the yard and whispered instructions to her. Doctor Plarr tried to hear what he was saying, but he could hear nothing until the voices rose.

'No,' Marta said, 'no, I will not leave you, Father.'

'Those are my orders.'

'Did you tell me I was your wife or your woman?'

'Of course you are my wife.'

'Oh yes, you say that, it's easy to say that, yet you treat me like your woman. You say "Go away" because you have finished with me. I know very well now I am only your woman. No priest would marry us. They all refused you. Even your friend, Father Antonio.'

'I have explained a dozen times to you a priest is not necessary for a marriage. A priest is only a witness. People marry each other. Our vow is all that counts. Our intention.'

'How can *I* tell what your intention was? Perhaps you just wanted a woman to sleep with. Perhaps I am your whore. You treat me like a whore when you tell me to go away and leave you.'

Father Rivas raised his hand as though he wanted to strike her and then he turned away.

'If I am not your sin, Father, why is it you will not say Mass for us? We are all in danger of death, Father. We need a Mass. And that poor woman in the *barrio* who died . . . Even the gringo in there . . . He needs your prayers too.'

The old schoolboy desire to mock at León came back to Doctor Plarr. 'It's a pity you ever left the Church,' he said. 'You see – they are losing confidence in you.'

Father Rivas looked up at him with the inflamed eyes of a dog who defends a bone. 'I never told you I had left the Church. How can I leave the Church? The Church is the world. The Church is this *barrio*, this room. There is only one way any of us can leave the Church and that is to die.' He made the gesture of a man who is tired of useless discussion. 'Not even then, if what we sometimes believe is true.'

'She only asked you to pray. Have you forgotten how to pray? I certainly have. I can never get further than Hail Mary, and then I mix the words up with an English nursery rhyme, "Mary, Mary, quite contrary."'

Father Rivas said, 'I never knew how to pray.'

'What are you saying, Father? He does not know what he is saying,' Marta told them, as though she were defending a child who had used some foul expression, picked up in the street.

'A prayer for the sick. A prayer for rain. Do you want those? Oh, I know all those by heart, but those are not prayers. Call them petitions if you want to give that mumbo-jumbo a name. You might just as well write them down in a letter and get your neighbours to sign it too and stick it in a post-box addressed to the Lord Almighty. Nobody will ever deliver your letter. Nobody will ever read it. Oh, of course, now and then there may be a coincidence. For once a doctor will give the right medicine and a child recovers. Or a storm comes when you want it. Or the wind changes.'

'All the same,' Aquino told them from the doorway of the other room, 'I used to pray in the police station. I prayed I would have a girl in bed with me again. You are not going to tell me that was not a real prayer. And it worked too. The first day I was out I had a girl. It was in a field while you were off buying food in a village. My prayer was answered, Father. Even if it was in a field and not in a bed.'

Like me, Doctor Plarr thought, he is a picador. He pricks the bull's hide to make the beast more active before he dies. The repetitions of the word 'Father' were like darts inserted to pierce the skin. Why do we so want to destroy him – or are we hoping to destroy ourselves? – it's a cruel sport.

'What are you doing out here, Aquino? I told you to stay and watch the prisoner.'

'The helicopter has gone. What can he do? He is only writing a letter to his woman.'

'You gave him a pen? I took away his pen myself when he was brought in.'

'What harm can a letter do?'

'They were my orders. If you all start disobeying orders there is no safety for any of us. Diego, Pablo, get outside again. If El Tigre were here . . .'

'But he is not here, Father,' Aquino said. 'He is somewhere in safety eating well and drinking well. He was not at the police station either when you rescued me. Is he never going to risk his own life like he risks ours?'

Father Rivas pushed him to one side and went on into the inner room. Doctor Plarr found it hard to recognize the boy who had explained the Trinity to him. In the innumerable lines of premature age which criss-crossed the face he thought he could detect a tangle of agonies, like a tangle of fighting snakes.

Charley Fortnum was propped on his left elbow. His bandaged leg stuck out over the side of the coffin, and he wrote slowly, painfully; he didn't look up. Father Rivas said, 'Whom are you writing to?'

'My wife.'

'It must be difficult to write like that.'

'It's taken me a quarter of an hour to do two sentences. I asked your man Aquino to write for me. But he refused. He's been angry with me ever since he shot me. He won't talk to me any more. Why? You would think I'd done him an injury.'

'Perhaps you have.'

'What injury?'

'Perhaps he feels betrayed. He did not believe you had the courage to trick him.'

'Courage? Me? I haven't the courage of a mouse, Father. I wanted to see my wife again, that's all.'

'Who is going to give her this letter?'

'Doctor Plarr perhaps. If you let him go after I am dead. He can read it aloud to her. She doesn't read very well and my handwriting is bad at the best of times.'

'If you like I will write the letter for you.'

'Thank you a lot. I'd be grateful if you would. I'd rather it was you than anyone else. A letter like this is a sort of secret. Like a confession. And after all you *are* a priest.'

Father Rivas took the letter and sat down on the floor beside the coffin.

'I've forgotten what I wrote last.'

Father Rivas read, '"Do not worry, my darling, about being alone with a child. It is better for him to be alone with a mother than with a father. I know that well. I was left alone with my father and it was never any fun. Always horses, horses . . ." That is all. You have written nothing after "horses".'

'In the situation I'm in,' Charley Fortnum said, 'I suppose you think I ought to find some way to forgive. Even my father. Perhaps he wasn't such a bad chap after all. Children hate too easily. Better leave out that stuff about the horses, Father.'

Father Rivas drew a line through the words.

'Put instead – but what? I'm damned unused to writing anything personal, that's the trouble. Give me a drop of whisky, Father. It may help the brain to tick, what there is left of it – my brain, I mean.'

Father Rivas poured him out a drink.

'I prefer Long John,' Charley Fortnum said, 'but this stuff you've brought me is not all that bad. If I stay here long enough I'll get quite a taste for Argentinian whisky, but it's more tricky than real Scotch to know the right measure. You wouldn't understand what I mean, Father, but every drink has its right measure – not water, of course. Water's not meant for drinking. It rusts the inside or gives you typhoid. It's not good for man or beast except those bloody horses. Is it any good asking you to have a small one with me?'

'No. I am, as you say, on duty. Do you want to go on with your letter?'

'Yes, of course. I was just waiting a while to let the whisky work. You've cut out that bit about horses, haven't you? What ought I to say next? You see I want to talk to her quite simply, as if we were alone together, on the verandah, at the camp, but words never come easily to me – not on paper, I mean. I expect you understand. After all you are married too in a way, Father.'

'Yes, I am married too,' Father Rivas said.

'But where I'm going there's no marriage, or so you priests always tell us. It seems a bit of a waste when I've found the right girl so bloody late in the day. There ought to be visiting days in heaven, so as to give us something to look forward to from time to time. Like they have in prison. If there's nothing to look forward to, it can't be much of a heaven. You see I even get theological with the right measure of whisky. Where *had* I got to? Oh, the horses. You are quite sure we left out the old bastard's horses?'

Doctor Plarr came in from the outer room; his feet made no sound on the earth floor, and neither man looked up. They were busy over the letter. He stood watching them in silence by the door. They looked to him like old friends.

'"Let the child go to the local school,"' Charley Fortnum dictated. '"But if he's a boy don't send him on to that grand English school in BA where I went. I was never happy there. Let him be a real Argentinian like you are – not a half and half like me." Have you got that down, Father?'

'Yes. Had you not better say something to her about the change in the writing? She may wonder . . .'

'I doubt if she'd notice a thing like that. And Plarr can always explain to her how it was. My God, writing a letter is a bit like getting Fortnum's Pride started on a rainy morning. One jerk after another. You begin to think the engine's beginning to run and then it cuts out again. Oh well, Father, write – "Lying here, I think of you most of the time, and the baby too. At home you are always on my right side, and I can put my right hand on your stomach and feel the little bastard kick, but there's no right side here. The bed's too narrow. Quite comfortable, of course. I've nothing really to complain about. I'm luckier than most men."' He paused, '"Luckier . . ."' and took the bit between his teeth. '"Before I knew you, my darling, I was a finished man. A man has to have some sort of ambition to live by. Even a millionaire wants to make another million. But before you lived with me there was nothing I could look forward to, except the right measure, of course. My maté was never exactly an exhibition crop. Then I found you and I had something I really wanted to do. I wanted to make you content and safe, and suddenly there was this child of ours. We were in business together. I didn't expect to live long. All I wanted was to make sure that those first years were all right – the first years are important to the child, they sort of set a pattern. You mustn't think though I've given up hope – I will find a way out of here yet in spite of them."' He paused. 'Of course that's only a joke, Father. How can I escape? But I don't want her to think I'm depressed. My God, Fortnum's Pride did begin to work for a while, we nearly got out of that ditch, but I can't manage any more now. Just write, "My darling girl, all my love."'

'Are you sure you have finished?'

'Yes. I think so. It's damned hard work writing letters. To think sometimes on a library shelf you see "Collected Letters" of somebody or other. Poor bugger. Two volumes of them perhaps. There *is* something I forgot. Just put it at the end. With a PS. You see, Father, this is the first child she's had. She hasn't any experience. People say a woman knows by instinct. I doubt it though. Write this – "Please don't give the child sweets. They are bad for the teeth, they pretty well ruined mine, and if you are in doubt about anything at all ask Doctor Plarr. He's a good doctor and a good friend." That's all I can think of, Father.' He closed his eyes. 'Perhaps I will manage something more later on. I'd like to add a word or two just before you kill me, the famous last words, but I'm too damned tired to think of any more now.'

'You must not give up hope, Señor Fortnum.'

'What hope? Since I married Clara, I've always been afraid of dying. There's only one happy way to die and that's together, and even if you hadn't interfered, I'd have been too old for it to happen that way. I can hardly bear it when I think she will be alone and frightened when her turn comes to die. I want to be there holding her hand and telling her it's all right, Clara, I'm dying too, don't be scared – it's not all that bad dying. I'm crying now, you can see for yourself that I'm not a brave man. All the same it's not self-pity, Father. I just don't want her to be alone when she dies.'

Father Rivas made a gesture – it might have been an attempt to sketch a blessing in the air which he had forgotten how to give. 'God will be there,' he said without conviction.

'Oh, you can have your God. Sorry, Father, but I don't see any sign of him around, do you?'

Doctor Plarr had walked back into the outer room in a state of unreasoning rage. It seemed to him that every word of the letter he had heard Fortnum dictate was a reproach aimed unjustly at himself. He was so absorbed in his anger that he strode straight towards the outer door until he felt the Indian's gun pressing into his stomach and stopped. The child, always the child, he thought, a good friend, don't give the child sweets, feel him kicking. He stood there with the gun stuck against his stomach and spat his bile upon the ground.

'What is the matter, Eduardo?' Aquino asked.

'I'm tired to death of being cooped up here. Why the hell can't you trust me and let me go?'

'We need a doctor for Fortnum. If you went away from here you could not come back.'

'There's no more I can do for Fortnum, and I'm in a bloody prison here.'

'You would not feel that way if you had been in a real prison. This is liberty to me.'

'A hundred square metres of dirt floor.'

'I was used to nine. So the world has grown a lot larger for me.'

'I suppose you can write your poems in any bloody hole, but I have nothing, nothing, to do. I'm a doctor. One patient is not enough.'

'I never write poems now. They were just part of the prison life. I wrote verses because they were easy to memorize. It was a way of communicating, that was all. Now I have all the paper I want and a pen and I cannot write a line. Who cares? I live instead.'

'You call this life? You can't even walk as far as the town.'

'I never cared very much for walking. I have always been a lazy man.'

Father Rivas came in. 'Where are Pablo and Diego?' he asked.

'On guard,' Aquino said. 'You sent them out yourself.'

'Marta, take one of them with you and go into the town. It may be the last chance we shall have. Buy as many provisions as you can. Enough for three days. Easily portable.'

'What is worrying you?' Aquino asked. 'You look as if you had heard bad news.'

'I am worried about the helicopter – about the blind man too. The ultimatum ends on Sunday night, and the police may be here long before then.'

'And afterwards?' asked Doctor Plarr.

'We kill him and we make a run for it. We must have food to take with us. We shall have to keep away from towns.'

'Do you play chess, Eduardo?' Aquino asked.

'Yes. Why?'

'I have a pocket set.'

'Then for God's sake let's have a game.'

They sat on the dirt floor with the tiny board between them. Setting out the pieces Doctor Plarr said, 'I used to play nearly every week at the Bolívar with an old man called Humphries. I was playing with him there the night you caught the wrong fish.'

'A good player?'

'He was better than me that night.'

Aquino was a slapdash player, moving too rapidly, and when Doctor Plarr hesitated over a move, he began to hum. 'Do be quiet,' Doctor Plarr appealed.

'Ha ha. I have got you, have I?'

'On the contrary. Check.'

'I can soon cure that.'

'Check again. And mate.'

He won two games in succession.

'You are too good for me,' Aquino said. 'I ought to take on Señor Fortnum.'

'I have never seen him play.'

'You are a great friend of his?'

'In a way.'

'And of his wife?'

'Yes.'

Aquino lowered his voice. 'That baby he is always talking about – is it yours?'

Doctor Plarr said, 'I am sick to death of hearing about that baby. Do you want another game?'

As they were putting out their pieces they heard the sound of a rifle shot, very far off. Aquino seized his gun, but there was no repetition. Doctor Plarr sat on the floor with a black rook in his hand. It grew damp with sweat. Nobody spoke. At last Father Rivas said, 'Only someone shooting at a wild duck. We begin to think everything has to do with our affair.'

'Yes,' Aquino said, 'even the helicopter might have belonged to the city council if you can forget the military markings.'

'How long is it before the next radio news?'

'Another two hours. There might be a special announcement though.'

'We cannot leave the radio on all the time. It is the only radio in the *barrio*. Too many people know about it already.'

'Then Aquino and I might as well have our game,' Doctor Plarr said. 'I will give you a rook.'

'I do not want your rook. I will beat you in a straight match. I am out of practice, that is all.'

Over Aquino's shoulder Doctor Plarr could see Father Rivas. A small and dusty object, he looked rather like a shrunken mummy dug out of the ground, together with a few treasured possessions which had been buried with him – a revolver, a tattered paper volume. Was it a missal? Doctor Plarr wondered. A book of prayers? With a sense of extreme boredom he repeated his old refrain, 'Check and mate.'

'You play too well for me,' Aquino said.

'What are you reading, León?' Doctor Plarr asked. 'Do you still read your breviary?'

'I gave that up years ago.'

'What have you got there?'

'Only a detective story. An English detective story.'

'A good one?'

'I am no judge of that. The translation is not very good, and with this sort of book I can always guess the end.'

'Then where is the interest?'

'Oh, there is a sort of comfort in reading a story where one knows what the end will be. The story of a dream-world where justice is always done. There were no detective stories in the age of faith – an interesting point when you think of it. God used to be the only detective when people believed in Him. He was law. He was order. He was good. Like your Sherlock Holmes. It was He who pursued the wicked man for punishment and discovered all. But now people like the General make law and order. Electric shocks on the genitals. Aquino's fingers. Keep the poor ill-fed, and they do not have the energy to revolt. I prefer the detective. I prefer God.'

'Do you still believe in him?'

'In a way. Sometimes. It is not so easy as all that to answer yes or no. Certainly he is not the same God as the one they taught us at school or in the seminary.'

'Your personal God,' Doctor Plarr said, teasing again. 'I thought that was a Protestant heresy.'

'Why not? Is it any worse for that? Is it any less likely to be true? We no longer kill heretics – only political prisoners.'

'Charley Fortnum is your political prisoner.'

'Yes.'

'So you are a bit like the General yourself, León.'

'I do not torture him.'

'Are you sure of that?'

Marta returned from the town alone. She asked, 'Is Diego here?'

'No,' Father Rivas said, 'surely he went with you – or did you take Pablo?'

'He stayed behind in the town. He said he would catch me up. He had to collect petrol. The car is nearly dry, he said, and there is no reserve.'

Aquino said, 'That is not true.'

Marta said, 'He was very frightened by the helicopter. By the old man too.'

'Do you think he has gone to the police?' Doctor Plarr asked.

'No,' Father Rivas said, 'I will never believe that.'

'Then where is he?' Aquino demanded.

'He may have been arrested on suspicion. He may have gone with a woman. Who knows? Anyway there is nothing for us to do. We can only wait. How long now before the news comes on?'

'Twenty-two minutes,' Aquino said.

'Tell Pablo to come in. If they have spotted us, there is no point in leaving him outside to be picked off alone. Better to keep together at the end.'

Father Rivas took up his detective story again. He said, 'The only thing we can do is hope.' He added, 'What a wonderfully peaceful world this one is. Everything is so well ordered. There are no problems. There is an answer to every question.'

'What are you talking about?' Doctor Plarr asked.

'The world in this detective story. Can you tell me what Bradshaw means?'

'Bradshaw?'

It seemed to Doctor Plarr that this was the first time he had seen León so relaxed since the long arguments they used to have when they were schoolboys together. Had he, as the situation grew darker, lost the sense of responsibility, like a roulette player who abandons his chart and no longer bothers even to watch the ball? He should never have tried to be a man of action: as a priest at a bedside he would have been most at his ease waiting passively for the end. 'It's an English family name,' Doctor Plarr said. 'My father had a friend Bradshaw who used to write to him from a town called Chester.'

'This one seems to be a man who knows all the trains in England by heart. The trains never take more than a few hours to go anywhere. And they always arrive on time. The detective only has to consult Bradshaw to know exactly when . . . What a strange world your father came from. Here we are little more than eight hundred kilometres from Buenos Aires and the train is supposed to take a day and a half to make the journey, but it is often two or three days late. This English detective is a very impatient man. He is pacing the platform of the station in London, waiting for the train from Edinburgh – that is nearly as far as Buenos Aires surely? – and the train is half an hour late, according to this man Bradshaw, and yet the detective thinks something must be wrong. Half an hour late!' Father Rivas exclaimed. 'It is like when I was a child and I would be late in coming home from school and my mother would worry and my father used to say, "But what could happen to the child between here and the school house?"'

Aquino said with impatience, 'And Diego? Diego is late too, and I tell you I worry.'

Pablo came into the hut. Aquino told him at once, 'Diego has gone.'

'Where to?'

'To the police perhaps.'

Marta said, 'All the way into town he talked about the helicopter. And when we came to the river – oh, he did not say anything, but it was the way he looked. At the ferry-landing he said to me, "That is strange. There are no police controlling the passengers." I said to him, "And the other side – can you see all the way across there? And can you tell a policeman when he is out of uniform?"'

Pablo said, 'What do you think, Father? I introduced him to you. I feel ashamed. I told you he was a good man to drive the car. And a brave man.'

Father Rivas said, 'There is no reason to start worrying yet.'

'I have to worry. He was my countryman. All you others come from across the border. You can trust each other. I feel as though I were Diego's brother and my brother had betrayed you. You should not have come to me for help.'

'What could we have done without you, Pablo? There is nowhere in Paraguay where we could have hidden the Ambassador. Even taking him across the river would have been too dangerous. Perhaps it was a mistake to include any of your countrymen in our group, but El Tigre never thought of us as foreigners here in Argentina. He does not think in terms of Paraguayans, Peruvians, Bolivians, Argentinians. I think he would like to call us all Americans, if it were not for that place up there in the north.'

Pablo said, 'Diego asked me once why there were only Paraguayans on your list of prisoners to be released. I told him – these are the most urgent cases. Men who have been in prison more than ten years. The next time we strike together perhaps it will be for our own people, like the time in Salta. There were Paraguayans who helped us then. I do not believe he will go to the police, Father.'

'Nor do I, Pablo.'

'We have only a little time to wait,' Aquino said. 'They must surrender – or we leave a dead Consul in the river.'

'How long before the news?'

'Ten minutes,' Doctor Plarr said.

Father Rivas picked up his detective story, but to Doctor Plarr, watching him closely, he seemed to be reading with unnatural slowness. He had fastened his eyes on one passage and he kept them there a long time before he turned the leaf. His lips moved a little. He might have been praying – in secrecy perhaps, because prayers by a priest at a deathbed are the last resort and the patient must not be allowed to hear them. All of us are his patients, Doctor Plarr thought, we are all about to die.

The doctor had no belief that things would turn out well. From a false equation you get only a chain of errors. His own death might be one of the errors, for afterwards people would say he had followed in his father's steps, but they would be wrong – that had not been his intention.

He wondered with an unpleasant itch of anxiety and curiosity about his child. The child too was the result of an error, a carelessness on his part, but he had never before felt any responsibility. He had considered the child to be a useless part of Clara like her appendix, perhaps a diseased appendix which ought to be removed. He had suggested an abortion, but the idea had frightened her – perhaps there had been too many unprofessional abortions in the house of Mother Sanchez. Now, waiting for the news bulletin on the radio, he said to himself: the poor little bastard, if only I could have made some sort of arrangement for it. What sort of a mother was Clara likely to prove? Would she go back to Mother Sanchez and have the child brought up as the spoilt brat of a brothel? That would probably be better than life with his mother in B A stuffed with *dulce de leche* in the Calle Florida among the international voices of the well-to-do. He thought of the tangle of its ancestry, and for the first time in the complexity of that tangle the child became real to him – it was no longer just one more wet piece of flesh like any other torn out of the body with a cord which had to be cut. This cord could never be cut. It joined the child to two very different grandfathers – a cane-cutter in Tucumán and an old English liberal who had been shot dead in the yard of a police station in Paraguay. The cord joined it to a father who was a provincial doctor, to a mother from a brothel, to an uncle who had walked away one day from the cane-fields to disappear into the waste of a continent, to two grandmothers . . . There was no end to the tangle which must constrict the tiny form like the swaddling bandages with which in old days they used to bind the limbs of a newborn child. A cold fish, Charley Fortnum had called him. What effect did it have on a child to have a cold fish for a father? It might have been better if they could have exchanged fathers. A cold fish would have been his own proper parentage rather than a father who had cared enough to die. He would have liked the little bastard to believe in something, but he was not the kind of father who could transmit belief in a god or a cause. He called across the dirt floor, 'Do you really believe in God the Father Almighty, León?'

'What? I am sorry. I did not hear. This detective is a very cunning man, so there must be a good reason why the train from Edinburgh is half an hour late.'

'I asked if you believed sometimes in God the Father?'

'You have asked me that before. You do not really want to know. You are only mocking me, Eduardo. All the same I will give you my answer when there is no more hope. You will not be ready to laugh then. Excuse me a moment – the story has become more interesting – the Edinburgh express is steaming into a station called King's Cross. King's Cross. Would that be symbolic?'

'No. Just the name of a station in London.'

'Be quiet, both of you.' Aquino turned the radio up and they listened to the international news which was beamed at that hour from Buenos Aires. The announcer described the visit by the Secretary General of the United Nations to West Africa; fifty hippies had been expelled with violence from Majorca; there was yet another rise in taxes on cars imported to Argentina; a retired general had died in Córdoba at the age of eighty; a few bombs had exploded in Bogotá, and of course the Argentine football team was continuing its violent progress through Europe.

'They have forgotten us,' Aquino said.

'If only we could believe that,' Father Rivas said. 'To stay here . . . forgotten . . . forever. It would not be so bad a fate, would it?'

Chapter 3

ON Saturday at midday the news came for which they had been waiting so long, but they had to listen patiently until the end of the bulletin. It was the policy of all the governments concerned to play down the importance of the Fortnum affair. Buenos Aires quoted moderate expressions of British opinion. *The Times* of London for instance had stated that an Argentinian novelist (whose name was not given) had offered himself in exchange for the Consul, and a BBC broadcast put the affair, as the Argentinian commentator remarked, in proper perspective. A Junior Minister had referred to the matter briefly when questioned in a television discussion on political violence occasioned by the tragic death of more than a hundred and sixty BOAC passengers. 'I know no more about this affair in Argentina than any of our listeners. I do not have time to read many novels, but before I came out this evening I did ask my wife's bookseller about Mr Savindra, and I'm afraid he was no better informed than me.' The Minister added, 'Much as I sympathize with Mr Fortnum, I want to emphasize that we cannot treat a kidnapping like this as an attack on the British diplomatic service with all that would imply. Mr Fortnum has never at any time been a member of the diplomatic service. He was born in Argentina, and so far as I know he has not even visited this country. When the unfortunate affair occurred we were about to terminate his engagement as Honorary Consul since he had passed the normal age for retirement and there was really no occasion to replace him as the number of British residents in that particular province has been very much reduced in the last ten years. I am sure you are aware that this Government is making every effort to economize in the Foreign Service.'

Asked whether the Government's attitude would have been the same if the victim had been a member of the diplomatic service the Minister said, 'Certainly it would have been the same. We don't intend to give in to this kind of blackmail anywhere, under any circumstances. In this particular case we have every confidence that Mr Fortnum will be released when these desperate men realize the complete futility of their action. It is for the President of Argentina in that case to decide whether he will treat these criminals with clemency. Now, if the chairman will allow me, I would like to return to the real subject of tonight's broadcast. I can assure you that there were no security men on the plane and so no question of an armed struggle . . .'

Pablo turned off the radio.

'What did all that mean?' Father Rivas asked.

Doctor Plarr said, 'They have left Fortnum's case in your hands.'

'If they have rejected the ultimatum,' Aquino said, 'the sooner we kill him the better.'

'Our ultimatum was not made to the British Government,' Father Rivas said.

'Of course,' Doctor Plarr hastily corrected himself, 'they have to say all that in public. We can't tell what pressures they may be exerting in Buenos Aires and Asunción privately.' Even to himself his words lacked confidence.

They all, taking turns with those on guard, spent the afternoon drinking maté, with the exception of Doctor Plarr who had inherited from his father a taste for tea. He played another game with Aquino and, by pretending a slip which lost him his queen, he allowed Aquino a victory, but there was a sullen lack of belief in the way Aquino pronounced 'Checkmate'.

Doctor Plarr visited his patient twice and found him sleeping on both occasions. He regarded with resentment the peaceful expression on the condemned man's face. He was even smiling a little – perhaps he was dreaming of Clara or the child, or perhaps only of the 'proper measure'. Doctor Plarr wondered what the years ahead might be like – in the unlikely event of there being any years ahead. He was not worried about Clara: that affair – if you could call it an affair – would have been finished soon in any case. It was the child's image, as he grew up under Charley Fortnum's care, which worried him. For no rational reason he pictured the child as a boy, a boy who resembled two early photographs of himself, one taken at four years and one at eight. His mother preserved them still in the over-crowded apartment, the silver frames tarnished from lack of care, among the china cockatoos and the junk of antique shops.

Charley, he was certain, would have the child brought up as a Catholic – he would be all the more strict about that because he had once broken the laws of the Church himself – and he could imagine Charley listening with sentimental pleasure beside the boy's bunk while the child stumbled through an Our Father. Afterwards he would join Clara beside the dumb-waiter on the verandah. Charley would be a very kind father. He would never make his son ride a horse. It was even possible that he would give up drink or at least severely reduce the proper measure. Charley would call the boy 'old fellow' and pat his cheek and turn over the pages of *London Panorama* before tucking him up firmly in bed. Doctor Plarr suddenly saw the boy sitting up in his bunk, as he had done, listening to the distant locking of doors, to the low voices downstairs, the stealthy footsteps. There was one night he remembered when he had crept for reassurance to his father's room, and he was looking down now at the bearded face of his father stretched on the coffin – four day's stubble had begun to resemble a beard.

Doctor Plarr returned abruptly to the company of Charley Fortnum's future murderers.

Guard duty had been resumed. Aquino was outside, while Pablo took the place of the Indian at the door. The Guaraní slept quietly on the floor, and Marta was clattering dishes noisily in the yard behind. Father Rivas sat with his back to the wall. He played with some dried beans which he tossed from hand to hand, like the beads of a broken rosary.

'Did you finish your book?' Doctor Plarr asked.

'Oh yes,' Father Rivas said. 'The end was exactly what I thought. You can always tell. The murderer went and committed suicide on the Edinburgh express. That was why it was half an hour late and why the man Bradshaw was wrong. How is the Consul?'

'Sleeping.'

'And his wound?'

'Doing all right. But will he live long enough to see it heal?'

'I thought you believed in those secret pressures?'

'I thought you believed in something too, León. Things like mercy and charity. Once a priest always a priest – that's the theory, isn't it? Don't start telling me about Father Torres or the bishops who went to war in the Middle Ages. This isn't the Middle Ages and this isn't war. This is the murder of a man who has done you no harm at all – a man old enough to be my father – or yours. Where *is* your father, León?'

'Under a marble monument in Asunción almost as big as this hut.'

'We all of us seem to live with dead fathers, don't we? Fortnum hated his. I think I may have loved mine. Perhaps. How can I possibly tell? That word love has such a slick sound. We take credit for loving as though we had passed an examination with more than the average marks. What was your father like? I can't remember even seeing him.'

'He was what you would expect, one of the richest of the bourgeoisie in Paraguay. You must remember our house in Asunción with the great portico and the white columns and the marble bathrooms and all the orange and lemon trees in the garden? And the *lapachos* covering the paths with their rose petals. Probably you never saw inside the house, but I am sure you came once to a birthday party in the garden. Friends of mine were never allowed inside the house – there were so many things they might break or soil. We had six servants. I liked them much better than my parents. And there was a gardener called Pedro – he was always busy sweeping up the petals – they were so untidy my mother said. I was very fond of Pedro, but my father threw him out because he stole a few pesos which had been left on a garden seat. My father paid a lot of money every year to the Colorado Party, so there was no trouble for him when the General came to power after the civil war. He was a good *abogado*, but he never worked for a poor client. He served the rich faithfully until he died, and everyone said he was a good father because he left plenty of cash behind him. Oh well, I suppose he was, in that way. It is one of the duties of a father to provide.'

'And God the Father, León? He doesn't seem to provide much. I asked last night if you still believed in him. To me he has always seemed a bit of a swine. I would rather believe in Apollo. At least he was beautiful.'

'The trouble is we have lost the power to believe in Apollo,' Father Rivas said. 'We have Jehovah in our blood. We can't help it. After all these centuries Jehovah lives in our darkness like a worm in the intestines.'

'You should never have been a priest, León.'

'Perhaps you are right, but it's too late to change now. What time is it? How tired to death I am of this radio, but we have to listen to the news – it is still possible they may give in.'

'My watch has stopped. I forgot to wind it.'

'Then we had better keep the radio on, however dangerous, as long as there is a chance . . .' He turned the sound as low as he could, but all the same they ceased to be alone. Someone was playing a harp almost inaudibly, someone sang in a whisper. They might have been sitting in a vast hall where they couldn't even see or hear the performers.

There was nothing to do but talk, talk about anything under the sun except about Sunday midnight.

'I've often noticed,' Doctor Plarr said, 'when a man leaves a woman he begins to hate her. Or is it that he hates his own failures? Perhaps we want to destroy the only witness who knows exactly what we are like when we drop the comedy. I suppose I shall hate Clara when I leave her.'

'Clara?'

'Fortnum's wife.'

'It *is* true what they say?'

'There's not much point in lying about anything, León, in the position we are in now. Dying is a wonderfully effective truth drug, better than pentothal. You priests have always known that. When the priest arrives I always leave a dying man so that he's free to talk. They most of them want to talk, if they have the strength.'

'Are you planning to desert this woman?'

'I'm planning nothing. But it will happen. If I live. I am certain of that. Nothing is for keeps in this world, León. When you entered the Church, weren't you sure in your heart that one day even your priesthood would come to an end?'

'No. I never believed that. Not for a moment. I thought the Church and I wanted the same thing. You see I had been very happy in my seminary. You might say that was the period of my honeymoon. Only there were occasions . . . I suppose it happens the same way in all honeymoons . . . there *was* a hint that something might be wrong . . . I remember one old priest . . . he was the professor in the moral theology course. I've never known a man so cut and dried and sure of the truth. Of course moral theology is the bugbear in every seminary. You learn the rules and find they don't apply to any human case . . . Oh well, I used to think, a little difference of opinion, what does it matter? In the end a man and wife grow together. The Church will grow nearer to me as I grow nearer to her.'

'But when you left the Church you began to hate it, didn't you?'

'I have told you – I never left the Church. Mine is only a separation, Eduardo, a separation by mutual consent, not a divorce. I shall never belong wholly to anyone else. Not even to Marta.'

'Even a separation brings hate often enough,' Doctor Plarr said. 'I have seen it happen many times among my patients in this damned country where no one is allowed a divorce.'

'It will never happen in my case. Even if I cannot love, I see no reason to hate. I can never forget that long honeymoon in the seminary when I was so happy. Now, if I feel any emotion for the Church, it is regret, not hate. I think she could have used me easily for a good purpose if she had understood a little better. I mean about the world as it is.'

The radio murmured on, and they listened with ears alert for the time-signal. In the room of mud, which might well have been some primitive above-ground tomb prepared for a whole family, Doctor Plarr no longer felt the least desire to torment León Rivas. If there was anyone he wanted to torment, it was himself. He thought: whatever we may pretend to each other, we have both given up hope. That is why we can talk like the friends we used to be. I have reached a premature old age when I can no longer mock a man for his beliefs, however absurd. I can only envy them.

Curiosity after a while drove him to speak. He remembered how at his first Communion in Asunción, dressed like a diminutive monk with a rope round his waist, he had believed – something, though now he could not remember what.

'It's a long time,' he told León, 'since I listened to a priest. I thought you taught that the Church was infallible like Christ.'

'Christ was a man,' Father Rivas said, 'even if some of us believe that he was God as well. It was not the God the Romans killed, but a man. A carpenter from Nazareth. Some of the rules He laid down were only the rules of a good man. A man who lived in his own province, in his own particular day. He had no idea of the kind of world we would be living in now. Render unto Caesar, but when *our* Caesar uses napalm and fragmentation bombs . . . The Church lives in time too. Only sometimes, for a short while, for some people – I am not one of them – I am not a man of vision – I think perhaps – but how can I explain to you when I believe so little myself? – I think sometimes the memory of that man, that carpenter, can lift a few people out of the temporary Church of these terrible years, when the Archbishop sits down to dinner with the General, into the great Church beyond our time and place, and then . . . those lucky ones . . . they have no words to describe the beauty of that Church.'

'I don't understand a word you say, León. You used to explain things more clearly. Even the Trinity.'

'Forgive me. It is such a very long time since I read the right sort of books.'

'You haven't the right audience either. I feel no more interested in the Church now than I feel in Marxism. The Bible is as unreadable to me as *Das Kapital*. Only sometimes, like a bad habit, I find myself using that crude word God. Last night . . .'

'Any word one uses from habit means nothing at all.'

'All the same, when you shoot Fortnum in the back of the head, are you sure you won't have a moment's fear of old Jehovah and his anger? "Thou shalt not commit murder."'

'If I kill him it will be God's fault as much as mine.'

'God's fault?'

'He made me what I am now. He will have loaded the gun and steadied my hand.'

'I thought the Church teaches that he's love?'

'Was it love which sent six million Jews to the gas ovens? You are a doctor, you must often have seen intolerable pain – a child dying of meningitis. Is that love? It was not love which cut off Aquino's fingers. The police stations where such things happen . . . He created them.'

'I have never heard a priest blame God for things like that before.'

'I don't blame Him. I pity Him,' Father Rivas said, and the time-signal struck faintly in the dark.

'Pity God?'

The priest put his fingers on the dial. For a moment he hesitated to turn it. Yes, Doctor Plarr thought, there is always something to be said for remaining ignorant of the worst. I have never told a cancer patient yet that there is no hope any longer.

A voice said as indifferently as if it were reading out a list of prices on the stock exchange, 'The following communiqué has been issued from police headquarters. "At seventeen hours yesterday a man who refused to give his name was arrested while attempting to board the ferry to the Chaco shore. He attempted to escape by plunging into the river, but he was shot by police officers. His body was recovered. It proved to be that of a lorry driver employed at the Bergman orange-canning factory. He had been absent from work since last Monday, the day before the kidnapping of the British Consul. His name was Diego Corredo and his age was thirty-five. Unmarried. His identification is believed to be an important step towards tracing the other members of the gang. It is thought that the kidnappers have not left the province, and an intensive search is now in progress. The commander of the 9th Infantry Brigade has put a parachute company at the disposal of the police."'

Doctor Plarr said, 'Lucky for you he was not interrogated. I doubt if Perez would have many scruples at this stage.'

It was Pablo who answered. 'They will discover soon enough who his friends were. I was employed at the same factory until a year ago. Everyone knew we were good friends.' The man on the radio was talking again about the Argentinian football team. There had been a riot with twenty injured when they played in Barcelona.

Father Rivas woke Miguel and sent him out to relieve Aquino, and when Aquino returned, the old arguments broke out anew. Marta had cooked the anonymous stew which she had served for two days now. Doctor Plarr wondered whether Father Rivas had endured the same meal every day of his married life, but probably it was no worse than he had been accustomed to eat in the poor *barrio* of Asunción.

Aquino waved his spoon and demanded the instant death of Charley Fortnum. 'They have killed Diego.'

To get away from them awhile Doctor Plarr carried a plate of stew into the other room. Charley Fortnum looked at it with distaste. 'I could do with a nice grilled chop,' he said, 'but I suppose they are afraid I would use a knife to escape.'

'We are all eating the same thing,' Doctor Plarr said. 'I only wish Humphries was here. It might give him an even greater appetite for the goulash at the Italian Club.'

'"Whatever the crime, the same meal's served to all."'

'A quotation?'

'One of that fellow Aquino's poems. Is there any news?'

'The man called Diego tried to escape to the Chaco, but the police shot him.'

'Ten little nigger boys and then there were nine. Will I be the next to go?'

'I don't think so. You are the only card they have left to gamble with. Even if the police discover this hideout they'll be afraid to attack it while you are alive.'

'I doubt if they would bother much about me.'

'Colonel Perez will bother about his career.'

'Are you as scared as I am, Ted?'

'I don't know. Perhaps I have a bit more hope. Or perhaps I have less to lose.'

'Yes. That's true. You're lucky. You haven't Clara and the baby to worry about.'

'No.'

'You know about these things, Ted. Will there be much pain?'

'They say when the wound's serious people feel very little.'

'And my wound will be the most serious of all.'

'Yes.'

'Clara will feel the pain longer than me. I wish it could be the other way round.'

They were still arguing in the outer room when Doctor Plarr returned. Aquino was saying, 'But what does he know of the situation? He is safe in Córdoba or . . .' He checked himself and looked up at Doctor Plarr.

'Don't worry,' Doctor Plarr said, 'I am not likely to survive you. Unless you give up this insane idea. You still have time to escape.'

'And admit failure,' Aquino said, 'to all the world.'

'You used to be a poet. Were you afraid to admit it when a poem failed?'

'My poems were never published,' Aquino said. 'No one knew when I failed. My poems were never read out on the radio. There were no questions asked about them in the British Parliament.'

'It's your damn *machismo* again, isn't it? Who invented *machismo*? A gang of ruffians like Pizarro and Cortés. Can't any of you for a moment escape your bloody history? You haven't learnt a thing, have you, from Cervantes? He had his fill of *machismo* at Lepanto.'

Father Rivas said, 'Aquino is right. We cannot afford to fail. Once before our people released a man rather than kill him – he was a Paraguayan Consul, the General cared no more about his life than Fortnum's, and when it came to the point we were not prepared to kill.

If we are weak again like that, no threat of death will be of any use on this continent. Until more ruthless men than we are begin to kill a great many more. I do not want to be responsible for the deaths which will follow our failure.'

'You have a complicated conscience,' Doctor Plarr said. 'Will you pity God for those murders too?'

'You have no idea, have you, what I meant?'

'No. I was never taught anything about pitying God by the Jesuits in Asunción. Not that I remember.'

'Perhaps you would have more faith now if you had remembered a little more.'

'Mine's a busy life, León, trying to cure the sick. I can't leave that to God.'

'Oh, you may be right. I have always had far too much time. Two Masses on a Sunday. A few feast days. Confessions twice a week. It was mostly the old women who came – and of course the children. The children were forced to come. They were beaten if they did not come, and anyway I gave them sweets. Not as a reward. The bad child received just as many sweets as the good one. I only wanted to make them feel happy while they knelt in that stuffy box. And when I gave them a penance I tried to make it a game we played together, a reward not a punishment. And they sucked their sweets while they said a Hail Mary. I could be happy too, for as long as I was with them. I was never happy with their fathers – or their mothers. I don't know why. Perhaps if I had had a child myself . . .'

'It's a long journey you've made, León, since you left Asunción.'

'It was not such an innocent life there as you think. Once a child of eight told me he had drowned his baby sister in the Paraná. People thought she had slipped off the cliff. He told me she used to eat too much and there was less for him. Less mandioca!'

'Did you give him a sweet?'

'Yes. And three Hail Marys for a penance.'

Pablo went out on guard in his turn, taking Miguel's place. Marta served the Guaraní with stew and cleaned the other plates. She said, 'Father, tomorrow is Sunday. Surely you could say a Mass for us on that day?'

'It is more than three years since I last said a Mass. I doubt if I can even remember the words.'

'I have a missal, Father.'

'Read the Mass to yourself then, Marta. It will serve just as well.'

'You heard what they said on the radio. The soldiers are searching for us now. It may be the last Mass we shall ever hear. And there is Diego – you must say a Mass for him.'

'I have no right to say a Mass. When I married you, Marta, I excommunicated myself.'

'No one knows you married me.'

'*I* know.'

'Father Pedro used to sleep with women. Everyone in Asunción knew that. And he said Mass every Sunday.'

'He did not marry, Marta. He could go to confession and sin again and go to confession. I am not responsible for his conscience.'

'You seem to suffer from an odd lot of scruples, León,' Doctor Plarr said, 'for a man who plans to murder.'

'Yes. Perhaps they are not scruples – only superstitions: You see if I took the Host I would still half believe I was taking His body. Anyway it's a useless argument. There is no wine.'

'Oh but there is, Father,' Marta said. 'I found an empty medicine bottle in the rubbish dump and when I was in the town I filled it at a *cantina*.'

'You think of everything,' Father Rivas said sadly.

'Father, you know I have wanted all these years to hear you say Mass again and to see the people praying with you. Of course it will not be the same without the beautiful vestments. If only you had kept them with you.'

'They did not belong to me, Marta. Anyway vestments are not the Mass. Do you think the Apostles wore vestments? How I hated wearing them when the people in front of me were all in rags. I was glad to turn my back on them and forget them and see only the altar and the candles – but the money for the candles would have fed half the people there.'

'You are wrong, Father. We were all glad to see you in those vestments. They were so beautiful, all the scarlet and the gold embroidery.'

'Yes. I suppose they helped you escape from everything for a little while, but to me they were the clothes of a convict.'

'But, Father, you won't listen to the Archbishop's rules? You *will* say a Mass for us tomorrow?'

'Suppose what they say is true and I am damning myself?'

'The good God would never damn a man like you, Father. But poor Diego, José's wife . . . all of us . . . we need you to speak to God for us.'

Father Rivas said, 'All right. I will say Mass. For your sake, Marta. I have done very little for you in these years. You have given me love and all I have given you has been a great deal of danger and a dirt floor to lie on. I will say Mass as soon as it is light if the soldiers give us enough time. Have we any bread left?'

'Yes, Father.'

A sense of some obscure grievance moved Doctor Plarr. He said, 'You don't believe yourself in all this mumbo-jumbo, León. You are fooling them like you fooled that child who killed his sister. You want to hand them sweets at Communion to comfort them before you murder Charley Fortnum. I've seen with my own eyes things just as bad as any you've listened to in the confessional, but I can't be pacified with sweets. I have seen a child born without hands and feet. I would have killed it if I had been left alone with it, but the parents watched me too closely – they wanted to keep that bloody broken torso alive. The Jesuits used to tell us it was our duty to love God. A duty to love a God who produces that abortion? It's like the duty of a German to love Hitler. Isn't it better not to believe in that horror up there sitting in the clouds of heaven than pretend to love him?'

'It may be better not to breathe, but all the same I cannot help breathing. Some men, I think, are condemned to belief by a judge just as they are condemned to prison. They have no choice. No escape. They have been put behind the bars for life.'

'"I see my father only through the bars",' Aquino quoted with a sort of glum self-satisfaction.

'So here I sit on the floor of my prison cell,' Father Rivas said, 'and I try to make some sense of things. I am no theologian, I was bottom in most of my classes, but I have always wanted to understand what you call the horror and why I cannot stop loving it. Just like the parents who loved that poor bloody torso. Oh, he seems ugly enough I grant you, but then I am ugly too and yet Marta loves me. In my first prison – I mean in the seminary – there were lots of books in which I could read all about the love of God, but they were of no help to me. Not one of the Fathers was of any use to me. Because they never touched on the horror – you are quite right to call it that. They saw no problem. They just sat comfortably down in the presence of the horror like the old Archbishop at the General's table and they talked about man's responsibility and Free Will. Free Will was the excuse for everything. It was God's alibi. They had never read Freud. Evil was made by man or Satan. It was simple that way. But I could never believe in Satan. It was much easier to believe that God was evil.'

Marta exclaimed, 'Father, you do not know what you are saying.'

'I am not talking as a priest now, Marta. A man has the right to think aloud to his wife. Even a madman, and perhaps I am a little mad.

Perhaps those years in Asunción in the *barrio* have turned my brain, so here I am waiting to kill an innocent man . . .'

'You are not mad, León,' Aquino said. 'You have come to your senses. We will make a good Marxist of you yet. Of course God is evil, God is capitalism. Lay up treasures in heaven – they will bring you a hundred per cent interest for eternity.'

'I believe in the evil of God,' Father Rivas said, 'but I believe in His goodness too. He made us in His image – that is the old legend. Eduardo, you know well how many truths in medicine lay in old legends. It was not a modern laboratory which first discovered the use of a snake's venom. And old women used the mould on over-ripe oranges long before penicillin. So I too believe in an old legend which is almost forgotten. He made us in His image – and so our evil is His evil too. How could I love God if He were not like me? Divided like me. Tempted like me. If I love a dog it is only because I can see something human in a dog. I can feel his fear and his gratitude and even his treachery. He dreams in his sleep like I do. I doubt if I could ever love a toad – though sometimes, when I have touched a toad's skin, I am reminded of the skin of an old man who has spent a rough poor life in the fields, and I wonder . . .'

'I find my disbelief a lot easier to understand than your kind of belief. If your God is evil . . .'

'I have had more than two years in hiding,' Father Rivas said, 'and we have to travel light. There is no room in our packs for books of theology. Only Marta has kept a missal. I have lost mine. Sometimes I have been able to find a paperback novel – like the one I have been reading. A detective story. That sort of life leaves a lot of time to think and perhaps Marta may be right and my thoughts are turning wild. But I can see no other way to believe in God. The God I believe in must be responsible for all the evil as well as for all the saints. He has to be a God made in our image with a night-side as well as a day-side. When you speak of the horror, Eduardo, you are speaking to the night-side of God. I believe the time will come when the night-side will wither away, like your communist state, Aquino, and we shall see only the simple daylight of the good God. You believe in evolution, Eduardo, even though sometimes whole generations of men slip backwards to the beasts. It is a long struggle and a long suffering, evolution, and I believe God is suffering the same evolution that we are, but perhaps with more pain.'

'I am not so sure of evolution,' Doctor Plarr said, 'not since we managed to produce Hitler and Stalin in one generation. Suppose the night-side of God swallows up the day-side altogether? Suppose it is the good side which withers away. If I believe what you believe, I would sometimes think that had happened already.'

'But I believe in Christ,' Father Rivas said, 'I believe in the Cross and the Redemption. The Redemption of God as well as of Man. I believe that the day-side of God, in one moment of happy creation, produces perfect goodness, as a man might paint one perfect picture. God's good intention for once was completely fulfilled so that the night-side can never win more than a little victory here and there. With our help. Because the evolution of God depends on our evolution. Every evil act of ours strengthens His night-side, and every good one helps His day-side. We belong to Him and He belongs to us. But now at least we can be sure where evolution will end one day – it will end in a goodness like Christ's. It is a terrible process all the same and the God I believe in suffers as we suffer while He struggles against Himself – against His evil side.'

'Is killing Charley Fortnum going to help his evolution?'

'No. I pray all the time I shall not have to kill him.'

'And yet you will kill him if they don't give in?'

'Yes. Just as you lie with another man's wife. There are ten men dying slowly in prison, and I tell myself I am fighting for them and that I love them. But my sort of love I know is a poor excuse. A saint would only have to pray, but I have to carry a revolver. I slow evolution down.'

'Then why . . . ?'

'Saint Paul answered that question, "What I do is not that which I wish to do, but something which I hate." He knew all about the night-side of God. He had been one of those who stoned Stephen.'

'Do you still call yourself a Catholic, believing all that?'

'Yes. I call myself a Catholic whatever the bishops may say. Or the Pope.'

Marta said, 'Father, you frighten me. All this is not in the catechism, is it?'

'No, not in the catechism, but the catechism is not the faith, Marta. It is a sort of two times table. There is nothing I have said which your catechism denies. You learnt when you were a child about Abraham and Isaac, and how Jacob cheated his brother, and Sodom was destroyed like that village last year in the Andes. God when He is evil demands evil things; He can create monsters like Hitler; He destroys children and cities. But one day with our help He will be able to tear His evil mask off forever. How often the saints have worn an evil mask for a time, even Paul. God is joined to us in a sort of blood transfusion.

His good blood is in our veins, and our tainted blood runs through His. Oh, I know I may be sick or mad. But it is the only way I can believe in the goodness of God.'

'It's much easier not to believe in a God at all.'

'Are you sure?'

'Well, perhaps the Jesuits left one germ of the disease in me, but I have isolated it. I keep it under control.'

'I have never spoken aloud like this before – I don't know why I do now.'

'Perhaps because you think there is no more hope?'

'Ted,' the voice which Doctor Plarr was beginning to hate called from the inner room, 'Ted.'

Doctor Plarr made no motion to rise.

'Your patient,' Father Rivas reminded him.

'I've done all I can for him. What's the good of mending his ankle if you are going to put a bullet through his head?'

'Ted,' the voice came again.

'He probably wants to ask me what vitamins Clara ought to give his baby. Or when he ought to be weaned. His baby! The dark side of God must be having a hearty laugh about that. I never wanted a child. I would have got rid of it if she had let me.'

'Speak lower,' Father Rivas said, 'even if you are jealous of the poor man.'

'Jealous of Charley Fortnum? Why should I be jealous?' He couldn't control his voice. 'Jealous because of the child? – but the child's mine. Jealous because of his wife? She's mine as well. For as long as I want her.'

'Jealous because he loves.'

He was aware of the way Marta looked at him. Even Aquino's silence seemed a criticism.

'Oh love! That's not a word in my vocabulary.'

Marta said, 'Give me your shirt, Father. I want to wash it ready for the Mass.'

'A little dirt will not matter.'

'You have slept in it for three weeks, Father. It is not good to go up to the altar smelling like a dog.'

'There is no altar.'

'Give it to me, Father.'

Obediently he stripped off his shirt; the blue was faded by the sun and stained with the marks of food and the whitewash of many walls. 'Do what you want,' the priest said. 'All the same it is a pity to waste our water. We may need all we have of it before the end.'

*

It was too dark to see and the negro lit three candles. He carried one into the inner room, but brought it back and nipped out the flame. He said, 'He is asleep.'

Father Rivas turned on the radio and the sad notes of Guaraní music came over the air – the music of a people who are doomed to die. There was a lot of static; it crackled like the machine guns of extinction. Up in the mountains beyond the river the summer was beginning to break up and the lightning quivered on the walls.

'Put out all the pans and pails you have,' Father Rivas told Pablo.

The wind came in a sudden blast, the leaves of the avocados swept across the tin roof, and then again the wind dropped. 'I shall have to wear a wet shirt at Mass,' Father Rivas said, 'unless I can persuade Marta that God does not mind a man's naked skin.'

Suddenly, as though someone were standing close at their elbow within the hut, a voice spoke to them, 'We have been asked by police headquarters to read the following statement.' There was a pause while the man found the right place. They could even hear the rustle of the papers he was carrying.

'It is now known where the gang of kidnappers are holding the British Consul captive. They have been located in a certain quarter in the *barrio popular* which . . .' The rain came sweeping down from Paraguay, beating on the roof, and drowned the announcer's words. Marta ran in, holding out a piece of damp cloth, the shirt of Father Rivas. She cried, 'Father, what can I do? The rain . . .'

'Hush,' the priest said, and he turned the radio louder. The rain passed over them towards the city, and the lightning lit the room almost continuously. Across the Paraná in the Chaco the thunder became audible, like a barrage which has lifted and moved on before an attack.

'You have no longer any hope of escape,' the voice continued slowly and ponderously, in an interval of static, speaking with extreme clarity like a teacher explaining a problem of mathematics to a class of children; Doctor Plarr recognized the voice of Colonel Perez. 'We know exactly where you are. You are surrounded by men from the 9th Brigade. Before eight tomorrow morning you must send the British Consul out of the hut. He must come alone and walk unmolested into the cover of the trees. Five minutes afterwards you must come out yourselves, one by one with arms raised over the head. The Governor guarantees that your lives will be spared and you will not be returned to Paraguay. Do not attempt to escape. If any man leaves the hut before the Consul has been delivered unharmed he will be shot down. No white flag will be respected. You are completely surrounded. I warn you that if any harm . . .' After that the static whined and shrieked through his words, making them unintelligible.

'Bluff!' Aquino said, 'only bluff! If they were out there Miguel would have warned us. That man can see an ant in the dark. Kill Fortnum and afterwards we will draw lots to see who leaves first. How can they tell on a night like this who it is that leaves the hut – the Consul or another?' He threw the door open and called out to the Indian, 'Miguel!' Like an answer to his question a semi-circle of floodlights flashed on – they flared from between the trees in an arc nearly a hundred yards across. Through the open door Doctor Plarr could see moths crowding away from him towards the lights to beat and shrivel against the reflectors. The Indian lay flattened on the ground, and the doctor's own shadow shot back into the hut and lay stretched there like a dead man on the floor. The doctor moved aside. He wondered whether Perez had seen him and identified him.

'They do not dare shoot into the hut,' Aquino said, 'for fear of killing Fortnum.'

The lights went out again. In the silence between the thunderclaps they heard a rustle no louder than the movements of a rat. Aquino stood at the edge of the doorway and turned his gun towards the darkness. 'No,' Father Rivas said, 'it's Miguel.' Another wave of water swept the roof and in the yard a pail was overturned and sent rattling away before the wind.

The darkness did not last. Perhaps the lightning had blown a fuse which was now repaired. The men watching from inside the hut saw the Indian rise to his feet to run, but the lights blinded him. He began to turn in a circle with a hand over his eyes. A single shot was fired and he fell to his knees. It was as though the men of the 9th Brigade had no intention of wasting ammunition on someone of so little importance. The Guaraní knelt with his head bent, like a pious man at the elevation of the Host. He swayed from side to side – he might have been enacting part of a primitive rite. Then with immense effort he began to raise his gun in the wrong direction until it pointed at the open door of the hut. It seemed to Doctor Plarr, who watched flattened against the wall, that the parachutists were waiting with a cruel and patient curiosity to see what happened next. They were not going to waste another bullet. The Indian was no danger to them, for how could he possibly see to shoot in the glare of the lights? Whether he were dying or not was immaterial to them. He could lie there till morning came. Then the gun sailed a few feet through the air towards the hut. It fell out of reach and Miguel was still on the ground.

Aquino said, 'We must pull him in.'

'He is dead,' Doctor Plarr assured him.

'How can you tell?'

The lights went out again. It was as though the men hidden in the trees were playing a cruel game with them.

'This is your chance, doctor,' Aquino said.

'What can I do?'

'You are right,' Father Rivas said. 'They are trying to tempt one of us to go out.'

'Your friend Perez might not shoot if *you* went out.'

Doctor Plarr said, 'My patient is here.'

Aquino edged the door further open. The automatic rifle lay just out of reach. He put a hand out towards it. The lights flashed on, and a bullet struck the edge of the door as he banged it shut. The man in charge of the lights must have heard the squeak of the hinge.

'Close the shutters, Pablo.'

'Yes, Father.'

With the glare of the lights shut out, they felt a sense of protection.

'What shall we do now, Father?' the negro asked.

'Kill Fortnum at once,' Aquino said, 'and if the lights go out again we can make a run for it.'

Pablo said, 'Two of us are dead already. It might be better Father, if we surrender. And there is Marta here.'

'But the Mass, Father?'

'It seems to me I shall have to make it a Mass for the dead,' Father Rivas said.

'Say any sort of Mass you like,' Aquino said, 'but kill the Consul first.'

'How could I say the Mass after I had killed him?'

'Why not if you can say a Mass when you intend to kill him?' Doctor Plarr said.

'Ah, Eduardo, you are still enough of a Catholic to know how to turn the knife in the wound. You will be my confessor yet.'

'May I prepare the table, Father? I have the wine. I have the bread.'

'I will say it at the first light. I have to prepare myself, Marta, and that takes longer than laying a table.'

'Let me kill him while you say your prayers,' Aquino said. 'Do your work and leave me to do mine.'

'I thought your work was writing poems,' Doctor Plarr said.

'My poems have all been about death, so I am well qualified.'

'It is madness to go on,' Pablo said. 'Forgive me, Father, but Diego was right to try to escape. It is madness to kill one man and make sure that five of us die. Father . . .'

'Take a vote,' Aquino interrupted with impatience. 'Let the vote decide.'

'Are you turning into a Parliamentarian, Aquino?' Doctor Plarr said.

'Keep to a subject you know, doctor. Trotsky believed in a free vote inside the Party.'

'I vote for surrender,' Pablo said. He put his hands over his face. The movements of his shoulders showed he was weeping. For himself? For the dead? For shame?

Doctor Plarr thought: the desperadoes! That is what the papers would call them. A failed poet, an excommunicated priest, a pious woman, a man who weeps. For heaven's sake let this comedy end in comedy. None of us are suited to tragedy.

Pablo said, 'I love this house. I had nothing else but the house left when my wife and my child died.'

Yet another father, Doctor Plarr told himself, are we never going to finish with fathers?

'I vote for killing Fortnum now,' Aquino said.

'You told us they were bluffing,' Father Rivas said. 'Perhaps you are right. Suppose eight o'clock comes and we have done nothing – they still cannot attack us. So long as he is alive.'

'Then what do you vote for?' Aquino asked.

'For delay. We gave them till midnight tomorrow.'

'And you, Marta?'

'I vote with my husband,' she said with pride.

A loudspeaker – so close that it must have been set up among the trees outside – spoke to them, again in the voice of Perez. 'The United States Government and the British Government have refused to intervene. If you have been listening to your radio you will know I am telling you the truth. Your blackmail has failed. You have nothing to gain by holding the Consul any longer. Send him out of the hut before 08.00 hours if you wish to save your own lives.'

'They insist too much,' Father Rivas said.

Somebody was whispering beside the microphone. It was unintelligible – a sound which grated like pebbles drawn back under a wave. Then Perez continued. 'There is a dying man outside your door. Send the Consul out to us now, and we will try to save your friend. Are you going to leave one of your own people to die slowly?'

No Hippocratic oath demands suicide, Doctor Plarr told himself. In his childhood his father had read him stories of heroism, of wounded men rescued under fire, of Captain Oates walking out into the snow. 'Shoot if you must this old grey head' was one of his favourite poems in those days.

He went abruptly into the inner room. He could see nothing in the darkness there. He whispered, 'Are you awake?'

'Yes.'

'How does your ankle feel?'

'It's all right.'

'I will bring a light and change the bandages.'

'No.'

Doctor Plarr said, 'The soldiers have us surrounded. You mustn't give up hope.'

'Hope of what?'

'There's only one man who really wants your death.'

'Yes?' the indifferent voice replied.

'Aquino.'

'And you,' Charley Fortnum said, 'you! You want it.'

'Why should I?'

'You talk too loud, Plarr. I don't suppose you ever talked so loud at the camp, even when I was out farming a mile away. You were always so damned discreet, weren't you, in case the servants heard. But the time always comes when even a husband has his ears open.' There was a sound of scrabbling in the darkness as though he were trying to pull himself upright. 'I always thought there was some code of honour for doctors, Plarr, but of course that's an English notion, and you're only half English, and as for the other half . . .'

'I don't know what you heard,' Doctor Plarr said. 'You must have dreamt it or misunderstood.'

'I suppose you thought to yourself what the hell does it matter, she's only a little tart from Mother Sanchez's house. How much did she cost you? What did you offer her, Plarr?'

'If you want to know,' Doctor Plarr said in a spurt of rage. 'I gave her a pair of sunglasses from Gruber's.'

'Those glasses? She was fond of those glasses. She thought they were smart, and now they've been smashed to bits by your friends. What a swine you are, Plarr. It was like raping a child.'

'It came more easily.'

Doctor Plarr had not realized how close he was to the coffin bed. A fist struck at him through the dark. It caught him on the neck and made him choke. He stepped back and heard the coffin creak.

'Oh God,' Charley Fortnum said, 'I've knocked the bottle over.' He added, 'There was still a measure left. I'd kept it for . . . ' A hand groped across the floor, touched Doctor Plarr's shoes and recoiled.

'I'll bring a light.'

'Oh no, you won't. I don't want to see your fucking face ever again, Plarr.'

'You are taking it too hard. These things happen, Fortnum.'

'You don't even pretend to love her, do you?'

'No.'

'I suppose you'd had her at the brothel, and so you thought . . .'

'I've told you before – I saw here there, but I never had her.'

'I'd saved her from that place and you've begun to push her back.'

'I never intended this, Fortnum.'

'You never intended to be found out. It was cheaper for you wasn't it, not having to pay for your fucks.'

'What good do scenes like this do? I thought it would be all over quickly and you'd never know. It's not as if she or I really cared for each other. Caring is the only dangerous thing, Fortnum.'

'I cared.'

'You'd have had her back. You would never have known.'

'When did it begin, Plarr?'

'The second time I saw her. At Gruber's. When I gave her the sunglasses.'

'Where did you take her? Back to Mother Sanchez?' The persistent questions reminded Doctor Plarr of fingers pressing the pus out of a boil.

'I took her to my flat. I asked her in to have coffee, but she knew very well what I meant by coffee, Fortnum. If it hadn't been me, it would have been someone else sooner or later. She even knew the porter at my flat.'

'Thank God,' Fortnum said.

'What do you mean?'

'I've found the bottle. It's not spilt.'

He could hear the sound of Fortnum drinking. He said, 'You'd better save a little for later in case . . .'

'I know you think I'm a coward, Plarr, but I'm not much afraid of dying now. It's a lot easier than going back and waiting at the camp for a child to be born with your face, Plarr.'

'It's not how I intended things,' Doctor Plarr repeated. He had no anger left with which to defend himself. 'Nothing is ever what we intend. They didn't mean to kidnap you. I didn't mean to start the child. You would almost think there was a great joker somewhere who likes to give a twist to things. Perhaps the dark side of God has a sense of humour.'

'What dark side?'

'Some crazy notion of León's. You should have heard that – not the things you did hear.'

'I wasn't trying to hear – I was trying to get off this damn box and join you. I was lonely, and your drugs don't work any more. I'd nearly got to the door when I heard the priest say you were jealous. Jealous, I thought, jealous of what? And then I heard and I got back on to the box.'

In a distant village Doctor Plarr had once been forced to perform an emergency operation for which he was not qualified. He had the choice of risking the operation or letting the woman die. Afterwards he felt the same fatigue as he felt now, and the woman had died just the same. He had sat down on the floor in his exhaustion. He thought: I've said all I can. What more can I say? The woman was a long time dying or it seemed so to him then.

Fortnum said, 'To think I wrote to Clara telling her you would look after her and the baby.'

'I know.'

'How the hell do you know?'

'You aren't the only one who overhears things. The joker again. I overheard you dictating to León. It made me angry.'

'You angry? Why?'

'I suppose León was right – I *am* jealous.'

'Jealous of what?'

'That would be another comic twist, wouldn't it?'

He could hear the sound of Charley Fortnum drinking again. Doctor Plarr said, 'Even one of your measures won't last forever.'

'I haven't got for ever. Why can't I hate you, Plarr? Is it the whisky? I'm not drunk yet.'

'Perhaps you are. A little.'

'It's an awful thing, Plarr, but there's no one else I can leave them with. I can't trust Humphries . . .'

'I'll give you a jab of morphine if you want to sleep.'

'I'd rather stay awake. I've the hell of a lot of things to think about and not much time. I want to be left alone, Plarr. Alone. I have to get used to that, haven't I?'

Chapter 4

IT seemed to Doctor Plarr that they had all been left completely alone. Their enemies had abandoned them: the loudspeaker had fallen silent, the rain had stopped, and in spite of his thoughts Doctor Plarr slept, though fitfully. The first time he opened his eyes it was the voice of Father Rivas that woke him. The priest was kneeling by the door with his lips pressed to a crack in the wood. He seemed to be speaking to the dead or dying man outside. Words of comfort, a prayer, the formula of conditional absolution? Doctor Plarr turned on his other side and slept again. When he woke a second time, Charley Fortnum was snoring in the other room – a dry-throated grating whisky snore. Perhaps he was dreaming of security in the big bed at home after he had finished the bottle on the dumb-waiter. Was Clara patient with him when he snored like that? When she was forced to lie awake beside him what had her thoughts been? Had she regretted her cell at Mother Sanchez's? There, with the dawn, she could sleep peacefully alone. Did she regret the simplicity of her life there? He had no idea. He could no more imagine her thoughts than he could imagine the thoughts of a strange animal.

The light from the projectors shining under the door lost brilliance. The last day had begun. He remembered an occasion years ago when he sat with his mother at a *son-et-lumière* performance outside Buenos Aires. The searchlights came out and went like a professor's white chalk, picking out a tree, under which someone – San Martín was it? – had sat – an old stable where another figure of history had tethered his horse, the windows of a room where a treaty or a constitution – he couldn't remember what – had been signed. A voice explained the story in a prose touched with the dignity of the unrecallable past. He was tired from his medical studies and he fell asleep. When he woke for the third time it was to see Marta busy at the table laying a cloth, while daylight seeped through the interstices of window and door. There were two unlit candles on the table stuck in saucers. 'They are all we have left, Father,' Marta said.

Father Rivas was still asleep, curled up like an embryo.

Marta repeated, 'Father.'

One by one, as she spoke, the others began to wake to the new day, León, Pablo, Aquino.

'What time is it?'

'What?'

'What did you say?'

'There are not enough candles, Father.'

'The candles do not matter, Marta. You fuss too much.'

'Your shirt is still wet. You will catch your death from cold.'

'I doubt that,' Father Rivas said.

She grumbled her disappointments as she laid out on the table in turn a medicine bottle full of wine, a maté gourd which had to serve as a chalice, a torn dishcloth for a napkin. 'It is not how I wanted it to be,' she complained. 'It is not how I dreamed of it.' She put a pocket missal which had lost half its binding open on the table. 'What Sunday is it, Father?' she asked, as she fumbled with the leaves. 'Is it the twenty-fifth Sunday after Pentecost or the twenty-sixth? Or can it be Advent, Father?'

'I have no idea,' Father Rivas said.

'Then how can I find you the right Gospel and the right Epistle?'

'I will take what comes. Pot-luck,' he said.

Pablo said, 'It would be a good thing to release Fortnum now. It must be nearly six, and in two hours . . .'

'No,' Aquino said, 'we have voted to wait.'

'*He* hasn't voted,' Pablo said, indicating Doctor Plarr.

'He has no vote. He is not one of us.'

'He will die with us.'

Father Rivas took his wet shirt from Marta. He said, 'We have not time to argue now. I am going to say Mass. Help Señor Fortnum in if he wants to hear it. I shall be saying Mass for Diego, for Miguel, for all of us who may be going to die today.'

'Not for me,' Aquino said.

'You cannot dictate to me whom I pray for. I know well enough you believe in nothing. All right. Believe in nothing. Stay in the corner there and believe in nothing. Who cares whether you believe or not? Even Marx cannot guarantee what is true or false any more than I can.'

'I hate to see time wasted. We have not so much of it left.'

'What would you prefer to do with your time?'

Aquino laughed. 'Oh, of course, I would waste it like you. "When death is on the tongue, the live man speaks." If I still had a wish to write I would make that verse a little clearer – I almost begin to understand it myself.'

'Will you hear my confession, Father?' the negro asked.

'Of course. In a moment. If you come into the yard. And you, Marta?'

'How can I confess, Father?'

'Why not? You are near enough to death to promise anything. Even to leave me.'

'I will never . . .'

'The parachutists will see to that.'

'But you, Father?'

'Oh, I will have to take my chance. There are not many people lucky enough to die with a priest handy. I am glad to be one of the majority. I have been one of the privileged too long.'

Doctor Plarr left them and went in to the inner room. He said, 'León's going to say Mass. Do you want to be there?'

'What time is it?'

'I don't know. Some time after six I think. The sun has risen.'

'What will they do now?'

'Perez has given them till eight to release you.'

'They are not going to?'

'I don't think so.'

'Then they'll kill me and Perez will kill them. You've got the best chance, haven't you?'

'Perhaps. It's not a big chance.'

'My letter to Clara . . . you'd better keep it for me all the same.'

'If you want me to.'

Charley Fortnum took a wad of papers from his pocket. 'Most of these are bills. Unpaid. The tradesmen all cheat except Gruber. Where in hell did I put it?' At last he found the letter in another pocket. 'No,' he said, 'there's not much point in sending it to her now. Why should she care to hear a lot of loving words from me if she has you?' He tore the letter into small pieces. 'Anyway I wouldn't want the police to read it. There's a photo too,' he said, searching in his wallet. 'The only one I've got of Fortnum's Pride, but she's in it as well.' He took a quick look and then he tore it also into minute pieces.

'Promise you won't tell her that I knew about you. I wouldn't want her to feel any guilt. If she's capable of it.'

'I promise,' Doctor Plarr said.

'These bills – you'd better look after them,' Charley Fortnum said. He handed them to Doctor Plarr. 'There may be enough in my current account to meet them. If not – the buggers have swindled me enough. I'm clearing the decks,' he added, 'but I don't want the crew to suffer.'

'Father Rivas will be starting Mass by now. If you want to hear it, I'll give you an arm in there.'

'No, I've never been what you'd call a religious man. I think I'll stay out here with the whisky.' He carefully measured what was left in the bottle. 'Perhaps one small one now – that leaves a real measure at the last. Bigger than a shipmaster's.'

A low voice was speaking in the other room. Charley Fortnum said, 'I know people are supposed to get a bit of comfort at the end – by believing in all that. Do you believe in anything at all?'

'No.'

Now that the personal truth was out between them Doctor Plarr felt a curious need to speak with complete accuracy. He added, 'I don't think so.'

'Nor do I – except . . . It's a damn silly thing to feel, but when I'm with that fellow out there, I mean the priest . . . the one who's going to murder me . . . I feel . . . Do you know there was even a moment when I thought he was going to confess to me. To me, Charley Fortnum? Can you beat that? And by God I'd have given him absolution. When are they going to kill me, Plarr?'

'I don't know what the time is. I have no watch. Some time around eight I suppose. Perez will send in the paras then. What happens afterwards, God knows.'

'God again! You can't get away from the bloody word, can you? Perhaps I'll go and listen awhile after all. It won't do any harm. It'll please him. I mean the priest. And there's nothing else to do. If you'll help me.'

He put his arm around Doctor Plarr's shoulder. He weighed surprisingly light for his bulk – like a body filled only with air. He's an old man, Doctor Plarr thought, he wouldn't have had long to live anyway, and he remembered the night he had met him first, when he and Humphries lugged him protesting across the road to the Bolívar. He had weighed a lot heavier then. They made only two steps towards the door and then Charley Fortnum stopped dead in his tracks. 'I can't make it,' he said. 'Why should I anyway? I wouldn't want to curry favour at the last moment. Take me back to the whisky. That's my sacrament.'

Doctor Plarr returned to the other room. He took up his stand near Aquino who sat on the ground, watching the motions of the priest with a look of suspicion. It was as though he feared that Father Rivas was laying some trap, planning a betrayal, as he moved to and fro by the table and made the secret signals with his hands. All Aquino's poems were of death, Doctor Plarr remembered. He wasn't going to be robbed of it now.

Father Rivas was reading the Gospel. He read it in Latin not in Spanish, and Doctor Plarr had long forgotten the little Latin he had once known. He kept his eye on Aquino while the voice ran rapidly on in the dead tongue. Perhaps they thought he was praying with his eyes lowered and a kind of prayer did enter his mind – or at least a wish, heavy with self-distrust, that if the moment came he would have the skill and determination to act quickly. If I had been with them over the border, he wondered, what would I have done when my father called for help in the police-station yard? Would I have gone back to him or escaped as they did?

Father Rivas reached the Canon of the Mass and the consecration of the bread. Marta was watching her man with an expression of pride. The priest lifted up the maté gourd and spoke the only phrases of the Mass which Doctor Plarr had for some reason never forgotten. 'As often as you do these things you shall do them in memory of Me.' How many acts in a lifetime had he done in memory of something forgotten or almost forgotten?

The priest lowered the gourd. He knelt and rose quickly. He seemed to be whipping the Mass to its conclusion with impatience. He was like a herdsman driving his cattle towards the byre before a storm burst, but he had started home too late. The loudspeaker blared its message in the voice of Colonel Perez. 'You have exactly one hour left to send the Consul out to us and save your lives.' Doctor Plarr saw Aquino's left hand tighten on his gun. The voice went on, 'I repeat you have one hour left. Send the Consul out and save your lives.'

'. . . who takes away the sins of the world, grant them eternal rest.'

Father Rivas began '*Domine, non sum dignus*'. Marta's was the only voice which joined his. Doctor Plarr looked around seeking Pablo. The negro knelt with bowed head by the back wall. Would it be possible, he wondered, before the Mass ended, while they were distracted by the ceremony, to seize Aquino's gun and hold them up for long enough to enable Charley Fortnum to escape? I'd be saving all their lives, he thought, not only Charley's. He looked back towards Aquino, and as though Aquino knew what was in his mind he shook his head.

Father Rivas took the kitchen cloth and began to clean the gourd, as punctiliously as though he were back in the parish church at Asunción.

'*Ite. Missa est.*'

The voice on the loudspeaker answered like a liturgical response, 'You have fifty minutes left.'

'Father,' Pablo said. 'The Mass is over. Better surrender now. Or let us vote again.'

'My vote is the same,' Aquino said.

'You are a priest, Father, you cannot kill,' Marta said.

Father Rivas held out the dishcloth. 'Go into the yard and burn this. It will not be needed again.'

'It would be a mortal sin for you to kill him now, Father. After the Mass.'

'It is a mortal sin for anyone at any time. The best I can do is to ask for God's mercy like anyone else.'

'Was that what you were doing up at the altar?' Doctor Plarr asked. He felt wearied out by all the arguments, by the slowness with which the short time left them dragged by.

'I was praying I would not have to kill him.'

'Posting a letter,' Doctor Plarr said. 'I thought you didn't believe in any reply to letters like that.'

'Perhaps I was hoping for a coincidence.'

The loudspeaker announced: 'You have forty-five minutes left.'

'If they would leave us alone . . .' Pablo complained.

'They want to break our nerve,' Aquino said.

Father Rivas left them abruptly. He carried his revolver with him.

Charley Fortnum lay on the coffin. His eyes were open and he stared up at the mud roof. 'Have you come to liquidate me, Father?' he asked.

Father Rivas had a look of shyness or perhaps shame. He moved a few steps into the room. He said, 'No. No. Not that. Not yet. I thought there might be something you needed.'

'I still have some whisky left.'

'You heard their loudspeaker. They will be coming for you soon.'

'And then you will kill me?'

'Those are my orders, Señor Fortnum.'

'I thought a priest took his orders from the Church, Father. Oh, I forgot. You don't belong any more, do you? All the same you were saying a Mass. I'm not much of a Catholic, but I didn't feel inclined to attend it. It's not exactly a holiday of obligation. Not for me.'

'I remembered you at the altar, Señor Fortnum,' Father Rivas said with awkward formality, as though he were addressing a bourgeois parishioner. The phrase came from a language which had grown rusty during the last years.

'I'd rather you forgot me, Father.'

'I shall never be allowed to do that,' Father Rivas said.

Charley Fortnum noticed with surprise that the man was close to tears. He said, 'What's the matter, Father?'

'I never believed it would come to this. You see – if it had been the

American Ambassador – they would have given way. And I would have saved ten men's lives. I never believed I would have to take a life.'

'Why did they ever choose you as a leader?'

'El Tigre thought he could trust me.'

'Well, he can, can't he?'

'I don't know now. I don't know.'

Does a condemned man always have to comfort his executioner? Charley Fortnum wondered. He said, 'Is there anything I can do for you, Father?'

The man looked at him with an expression of hope, like a dog who thinks he has heard the word 'walk'. He shuffled a step nearer. Charley Fortnum remembered the boy at school with protuberant ears whom Mason used to bully. He said, 'I am sorry . . .' Sorry for what? For failing to be the American Ambassador?

The man said, 'I know how hard it must be for you. Lying there. Waiting. Perhaps if you could prepare yourself a little . . . that might take your mind off . . .'

'You mean confess?'

'Yes.' He explained, 'In an emergency . . . even I . . . '

'But I'm no good as a penitent, Father. I haven't confessed in thirty years. Not since my first marriage anyway – which wasn't a marriage. You'd better look to the others.'

'I have done all I can for them.'

'After such a long time . . . it's impossible . . . I haven't enough belief. I would be ashamed to speak all those pious words, Father, even if I remembered them.'

'You would feel no shame now if you had no belief. And you need not say them to me aloud, Señor Fortnum. Only make an act of contrition. In silence. To yourself. That is enough. We have so little time. Just an act of contrition,' he pleaded as though he were asking for the price of a meal.

'But I've told you, I've forgotten the words.'

The man came two steps nearer, as if he were gathering a bit of courage or hope. Perhaps he hoped to be offered enough cash for a piece of bread.

'Just say you are sorry and try to mean it.'

'Oh, I'm sorry for a lot of things, Father. Not the whisky though.' He picked the bottle up, scrutinized what was left and put it down again. 'It's a difficult life. A man has to have one sort of drug or another.'

'Forget the whisky. There must be other things. I only ask you to say – I am sorry for breaking a rule.'

'I don't even remember what rules I've broken. There are so many damned rules.'

'I have broken the rules too, Señor Fortnam. But I am not sorry I took Marta. I am not sorry I am here with these men. This revolver – one cannot always swing a censer up and down or sprinkle holy water. But if there was another priest here I would say to him, yes I *am* sorry. I am sorry I did not live in an age when the rules of the Church seemed more easy to keep – or in some future when perhaps they will be changed or not seem so hard. There is one thing I can easily say. Perhaps you could say it too. I am sorry not to have had more patience. Failures like ours are often just failures of hope. Please – cannot you say you are sorry you did not have more hope?'

The man obviously needed comfort and Charley Fortnum gave him all he could. 'Yes, I suppose I could go about as far as that, Father.'

Father, Father, Father. The word repeated itself in his mind. He had a vision of his father sitting bewildered, not understanding, not recognizing him, by the dumb-waiter, while he lay on the ground and the horse stood over him. Poor bugger, he thought.

Father Rivas finished the words of absolution. He said, 'Perhaps I will have a drink with you now – a small one.'

'Thank you, Father,' Charley Fortnum said. 'I'm a lot luckier than you are. There's no one to give *you* absolution.'

*

'I only saw your father for a few minutes once a day,' Aquino said, 'when we walked around the yard. Sometimes . . .' He broke off to listen to the loudspeaker from the trees outside. The voice said, 'You have only fifteen minutes left.'

'The last quarter of an hour has gone a bit too quickly for my taste,' Doctor Plarr commented.

'Will they begin to count out the minutes now? I wish they would let us die quietly.'

'Tell me a little more about my father.'

'He was a fine old man.'

'During the few minutes you had with him,' Doctor Plarr asked, 'what did you talk about?'

'We never had time to talk of anything much. A guard was always there. He walked beside us. He would greet me – very formally and affectionately like a father greeting his son – and I – well, I had a great respect for him, you understand. There would always be a spell of silence – you know how it is with a *caballero* like that. I would wait for him to speak first. Then the guard would shout at us and push us apart.'

'Did they torture him?'

'No. Not in the way they did to me. The C.I.A. men would not have approved. He was an Anglo-Saxon. All the same fifteen years in a police station is a long torture. It is easier to lose a few fingers.'

'What did he look like?'

'An old man. What else can I say? You must know what he looked like better than I do.'

'He wasn't an old man the last time I saw him. I wish I had even a police snap of him lying dead. You know the kind of thing they take for the records.'

'It would not be a pleasant sight.'

'It would fill a gap. Perhaps we wouldn't have recognized each other if he had escaped. If he had been here with you now.'

'He had very white hair.'

'Not when I knew him.'

'And he stooped badly. He suffered very much from rheumatism in his right leg. You might say it was the rheumatism which killed him.'

'I remember someone quite different. Someone tall and thin and straight. Walking fast away from the quay at Asunción. Turning once to wave.'

'Strange. To me he seemed a small fat man who limped.'

'I'm glad they didn't torture him – in your way.'

'With the guards always around I never had a proper chance to warn him about our plan. When the moment came – he did not even know the guard had been bribed – I shouted to him "Run" and he looked bewildered. He hesitated. That hesitation and the rheumatism . . .'

'You did your best, Aquino. It was no one's fault.'

Aquino said, 'Once I recited a poem to him, but I do not think he cared much for poetry. It was a good poem all the same. About death of course. It began. "Death has the taste of salt" Do you know what he said to me once? It was as if he were angry – I do not know who with – he said, "I am not unhappy here, I am bored. Bored. If God would only give me a little pain." It was an odd thing to say.'

'I think I understand,' Doctor Plarr said.

'In the end he must have got his pain.'

'Yes. He was lucky at the end.'

'As for me I have never known boredom,' Aquino said. 'Pain yes. Fear. I am frightened now. But not boredom.'

Doctor Plarr said. 'Perhaps you have not come to the end of yourself. It's a good thing when that happens only when you are old, like my father was.' He thought of his mother among the porcelain parrots in

Buenos Aires or eating éclairs in the Calle Florida, of Margarita fallen asleep in the carefully shaded room while he lay wide awake watching her unloved face, of Clara, and the child, and the long impossible future beside the Paraná. It seemed to him he was already his father's age, that he had spent as long in prison as his father had, and that it was his father who had escaped.

'You have ten minutes left,' the loudspeaker said. 'Send the Consul out immediately and afterwards one at a time with your hands raised . . .'

It was still giving careful instructions when Father Rivas came back into the room. Aquino said, 'The time is almost up. Better let me kill him now. It is not the job for a priest.'

'They may still be bluffing.'

'By the time we know for sure it may be too late. These paras are well trained by the Yankees in Panama. They move quick.'

Doctor Plarr said, 'I am going out to talk to Perez.'

'No, no, Eduardo. That would be suicide. You heard what Perez said. He will not even respect a white flag. You agree, Aquino?'

Pablo said, 'We are beaten. Let the Consul go.'

'If that man passes through the room,' Aquino said, 'I shall shoot him – and anyone who helps him – even you, Pablo.'

'Then they will kill us all,' Marta said. 'If he dies we shall all die.'

'At any rate it will be a memorable occasion.'

'*Machismo*,' Doctor Plarr said, 'your damned stupid *machismo*. León, I've got to do something for the poor devil in there. If I talk to Perez . . .'

'What can you offer him?'

'If he agrees to extend his time limit, will you extend yours?'

'What would be the good?'

'He *is* the British Consul. The British Government . . .'

'Only an Honorary Consul, Eduardo. You have explained more than once what that means.'

'Will you agree if Perez . . .'

'Yes, I will agree, but I doubt if Perez . . . He may not even give you time to talk.'

'I think he will. We have been good friends.'

A memory came back to Doctor Plarr of the back reach of the river, of the great horizontal forest, of Perez moving without hesitation from dipping log to dipping log towards the little group where the murderer awaited him. 'They are all my people,' Perez had said.

'Perez is not a bad man as policemen go.'

'I am afraid for you, Eduardo.'

'The doctor is suffering from *machismo* too,' Aquino said. 'Go on . . . get out there and talk . . . but take a gun with you . . .'

'It's not *machismo* I'm suffering from. You told me the truth, León. I *am* jealous. Jealous of Charley Fortnum.'

'If a man is jealous,' Aquino said, 'he kills the other man – or gets killed. It's a simple thing, jealousy.'

'Mine is not that kind of jealousy.'

'What other sort of jealousy is there? You sleep with a man's wife . . . And when he does the same . . .'

'He loves her . . . that's the trouble.'

'You have five minutes left,' the loudspeaker announced.

'I'm jealous because he loves her. That stupid banal word love. It's never meant anything to me. Like the word God. I know how to fuck – I don't know how to love. Poor drunken Charley Fortnum wins the game.'

'One doesn't surrender a mistress so easily,' Aquino said. 'They cost a lot of trouble to win.'

'Clara?' Doctor Plarr laughed. 'I paid her with a pair of sunglasses.' Memories continued to return. They were like tiresome obstacles which he had to work around, a blindfold game with bottles, before he reached the door. He said, 'There was something she asked me before I left home . . . I didn't bother to listen.'

'Stay here, Eduardo. You cannot trust Perez . . .'

For a moment after he opened the door Doctor Plarr was dazzled by the sunlight, and then the world came back into sharp focus. Twenty yards of mud stretched before him. The Indian Miguel lay like a bundle of old clothes thrown to one side, sodden with the night's rain. Beyond the body the trees and the deep shade began.

There was no sign of anyone alive. The police had probably cleared the people from the neighbouring huts. About thirty yards away something gleamed among the trees. It might have been a drawn bayonet which had caught the sun, but as he walked a little nearer and looked more closely, he saw it was only a piece of petrol tin that formed part of a hut hidden among the trees. A dog barked a long distance away.

Doctor Plarr walked slowly and hesitatingly on. No one moved, no one spoke, not a shot was fired. He raised his hands a short distance above his waist, like a conjuror who wants to show that they are empty. He called, 'Perez! Colonel Perez!' He felt absurd. After all there was no danger. They had exaggerated the whole situation. He had felt more insecure on the occasion when he followed Perez from raft to raft.

He didn't hear the shot which struck him from behind in the back of the right leg. He fell forward full length, as though he had been tackled in a rugby game, with his face only a few yards from the shadow of the trees. He was unaware of any pain, and though for a while he lost consciousness, it was as peaceful as falling asleep over a book on a hot day.

When he opened his eyes again the shadow of the trees had hardly moved. He felt very sleepy. He wanted to crawl on into the shade and sleep again. The morning sun here was too violent. He was vaguely aware that there was something he had to discuss with someone, but it could wait until his siesta was over. Thank God, he thought, I am alone. He was too tired to make love, and the day was too hot. He had forgotten to draw the curtains.

He heard the sound of breathing; it came from behind him, and he didn't understand how that could be. A voice whispered, 'Eduardo.' He did not at first recognize it, but when he heard his name repeated, he exclaimed, 'León?' He couldn't understand what León could be doing there. He tried to turn round, but a stiffness in his leg prevented him.

The voice said, 'I think they have shot me in the stomach.'

Doctor Plarr woke sharply up. The trees in front of him were the trees of the *barrio*. The sun was shining on his head because he had not had time to reach the trees. He knew that he would not be safe until he reached the trees.

The voice which he now knew must be León's said, 'I heard the shot. I had to come.'

Doctor Plarr again tried to turn, but it was no use – he gave up the attempt.

The voice behind him said, 'Are you badly hurt?'

'I don't think so. What about you?'

'Oh, I am safe now,' the voice said.

'Safe?'

'Quite safe. I could not kill a mouse.'

Doctor Plarr said, 'We must get you to a hospital.'

'You were right, Eduardo,' the voice said. 'I was never made to be a killer.'

'I don't understand what's happened . . . I have to talk to Perez . . . You have no business to be here, León. You should have waited with the others.'

'I thought you might need me.'

'Why? What for?'

There was a long silence until Doctor Plarr asked rather absurdly, 'Are you still there?'

A whisper came from behind him.

Doctor Plarr said, 'I can't hear you.'

The voice said a word which sounded like 'Father'. Nothing in their situation seemed to make any sense whatever.

'Lie still,' Doctor Plarr said. 'If they sce either of us move they may shoot again. Don't even speak.'

'I am sorry . . . I beg pardon . . .'

'*Ego te absolvo*,' Doctor Plarr whispered in a flash of memory. He intended to laugh, to show León he was only joking – they had often joked when they were boys at the unmeaning formulas the priests taught them to use – but he was too tired and the laugh shrivelled in his throat.

Three paras came out of the shade. In their camouflage they were like trees walking. They carried their automatic rifles at the ready. Two of them moved towards the hut. The third approached Doctor Plarr, who lay doggo, holding what little breath he had.

Chapter 5

IN the cemetery were a great number of people whom Charley Fortnum did not know from Adam. One woman in a long old-fashioned dress of black he assumed to be Señora Plarr. She held tightly to the arm of a thin priest whose dark brown eyes turned here and there, to left and right as though he were afraid of missing an important member of the congregation. Charley Fortnum heard her introduce him several times – 'This is my friend Father Galvão from Rio.' Two other ladies wiped their eyes prominently near the graveside. They might have been hired for the occasion like the undertakers. Neither of them spoke to Señora Plarr, or even to one another, but of course that might have been a matter of professional etiquette. After the Mass in the cathedral they had come separately up to Charley Fortnum and introduced themselves.

'You are Señor Fortnum, the Consul? I was such a great friend of poor Eduardo. This is my husband, Señor Escobar.'

'My name is Señora Vallejo. My husband was unable to come, but I could not bear to fail Eduardo, so I brought with me my friend, Señor

Duran. Miguel, this is Señor Fortnum, the British Consul whom those scoundrels . . .'

The name Miguel called up immediately in Charley Fortnum's mind the image of the Guaraní as he squatted in the doorway of the hut, tending his gun with a smile, and then he thought of the bundle of rain-soaked clothes past which the parachutists carried him on a stretcher. One of his hands in passing had dangled down and touched a piece of wet material. He began to say, 'May I introduce my wife . . . ?' but Señora Vallejo and her friend were already moving on. She held her handkerchief under her eyes – so that it looked rather like a yashmak – until her next social encounter. At least, Charley Fortnum thought, Clara does not pretend grief. It's a kind of honesty.

The funeral, he thought, very much resembled two diplomatic cocktail parties he had attended in Buenos Aires. They were part of a series given for the departing British Ambassador. It was soon after his own appointment as Honorary Consul when he was still regarded with interest because he had picnicked with royalty among the ruins. People wanted to hear what the royals had talked about. This time the second party, with the same guests whom he had seen in the church, was held in the open air of the cemetery.

'My name is Doctor Saavedra,' a voice said. 'You may remember we met once with Doctor Plarr –'

Charley Fortnum wanted to reply, Surely it was at the house of Mother Sanchez. I remember you well with a girl. I was with María, the one whom somebody stabbed.

'This is my wife,' he said, and Doctor Saavedra bowed with courtesy over her hand; her face must have been familiar to him, if only because of the birth-mark on her forehead. He wondered how many of these people knew that Clara had been Plarr's mistress.

'I must go now,' Doctor Saavedra said. 'I have been asked to say a few words in honour of our poor friend.'

He moved towards the coffin, pausing on the way to shake hands and exchange a few words with Colonel Perez. Colonel Perez was in uniform and carried his cap in the crook of his arm. He had the air of being the most serious person present. Perhaps he was wondering how the doctor's death would affect his career. A lot depended, of course, on the attitude of the British Embassy. A young man, Crichton, who was a new face to Charley Fortnum, had flown up from BA to represent the Ambassador (the First Secretary being in bed with flu). He stood beside Perez close to the coffin. You could estimate the social importance of a mourner by his closeness to the coffin, for the coffin represented the guest of honour. The Escobars were worming their way towards it, and Señora Vallejo was almost near enough to put out a hand. Charley Fortnum with a crutch under his right arm stayed on the periphery of the smart company. He felt it was absurd to be there at all. He was an impostor. He only owed his position there because he had been mistaken for the American Ambassador.

Also on the periphery, but far removed from Charley Fortnum, stood Doctor Humphries. He too had the air of being out of place and knowing it. His proper habitat was the Italian Club, his proper neighbour the waiter from Naples, who feared he had the evil eye. When he first noticed Humphries Charley Fortnum had taken a step in his direction, but Humphries had backed hastily away. Charley Fortnum remembered telling Doctor Plarr, in some long distant past, that Humphries had cut him. 'Lucky you,' Plarr had exclaimed. Those had been happy days, and yet all the while Plarr had been sleeping with Clara and Plarr's child was growing in her body. He had loved Clara and Clara had been gentle and tender to him. All that was over. He had owed his happiness to Doctor Plarr. He took a furtive look at Clara. She was watching Saavedra who had begun to speak. She looked bored as though the subject of the eulogy was a stranger who did not interest her at all. Poor Plarr, he thought, he was deceived by her too.

'You were more than a doctor who healed our bodies,' Doctor Saavedra said, addressing his words directly to the coffin which was wrapped in a Union Jack that had been lent on request by Charley Fortnum. 'You were a friend to each of your patients – even to the poorest among them. All of us know how unsparingly you worked in the *barrio* of the poor without recompense – from a sense of love and justice. What a tragic fate then it was that you, who had toiled so hard for the destitute, died at the hands of their so-called defenders.'

Good God, Charley Fortnum thought, can that be the story Colonel Perez is putting out?

'Your mother was born in Paraguay, once our heroic enemy, and it was with a *machismo* worthy of your maternal ancestors who gave their hearts' blood for Lopez – not seeking whether his cause were good or ill – that you walked out to your death from the hut, where these false champions of the poor were gathered, in a last attempt to save their lives as well as your friend's. You were shot down without mercy by a fanatic priest, but you won the day – your friend survived.'

Charley Fortnum looked across the open grave at Colonel Perez. His uncovered head was bowed; his hands were pressed to his sides; his feet were at the correct military angle of attention. He looked like a nineteenth-century monument of soldierly grief while Doctor Saavedra continued to establish by his eulogy – was it about that they had spoken together? – the official version of Plarr's death. Who would think to question it now? The speech would be printed verbatim in *El Litoral* and a resumé would surely appear even in the *Nación*.

'Except for your murderers and their prisoner I was the last, Eduardo, to see you alive. Your enthusiasms were so much wider than your professional interests, and it was your love of literature which enriched our friendship. The last time we were together you had called me to your side – a strange reversal of the usual role of doctor and patient – to discuss the formation in this city of an Anglo-Argentinian cultural club, and with your usual modesty you invited me to be the first president. My friend, you spoke that night of how best to deepen the ties between the English and the South American communities. How little either of us knew that in a matter of days you would give your own life in that cause. You surrendered everything – your medical career, your appreciation of art, your capacity for friendship, the love you had grown to have for your adopted land – in the attempt to save those misguided men and your fellow countryman. I promise you with my hand on your coffin that the Anglo-Argentinian Club will live, baptized with the blood of a brave man.'

Señora Plarr was weeping, and so, more decoratively, were Señora Vallejo and Señora Escobar. 'I am tired,' Charley Fortnum said, 'It's time to go home.'

'Yes, Charley,' Clara said.

They began a slow walk towards their hired car.

Somebody touched Fortnum's arm. It was Herr Gruber.

Herr Gruber said, 'Señor Fortnum . . . I am so glad you are here . . . safe and . . .'

'Nearly sound,' Charley Fortnum said. He wondered how much Gruber knew. He wanted to get back to the shelter of the car. He said, 'How is the shop? Doing well?'

'I shall have a lot of photographs to develop. Of the hut where they held you. Everyone is going out there to see it. I don't think they always photograph the right hut. Señora Fortnum, you must have had an anxious time.' He explained to Charley Fortnum, 'Señora Fortnum has always bought her sunglasses at my shop. I have some new designs in from Buenos Aires if she would care . . .'

'Yes. Yes. Next time we are in town. You must forgive us, Herr Gruber. The sun is very hot and I have stood too long.'

His ankle itched almost unbearably in its plaster case. They had told him at the hospital that Doctor Plarr had done a good job. In a matter of weeks he would be driving Fortnum's Pride again. He had found the Land Rover standing in its old place under the avocados, a little battered, with one headlight gone and the radiator bent. Clara explained it had been borrowed by one of the police officers. 'I shall complain to Perez,' he had said, supporting himself against the car while he pressed his hands tenderly upon a wounded plate.

'No, you must not do that, Charley. The poor man would be in trouble. I told him he could take it.' It wasn't worth an argument on his first day home.

They had driven him straight back from the hospital through a landscape which seemed like the memory of a country he had left for ever – the by-road which went to the Bergman orange-canning factory, the disused rail track of an abandoned camp which had once belonged to a Czech with an unpronounceable name. He counted the ponds as he passed – there ought to be four of them – he wondered how he ought to greet Clara.

There was no real greeting apart from a kiss on the cheek. He refused to go and lie down on the excuse that he had been on his back too long. He couldn't bear the thought of the large double bed which Clara must so often have shared with Plarr when he was out farming (because of the servants they would have been afraid to disarrange the bed in a guest room). He had sat with his foot propped up on the verandah beside the dumb-waiter. He had been away less than a week, but it seemed a long slow year of separation, long enough for two characters to grow apart – he poured himself out a shipmaster's measure of Long John. Looking up at Clara over the right measure, he said, 'Of course they have told you?'

'Told me what, Charley?'

'Doctor Plarr is dead.'

'Yes. Colonel Perez came here. He told me.'

'The doctor was a good friend to you.'

'Yes, Charley. Are you comfortable like that? May I fetch you a pillow?' He thought that after all their love-making and deception it was hard Plarr had not earned a single tear. The Long John had an unfamiliar taste, he had become so accustomed to Argentinian whisky. He began to explain to Clara that it would be best if for the next few weeks he slept alone in one of the guest rooms. The plaster round his ankle made him restless, he said, and she must sleep well – because of the child. She said yes, of course, she understood. It would be arranged.

Now as he shunted on his crutch away from the cemetery towards the hired car, a voice said to him, 'Excuse me, Mr Fortnum . . .' It was the young fellow Crichton from the Embassy. He said, 'I wonder if I could come out to your camp this afternoon. The Ambassador has asked me . . . there are certain things he wants me to talk over with you . . .'

'You can have lunch with us,' Charley Fortnum said. 'You will be very welcome,' he added, thinking that anyone, even a man from the Embassy, would help to preserve him from the solitude he would otherwise have to share with Clara.

'I am afraid . . . I would very much like to . . . but I have promised Señora Plarr . . . and Father Galvão. If I could come about four o'clock. I am catching the evening plane to BA.'

When he got back to the camp Charley Fortnum told Clara that he was too tired to eat. He would sleep a bit before Crichton came. Clara made him comfortable – she had been trained to make men comfortable as much as any hospital nurse. He tried not to show that the touch of her hand irritated him when she arranged the pillows. He felt his skin tighten when she kissed his cheek and he wanted to tell her not to trouble. A kiss was worth nothing from someone who was incapable of loving even her lover. And yet, he asked himself, what fault was it of hers? You don't learn about love from a customer in a brothel. And because it was not her fault he must be careful never to show her what he felt. It would have been a lot simpler, he thought, if she had really loved Plarr. He could so easily picture how it would have been if he had found her heartbroken, the gentle way in which he would have comforted her. Phrases from romantic novels came to his head like 'Dear, there is nothing to forgive.' But as he played with the fancy he remembered she had sold herself for a gaudy pair of sunglasses from Gruber's.

The sun through the jalousies striped the floor of the guest-room. One of his father's hunting prints hung on the wall. A huntsman held a fox above the ravening hounds. He looked at the picture with disgust and turned his face away – he had never killed anything in his life, not even a rat.

The bed was comfortable enough, but after all the coffin with the blankets had not really been very hard – better than the bed in his nursery when he was a child. There was a deep quiet here, broken by an occasional footstep from the kitchen region or the creak of a chair out on the verandah. There was no radio to announce the latest news, no quarrelling voices from an inner room. To be free, he discovered, was a very lonely thing. He could almost have wished the door to open, to have seen the priest come shyly in, carrying a bottle of Argentine whisky. He felt an odd kinship with that priest.

There had been no ceremony at the priest's funeral. He had been shovelled quickly away in unconsecrated ground, and Charley Fortnum resented that. If he had known about it in time he would have stood by the grave and said a few words like Doctor Saavedra, though he could not remember ever having made a speech in his life: all the same he could have found the courage in the heat of his indignation. He would have told them all, 'The Father was a good man. I know he didn't kill Plarr.' But his only audience, he supposed, would have been a couple of gravediggers and the driver of the police truck. He thought: at least I'll find out where they stowed him and I'll lay a few flowers there. Then he fell into a deep sleep of exhaustion.

Clara woke him because Crichton had arrived. She found his crutch and helped him on with his dressing-gown, and he went out on to the verandah. He lowered himself down beside the dumb-waiter and said, 'Have a Scotch.'

'It's a bit early, isn't it?' Crichton asked.

'It's never too early for a drink.'

'Well, a very small one then. I was saying to Mrs Fortnum what a terribly anxious time she must have had.' He put the glass down on a small table without taking any.

'Cheers,' Charley Fortnum said.

'Cheers.' Crichton took his glass up again with reluctance. Perhaps he had hoped to leave it untouched on the table until the canonical hour. 'There are things the Ambassador wanted me to talk over with you, Mr Fortnum. Of course I needn't tell you how very very worried we have all been.'

'I was a bit worried myself,' Charley Fortnum said.

'The Ambassador wants you to know we did everything in our power . . .'

'Yes. Yes. Of course.'

'Thank God things turned out all right.'

'Not everything. Doctor Plarr's dead.'

'Yes. I didn't mean . . .'

'And the priest too.'

'Well, he deserved what he got. He murdered Plarr.'

'Oh no, he didn't.'

'You haven't seen Colonel Perez's report?'

'Colonel Perez is a bloody liar. It was the paras who shot Plarr.'

'There was a post-mortem, Mr Fortnum. They checked the bullets. One in the leg. Two in the head. They were not army bullets.'

'You mean the surgeon of the 9th Brigade checked them. You can tell the Ambassador this, Crichton, from me. I was in the next room when Plarr went out. I heard all that happened. Plarr went out to try to talk to Perez – he thought he might save all our lives. Father Rivas came to me. He said he had agreed to postpone the ultimatum. Then we heard a shot. He said, "They have shot Eduardo." He ran out.'

'And gave him the *coup de grâce*,' Crichton said.

'Oh no, he didn't. He left his gun where I was.'

'With his prisoner?'

'It was out of my reach. He had an argument with Aquino in the other room – and with his wife. I heard Aquino say, "Kill him first." And I heard his reply . . .'

'Yes?'

'He laughed. I heard him laugh. It surprised me because he wasn't a man who laughed. A shy sort of giggle sometimes. Not what you'd call a laugh. He said, "Aquino, for a priest there are always priorities." I don't know why, but I started to say an "Our Father", and I'm not a man who prays. I only got as far as "thy Kingdom" when there was another shot. No. He didn't kill Plarr. He hadn't even reached him. They carried me past the bodies. They were ten feet apart. I suppose if Perez had been there he would have thought of rearranging them. To make the distance right for a *coup de grâce*. Please tell the Ambassador that.'

'Of course I'll tell him what your theory is.'

'It's not a theory. The paras scored all three deaths – Plarr, the priest and Aquino. It's what they call good shooting.'

'They saved your life.'

'Oh yes. Or Aquino's bad aim. You see he had only his left hand. He came nearly up to the coffin I was on before he fired. He said, "They've shot León." He was too excited to keep the gun steady, but I don't suppose he would have missed a second time. Even with his left hand.'

'Why didn't Perez get your story?'

'He didn't ask me for it. Plarr said once that Perez always has to think about his career.'

'I'm glad they got Aquino anyway. He was a murderer – or wanted to be.'

'He'd seen his friend shot. You have to remember that. They'd been through a lot together. And he was angry with me. I made friends with him and then I tried to escape. You know he fancied himself as a poet. He used to recite me bits of his poems and I pretended to like them, though they didn't make much sense to me. Anyway I'm glad the paras were satisfied with three deaths. Those other two – Pablo and Marta – they were only poor people who got caught up in things.'

'They had more luck than they deserved. They needn't have been caught up in things.'

'Perhaps it was love of a kind. People do get caught up by love, Crichton. Sooner or later.'

'It's not a very good excuse.'

'No, I suppose not. Not in the Foreign Service anyway.'

Crichton looked at his watch. Perhaps he was satisfied now that the proper hour had been reached. He raised his glass. He said, 'I suppose you'll be out of action for quite a while.'

'I haven't much to do here anyway,' Charley Fortnum said.

'Exactly.' Crichton took another drink.

'Don't tell me the Ambassador wants another report on the maté?'

'No, no. We just want you to get well in your own good time. As a matter of fact the Ambassador is writing to you officially at the end of the week, but he wanted me to have a word with you first. After all you've been through, official letters always seem – well, so official. You know how it is. They are written to go on the files. Top copy to London. You have to be so – cautious. Someone at home might possibly look at the files one day.'

'What's the Ambassador got to be cautious about?'

'Well, for more than a year, London has been pressing us for economies. Do you know they are cutting us down ten per cent on official entertainment and we have to show chits now for the least expenditure? And yet those damn MPs keep on coming out and expect to be invited to lunch at least. Some of them even think they rate a cocktail-party. Now you, you know, you've had a pretty long innings. If you were in the Service you would have passed the retiring age quite a while ago. In a way the office forgot about you – until this kidnapping came along. You'll be much safer – out of the front line.'

'I see. That's it. It's a bit of a blow, Crichton.'

'It's not as if you ever got more than your expenses.'

'I could import a car every two years.'

'That's another thing – as an Honorary Consul you hadn't really the right.'

'The Customs here don't distinguish. And everyone does it. The Paraguayan, the Bolivian, the Uruguayan –'

'Not everyone, Fortnum. We try to keep our hands clean at the British Embassy.'

'Perhaps that's why you'll never understand South America.'

'I don't want to bear only bad news,' Crichton said. 'There was something the Ambassador asked me to tell you – in strictest confidence. Have I your promise?'

'Of course. Who would I tell?' There isn't even Plarr, he thought.

'The Ambassador proposes to recommend you for an honour in the List next New Year.'

'An honour,' Charley Fortnum repeated incredulously.

'An OBE.'

'Why, that's really kind of him, Crichton,' Charley Fortnum said. 'I never thought he liked me . . .'

'You won't tell anyone, will you? In theory you know all these things have to be approved by the Queen.'

'The Queen? Yes. I understand. I hope it won't make me too proud,' Charley Fortnum said. 'You know I guided some members of the Royal Family once – round the ruins. They were a very nice couple. We had a picnic like I had with the American Ambassador, but they didn't expect me to drink Coca-Cola. I like that family. They do a wonderful job.'

'And you'll tell no one – except your wife, of course. You can trust her.'

'I don't think she'd understand anyway,' Charley Fortnum said.

During the night he dreamt he was walking up a very long straight road with Doctor Plarr. On either side the *lagunas* lay like pewter plates which grew more grey every moment in the evening light. Fortnum's Pride had broken down and they had to reach the camp before it was dark. He was anxious. He wanted to run, but he had hurt his leg. He said, 'I don't want to keep the Queen waiting.'

'What's the Queen doing at the camp?' Doctor Plarr asked.

'She's going to give me the OBE.'

Doctor Plarr laughed. 'Order of the Bad Egg,' he said.

Charley Fortnum woke with a sense of desolation, and the images wound themselves quickly up like a strip of scotch-tape, so that all he could remember was the long road and Plarr laughing.

He lay on his back in the narrow guest-room bed, and he felt his age weigh heavily on his body like a blanket. He wondered how many more years he would have to lie alone like that–it seemed a waste of time. A lamp passed the window. He knew it was carried by the *capataz* going to work; in that case it must be nearly dawn. The lamplight moved along the wall and lit his crutch which looked like a big carved initial letter against the wall, and then dimmed and passed away. He knew exactly what the lamp would be lighting now – first the avocados, then the sheds and afterwards the irrigation ditches; from here and there the men would be gathering for work in the gun-metal light.

He swung his good leg out of the bed and reached for the crutch. After Crichton had gone he had told Clara the bad news of his retirement – he could see it meant nothing to her. In the eyes of a girl from Mother Sanchez's house he would seem always to be a rich man. He had said nothing about the OBE. As he had told Crichton, she wouldn't understand, and he feared that her indifference might make it seem less important even to himself. And yet he wished he could have told her. He wanted to break the wall of silence which was growing up between them. 'The Queen is going to give me an honour,' he could hear himself saying to her, for the words 'the Queen' would surely mean something even to her. He had often told her about his picnic with royalty among the ruins.

He moved on his crutch diagonally like a crab down the passage between the sporting prints, then put his hand out in the dark to open the door of the bedroom, but the door wasn't there and he moved forward into what he felt certain was an empty room. There wasn't even the faintest sound of breathing to break the silence. He might have been walking alone through another ruin. To make sure he passed his hand back and forth over the pillow, and he felt the coldness and cleanness of a bed which had not been slept in. He sat down on the edge of the bed and thought: she's gone away. Right away. Who with? The *capataz* perhaps? – or one of the workmen? why not? They were more her own kind than he was. She could talk to them as she couldn't talk to him. He had been alone a great many years before he found her and there was no reason to be afraid of the few years likely to be left. He had managed then, he assured himself, and he could manage again. Perhaps Humphries would no longer cut him in the street after his name had appeared among the New Year Honours. They would eat goulash again at the Italian Club and he would invite Humphries to the camp; they would sit together by the dumb-waiter, but Humphries was not a drinking man. He felt a pang of pain because Plarr was dead. By her absence she seemed to be betraying Plarr as well as himself. He felt a little angry with her for Plarr's sake. Surely she could have been faithful for a short while to a dead man – it would have been like wearing something black for a week or two.

He didn't hear her come in, and he was startled when she spoke. She said, 'Charley, what are you doing here?'

He said, 'It's my room, isn't it? Where have you been?'

'I was afraid of being alone. I went to sleep with María.' (María was the maid.)

'What were you afraid of? Ghosts?'

'I was afraid for the child. I dreamt I was strangling the child.'

So she cares for something he thought. It was like a glimmer of light at the end of his darkness. If she is capable of that . . . If she isn't all deception . . .

She said, 'I had a friend at Señora Sanchez's house who strangled her baby.'

'Sit here, Clara.' He took her hand and pulled her gently down beside him.

'I thought you did not want me to be near you.' She said the sad truth like a fact of no importance, as another woman might say, 'I thought you preferred me in red.'

'I have no one else, Clara.'

'Shall I put on the light?'

'No. It will be daylight soon. Just now I saw the *capataz* going by to work. How is the baby, Clara?' He knew he had hardly mentioned the baby since he came home. He felt as though he were relearning a language he hadn't spoken since a childhood in another country.

'I think he is all right. But sometimes he is so quiet I feel afraid.'

'We shall have to find you a good doctor,' he said, speaking mechanically without thought. She made a sound like a dog does when you tread on its paw, an exclamation of shock – or was it pain?

'I am sorry . . . I didn't mean . . . ' It was still too dark to see her. He raised his hand and found her face. She was crying. 'Clara . . .'

'I am sorry, Charley. I am tired.'

'Did you love him, Clara?'

'No . . . no . . . I love you, Charley.'

'There's nothing wrong in love, Clara. It happens. It doesn't much matter who with. We get caught up,' he told her, and remembering what he had said to young Crichton, he added, 'we get kidnapped,' attempting a feeble joke to reassure her, 'by mistake.'

'He never loved me,' she said. 'To him I was only a girl from Señora Sanchez.'

'You are wrong.' It was like pleading a cause; he might have been attempting to bring two young people to a closer understanding.

'He wanted me to kill the baby.'

'You mean in your dream?'

'No. No. He wanted it killed. He really wanted it. I knew then he could never love me.'

'Perhaps he'd begun, Clara. Some of us . . . we are a bit slow . . . it's not so easy to love . . . we make a lot of mistakes.' He went on for the sake of saying something, 'I hated my father . . . I did not much like my wife . . . But they were not really bad people . . . that was only one of my mistakes. Some of us learn to read quicker than others . . . Ted and I were both bad at the alphabet. I am not so good at it even now. When I think of all the mistakes there must be on those files in London,' he rambled on, making a little human noise in the darkness in the hope that it might reassure her.

'I had a brother I loved, Charley. One day he wasn't there any more. He got up to go cane-cutting, but no one in the fields saw him. He went away just like that. Sometimes at Señora Sanchez's house I used to think, Perhaps he will come here looking for a girl and then he will find me and we will go away together.'

There seemed at last to be a sort of communication between them and he tried hard to keep the thin thread intact. 'What shall we call the child, Clara?'

'If he is a boy – would you like Charley?'

'One Charley's enough in the family. I think we will call him Eduardo. You see I loved Eduardo in a way. He was young enough to be my son.'

He put his hand tentatively on her shoulder and he felt her body shaken with tears. He wanted to comfort her, but he had no idea how to do it. He said, 'He really loved you in his way, Clara. I don't mean anything wrong . . .'

'It is not true, Charley.'

'Once I heard him say he was jealous of me.'

'I never loved him, Charley.'

Her lie meant nothing to him now at all. It was contradicted too plainly by her tears. In an affair of this kind it was the right thing to lie. He felt a sense of immense relief. It was as though, after what seemed an interminable time of anxious waiting in the ante-room of death, someone came to him with the good news that he had never expected to hear. Someone he loved would survive. He realized that never before had she been so close to him as she was now.